BLACK BLADE

ERIC LUSTBADER

BLACK BLADE

HarperCollins*Publishers*

HarperCollins*Publishers*
77–85 Fulham Palace Road
Hammersmith, London W6 8JB

Published by HarperCollins*Publishers* 1992
1 3 5 7 9 8 6 4 2

A catalogue record for this book
is available from the British Library

ISBN 0 00 223930 2

Set in Baskerville

Printed in Great Britain by
HarperCollinsManufacturing Glasgow

ACKNOWLEDGEMENTS

Washington unit:

Martha Pattillo Siv, The World Bank Library Data Center

Sichan Siv, Deputy Assistant for Public Information to the President of the United States

Mya Shaw (Molly) Shin, attorney for the Library of Congress

Sue Anna Brown, Collins Australia, for research on Lightning Ridge and Australian opal prospecting

Kerry Sharkey-Miller and Ray Tracey, for introducing me to their love of American Indian culture

Tomomi Seki, the Ronin Gallery, for Japanese translations and advice

Virgil England, master armourer, for the design for Suma's flail

Bob Kunikoff, Mark Allan Travel, for character travel arrangements

Sara Davison, Director, South Fork Shelter Island Chapter of the Nature Conservancy

Thank you to:

My wife, Victoria, for tireless editorial assistance, above and beyond

Kate Medina, for all her expertise, editorial and otherwise

My father, for stellar proofing

Everyone at Collins Australia and New Zealand, for inspiration. I love you!

This is for Victoria
And
The Piranhas & W.A.

A shrine: here, keeping
far from the garden lights,
float wild birds, sleeping.
Shiki

The strongest poison ever known
came from Caesar's laurel crown.
William Blake

The Shrine

Tokyo/New York

The Water-spider traversed the small, still pond, moving from rock to rock without a sound or even a sensation of motion. The emergence of the Water-spider from out of the blue winter shadows on the far side of the pond was beautiful to behold – and quite terrible.

The flat, grey rocks were covered in moss, brown and crunchy at this time of the year, but the Water-spider seemed to disturb the living nap not at all.

The pond was in a small but exquisitely composed garden around which, on all sides, the steel skyrises of Tokyo loomed like a futuristic forest. There were two people in the garden: a man dressed in a dark-grey chalk-stripe suit, black loafers, thin gold wristwatch; and a woman in a silk kimono. The man stood near the side of a muscular boulder, at the crest of a small knoll covered with sleeping azalea. Behind him, and to the right, the woman in the silk kimono knelt, head bowed, snow-white hands folded obediently in her lap, her eyes closed as if in the same hibernal slumber that gripped the azalea. Before her sat a black lacquer tray with the ingredients for the *chado*, the formal tea ceremony. The kimono that wrapped her in lush comfort was a silver that smouldered in the wan sunlight. It was embroidered with phoenixes, their red and black plumage quivering whenever she stirred.

Leave it to Nishitsu to have a beautiful woman at his side at all times, the Water-spider thought.

Naoharu Nishitsu was a trim, well-muscled man in his early sixties with a neat moustache, shaggy eyebrows and an iron disposition. The iris of his right eye was entirely white, not milky-white, as one sometimes saw in blind people, but a lustrous hue similar to that of a pearl.

Beyond Nishitsu and his female companion, in the tatami room that looked out on this improbable urban glade, dark-suited, sun-glassed men prowled, no doubt illegally armed, with the glowering faces of all professional goons. Nishitsu was never without a set of bodyguards, even here at Forbidden Dreams, where his word was law.

It was said that this man never raised his voice, but then again he had no need to; his anger could manifest itself in such a palpably physical

11

way. While it was true that this was part of Nishitsu's frightening mien, it was also true that he possessed an intensity that was best equated to a gathering of gravity around the energy of a black hole.

'You summoned me, and I have come,' the Water-spider said as he came to rest in front of Nishitsu. His name was Mizusumashi Kafu, his given name meaning 'water-spider', but he was known to his friends and enemies as Suma. He had the face of a predatory raptor, a creature beyond the bounds of gravity, whose scars came from wind and salt and sun. His hatchet face was crowned by salt-and-pepper hair and, below that, heavy brows, eyes that seemed more like holes in his flesh because they never appeared to move. And yet they took in everything in his immediate environment.

Suma was dressed in black slacks, shoes with paper-thin soles, a black form-fitting T-shirt that displayed his sculpted torso. The extraordinary thing about him was how well he masked the sense of menace that was, at times, so tangible as to be painful. Perhaps this had something to do with his size, so small, even for a Japanese. In all ways he had used his lack of size as an advantage, and it was Nishitsu's opinion that the Water-spider embraced his smallness because it had about it a vaguely feminine cast. The Water-spider had that rare confluence of *koha* – an eagerness to experience the spiritual tests of manhood – and *ninkyo* – a personal code of honour. *Ninkyo* was wholly unlike the Western definition of justice, which was impersonal, objective; rather it depended solely on his relationships within the Black Blade Society.

Tea was forthcoming, the ritual long, complex, and relaxing for the two men because it acknowledged more profoundly than any words the respect they had for one another. Though the Water-spider was not a man comfortable with social amenities, nevertheless he, like Nishitsu, relished the ceremonies of respect. Also, he could appreciate the deft, precise manner in which the woman made the tea, served it, folded herself like a stunning origami, silent, waiting for their cups to empty so she, unbidden, could refill them. He envied Nishitsu this woman; her there-not-there attitude rare in these modern times.

'The Toshin Kuro Kosai – the Black Blade Society – welcomes you back to its bosom, Suma-san.' Nishitsu put down his cup.

Suma inclined his head just a fraction lower than Nishitsu's, all that was required to show his obeisance. 'You summoned me,' he said. 'Something has happened.'

'Something, indeed,' Nishitsu said.

What outsider would believe the power secreted within this shrine like the ghost of a whisper? Nishitsu thought. The Toshin Kuro Kosai

12

– the Black Blade Society – hidden away from the world at large, was protected, as we gifted people at its hub, busily spinning our webs of power, schemed in shadows the conquest of the world.

No one would believe it, of course, which is our ultimate strength. No interference, and none to oppose us.

But, even for us, it seems, times change. Once, we had so much time – far more than a mere human lifetime – to formulate the perfect plan to stretch the wings of our influence to the ultimate, unimaginable to minds more limited than ours.

But now Time – a finite boundary whose leash we had traditionally slipped – has become a factor, a hideous spectre stalking us as if we were mere mortals. The implications were appalling. All our dreams, built in darkness for decades, would crumble to so much dust as Time's great scythe cut us down.

None of this, of course, was told to Suma. What Nishitsu said was, 'Suma-san, it appears as if we need the benefit of your skills in America.'

There was a humming in the air, as of cicadas, but this was wintertime and there were no insects. In a moment, Nishitsu became aware that the humming was emanating from Suma.

'You have only to ask,' the Water-spider said.

'The task is complex,' Nishitsu said, 'and may take several months.'

'All the better,' Suma said. He looked as if he were licking his chops.

'There is one caveat,' Nishitsu said. 'You will need to coordinate with an agent already in place.'

Suma frowned. 'This is not my agreed-upon methodology.'

'Different times dictate different methodologies,' Nishitsu said firmly. 'It is our duty to adapt as the willow adapts to the changing weather.'

'*Hai!*' Suma bowed. 'I understand.'

'I truly hope so,' Nishitsu said, 'because the storm is upon us. Circumstances beyond our control have dictated that we enter into our final stage, and every step we make now is critical.'

'I will not fail you, Nishitsu-san.'

'No,' Nishitsu said, looking at the Water-spider's bowed head. 'I do not think you will.'

Lawrence Moravia was lying on carpet that cost more than many people's yearly salary. That was okay with him, because he saw it as a symbol, one of many he collected like a legion of personal guards. A billionaire, he felt strongly that he had a duty to help keep in business the shrinking number of true artisans and artists left in the world.

13

As a self-made billionaire he had learned that having so much money forced you out of the mainstream of everyday life. People, unattractive and venal, beautiful and predatory, were attracted to the scent of money the way a bear is to honey. He supposed they couldn't help it; like Pavlov's dogs, they were highly programmed, hooked on the junk of wealth.

He had dealt effectively with these sharks, just as he had dealt with the changing face of his business, which was commercial real estate development. Of all of New York's super-developers, Lawrence Moravia alone had had the foresight in the runaway eighties to salt away huge contingency funds for what he foresaw would be lean times at the beginning of the nineties. No party ever lasts, was the first and only rule drummed into him by the man who had taught him the urban real estate business.

While every other developer was either living on a shoestring or testing the waters of bankruptcy court, Moravia continued to make money.

Money. It was so easy to say money didn't matter when you had so much you couldn't possibly spend it all in this lifetime or, the way it continued to amass, possibly even the next. But, several years ago, the fact had become clear to him that what he was doing no longer lit a fire under him.

In the end, that was what had made the proposal so intriguing, because he could see right away that what he would be involved in would deliver the excitement he craved. And he could see their point: he was the perfect man for the job they had in mind. He was a man with an innocuous business, who had spent many years in Japan, spoke the language fluently, had made many contacts and friends over here, had used Japanese production and marketing techniques and so was fully versed in the Japanese mind. He was also rich enough to attract the attention of the right people in Tokyo and, thus, gain an invitation to Forbidden Dreams.

And, of course, the kicker was that he already knew Naoharu Nishitsu, the leader of Japan's all-powerful and incredibly wealthy Liberal Democratic Party. The two had had a number of business dealings that had helped make Moravia rich and which had given Nishitsu access to certain contacts in New York, where these days he often found it difficult to conduct business.

Nishitsu was apparently more than he seemed; was, in fact, the key into the world Moravia was meant to investigate clandestinely. It was proposed that he become a spy; an offer he found utterly irresistible.

Besides, he felt no compunction about conspiring to bring Nishitsu down. Nishitsu had destroyed so many people it was no longer possible to keep a body count. And, beyond that, through his control of the political climate of the country, he had warped the lives of countless others without their ever becoming aware of it.

Nishitsu had a secret life, just as Moravia himself did, and now Moravia had been charged with unearthing those secrets. Dangerous work, undoubtedly, but all the more exhilarating because of it.

Moravia watched now as a beautiful Japanese woman, almost a girl, yes, but not quite, brought over a refill of his drink. She had done this without him asking. That was the Japanese way, one of the reasons why he had been so drawn to Japan as a young man.

As she sat, naked, beside him in the tiny, windowless room, she became another piece of art with which this room was furnished. She was smiling that sincere but empty smile that was the symbol of modern-day Japan; he considered in what ways she reminded him of that first Japanese girl he had met in New York, when he was a young man. She had been so fresh-faced and, in the arena of sex, so willing to do anything he wished. She had beguiled him, luring him back to Japan, and she had almost convinced him to marry her. But just in time, he had backed out and, since then, he had never considered marriage again.

Once, he had imagined it was his great wealth that was an impediment to a lasting relationship with a woman. Now he knew better. It was his secret life, the one that opened up for him at night like a poppy, whose kiss could bring all his delicious dreams alive. And there was no better place than Tokyo for him to indulge his appetite for sexual excess.

He picked up the red silk cord, wound it around his hand. He tugged gently at it, and the woman, the other end of the cord tied around her ankle, was pulled closer to him. He got up and, stepping away from the comfort of the sofa, brought her over to the restraint of a hard, armless ladderback chair. He jerked on the silk cord, and she straddled the chair, facing the back.

He knelt, tied first one ankle, then the other to the chair legs. Now he began the most enjoyable work, using other lengths of silk cord. When he was finished, she was bound around neck, wrists, waist, breasts, across eyes and open mouth in a kind of complex puzzle of tight loops and knots that, in concert with her smooth, firm flesh created a kind of artwork, a living sculpture that was as aesthetically pleasing as it was sexually arousing.

Her helplessness – and her enjoyment of that helplessness – was an irresistible erotic magnet to Moravia. He stood, naked himself, with his

15

hands on her shoulders, knowing that she could not move even if she wanted to. Of course, she did not want to.

His hands slid down her bound back, caressing her flanks, then gripping her pelvis. His knees bent until he was at the correct height, then, pulling on the tightly bound cords, he entered her.

She gasped through the silk, her head falling back onto his chest, sightless and, therefore, feeling him all the more deeply. But this kind of heightened pleasure could not last long, and it was over for both of them too quickly. Well, he thought, gripping her hard-nippled breasts, there would be more to come after his requisite interval of rest and recovery – he knew that she was ready to go on now.

Moravia, just returned from his latest trip to Tokyo, was assaulted by memories of his last night there, spent with a girl named Evan. In all ways, he realized, he had just now attempted to duplicate his inchoate coupling with the extraordinary Evan. Together, they had celebrated his new-found endurance well into the small hours of the morning. It was only when he had finally been sated, that a discreet knock at the *fusuma* had announced the arrival of Naoharu Nishitsu.

Moravia had noticed that, as Nishitsu passed her, Evan bowed so low her forehead touched the tatami, just as if Nishitsu had been the Shogun of feudal Japan. When she raised her head, Moravia signed to her to close the *fusuma*. Much to his annoyance, she had looked to Nishitsu for confirmation of this command. A minute incline of his head, and she shut the sliding door.

The incongruity of the situation had not been lost on Moravia: Nishitsu, the traditionalist, in neat Western suit and tie, and he, a Westerner, in traditional silk kimono.

Nishitsu had turned that eerie opaline eye on Moravia and they went through the ritual of a formal greeting. Evan brought tea. Though it was not green tea and had not been hand-whisked to a froth, Nishitsu nevertheless gracefully accepted a cup.

'Moravia-san, my friend,' he said, when the tea had been drained and Evan had refilled their cups, 'my apologies for disturbing your relaxation, but it has been put to me that in a few days it will be your birthday.'

'This is true, Nishitsu-san,' Moravia said, using the most respectful syntax. 'But I am amazed that such an insignificant event would be of interest to you.'

Nishitsu had sat as still and erect as a toy soldier. The teacup was lost in the palms of his calloused hands. Hands that, if one were any kind of a student of Japan, it was apparent had been assiduously exercised for years on karate's wood, stone, metal and hot sand practice stations.

'As you must be aware,' Nishitsu had said, 'markers of time passing

16

have great significance for us. And what more important marker is there than the day of one's birth. We will have a night of celebration.'

Moravia bowed, very pleased indeed. 'Thank you, Nishitsu-san.'

Nishitsu gave the smallest of bows, then rose, and exited the room, leaving the atmosphere charged with the residue of his presence.

And what a celebration his last night in Tokyo had been! Evan had only been the appetizer. He had been wined and dined by Nishitsu and some of the inner circle of Forbidden Dreams. Then, when the sky was turning from pink-black to nacre, the other members of their party either departed or dead drunk, Nishitsu had pulled him to his feet, saying, 'The celebration is not yet over, Moravia-san.'

He and Nishitsu had wrapped themselves in overcoats and had gone out into Tokyo proper. A taxi was waiting for him, its automatic doors opened for him and he climbed in. Half-drunk, he had turned to see Nishitsu standing at the kerb.

'Aren't you coming?'

'Not this time.' Nishitsu had given him a rare smile. 'Enjoy yourself, Moravia-san. Happy birthday!'

The doors closed and they took off. The wind, whipping in through the partially opened windows, began to revive him, so that by the time they slid to a stop he felt more himself.

He exited the taxi, saw he was in a warehouse district near the Sumida. The smell of fish was very strong, great lights burnishing the newly coloured sky just beyond the warehouse rooftops, and he assumed he was near Tsukiji, Tokyo's mammoth fish market.

There was a woman waiting for him at the entrance to a warehouse. One lone bare bulb dropped gold light at her feet.

'Lawrence-san.'

He walked towards the woman, recognizing her now. 'Minako-san.' She was a beautiful woman of indeterminate age, whom Nishitsu had introduced him to one night perhaps a year ago at a glittering restaurant high above the Ginza. She seemed unattached and curious about getting to know an American first-hand. He had been flattered, and, in the manner of the Japanese, they had become friends. There had been no sex but, rather, the comfort of trust far from home.

Minako laughed when she saw his bewildered face. 'Poor Lawrence-san,' she said, 'being led from temple pillar to gatehouse post.' She took his arm companionably, led him into the warehouse. 'How has your birthday celebration been?'

'Memorable,' he had murmured.

'Good. Then we mustn't disappoint you now.'

They went up in a gigantic steel and chrome elevator, the servos

17

almost silent. He could smell oil and disinfectant, and wondered where he was.

The elevator deposited them on the third floor, and Minako took him down a hallway smelling of sawdust and hot machinery.

In a room rather smaller than he had expected in such a structure, he saw a matte-black cube on a dolly. Unaccountably, he was reminded of an illustration he had once seen of Humpty Dumpty sitting on his wall.

The cube was set with all manner of interfaces and a kind of LED panel in front.

'Lawrence-san,' Minako said, 'I would like you to meet the Oracle.' With that, she pressed a miniature remote in her hand, and, as if at the unseen behest of a prestidigitator, the Oracle came to life.

'GREETINGS, MORAVIA-SAN,' came a voice that undoubtedly emanated from the matte-black cube. 'I HAVE AWAITED THIS MOMENT FOR SOME TIME.'

Moravia had tried not to look startled. Out of the corner of his eye he could see a tiny smile curl Minako's pressed-together lips. Then he grunted, annoyed at his momentary discomfort. 'It's some kind of recorded tape.'

'I MUST CORRECT THAT SURMISE,' the Oracle said. 'ALTHOUGH I AM EQUIPPED TO TAPE CONVERSATIONS AND PLAY THEM BACK ON REQUEST.'

Moravia stared at the thing, trying to fathom it. But, in truth, he was struggling to understand the unknowable.

He had walked towards it. 'Tell me more about this thing,' he said to Minako.

The Oracle supplied the answer. 'I WAS CREATED FROM A COMBINATION OF HEURISTIC NEUROLOGIC CIRCUITS AND AN ENTIRELY NEW TECHNOLOGY CALLED LAPID. LAPID IS AN ACRONYM FOR LIGHT WAFER/PRISM GATE IMAGE DATA. IN OTHER WORDS – '

'Enough!' Minako said sharply, then smiled. 'These explanations are wearisome to everyone but the most fervid scientists.'

Moravia took another step forward, peered into the face of the cube. 'But what *are* you?'

'JUST WHAT YOU ARE THINKING,' the Oracle said. 'A LIFE FORM.'

Out of the silence that ensued, Moravia said, '*I* am a life form. You are not.'

'I SUPPOSE WE CAN ASSUME THAT YOU NO LONGER BELIEVE YOU ARE CONVERSING WITH AN AUDIO TAPE MACHINE.'

Moravia didn't know whether to laugh in secret joy or at his own cupidity. He stared, silent, at the Oracle.

'IN ANY CASE, IT SEEMS CLEAR WE *ARE* HAVING A CONVERSATION,' the Oracle said pleasantly.

18

'A conversation, yes.'

'WITH WHAT?'

Moravia, stupefied at being outwitted by the Oracle, could not bring himself to utter a sound.

'ARE YOU TALKING TO A ROCK, A TREE, A BLADE OF GRASS, MORAVIA-SAN? HAVE YOU LOST YOUR MIND, PERHAPS?'

'Don't be ridiculous,' Moravia had said before he could stop himself. He bit his lip, his face dark with the implications of this discussion.

'I AM A LIFE FORM,' the Oracle said.

'But you aren't *life*,' Moravia had said. 'You have no living tissue or organs inside you.'

'I THINK. THEREFORE I AM,' the Oracle said with simple but profound logic. 'BUT, IN ANY CASE, YOU ARE WRONG HERE, TOO, MORAVIA-SAN. THE LAPID TECHNOLOGY DEVISED FOR ME CONTAINS A QUANTITY OF HUMAN DNA, WHICH I CONTINUE TO BREAK DOWN AND ANALYSE. SO, YOU SEE, I *DO* HAVE LIFE AS YOU KNOW IT INSIDE ME.'

'Fluttering like a butterfly inside a belljar,' Moravia had said softly.

'What?' Minako said, because she hadn't heard.

'PRECISELY,' the Oracle said, because it had.

Now Moravia did smile. 'So,' he said, standing before the black cube as forcefully as a sumo, 'what is it you think you can do for me?'

'WHAT YOU WANT HAS ALREADY BEEN DONE,' the Oracle said with the air of a mischievous child.

And now here he was back in New York, a spy in amber, clinging to deliciously warm flesh, awaiting his master's call, making the best of his down time. Unwittingly, Nishitsu had opened the doors to an inner sanctum, and Moravia had absorbed all the information he could. And still there had been more! So much, in fact, that he had sent a coded fax demanding a face-to-face debriefing. This was a dangerous precedent, certainly, and against the strict regulations that had been explained to him upon his recruitment, but, he felt, justified given the extraordinary nature of his latest information on the Oracle.

That was when he felt something, surely no more than a shadow, fall across the periphery of his vision. It was akin to the sensation one experiences falling asleep during the day and awakening at night. Perhaps he felt the prick of a needle, but if so it seemed dull and far away, nothing to do with him.

His eyes, hooded and dulled in the aftermath of sex, made out only a vague darkness, as if, out swimming in deep water, he had been abruptly pulled downwards into a darkness, thicker and more silent than he could imagine.

He awoke, dizzy and sick to his stomach. He had sampled enough drugs in his lifetime to know that something very powerful was swimming in his veins. He tried to struggle against it, but it was no use.

He turned his head, noticed with a dull surprise that he was no longer at home, but had been taken to his office. Abducted – but surely one was not abducted to a place one already owned.

Becoming aware of movement, he turned his head again, was rewarded by a slosh of vectors, a wobbling of direction and dimension. He *was* going to be sick. He gagged, tried to puke, but he lacked the strength even for that. It was a wonder the air was going in and out of his lungs.

He saw someone swimming like a manta towards him. 'Who –?' Great wings undulating, wicked barbed tail fluttering, up, down, up, down. Moravia tried to scream, then, but there was something stuck in his throat – no, his mouth, filled with soft cotton, so much he could not bite down. He tried to get it out, gagged reflexively again, could not manage to budge it.

'How does it feel now?' a voice said – male? female? he couldn't tell. 'To be helpless.'

Moravia closed his eyes, tried to use some of his new-found strength, vitality, endurance to break whatever interior bonds were holding him fast, but succeeded only in accelerating his heartbeat to the point where the muscle began to pain him. He squinted up at the manta's terrifying, amorphous shape, blinking again and again to clear his vision.

'Here, let me help you.' Lifted like a baby, head cradled in a lap. 'Do you want to know who I am, Moravia? Then I'll tell you, just like I tell all of them.' All of who? Moravia thought dazedly. 'Every morning I pray to the gods for enlightenment, because enlightenment breeds success. There are those who would tell me that the gods will spurn me because I am unclean, stained as I am by blood spilled at my own hands. To them I say, let the gods do what they may – I have no control over what they may think or do. But I will not cease my prayers; in that, I am pure.' A hand tenderly stroked his cheek. 'And I am right, Moravia, because I have known nothing but success.'

He was rocked as he had been when he was a child. 'This is all that I am, what I have just told you. The rest is just a gloss, two arcs of rouge brushed into the cheeks before performing the important occasions in one's life – ' A brush, delicate as a butterfly's passage, against one cheekbone then another '– One's birthday, perhaps . . . or one's death.'

Lips, soft as butter, cold as a dewdrop, pressed against his, and then something as concrete as a fist had seized his heart, clamping down on it with the strength of a god.

Moravia screamed – or, rather, struggled to scream. His mind, shredding like clouds before a chill north wind, commanded him to scream, but nothing appeared to work. There was only the pain, and now a pressure – inside out, insupportable – that stilled, one by one, every element inside his helpless form that pumped, sighed, pulsed and, finally, thought.

BOOK I

Inbetween Days

Three can keep a secret,
if two of them are dead.
Benjamin Franklin

ONE

New York City

On a night when thick, ugly clouds hunkered across the full moon of late February, Wolf Matheson was crouched on a rubble-strewn rooftop six storeys above the fetid swamp of East Harlem.

It had been a long run, nearly seven weeks, longer than he'd ever been on a case, but now, on this dank, malodorous night Wolf was certain he had run his quarry down, just as he had brought to justice the three other serial killers whose cases had been handed to him by Hayes Walker Johnson, the commish, a year ago when he had appointed Wolf head of the NYPD's Special Homicide Task Force. The Werewolves, as the force was quickly dubbed out of a mixture of respect and fear inside the department, was an elite unit created specifically 'to direct' Wolf's talent for tracking down the worst form of psychotic murderer who could, from either guile or utter randomness, sometimes, God help them all, a combination of the two, otherwise frustrate whole divisions of overworked city detectives.

Wolf had first come to the commish's attention when he solved the murders of two prostitutes – a mother and daughter. The savagery of their particular deaths was grisly enough to get the attention of even the most jaded street bull but, typical of the overworked department, nothing was done until a tourist – more or less the same age as the demised daughter – was offed with the same MO. Prostitutes were so much street fodder, but a tourist was, after all, a tourist, and still represented the lifeblood of a city stumbling, without the knowledge of those who ran it for their own benefit, straight from first world to third world status. The swiftly following meeting with the publicity-minded Hayes Walker Johnson, as canny a black politician as ever held the office of commissioner, confirmed what Wolf already knew: the case had become a top priority.

Trouble was no one had a clue as to where to start the search for the killer. But Wolf, at the end of that long day of visiting the scene of the second crime, lying alone in his bed, had known. Watching the flickering streetlight, which in this city passed for starlight, seep through his bedroom skylight, he had slowly closed his eyes, but not into darkness.

Within the pellucid red glow of an inner heat he had seen the face of the murderer, could smell his sourish stench, sense his peculiar tread as light as a dancer's, had felt the insistent demand – as debilitating as the pressure of an abscess – of alien voices just as he had known the murderer did.

How he knew these things he could not say. But he found his murderer within seventy-two hours and, although already a lieutenant of some wide renown throughout the five boroughs of New York City, Wolf was instantly thrust into a media spotlight, arranged to promote the commish. The Special Homicide Task Force was a direct result of the publicity fallout of the successful conclusion of the case. The commish had had to do something visible with his hero – in fact, to be perfectly fair, he had *wanted* to reward Wolf in some special way for sending his Q-rating – his recognition among the populace – soaring.

The nuts and bolts of forming the unit had given Wolf time to think about his bizarre talent which, considered in the new light of his rapid advancement, must have been with him in some form or other all his life.

Now, alone on the rooftop, waiting for his quarry to emerge into the darkness, Wolf crouched as still as one of those stone gargoyles guarding the rich, safe in their oversized pre-war apartments on the West Side. It was nearly four in the morning, that time when all colour had drained out of the city, a time when he and his quarries existed, listening to the cacophony of voices and acting on their cries.

His tour of duty would not be over until he brought in his man, or one of them was dead. A far cry from his childhood games of hide-and-seek, his favourite because he had never lost. Or was it?

He was on the edge of El Barrio, a burned-out, festering canker that was nominally a part of New York City but which might just as well have been a section of Calcutta for all its resemblance to any place in the modern metropolis that contained Bloomingdale's and St Patrick's Cathedral.

Swirling precipitation littered the sky. In another, less inimical clime it might have been snow, but here it had picked up so many kinds of noxious hydrocarbons on its way down that the waxy flakes disintegrated on contact with the ancient iron and the pot-holed macadam.

Nothing much was happening on the pavement below him. Sirens rose and fell streets – worlds – away, dogs barked, skirmishing with the homeless for scraps of food in the piles of litter along the gutters. Garbage-can fires burned here and there, huddled shapes bent over them, surrounded by supermarket carts piled high with scrounged junk. Further away, a razed lot had been turned into a permanent

26

reservation of cardboard tents, their lopsided, conical shapes throwing shadowy fingers into the clogged gutter. An old man, bare feet as white as maggots under the fizzing sodium lights, picked his way through the broken green glass that served as the reservation's border. Spying a rat in his path, he hawked and spat a thick gob of phlegm, guffawing as the rat went tumbling back into the darkness. A pieced-together black Firebird waited at a No Loading zone, its exhaust rumbling softly. Opposite, an old souped-up Chevy with stylized flames painted on its sides revved, then roared away from the kerb, adding to the stink of the night air.

Somewhere within that jungle of iron and fire his men, Bobby Connor and Junior Ruiz, were hidden. In the specifics of his job Wolf worked alone, but he always had backups in the immediate environment in the event his quarry outran the perimeter of his own personal defence – or, of course, killed him. With men such as those he had been given a mandate to find, one was obliged to consider all the worst possibilities.

Wolf did not need to look at his watch. Time had become insubstantial, irrelevant; he was living inbetween days: immersed in the inner language used by his quarries as they went about trying to make sense of a disordered and dysfunctional universe.

This time his quarry was a Colombian named Chucho Arquillo, a major player in narcotics bought from the Cali Cartel, and arms which he had cleverly siphoned out of US military bases. Had Arquillo graduated out of big-time conduit to big-time assassin, or had he simply gone stone loco? This was a question, though intriguing, not sufficiently central to the problem of locating him and bringing him in, so that while Wolf had turned it over in his mind like a crystal, its facets had remained opaque; much like the enigma of his own talent for unearthing the whereabouts of the city's most unappetizing – and dangerous – denizens.

There was no set *time* when Arquillo would appear; he would come when he would come, and Wolf would sense his approach. As always, after he had identified his quarry, Wolf knew the identity of Arquillo's next victim. There was a synchronicity between victim and murderer, he had found, as if the stalker was somehow able to tap into the life pulse of the victim – as unique as an individual's fingerprints – and match his own pulse to the other, identifying in some way with the victim, with what was to come, the cessation of breath, sound, heat: life.

Wolf closed his eyes, thought he could sense both Bobby and Junior, although in truth he couldn't be sure, and wondered not for the first time whether his talent was genuine – or merely some form of eerie parlour trick beyond his ken.

'Kill you, *maricone!*'

Wolf turned his head towards the barked shout, the movement in

27

the street below, saw a squat Puerto Rican with a barrel chest running after a lithe young man, skin so black it glistened like oil in the light reflected off the rutted pavement. The two men raced diagonally across the street, through the sulphurous steam billowing up through an iron manhole cover and out the other side, around the black Firebird. In their wake, laughter rather than concern over the murderous intent from the spectators who lived in this Brechtian theatre, who had nowhere else to go when the curtain came down on the last act.

Wolf felt something, as of a puff of wind inside his mind, as he became aware of Arquillo. He heard the *snik!* of the gravity blade. Even though it came from very close at hand, he did not turn his head; he had the vivid premonition that, as with a shark that had tasted blood, any movement on his part would result in the commencement of an attack with which he could not effectively deal.

Arquillo was crouched behind him, a big man, muscular, with a sense of subliminal menace that, like an ocean's tide reducing cliffs to boulders and thence to the rubble of sand, caused in those close to him the surge of primeval fear.

Arquillo crept towards Wolf's back, secure in his safety in the shadows of the roof, the stealth of his attack. Wolf felt the murderous intent as Arquillo leaned forward, tongue licking dry lips.

Wait, Wolf whispered to himself. *Wait.*

At the last instant, he spun, already in a crouch, and there was Arquillo in motion, handsome moustachioed face like a bull, with the square shoulders and majestic bearing of a matador, lunging towards his kidneys.

Everything and everyone else was still. Wolf was acutely aware of a suspension of the snow swirling, the bonfires in the reservation of New York's damned, the hiss of traffic over slick pavement, the continuing altercation that might possibly be resolved by murder, the bark of a dog denied its meagre scavenged meal.

In the slowness of time came magnification. Wolf swung to the side, saw Arquillo's face distorted by hatred and the killing effort. He saw his own reflection miniaturized in a bead of sweat hanging at the end of Arquillo's sideburn.

Then from stillness, there was motion. An instant before the point of the knifeblade would have punctured his flesh, Wolf's right elbow crashed into Arquillo's forearm. For a time, they were locked in an almost immovable struggle, veins popping, hearts pumping desperately, lunging, surging with inhalation and exhalation, muscles knotted, pitted one against the other, as bull and matador, in the end, come together, locked in a dance of death. The viscous snow whirled down all the harder,

28

hanging from his brows and eyelashes, tasting of iron and cinders, and then he gritted his teeth, applied the last ounce of leverage he could manage. In that next heartbeat, the sharp, sickening crack as the radius, then the ulna splintered.

Arquillo's handmade gravity knife, with which he had disembowelled three effete men – the mules of a rival drug dealer? Ex-lovers? Or the connection between the four something unfathomable except in madness? – lay on the dark rooftop empty of menace, as innocent as a child's finger. Arquillo slammed the heel of his good hand into the bridge of Wolf's nose with sickening impact.

Wolf took off after Arquillo, thinking of alerting Bobby and Junior via his throat mike, but changing his mind as he swung open the metal door to the roof, listened for five seconds, gauging distance and direction of his quarry's flight, took the iron stairs three at a time. Selfish of him to want Arquillo himself, but there was something undeniably *intimate* between the two of them now, the stealthy approach, the slow dance of death on the rooftop a personal challenge, that swing at the kidneys the slap in the face that signals the intent to duel, an affair of honour now. The killing effort on Arquillo's face etched into Wolf's memory; the dark pupils fixed on death was what Wolf imagined those three effete men had seen in the instant before Arquillo had taken their lives.

The girl Arquillo had been after this time lived on the fourth floor, in a half-abandoned apartment, scoured by fire, more suited to the rats and roaches that nested in its darkest corners. And yet, Wolf had discovered earlier tonight, this girl had three mattresses stuffed with cash, nothing smaller than fifty-dollar bills. Evidence that Arquillo wasn't stone loco, but was motivated by business concerns? Perhaps. But then why didn't he hire someone to off the competition; why take the risk of doing the wet work himself? Unless it kicked him into gear.

Wolf hit the door to the girl's apartment at a run, the wood not giving him as much resistance as the awful stench within of a graveyard overturned by an army of bodysnatchers. His eyes watered as profusely as if someone had thrown formaldehyde in his face.

He heard the girl screaming and he thought: this is what Arquillo wanted, to kill her after he had warned me of his presence. Once again, he did not know how he knew this, did not question the truth of it. And just how Arquillo had become aware of him was another question to ponder, after Arquillo had been taken into custody. It was discomfiting, to say the least, for the watcher to be made aware that he had become the watched.

Like a hound he could smell the blood, thick and cloying, like confetti at New Year's. The taste filled his mouth, making him want to gag. He went swiftly from room to room, dizzy with a surfeit of stenches and the mirror of the girl's imminent death held up to him by Arquillo, as if the bastard knew – how *could* he know? – of the link that drew Wolf to him as surely as sonar brings a destroyer to a submarine.

Rotting burlap, used to keep the cold out of a heatless apartment, slapped dolefully, like the fitful thrashing of a child with night terrors. Wolf rounded a corner, saw the thin cocoa hand, fist, really, clutching burlap to bring it down or the body that belonged to it up.

He became aware of a rhythmic sound, as of an engine labouring beneath a load too great for it, but there was an obscene quality to it that he recalled from rookie days patrolling sleazy peep-shows on Eighth Avenue, cheap plywood floor and walls sticky with ejaculate and Vaseline.

He was aiming for the body because a shot through the head would mean *finis* for them both, Wolf and Arquillo, because he very much wanted to take this one back alive, even knowing that it was pride that pricked him now like a thorn, a desire to drag this beast among miserable beasts into One Police Plaza like a trophy, and make of him if not a spectacle then at least an example for the other monsters out there.

He thought of the Romans then, great warriors, undefeatable in their heyday, with their massive shields, because Arquillo was using the girl, draped over him from shoulder to shin, in just that way. Arquillo's expression made him seem even more the bull. His lips were pulled back from his teeth, his breaths were coming in small, excited pants and his eyes had that look people get when they are engaged in a private act. His broken arm held the girl tight and, on his face, Wolf could see that surge of endorphins killing any pain he might feel from the pressure he was exerting on it. He didn't care about his own pain – he had other things on his mind.

Wolf hesitated – fatal because maybe, just maybe, he had had a split-second when Arquillo's right temple was exposed, and for a NYPD-certified sharpshooter like Wolf, a high percentage risk even in this low light. Then the girl, her face pale and pinched with pain and fear, moaned, and Wolf saw that she was exsanguinating.

How far had Arquillo gone with his butcher's work? It was impossible to say, but the moral dilemma facing Wolf was what if she had already lost so much blood that she would be DOA no matter what action he took, if he put his gun up, put three shots into the human shield at close range to get at least one bullet into Arquillo. But that kind of thinking would never do, no matter the circumstances.

Arquillo gave him a wide grin, just as if they had engaged in a hard-fought but friendly round of golf and, exposing a homemade hand

30

scythe formed from three razor blades, held the girl up by her hair, sliced right across her, throat-neck-spine, one-two-three, just like that, severing her head from the rest of her and, with a laugh, tossing it like a bloody ball at Wolf.

Blood all over him, Wolf leaped past the decapitated girl, reaching the window through which Arquillo had exited. He was on his way down, already two floors below on the rusty fire escape that ran along the tenement's spine like a scar that would never heal. Wolf moved, but this time he raised Bobby and Junior on the mike, gave them Arquillo's likely egress point from the building.

'*Got him!*' he heard Bobby's tinny voice from the receiver in his ear canal.

He was almost to the second storey when he heard the shots, a flurry of eruptions not so very out of place in this unquiet and unfriendly neighbourhood.

Wolf hit the pavement running, bent his shoe soles to the concrete of the garbage-piled alley. He rounded a corner, saw Bobby Connor kneeling over the prostrate form of Junior Ruiz, said, 'Shit!' under his breath, and then, when he recognized the blank look in Junior's eyes, said more loudly, 'Where is he?'

Bobby stood up. His hands were covered with Junior's blood. The two men looked as if they belonged in an abattoir. He pointed, mute with shock, to a corner of the alley. Wolf went across, kicked the body over. Chucho Arquillo's mahogany matador's face was covered with blood.

'Good work, Bobby,' he said.

'I – I didn't do anything, Lieutenant.'

Wolf, hearing some hoarse and semi-hysterical note, looked back at Bobby.

'What the hell is it?'

'Look,' Bobby said. Then, swallowing hard, 'Look at the bastard's face.'

Wolf turned back to Arquillo's corpse, the dark face made so familiar to him over the past seven weeks as it hung in his mind like a black moon. The blood still seemed to be bubbling out of wounds he could not see. He knelt, looked more closely. *Really* bubbling, as if with a terrific heat that emanated from the inside of Arquillo's body. He started. Had he seen the flicker of a flame dancing along the edge of the cheekbone? But, no, that was impossible. Still . . . He put a hand out, over the face, and felt a heat he could not explain.

Wolf stood up and, acknowledging Bobby's reluctance to approach Arquillo's corpse, came over to where he stood, shivering. Bobby, in his early thirties, broad-shouldered and strong, with an open Midwestern face, pale-blue eyes and sandy hair, looked like he could use several stiff drinks. Wolf put a steadying hand on his shoulder. 'Just tell me what happened here.'

He could see Bobby struggling to maintain his composure, said, 'If you're gonna be sick, do it, there's no shame in it.'

Bobby nodded, wiped the cold sweat from his brow, said a bit shakily, 'I'm all right, Lieutenant.' And, when Wolf nodded encouragement, began again. 'Junior and I saw Arquillo coming down and we identified ourselves. He was already in shadow. There's so much of it in here.' He shivered again as he looked around the black alley. 'Anyway, after Arquillo hit the ground everything seemed to happen at once, and I don't know – I'm not sure what happened. We both had our guns out. Junior fired first, and he thought he'd gotten him. He went into the shadows and I covered him. Then I heard two shots and Junior was thrown back almost into my face.' He stopped there, as if come to the end of his debriefing.

'And then you saw Arquillo,' Wolf prompted.

Bobby shook his head. 'I saw *something* but I don't know what it was. It was like a – I don't know – a fireball, a blue fireball. I heard a sizzle, smelled – Jesus, the smell was sickening. Then someone screamed – Arquillo, I'm sure, and he came staggering out of the blackness. One arm was hanging like it was broken, but the other hand was held to his face. His *burning* face.'

Bobby blew out air very fast as if by these hearty exhalations he could rid himself of the memory.

Wolf, thinking of the heat, the hint of a flame flickering along Arquillo's cheekbone at the periphery of his vision, said, 'I want you to think about this carefully, Bobby. Arquillo was on fire, is that right?'

Bobby looked at him. 'His face. Only his face.'

Sirens coming. Wolf could hear their familiar clamour even this far off. He said gently, 'Then what happened?'

'Then something went past me.'

'You mean someone.'

'Yeah, I guess. To be honest, Lieutenant, I don't know what the fuck it was. It was dark and thick.'

'Heavy, you mean.'

'No.' Bobby shook his head. 'Thick, like syrup, like a stew, filling the alley. It felt like it had suddenly got *darker* in here.'

A cold sensation began to wind itself like a viper through Wolf's belly. He used his mind to search the vicinity for a new aura, perhaps stronger even than Arquillo's, but there was nothing, not even a lingering

32

afterscent. The viper, already having been awakened, began to stir, coiling and uncoiling restlessly.

Bobby took another breath. 'Then the darkness lifted, like, and I turned, saw *someone* heading out of the alley. The guy – I guess it was a guy – had a car, Lieutenant. A black '87 Firebird. Pieced together, looked like shit beneath the shine. Someone was waiting for him to get by us.'

Wolf recalled seeing that car from his rooftop perch, part of the background environment in motion.

'Any description at all on this person, Bobby. Think now.'

'I have, Lieutenant, but I can't come up with anything. I mean, if I had to swear to it I wouldn't even know whether it was a man or a woman.' Bobby sighed. 'Got a partial on the licence, though.'

'That was great work.' Wolf appreciated Bobby's discerning eye, but he also recognized the young man's need for positive reinforcement now – not to mention his need to be busy. 'Get onto DMV now. Get them to clear the computers. Tell them to run the partial with your description of the car. I want an answer inside an hour.'

Then he knelt beside Junior Ruiz. Afterwards, Wolf would remember that Bobby's face was as pale and pinched as that of the girl Arquillo had decapitated. Toughminded and as loyal as any terrier, he had nodded, darted away into the sharp, acid-white false dawn made by the revolving lights of the blue-and-whites he – or maybe Junior, his last call in – had ordered up. The lights bloomed and faded like nuclear flowers born and dying in the same brief moment. At Wolf's shouted commands, the uniforms began to seal off the area, some of them trooping dispiritedly into the tenement to hit the crime scene and round up any witnesses. Even so engaged, they haphazardly broke windows, rousted drunks, and brought out their burnished nightsticks, mainly, he supposed, because they were bored, scared or both. They had a life, it was true, but it was another kind of life, unimaginable to civilians, where the fear of being a target filled the days and nights like decay fills a rotten tooth.

Through it all, Wolf still knelt, holding Junior Ruiz's wet head in his hands, keeping it raised even when the ME's men arrived, as if even in death his man needed protection from the street.

The Werewolves were headquartered in a run-down movie theatre in Chinatown that had shown a stultifying succession of cheap, racist Kung Fu films (the villains were invariably Japanese, scrutable, wholly evil) until a teen tong war, more violent than any of the films, had closed the place down.

Its decomposing exterior hunkered on the decayed thoroughfare of East Broadway like a ragged dog beneath the vibrating steel underside

33

of the Manhattan Bridge. There were large gaps now in the bridge, where girders had rusted away, leaving exposed timbers which were spirited away in the middle of the night to fuel the bonfires in the burgeoning communities of the homeless under the East River Drive and elsewhere around the city.

Wolf liked the anonymity of the location, although he had been somewhat surprised that he hadn't been afforded space at One Police Plaza, southwest of the theatre. In fact, Commissioner Hayes Walker Johnson had requested just such a spot, and the Werewolves would have been assigned a suite of offices there had it not been for the clandestine interference of Chief of Police Jack Breathard, who did not like Wolf or his swift accession into the stratosphere of the NYPD. Breathard saw Wolf as his one true rival in the department and, as such, deserving of every administrative snafu Breathard's Machiavellian brain could throw at him.

Seeing the interior of the dilapidated theatre for the first time, Wolf had decided to simply pull out all the seats, plywood over the rotting, threadbare carpeting and treat the space as if it were a loft, dividing off cubicles for each of his staff, providing a larger space near the front where the movie screen still hung, as glossy as the hair of a forties film noir heroine. The other walls, however, were still as dark as pitch with the spilled blood of young Chinese; Wolf's repeated requests for a paint crew were still being rerouted by Breathard.

After a necessary detour, it was to this odd office that Wolf and Bobby Connor headed when they had wrapped things up at the crime scene. By that time, DMV had got back to them. There was no match between the partial licence plate number and the black '87 Firebird. Naturally. Stolen plates. It was to be expected, but you needed to run down every lead.

Wolf and Bobby went to see Junior's wife and kid, and Bobby had watched mute and numb while Wolf held the sobbing woman in his arms and had gently rocked her. The kid, eight years old, had sat on a corner of the shiny couch, holding a baseball bat in his hands, saying nothing at all; Bobby had wondered what the kid might be thinking, maybe smashing in the side of their heads for taking his daddy away from him.

'This may not mean anything to you now, Maria,' Bobby overheard Wolf talking softly in idiomatic Spanish to Junior's widow. 'But your man was brave. He was doing something important, making his force felt on the street. That's something you'll be able to tell Julio when he's old enough to understand, and it will change his life.'

'I don't know how you do it, Lieutenant,' Bobby had said in the car, on their way to the theatre. 'I wouldn't't've known the right words to say.'

'Were they the right words, Bobby?' Wolf had stared straight through

34

the windshield, oblivious to Bobby's weaving in and out of early morning truck traffic. 'I'm glad you thought so.'

'Weren't they? You calmed her down.'

Wolf had made no move; it was this uncanny ability to lapse into utter stillness that often unnerved Bobby as it unnerved Wolf's quarries. 'I don't know any more whether I believed what I said or whether it was just bullshit.'

'But you were right what you said.'

Wolf, his mind on other matters – burning faces, the thickness of the dark, vipers uncoiling in his gut – said, 'Maybe, in time. But for right now the only thing that matters is that Junior's dead.'

Bobby had waited a moment, thinking as he steered around a newspaper van. 'No, Lieutenant,' he had said at last, 'what matters is that Junior's dead and his murderer is still at large.'

There was an overpowering sense of gloom at the office. Someone had thrown Junior Ruiz's photo up on the screen as a kind of memorial. He looked wide-eyed, considerably older than his twenty-nine years, and so serious you'd never know without having spent time with him how funny he could be. Wolf went to his cubicle, sat back in his metal-and-vinyl swivel chair and thought about just how much he despised his life.

When had he come to the conclusion that the city was no place for him: last week, last month or last year? He was sick of living in the soft yellow underbelly of a rotting metropolis, patrolling its filth-strewn byways inbetween days, his head filled with the monstrous voices of his quarry. My God, he wondered, how had a boy who had grown up in Elk Basin, Wyoming, got himself into this particular sewer? He closed his eyes. He knew why he had fled Elk Basin. The truth was he didn't want to think about it. The reality was he was here now and he damn well better decide what he was going to do about it. Live in the sewer all his life or . . . Or what?

'Lieutenant?' Bobby Connor's voice.

'Not now.'

Bobby backed off. Rank aside, there was something uniquely for-midable about Wolf Matheson, with his high-cheekboned face, straight, brushed-back hair and curiously shaped eyes the colour of cinnamon. Beyond anything physical, however, he possessed an intensity of – Bobby was not sure of the right word – stillness, maybe?, that set him apart from anyone else Bobby had come in contact with.

Wolf, his breathing slowed, deepened, had too much to think about. Such as who had killed Arquillo – and Junior Ruiz, for that matter? It was easy to say that in the dark Arquillo had wrestled Junior's piece from him and had shot him, but was that what had really happened?

35

Wolf, projecting himself back into the alley, Junior Ruiz's blood covering him, had, in fact, felt the residue of his slain man's aura like a teardrop left behind on a jilted lover's cheek. And he knew – *knew* – that Junior had not been shot by Arquillo.

Who, then, had taken his piece from him, turned it on him point-blank? Bobby's anthropomorphic shadow figure, thick as syrup, scary as shit.

· And who had been waiting for the shadow in that pieced-together black '87 Firebird? And how in the hell had this shadow managed to conceal its aura from him?

It was becoming clear to him – as it should have in the instant he had seen the blood bubbling as thick as syrup upon Arquillo's proud, mad matador's face – that this investigation was something more than any of his others.

He tried to think, but his mind was cluttered with images of the girl Arquillo had decapitated – not innocent, surely, but what sin was grievous enough to deserve such butchery? Images of Junior's eyes like copper pennies, already patinaed; images of his widow who had known – because every cop's wife waits for it, fears it – why he had appeared at her front door in the grim light before dawn. And, most vividly, images of the eerie fire that had come simmering up from inside Arquillo.

He had better listen to himself, the clutter a clear indication of how far this mystery was pushing his emotions around . . .

'*Here is your mind*' – held in one gnarled, weather-beaten hand. '*– And here is your body.*' The other hand held a forearm's span from the first.

The young Wolf had watched with a combination of fascination and dread as the old man had brought his two hands together. At first, they seemed to be moving so slowly, but at the end they came together so swiftly and with such a force that the resulting sound, as sharp, startling as a sudden thunderclap, had caused Wolf to jump. And, in the aftermath, the familiar jingling of the carved animals – bear, bison, hawk and wolf – on the old man's beaded bracelets.

The old man had smiled, as if he enjoyed startling his grandson. In the place where he dwelled, the smells, heady and pungent, of hide tanning into leather, the ashes of a fire, and herbal oils too exotic and complex for the child to identify, combined to make Wolf lightheaded.

The old man's smile had turned benevolent. '*You do not believe me. That is good. Belief in anything – especially yourself – can only come over time.*' He had reached out so that his thin, long fingers settled over Wolf's shoulders. They were strong, those fingers, and Wolf remembered their strength as he remembered few other things in his past.

'*Now settle yourself,*' his grandfather had said, fixing the boy in his

36

careful gaze. *'No. This way. Keep your back still, like that, yes, very still.'* He was a tall, handsome man and, though not particularly bulky, Wolf imagined him to be the largest man on earth. Perhaps the child was responding to the old man's aura, which was formidable. *'Now observe, soon you will cease to feel your body. In a moment, there is only your mind, gorged with the chaos of youth. Are you happy with this: running, running and never thinking? How could you be? Only in the stillness of thought can decisions be properly made. Think of a mountain or a tree, how still they are. When you become as still as a mountain or a tree you will at last be able to think.'*

It had taken the young Wolf a long time to understand what his grandfather had meant. Kineticism was such an integral part of his life – as it was his father's – Wolf always playing baseball, hide-and-seek, running races, seeing his endurance and strength multiply as he ran with the Wind River Shoshones on the marathon races so important to them, a reminder of a past they could no longer remember . . .

Wolf started, opening his eyes. Had he fallen asleep or was he still being haunted by the old man? Haunted by something, for certain.

'Matheson – '

Wolf stared up at the wide, black, moustachioed face of Jack Breathard, Chief of Police, and in Wolf's estimation, an exceedingly dangerous man. Breathard's small yellow eyes were as cold as a meat locker, though his wide mouth was smiling in that practised expression only those in media or comfortable with it could muster. Breathard, a big man by any standard you cared to name, loomed over Wolf like the ogre just slid down Jack's beanstalk.

'How's it goin'?'

'Going just fine, Chief.' This said neutrally but somewhat warily because Breathard was far too busy to waste his time with idle chatter.

'Heard you lost a man this morning, shot with his own service revolver.' His face had taken on the expression of a stern schoolmaster. 'That's not the kind of news we like to disseminate to the press.'

'I'll pass your rebuke on to Junior Ruiz's widow.'

Breathard's tree trunk arms went rigid as he leaned over, pressed his palms onto Wolf's desk. 'Now, look here, wise ass, I don't take shit like that from anyone, hear? Any time a man of mine is killed in the line of duty it's bad enough; killed with his own gun, stinks. You know my meaning. It makes us seem incompetent. We already have enough shit shovelled at us by civilians in the way of charges of brutality, racism, graft and protectionism, without this kind of crap.'

'I can see your point,' Wolf said while grinding his teeth.

'No, you fucking well can't, Mr Big-Shot-Bring-'Em-In-Dead-Or-Alive.' He lifted his hands off the desk, pointed a sausage-like forefinger at Wolf. 'You may be the Commissioner's fair-haired white boy, but you ain't mine. I got my eye on you, Matheson. I'm just waiting for you to fuck up so I can get you out of here, fill this place with my people. You got any of my people here?'

'You know Squire Richards works for me.'

'One.' Breathard lifted the forefinger, as if by this gesture he could test the tenor of the atmosphere. '*One* of my people on a staff that's how big?'

'Six, all told,' Wolf dutifully provided, though he knew damn well Breathard was the first to keep track of such things.

'One in six, Matheson, not a justifiable percentage of Afro-Americans. Not fucking justifiable at all.'

'I pick the best people, Chief, you know that.'

'I know that's the bullshit you put out, I know the commish buys it,' Breathard said. 'But I don't.' He nodded. 'I got two of my best people, Washington and White, just waiting to get in here, even out the odds.'

'I know them both,' Wolf said. 'One's failed his detective's exam twice; the other, I hear, was caught by his precinct captain shaking down store owners.'

'That's a lie. Honky shit – '

'Detective exam results are a matter of record,' Wolf said. 'And White's precinct commander is a friend of mine. I know who bullied him into burying the shake-down.' He leaned back in his chair. 'Besides, my manpower manifest is full.'

Breathard's yellow eyes darkened. 'Sure as shit, Matheson, something's gonna happen here, and when it does, I'm goin' to be the one who comes in, cleans up this mess.' He gave Wolf his best sneer. 'Who knows? Maybe this Ruiz fiasco's just what I've been looking for.'

He didn't wait for Wolf to reply, but turned on his heel and went out.

Wolf, watching Breathard's linebacker figure disappear into the theatre's haze, let his breath out in a hiss. He supposed the man, as corrupt as the mayor, the city council and all the rest of the macho politicos who ran the city, hated the fact that Wolf was directly responsible to Hayes Walker Johnson, the commish. Being out of the chain-of-command loop in this one instance didn't sit well with him.

His virulent racist leanings, needless to say, never made it up to the commish's or the mayor's level. With them, he was the very model of an impartial arbiter, the calm voice of reason. He was a cool customer. Like a moray eel, he would be passive, invisible for long stretches of time, until you just about forgot he existed. That's when he took his opportunity to pop up like a death's-head and tried to put the fear of God into you.

38

Wolf pushed himself away from the desk, stood. He found himself looking up into the larger-than-life face of Junior Ruiz up on the movie screen. 'Take that down,' he said sharply, because it was reminding him of how much there was left to do. Even after he had run Arquillo down, there was still the same shit to deal with, the ever multiplying amount of work. It never ended. On the contrary, it continued to grow like a cancer out of control and, for the first time, he found that idea intolerable.

The confluence of body and mind, the inner stillness necessary for both thought and action of consequence, began, for Wolf, with aikido. Being by nature kinetic he required a conduit for his energy, but he also needed a discipline so that he could discern the essential stillness within even the most violent burst of movement.

This discipline he found within aikido, a harmony of mind and body control that revealed to him the form of intrinsic energy, the circular forces within everyone that could be used against an opponent. The essence of martial arts for Wolf was not in being able to put his fist through a concrete wall, but in being a practitioner of Ken, the stillness of the mountain, to harness intrinsic energy, bringing to heel the agents of chaos.

His mind weary with questions without answers, his body not tired – remarkably, never tired no matter how hard he pushed it – he purged himself with aikido. He put himself through a rigorous set of movements of centralization, extension and evasion, the trine of the discipline's function of self-defence. Aikido actually refined such instinctive responses as heading directly into an attack to finding ways to evade the attack while using its energy to guide it away from you.

He took on as many of his Werewolves as he could cajole onto the hardwood floor he had had installed in the balcony. Since most were either leaving their night shift or coming in for the day shift his opponents were limited to three: Bobby Connor, Squire Richards and Tony Three Times.

Tony Three Times – his real name was Pugnale, but since he had stuttered as a child, no one called him that – was strong but impulsive, given to taking chances even when he suspected he was being suckered into reacting. He had almost as much stamina as Wolf, but in the end Wolf took him down by feinting a blow to the left side of his head. When Tony reacted, grabbing at Wolf's shirt as he extended himself forward, Wolf used two *tenkan*, spinning first to his right, pulling Tony momentarily off-balance, then to his left. As he did so, he grabbed Tony's right wrist with his left hand and bowed low, pulling Tony up and over him, so that he flipped over, sprawled on the floor, immobilized by Wolf.

Squire Richards, a black man as big as any stevedore, was as lithe as a panther. His bulk was deceiving; he could outrun any of the Werewolves with the exception, perhaps, of Wolf. Squire liked contact so much that he could wear down an opponent who might otherwise be able to figure out a way to defeat him. Wolf worked with him for perhaps ten minutes before it appeared to Squire that Wolf was tiring. Squire took the opportunity presented him, grabbing Wolf's right wrist with both hands for an immobilization.

Wolf waited until the last split instant before pivoting to his left. This dragged Squire with him, his momentum carrying him forward, lifting Wolf's arm up over his head. Wolf planted his left foot, transferring his balance as he turned his lower body to the right, sliding beneath Squire and, dropping to one knee, reaching up and back for Squire's hands locked on his wrist and pulling hard forward. Squire's feet left the floor as he tumbled over Wolf's ducked head onto the floor in front of Wolf.

Bobby was another matter entirely. Not as strong as Wolf, he was a serious thinker, who conceived the most remarkable combination of moves to defeat opponents even more advanced than he was. Wolf got him down by using the *ikkyo*, the first and simplest of immobilization techniques, using a first-level circular *irimi* on Bobby's left arm to twist it up over his head, bringing him to his knees.

Wolf spent the next hour instructing the three of them on how he was able to use their own weaknesses to defeat them. By the time he showered he found that he was famished. He was about to take Bobby out to breakfast when a call came in from the commish, who wanted to set up an immediate briefing.

'I'm not at the office,' Hayes Walker Johnson said in Wolf's ear. 'Come to my brownstone, but not the front way. In fact, I want you to use the entrance I use when I'm ducking reporters. No one knows about it, except a few of the brass so keep it to yourself.'

Wolf and Bobby took one of the unmarked Werewolf cars, a medallioned yellow cab, its top spray-painted with infra-red dye that could be tracked by a helicopter. That innovation was Wolf's idea, and he could think of at least two times they would have lost their quarry had it not been for this link, invisible to the human eye, between types of police vehicles.

As Bobby drove, Wolf speculated on the meet. Usually, the cases the commish wanted Wolf to work on were faxed over from his office; a face-to-face briefing was rare. The same thing must have been on Bobby's mind, because he said, 'Must be some important murder victim involved – probably something political that the commish can make headlines with.'

The commish's brownstone was in the east eighties, a perk he had insisted on when James Olivas, the mayor, wooed him to NYC from Houston. Wolf directed Bobby to swing around onto the street one block south of the building, and he pulled over, parked without putting out the POLICE BUSINESS sign – commish's orders. This meet was strictly hush, which was no doubt why the commish was going to get to the office late this morning.

Wolf led Bobby into the basement entrance of a sedate, well-groomed greystone. As Johnson had predicted, the black iron gate was closed but unlocked, and they went through it. The door just beyond in the minuscule cement courtyard was the same, and they took a long walk down a perfectly straight, dimly lit corridor smelling pleasantly of aromatic pipe smoke and some heavy cloth, perhaps velvet.

At the end of the windowless corridor was an old-fashioned wooden door with a glass panel, frosted and etched, that allowed what appeared to be outdoor light inside.

Wolf opened the door, found himself in the rear garden of the house. A pair of bald English plane trees arced overhead, guarding privet and boxwood. White-painted boxes for annuals rimmed the perimeter, their earth turned over, waiting for the sun.

At the far end of the garden, a twelve-foot fence of some basket-like material had been erected. There was a door in this fence, but had Johnson not described its location to Wolf he would not have known it was there. He pushed the door open, Bobby following close behind, and they found themselves in the back yard of Hayes Walker Johnson, the commish. Mature honey locusts, their long branches reaching upward, were underplanted with sheared ilex and holly, still glossy green. Beyond, an ancient wisteria, as gnarled as a brawler's fist, wound itself up the brownstone's four-storey facade.

The commish was waiting for them at his back door, beckoning them across the brown grass and fieldstone pathway. A bandy-legged man with skin the colour of milk chocolate, his cheeks were dusted with black birthmarks. He had small, inquisitive eyes offset by a telegenic smile that could put Anglos, if not Latinos, at ease. This was, no doubt, more due to the colour of his skin than it was to his manner. In his dark suit, white shirt and regimental striped tie, he looked quite formidable.

He ushered them into a kitchen area, sunlit and homey, with that lived-in and loved air that could not be replicated by money or an interior designer.

'Good of you to come,' the commish said, just as if he had issued an invitation that had been in jeopardy of being refused. 'Heard about your man going down, Wolf. Sorry about that.' Then added, 'It's always

41

hard, isn't it?' without expecting an answer. 'But at least Arquillo's taken care of.' He waved them to a dark wood refectory table that dominated this section of the wood-panelled kitchen. It was covered with food, hot and cold, the commish mindful of the hour, considerate of his heroes just coming off shift.

As they sat, Wolf thought, apparently, word had not got out about the strange fire that had consumed Arquillo's face. He had told Bobby not to include that strange bit of info in his written report, and to say nothing of it to anyone, which was just fine by Bobby. He was too busy right now to wonder why he had ordered Bobby to do those things.

Standing at the head of the table like a patriarch at Thanksgiving, Johnson, apparently anxious to show his avuncular side, loaded up their plates with smoked salmon, curried chicken, lobster salad. From a drawer hidden at his end of the table he took a bread knife, sliced a loaf of fresh-baked seeded rye. 'Help yourself to juice and coffee. Or I can make you decaf espresso,' he said. Wolf noticed he made himself a double espresso, but no food at all. He allowed them perhaps ten minutes to make appreciative noises over his breakfast before he got down to business.

'I, for one, am damn glad this Arquillo thing is wrapped up,' he said, 'because what I've got now for you is top priority.' He handed over a buff folder. 'Someone iced Lawrence Moravia last night. In his own office no less. Pranced right through Moravia's vaunted security, did the deed and split without a trace. The autopsy's being done even as we speak.' He nodded at the folder. 'Tell me what you think.'

Hayes Walker Johnson slowly drank his way through three cups of his double espresso while Wolf and Bobby read the file. This is what they learned:

Lawrence Moravia, a multi-millionaire before he turned twenty-five, was an anomaly in New York City. A self-made man from Brooklyn, Moravia, whose immigrant parents never spoke fluent English, had built himself a burgeoning real estate empire to rival those of the Helmsleys and the Kalikows.

But Lawrence Moravia was the exception to the rule: instead of making deals with the city to infringe on its already diminishing air space, he took his tax breaks and created desperately needed middle income housing. In part, he could do this with a good deal of cost-effectiveness because of his ties to the Japanese. He had spent a number of years in Tokyo learning alternative construction and management techniques and, up until his murder, had continued to shuttle back and forth between New York and Tokyo with some frequency, to keep himself current and to fulfil the complex but enigmatic obligations of friendship so important to the Japanese.

Increasingly polarized into a city of the elite rich and the abject poor, New York in the decade of the eighties and the early nineties was dying from an exodus of the middle-class, who were fed up with the escalating costs of rents, essential services and taxes, frightened by dark and forbidding neighbourhoods overrun by teenage drug pushers and the homeless.

Moravia sought to change all that on a scale that could make some real difference until, last night, he was murdered in his office on the top floor of a Fifth Avenue skyscraper he owned. He had been shot twice in the back of the head with what appeared to be a 9mm gun (ballistics being run) in classic execution style, and the only fact immediately apparent was that it had been a thoroughly professional hit. No murder weapon had as yet been found; no fingerprints except those of the deceased and those of his assistant and secretary. Moravia's security people, who had discovered the body, had been careful not to touch anything. On first glance, the only thing close to being odd was that Moravia had been found with his cheeks rouged. But this was New York and, after a while, almost nothing seemed odd.

Bobby was still scanning the last page of the report when Wolf said, 'There must be more to it than just this. Otherwise you could've faxed me this file.'

Hayes Walker Johnson put down his cup. 'On the surface this guy was golden – and I do mean golden. He probably meant more to the revitalization of this city than anybody else I can think of. But something wasn't kosher with him. I got a call from the CME himself early this morning. On prelim, he says Moravia didn't die from the bullets in his brain – maybe. He's got to do some sophisticated toxicological tests.' The commish sighed. 'In any event, this isn't the clean hit it appears to be. And I want you to find out what is going on before the shit hits the fan – and, believe me, unless you can close this down immediately, it's going to in a big way. Because – and let's take the simplest answer – if Moravia was a user, his close ties with high-ranking members of the city government are going to rock the area's economy to its foundations. Given Moravia's rep and influence as a deal-maker, I can guarantee you that his shit is going to become our shit, and it will cast a long, ugly shadow. The pull-out of new business we've been trying to coax back into the city will take on the impetus of a stampede. We can't allow that. Our economic survival is in the hands of these people.'

Wolf sat back while Bobby returned the last page to the folder and closed it. The commish took it out of Bobby's hand. Wolf, watching how

43

carefully Hayes Walker Johnson guarded the file, imagined he knew why he hadn't received it by fax.

'In other words, you want this covered up,' Wolf said.

'I want it *cleaned* up.' The commish held up his hands. 'Do it any way you want, Wolf. Just make sure you get to the bottom of it ASAP. I don't want the media to get wind of any dirty laundry.' His watch beeped and he glanced at it. 'I got a meeting in five. Any other questions?' as he got up.

'I want a paint crew,' Wolf said. 'I'm sick of seeing the blood on my office walls.'

'You got it,' Hayes Walker Johnson said. 'Just call my office and – '

'No,' Wolf said, pinning him with his eyes. 'Tomorrow morning. First thing. I'm not handing any more requisitions to your office. Handle this yourself.'

'I'll do that,' the commish said. His telegenic smile almost wiped away the chronic apprehension in his eyes. 'Just get this job done quickly, neatly and on an eyes-only basis so we can all breathe a little easier, okay?'

Back on the street – having left via the circuitous way they had entered – Bobby, climbing in behind the wheel of the cab, said, 'What do you think the real story is?' He fired up the engine to get some heat into the interior.

Wolf, about to answer, paused. It occurred to him that he didn't really much care what Johnson's own motivation was, and this concerned him. Even a month ago, it would have been an intellectual puzzle he would have pored over until he had unearthed the answer. He wondered what was happening to him – whether he was going a little crazy. The power he had been given was sought after by every member of the NYPD. He regularly gave audiences not only to the city's chief prosecutor but to the state's attorney general, both of whom treated him as if he were some sort of guru, giving them advice on how to pursue the convictions of the most dangerous felons. In short, he was living the dream of every person who entered law enforcement. He had worked hard to get to this place of privilege. And yet now that it was his, he was beginning to realize he no longer cared about it. What was the matter with him? Maybe he just needed some sleep. The Arquillo hunt had been in its final stages and he hadn't slept in thirty-six hours. Now this.

'Let's get over to Moravia's apartment,' he said as Bobby threw the cab in gear.

'But Moravia was iced at his office.'

'I think we'd better get a sense of the man before we visit a crime scene that's likely to be sterile.'

*   *   *

Lawrence Moravia had lived on the top floor of a new condo he had built on Central Park South. The building catered to Arabs and Japanese; his quarters took up the entire floor.

'Holy Jesus!' Bobby exclaimed when a uniform guarding the door let them in. Wolf said nothing; Bobby had said it all.

Moravia's apartment – house was a better description, though somewhat less than adequate – seemed endless. Room after room replicated itself before them, all decorated in the most exquisite and expensive taste, all looking out on one half of Manhattan island. From up here, Wolf thought, you could almost convince yourself that New York was as glittery and majestic as it appeared in this picture postcard view, that there were no monstrous deeds being perpetrated even as you looked out on its streets. You were so high up, you wouldn't even hear the squad car sirens. But, in truth, the panorama sickened Wolf; he had had experience in the pyrrhic value of a lofty, dispassionate perspective of monstrous deeds.

Bobby ran his hand along the Missoni fabric covering a vast semi-circular couch. 'I don't know about you,' he said, 'but I wouldn't mind having a tenth of this guy's dough.'

Wolf stared out of the windows at the gleaming towers of Manhattan. The stink of El Barrio might have been on another planet. 'See what you can turn up here. I'll hit the rear of the apartment.'

Wolf made no sound as he went from room to room. The place had that decorated look that made the rooms appear as if no one lived in them. The perfection and harmony of the colours, patterns, styles of furniture set his teeth on edge. So much money had been spent in furnishing this vast space, but it was a place to look at rather than to inhabit. It occurred to Wolf that he was looking at a video image, an advertisement, perhaps, meant to sucker you into parting with your hard-earned bucks.

He tried to imagine Lawrence Moravia moving through these rooms: what did he do here? Did he put his feet up on the highly polished mahogany burl deco table? Did he drip ice cream on the $250-a-yard fabric of this stylish but uncomfortable-looking chair? Did he leave hair and dandruff in the hand-carved jade Sherl Wagner sink? Who cleaned this place? – it was a job for Hercules.

The master bedroom seemed as large as half a football field. Like the other rooms, it was filled with artwork by minimalists whose names – Flavin and LeWitt – meant nothing to Wolf; neither did their work. There was a circular whirlpool spa set in the floor near the window that looked north over the bleached bare trees of Central Park, a vast skeleton dropped down into the centre of bleak Manhattan.

Wolf climbed into the spa, stared out the window. What had Lawrence

45

Moravia thought of while he had soaked in the steaming water? Perhaps, if he was not alone in the spa, he had thought of nothing.

Wolf got out, went over and stretched out on the bed. It faced a blank wall, not the picture window. Why? It was important, before the data of any murder case began to accrete, to scope out the victim's psychological profile. Without knowing what was important to the victim, the incoming data could be ineffective or, worse, lead you in the wrong direction.

What did Moravia look at when he was in bed?

Wolf got off the bed, looked at the blank wall. It was perfectly featureless, different somehow from the other painted wall in the room, as if someone had sanded it down for some reason.

Between the wall and the bed was a small table. On it was an electronic object of some kind. Wolf switched it on, saw it was a Sharp flat-vision TV that projected its picture onto the smooth wall. Below it was a VCR and a laser-disc player. Wolf bent down, extracted the first half-dozen laser disc titles. These would be Moravia's favourites, being on the top. *Eyes Without a Face, In the Realm of the Senses, Mädchen in Uniform, The Mask, Psycho, Woman in the Dunes*. Wolf knew some of the films, read the synopses on the jackets of the others. The bizarre themes of dual personalities and kinky sex linked them all. Not your typical home film library, he thought, replacing the discs. But already he had a better sense of Lawrence Moravia than he had got from reading the avalanche of police paperwork on the case.

He went to the wall that contained Moravia's wardrobe and slid open one mirrored door after another.

Suits from Brioni and Armani, handmade shirts from Ascot Chang, off the rack from Comme des Garçons, ties from Sulka and Frank Stella. Wolf paused, curious. It was as if he were looking at the wardrobes of two distinct men, one conservative, the other loose, high-fashioned. He thought about the duality theme that ran through the storylines of the films Moravia obviously liked best to watch; he felt it now; it was as if this place had been inhabited by two men, not one.

He moved on, encountered a series of Japanese kimonos exquisitely embroidered with feudal devices, cranes, peony blossoms, pine trees, the snaking path of a shimmering river. Something here; what?

The fantastic images seemed to shiver as a small breeze stirred the silks, and Wolf turned back into the room to find the source. His hand went to his gun and he pulled it out.

He went all around the perimeter of the bedroom. He stuck his head into the adjoining marbled bathroom. He was alone. What was out of sync? What was he missing? Or was he imagining things? He closed his

46

eyes, not into darkness but into the glow from the heat emanating from the core of him.

He could see Lawrence Moravia, see the muzzle of the gun as it was placed against the back of his neck. But there was no struggle, no wildly beating heart. In fact, there was nothing at all, no emanation, no aura, no face to go with the killing. Again, he thought of kneeling in the alley with the corpse of Junior Ruiz, knowing Junior hadn't been killed by Arquillo but finding no trace of any other aura, feeling nothing but the slither of the vipers, cold and clamorous for attention.

So in this the commish's info had been correct: the two bullets to the base of Moravia's head had penetrated an already dead brain. Who had murdered Moravia and why? Why make it look like a mob hit? From which world had his murderer come: the straight-and-narrow world of Brioni suits and business lunches at the staid Four Seasons or the twilight world of the sexually bent *In the Realm of the Senses*? Wolf had got no clear signal, but on instinct he was willing to bet on the latter.

He returned to the bedroom. Back inside the wardrobe, he stood for a moment, feeling again the press of cool air. He went past the suits, stared hard at the kimonos, felt again the small but discernible pulse of air. On impulse, he passed his palm across the kimonos' silken fronts. They moved. He pushed them aside, felt the breath of air more clearly. He knelt down and saw what before he had missed.

Behind them was a crack of dim light.

Putting his hand against the crack, he felt the stirring of air, knew this was what had ruffled the edges of the kimonos. He reached out, opened an almost seamless doorway set into the back wall of the wardrobe. Stooping, he went through.

And found himself in a small room, no more than a rather large cell. There was a distinct scent, faint but still discernible. It was musky, herbal, unfamiliar but not at all unpleasant. His hand found a light switch, and he flipped it on.

The room was so sparsely furnished it could have doubled as a monk's cell: a reed mat sunk flush with the floor in one corner, an antique carved standing mirror against the opposite wall, a hibachi – a Japanese wood and copper grill – nearby, charcoal residue in it showing that it had been used. A seemingly authentic knight's armoured helmet and a pair of long doeskin gloves sat on one corner of the hibachi, an antique Oriental rug was rolled up along another wall. There were no windows, no doors, but the walls were hung with large black-and-white photographs, blowups meticulously and lovingly printed as if they were themselves artwork. The photos were variations on a single theme: sexual bondage.

Nude female forms – one could not accurately say bodies since the faces were never shown, but were always twisted away from the camera lens – were tied with cord, not merely wrists and ankles, but artfully patterned cords striping the flesh of breast, belly, thigh and crotch. The lighting caressed the naked flesh as would a lover, lending a three-dimensional quality, a kind of innocent yearning to the images, as if there was hidden amid these grotesque fleshscapes a hunger for forbidden knowledge. All the photos were highly charged with either erotic or pornographic content, depending on your point of view. In any case, they were shocking. Were they insulting, alarming or merely outrageous? Wolf suspected that a coherent case could be made for any one of the three.

But, in a sense, Wolf took in all of these eerie, sadomasochistic elements with only a portion of his mind, filing them away for future reference; in the end, he was obliged to concentrate on the object in the centre of the room.

An eight-foot sculpture hulked there, seeming even larger and more hideous in the close, dense atmosphere of the cubicle. It was constructed of trapuntoed fabric – kimono silks, Wolf noted, almost absently – and black leather strips affixed to sheets of burned twisted metal.

Like the photos, it was disturbing and fascinating all at once, like witnessing some disaster, bringing out all the worst instincts in the human soul.

It had a title, engraved on a small brass plaque: *Art or Death*. Or, Wolf thought, in Lawrence Moravia's case, Art *and* Death.

He bent down to take a close look at the plaque, noticed a tiny corner of white wedged beneath the sculpture. He pulled it out without difficulty. It was a bill for the piece, very recent, a week ago; on top was the name of an art gallery down on the Lower East Side, Alphabet City. He folded it, put it in his pocket.

Wolf took the unmarked cab uptown to Morningside Heights, parked illegally on Broadway near 116th Street.

'I've got to get out of here,' he had told Bobby back at Moravia's. *'Get back to the office and brief Tony. Send him to sit on the ME; get everything he can from him. Meet me back here at nine tonight.'*

Now he slapped the POLICE BUSINESS sign on the dashboard, climbed the steps onto the campus of Columbia University. He had come to love this oasis of plazas, ivied walls, narrow walkways smelling of bricks and books, not the least of the reasons being that Amanda taught here.

As he approached the red brick building she taught in, he thought about their first meeting just over a year ago. He had caught sight of her as she rushed across the campus, notebooks crammed under her left arm, a battered pigskin courier case clutched in her right fist. He had been up here investigating the murder of two Barnard girls who had been strangled and raped, in that order, the ME had confirmed. He had followed her to a classroom and had stopped a student on his way in. Minutes later, in the Registrar's office, he had produced his badge, asking for the class schedule of Professor Amanda Powers.

It wasn't until he had tracked down the Morningside Heights Monster, as the New York tabloids called him, that he had had a chance to take the time to return to her classroom. He had waited for the end of the seminar she was teaching, then had contrived to bump into her as she was emerging from the classroom.

In order to properly apologize (he said) he asked if he could buy her a cup of coffee. He could remember the coffee and doughnuts ordered at a nearby restaurant, the laughs they had shared. She had surprised him. Attracted to her physically, he had perhaps expected her to be an utterly serious-minded academician. Instead, he had found a fun-loving free spirit, fearless in questioning academic tradition, who was therefore constantly in trouble with her departmental head, but her transgressions were always excused because of her success with her students.

He went into her classroom now, sat down in the last row, watched her as she lectured to her students on the social responsibilities of mass communication. Amanda had a PhD in sociology, and the post-modern extrapolations of her field never ceased to fascinate her. Her ability to bring her subject alive was evidenced by the fact that her courses were among the first to be fully subscribed at the beginning of each semester. Wolf often thought that she was far too clever to spend her life teaching, but then he would visit her seminars and witness the galvanizing effect she had on her students and he would have to change his mind.

Amanda was of medium height, blonde hair blunt cut just above her square shoulders. She had a wide, laughing mouth, searching grey eyes and the kind of peachy complexion most New York women would kill for. He was certain when they had met that she was in her early thirties, and had been somewhat astonished to discover subsequently that she was a decade older than that. She lived in a university apartment in Morningside Heights that was pleasant enough, high-ceilinged, with lots of light from the south and west, but Wolf did not trust the neighbourhood. Despite attempts at gentrification in the eighties, it had slipped back into the 'armed and dangerous' category as far as the NYPD was concerned.

The seminar over, the students began to file slowly out. There was already a line to talk to Amanda but, as Wolf stood up, she saw him, made her excuses to the students, and came up the central aisle. Smiling,

49

she put her arm through his, leaned happily against him as they walked out onto the campus grounds. He put her coat around her shoulders. The weather had cleared and it was mild for February, the sunshine less watery than any New Yorker might expect.

'What a surprise,' she said, kissing him now that they were out of sight of her students. 'I thought you'd be home in bed at this hour of the morning.'

'The only bed I'd like to be in now,' Wolf said, 'is yours.'

She laughed, quickening her pace past the ivy-clad brickwork. 'I'll race you there.'

'This must be the world's oldest dance,' Amanda whispered.

Light, as pale and thick as milk, spilled through the old-fashioned venetian blinds, striping them both. A shadow arched over one naked breast, spilled down her belly, where Wolf's mouth moved in concert with the beat of her heart. She stood on tiptoe, knees bent, still and shivering at the same time, ice and fire churning through her while she whispered to him words only he understood. Hips canted forward, she bit her lip, wanting this to go on and on, but she wanted something more, and she curled down, twining herself with him, bringing them both up together.

Already her thighs were trembling so strongly she had to reach up, grab hold of him. Her breasts rose, and he took first one, then another in his mouth, laving the nipples until she gasped.

He pulled her off her feet, turning her slowly as she let go of him so that her back arched like a cat's and her buttocks curved into his groin. Wolf curled one arm around her waist, the other across the swell of her breasts. Her thighs opened and she locked her ankles behind his knees. She reached down, rubbing him against the hot, liquid core of herself, using both hands to stroke him until she felt a shudder ripple through his heavy muscles. Then she fitted him to her, felt him arch his hips up and the wet connection sliding all the way up her so that she felt a rush of blood radiating up through her chest into her brain.

She convulsed on him and, groaning, closed her eyes, letting her head fall back onto the rock of his shoulder while he jolted her over and over with a pleasure she could feel all the way to her fingertips.

'Oh, my God!'

She heard her voice escaping from her like helium from a balloon, an odd sound, erotic in its own right so that she heard herself whispering, 'More, more, don't stop, ohhh!'

Then she felt it, rising like a wind before the onset of a storm because in her mind she was standing in a Midwest plain, watching a black funnel descending from heaven, heading her way. She could feel it moving like

50

an animal or at least something animate, this mysterious, ecstatic force emanating from her lover, and it transformed her world. She was dimly aware of the curtains billowing like clouds on a summer's day, the sweep and curl of her bedspread like surf on a brilliant beach, the door to her closet half-open, the interior bathed in the soft twilight of a long, languorous September's day. All images from her past stamped with the sweaty heat of the moment's eroticism, all extensions of the ecstasy welling in waves through her, so that her immediate environment was transmogrified, her pleasure increasing exponentially until she reached down, dizzy with lust, and cupped him, drew him up inside her even more, that last inch bringing a sharp cry from her half-open lips, a deep, heart-felt moan from him that took her over the top.

On the bed, he stayed inside her a long time, as he always did, because she liked to feel his strength, his pulsing – the ebbing of that thrilling force, the whirling funnel on the horizon sweeping her up in its dark arms that came only from him, she imagined unconsciously because he had never mentioned it to her – and, gradually, the softening that, often, she could do something about.

This time, however, she turned him over on his back, knelt astride him, friendly as a sister now, and gently stroked his forehead. The warm colours of the apartment enclosed them, the curtains and blinds obscuring the grille-like extension of the fire escape just beyond.

'Panda,' he said softly. It was an old family nickname, given her by accident by her younger sister, Stevie, who, early on, had had difficulty pronouncing the 'Am' sound in her name.

'What's the matter?' She kissed his cheek.

He looked up at her with his heavy-lidded cinnamon eyes. 'How do you know there's anything the matter?'

She smiled. 'For one thing, you came onto campus while I was working. You haven't done that since we first met.'

'What do you mean? I ran into you by accident.'

'Oh, come on, Wolf. Don't you think I have friends in the Registrar's office?'

He was genuinely surprised. 'You mean you knew all along – '

'That our first meeting was a set-up?' She nodded.

'And you never said anything?'

'I thought it was sweet.' She kissed him lightly again. 'And terribly romantic. Besides, I didn't want to spoil your triumph.'

'And I thought I'd been so clever.'

Seeing his expression, she laughed again. 'You shouldn't have used your badge. People tend to remember that kind of thing, especially on campus.'

He grunted and she knew he was filing the information away in that very clever brain of his.

She smiled, not unkindly. 'Men are so vain. They think the world revolves around them, that the secret of life is to control everything.'

'That's not what I want.'

Amanda put her palms against his chest, lowered herself so that her face was very close to his. 'What *do* you want to control?'

'Why should I want to control anything?'

'Because, darling, that's what men find most exhilarating – and most fearsome.'

'And what are women most afraid of?'

'That's simple,' she said. 'Age.'

'You're kidding.'

'That's one thing women never kid about.'

'I never considered it a subject to think about.'

'You wouldn't. It's easier for you men, isn't it? You grow old and all you need do is look for a young woman to hang on your arm.' She tossed her head. 'And what happens to us?'

Wolf, thinking of his father, touched her firm body, skin as smooth as satin, breasts as firm as a twenty-year-old's. 'Well, you have nothing to worry about; you're certainly not growing older.'

'We all are.' She twisted her fingers through the spaces between his. 'I'm no longer young. I look at myself in the mirror sometimes and wonder – I don't know, maybe what I feel is the years rushing away from me like a river and what I really want to do is reach out and hold back the flow.' She gave a little laugh but, just the same, she buried her face in the hollow of his shoulder.

Wolf stroked her hair. 'You can't do that, Panda,' he said, kissing her gently. 'No one can.'

'Of course, I know that. But still ... I want, oh, I wish I was younger.'

'Maybe what you need is a good hot affair with a younger man.'

'That's just what I have.'

'I'm three years older than you are.'

She passed a finger over the line of his jaw. 'Wolf,' she whispered hoarsely, 'you look so beautifully young – no older than thirty.'

'That's ridiculous. Panda, listen to me, time passes for everyone. Be happy you're here. Three hundred years ago, you might have been dead already.'

'Now there's a comforting thought.' She sighed, closing her eyes so that he felt the butterfly brush of her lashes against his skin. Then, in a furred voice, 'Still, what a dream it would be to be eternally young.' In

52

a moment, she rolled off him, snuggled into his side. 'Now tell me why you came up here to see me when you should be sleeping.'

'I don't want to sleep.'

'No,' she said softly. 'You want to talk.'

He was silent for some time. White pillars striped the cream-coloured ceiling, their edges as diffuse as gauze, light reflected through the blinds. Because the windows were closed, the traffic sounds were as muted as a domestic quarrel in the next apartment.

'Panda, what am I doing with my life?'

She put a hand over his heart. 'What answer do you want, practical or philosophical?'

'Maybe neither,' he said. 'I think right now I need a metaphysical answer.'

'Mmm, I think you're on your own then. Metaphysics is more your field than mine.'

He knew what she meant. He had told her enough about his grandfather so that she knew that much of Wolf's early schooling had been in a kind of metaphysics, though it would no doubt be unrecognizable as such to the Columbia academicians in that field. But she didn't know it all, not even Wolf's parents did.

'There is a way things should happen in the world,' he said slowly as if trying to translate thoughts in another language into English. 'The way a tree grows, a river flows, a leaf dies in winter. But if, for example, you see a leaf shrivelling in summer, you know instinctively that something is amiss.'

He took several long slow breaths, so that Amanda was aware of just how deeply he was being affected. 'I feel as if – I don't know how to say it – there's something growing out of season.'

'Do you know what it is?' Then, because she could feel the words congested like lead in his throat, she took his hand in hers, said, 'If you want my opinion, this is not a matter of metaphysics. Something has disturbed you, and that, great sex or no, is why you came onto campus today.' She pressed close to him. 'Is it Breathard?'

'It's always Breathard,' Wolf said. 'But, in a curious way, now it's becoming what he stands for. He and I are members of an exclusive club. But I never bought into using my badge as privilege. For guys like Breathard, it has become second nature. It's symptomatic of how they see themselves: different, apart, a member of an elite group, above the law.

'It's a disease, Panda, I've seen it in action. The first step – and, believe me, it's only the first – is flashing your badge to get special attention. The next step is using it to cadge free meals when you're on the run, then expensive free dinners just once in a while as a return for a favour done for a restaurateur, then getting some criminal off a bust charge because he's part of your snitch network or important to you in some other way.

'Cops like to say they make their own perks, but they're not, in fact, perks at all. What they are are bendings of the law, cops saying to themselves, we're a brotherhood apart, we take risks, and we don't get paid shit for taking those risks, we've got to have some other compensations. But those compensations are dangerous because they're by definition amoral, and so represent a special corruption of their own: a contempt for the law. You bend the law once, Panda, and it only gets easier to bend it just a little bit further until you no longer realize you're bending the law at all.'

'So it's the system that's getting to you, right?'

He said nothing, and she waited patiently beside him, knowing he was used to the vast silences of Elk Basin, Wyoming, that he needed the silence to build now before he could get to the core of his distress.

At length, he nodded. 'After seven months, we were closing in on this madman who had already killed three times before. I had him, but I allowed my need to get to him alone get in the way. In the process, a girl was killed, and so was one of my men.'

Amanda's eyes were deep and as dark as amber. 'Of course that's tragic, Wolf. I'm terribly sorry. But to be brutally frank I doubt that you were negligent in any way, I know you too well. Something else entirely has disturbed you so.'

Vipers uncoiling. 'I don't know who killed Junior; I couldn't feel him,' he said in a rush. 'Then, later this morning, the commish dropped the Moravia murder in my lap. I came here from Moravia's apartment. I couldn't get any hint of who had murdered him. There was no psychic trail at all.'

Amanda said, 'What you really mean is you're afraid that in both instances the psychic trail was there and you couldn't detect it.'

He nodded.

She caught his eyes, held them with her own. 'Wolf,' she said, 'whatever mysterious thing is inside you has not abandoned you. I felt it before as I always do when we're making love.' She squeezed his hand. 'Nothing's changed.'

'But it has,' he said, sitting up abruptly. 'I feel as if I'm a dog chasing its tail, like I should be carrying a white stick.'

'Then there's a bigger mystery to solve than just two murders,' she said. 'Have you considered the notion that whoever killed your man might also be the one who murdered Moravia?'

54

'Why? There's nothing to connect the two.'

'Perhaps not on the surface,' Amanda said, 'but what about the lack of a psychic trail? You said in both cases you felt nothing. Do you think that can be explained away by coincidence?'

Wolf felt the vipers climbing his spine. It was such an obvious conclusion, standing there in plain sight, but he had missed it.

'Poor Wolf,' she said, not unkindly, and she kissed him hard on the lips. 'Do you want my suggestion? A little R and R. Stevie is hosting a party tomorrow night downtown in Alphabet City, for a group of new artists. She promises it's going to be a lot of fun. I want you to come with me.'

'I can't, Panda. The commish made it clear that this new case is politically explosive. I've got no time for – '

She put a hand over his mouth. 'If I know anything at all about you, you're already doing everything you can. But you can't work it twenty-four hours a day – even you, Mr Iron Man Wind River Shoshone.'

'Is that how I appear to you?'

She laughed softly, hugging him affectionately. 'That's who you are. But since even you are made out of flesh and blood, a brief time away from work will do wonders for your concentration – ' She reached down between them, stroked him softly. '– Not to mention your mood.' She laughed again as he grew in her hand. 'Here's a case in point staring me right in the face.'

TWO

New York City/Tokyo

Vernon Harrison, the Chief Medical Examiner for New York, was an exceptionally tall, stoop-shouldered man with the dolorous face of a basset hound. His thick glasses attested to his poor eyesight, but that was about the only thing poor about Harrison, Wolf had found. He was a man who always seemed calm and cool in the midst of the kind of political, administrative and forensic chaos that could only be engendered by a metropolis on the verge of collapse.

They were in the basement of the CME's building on First Avenue and 30th Street, in one of the autopsy cells that adjoined the cold room where the city's corpses awaited disposition. It was almost three o'clock in the afternoon, Wolf having spent the morning going over forensics on Moravia's office and apartment, catching up with ballistics reports (nothing, so far) and past due paperwork. A Chief of Police Breathard memo had been waiting for him, the gist of it being that he was continuing the internal investigation into the manner of Junior Ruiz's death, and he would advise Wolf of the disposition of the matter at his (Breathard's) convenience. More intimidation; Breathard was a master shake-down artist.

'You get to Arquillo, the drug dealer yet?' Wolf asked.

'What a mess!' Harrison said, snorting. 'Looked like some lunatic took a blowtorch to his face.' He shrugged. 'Well, as the Romans so eloquently put it, you live by the sword, you've got to expect to die by the sword, eh?' He put down his bone saw. The smell of human tissue hung in the air like a pall.

'So the blowtorch snuffed him?'

'Looks that way,' Harrison said, lining up his instruments. 'Someone did a nice job on his right arm, too.'

'That was me.'

'Chalk up one for our side.'

Wolf, unaccountably relieved that the CME had found nothing suspicious in Arquillo's death, decided to change the subject. 'About Moravia.'

'Ah, now you've given me something to sink my teeth into,' Harrison said, as he pulled back the tallowy skin on Junior Ruiz's chest. 'Except I honestly don't know what to tell you.' He wielded his chrome tools as if they were batons, and he the drum-major at the head of a parade. 'The whole thing is beginning to give me *agita*. Blood samples, tissue cross-sections, the whole nine yards are being run through every toxicological test I can think of. So far what I got is *bupkis*.' Wolf had noticed that Harrison, very much a WASP, must in some way be self-conscious about his status, immersed as he was in the rich ethnicity of the city; his speech was peppered with idioms from as many different cultures as he could pick up.

'You check out the rouge on his cheeks? Anything there?'

'Not unless you're Estée Lauder,' Harrison said. 'Ingredients were choice quality stuff but just what you'd expect in a premium rouge.' He looked up. 'No exotic poisons, if that was what you were thinking.'

Wolf shrugged. 'I need some answers and soon.'

'*Madre de Dios*, I'm dancing as fast as I can,' Harrison grunted as he peered into Junior Ruiz's open chest cavity. He pointed. 'Now this guy is different. *O-yasui koto desu*, no trouble at all – he got whacked with two thirty-eight slugs at point-blank range that just about tore his lungs and heart out.'

Wolf was having difficulty looking at the yellow corpse, mottled by purple bruises and red-black patches of dried blood, that had been Junior Ruiz. 'Back to Moravia,' he said now to Harrison, forcing himself to focus. 'Any sign of drug addiction?'

'Good question,' the CME said as he began to sew up the long vertical incision with a thick suture. 'He was shot full of coke, no doubt about it. Was he a long-time user? No. Was he a user, period? *Quien sabe?*'

Wolf waited while Harrison finished dictating his post-mortem report into the steel microphone. Wolf wished he would set the sheet back over Junior Ruiz.

'So what killed Moravia?' Wolf said at last.

'The billion-dollar question,' Harrison said, then paused, frowning. 'I'll tell you what *didn't* kill him. He was already dead when he was shot. And as for the coke, we found none of the telltale signs of an OD. The coke was okay and the levels we found in his system were not consistent with a lethal OD.' He pulled the sheet up over Junior Ruiz at last, turned to Wolf. 'I'd say we've got a helluva mystery on our hands, *kahuna*.'

Wolf was on his way out when Harrison stopped him. 'One funny thing about this guy Moravia.'

Wolf turned. 'What's that?'

57

Harrison rubbed the side of his nose. 'Well, you ever hear of an adult lying about his age to make himself seem *older*?'

'No. What would be the point?'

'Exactly,' Harrison said. 'According to his birth certificate, Moravia was forty-eight years old. And yet, when I did the autopsy, it was clear to me that I was looking at the insides of a man who was no more than thirty.'

Naoharu Nishitsu lay in utter darkness. Behind him, across the tatami mats, through the sliding doors out to the snow-covered garden that was, to him, something of a shrine, he heard the frail clatter of the moso bamboo. Because the sliding doors were partially open, it was very cold in the room. Nishitsu, naked, did not mind.

He heard a gentle stirring – felt it, really, as one catches the whiff of a scent – and he stretched upon the futon. In a moment, Evan was kneeling beside him, her slim girl's body warm and smelling of a certain kind of exotic fruit.

'Tell me, Evan,' he said, as she served him bitter green tea, frothy and pale, 'are you happy here?'

'I never considered it, Nishitsu-san,' she said, settling herself on her haunches. 'Forbidden Dreams is my home, it always has been. It is my duty to be here, to serve you.' Her voice was like cotton that you could pull apart with your hands, mould back together in another shape at whim.

'Then, can you tell me whether you have ever been happy?'

'I am content, Nishitsu-san.'

He grunted. 'I am not, Evan.'

That statement hung in the air like a straight razor about to fall off a shelf.

'There is a growing sense of dissent.'

'Dissent?'

'Yes,' Nishitsu said, lying quite still. 'I am speaking now of loyalty. Something that, up until now, did not seem to be an issue.' He watched her, a dim charcoal outline in the blackness of the room. 'Historically, from the time of the Shoguns, we of the Toshin Kuro Kosai have always been of one mind, set on one path, and that path was secure. Now I believe it is not.'

'Are you speaking of a traitor, Nishitsu-san?'

From utter stillness, he shot up on one elbow, his left hand gripping her right wrist so hard he could feel her bones give. 'Clever girl.' Evan made no sound, but he sensed her head had swung around and, a moment later, he could smell a change in her scent, slightly acrid, musky, less delicate. His nostrils dilated as he feasted on the odour, complex and heady, of her fear.

'Yes, a traitor.' His voice was a harsh whisper. 'I believe that someone close to us has turned against us, is working from within to undermine our plan.'

His other hand came up, cupped her breast. He clamped down so hard that now, despite her iron discipline, he heard a distinct whimper come from between her lips. 'You wouldn't know anything about this, would you, Evan?'

'What?'

He had startled her, surely, and this was good because it meant he could trust her, but he did not relax his painful hold on her. On the contrary, he ground down harder on wrist and breast until he could feel her vibrating with the pain, until, bending over, he could taste her pain in the bitterness of her newly produced sweat.

'Someone, Evan, and it could be you,' he said, rolling the taste of her around his mouth, no less precious than the finest wine. 'Someone we know well is betraying us or thinking of betraying us, and it could be you, who slept with the spy Lawrence Moravia again and again.'

'But I did not know he was a spy; if I had I certainly would have tried to discover who he worked for.'

Nishitsu was grateful for the darkness because he could not stop himself from smiling. It was true what he had learned about the sexes: men were duplicitous, but women knew how to discover their duplicity.

It did not matter that Nishitsu already knew who Moravia's masters were, that he had known from the moment the amateur had sent his coded fax from the American Express office on the Ginza. It had not mattered to Nishitsu that he could not read the message, only that his people there had reported to him the destination of the fax.

Evan need know nothing of this; it was his experience that too much information could become an insupportable burden. In any event, he had a more important use for Evan. He loosened his grip on her, felt in response a lessening of that odour he loved so completely. 'Who would betray us?'

'I don't know.'

His mouth was so close it brushed the skin of her cheek, the corner of her lips. 'The suspects are limited. There are only a few people with enough power, experience and guile.' There was a thin line of saliva sealing her lips, and he wanted it. 'A male has the strength of ego required to oppose us, a woman the subtlety of character. What is your sense? Which one?'

'A man.'

'I would have said a man. Shoto Wakare, in fact, is my prime suspect.'
He let go of her wrist and was gratified to see that she did not move it. 'I
know how your gift works and I give it full credence in these matters.'

'I have always done what you have asked, Nishitsu-san.'

He could not help himself, tasted the wetness between her lips.
'And you will do so again,' he said throatily. 'You will help me find
our traitor.'

In answer, Evan lifted her head, revealing the long arch of her neck.
Nishitsu felt a commingling of poignancy and lust at the sight of that
tender flesh, at how she so willingly exposed it to him.

He moved over her, his powerful legs spreading her thighs. In a
moment, she was crying out, but it was a different sort of cry from her
whimpers of before.

Wolf had decided not to tell anyone about the door in the back of
Moravia's wardrobe, the cell behind it or its bizarre contents, including
the photos and the sculpture. He couldn't even bring himself to tell
Bobby. Why not? He didn't know, except some instinct told him to keep
that part of the investigation to himself for now.

The late afternoon was cold and still, as if there was no weather
at all, only a vast frozen grey pall that threatened to smother the
city in nothingness. He parked on East Third Street, opposite an
old brownstone. The ground floor was given over to an art gallery,
if you could call fabric and black leather strips affixed to sheets of
burned twisted metal art. The huge pieces were visible in the window
behind reinforced steel gates painted hideous shades of green, purple and
yellow, like a raw bruise, upon which was scrawled like elegant graffiti,
Urban Decay.

At least they got the name right, he thought. The painted iron gates
were drawn back, but even so the sculptures in the windows seemed to
drink in the acrid winter light, absorbing all illumination.

Inside the gallery, it seemed as dark and drear as midnight. The
dreadful gallery was presided over by a painfully thin young woman
with the figure of a coat rack, long, lank hair as red as a fire engine and
a repellent blue-white complexion. Her eyes were circled by thick rings
of kohl, and her lipstick and nail lacquer were as black as the walls of the
gallery. All of this made her appear closer to death than to life which, Wolf
supposed, was the point. Charming, he thought. Or very hip, depending
on your point of view.

The young woman's name was Moun which, she informed him in
words clipped out between tiny sharp teeth, rhymed with noun. Wolf
told her he was an attorney representing the estate of the late Lawrence

60

Moravia. When Moun looked at him blankly, he pulled out a snapshot of Moravia, showed it to her.

'Oh, Larry,' Moun said. 'He's dead? Gee. Gross.' Then she shrugged off whatever grief had momentarily seized her. 'Sure, he came in here a lot, he liked to look around. I played this game I always do, you know? At first, I was sure he wasn't interested in the art, just, you know, taking a friend from out of town around a kinky neighbourhood, playing Mr New York. But then I got to know him better, and eventually I knew he'd buy a piece.' She opened a wad of Bazooka bubble gum, crammed it in her mouth. 'You usually get a feel from people, you know? Like I knew when you walked in you weren't here to buy.'

'Like why did you think I was here?'

If Moun had any idea that he was mocking her she gave no sign of it. She cocked her head to one side as if he were a sample a new artist was bringing her to evaluate. She chewed reflectively, then popped the biggest bubble Wolf had ever seen. 'I thought you'd made a mistake. There's a boutique down the block called Urban Design, sells, you know, like trendy stuff.'

'Isn't this trendy stuff?' Wolf said, spreading his hands.

'Is art trendy?' Moun asked seriously. 'It's not meant to be bought then thrown out next season. No, no, it's timeless. That's what makes it art.' She watched him as he moved around the gallery, popping bubbles now one after another. 'All these pieces are made by one artist, Chika,' she said, trying to be helpful. Then, nervously, 'You aren't going to ask for Larry's money back.'

Wolf turned to look at her. 'Why would I want to do that?'

'Gee, I don't know,' Moun said, 'but, well, since Larry's dead, I thought your being here and all, that, well . . . ' She lapsed into an uncomfortable silence.

'How come you call him Larry?'

Moun shrugged. 'That's his name, isn't it?' She popped another monstrous bubble. 'Anyway, Larry and I . . . ' She hesitated. 'I think that's why he came in so much. It wasn't anything, just – Well, one Saturday afternoon we went back behind there' – she indicated a matte-black door at the rear of the gallery – 'and, you know, fucked.' She giggled. 'It was kind of cool because there were customers in the gallery and we could hear them, you know, moving around and talking while we fucked. It was *very* cool.'

I'll bet it was, Wolf thought. He said, 'When did Mr Moravia – Larry – buy his . . . Chika?'

'At the opening,' Moun said. 'He came for the party. Chika was here, and he bought the piece after talking to her. That would have

61

been, gee, about a week ago. That's why I thought, well, you know . . .'

'That the estate wanted to return the sculpture.'

'Yeah.' Moun made a face. 'Well, you know, Chika's stuff isn't for everyone. In fact, I really didn't think it was for Larry, but he flipped over it; he was talking a blue streak to Chika.'

'The artist.'

'Uh huh.'

'Do you think he fucked her, too?'

'I don't know.' Moun popped a bubble. 'Maybe. I think he liked that kind of thing.'

'What kind of thing?'

Moun made a moue with her black lips; the effect was frightening. 'Are lawyers always so dense? Trip up. Larry liked to fuck, but I got the impression he didn't want any, you know, entanglements.'

'Relationships, you mean. Wham, bam, thank you, ma'am, that was Larry.'

That made Moun laugh. 'They're all like that, aren't they?'

'All who?'

'Oh, you know, guys like Larry. I got to understand him after a while. He was a big shot, lots of money, I bet he ate all his meals at places like the Four Seasons and Lutece. I mean in that life he was a suit like all the rest of the suits, only deep down inside he was laughing at them, the other suits, you know. He hated that kind of life, it wasn't him at all.'

'What was him?'

Moun looked at him. 'Larry was bent – I mean *seriously* bent.'

'Sexually.'

'Like what else?'

He said, 'Did Larry ever tie you up?'

Moun popped a bubble. 'Are you Larry's lawyer or his shrink?' She gave a delicious little shiver. 'He never did, no, but I wouldn't have minded.'

'You wouldn't?' Wolf said, surprised despite himself. It was impossible to think of this bizarre creature as being someone's daughter.

She came up close to him, and he could smell her scent, a combination of neroli and cloves, sharp and exotic and without the slightest nuance. 'Are you a control freak?' she asked. 'Most men are, I know, but, see, there's a pleasure in loss of control – it's powerful, I mean, it could kind of control you if you let it, and that in itself heightens the pleasure.' She looked up at him. 'Do you like pleasure? Do you even understand it?'

Wolf had the irrational notion that she was about to ask him back into that noisome inner room for a bout of tie up the princess; part of him was wondering what it would be like, another part was appalled that he was even fantasizing about it.

'You mentioned before that Larry came in with a friend.'

Moun popped her bubble. 'What?'

'You said a friend from out of town – that Larry was playing the big shot with him. He also bent?'

She laughed. 'Oh, no way, man, not *him*. He was uptight and not a bit all right.'

'How so?'

She cocked her head; it made her look like some kind of futuristic fighting cock. 'You know the type: a suit, a crew, a tight-ass.'

He didn't bother asking her for a better description. Within the red glow coming from the core of him he saw the face of a handsome young Ivy-Leaguer, no doubt Yalie, blond, inquisitive blue eyes – pulled from Moun's memory like a trout from a lake. He said, 'From out of town.'

'Yeah, right.'

'How'd you know that?'

'He kept saying things, like "back in DC", things like that. Also – ' here she squinted at him, the ultimate test of his New Yorker-dom, whether he could get this '– he had that Martha, Wouldja Look At-all Them Tall Buildin's look.'

'You mean he had an accent.'

Moun grinned at him, a truly horrifying sight, like something you'd see in a *National Geographic* special on New Guinea cannibals. 'Uh huh.'

'What kind?'

'Kinda Southern, kinda.'

'By that I take it you mean not a broad You-all, but a soft one.'

'Right.'

DC for sure, Wolf thought. 'He have a name, this friend of Larry's?'

'Sure did,' Moun said, enjoying this interview plenty. 'The only interesting thing about him. McGeorge Shipley.' She nodded. 'Worked for the government, too.'

'The Federal government?'

'Uh huh. Larry asked him a question, I couldn't hear what, and Shipley took out a business card. His pen was out of ink so he asked me for mine – to write something on the back. That's when I saw his name on the card. And the seal. The card said he worked for the Department of Defense.'

Interesting, Wolf thought. Moravia, who shuttled back and forth between New York and Tokyo, palling around with some heavy hitter from Defense. Now what could that be all about? Nothing in his file mentioned any ties to the Feds. All of a sudden, Lawrence Moravia began to increase in importance.

He took a quick stroll around the gallery again, said to Moun in the most casual way, 'You get a look at what Shipley wrote on the back of his card?'

'Yeah.' Moun's tongue, seeming almost a neon pink against her shiny, black lips, swept briefly up and out. 'Want to know what it was?'

For a dizzying moment he thought she was going to ask for his services in that dank back room, small, thin body pushed sweatily up against his, her avid fingers loosening his belt. Some quid pro quo.

Then she laughed. 'You should see your face.'

Wolf laughed with her, liking her despite her bizarreness. It occurred to him that there was more to her than the rebellious child wanting merely to shock her elders.

'It was a phone number, a two-oh-two area code.' She recited the number as if she had used a mnemonic to memorize it.

'How come you remembered it?' he said, writing the DC number down.

Moun shrugged her thin shoulders; every time she moved he could scent the cloves and neroli drifting off her like pollen. 'I remember everything. Especially about Larry. He was like that, God, I don't know why.' She seemed abruptly sad, as if only now the news of his death had reached her.

'What can you tell me about the artist Chika?' he said to change the subject.

Moun put her hand lovingly on one of the sculptures, a gesture that in its innocence reminded Wolf of the disturbing photos in Lawrence Moravia's inner sanctum. 'You mean what's in the brochure or what I know?'

'They're not the same?'

Moun giggled. 'Well, you know what artists are like, everything's a mystery – in fact, the more mystery the better because they think the bio stuff about them only gets in the way. You see, they want their art to speak for them. What they want most is for the viewer to come to their art without any preconceived notions about what it is they should be seeing.'

'I thought what artists wanted most was to sell their art. Aren't most of them starving in some garret somewhere?'

Moun giggled again. 'Some, maybe, but not Chika. I don't think she has to worry about whether or not her art sells.'

'Why not?'

Moun blew another bubble; it took a long time to pop. 'You ask an awful lot of questions for a lawyer.'

'The estate pays me to ask a lot of questions. No one's heard of Chika before.'

'As always with art,' Moun said, 'you have to find the right people to ask.'

'About the artist Chika. Would you say she and Larry were good friends?'

'They liked each other, you could tell that just by looking at them. I think they had a history.'

'Either of them mention something that would give you that impression?'

'I overheard them talking about Tokyo a lot, like they'd been to places together.'

'Like what places?'

Moun shrugged, another cascade of scents. 'They spoke of something called Forbidden Dreams. Sounds like a club to me. Maybe a kinky sex place, knowing Larry.'

'I think I'd like to talk to Chika,' he said slowly, reminded again of Moravia's disturbingly erotic photos. 'She live in Manhattan?'

'Sure.' Moun nodded. 'In fact, she's got the second-floor apartment in a building three blocks from here but – ' she glanced at a desk calendar '– I can tell you she's out of town and won't be back till tomorrow.'

'We never should have tried it so soon,' Yuji Shian said.

'I doubt we had a choice.'

'But to kill a human being . . . '

'It was an accident. An honest mistake.'

Yuji looked at his mother, Minako. It was just coming on dawn, and an oyster-grey light filled the sky over Tokyo. To their left, Tsukiji's forest of bare-bulb lights illumined lines of glistening fish. As they stood there, men in high rubber boots passed by, holding hoses, methodically spraying the fish to keep them fresh. The sharp smells of fish and brine came in waves, heady as foaming beer. Behind them, in the last vestiges of the shadows of night, hulked the unmarked warehouse where the Oracle was stored.

'I am a scientist, Mother,' Yuji said now. 'I should have known better. Procedure dictated that I wait for – '

'For what? Clinical trials? You know that in this case, standard procedure would be useless,' Minako said. 'Testing on lower forms of life would tell us nothing.'

Yuji turned his head away, towards the river. Steam rose from it, and now and again the mournful hoot of a passing boat hung in the air like frost.

He nodded. She was right, of course. They had had no choice. As a scientist, he knew this. The technology demanded testing. But as a human being, he was appalled at the outcome.

'Yuji-san,' Minako said gently, 'let me bring you some tea.'

At one of the many stands selling sushi and soba, Minako turned back to look at her son. He stood there on the fringes of the great fish market's hubbub, shoulders hunched against the early morning chill, alone in a crowd. Her heart ached for him. All her children were precious to her, but Yuji was her only son. That, alone, would have made him special to her, but his genius in the biosciences made him even more so. Minako ordered tea, and thought of her son, and how she had fought to keep him innocent of the dark side of the world. Now, that would have to change. That was his karma – and hers.

Yuji waited patiently for his mother to return, his mind racked with guilt. He could not have known, of course, what the Oracle would do to Moravia. But wasn't that the point? He thought of the risk they had all taken, and was again swamped with grief. He looked out on a sea of flat, colourless eyes. Here and there, the soft thud of a tail beating against the wet concrete was enough to confirm the fish were still alive.

'Tea,' Minako said, handing him a steaming cup. All around him he could feel the city awakening, moving by increments towards the inchoate roar of rush hour. They had deliberately set up the Oracle labs at this ancillary warehouse far from Shian Kogaku's Shinjuku headquarters, so that late-night sessions would go unnoticed in this area where fishermen laboured through the night and dawn.

'Does this mean that we will have to begin all over again?' his mother asked.

Yuji considered this for some time. It had been a question that had plagued him ever since she had told him of Lawrence Moravia's death.

'I don't think so,' he said at last. 'It isn't as if we were on the wrong path. But we are missing a vital piece of the puzzle. The problem is akin to a generator with one On switch that blasts so much power it lights up the city, then blows the generator.' He turned to her. 'No, we won't have to start anew. What we have to do is modify the On switch.'

Minako nodded. 'I feel at fault, Yuji-san. It was I who pushed you into creating the Oracle. It was I who brought Moravia to you, who urged you to use him as a guinea pig.'

'But, Mother, he consented. He knew the risks.'

Minako smiled sadly. 'Then do not blame yourself, Yuji-san. Moravia's karma was his own doing.'

'You're right, Mother,' Yuji said. 'But, still, I feel compelled to go to Senso-ji.'

Minako nodded. 'It is only right. We will go together.'

They went down to the Sumida river, caught a water taxi to the Asakusa district, where the Senso-ji temple stood. It was dedicated to Kannon, the Buddhist goddess of mercy, and was the holy place where Minako had taken her children on festival days.

They went down the long lane, lined with a profusion of stalls selling anything and everything, from rice paper parasols and traditional wooden combs to wind-up robots and sake. They paused at the mammoth incense burner in front of the entrance and, cupping their hands, drew the aromatic smoke to them, covering themselves with it, thus ensuring continued good health.

They climbed the steps, went into the temple itself. Echoes filled the otherwise still air. They were surrounded by phalanxes of huge columns, and lanterns, which hung like pine cones in this stylized forest. High above their heads, like the distant swirl of clouds, the ceiling was decorated with complex dramas out of Japanese legend – or history, depending on your point of view.

They said a Buddhist prayer for the dead, lighting sticks of incense, chanting as the thick smoke curled like adders' tongues in the still, cold air of the temple.

This ritual, so familiar it was comforting, calmed Yuji, but, glancing over at his mother as they left Senso-ji, he saw that she was still troubled.

Outside, the sun was up, struggling through the thick industrial haze that blanketed the metropolis. Asakusa seemed a dream, a painting from the brush of a pointillist like Seurat.

Minako shivered. 'I feel a change in the air,' she said in a whisper.

Yuji, by now used to his mother's presentiments, said, 'It will be a change for the better.'

'No,' Minako said. 'We are on a precipice, and below us, in the darkness, is an abyss.' Her clasped hands twisted this way and that. 'And, Yuji-san, something is moving in the abyss. Something even I cannot guess at.'

Rain, hard as a fighter's fists, drummed against the roof of his car. Wolf, parked within sight of Urban Decay, was watching steam come cannoning through a hole in the tarmac of Avenue C while a slickered Con Ed crew tried to find some way to stop it.

He had dialled the main number of the Department of Defense in DC and had already been bounced more times than a basketball from department to department in a search for the seemingly elusive McGeorge Shipley, Moravia's out-of-town buddy. No one, it seemed, wanted to take responsibility for Shipley's existence, which meant that either he had run afoul of the Federal government's vaunted bureaucratic inefficiency or Moun had given him the Warhol, the wrong information.

With a grunt, he checked out of the Defense's electronic tangle, phoned an acquaintance at the NYC headquarters of the FBI. No one at NYPD was ever what you might call friendly with a Fed but, from time to time, favours were grudgingly done on either side, resulting in a kind of sand castle relationship that might hold up as long as too much pressure wasn't brought to bear.

Wolf hung on the line, while Fred the Fed waited for his computer to come back on line. 'Fuckin' Con Ed,' Fred said. Staring out of his windshield at the great gout of steam rushing from the bowels of lower Manhattan, Wolf could sympathize, if only fleetingly, with this minion of bureaucracy.

'Okay,' Fred said at last, 'I'm into the Defense personnel program. What'd you say this guy's name was?'

'McGeorge Shipley.'

'Yeah, right. Hold on.' Across the street, the foreman of the Con Ed crew was on the phone in his truck; calling for reinforcements, Wolf guessed. Then he became aware of a woman.

She was standing at the kerb, rice paper umbrella sitting on her shoulder. Wolf peered at her face, but the curtain of rain made it impossible to make out her features. The woman wore black shoes, their chrome high heels flaring in the light from the traffic headlights. She wore a black micro skirt that showed all of her luscious thighs. An oversized black wool and metallic-looking leather bomber jacket covered her from waist to neck. She stepped down, across the gutter rushing with sludgy water, and Wolf had an instant's flash of her pale face, black-eyed, extraordinarily beautiful, unmistakably Oriental – Japanese? Then a truck lumbered by, black rain sluicing from its mudguards, and she was gone.

He blinked, but the sight of the Japanese girl's thighs was imprinted on his retinas, just lying there, refusing to go away, like a latent print on a murder weapon.

'Okay.' Fred's reedy, smoke-broken voice was back on the line. 'Sorry, bud, no McGeorge Shipley anywhere on file.'

'You sure?' Wolf closed his eyes, but the extraordinary-looking woman refused to disappear; instead, moved there in the darkness, stepping down into the street, her thighs stretched taut.

'There's a Shipley, William H. in Procurement, another Shipley, lessee, Donald R. in Accounting. That be it.'

68

'He's got to be there,' Wolf said.

'Well, he could be there,' Fred told him, 'but I can't see him.'

'How's that?' All thought of the Japanese woman was driven from his mind.

'Blind files, bud. All the Government directories carry 'em. In case it's slipped your attention there's a lot of covert shit happenin' out of DC. Guys into that don't get carried on the directories just anybody – even FBI – can call up.'

'So, what you're saying is this Shipley doesn't exist or he's a spook.'

'That's about the size of it,' Fred the Fed said. 'Hey, now we're even, bud. I gotta go. It's been real.'

Wolf hung up, stared for a moment at the thunder of the steam rising up to meet the cold, metallic rain. His car roof had become a drumhead. What the hell was Lawrence Moravia doing with a Defense spook? Or had Moun, enjoying a game of Bait the Square too much to stop, slipped him the Warhol?

He pulled out a pad, stared at the DC phone number she had recited to him, the one the phantom Shipley had allegedly given to Moravia. He took a breath, dialled it.

It rang seven times, and he was about to hang up, waiting this long, perhaps, for an answering machine's tinny voice, when he heard a brief pause, the ringing begin again, and someone at the other end said, 'Shipley here.'

Wolf felt his heart give a quick thud. 'McGeorge Shipley?'

'Yes. Who is this?' The light tenor of a young man; Wolf thought of Moun's mental picture of Shipley.

Wolf told him. 'You were acquainted with Lawrence Moravia?'

'You don't mind if I verify this with your commander, do you?' Shipley said. 'Give me your badge and phone number. If this is legit I'll call you back within ten minutes.'

Wolf gave him the information, then disconnected, waiting to be legitimized as real by a spook. Some situation. He wondered what Moravia had really been up to on his shuttle trips to Japan. If Shipley was a Defense spook, then he dealt in high-level secrets, and those were apt to get you killed. Wolf realized all at once that he might now be in an entirely different league.

Through the rain, he could see two more Con Ed trucks rumbling up, more slickers piling out, more disorder as the saw horses were unloaded, the traffic starting to build as the hour got later and the disruption more intense. The next – and final – step was to block off Avenue C entirely.

He thought about the call to Shipley, the slight pause after the seventh ring, the phone call undoubtedly being rerouted to wherever Shipley was at this moment, could be anywhere.

The phone ringing made him jump. He picked up the receiver. 'Matheson.'

'Yes, you are,' Shipley's familiar tenor said, as if he were an alienist brought in to reassure a patient. 'To answer your question, I was acquainted with Lawrence Moravia.'

'Was he working for you?'

'Mr Matheson,' Shipley said, ignoring Wolf's rank, 'I think it would be better if we met face to face. Take the eleven o'clock shuttle tomorrow morning. Take a cab to H Street in Chinatown and find a restaurant called Phoenix Chinatown. I'll see you at one.'

The saw horses were up all along the width of the tarmac; in a sea of headlights and whacking wipers, traffic was at a standstill, waiting wearily for the cops to set up an alternate route. But for the moment there was no exit.

Chief of Police Jack Breathard was a career cop, smart in every way it was essential for a career cop to be: he was streetwise and publicity-minded. He managed to keep the commissioner and the mayor in a good light with the TV people – who terrified just about everyone else in the department. Not an easy task considering that under the carefully manufactured public veneer the commish and the mayor would cheerfully duke it out in any back alley. The mayor, James Olivas, a second-generation Puerto Rican with everything to prove, had been forced by malignant political circumstance to appoint Hayes Walker Johnson, a hard-nosed black, as his Commissioner of Police. The two saw eye-to-eye on nothing and, away from the public eye of the television cameras, their clash of egos was already the stuff of legend.

Breathard could dance through this volatile ethno-political minefield better than anyone in the department, which meant he knew every way there was to use the enmity of his superiors to his own ends. He had, for instance, made himself indispensable to Olivas's precarious media image, no easy task since the mayor was apt to see him and Hayes Walker Johnson, two blacks, peas in a pod, in the same corner.

Breathard's dream, of course, was to replace first one, then the other. And this dream had been right on track until the advent of Lieutenant Wolf Matheson.

Breathard had never liked Wolf. He distrusted the talent, which, he told himself, he saw as a shortcut to the hard work and perseverance he recognized as the hallmark of all the best police work. This myopic view was no doubt reinforced by his envy of the attention Wolf received every time he brought in a collar. The way Breathard saw it, that was media awareness that should have been given to him.

It was Breathard who had cleverly rerouted the commish's request for office space for Wolf and his people down a black hole from which it never reappeared. And it was he who first heard about the murder of Lawrence Moravia and diverted the report just long enough for him to be brought up to speed on it before it was sent on to Wolf. It rankled Breathard no end that the commish had had an early morning meet with Wolf – he'd checked the office sign-out logs, the commish not bothering to inform him – and had left him in the dark on this Moravia thing. Breathard could see the media attention such a spectacular case would bring the man who took credit for collaring Moravia's murderer. Fuck the commish and fuck Matheson, Breathard was determined to be that man and, in the process, screw Matheson.

Breathard was sitting in the dimness of Clancy's, one of those Irish pubs downtown where the smell of beer was so strong you could almost quench your thirst just by taking a few deep breaths.

Breathard liked this place, since few of his brethren ever stepped inside, except to shake down a selection of the more notorious potatoheads who frequented the joint, and at this hour he just about had the bar to himself.

The big black man was nursing a beer when the front door opened and Squire Richards came in. He squinted into the dimness, then headed over to Breathard's table.

'Buy you a beer, blood?'

'Why not?' Squire Richards said as he shook rain off his shoulders, shrugged out of his coat and dropped onto a rickety chair.

Breathard signalled the waitress, a heavy heifer with dyed hair and false eyelashes who looked like she had time-warped in from the 1970s, and a couple of minutes later two beers hit the scarred plywood table.

'What you got for me?' Breathard said, automatically falling into street argot. It was something of a relief; the strain of catering to a spic and an oreo more white than black was beginning to tell on him.

Squire Richards took a mighty gulp of his beer. 'Wish I could feel a hundred per cent okay 'bout what I'm doin'.'

'What you mean, whatchew doin',' Breathard said. 'If we bloods don't hang together, who's gonna take care of us? Whitey? He done gone from this burg; Olivas? He busy coverin' his ass, lookin' out for the greasers got him into office; and then there's Mr Muthafucka Hayes Walker Johnson, Mr My-Shit-Don't-Stink-Like-You-Otha-Niggas, Mr My-Job - Makes - Me - As - Good - As - Any - You - Whiteys - So - Please - Let - Me - In - I - Be - A - Good - Little - Nigga. Huh!' This last, an explosive outburst.

71

Breathard thrust his head out, like a great snapping turtle, said, 'So now what you got to tell me, blood? Your boss, Wolf Matheson, be the only otha muthafucka who can stop me from moving up, from getting rid of Johnson and Olivas, and I want his ass right heah on a platta, that clear?'

Squire Richards nodded. 'Don't have much hard yet. But as far as the Moravia case goes, there sure is some weird shit coming down. Like, for instance, Bobby Connor acting funny. 'Course he was there when Junior Ruiz bought it, but there's something ain't natural about him now, like he saw something he shouldn't.'

'Interesting,' Breathard said, stroking his bristly black moustache. 'You passed me the written report of the killing of that girl, Arquillo and Ruiz. Nuthin' extr'ordinary there.'

'Just my point,' Squire Richards said, burying his face in his beer. 'And then there's the Lieutenant hisself. I mean, he be a strange dude, sure 'nuf, but he's gotten major weird since Junior be offed. He's talking to nobody, he's out doin' shit on his own, ain't be logging hisself in. Nobody know where to find the dude these days. He becomin' very uncool all of a sudden.'

'More interesting still.' Breathard considered this while he downed his beer. 'I sure do want to catch that muthafucka with his hand where it don't belong, bring him down hard once an' for all, don't have to consider his bad self no more.' He winked at Squire Richards. 'Maybe I put a tail on him, I catch myself one white fish.'

Squire Richards was shocked. 'Don' care what you do, long's you don' make me part of it. You don' know, this dude's bad. You put someone on him you betta make damn sure he knows what he's about or he's liable find hisself eatin' outta the wrong side his head.'

Breathard stroked his moustache, grinned. 'Don' you worry none, blood, I won' do nuthin'll jeopardize your position with Matheson.' He laughed. 'You far too valuable a muthafucka t'lose.'

THREE

Washington/Tokyo

The New York–Washington shuttle deposited Wolf at National Airport fifteen minutes late. It was a short but uncomfortable ride, reminding him of being wedged inside a cattle car. He deplaned, stretched his muscles as he strode through the terminal and, slipping on his leather flight jacket, went out into a misty rain to hail a cab.

There was already a queue and Wolf joined it. He used the large areas of glass to give him reflections of the immediate environment, but he saw no one suspicious. Still, as he got to the head of the line, he made frantic motions as if he had forgotten something in the terminal, turned and hurried back inside. He waited five minutes before he reappeared outside. The queue had disappeared and he grabbed the first cab in line from the dispatcher.

Chinatown in Washington was smaller than the one in New York, just as dismal, though somehow less filthy. On the other hand, H Street seemed to contain almost as many stir-fry joints as Hong Kong.

Phoenix Chinatown seemed no different from the restaurants on either side of it, except for the pair of peeling plaster Foo Dogs flanking its otherwise unprepossessing entrance. Inside, it was pleasantly dim, the walls and atmosphere mahogany with the sticky residue of heated rice vinegar, chilli oil and soy sauce.

It was just before one, and the place was crowded enough. Wolf found an open table, slipped onto a vinyl banquette that once must have been red.

A hyperactive waiter dropped a slippery menu on the table, splashed hot tea into a cafeteria-style glass, dropped a metal carafe beside it. At one o'clock Wolf, being hungry, ordered hot and sour soup; at five after it was served, along with a bowl of dried noodles and a small plate of pickled cabbage.

He had just finished the soup – good, had tried some noodles – not, when a tall, slim Oriental rose from a table across the restaurant and approached him.

'Mr Matheson, Mr Shipley apologizes for the delay.'

73

The Oriental seemed to have more on his mind, but seemed rooted to the spot, silent.

Wolf extended a hand, poured tea into a second glass. The Oriental nodded, slid onto the banquette opposite Wolf.

'You're not Chinese,' Wolf said.

'No, I'm Japanese,' he said. 'But I like Chinese food. I also seem to have developed a taste for cheeseburgers.' He reached a hand across. 'Jason Yoshida.'

Wolf eyed him. 'How long have you been watching me, Mr Yoshida?'

'Not watching *you*, precisely. Watching everything around you.'

'I wasn't followed here,' Wolf said, 'if that's your concern.'

'It's always my concern,' Yoshida said as he downed the tea. 'Shall we go? Mr Shipley is waiting.' He waved a hand as Wolf reached for his wallet. 'Already taken care of, Mr Matheson. It's all part of the service.'

Instead of heading for the front door, Yoshida led Wolf back through the restaurant, down a narrow corridor, past a public phone and the rest rooms, and out into a back alley. They turned left, then left again. There was a black Taurus with Government plates parked at a NO PARKING sign. Yoshida unlocked it and they got in.

Yoshida made a couple of turns and they were on H Street, heading west.

'You work for Shipley?' Wolf asked.

'Something like that,' Yoshida said in a tone of voice that exhibited his distaste for further conversation.

He made a right onto Massachusetts Avenue, took it all the way to Dupont Circle, then swung onto Connecticut Avenue, heading northwest into Rock Creek Park. At the northern edge of the park, Yoshida made a right onto Tilden Street, then a left onto Linnean Avenue.

'The Hillwood Estate belonged to Marjorie Merriweather Post,' Yoshida said, suddenly becoming loquacious as they swung through high black iron gates, 'but it was originally part of a two-thousand acre plot of land owned by Isaac Pierce near the beginning of the eighteenth century.' He nodded to an ancient black man in a uniform Wolf could not identify, perhaps that of a private security firm.

They went up a long twisting drive towards the ridge of a low hill. Upon its summit crouched a large red-brick Georgian mansion; Yoshida was thoughtful enough to tell him it was built in 1926.

They pulled up but Yoshida did not turn off the engine nor make any attempt to get out. 'Behind the main residence is a path that will descend over a slight knoll,' he said. 'Take it and at the fork, bear left past the miniature Russian dacha. The next structure you come to will be a log cabin.'

Wolf waited for him to continue, and when he did not, said, 'Is that all?'

Yoshida turned to him and for a split instant Wolf felt something in the core of him stir uneasily. 'Mr Shipley is waiting,' he said just as if Wolf had not been made to wait for the spook.

Just like something out of a fairy tale, there was, indeed, a miniature dacha and, just down the path, an honest-to-God log cabin. Wolf opened the door, felt immediately that change in temperature and humidity that presaged entrance into a hermetically sealed environment.

He could immediately see why. The interior of the log cabin had been transformed into a museum housing Mrs Post's impressive collection of American Indian artefacts, including buckskins, beaded moccasins, painted war drums, weavings – a wealth of the stolen history of the great American plains.

Wolf was so thunderstruck by the displays that he almost failed to see the young man come up to him. He matched the mental image he had pulled from Moun's memory: his blond hair cut short, his long, pleasant face dominated by porcelain-blue eyes that compensated somewhat for his underdeveloped chin. He was in DC mufti: dark-blue suit, starched white shirt, regimental striped tie, and so could walk unnoticed down any corridor in any Federal building in the District.

He stuck out his hand. 'Mr Matheson.' His smile was so healthy it might have cured the common cold. His grip, firm and dry, was meant to be reassuring.

'Mr Shipley, I presume.'

Shipley grinned, and he suddenly seemed as guileless as a boy. 'I apologize for the shift in venue but it was a necessary precaution.'

Wolf had to remind himself that all spooks were paranoid.

'Your Mr Yoshida seemed concerned I had been followed to Chinatown. Who would do that?'

'Will you step this way?' Shipley said, as he guided Wolf to the left, up a flight of wood and metal steps to a small balcony from which one could see close-up a pair of magnificently woven Tlingit blankets. One also had a commanding view of the entire interior from this eyrie.

Wolf put his hands on the polished wood rail, said, 'The first question I want to ask is if Moravia was an agent working for Defense, why weren't Feds crawling all over his murder site, mucking up my investigation? We could have made a good B movie out of that conflict.'

Shipley gave off a tiny laugh, like a puff of breath on a winter's day. 'I like you, Mr Matheson. There's nothing between your ears but brains. That's what I'd been told, but it's always helpful to get first-hand confirmation.'

75

Wolf squinted hard. 'You'd been *told* I was smart? By whom?'

Shipley took a deep breath, stared out and down at the exhibits, painstakingly maintained beneath glass. 'Look at this place, Mr Matheson, it's a kind of shrine, don't you think?'

'What I think is that it doesn't tell the whole story.'

Shipley nodded. 'Too little, too late, eh?' He nodded. 'I can sympathize.'

'I doubt that you can,' Wolf said.

Shipley absorbed the rebuke. 'But there were some who grew to love these Indians. Your father, for one.'

Now Wolf knew why the spook had brought him here, to a museum housing artefacts from members of the Nation. It told him with more immediate impact than words or a dossier with his name on it that these people – whoever they may be – knew who he was, what he was, as well as what might be important to him. Or, at least, they thought they did.

'There's no need for you to see our file on you, is there?' Shipley said conversationally.

'No.'

He nodded, apparently satisfied with how the interview had gone so far. 'Lawrence Moravia was working for us, Mr Matheson, though on a strictly unofficial basis.'

'Put a fine line on that, would you?'

Shipley turned to him, his blue eyes seeming unnaturally bright in the log cabin's overhead lights. Wolf suspected him of wearing contact lenses. 'Moravia's name appears on no departmental books, ledgers, files or microfiches. He was paid in cash, from what is known in-house as "appropriated field funds". Do you copy that?'

'In other words, untraceable coin lifted from opposition units.'

Shipley's smile was almost a smirk. 'Head of the class, Mr Matheson. By the way, did you learn your tradecraft overseas in 'Nam?'

'You had a spotter at the airport?'

'Right,' Shipley said. 'But, as you have noted, no one followed you to Chinatown – even us. You did very well; Mr Yoshida needn't have been concerned.'

Wolf let out a breath he realized he had been holding for some time. He *was* in a very different arena than NYPD homicide, and he found himself wondering how long these spooks were going to allow him to remain in it. In that regard, he had a surprise coming.

'To answer your question,' Shipley said, 'we did not send people in, precisely because we did not want to – how did you put it? – muck up your investigation.'

76

'Well, this must be a first, the Feds not wanting their piece of the action. I mean Moravia was your pigeon.'

'Unofficially, yes.' Shipley stepped closer to Wolf, lowered his voice accordingly. 'And *unofficially* is the operative word here. Since Moravia was an eyes-only agent on special assignment, he is *officially* considered a civilian. Can you imagine the questions we would have to endure if we sent our people in to handle the investigation of his murder? No, no, that wouldn't work at all.' He moved slightly along the rail, as if to keep a better eye on who was coming in downstairs. Wolf followed him.

'Now you answer one for me,' Shipley said. 'How did you get my private number?'

Wolf told him about his visit to Urban Decay, how Moun had remembered him coming there as Moravia's guest.

Shipley nodded, his face becoming mournful. 'There's a damn good reason why we're officially forbidden to make use of civilians. This is an example: you lie down with civilians, you tend to be lax in your tradecraft.'

Wolf leaned in. 'What was Moravia working on?'

Shipley shook his head. 'National security. You know I can't tell you anything about that.'

'Then you're deliberately tying my hands on this investigation. It's already got enough bizarre aspects to it for me to be certain that he wasn't iced by a business rival, personal enemy or some burglar caught in the attempt. Surely you can tell me *something*. A direction to head in.'

'You can see the pity of it, Mr Matheson.' Shipley sighed, his face taking on an even more mournful cast. 'It's really too bad, because you *would* work.'

'Come again?'

'Oh, come on, Mr Matheson. You're everything we require: a civilian with smarts, a cop, a detective with an unparalleled reputation for running down murder perps, with your own semi-autonomous unit and the full backing of the NYPD. But the fact is after what you've just told me I wouldn't use another civilian if my life depended on it.'

Wolf had a feeling that his time on the Moravia case was just about to run out and he found that he very badly did not want that to happen. 'I'm hardly a civilian,' he pointed out.

'As far as my department is concerned – '

'In the most elemental sense, we're both cops, aren't we?'

Shipley stared hard at him, those eyes like bright blue chips, betraying for an instant the spook's need, as shrill as a cicada's buzz, for Wolf's help. Then the porcelain quality returned like an opaque curtain, shutting him off from all but the fastidious facade. Still, like the afterscent of an overripe fruit, he could smell Shipley's need. Surely there was a way to capitalize on that.

Wolf said, 'You and I belong to a kind of fraternity. We're outsiders, always in danger, walking a tightrope between the shadow and the light, living inbetween days.'

Shipley gave him that wide, megawatt smile. 'I see what you're doing, Mr Matheson – '

'Lieutenant.'

Shipley nodded. 'That's right, I forgot. But it makes no difference, *Lieutenant* Matheson. Your attempt to link us together just won't work. You might be a cop, yes, but you're sworn to uphold the law, isn't that more or less how your oath goes? I am bound by no such oath. I am sworn to uphold the sovereignty of the United States of America. Whatever that takes.'

'Is that how *your* oath goes, Mr Shipley?'

'Ha ha! Yes, sir, the oath we swear in private goes very much like that.' He shook his head. 'But, like I said, it sure is a shame we couldn't work together.'

Shipley turned to go, but Wolf said, 'Without me you'll have no handle at all on the Moravia hit. What will you do then?'

Shipley shrugged. 'I'll just have to limp along as best I can. Adios, Lieutenant. This will be the last time we see one another.'

Wolf waited until he was at the head of the stairs before he said, 'Tell me just one thing, Shipley. What year was Moravia born?'

Shipley turned, regarded Wolf with a curious eye. 'Nineteen forty-four, I believe, November twenty-third.'

'You're sure of that?'

He could sense Shipley becoming more curious than ever.

'If you have a point, you'd better make it now.'

'I do have a point,' Wolf said, walking towards Shipley. 'And it's this: if Lawrence Moravia was forty-eight, how come the CME of New York City swears his organs are those of a man thirty years old?'

For a long time Shipley said nothing. All around them the spirits of the American plains, preserved under glass, darkened the air with the power of their worldsong.

At last, Shipley stirred, as if coming out of a deep sleep. He lifted his arm in invitation. 'Lieutenant, I believe you'd better come with me.'

Nishitsu was feeling refreshed, ready for business. He was not normally one to gloat over his own cleverness – the world being too full of dangerous pitfalls for the unwary – but in this case he allowed himself to feel very pleased by his recruitment of Evan. Everyone at Forbidden

78

Dreams loved her and, more importantly, trusted her. Perhaps that was because she was the only one of them who had never stepped outside its walls. In that regard alone, Evan was a special creature, but she had so much more to offer him. She exuded the guilelessness of a child – she looked like a child, for that matter – but her mind was razor sharp, fuelled by the wisdom of age.

He thought of these things as he crossed the small garden, a touch of snow built in its corners like spider webs. He looked upward, at the towering spires of Tokyo. The Toshin Kuro Kosai, the Black Blade Society, had come so far, so fast, and soon it would all be over, the fruition of their decades of scheming. But now they were all walking a knife-edged tightrope, the infiltration of Moravia was proof of that – as was the existence of a potential traitor.

In the precise centre of the garden, he paused, recalling the moment when the Reverend Mother had opened her eyes, pale as diamonds, and seemingly as faceted, and said to him, 'Someone will move against us, will or has already, planning, doing, it is all the same now because the thought and deed are moving in concert.'

He always listened to the Reverend Mother because this was her gift, and she was almost never wrong. She saw what she saw, in what kind of shimmering, darkling future, piercing her mind like a black blade, he could not begin to imagine. But he had listened to her dire warning, his blood running cold, and then he had acted. And, surely, Evan would find the traitor.

He moved on, a bit chilled without his overcoat, and, pulling aside another sliding door, removed his shoes. Kneeling, he entered the room in the traditional fashion, on his hands and knees.

He saw Minako Shian first. She was the mother of Yuji Shian, chairman of Shian Kogaku, Japan's foremost *keiretsu* – multi-industrial conglomerate – and a man who, above all others, Nishitsu needed. Minako was a magnificent creature, as desirable now as any woman Nishitsu had met half her age. Her eyes were luminous, her long, glossy hair, black as a raven's wing, coiffed in complex swirls above her sculpted face. All the power one traditionally felt in a woman's body was in her face, and the force of it was akin to putting one's hand near the open door of a furnace.

Behind him, he could feel the presence of another woman, would have done so had she been at the other – more public – end of Forbidden Dreams. He did not look directly at this woman, known as the Reverend Mother, had every reason to feel good about not having to do so since, often, that was like peering too long into the sun.

79

'I am sorry about your friend Moravia-san,' Nishitsu said, not meaning a word of it. Moravia had got just what he deserved.

Minako nodded. 'I suppose it was careless on my part not to have seen through him.'

'In that, we can all share the blame,' the Reverend Mother said in a tone not unlike the reverberation of a distant avalanche.

'And, in a very clear way, it was fortuitous,' Nishitsu said. 'The innocence, as it were, allowed us to deal with him totally without suspicion, and that freedom made him careless.'

'We know who his masters are,' the Reverend Mother said, 'and we will deal with them accordingly. Today, however, we have more pressing matters to attend to right here in our own back yard.'

Nishitsu nodded. 'Your son Yuji-san. Minako-san, we understand – have understood all along – your desire to keep your son apart from – us – from what we do. Up until now we have indulged this desire.'

'This is, unfortunately, no longer possible,' the Reverend Mother said.

'What has happened?' Minako asked.

Nishitsu rose, walked on stockinged feet to the rear of the room, and there stood looking out at the garden, bathed in light filtered by delicate bamboo and urban monolith. He was a man both of high energy and great stillness, and it was said that this garden had been built to his specifications, that he drew his seemingly inexhaustible strength from its many elements – boulder, bamboo, gravel, water, maple, stone, azalea. Perhaps, Minako thought, this was because (so the story went) he had had the garden's architect put to death so that he could not recreate this space – this shrine – for anyone else. Buried there in the garden, and bound by its perimeter, the architect's spirit continued to nourish Nishitsu like the rice and fish he daily ate.

'What has happened,' Nishitsu said, 'is that we are faced with an enemy or enemies from within.' He watched Minako carefully with his opal eye, to divine any quickening of pulse or breath, any sheen of sweat or small galvanic response occurring subcutaneously. There was none.

Minako said, 'Can this new development in some way be traced back to Moravia?'

'A good question, and I can see how it would be of interest to you.' Nishitsu, through with his visual survey of her, turned back to contemplate the garden. 'For the moment, I have no adequate answer. I only know that we have now been put on notice. We no longer have the luxury of time. Accordingly, the final stages of your plan have been set in motion. All that remains unfinished is to bring your son, and those who follow him, into line. We will need you for this, Minako-san.'

80

'I understand,' Minako said.

'Do you?' Nishitsu whirled on her. 'I don't know. Were it *my* son we were speaking about, I think I would need to clarify the conflict between *giri* and *ninjo.*'

'Just like in the Yakuza movies, eh?' Minako said with intended irony. She knew what he meant. *Giri* was that sense of ultimate obligation to family or group without which life itself had no meaning. *Ninjo* was that sense of decency against which *giri* almost always pushed. It was this very sense of conflict that gave such situations special poignancy, so that they could be remembered for centuries, recounted over and over, the listeners weeping openly at the suffering and the nobility of the heroine. It might be so with her and Yuji. She felt *giri* towards the Black Blade Society, had in fact over the decades sacrificed much for them. But now with her son, Yuji, Nishitsu was calling into question her loyalty because of her sense of *ninjo* towards the son she had, until now, kept sacrosanct from her life within the Black Blade Society.

'I do not deny the conflict,' Minako said, 'but it is internal and need not concern you. I am Toshin Kuro Kosai. My sacrifices for the cause are well documented, eh, Nishitsu-san?'

'That they are,' Nishitsu said, nodding slowly. 'However, we are aware of the special regard you place on your son. He is, after all, the only one of your four children unaware of the Toshin Kuro Kosai and your involvement in it. You yourself have put him in a sacrosanct place, beyond our reach.'

He came back across the room, sat opposite her on the tatami. 'Now all that must change. We are asking you to make the ultimate sacrifice.'

'Asking me?' Minako smiled, letting the silence gather at her feet before she said, 'I was called to make the ultimate sacrifice as a small girl when I agreed to the summoning. From then on it was understood that whatever the Toshin Kuro Kosai asked of me I would do. Nothing has changed.'

Nishitsu nodded. 'It was important for us to speak of this openly.'

'I understand,' Minako said.

'Then you will present your son, Yuji Shian, to us two weeks from today.'

Minako said nothing, and the silence built again, though this time it was not of her making. At length, the Reverend Mother stirred. 'Tell me, Minako-san, how will you accomplish your son's conversion to a philosophy he now finds abhorrent?'

'I have no choice,' Minako said. 'I will have to use his best friend, Shoto Wakare.'

* * *

81

At Hillwood's main residence, Wolf saw Jason Yoshida behind the wheel of a dark-blue Lincoln Town Car with Government plates. What had become of the black Taurus? he wondered. Yoshida opened the near-side rear door for them and they got in. Shipley immediately pressed a button and the privacy screen blotted out the back of Yoshida's head. They began to move, but the Town Car's windows had been blackened so effectively that Wolf had difficulty seeing through them. Soon he gave up trying.

'What do you know of Japan, Lieutenant?'

'I'm an expert in aikido,' Wolf said.

'Of course you are. But that's something cultural, spiritual. I was speaking of the current political climate.'

'Only what I read in the papers.'

'That's not enough, Lieutenant. Not nearly enough.' Shipley reached over, pressed another button, and a portion of the burlwood fascia flipped down to expose a safe. He opened it with a couple of deft twists, extracted a grey-coloured file. It was bound with a wide royal-blue ribbon that was stamped in gold with the seal of the President of the United States. Just below it, in bold red capitals, was stencilled: EYES ONLY.

Shipley unbound this file as reverently as a priest handles a communion grail. 'Here,' he said, placing the flat of his hand on the cover sheet, 'is everything you need to know about the Japan of today. About its future and ours. And about the death of Lawrence Moravia.'

Shipley drew out a photo – a publicity still, from the polished look of it – of a menacing-looking individual with a determined jaw and one cloudy eye. 'This is Naoharu Nishitsu. As you must know from reading the papers, he is the boss of the Liberal Democratic Party, to all intents and purposes Japan's one true political party. The LDP is wealthy beyond our wildest dreams. They are funded by annual contributions of enormous size from the country's leading industrialists.

'What has been kept a deliberate secret is that Nishitsu runs the LDP's powerful – and dangerous – ultra-conservative wing. Recently, we received an intelligence report that indicated many demonstrations and violent clashes attributed to a number of Japan's fanatical right-wing nationalist splinter groups are really conceived, funded and condoned by this faction. This means two things: one, that these groups, previously thought unconnected, underfunded and of no real consequence, are, in fact, just the opposite; and, two, that Nishitsu is a major player in these escalating terrorist tactics. Subsequently, this report was confirmed by another . . . source.'

Wolf saw that Shipley was watching him carefully, he supposed for any sign of a lapse in attention.

'This is serious business, Lieutenant, I cannot emphasize that enough.

In 1990, for instance, the mayor of Nagasaki was assassinated for daring to hint that the Emperor of Japan could in part be held responsible for World War Two; just eight months ago, the prime minister was severely wounded just after he had called for a further opening of Japan to American business interests. The fanatics call these murderous attacks "acts of justice"; Nishitsu privately calls them "heaven's punishment".

'The fact that these outright murders are being paid for by legitimate corporate Japan is . . . well, we would have considered it absolutely unthinkable – until our recent intelligence proved otherwise.'

'If you have the hard intelligence,' Wolf said, 'why not bring the evidence to the Japanese government?'

'Two problems there,' Shipley said. 'The Japanese government currently has no idea of the extent of our intelligence network over there; we have no intention of tipping them off to it. Also, Nishitsu's people have so deeply infiltrated all levels of Japanese government that we can no longer be certain who to trust over there.'

'This sounds like heavy weather.'

'It gets worse, believe me. Over the prior eighteen months, a number of prominent liberal members of the LDP have died: a car crash here, an apparent heart attack there. Others have been dogged by scandal, and resigned in disgrace. We did some further digging, and now strongly suspect Nishitsu of clearing out the liberals from the top of the LDP hierarchy, so that now, in each ensuing election, the traditionalist, the ultra-conservative, even, most alarmingly of all, the radical LDP candidates are being elected to office. If the trend cannot be reversed and soon, the entire tenor of Japan's political outlook will move further to the right than it was on the eve of Pearl Harbor.'

Shipley replaced Nishitsu's photo, brought out a second one, this also a publicity still. But he did not yet give it to Wolf. 'This situation would be worthy of our most immediate attention, even if that were all there was to it. Unfortunately for all of us, it isn't.'

'Hold it right there,' Wolf said. 'I might have rubbed elbows with some spooks in 'Nam but that was a long time ago and the jargon's changed. Just what does "most immediate attention" connote?'

'It is, Lieutenant, just one small step below covert war status.'

Wolf turned away for a moment, looking blindly out of the blackened windows, recalling one by one the contents of the log cabin at Hillwood: the buckskins, war bows, weavings, tomahawks. He needed time to digest not only what Shipley was telling him, but the consequences of it. At last, he turned back. 'I want to get this straight. By "covert war", are you speaking of a status similar to the cold war relationship we had with the USSR?'

'Yes, I am.'

Christ, Wolf thought, what the hell am I getting myself into? He wondered whether he should tell Shipley to stop the car right there and let him out, never see him again. But he knew he never would. There was a familiar fire inside him now that would take him through to the end of this rapidly expanding investigation.

'Shall I continue?'

Wolf nodded.

'It happens that there is more to Nishitsu than even his terrorist funding,' Shipley said. 'Most recently, intelligence – supplied by Lawrence Moravia, by the way – confirmed that Nishitsu was also the leader of the Toshin Kuro Kosai, an organization known as the Black Blade Society. It is so clandestine that even most Japanese have never heard of it. It's a cabal of – and from now on I must say that we are dealing with speculation only – influential people from all walks of Japanese life: business, political, bureaucratic, Yakuza, whose purpose was and always had been to conquer the world – but in their own way and in their own time.

'It is said that in 1937 the Toshin Kuro Kosai had argued against an aggressive imperialist Japanese policy, had argued, some years later, against attacking Pearl Harbor. They, it is further said, knew enough not to underestimate the military strength and resolve of the United States.

'But they were not as strong then as they are now, and they were overruled by the all-powerful military-industrial complexes of the day known as *zaibatsu* that ultimately led their country to defeat in the war in the Pacific.

'Accordingly, the Black Blade Society pulled in its horns, went deep underground until after the post-surrender war crimes trials during the American Occupation of their country had run their course. Then they emerged, slowly, in ones and twos, stronger, more influential than ever before. We know that Japan's high-speed economic growth in the decades after the war was directed by members of the Black Blade Society within the powerful Ministry of International Trade and Industry and the heads of the new, emerging industrial *keiretsu* – their new name for the old *zaibatsu*. Think of it, Lieutenant. This cabal conceived and executed economic policy for the entire country that would be dynamic – not static – for decades to come.' Shipley's obvious admiration had been coerced out of him, and that made his fear of these people all the more concrete. 'Can you imagine formulating such complex concepts in 1947 that would work well into the twenty-first century? Our best minds still can't fathom it all. Look what the Black Blade Society has fashioned Japan into today: an economic and technological colossus of previously unimaginable clout.

84

'This is what we are up against, Lieutenant. And now, we have intelligence, absolutely reliable, independently corroborated, that the Black Blade Society is finally on the verge of gaining enough power to fulfil their dream: the economic domination of the world.'

Now Shipley handed over the second photo. 'This is Yuji Shian, the one man with influence enough to stop Nishitsu's rise to power.' It revealed a man with a thin, unlined face, his hair, a glossy black, worn unconventionally long so that it swung against his shoulders. His eyes seemed as soft as a favourite uncle's, but in their depths Wolf could see burning the fevered light of a strange, unreadable emotion . . . not rage, not obsession, but something just as hot.

'Naoharu Nishitsu and Yuji Shian. The one represents its entrenched radicals, dreaming the traditional Japanese dream of global domination, the other, the emergence of Japan's globally responsible new order.

'The influence-peddling scandals of the last several years that have rocked the entire political-economic infrastructure of Japan have been a personal affront to Shian, and his has been the lone voice that, time and again, was raised in outrage against the traditional trading of confidential information and money that's a tacit part of almost every business and political arrangement in Japan.

'There is a whole new territory that Nishitsu must conquer: the powerful technocrats whose inventions will ensure the future economic security of Japan in the twenty-first century. Because of Shian's unparalleled stature among them, his influence is of incalculable worth to Nishitsu. Up until now, Shian has remained unmoved by Nishitsu's overtures. But Nishitsu's power and influence are growing exponentially. Though Shian is still scheduled to come here within the next six months on a lecture tour to try and persuade Americans to see the new Japan as it really is, we can no longer rely on him.'

Shipley put the photo of Yuji Shian away.

'It was Moravia's assignment to gather enough hard evidence against Nishitsu to stop the Toshin Kuro Kosai's growing dominance in Japan. To bring Nishitsu down. Once Nishitsu is gone, we can take our time in helping the new order in Japan to dismantle the Black Blade Society.'

'But someone got in Moravia's way.'

Shipley nodded, grim-faced. He pulled out a third photo, this one grainy, a black-and-white with no depth of field, surely a surveillance snap, of a hatchet-faced Japanese with short salt-and-pepper hair, beetling brows, eyes that, even caught in shadow by the voyeur's lens, seemed like holes punched in the fabric of the universe.

'The man you're looking at is Mizusumashi Kafu, the Water-spider. That's what his first name means, but he's known as Suma. He's deceptively small for an assassin, but don't let his size fool you.' Shipley grunted. 'Water-spider. Jesus, think of parents who would name him that.'

The face in the photo had death written like a tattoo across it, Wolf thought. He said, 'You think Suma iced Moravia?'

'Could be,' Shipley said, sliding the photo back into the dossier. 'He's Toshin Kuro Kosai and he's here in the US.'

'Can you be more specific?'

'If I could, I would,' Shipley said a bit stiffly.

At that moment, the Lincoln lurched to the left, rocking on its heavy-duty shocks, and Shipley's file shifted on his lap. Another surveillance photo came into view, and Wolf, catching the wedge of an image, asked to see it.

Shipley complied. It was another grainy snap with a long lens of Suma, the Black Blade Society's assassin, and now Wolf could get a sense of how small the man was. He was crossing the street – a street, Wolf could see by a sign in the background, somewhere in Tokyo. However, he seemed not to be alone, because his face was turned slightly off true front, as if he were in the midst of a conversation with the person next to him.

Wolf looked again, and a third time, just to be sure. But he was sure. Mentally, he removed Suma from the picture, added a rice-paper umbrella. Despite the graininess, despite the angle and not being able to see all of the person walking next to Suma, he recognized the face. He was looking at the exquisite Japanese woman he had seen last evening when he was parked outside the art gallery, Urban Decay.

'Anything special I should know about this photo?' Wolf asked.

'Standard surveillance photo. Suma in Tokyo, fall of last year,' Shipley said. 'That's about it.'

Wolf wondered whether he should tell Shipley about the girl, decided not to. He knew nothing about her – and it was a sure bet that either Shipley knew the same nothing or he wasn't telling Wolf everything he knew. Spooks were like that, they couldn't help themselves. Either way, it paid to keep this to himself, at least for the time being.

He handed back the photo, said casually, 'Is Suma the Black Blade Society's only assassin?'

'Hardly,' Shipley said, rebinding the file, putting it carefully away in the safe. 'We have no clear estimate of how many they could have, and so cannot trace all their movements. But it's a certainty that one of them murdered Lawrence Moravia.' He rubbed his forehead. 'In that regard, remember I told you we knew that Nishitsu was getting rid of his opposition inside the LDP? Well, we now have

evidence – slim but accurate – that he has begun the same process here.'

'What?' Wolf sat up as if he had been hit by a bolt of lightning.

'Over the past six months two legislators have died, both under
mysterious circumstances – hit-and-run car, a malfunctioning elevator
– and both were liberal in their stance on Japanese economic restrictions
– Yuji Shian's people, so to speak. Now the hard-liners are gaining power,
and we believe it is all part of the Toshin Kuro Kosai's plan.'

'I don't follow you.'

'How clever Nishitsu and his Black Blade Society are! Just imagine,
Lieutenant, the oh-so-delicate economic detente the two nations have
now will be ruptured, perhaps irretrievably. For some time, there has
been a solid base in the US Congress to take a hard line with Japan.
Now, between the radical shift in Japanese policy and the consolidation
of power of our hard-line legislators the consequences will be dire: major
trade barriers will form, blocking Japanese imports of cars, electronics,
home computers. And then, the retribution will come: the flow of vital
computer technology will dry up. The armed forces, the Pentagon, CIA,
DEA, Defense, our nation's entire security network depends on Japanese
computer chips. What will happen to us when we can no longer get them?
When Japan sells them to the Western European nations, even the former
Eastern Bloc countries, but not to us?'

He leaned close enough for Wolf to suspect he was wearing coloured
contact lenses. 'We do not believe that America would long remain
competitive on a worldwide basis without the help of the cutting edge
Japanese technocrats. And, falling from competition, we would surely
experience a debilitating and humbling economic decline so rapid that
only Nishitsu's people, already being salted among the CEOs of the
world's largest multi-national conglomerates, could save us. But at what
price? They would own us, lock, stock and computer chip. We would be
under their economic thumb for ever.'

The Town Car slid to a halt, and the door opened. Wolf climbed out
after Shipley to find himself back at the terminal of National airport.
Yoshida stared at him for a moment, before looking away. The sky had
lightened a little, but the air was heavy with the incipience of a storm.

'You've come this far on your own, Lieutenant,' Shipley said, 'so it's
only fair to warn you. If you're going after the Black Blade Society, you'll
be going after everything.' He guided Wolf away from the kerb and its
crowd of people. 'Take it from me; I know these people. Think very
clearly. If you take one more step in this investigation, they will not
allow you to back out. They'll come after you as they did with Moravia.
But you have an advantage. As you said, you're not a civilian.'

'What is it you're not telling me, Shipley?'

'I beg your pardon?'

'Back there at Hillwood, you didn't want any part of me because you thought I'd be a security risk. Then I mentioned the CME's report on Moravia and you couldn't wait to brief me. Why?'

Wolf could tell that Shipley did not want to go on.

'I promise you I won't leave until you tell me what it is.'

Shipley nodded, a brief, painful acquiescence. 'A rumour,' he said. 'It is said among those who know Toshin Kuro Kosai members that there is something subtly different about them. No one knows precisely what it is. But they do not seem at odds with the ravages of time.'

Wolf, not certain he had heard correctly, said, 'Can you translate that?'

'The stories – circulating much like those of vampires and werewolves – indicate that those within the Black Blade Society age at a slower rate than you or I.'

'That's nonsense,' Wolf said, but the vipers were again uncoiling in his gut. 'There are people all over the world who don't look their age.'

'We're both sceptics, Lieutenant,' Shipley said. 'Imagine, then, my interest when you told me of the CME's report on Moravia.' He looked quickly around, saw Yoshida standing watch, turned back to Wolf. 'I have no choice now but to ask you to work with me. We need your help, Lieutenant. Desperately. If there is even a shred of truth to the rumours of their longevity . . . ' He paused as if the notion had robbed him of breath. 'The consequences of their rise to power would be multiplied a hundred-, a thousand-fold. They must be stopped, Lieutenant, and you must stop them.'

'Wait a minute,' Wolf said. 'This sounds as if I'm going into a final mission.'

'Maybe you are,' Shipley said, his breath coming in hard, little bursts. 'By taking down two of our senators, Nishitsu and his crowd have crossed the line.' His eyes, sharp pebbles, were now glossed over by the reflection from their coloured lenses. 'I know what you're thinking, Lieutenant, and you've made the correct deduction. We've gone to covert war status with Japan.'

FOUR

Tokyo/New York City

Shoto Wakare received his encoded instructions while he was in the shower. He emerged, beads of chill water on his superbly toned, hairless flesh, to see the seven sheets lying in the receiving bin of his portable fax machine. Padding across the room, he stared down at the series of numbers which would mean nothing to anybody without the electronic decoding device with which Yoshida had provided him.

His morning routine never varied. He arose at four, slipped into workout clothes, drove his body as hard as he could for exactly two hours. By that time his flesh was shiny with sweat and his muscles were pumped up to a point where he felt justified in spending fifteen minutes admiring their definition in just the way he went once a week to a museum to admire modern Japanese works of art.

In a warm shower he shaved arms, underarms, legs, then, with a violent twist, turned the water cold, cleansing himself in the icy stream until his teeth chattered and the skin beneath his fingernails was blue.

Always, then, he stood naked and dripping in front of yet another full-length mirror, staring at his penis which the intense cold had made small. He bent his knees and beat upon the flexed muscles of his thighs until the skin turned red and he was vibrating from the pain.

The first thing he saw upon emerging from the bathroom was a framed photo of Yukio Mishima, the samurai-poet who had committed hara-kiri in 1970 in order to dramatize to an uncomprehending nation a death of uniqueness: the dissolution of traditional Japanese values in the noisome cauldron of the ethos of the West.

In the photo, Mishima, naked, in the position of crucifixion, phallus-like arrows sticking out of him, had studiously aped the famous painting of the death of St Sebastian, to whose life he was so strongly drawn. And no wonder. Sebastian had been a member of the Roman Praetorian guard while secretly a Christian. When his secret was revealed to the emperor, Diocletian ordered his archers to execute the soldier-saint. The secret mystic existing within the warrior's body, whose fate was to become a

89

martyr, seemed to Wakare to be the ultimate symbol of Mishima's brief tortured life.

Now, as Wakare, naked and powerful, bent to his task of deciphering his latest instructions, he had cause to think of Mishima and St Sebastian. Wakare, too, worshipped the human body. The eroticism of the male form was not lost on him as it was on so many more ordinary men. With a pang as sharp as any pain, Wakare placed his palm across the array of number series on the seven pages that had been sent him. They were oblivious, unmoved by his passion, but he, involved in such dispassionate work as this, could feel the blood surge in his veins as he thought about his friend, Yuji Shian, who he was terrified to approach on such a matter. Yuji, who was such a master of the post-modern world, yet was possessed of the special fire Yukio Mishima marked and made immortal in the poetry of his fiction.

Wakare blinked, took his hand away, saw the stain of his sweat like stigmata upon the stark mathematics of the encoded message. A stigmata he was terrified Yuji would see appear on his face should he tell him of his desire.

Yet it wasn't only men that Wakare longed for; sex in any form fascinated him. He adored, for example, the Japanese female impersonators who were intelligent, sensitive, perfect. They were not the mincing, high-camp performers of execrable standards with which leering Westerners were familiar. No, as Mishima understood, these Japanese were artists of the highest rank. Only a man, freed from the impurities of the female personality, could accurately portray a woman with such exquisite perfection, creating an ideal that was far beyond life itself to create.

If the truth be known, Wakare despised life – as he suspected Mishima had done – because it was so imperfect. He lived for the imminence of the ideal. In his body, as in almost all other things, he was to be disappointed; the chaos of the universe worked continually against perfection, eating away at all creation which, he was certain, must begin in some unseen and unknowable state of flawlessness.

Wakare longed to be witness to that blinding instant of perfection, the one moment of the paradigm before the inexorable trine of chaos – time, random chance, entropy – commenced their revolution of destruction. And, as he grew slowly older, he suspected with more and more certainty that that moment would be up to him alone, and that it would involve his death. Because, as Mishima had realized, death was its own purification, being at once the final release from the tyranny of the group that bound all Japanese, and the ultimate indemnity of the debt one owed to the group.

It took him five minutes to decode his instructions, forty-five minutes to encode the weekly intelligence digest on the latest movements of Black Blade Society operatives worldwide: their postings by country, city and corporation. He looked at the list. Very impressive, even to him. Scary, even, he supposed, to the opposition. Very good. He sent the encoded fax, then took the sheets into the bathroom, set fire to them and, when he felt the flames on his fingertips, dropped the ashes into the toilet, flushing them away.

He met Minako in a theatre where a choir of young women, dressed as samurai-in-training, sang with an angelic fervour and danced with a ethereal grace that brought tears to the eyes of the audience, almost all men.

When the show was over, Wakare and Minako strolled through the neon bustle of the Ginza, the two of them dwarfed by the enormous signs and billboards, the even more stupendous buildings.

'Thank you for meeting me. I have nowhere else to turn,' Minako said. 'As my son Yuji's closest friend, you hold a special place in his world, which is why I must speak candidly with you.'

'It is true that Yuji-san and I are close,' Wakare said carefully, 'but our relationship is a precarious one at best. It's a wonder to me we are still friends.'

'A testament to the two of you,' Minako said.

Wakare smiled. So like a woman, he thought, to believe our bond is a matter simply of our maleness. To Minako, he said, 'Perhaps. But, then, we, too, have a special friendship, eh? I could not imagine taking any other woman to the show we have just seen.' He smiled. He seemed to be enjoying the sunshine, even winter's wan rays, being out of his office for the day.

Wakare was vice-minister of the Industrial Policy Bureau of MITI. MITI was Japan's all-powerful Ministry of International Trade and Industry. It would be impossible to overvalue MITI's influence on all phases of life in Japan. It was this ministry, for instance, which dictated industrial policy for the entire country during Japan's period of high-speed growth from the mid-fifties all the way into the 1980s. By giving incentives to companies willing to invest in the new emerging industries of electronics and computers, MITI was able fluidly to guide Japan to the astounding economic dominance it currently enjoyed.

'The fact that I am head of the Chosa-ka, the Research Section of the Bureau, and could make or break any one of Yuji's lab discoveries, is enough to make our friendship potentially dangerous,' Wakare said. 'Then there is the matter of my being Toshin Kuro Kosai.'

'That is a bond between us,' Minako acknowledged. 'Certainly, it was why you were chosen to head up the Chosa-ka.'

'But it was you, personally, who got me the job, Minako-san. For that, I owe a debt I can never adequately repay,' Wakare said. 'But since we are speaking candidly, excuse me if I say that I have wondered whether any personal motives were at play in my appointment. After all, I could be of immense help to Yuji.'

'Do you believe me that devious?'

He shrugged. 'It hardly matters. Your son is incorruptible. He would no more accept a favour from me than he would shove someone off a bridge. To him, both actions constitute an act of lawlessness.'

'I truly hope you are wrong.' Minako sighed. 'You cannot understand the pain I feel in asking you to help me. But I have no choice. We must somehow get Yuji to agree to join forces with Nishitsu and his Liberal Democrats.'

'Of course, I will do whatever you ask of me, Minako-san. But you know you are asking the impossible.'

'Perhaps,' she said, then inclined her head. 'But perhaps not.' Her lips curled into a tiny smile. 'This is what I will propose. I want you to enter into a kind of conspiracy with my son.'

'I – What? – I don't follow you.' Wakare seemed startled. 'I mean to say, that's not – I don't know whether I'm cut out for conspiracies.'

'You will like this one,' Minako said confidently. 'I guarantee it. I want you to approach Yuji. Do it in a neutral setting – outside the scope of business – go out to dinner and a show, perhaps. When he is at his most relaxed I want you to confess.'

Wakare felt his heart lurch again. 'Confess what?'

'That you are a member of the Black Blade Society.'

'What? Forgive me, Minako-san, but that will surely mean the end of my friendship with Yuji.'

'If you believe that, you've seriously underestimated my son,' Minako said. 'Consider, Shoto-san, he knows of your fondness for Yukio Mishima and all he stood for – and I think he respects you for it. Yuji knows your heart is pure. That is what is important to him.'

'But telling him I am Toshin Kuro Kosai – '

'Will intrigue him,' Minako finished for him. 'You must understand, Yuji is in many ways a naif. In his mind, the Black Blade Society is a purely political organization whose membership is unknown. He has no sense at all that only those gifted with the sight are members – and hopefully he'll never learn that.'

'But even as a purely political organization, Yuji would find the Black

92

Blade Society's virulently reactionary posture abhorrent, not to say dangerous to everything Yuji believes in.'

'I'm counting on that,' Minako said. She smiled. 'Imagine how intrigued he will be once you reveal your plot to replace Nishitsu with yourself.'

'I'd be mad to say such a thing!'

'To anyone but Yuji, yes,' Minako said. 'But telling him is like telling a dead man.' She waited while several punks ran by, black boots clattering, coloured Mohawk haircuts bobbing. 'And telling him you want to bring him into the Toshin Kuro Kosai will make sense to him. The two of you, together, will have enough power to effect changes in the society. He'll see that right away.'

Wakare considered this. 'But to do that I will have to reveal Nishitsu-san's involvement in the Black Blade Society.'

'Again, I urge you to have faith in your friend, Yuji. He is a powerful man with a powerful mind. The very fact of Nishitsu's involvement will act as a magnet for him.' Minako stopped, looked at Wakare. 'Trust me, we'll get Yuji and Nishitsu together. Yuji will believe he is working on your behalf to destroy Nishitsu, and Nishitsu will be content with Yuji's presence.'

'For the time being,' Wakare said dubiously.

Minako nodded. 'Events are moving very fast now. That's all the time we will need.'

There was a crew busily stripping off bloody plaster, respackling and painting his office when Wolf returned from DC. It was just after seven and he was scheduled to pick Amanda up at ten for the party her sister Stevie was throwing at a downtown club. He was about to phone her to cancel when he thought better of it. He was tired, but too wound up to sleep. And maybe Amanda was right. A little R and R in the midst of the bedlam coming down sounded pretty good to him.

He checked in with Squire Richards, who brought him up to date on calls, but the only one he was looking for, from Harrison, the CME, hadn't materialized. He put in a call, was told Harrison was currently not in the building, though he was expected to return.

Wolf went back down the drop-clothed corridor to the shower he'd had installed in the public-sized men's toilet. They were painting here, too. Christ, the entire place was crawling with them, Hayes Walker Johnson flexing the mighty muscles of his authority.

The lone painter here was a Japanese, as compact and burly as a miniature sumo, working high up on a spackle-encrusted ladder. He wore torn overalls hooked over bare shoulders, adamant with dense muscle.

Though his steely hair and the lines in his face indicated that he was decades older than his fellow workers, the lines of his body seemed ageless. He nodded to Wolf, went back to his work on the muddy plaster of the ceiling. Wolf's shower was punctuated by the soft booms and slaps occasioned by chunks of rotting plaster crashing to the drop-cloth spread over the black-and-white tiled floor.

Drying off and dressing in new clothes pulled from his locker, he stared up at the painter, thought, I'll never look at a Japanese the same way again.

'Have you been with the department long?' he called out.

The painter stopped his work with the plaster, looked down at Wolf. 'Not long,' he said. Then, 'Is there a problem?'

'How long?' Wolf asked him.

He put down his tool, came down the ladder. 'Maybe you think of me as a potential security risk,' he said as he wiped his hands on his overalls. 'Is it because I'm Japanese?' He turned away, began to clean up. 'Well I get that all the time. That doesn't make it right, but I guess it's a fact of life I'll have to live with if I want to stay in America.'

Wolf, thinking of his mother, of the Wind River Shoshone, his own childhood, was abruptly ashamed. His talk with Shipley had made him paranoid – he'd forgotten how proximity with a spook could do that to you. It had also, he thought now, scared the hell out of him. Was it any wonder he was seeing spooks in every dark corner? He'd have to watch that.

'Forget it,' he said. 'I was just curious. And it had nothing to do with you being Japanese.'

The painter turned back, ran his hands down the legs of his overalls again. He made a motion – more than a nod of his head, perhaps a modern-day formal bow. 'Okay if I get back to work?'

'Sure,' Wolf said, throwing his damp towel into the wire basket against the wall. 'Don't let me get in the way.'

He went back down the hall, still slightly disturbed by his newly acquired prejudice, found Squire Richards looking for him. 'Just got a message, Lieutenant,' he said, trotting up. 'Tony's found the black '87 Firebird.'

Tony Three Times was waiting for them on a pier at West 43rd Street. The oily, dark Hudson slapped at the rotting timbers, and the smell of sulphur was intense. Wolf looked out at the water, saw yellowish snowflakes disappearing into it as if into a vat of acid.

Behind them, burned out tenements, abandoned to the wrecking ball of some contractor now in Chapter 11, were filled to overflowing with families, filthy and destitute, who had abandoned all hope of looking for the American dream. It was another of the crack cities that had grown up like cankers throughout the city. And, as if to underscore the insufficiency of these brownstone husks, the side streets debouching onto the piers that, a century before, had helped make New York the premier seaport on the East Coast, were clogged with makeshift shanties of cardboard and pressed tin. Fires burning before their cave-like entrances gave the whole the aspect of a medieval village.

Tony Three Times led them out onto the pier where the black '87 Firebird hulked like some prehistoric monster, its shell throwing back in distortion the night lights of the city. The interior was scorched, and some of the paintwork on the hood and the roof was scarred by heat, blackened with soot.

'Looks to me like someone started the fire after the car was dumped here, Lieutenant,' Tony Three Times said, training his flashlight on the car.

'Fuckin' kids, high on junk, torching it,' Squire Richards said, flicking on his own flashlight.

'Maybe,' Wolf said, ducking into the interior. But, if it was kids, he thought, why did they torch something as valuable as a set of wheels? More kicks to be had driving it down the Sawmill River Parkway at one hundred miles per.

He sniffed, thought immediately of Bobby Connor's story of a blue fireball, the heat coming off Arquillo's stone-dead face, the flicker of a phantom flame along his cheekbone. He sniffed again, found no traces of lighter fluid or gasoline, the first signs of arson.

He took out a steel stylus from his leather aviator's jacket pocket, poked around the blackened rubble of the front seat and dashboard. The glove compartment had been melted shut by the fire, so he asked Tony Three Times, who made a speciality of getting into locked things, to pop it.

Inside, he found burned crisps of paper, black flakes of the interior material. He poked the stylus in deeper until he encountered the back wall. Nothing in the right corner, nothing along the rear perimeter, but the tip of the stylus punctured something wedged into the left corner. He drew it out, brought it into the snowy night. Tony Three Times shone his flashlight onto it.

'What the hell is that?' Squire Richards said.

'A piece of trapunto,' Wolf said, turning the square of woven fabric around, one side singed, yes, but the rest of it, though stinking of smoke, whole and recognizable as material used by the Japanese artist Chika.

Yuji Shian signed off on a memo that would create 100,000 Shian

95

Kogaku telephone cards. These plastic wafers would be distributed to the company's best accounts, political and bureaucratic allies, giving them prepaid time from any public phone. A hologram of the Shian Kogaku logo filled the centre of the cards and, when the telephone time was used up, would turn them into valuable collector's items. Great marketing idea, Yuji thought, another example of the reality of our advertising tag line, SHIAN KOGAKU: WE ARE ALWAYS WITH YOU.

Yuji took, in succession, calls from Singapore, Taipei, Silicone Valley, and, lastly, Hong Kong.

When he was finished, he pushed back his chair, laced his fingers behind his neck, stared out at the gleaming towers of Tokyo. Although Yuji was so high up he could still see the summer sun, bloated and reddened by pollution, the streets surrounding the Hammacho Station were plunged into shadow so deep he knew it must seem like evening to the hordes of people rushing by so far below him.

Yuji grunted. He wondered what it was like to be down there in the artificial twilight, running, running, always running; he wondered what it was like to live in one room with three roommates, to eat soba – buckwheat noodles – from sidewalk stalls at every meal because that was all you could afford, and some nights going without food at all.

It had taken him many years to understand this as the basis for his friendship with Shoto Wakare. *'Though it seems like so long ago that destitute wretch might have been another me, living another life, I have not forgotten what it is like to be poor in Tokyo,'* Wakare had once told him, the two of them on an all-night drunk. *'It would be shameful to allow myself to forget such an important lesson: having nothing prepares you for nothing save having nothing again.'*

Having nothing had never been Yuji Shian's problem. He had been born into a family with a thriving mercantile business, generations old, that had been passed down on his mother Minako's side from daughter to daughter. Traditionally, these matriarchal firms were run from behind the scenes by the women while the men they had chosen in marriage fronted them, even to the point of taking their family name as their own.

Yuji's father had been something different. A banker by profession, he had agreed to marry Minako and take the Shian name. But he had quickly grown discontented with the restrictions inherent in a mid-sized mercantile firm. Accordingly, he proposed moving Shian Kogaku from Osaka to Tokyo, buying a nearly bankrupt commercial bank as their core *kobun* or company, turning it around, and using its new-found strength to buy other *kobun*, to build Shian Kogaku into a *keiretsu* of the first rank.

Minako, as ambitious as her new husband, had agreed, but it was only afterwards, when the deed was done and all her assets had been ploughed into the bank to help it turn around, that Yuji's father told her that she

96

could no longer run Shian Kogaku, even behind the scenes. If even a hint that she was involved should get out to his business contacts, he told her, the company would be dead. No one would want to do business with a company run by a woman; no one would take such a venture seriously.

Minako had come from a long line of businesswomen, accustomed to skilfully handling their own affairs without male interference. Perhaps there were some who might have said, this will kill her. But it did not kill Minako. As had always been the case in her life, men – even the ones closest to her – had underestimated her. The exquisite exterior hid a tough shrewd interior, one that was resilient and held its own secrets.

'*I understand,*' Minako dutifully said when her husband had told her of his decision and, without a word of protest, had given up all involvement in her own company.

'*This was my punishment for being a woman,*' Minako had once told Yuji. But, years later, it occurred to Yuji that she had not taken her punishment lying down. From that day on her relationship with her husband had changed drastically. And when, at length, he died of a heart attack, having seen his dream for Shian Kogaku come true, Yuji was unsure what had killed him, overwork or his wife's coldness. In truth, Minako shed no tears for him. And as for him, several years before his premature death, he said to Yuji during a drunken bout, '*If you trust a woman, you will eventually be disembowelled.*'

Yuji shivered, thinking of how this poison had affected his own life. He had married a woman as weak as his mother was strong. This irony was hardly lost on him, but he felt unable to change course. Had he even fallen in love with her? Who could tell? Yuji was consumed by his work. He delighted in the knowledge that he had turned his love of biogenetics into a full-blown business venture that added to what his father had given his life to build. Shian Kogaku now boasted successful *kobun* in computer hardware, advanced laser technology and the budding biosciences.

Yuji's wife was beautiful, delicate and fragile, a porcelain doll whom he could admire as all his associates admired her. In a way, she was another symbol of his burgeoning success, having come from a prominent samurai family whose lineage could be traced back to Edo, the capital, in the 1600s.

Yuji had had only one child, a son. And, quite naturally, Yuji drove him in his studies as he had been driven by his father. The boy grew strong and handsome and, if he was not quite first in his class, Yuji had high hopes that he would be first before he graduated.

But last year, Yuji and his wife were suddenly called to the school his son attended. Sallow-faced school officials conducted them to the critical ward of the nearby hospital where Yuji's son lay in an irreversible coma; he had tried to commit suicide by hanging himself from a beam in his room.

It took him three weeks to die; it took Yuji's wife three months. Heartbreak can do that to you, he had read. He had never believed it, however, until he saw it happening to his wife. She stepped in front of a subway train at the height of rush hour.

When pressed, city officials politely said they had adequate safeguards against such an occurrence. A tragic accident, the police called it, but he knew better. She walked off that platform as surely as he was sitting here watching the industrial haze strangle Tokyo. All his influence and he could do nothing to save her. At that point, Yuji suspected his wife had been particularly determined.

Watching her being buried, it occurred to him that he had never before been aware that she could be so in control of her life. For the first time, she reminded him of his mother, and he hated her for secretly harbouring this hideous strength in her bosom like a poisonous viper.

In the weeks and months that followed, he found himself gripped by an odd manic mood he could not dispel. He hit all the night spots, drank, gambled, fornicated. And wherever he was seen there were always two nubile women on his arm. His half-sister Hana could see what he did not: that this mania was merely a manifestation of the guilt and self-loathing he felt – but could not face – for his role in his son's death. She told him this later, when she saw the mania burning itself out and she felt confident about reaching into the psychic fire without getting burned herself.

Hana had saved him from himself. Hana and his work on the Oracle.

'Hana,' he had said, one sorrowful night, *'what did you think of my wife?'*

Hana's eyes moved slowly to settle on his face. *'From the first day of your marriage your wife had her life, and you had yours,'* she had said in that direct way of hers that he found almost painful.

'Were we really estranged from the very beginning?'

'That was the way you wanted it.'

'No,' he said slowly, *'I didn't. I couldn't.'*

'You seem to forget that you always get what you want, Yuji-san.'

He had thought a moment, feeling her hand warm and pulsing in his. *'She was beautiful, though, wasn't she?'*

'Beauty,' Hana had said, *'is like a curtain or a frieze, a facade that only hints at the life behind the surface.'*

'You understand about that. I wish you could tell me what it's like to absorb life in that way.'

'I think it's impossible to communicate, in any language,' she said. *'But that really doesn't matter, since you already possess the ability.'*

98

'My curse.'

'Why do you call your sight a curse?'

'Isn't it?' he said. 'I did not see my son's . . . death nor my wife's. I can neither see the future nor predict it. I can on occasion see possibilities, many paths branching from the single moment of the present. Can't you understand how something like that could drive you insane?'

'If you could look at your life from death to birth, it might drive you insane, too,' she said. 'But suppose that you were misunderstanding this ability?'

'What do you mean?'

'Imagine that the present was not, after all, a "single moment", as you have defined it, but instead a multiplicity of choices, like an explosion at each fraction of a second. In that event, seeing the many paths created by such explosions would have a kind of logic and, once you began to learn the vernacular of that logic, they might even start to have meaning for you.'

'I don't understand.'

'Not yet, perhaps.'

What would he do without her? Yuji rubbed his eyes, looked at the time. Then, grabbing his coat, he left the building. He ducked into his waiting BMW, said to his driver, 'Hana's.'

It was dark by the time Wolf arrived at the graffiti-blanketed red-brick tenement on East Sixth Street just off Avenue C. The snow had changed to sleet, then back again to snow. Downstairs was a clothing store called La Mort C'est Moi. Very pleasant. Wolf peered through the steel gates – every item in the window was black and looked as if it was made to fit Frankenstein's monster. Perhaps it was closed because no one wanted to wear that stuff any more, but he doubted it.

He went around the corner, and put his foot to the accelerator, swung around west on East Fifth, then north to the corner of East Sixth. He pulled over, killed the engine and the lights. He got out and went cautiously down the block.

Lights were on in the apartment Moun had said belonged to Chika, but Wolf could not see through the opaque shades. Keeping to the shadows, he headed for the tenement doorway. He popped the lock, went inside.

The tenement hallway was lit by a fly-specked fifteen-watt bulb. The feeble light, exaggerating shadows, obscuring corners, hid more than it revealed. The stink of urine and excrement was nauseating. A huge old German shepherd with the worst case of mange Wolf had ever seen sat curled at the foot of the stairs, licking the bare pink patches on its flanks. Its head came up, yellow eyes luminous as it stared at him. Wolf saw its nostrils flare as it scented him, then its head lowered, the tongue came out, and it went back to work. The rhythmic lapping sound was grating.

He stepped over the dog, went up the filthy stairs. The bannister was greasy and, at the first landing, he was certain the dark brown stains on the wall were dried blood. He wondered briefly whose head had been busted here and by whom.

Oddly, for a bottom of the barrel tenement, there were only two doors on this floor, for, it appeared, oversized front and rear apartments. He checked out the one filthy window that led onto an iron fire escape. He ran his hand along the rough plastered walls, feeling places where doors to the other apartments had once been; despite the stink and slime downstairs, someone had been doing a lot of renovating up here.

He stood for a moment, listening to the ambient sounds of the old building. It was important to get a sense of the natural sounds of the environment so that when some new noise was introduced you could pick it up immediately.

He went to the front door of Chika's apartment, put his ear to the door, but could hear nothing. Once, he would have just gone up to the door and knocked, using the same cover he'd put on Moun. But not after Washington, seeing Chika in the company of Suma, the Water-spider, and certainly not after finding a piece of her trapunto in the black '87 Firebird.

If she had driven the getaway car for Suma or, even worse for him, if she had been the one to off Junior Ruiz and Arquillo, he would not want to approach her frontally. She'd already know who he was – and, he reminded himself, if she *had* been responsible for the double homicide, he would not be able to read her aura. He moved away from the door; there was no way in here.

He put his ear to the door of the rear apartment, heard Skinny Puppy grinding out a gut-wrenching monotone song on the tenant's stereo. No entry here, either, he thought.

Abruptly, he twitched, knelt, and his piece came out, aimed down the black stairwell. He heard something: soft sounds on the stairs, ascending. He tried to find an aura, failed. Suma?

Crouched down, waiting, he thought of Suma's face, the Water-spider's eyes like pits into infinity. He blinked, concentrated on the black hole leading down to the first floor, his finger taut on the trigger. Waiting for Suma.

C'mon, you sonuvabitch, he thought, come up here and take a bullet through the heart.

In a moment, the old shepherd padded laboriously into view. One of its rear legs must have been broken at one time, because the dog

100

was limping badly. The shepherd stared at him, then began to lick the muzzle of his service revolver.

He let out a long-held breath, his mouth jerked in the semblance of a smile, then he holstered his gun, got back to work. He prised open the window that led out onto the fire escape, climbed out into the dank night. He stood for a moment on the fire escape, listening to the city pulse on around him. It was like a leviathan whose heart throbbed on despite its grubby, decaying flesh; there was life, Wolf thought, even in the moment of dying.

The greasy snow had collected on the iron runners of the fire escape, and he had to make his way carefully. It had turned colder, and his exhalations emerged as puffs of steam.

Wolf turned his attention to the pair of double windows of Chika's apartment. What he had thought from the street were shades he saw now was a form of pigment smeared on the glass of the new panes from the inside. Swirls of iridescent black paint turned the glass translucent: light streamed through it but it was impossible to make out details of what or who was inside.

Wolf crouched down, testing one window after another. The first three were locked, but the last one was open a crack. He lifted the window an inch at a time; it made no noise. Then he ducked into a horizontal position, slipped inside the apartment.

He was in a dark room. At first, he heard nothing. Then slowly, as if his ears had to adjust to a different environment, he heard the heavy thrumming as of an engine or a compressor. Slowly and carefully, he made his way through the room. He was aware of shapes, as of massive furniture covered by drop-cloths used when painting or leaving a place vacant for a long time. Cautiously, he lifted a corner up, saw jagged pieces of burned metal covered with trapunto. Sculptures being born.

Careful, he thought. Be patient.

He crept towards a door. Beyond, was the living room; he could see no one in there so he went through the door. The walls of the living room were bare except for one painting in an ornate gilt frame. It was large, and set into the bottom of the frame was a plaque with its title, *The Salon in the Rue des Moulins*. Wolf stared at the painting, powerful and erotic, of the whores of Paris. In their shabbiness, in the informality – the naturalness – of their nakedness, in their acceptance of fornication resided their humanity. He had never before seen whores depicted as human beings, never before considered that motherhood and scandalous sex could co-exist in one person, and he found himself drawn to the moral paradox the painting presented. At length the signature in the corner of the painting drew his eye: Henri de Toulouse-Lautrec. Christ,

101

he thought, could this be the original? He peered more closely, but he was no art expert. What would it be worth if it was the original? Millions? Hundreds of millions, more like it. He left the living room not because he wanted to but because he had to.

In the kitchen, he found the source of the thrumming: an enormous generator. Behind a door with no lock or knob he found a professionally equipped darkroom, a battery of Nikon, Leica and Hasselblad cameras, lenses, tripods and spotlights. A small refrigerator held boxes of film; on top of it, stacks of round plastic containers housed filters of every variety. Wolf thought of the photos in Moravia's cubicle. Could Chika have been the photographer; could she have been the model; could she have been both?

He went back across the living room on the outside of his soles. The newly laid wooden floor was so shiny he could see his imperfect reflection in its surface.

Another door, this one half opened. Wolf stood so that his shadow would not cross the threshold. In this way he could see a good wedge of the room beyond. There was a distinct scent emanating from the room. It seemed vaguely familiar, but Wolf could not remember where he had smelled it.

Abruptly, there was movement, and he had to fight the instinct to move in response. He felt a prickling along his spine as he watched the silhouette of the exquisite Japanese woman he had seen across the avenue from Urban Decay, who had shown up with Suma in the Defense Department surveillance photo. This was Chika, the artist who, in some way, had insinuated herself into Lawrence Moravia's life. Was she an innocent, who happened to be at the wrong place at the wrong time or was she the assassin the Black Blade Society had sent to take care of Moravia?

He continued to watch, transfixed. She was staring at something on the side of the room that Wolf could not see. She turned her body and the silhouette resolved into three-dimensional flesh. Warm lamplight flowed slowly, sinuously over Chika's flank, throwing her high, hard breasts into prominence. She stretched her legs as if readying herself for a strenuous exercise.

She was naked. The light was strange, as if it had been combined with mist or syrup, as if Wolf could actually see it moving, coiling and dripping in attenuated tears. She ran a hand over her breast, down her rib cage, over her flat belly. The hand, lowered further, disappeared into a triangular forest of shadow.

He could smell that scent, foreign and yet peculiarly familiar. He drank it in, trying to recall where he had first smelled it. Her lips parted

102

as she altered her stance subtly; it was now more erotic, as if she were opening herself in some unfathomable way. Then, with her other hand, she pressed a spot low on her spine and her hips canted forward; her hand moving, moving, she made a tiny moan.

Wolf could feel the feral beating of his heart, as heavy as the thrumming of the engine somewhere in the apartment. He knew he should turn around and, as Bobby would say, get outta there, but he could not move. His felt as if his feet were nailed to the floor, as if his lungs were breathing liquid oxygen. There was sex here, to be sure, powerful and magnetic, but he knew there was something more, an aspect hidden, as significant as it was seductive.

There was a sense about this of a performance – disturbing in the manner of the photos of female bondage, of her sculptures – but for whom, and why?

Those thighs. Luscious meat moved beneath taut skin the colour and intensity of bronze. The long, developed muscles began to bunch and knot, and abruptly, there was a line of tension that marred the side of her neck. Curiously, this marring – like a scar – became an added excitement, as if Wolf were seeing a secret part of her inaccessible to the outside world.

Those thighs were trembling now, Chika almost rocking in the last throes of her self-induced ecstasy. He could hear the soft 'uh-uh-uh!' as the primitive sounds were pushed up through her diaphragm, out of her mouth.

Her eyelids fluttered, but her gaze never wavered. Wolf, rapt as he was, still longed to see what she saw, to know what she was thinking, to understand the nature of her performance – if it was a performance at all. What would the answers tell him?

And, then, as abruptly as a shark's dorsal fin rising from water, he entertained the mad notion that Suma was actually in the room with Chika, that, together, they had lured him here in order to set him up for a kill. Here in this strange apartment with this eerie Japanese woman to whom he was curiously and powerfully drawn and of whom he was inexplicably afraid, he abruptly felt more naked than she, so exposed that he shivered. He should have been able to feel Suma's – or anyone else's – aura, but he encountered only impenetrable blackness.

Abruptly overcome by the cloying fetor of the chaos that was destroying his understanding of the world, he retreated out onto the snow-covered fire escape, ducked back inside the second floor hallway. He put his hand on the sweaty bannister – or perhaps it was his hand that was sweating.

He shivered; the cold seemed to pierce to the core of him all of a sudden. Still, he could not leave. He stared at the second-floor apartment. His instinct told him that he had managed to avoid a cleverly set trap, that he now had a unique chance to trap the would-be trappers.

Wait, he thought. Be patient. See who comes out.

Within twenty minutes, the lights were extinguished in the second-floor apartment and, several moments later, Chika emerged from the tenement. No one was with her, and somehow now he was certain she had been alone up there. It was as if, with her on the street, he encountered no trouble scanning the apartment and feeling its lack of human aura.

She was dressed much as she had been yesterday: high heels, black micro skirt, oversized bomber jacket. Her black leather bag was thrown over one shoulder; she searched in it for a moment before heading east, away from where Wolf was hidden in the shadows of a doorway. Her heels made dull sounds against the slush-covered pavement.

He started after her. The snow was coming down harder again. The sky had a fragile, powdery look like old gums into which the rotting teeth of the city's pest-infested tenements were loosely set.

Around the corner, two blocks south, he saw her striding down the avenue. She passed through steam venting from the sewers, disappeared, reappeared in silhouette. He did not have to keep her in sight; the sound of her chrome heels striking the pavement was enough to lead him on.

At East Second Street she turned back west. He was struck by how she walked with complete confidence, as if she had no fear of anything or anyone around her. He dropped back, suddenly aware that he was closing the distance between them.

When he got her in sight again, he saw that she had been stopped by a pair of slum kids. They wore baseball jackets, high-topped sneakers, black jeans – the uniform of the streets. The sides of their heads were shaved but elsewhere there were great bristly thickets of hair, shiny with gel. One carried a pig-sticker, a crude knife with a foot-long blade, the other held a hockey stick with razor blades affixed with black electrician's tape to its curved blade.

The kid with the doctored stick was tapping it impatiently on the pavement while his buddy swung the pig-sticker through the snowy night in one arc parallel to her breasts, a second parallel to her groin. The kids laughed wildly. Wolf wondered what combination of drugs they were on.

104

The kids were close to Chika now, and Wolf knew he had to make a decision. He did not want to show himself, but he could not let the punks hurt her. He was working on a cover story she might believe about why he was where he was at this time of the night when she took the decision out of his hands.

Chika withdrew her left hand from her pocketbook, and Wolf could see the glint of a gun. It was made of blued steel, the reliable workmanlike model of a professional. It was clear by how she stood, legs spread, how she aimed the pistol first at the head of one punk, then the other that she knew precisely what she was doing. She said something to the kids that must have unnerved them even more than the weapon because the kid with the pig-sticker let it drop as the two of them turned and ran.

She stayed in her marksman's position until she was certain the punks would not return, then she replaced the gun in her pocketbook but did not withdraw her hand. Wolf guessed that she had had hold of the pistol from the moment she had left the tenement on East Sixth Street.

He followed, saw her turn north when she got to Second Avenue. She stopped in front of the facade of a funeral parlour. It had some unreadable name, being square in the middle of the Ukrainian district. Light streamed through the thick yellow pebbled glass on either side of the wooden front doors.

The sidewalk was jammed with street people, shuffling, muttering or just staring into space as they waited in some kind of line. Wolf watched the head of the line as it wound up at the front doors to the funeral parlour where people were being served food by a corpulent, sweating funeral director. For a moment, Wolf watched his face, as expressions flitted over the flat planes: distaste, pity, relief, satisfaction. It was strange, thinking of this man tending the dead by day, then feeding the living by night, but there was a cruel symmetry that seemed to fit this granite-edged city, a kind of rough justice.

Wolf pulled back into the shadows of a doorway just before Chika looked quickly around, cursing as he stumbled over a man wrapped in newspapers. The stench of Sterno was overpowering.

'Git outta my house,' the newspaper-wrapped man growled thickly. 'Find yer own place t'flop.'

Wolf glanced back down the avenue in time to see a hearse without a rear licence plate pull up in front of the funeral parlour. It was new, metallic charcoal and chrome, shining like a cue ball in the lurid yellow light.

The newspaper-wrapped man began batting ineffectually at Wolf's shins. Chika stepped smartly off the kerb and, to Wolf's amazement, opened the back of the hearse with a practised twist of her wrist and climbed in. The hearse took off.

'Son of a bitch,' Wolf said, stepping out into the street as the hearse disappeared into the truck traffic rumbling uptown.

FIVE

New York City/Tokyo

Wolf and Amanda arrived at La Mentira, a rock club between Avenues B and A, just after eleven. On their way downtown they had to detour off Park Avenue South because an enormous granite tower had collapsed inwards. The structure, ironically the home office of a giant insurance company, was surrounded and supported by a complex spiderweb of wooden scaffolding crawling up its bottom half. The naked light bulbs draped in tiers threw an eerie blue light upon the disaster, but the new aluminium street lights were nowhere in evidence, having been uprooted by looters to be sold on the flourishing black market for scrap metal.

It seemed to Wolf that there was little sense of the modern world here; the cracks and fissures, the canted outer walls gave the building an entirely new aspect: it was as if he were looking at the decaying remnants of the hanging gardens of Babylon.

'They say there's a hole under there as big as the Holland Tunnel,' Wolf said, nodding in the building's direction. 'You can bet traffic will be screwed up around here for at least a year, and forget about using the Lex subway in our lifetime. The only ones not suffering are the street people; they've got miles of new warrens to explore and settle into.' He looked over at Amanda, scrunched into the far corner of the seat, but she said nothing.

Downtown, the street along which La Mentira was set was ankle deep in litter, blowing here and there in tiny wind-lashed spirals. The ancient tenements that long ago had forgotten their first tony owners had that carapace of black grit peculiar to New York that even steam cleaning would not penetrate.

Young people as thin and bent as whippets clattered down the filthy, disintegrating sidewalk in their black boots, black jeans or tights, black chrome-studded leather jackets, thick chains and spiked spurs jingling rhythmically. All of them – boys and girls alike – had multiple earrings; many had nose studs or rings.

A city sanitation truck, so covered with graffiti Wolf could not tell what colour it had originally been painted, rumbled down the street.

Although there were plenty of dented garbage cans filled to overflowing, the truck passed them all by. Two thin black urchins with Reeboks on their feet and Walkman earphones around their heads sat in the enormous hopper at the back, picking through unmashed trash. They could not have been more than eight or nine years old. At the end of the block, the urchins leapt out and, clutching their loot, ran screaming around the corner onto Avenue B.

He parked the car illegally, and they got out. Arching above their heads he could see La Mentira's mud-spattered black and yellow awning with its rather too explicit painting of a big-breasted Egyptian queen holding a skull in one hand, a shape that looked suspiciously like a male member in the other.

Seeing several Japanese in the throng filing in, Amanda said, 'I hear a lot of stories on campus about the Japanese.'

She had been utterly silent on the way downtown, but when he had commented on it, she had merely turned her head, looked out of the window. He had never quite got used to this closed side of her. Perhaps the detective in him was disturbed by her refusal to talk about these odd black moods, conjured up malevolent conspiracies, whole other lives as explanation. In any case, he was happy she was talking again. 'What kinds of stories?'

'Oh, you know, so many people these days even in academia seem prejudiced against them, so there's always some juicy bit of catty gossip about the Japanese professors. They don't mingle too well, and many of my colleagues think of them as having a superior attitude.'

'And what do you think?' Wolf asked.

Amanda sighed. 'I haven't been able to make friends with any of them. But, on the other hand, it seems to me they're appalled at what they see in New York. I think many of them believe in a kind of purity of breeding – you know, Japan for the Japanese – and come to think of America as a second-class nation because of what they see as the mongrelization of our blood.' She shrugged. 'For all I really know of them, they may see a posting to America the way I would view a job in Africa. It's great for the résumé but I wouldn't want to live there.'

She took his arm as they squeezed through the entrance, so they wouldn't be separated by the crush of people. 'For years my ivory-tower colleagues liked to use this bigotry against the Japanese, to show off how America's melting pot was what made us great. But, lately, though they won't admit it even to one another, they look around them at what's happening to the city – the increasing polarization of economic classes, the inflammatory hatred, the escalation of race bias; in short, the fracturing of our Republic – and they are secretly ashamed. They no longer know how to respond to the Japanese criticism of us, and they hate the Japanese all the more for it.'

Wolf was intrigued. He wondered how Shipley the spook would respond to Amanda's thesis – or, for that matter, how Amanda would react to Shipley's all-too-possible doomsday scenario of America's near future.

'One thing's for sure, though, the Japanese *are* different from us in many ways,' Amanda continued, looking this way and that for her sister Stevie. 'Their idea of sex, for instance, is not ours.'

'Did you get this hot off the campus grapevine?'

She laughed. 'Not in the least. There was a film, did you see it? *In the Realm of the Senses*, where a couple try to strangle each other just as they come. I think they were trying to elicit the best orgasm ever. It's considered a classic of its genre in Japan.'

Wolf was thinking of the laser disc in Lawrence Moravia's apartment: *In the Realm of the Senses.* And that led, inexorably, to a mental image of Chika's strong thighs, scissoring as she stepped down into the street, the rain beating against her bomber jacket, beading over her rice-paper umbrella; Chika, thighs bent, hips canted forward, hot breath rushing out of her open mouth as her fingers disappeared between her legs; Chika, naked and wet, coming with a soft, perfumed cry.

'Wolf?'

'What?'

'You had the oddest look on your face.'

'These people . . . '

Watching how these so-called patrons of the arts dressed was a show in itself: gowns by Mizrahi and Ferre, weird spangled bustier-type items by Lacroix and leather sweep dresses by Montana, nothing less bizarre than what the trade on the street was clad in, just more expensive. Amanda, with Wolf in tow, cleaved through sweating clumps of these people, who, like Victorian vampires, ventured out only at night.

La Mentira was made up of three cavernous rooms, the first a kind of new-wave lounge with uncomfortable-looking banquettes that snaked across a floor paved in thick translucent glass tiles. Under the tiles, coloured lights turned everyone's legs sickly shades of red, blue and violet. Along one wall was a kitschy tiger-striped bar with a copper top and, on the wall behind it, Kewpie dolls from the forties and fifties lined up where bottles of liquor would normally be.

The second room, the largest of the three, was normally where the dancing took place. Tonight, the polished hardwood floor contained the paintings and sculptures of the artists being promoted by the party. The place was jam-packed with people and music was pouring out of every speaker, of which there were ten times too many.

How Stevie found them in the madhouse Wolf never knew, but she appeared out of the throngs of people to kiss her sister on both cheeks, squeeze Wolf's hand. Stevie Powers was a psychotherapist and also a member of the board of the most prestigious arts and science councils of the city. One group or another was always sponsoring society bashes such as this one. It was, Wolf supposed, Stevie's way of contributing to society. She and her husband, Morton Danaher, had a five bedroom co-op on Fifth Avenue as well as a house in East Hampton. God knows how much money they had. They were like a golden couple, perfect together.

Stevie looked nothing like her older sister. She was dark-haired, dark-eyed, her figure voluptuous where Amanda's was slimmer. She had delicate, long-fingered hands – artist's hands – which always seemed in motion. Her lush body moved in quick bursts with the kind of precision reserved for actors or surgeons. It must have been her husband who had moved her into the elite circles of New York society because Amanda knew none of the old monied family scions with whom Stevie hung out.

'God, I'm so happy you made it, Panda,' Stevie said. '*Everyone* who's anyone is here tonight. There are so many people I want you to meet!'

Wolf supposed that she did not mean to be deliberately rude to him, but he was also aware that she was, though never less than polite, always cool to him. Perhaps she disapproved of what he did for a living. Who knew with siblings?

Amanda kissed him quickly on the cheek as Stevie began to pull her into the fray. She gave him a sorrowful look, but he knew better. She adored meeting Stevie's list of the rich and famous.

He drifted on his own into the main room, looked at the artwork. Most of it was abstract to the extreme. He wondered whatever happened to Expressionism. It seemed to him that too much of what was considered 'modern' by the art world was devoid of either sense or feeling. He did not believe that space necessarily needed to be filled. Having been exposed to Japanese culture in the form of the martial arts, he could appreciate what was essentially negative space – emptiness that formed the context for a single concise image, for instance. Meaning could manifest itself in many strange and unexpected forms.

As he moved around the ellipse of artwork, he came to the end of the paintings, the beginning of the sculptures: metal armatures upon which had been affixed globs of cooled bronze the colour of honey, African hardwoods, as vividly striped as a zebra's skin, plaster lacquered shades of brown. They were all mute, impassive, their lifelessness awkward and

110

coarse. Even in death, Wolf thought, objects such as a Pharaoh's mummy could be eloquent.

All except the last sculpture, which rose above his head. He stopped in front of it, and perhaps because he was already familiar with the disturbing style he found the confluence of the black twisted metal, the bright tribal trapunto fabrics, had a voice all its own.

He was looking at another example of Chika's artwork, and now he turned, moving methodically through the crowd, searching for her.

He made a full circuit of the main room without spotting her, so he headed towards the smallest of the rooms, a dizzying mirror-lined restaurant with fake fur-covered chairs and postage stamp-sized tables that seemed to lurch with every crash of bass, percussion and drums of the wildly amplified music of Redbox and the Pet Shop Boys.

His mind was filled with Chika. What was it about her? She was beautiful, yes, and exotic but he had come in contact with other beautiful women without experiencing this feeling of – *what*?

Déjà vu? Could that be it? But surely he had never seen her before. And yet, staring into those huge black eyes he heard the worldsong of White Bow, felt again the elation and terror he thought only his grandfather could elicit from him. He felt the triphammer beat of his heart, the surge in his pulse and, for just an instant, the impossible happened: he forgot about Suma and Lawrence Moravia.

He scanned each table as he moved through the aisles, dense with people. He quartered the room from front to back, turning back every fifteen seconds or so to monitor who was coming into the restaurant. In the rear, he paused, eyeing the entrance one more time before pushing his way through the swinging doors into the kitchen area.

It was a madhouse in there as well: cooks, assistants, waiters, busboys. The air was humid with food and steam. Wolf took a tour around the islands of stainless steel sinks, counters laden with chopped vegetables, slabs of raw meat, the huge stoves, singing with bubbling vats of soup, deep fryers for French fries and onion rings.

At the back, out of sight of the main part of the kitchen, was an alcove against which was set the thick metal door to the meat locker. Wolf glanced over there and stood rooted to the spot at the scene in front of him.

Squire Richards, his black skin turned blue by the bright fluorescent bars overhead, had hold of a thin, handsome man in shirtsleeves and tie, his fists clutching the man's shirtfront as he bent him up against the door to the meat locker.

'You're late with the payment, Dickie,' Squire Richards growled. 'I'll take your money now or I'll take my shiv to that gorgeous face of yours.

111

And what would you be without that? You'd have to sell this club when all your fag friends abandoned you.'

'Okay, okay,' the handsome man said in a high-pitched squeal more appropriate to a terrified woman. 'I'll give you your damned money. Just don't cut me.'

Wolf waited until Squire Richards dropped the club owner and the money had changed hands.

'Mr Sansone, take your money and get out of here,' Wolf said.

Both men turned, transfixed with shock and fear. Wolf went over, took the money from Squire Richards, slapped it into Sansone's hand. 'My sincere apologies for this misunderstanding,' he said. 'I promise you this will not reoccur.' He gave him his card. 'If you ever have any problems please call me. My direct number is on the card, you can reach me day or night.'

Sansone, still slightly stunned, nodded, pocketed the money and the card. Then he gave Wolf a tentative smile and, taking a handkerchief to wipe the sweat off his face, hurried out to the party.

Wolf turned to Squire Richards. 'Just what the hell did you think you were doing?'

The black detective said nothing. He seemed to be biting his lip.

'What is the matter with you? You know I won't tolerate corrupt cops on my staff.'

'I'm not corrupt,' Richards said stolidly.

'You think not? Internal Affairs will not, I assure you, take that point of view.'

'Is that what yo' gonna do with me, turn me over to IA?' It was said as an accusation, the tone not lost on Wolf.

'Squire, I'm asking you for an explanation.'

Richards turned away, went over to a sink, got himself a glass of water. Wolf stood next to him, as patient as Amanda was with him, waiting. Finishing his water, Richards put his glass down, looked nervously at the kitchen staff who, busy as they were, seemed to be watching them out of the corners of their eyes. Assured that, at least, no one could hear them, he said at last, 'I needed the money,' and left it at that, as if that was all Wolf needed to know.

'And?'

Richards looked at him. 'Weren't no big thing, man. These sleazeballs are used to doling out the bread, health inspector, liquor licence board, Mafia deliver their fish ev'ry day for a price. Payoffs, all of 'em, that's how these bastards stay in business, you know that. I was just getting a piece of mine. This guy's rich, bread I ask for he won't even miss.'

112

Wolf stood very close to Richards. 'Think some of that belongs to you, do you?'

'Needed the bread, man, I tol' you.'

'Squire, I *will* turn you over to IA unless you're clean with me.'

'I needed money to bail my brother outta the loan sharks he got hisself into,' Richards said, his voice rising. 'Okay? Got it, bossman, now get outta my face!' He reached out, shoved Wolf back into the door against which he had held Dick Sansone, then turned, began to make his way through the kitchen. Wolf went after him, spun him around. 'You're a good cop, Squire, but you've got to learn the limits of your badge. You've got power, but you can't just use it indiscriminately whenever it suits you.'

'I said why I did it.'

'That's not good enough,' Wolf said. 'No reason can justify a felony, which is what you committed tonight.'

'You *are* gonna turn me in. Serves me right bein' loyal to a honky. You're just like all the rest, you had your mind made up 'bout me from the beginning. Now what am I goin' do about my brother? They break his legs, sure as shit, he don't have the bread.'

Wolf felt the eyes of the kitchen staff on him, and knew he had to defuse the situation now.

'We'll talk about this first thing in the office tomorrow.'

'Like fuck we will,' Squire Richards said, sending a long, looping right fist at Wolf's ear.

Wolf ducked, spun, used an *irimi* to pull the extended Richards around the way his haymaker had taken him, rolled him over and down, put a knee on his neck.

Looking down at Squire's face, black with rage and humiliation, aware of the spectacle they had put on for the civilians, he felt another spurt of hatred for the life he lived. The stink of corruption was so foul it had infected this essentially honest cop, giving him false sanction to procure money any way he could to bail his brother out of hock and possible serious harm with shysters.

Wolf let go of Richards, said, 'Get up, Squire, and go home.'

Hana had about her the stillness of the blue heron.

The heron was a very special creature inasmuch as it was a solitary bird, quietly stalking its prey, which it speared with its long, curved serrated beak. And when the heron took off, it flew with its head majestically back on its shoulders, not extended out like its remote cousins the ibis and the crane.

Yuji thought the blue heron was the most beautiful of all these exquisite birds because it could, in those enchanted moments during sunrise and sunset, merge with the sky, the colour of its plumage exactly matching that of the firmament, so that when it rose from the water it appeared to vanish like a sorcerer into thin air.

Hana had a house in a suburb of Tokyo. Only six miles from the centre of the city, but in all other ways a million miles distant. This was where Yuji's half-sister preferred to spend her time. She was younger than he by thirteen years, a product of his mother Minako's second marriage.

Her house was ferroconcrete on the outside, black granite and black and white tiles on the inside. The rather stark skeleton, then, made a dramatic backdrop for her richly coloured, patterned and textured collection of *mai ogi*, stage fans used by dancers. These were without exception intricately painted, etched and lacquered. Since the *mai ogi* were often the only props allowed on stage, they took the place of a samurai sword, a pine forest, the moon in autumn, a staircase to the attic, a storm-roiled sea or a simple teacup. But there was nothing simple about these fans, their labyrinthine symbology tumbling out upon the hard-edged surfaces of Hana's house.

'Hana,' Yuji said now, taking her hand in his, 'it's always so good to see you.'

Beneath the surface, Hana was in all ways unlike her mother. Minako had about her that traditional air of fragility so many women of her generation sought to cultivate. It came as a shock to Yuji when he had discovered that she was utterly self-sufficient.

Hana, so pleased to be with him, followed him with her luminous eyes wherever he went in the room. Her eyes held her emotions like an amphitheatre holds sound, amplification and nuance generated together.

'When I am here with you, it seems as if all my anxieties are far away.'

Hana was like a great psychic engine. At times Yuji was certain that he could hear the thrumming of her heart, the singing of her blood, and that he could converse with these things as if they were true voices inside her. At other times she could be as impassive and impervious to exploration as a stone wall.

When she was six Hana had had a rare type of brain fever so resistant to treatment that it had been given her name. To this day experts differed on what the effects of the fever had been on her. Some said it was only her speech centre that had been affected, others insisted that her memory and even other, more esoteric functions had been impaired. The doctors could not even agree on whether these facilities had been crippled or altered in some way impossible to

114

calculate. In any case, Hana had not spoken a word until she was twelve.

Finally, Minako had had enough; Hana had spent years being probed by batteries of sophisticated tests, all to no avail. She had taken Hana away from the stainless-steel medical centres that had virtually been her home, bringing her here to this sanctuary.

Hana had inherited all her mother's ephemeral beauty: porcelain skin, heart-shaped face, deeply etched, sensual lips. But she had added strengths, an enviable mastery of language and art, a more profound impression of the mysterious than even Yuji's mother had. Her father was long gone, driven out by Minako at the first hint that he was after her money. He either did not want to see his daughter or was prevented from doing so by Minako who, Yuji had observed, was fiercely protective of her younger daughter.

In truth, he suspected that he was the only one who finally understood Hana. Minako tried to understand her daughter but she was doomed to see her as a cripple, because she had spent too many years judging her progress against that of other children. Yuji saw his half-sister as merely different, and so besides loving her, he was intrigued by her. Hana, for her part, felt his interest (he was absolutely certain of this, though she never chose to communicate her feeling in any concrete fashion) and returned it. They were like a battery, anode and cathode, creating a current of unknown origin and energy.

Yuji was duty bound to love his half-sister, but he liked her as well. She was quick-witted and often very funny, although it was rare that he saw her laugh. She was always clever even when her unhappiness turned her cleverness into barbs too bitter for most people to bear. Her frequent depressions, abrupt and severe, concerned Yuji, principally because he could not understand what triggered them; he was often afraid they were a symptom of the baffling changes caused by her fever, as beyond her control as her monthly periods.

Being with Hana often brought to mind a haiku by his favourite poet, Taniguchi Buson: *Morning haze:/as in a painting of a dream/men go their ways.*

When he left her it was with the understanding that there was more to the world than the empirical methodology he had learned at school, that there existed other universal constants science could not even guess at. And he was hard put to say which was the right path through the haze, which was the painting of the real world and which was the dream.

'What anxieties are eating at you now?' Hana asked.

Yuji sighed, relaxing into the peace and depth of her extraordinary aura. 'The Oracle,' he said.

115

Outside the windows of the living room was a forest of green moso bamboo Hana had planted in a stone courtyard whose walls reflected light in seemingly endless ways. Some of the bamboo were vertical, others set at angles, so that a complex pattern was always forming. At times, the courtyard, only twelve feet square, could seem as immense as a hillside in Nara. Yuji loved to stare out these windows for they seemed to foster in him the ability to dream.

'I am beginning to regret we ever began this project,' Yuji said.

Watching him carefully, Hana said, 'Who told you about Moravia's death?'

Yuji shrugged. 'What difference does it make? I know the Oracle is responsible, that's the only thing that matters. I never thought I'd be capable of creating something that would be responsible for the death of a human being.'

'Yuji-san, you're talking as if the Oracle murdered Moravia.'

'Isn't that just what happened?'

'Oh, no, no.' And, seeing the anguish on his face, she reached out, closed his hand in hers. 'Come here.' She drew him down to sit beside her. 'Moravia was a test case. We all believed the Oracle, but the errors here prove that even the Oracle is fallible.'

Yuji grunted.

'You must not give up because of one mistake,' Hana said. 'The Oracle is so important. Can you understand that I believe there must be more out there in the universe. Sometimes I feel as if my body is a cage I am forced to inhabit like an animal in the zoo, that by its very flesh and blood I am made an inferior being.'

Hana was still, but in the silence she projected, Yuji could read portents like shadows thrown upon a wall. What metamorphoses were occurring within her? He wanted to ask her: who was she, what was she becoming, what was her psychic presence doing to the Oracle? He was about to do so, overcoming his embarrassment (accusing himself of invading her privacy) and his fear (of her answer as much as her silence), when she said, 'Death,' in a wholly different tone of voice.

He shivered as the word reverberated through him. He knew she received wavefronts – she refused to call them visions because she said they were not visual at all but, rather, visceral. They seemed to come not from a source outside but from some place deep inside herself, a space created – or at least accessed – by the fever. *'There is an infinite hole inside me,'* she had said to him long ago. *'From its depths images emerge, not visions, I don't see anything at all, but I know they are there and what they are, as if while asleep I had been taught an ancient language.'*

'Hana! What have you seen?' he asked now.

116

Her luminous eyes were as dull as dust, and he knew that she could not see him. She said, 'I see you and Naoharu Nishitsu locked in a monumental struggle while a great black bird hovers over your heads.'

'You mean Death with a capital D?' He tried to laugh, but the sound got caught in his throat. 'This sounds like a scene from an Ingmar Bergman film.'

'No, no, you don't understand. Not death.' Hana suddenly gripped him, her eyes luminous again, focused on him. Her mouth was trembling. 'There is someone else, someone unknown. Someone who would kill you both.'

Wolf, sitting in silence in Lawrence Moravia's apartment, was thinking of that cubicle and its strange contents behind the wardrobe. After the incident with Squire at La Mentira, he had found the forced gaiety of the party cloying. He had found Amanda, had made his apologies. Stevie had offered to drive her home, and Amanda, seeing the look on his face, had not protested, had kissed him hard on the lips before being whirled away by her sister.

Wolf, sitting on Moravia's curved couch, thinking of Moun saying to him, *Larry was bent – I mean* seriously *bent*. Thinking *In the Realm of the Senses*. Thinking: Chika with Moravia a week ago, Chika with Suma last fall, Moravia killed yesterday. One of his men down for the count. Thinking of everything Shipley the spook had made him privy to. Thinking he could still get no fix on Suma's aura – or Chika's; could get no fix on Moravia's murderer, either. Was Chika a member of the Black Blade Society? More to the point, was she one of their assassins?

Either way, he felt certain that she was the nexus point. Despite himself, he felt again a stirring in his loins. The image of her shuddering in ecstasy fired against his retinas. He remembered her scent. And then it hit him: this was the scent he had picked up in the secret cubicle in Moravia's apartment. Chika had been there. Scents did not last that long even in a small windowless room, which meant that Chika had been in Moravia's apartment only hours before Wolf was. Why? And just as importantly how had she gained entrance? The place had been under a Homicide Division seal since the time the police had been summoned to the murder scene.

By three a.m. the intermittent snow had become a cold hard sleet, littering the teeming sidewalks and the steaming grates with a treacherously slick veneer. Wolf was fed up with work; he longed to see Amanda's face, to feel her body close against his, warming his flesh and his bones which, over the course of this day and a half, had come to seem as if they would never feel warm again.

117

Wolf left Moravia's apartment, took off in the unmarked car for Amanda's apartment in Morningside Heights. Here, most of the street people were from the Caribbean islands or Africa, and the park was filled with their makeshift hovels, the pathways smeared with the bloody excrement of their primitive necromantic rites. Amanda abided these dangers for the same reason all New Yorkers did: economics. She simply could not afford to live in a better section of the city. Plus, she was quick to remind Wolf, there was all that space of the oversized two-bedroom apartment, which was perfectly safe once you were inside thanks to the police dead-bolt Wolf had affixed to the front door and the padlocked steel gates across all the windows. Why was it, Wolf had wondered more than once, that her talent for teaching also made her a superb rationalizer?

The sleet, turned fluorescent by the neon of the Manhattan night, hit the windscreen like the flailings of a madman; the wipers proved of little help. Wolf dialled Amanda's number. Was she home yet from the party? He didn't think he'd wake her up, she had no classes today.

'It's me,' he said into the phone when he heard her voice. 'I'm on my way uptown.'

'The apartment's a mess,' Amanda said. 'Let's go somewhere else.'

'How about my place?'

'As long as it's not here.'

He pulled up in front of her building fifteen minutes later. The sleet, increasing in ferocity, had slowed him down some. He eyeballed the three or four figures slumped beneath the sagging canopy, shreds of cardboard pulled up against the cold and wet. As far as he could tell, all of them were asleep. The sleet hammered against the car, the noise reverberating in his ears.

In a moment, he caught movement in the building lobby. Amanda, wrapped in her heavy raincoat, dashed out, making her way around or over the street people, opening her stride as she sought to avoid the water rushing along the gutter.

As she did so, something buzzed in Wolf's mind, something not right, and the hair at the back of his neck stirred in anticipation or in foreboding. That stride – was it Amanda's? It seemed familiar, yet subtly out of place in this context. He looked at her face but the harsh shadows flung down from the sodium street lights made her features indecipherable.

Wolf rubbed his eyes, thinking, I've been working too hard, I'm a bit loopy. He leaned over to open the door for Amanda, found himself abruptly looking up into the face of the beautiful Japanese woman, the artist, Chika.

Her look was full of contempt as, in an almost lazy manner, she

118

brought her right hand up. In it was the blued steel pistol Wolf had seen her produce that night against the street punks. Her lips, red turned black in the narrow-spectrum light, opened and she seemed to be saying something but, perhaps because of the closed window and the noise of the sleet, he could not hear what she was saying. Then, an explosion bloomed from the muzzle of the pistol; noise rocketed through the interior of the car like a crack of thunder.

'No!' Wolf said as the glass pane shattered inwards. He felt an impact, slamming him into the door on his side of the car. There was the taste of iron and blood in his mouth. Then the pain began . . .

Wolf awoke with a start. He sat up hard, looked around, bewildered for an instant. He was in his own bedroom. His heart pounded in his chest, and he could still feel the pain – the dream pain – where the bullet had entered his body. Stupidly, he rubbed the spot to make sure he was whole and unharmed.

He turned on the ceiling light, stared at the reflection of the rain on the skylight, rolling off its copper shade. It seemed suspended in time, and he felt no small kinship, suspended as he was between his father and his grandfather. And always his mother inbetween.

He could see his mother's face in his mind as clearly as if she were sitting beside him: her expressive black eyes hooded by the characteristic thick folds of the upper lids, her prominent cheekbones, strong, almost savage, sculpted nose and jaw and wide mouth, the thick dark hair shot with silver she wore to the tops of her buttocks, studded with tiny coral-eyed Sleeping Beauty turquoise and lapis beads made for her by White Bow. Every line in her face added to the strength of her presence.

She was a holy person in her own right, a Dream Collector, as she was known, and many people came to her for guidance when they were sad or afraid or psychically vulnerable.

And yet her strength must have lain in her passivity (so Wolf believed) because in the male arena of her family she had allowed the skein to be played out without interference.

He lay back down, closed his eyes. He dreamt again. In his dream he awoke, sat up and went to the American armoire across the room. He pushed aside his hanging clothes, behind which he took out a bow. It was made of caribou horn and had belonged to his grandfather.

He had made this caribou horn bow when he was a very young man, not more than fourteen or fifteen. It was a very difficult task. Most of the Nation's bows were made of stout wood staves, wrapped with dried animal sinew, glued with a substance called asphaltum. These wooden bows were relatively easy to manufacture, but the horn bows were where real power resided and so were prized within the Nation above all others.

Gripping the pale caribou bow in his dream, looking upwards as it arched over his head, feeling its toughness, its pure tensile strength, Wolf felt the song of his life with his grandfather gathering around him like the swell of a choir . . .

Wolf opened his eyes. He looked at his watch. It was just after midnight. Above him, the rain had changed to sleet, clattering wildly against the skylight's sixty-year-old glass panes. A wan blue light dribbled through, leaking like noxious radiation from a wornout factory.

He put his head in his hands. His pulse rate was still accelerated, and he thought, Jesus. Then he thought of Amanda. Was she all right? Why wouldn't she be all right? he asked himself. And yet an irrational fear was growing inside him, fuelled, perhaps, by the first dream.

He threw on some clothes, went hurriedly out the door. It was only when he was in the car heading uptown that it occurred to him that he should have called Amanda from home. He wasn't thinking clearly; it was as if he were still somehow enmeshed within his dream.

Water streamed wildly from the windshield, and it seemed as if all the lights were running against him; he decided to ignore them. He had to detour off Amsterdam Avenue because from 73rd to 79th the street was a gaping hole where, last week, macadam, rotting water pipes, sewage and enormous bundles of electrical cables collapsed into the subway tunnels, victim, so the city engineers said, of age, constant vibration and a volume of traffic unforeseen by the city fathers of seventy years ago. Someone had spray-painted along one plastic tarped edge of the disaster, DIE, YUPPIE SCUM!

On Broadway, clots of sleepless Senegalese milled beneath awnings of darkened stores, undeterred from selling their casbah-like array of goods to the pedestrians hurrying by, hunched over against the chilly downpour.

Wolf dialled Amanda's number. 'It's me,' he said into the phone when she answered. 'Are you okay?'

'Sure,' she said. 'Why?' There was so much static on the line it was impossible to say whether he had woken her up or what kind of mood she was in.

'I'm on my way uptown.'

'Oh, God, I just got home and the place is a mess. Can we go somewhere else?'

Wolf's mouth was dry; he wanted to swallow but couldn't. He seemed to be reliving his dream. 'How – ' He stopped, hearing something, then the line broke up, crackling in his ear. 'What did you say? Amanda?'

Wolf was abruptly gripping the receiver so hard his muscles knotted. Had he heard a laugh? 'Amanda?' The line was dead. He hung up, pressed the redial key. Busy signal. Jesus, what had he heard just before the line broke up? His dream, on top of his briefing with Shipley, had made him paranoid. He began to wonder – was it someone else's voice on the other end of the line? With all the interference, could he be sure it was Amanda he had been talking to? *Think very clearly*, Shipley had warned him. *If you take one more step in this investigation, they will not allow you to back out. They'll come after you as they did with Moravia.* Dear God.

He jammed the accelerator to the floor, and the car leaped forward; he spun the wheel, dodging traffic. The sleet pelted down with a furious, almost malevolent purpose. He hunched forward, his wipers on high, peering through the clouded windshield.

He screeched to a stop outside Amanda's building in Morningside Heights, bolted out of the car. Freezing water lapped over his ankles, sopping his feet as he stepped through the gutter. A young woman with twins sat in the vestibule huddling them against the cold and wet. They were asleep, but she was not, and she watched Wolf with old, disinterested eyes as he dashed in, picked the lock on the inner door, sprinted through the dimly-lit lobby.

Amanda's apartment was on the fourth floor. Like most such old buildings, the elevator here was old and slow; Wolf took the stairs, three at a time. He felt as if he were losing his grip on reality. Even as he raced upwards he was seeing again the scenes of blood and pain from his dream. These images seemed more and more real to him until they had gained the power of a film montage or a piece of art, until what he saw with his eyes was overlaid with what he had seen in his mind. He felt a pain, and began to unconsciously massage the spot where in his dream he had been shot. He drew his service revolver.

The door to Amanda's apartment was slightly ajar. Wolf felt a coldness seeping through him. His gun at the ready, he pushed the door inwards with his fingertips and, as it gaped open, rolled into the long hallway in a tuck. He came to rest with his back against one plaster and lath wall. He saw the dead bolt leaning against the wall near the open door.

'Amanda?'

'Wolf. I left the door open for you. I'm almost ready.'

Wolf came out of his crouch. He was sweating. Get a grip on yourself, he thought. This is not your dream. He holstered his gun, said, 'Where are you? Why did you hang up on me?'

'We got disconnected. It's those damn car phones; I could hardly hear a word you said. Didn't you hear me say goodbye?'

'No.' The hallway was dark, but in the living room lamplight warmed the apartment. She didn't ask why he hadn't buzzed from downstairs.

Wolf leaped across an ottoman, crossing the living room with lightning speed, threw open the door to Amanda's bedroom, and let out an involuntary snarl of pain, shock, rage.

Blood was sprayed all over the walls and floor; it was pooled on the bed where Amanda lay naked and spreadeagled. She stared sightlessly up at the ceiling; there was a black-red line across her throat from which a combination of blood and air escaped in a profusion of bubbles.

Wolf put a hand over her heart, two fingers against her carotid artery. They were useless gestures – so much blood all over – but necessary because this was Amanda, not some unknown victim, one more new case he had been called to investigate.

'We got disconnected. It's those damn car phones; I could hardly hear a word you said. Didn't you hear me say goodbye?'

Wolf jumped as he heard her voice. Absurdly, he could not stop himself from looking at her still, blank face. Then he saw the cassette player tucked neatly into the sheets beside her head. Blood had leaked into the mechanism.

'We got disconnected. It's those damn car phones; I could hardly hear a word you said. Didn't you hear me say goodbye?'

With a curse, Wolf reached over, switched it off. He looked up, saw the open window; the steel gates had been unlocked, and now swung uneasily in the wind. Beyond was the fire escape. Sleet sluiced down, bouncing off the sill. Just a spattering covered the floor, which meant that the window had been opened only moments ago.

Wolf snatched at his gun, vaulted over the bed, went out onto the fire escape. A wall of water smashed against him, almost bringing him to his knees. His first instinct was to peer downwards, but nothing moved on the fire escape below him or on the street. He raised one hand to shield his eyes, looked upwards. A shadow . . . movement? Wolf sprang upwards, taking the rungs two at a time.

Up and up he went. Above him, he could see the shadow pour itself over the side of the building, onto the roof. Suma? Chika? There was no time for coherent thought. The sight of Amanda's pale corpse, her blood, her life soaked into the room all around her was like a knife twisting between his ribs. Grief transmuted into rage, fuelled by a sense of frustration that he, with all his skills, all his honed instincts, had not been able to protect her.

Over the parapet, onto the slick tarred surface of the roof. He could see the building's water tower, the rectangular bulge of the top of the elevator shaft, the various vents for furnace and compressors, fans, a skylight similar to the one in his own apartment, auxiliary electrical shed, a locked and alarmed access from the building itself. He could feel no aura, but somewhere in this urban jungle, he knew, was Amanda's killer.

The sleet continued to crash down with such fury he could scarcely breathe. He crept forward, then stopped, considering. He went back to the edge of the parapet, began a coordinated search along the perimeter of the roof. He wanted to do this for two reasons. The first was to try to flush out the killer, who would expect him to approach in line with the top of the fire escape, the way they had both come. The second was to get a full sense of the confined topography of the roofscape. When Wolf flushed his quarry it would be helpful to have an image in his mind of the various structures – potential hiding places – from all angles, and thus be able to cut off his quarry's escape.

He was three-quarters of the way around the roof when he caught a change in shape in the auxiliary electrical shed. It was so slight that he almost missed it. He looked away for a moment to stabilize his vision, then back. There it was! Got you! he thought. But who was it, Suma or Chika?

He headed towards the shape, only to see it detach itself from the shed, come hurtling towards him so fast that it was inside his range before he had a chance to aim. He pulled the trigger even as he felt the shape slam into him.

Wolf went down on one knee, lashed out with the barrel of his gun. Something went into his diaphragm just below the sternum, and he flew backwards, fetching up against the crumbling brick and concrete wall of the parapet. The shape was immediately upon him, and Wolf rolled into a defensive ball, tumbling along the perimeter of the roof.

The shape followed him. Wolf was up, already pointing his gun at where he thought the shape would be only to find empty roof. Then a blow struck him from behind, and he groaned as he was slammed against the top of the parapet. The taste of iron and blood was in his mouth. He felt himself being lifted, and he struggled. He was so close to the edge, and the pavement loomed in lethal attraction six storeys below him.

He got a lock, thought he had the leverage, then to his astonishment, found it reversed, the leverage somehow working against him, and he felt himself being forced over the parapet. He could see the street glistening evilly below him, and he began to pant in effort and fear. He struck out once, twice with blows that would knock a normal man to his knees. Nothing worked. Wolf was thrown into the night.

Over the parapet he went, the street rushing up to meet him. With a desperate effort, he reached out, was brought up short as his hand clamped wet iron. He grunted as he felt the full weight of his body hanging from his left arm socket, let his gun go in order to get the fingers of his right hand against metal, held on hard, the pressure easing somewhat. He was hanging head first from the top platform of the fire escape. His breath was like fire in his lungs, unconsciousness lapping at the edges of his vision. He shook his head hard to clear it, and became aware of the black shape making its way over the parapet, coming after him.

With a superhuman effort, he swung upwards, once, twice, his fingertips slipping on the ice-slick iron, then he made firm contact and he was crouched, gasping and dizzy, on the fire escape. His hands were bloody, but he could not think of that now. The shape was upon him, cutting his legs out from under him as he attempted to rise.

Wolf fell hard onto the iron bars of this prison eyrie, ignored the ache in his arms and shoulders. He lashed out with a kite, felt the blow intercepted, then made the supreme effort, surprising his adversary, grabbing the shadow's left wrist with his right hand as it lunged in on him for the kill, pulling it hard, towards him and down, past him then, as the shadow's own momentum, magnified by Wolf's use of force, worked against it. Wolf used his other hand to jam the other's elbow upwards, slamming the upper torso to the iron-barred floor of the platform.

Then he was up and running, leaping for the ladder upwards, hauling himself back over the low wall of the roof parapet. He stumbled to the wet tar of the rooftop. But now a peculiar lassitude was stealing through him, making him want to sit down and close his eyes: shock. He fought it. Endorphins pumped through his system, numbing the pain, but also interfering with thought and coordination. He'd be better off with the pain. Wolf focused his mind.

He felt something inside his mind, turned to find the shape waiting for him. It took him in its arms, threw him down to the tarred roofbed. It crouched close to him. The sleet beat at his eyes, and he strained to make out the nature of the shape: was it large or small? Suma or Chika? He could not tell; the air seemed filled with unnatural shadows. There was a blackness that, impossibly, seemed to hurl the sleet away from him, then the streetlights winked out and, finally, all air. He had the eerie sensation of being suspended in time and space. The nature of chaos was upon him, blotting out all vestiges of the worldsong he had learned from White Bow.

He almost gave up then, the shock reasserting itself, swirling through his system, turning his thoughts woolly, threatening to shut down all coordination and motor function. But then, superimposed on the night, the horrific sleet beating against him, the creeping numbness chilling him to the marrow, was the image of Amanda's inert, blank face, the smell of her blood rising up to engulf him, the last pink bubbles of her life leaking out her rent neck, and it was too much to bear, there was too much still left undone to allow the systems to shut down, so he fought as he had always fought, against family and adversity and the enemy, seen and unseen alike.

Wolf gritted his teeth, reached up, out through the unnatural darkness, struggling in the airless space in which he was bound, until he had grabbed hold of the shape. He pulled it violently while he threw his head forward, butting his forehead hard against the face of the shape. There were sounds, but perhaps only of the downpour drumming against tar and brick and concrete and metal.

Wolf pulled again, but that was a mistake, to repeat a move – any move – against this enemy, and he felt a searing pain down his thigh, saw a black boot scoring a gash in his flesh. A piercing pain as the boot continued to grind down trying to find the bone, to break it.

He screamed, slammed his elbow twice into flesh, used first the heel then the edge of his hand in kites meant to maim. The shape grunted heavily, the boot came mercifully away and the shape retreated.

He went right after the shape, lunging in a killing rage, the pain of Amanda's death beating at him like dark wings. He saw an opening, and took it. But as he closed with his quarry he began to slow. The world became indistinct, as if he was underwater. Breath laboured in his lungs, his pulse decelerated sharply. The blackness, a viscid living thing, pressed in on him as if it had shape, form, and an insupportable weight.

Then the fire started. It was terrifying, and yet there was about it some preternatural familiarity, as if he had glimpsed an old, long forgotten acquaintance through the interstices in a fence.

Blue fire began to consume him and, thinking of Arquillo's face, he threw his arms across his own. In that moment, he found himself lifted, hurled high into the night, as the shape used his own momentum against him, to draw him up and over, into the air.

Light flooded his blurred vision, then was extinguished; sleet stung him, then ceased; wind rushed in his ears, then only silence.

Burst of sound and motion.

He hit the skylight with his left shoulder and hip, breaking through the grimed panes of glass in a shattering instant, his left leg scored by a long, jagged shard held like an arrow in the bow of the frame. Then he was plummeting through darkness and light, his life falling away from him, angry spirits hissing in his ears, Amanda whispering, *'We got disconnected. It's those damn car phones; I could hardly hear a word you said.*

Didn't you hear me say goodbye?' Wolf whispering her name, tears whipped from the corners of his eyes as he hurtled downwards, consciousness and unconsciousness blending, memory snatched from him, thought dissolved into emotion, until pain blotted out everything, even his own scream.

WOLF

Elk Basin/Lightning Ridge 1957/1964

Wolf's father's name was Peter Matheson. Like his son, he had belonged to an elite male club – the Texas Rangers. He had revelled in its elite status, and had gone into a deep depression when, in 1935, it had been ignominiously folded into the highway patrol, turning out like trained dogs in full regalia for state holidays, bastardized into a basically political animal. But was this the only reason that had caused him to leave his wife and Wolf? Peter Matheson, as macho and prideful as a matador, had been steeped in *konjo*, a Japanese word Wolf had learned many years later from his aikido *sensei*, which meant a distinctly masochistic obsession for physical acts that involve an enormous degree of hardship and pain. *Konjo*, his *sensei* had stated flatly, was impossible to attain without suppressing one's innermost emotions. And so, without at first having realized it, he had discovered something basic about his father's personality.

Peter Matheson had been a Texas Ranger for twelve years. He had tried to fight against the encroachment of time and the modern age on this last elite band of lawmen. He often recounted their proud birth a century before as guardians of the republic of Texas's frontier during the statewide revolution. In the course of their heroic history, they had fought fierce battles with the Comanches, had served with distinction and valour in the Mexican and Civil Wars. Peter Matheson had, of course, never done any of those things, although he had spent time bringing to justice Mexican banditos and outlaws of every imaginable variety. He had joined the Rangers because they were unique in the annals of American lawmen, never required to wear a uniform or salute an officer, never having to drill or answer to a higher authority. At least, that's what they had been in their heyday, and Wolf's father had spent more than a decade trying single-handedly to bring them back to their glory years. As such, he was looked upon by many as a hero, a larger than life figure, respected for his valour and his personal philosophy that Wolf would later identify as *konjo*, his dedication to getting the job done no matter the suffering and torment inflicted on himself.

127

To those who did not know him well, it seemed more than a little curious that Peter Matheson had married an American Indian, but Wolf's mother, Open Hand, was in all ways an exemplar of her Wind River Shoshone forebears, and Peter was drawn to distinction in every aspect of his life. She, far more than her husband, had been pragmatic enough to have resigned herself to the advent of the modern world, the inevitability of taming the wild ranges for the hordes of immigrants teeming westwards from the northeastern states. And perhaps, after all, this was the answer to why she had married him, a white man, a Texas Ranger. She could feel the power of the new world and she did not want to be left behind to falter, turned drunkard, bitter and old before her time in the mean reservations. Once, he overheard her tell White Bow that she could see the future – the advent of the modern world – in her husband's piercing blue eyes, feel it emanating from the bearing of his sharp, handsome countenance. For his part, White Bow had his own opinion as to Peter Matheson's demeanour.

Wolf remembered one evening asking his father if it was true, as he had heard at school, that in Texas the Rangers had written the law.

'No,' Peter Matheson, tall and lanky, wind- and sun-burned, powerful in body as well as spirit, had said, looking sternly down at his son. 'We *were* the law.'

This arrogant response so perfectly exemplified an aspect of Peter Matheson that Wolf could never forget it. It was also the reason why White Bow could not abide the man. 'Man is not the Law. The Law is of the World,' Wolf's grandfather had said to him shortly thereafter, 'and the voices of the World, Spirits which must be heeded, even though Their words are often difficult to discern.'

The wisdom of these words was never more apparent than when Peter Matheson came home one day, white-faced, short of breath. He waved away his wife's concerned queries, but finally collapsed at the dinner table. Instead of calling a doctor, Open Hand had summoned her father.

White Bow took one look at Peter Matheson and bade his daughter to spread out one of her hand-woven blankets. When she had done so he produced bits of woven material dyed to the colours of the four cardinal Directions. These he placed on the appropriate corners of the blanket, then crushed fresh sage between his thumb and forefinger, so that the pieces fell onto the centre of the blanket and the oil perfumed the room.

White Bow who, it was said by many, possessed more power than even Black Elk and Fools Crow, was the high shaman of the Wind River Shoshone. But unlike other tribal shaman, his philosophy was not limited to his particular tribe, but was rather a synthesis of myth, philosophy and

128

ethics drawn as well from many of the other Indian tribes. In his time, he had been exceedingly well travelled and, it was said, had been welcome even in the communities of the Nation who were normally the enemy of the Wind River Shoshone and their cousins, the fierce and violent Comanche of West Texas.

Wolf and Open Hand settled the unconscious Peter Matheson on the blanket. Kneeling beside him, White Bow produced two hawk feathers. He placed one over the patient's throat, the other over his lower belly. Then he began to move them over the entire torso. All the while he chanted in a voice so low Wolf could not hear his words.

Abruptly, one feather paused over Peter Matheson's abdomen; the second one joined it; they crossed at the tips. 'There is poison in his stomach,' White Bow said. 'Hurry now, he is dying.'

With liquid indigo he drew a circle at the spot where the feathers had crossed, then he placed a smooth stone within the circle. He began a chant that filled the room with the movement of its melody and words. Soon, the stone began to emit heat, glowing red just as if it were the coal of a fire.

Now White Bow bade them draw Peter's head back, open his mouth fully. He held the tongue in place with a strip of dried buffalo tongue, then he produced a long, hollow quill, wrapped in the centre with sinew dyed deep blue. He placed one end of the quill in Peter's mouth, began to push it carefully down his oesophagus. Then he put his lips to the other end and sucked. He did this until the quill was filled, then he removed it, allowed the contents to dribble into a plate his daughter had provided. He repeated the process seven times until, sniffing the contents of the quill, he was satisfied. He took up his feathers, bowed his head, chanting another song. Then he put them away, along with the quill. Lastly, he removed the smooth stone, now returned to its cool, original state, from Peter Matheson's abdomen. Within the blue circle was a mark, like a bruise, that Peter would carry for the rest of his life.

White Bow sat back; he appeared tired. 'He sleeps now,' he told them. 'The poison is gone, white man's poison that contaminated his food, the kind I have heard was used many times against the Nation.' He made no more comment than that but, many years later, Wolf would suspect the irony of the incident had not been lost on him. 'When he awakens, he will be well again.' Open Hand bowed her head in gratitude.

Then White Bow turned to Wolf and said softly, 'The Spirits of the World came when they were summoned. Here is the Law. Now you have seen it with your own eyes.' . . .

So many aspects of his grandfather were opaque then, Wolf had finally

129

come to the conclusion that this impression was a deliberate part of the old man's persona. At first, he believed his grandfather was merely being wilful, but later he found himself wondering whether the old man had had deeper, less selfish motives for presenting the enigmas of himself to Wolf.

One day, the old man said to him, 'You are going to stay with me for some time now. Your mother has given her consent.' He never spoke of Wolf's father, an unbeliever in his ways, who, for him, did not exist. 'We are going to go away, but before we do I will tell you a story. Once there was a young boy. He had no friends but the rivers and the mountains, the trees and the sky. Still, he was a lonely boy and longed for companionship. One day, as the boy was picking nuts and berries in the bushes by the edge of the plain where he lived he heard a cry.

'He rushed toward the sound to find a hawk lying in the dust. Its wing was broken. The boy crouched beside the bird, tried to touch it, but the hawk almost bit his finger off. Then the boy spoke to the bird, and at last the hawk consented to be lifted out of the broiling sun.

'Beneath the shelter of a tree, the boy ministered to the bird, giving it first water and then some berries, which the hawk, preferring meat, did not like but ate anyway. Then the boy set about putting a splint on the hawk's broken wing.

'In time, the hawk recovered and soon, because his sense of adventure was greater than his companion's, had led the boy away from the plains of his youth, through a valley so dry its floor was compacted salt, up into umber foothills, and then along the steeply rising spine of a mountain. This was the mountain that the boy had seen every day of his life – when it was clear enough – the mountain that formed the backdrop to his young life, the mountain he sometimes dreamed about but never dared think he would reach.

'Now he was there, nearing the summit, and he felt a sense of great elation, as if, somehow, coming here, had been the hawk's gift to him for saving its life.

'At the summit of the mountain, the boy saw a tree, gnarled, twisted by wind and lashing rain, old and sturdy. He went up to the tree and put his arms around it as if embracing a long-lost ancestor. As for the hawk, it flew off the boy's shoulder and onto the very topmost branch of the tree. It craned its neck this way and that, searching all it saw around it. Then it gave one piercing cry, as if in farewell, and launched itself into the clear, blue sky.

'The boy, delirious with joy at being atop his mountain, pushed himself away from the tree and, shading his eyes, watched the flight of the hawk. The boy had superior vision, and he watched as the bird spiralled higher and higher, not drifting away in any horizontal plane, but rising vertically as if through a tunnel, invisible to anyone but the hawk itself, above the crown of the tree.

'The boy continued to watch as the hawk dwindled in his vision, still rising, so that the boy was certain that at any moment the bird would pierce the floor of heaven. Then it was gone, and in that moment he saw floating down three feathers – hawk feathers – which he plucked out of the sky and placed in his thick black hair. And, years later, when he had made his home in the foothills of the mountain, when he had wed and had sired children, he told his family of the hawk and used the sacred feathers in ceremonies consecrating heaven and earth and the implicit connection between them.'

White Bow stared at Wolf with his black crow's eyes: that fierce, independent look that was nevertheless without the peacock's pride he so despised. 'We will go now. Are you ready?'

Ready for what?

Wolf did not know, but he was frightened: of the old man's witchy aura, of his enigmatic statements, of the overriding sense that something – what? *what?* – was expected of him. The old man would not tell him, and Wolf could not work it out by himself.

On the other hand, it never occurred to him not to go. Whatever his grandfather demanded of him he did without thought or question. This blind obedience he had learned – like the language of her people – in his mother's lap, perhaps had ingested along with her breast milk, a loyalty that, as he progressed from toddler to child, increasingly infuriated his father, who demanded of his only son a fealty second to none.

In deep snow, they left Elk Basin by horse, his grandfather's favourite means of travel. The Wind River Shoshones, he had once told Wolf, had been among the first of the tribes to understand the nature of the horse and to use him (he never called animals 'it'). It was very cold, Wolf wrapped in skins and blankets woven by his mother – White Bow would allow no modern dress when his grandson was with him – but the old man, seemingly impervious, in only a beaded shirt and breeches of soft deerskin he had tanned himself and which Wolf had seen him wear in summer. On his feet were buckskin moccasins with stiff rawhide soles, the tops beautifully decorated with beads of coloured glass and enamelled metal.

Wrapped in blue twilight, they camped in the desolate wilderness of the playa, the salt flats, where the wind was merciless, its cry echoing for miles in every direction. White Bow chose a spot in the lee of a snaking bank of the icebound Sevier river. They were near the end of it so that Wolf could see the salty lake into which it flowed.

'You are lucky,' he said to Wolf as they set up the tepee painted with curious symbols that appeared to Wolf like war shields. 'When I was your age I was stricken with a great sickness.' And then White Bow had described how he had been afflicted by epilepsy. 'The attacks were very bad; I was incapacitated for days afterward. I slept as the dead sleep and, gradually, into my sleep crept the spirits of the creatures around me: the bison, the wolf, the bear and the hawk. It took me some time to understand that these were the spirits of slain animals and that their message to me was that I was special and had been chosen to be shaman.

'"How is such a thing possible?" I said to the spirits. "I am ill." And they replied, "As shaman you must heal illness. Before that can be done, you must understand the nature of illness." And then,' White Bow said, 'I awoke from my sleep and knew that I must learn to heal my own illness for only in so doing would I learn to heal others.'

Wolf was just wondering how in the world his grandfather had managed to do that when the old man reached out a bow from a long mottled cowhide sheath. It was made of some kind of horn or bone; it had a magnificent double arch to it. The sinew wrapping it had first been dyed a rich burnished blue by immersion in liquid rendered from the indigo plant. The ends just above the nocks where it was strung were decorated with hawk feathers and, from a rawhide strip, there dangled from the lower end what Wolf could only imagine was the yellowed talon from that same bird.

'This bow is made from caribou antlers,' the old man said, settling himself comfortably. 'There is power in such a weapon, as I have no doubt you have been told. But I will now tell you a secret. The power comes from here – ' he struck his chest just over his heart '– and not from the antlers themselves as many believe. Instead, the antlers serve as a kind of storehouse of this power. Do you understand?'

Wolf nodded his head, terrified to admit he did not understand. What power? Power wasn't tangible, and that being the case he could not see how any tangible object could hold such an ephemeral thing.

His grandfather smiled at him just as if he knew what was turning over in his mind, but that was impossible, wasn't it?

'Objects of veneration, such as horn bows, are most useful,' the old man went on, 'because they also serve as mystic markers, talismans from which one comes to recognize one's own power.' Seeing the look on his grandson's face, he bent forward. 'Think of a mirror, Wolf. How could you recognize yourself without having looked into one? By a photograph? But

132

how would you know that was you? No, the reflection is your guidepost, your marker.'

Hours later, after all the chores had been seen to, after they had eaten a meal of dried beef jerky and roasted corn, had relieved themselves into a nearby depression and were ready for bed, White Bow returned to the subject.

'The bow,' he said, 'is how I healed myself.' In the firelight his lined face was as dark and tough as the hides he painstakingly cured. 'In the making of it I found myself: I discovered my power and healed myself. The caribou came to me in a dream and the next morning I set off after him. It took me more than a week of tracking, but once I found his spoor I knew he would not get away. In fact, in hindsight, I see that he did not want to get away. On the contrary, his spirit had called me to him.

'I came upon him in a forest glade. I was far to the north by then – there are few caribou where we come from. He was an enormous beast, even by the standard of his kin, his antlers huge curving arcs like the arms of a white crescent moon. He turned his great head, saw me and shook his antlers. I could see that he was ready to shed them. It is so obvious now that the creature was sent to me so that I could take his antlers and make my white bow.'

The old man was sitting crosslegged, smoking a long bone pipe. Wolf, lying next to him, bundled in his buckskins and blankets, liked the aromatic scent of the tobacco, the way the blue smoke wreathed his grandfather's head as if it were a mountain seen through clouds. He was growing drowsy, the old man's words, in the sing-song language of the Wind River Shoshone, acting as a kind of lullaby.

'Now it happens that my father was a great bow-maker, and he had instructed me in his art from the time before I could speak in sentences. I knew that cutting the antlers was not nearly so critical as boiling them to rid them of their inner core which would grow brittle and cause the bow to break under the stress of being drawn. I also knew that only such sustained heat would cause the antlers themselves to be moulded into the proper shape to make a bow.

'The reason there are so few bow-makers who can make a horn bow is simple. Boiling the antlers in water deprives the horn of the natural glue and gelatin that makes it pliable. My father put a combination of herbs into his water to keep these elements within the horn. I, however, had none, nor did I know what they were. I was alone, with no one to help me. And yet I made this bow.'

He waited until Wolf's eyes opened and the boy said, 'But how did you do it?'

'Heat,' White Bow said. Then, acknowledging that same look on his

133

grandson's face, he held out his hand. Wolf's hand disappeared within the old man's fist as he was pulled to his feet.

White Bow took him outside. It had cleared, and the sky was a frosty black. The full moon was so sharp Wolf imagined he could cut himself on it. All around them a thick crust of ice had formed over the playa.

'Here,' the old man said, as he knelt on the bank of the river, 'this is how.' And, making a fist, he thrust his left arm elbow deep into the ice that had formed over the water.

Wolf, still with his hand buried in his grandfather's huge, horny palm, felt a curious sensation, as if he were somehow hooked into a current. He jerked his hand away, as if burned, but even so disengaged felt something else so terrifying that even in a dream he could not remember what it was.

That was when he saw the water running from the spot where White Bow held his arm in the frozen river. A moment later, water gushed like a swollen spring river and, not long after, steam rose, hissing, from that hot black hole in the ice . . .

And so, when he slept, which he did a great deal on that Thursday afternoon, he dreamt of a time long ago, when White Bow's worldsong was everything . . .

The floor of the great basin – the playa – was as hard and flat as concrete. It was like the city to which, years later, Wolf would flee. On the furthest edge of the playa, so distant they were almost colourless, were the Sierra Nevada mountains. It was dangerous here; it was dangerous in the city. Somewhere, in Wolf's unconscious, there must be a connection.

'We – and by we I mean the Nation – are not native to this country – no one is,' White Bow said to the young Wolf. They were seated in the tepee they had pitched on the great salt flats. In the pale moonlight, the playa was preserved with an iridescent rind of ice and hoarfrost. 'Our own family, as I trace it back with the help of the Spirits, came from Asia, trekking for months across the ice steppes of Siberia. They were undaunted by the tongue of almost solid ice that is now the Bering Straits, when the two continents of Asia and the Americas were one, when there were only pockets of lakes where now there is frigid water. They moved through Alaska and then south, ever south. What drew them? I wonder. Perhaps it was the never-ending ice. In truth, though, even the Spirits have no single answer so perhaps I will never know until I cross over into the Other Side and I will know everything.'

As he spoke, White Bow's fingers worked on wrapping wet sinew around an obsidian arrowhead, chipped by his hand to a wicked point. He was affixing it to a polished shaft of wild currant, his favourite wood for this purpose because it was flexible and so strong that if even a bison

134

rolled over on it it would slide deeper into the animal's flesh rather than break off.

'Surely, in those days,' White Bow continued, 'we were Chinese; perhaps we were not so very different from those immigrants who would become the modern-day Japanese.'

At this point, White Bow raised the unfinished shaft of the arrow, measured it against Wolf's right arm, from the elbow to the end of his middle finger. White Bow marked this dimension on the shaft with a bit of charcoal, then with a length of jute, he measured the distance from Wolf's right wrist to the first knuckle of that same middle finger. Wolf watched as his grandfather added this measurement to the first, which would constitute the length of the arrow. This was how the great arrowsmiths custom-manufactured weapons for the men of prestige of the Nation. Wolf, surprised, saw that White Bow was making this arrow for him.

Wolf loved to watch his grandfather's hands, so large, so capable and, unlike the whole man himself, unintimidating. There was nothing enigmatic about those hands – they were simply instruments of invention and healing.

It was cold, and getting colder. Each day they remained upon the vast plain of icy salt Wolf felt the chill insinuating itself through his bones. He moved more slowly and with more difficulty, as if he were required to unfold like some two-dimensional construction. For his part, White Bow seemed to be completely unaffected by the cold. In fact, some days he went out without a shirt on at all. On those occasions, Wolf would watch to see what effects the frigid temperature would have on his bare skin. None, it appeared. And at those times, he would recall how the old man had thrust his fist into the ice and had turned it to water and, thence, to steam.

One night, he said, 'Grandfather, where does so much heat come from?'

White Bow nodded, as if he had been expecting this question. 'The healing power of the shaman is connected with that of fire. Fire, Wolf, is the eye of the sun, brought down to this world a very long time ago by one of the Spirits. Fire is energy; fire is power. It has many manifestations, and it is the duty of the shaman to decide which manifestation fits the moment.' He cocked his head, peering down the length of the shaft of wild currant. The broader end was where he would put the nock in which the bowstring would sit because the arrow must fly in the same direction in which the limb that became the shaft grew on its tree. 'This, after all, is the most difficult decision a shaman must make: when to use the fire and in which way. And it is this inner fire that makes one impervious

135

to the deepest cold that comes not only in the dead of winter but on the very point of death.'

Several nights later, after White Bow had finished three arrows of remarkable workmanship, the young Wolf had a dream. In it, he was visited by a bear so immense he blotted out the sun, his fur so black it appeared as if the sky had turned from day to night. This immense black bear taught Wolf his language, then spoke to him earnestly for a long time, and, beckoning led him outside the tepee onto the playa. But when Wolf awoke he had lost the knowledge of the bear language and so could not remember what the creature had told him. He related this dream to his grandfather, and the old man had smiled.

'It is time,' White Bow said, nodding. He took up his bow and trio of new arrows, and led Wolf outside, where a low, red sun had turned the salt flats to stained glass. 'Can you recall the direction in which the bear was leading you?'

Wolf pointed west, and they set out into the light of the dying sun. Ahead, in the hazy distance, lay the Sierra Madre, at this time of day enrobed in regal purple. The lowest arc of the solar disc touched them, and the sun seemed to flatten like a vessel being born in a potter's hands. Blue shadows strode behind them, lengthening with every step they took.

The air was exceedingly dry; it sought out every opening in Wolf's clothing with the precision of a surgeon's scalpel. White Bow, in summer weight doeskins, seemed oblivious, and Wolf thought with no little terror of his mastery over fire.

After several miles, a dark lump appeared in their field of vision. Even at this distance, Wolf sensed that it was a human being. He was correct, of course.

A young man, perhaps three or four years older than Wolf, lay on his side in the rimey crust of the playa. Wolf squatted down, felt the side of his neck where his father had taught him the carotid artery pulsed.

He glanced up at White Bow. 'He is alive, Grandfather. But just barely.' He ran his hands carefully over the boy's body, then turned him over. 'There is no blood, no wound. Not even a bruise. What is the matter with him?'

Impossibly tall, terrifying in his imposing presence, White Bow held out his hand, said, 'This stone is for you. Use it.'

Wolf reached upwards for the small, speckled stone, as smooth as his mother's breast. It was warm, and warmed Wolf from the instant he took possession of it. Giving his grandfather one more brief glance, he placed the stone in three spots on the boy's body: his lower belly, his heart, his forehead. He touched the stone with the tip of his middle finger

136

each time. In the first two instances, he felt nothing amiss, but when the stone came in contact with the boy's head, Wolf started. He shivered and closed his eyes.

'What has the stone told you?' White Bow asked.

At first, Wolf said nothing, so filled with dread was he. Then he swallowed something thick that seemed stuck in his throat, said, 'The boy suffers from no physical illness. Someone has stolen his soul.'

'Yes.' White Bow nodded, as if he had somehow already known. 'This is why the spirit of the black bear came to you in your dream. This boy is protected by the black bear, and its spirit sought out a shaman.'

'But I am no shaman, Grandfather.'

'Take the stone from the boy's forehead,' the old man said. He took up one of the arrows he had made for Wolf, thrust the great bow with its deadly missile into Wolf's hands. 'This is what has happened,' he said. 'A man has died. A cowardly creature who, lacking the courage to walk the path of the dead alone, has stolen the boy's soul to accompany him on his journey.' He stared down at Wolf. 'When you touched the healing stone the third time you could feel the interruption of the worldsong.'

'Yes,' Wolf whispered, trembling, dreading what he knew must come next.

'We must return that which was wrongfully stolen,' White Bow said. 'We must walk the path of the dead.'

It was dark now, but that did not seem to matter to White Bow. He took Wolf south, until they came to the bank of the Sevier.

'Rivers are gateways,' he said to his grandson. He sat himself down cross-legged on the riverbank and produced his pipe. He filled it with some dark substance that did not smell anything like the tobacco he smoked. He lit it, sucked at the pipe several times, passed it to Wolf. Wolf took the smoke into his lungs. It was highly aromatic, surprisingly light, and did not make him cough or choke as his one stab at tobacco had. The two passed the pipe back and forth until its burning contents were used up.

'Now we go.'

Wolf rose with his grandfather and, together, they slid into the river. It was so cold that Wolf felt immediately numb, and it was so deep he could not feel the bottom with the tips of his moccasins.

He needed to get air into his lungs, but his grandfather was holding him, keeping him beneath the water. He struggled briefly, panicking, but his perception of reality was already shifting. The darkness of the river had metamorphosed into a deeper darkness; the chill fading from his flesh and bones. Also, he seemed able to breathe. But, far from reassuring him, all of this merely increased his panic.

137

He felt a tug on his arm, saw his grandfather gesturing. Ahead, lay a series of stones glowing faintly a bone white. The pathway of the dead. Only steps ahead of them was an old man. Beside him, was the boy they had found on the playa. The boy, suddenly aware of them, turned his head in their direction, but the old man, his grip firm, did not, so intent was he on his dread journey.

'Quickly, now,' White Bow whispered to Wolf, 'before they get too far along and it is too late. Use the bow.'

'I am afraid,' the young Wolf said. 'It takes a shaman to do this. I am no shaman.'

'Use the bow,' his grandfather said urgently. 'Loose the arrow.'

With trembling hands, Wolf nocked the arrow to the bowstring, put the bow up. Sweat was rolling down his face, and his fear had turned his stomach inside out. He imagined himself weeping as he drew the bow into its magnificent arc. It was very difficult, the bow being strung for his grandfather's prodigious strength. But he thought of the poor boy, lying on the playa, suspended between life and death, and, gritting his teeth, swallowing his nausea, he drew the bow to the full extent of its arc, aimed down the shaft, let the arrow fly straight into the old man's back.

There was a sharp, unearthly scream; the boy vanished. Then water was rushing into his mouth, his eyes were burning, and he was vomiting up salt . . .

In the centre of the tepee, Wolf opened his eyes. He was dry, and all about him everything was as it had been when he and White Bow had left it before they had gone in response to the summons of the spirit of the black bear, except all his senses seemed to be heightened, the new acuity imprinting itself on him with every move he took. He recalled the pipe his grandfather had given him, and for some time, then, he was convinced the journey had simply been some kind of peyote-induced hallucination. Then he felt the rime of salt on his skin, a residue, surely, of his dunking in the salt-choked Sevier.

He was paralysed with terror. Then it was all true. He had plunged through the portal of the river into the land of the dead.

Half-dazed, he got up, then, searched inside and outside, but there was no sign that White Bow had ever been there. In the middle of the playa in winter, Wolf was totally on his own. Except for the two remaining arrows White Bow had fashioned for him.

Three hours later, with the light failing, and the chill creeping through the tepee, Peter Matheson found Wolf, having threatened White Bow with bodily harm if he did not divulge the location of his son.

'He should not go,' Peter heard the old man say to Open Hand as

138

he mounted his horse. 'It has begun, and what Wolf must do he must do alone.'

Peter had spat on the ground and, pulling on the reins, had dug his spurs into the flanks of his horse, wheeling him, and had taken off for the salt wastes of the playa where the senile creature had left his son to die.

Wolf should have been delighted to see his father appearing out of the indigo dusk, but in fact he contemplated hiding. In truth, if he could have found someplace on that plain to secrete himself he would have done so. But the only place he could think of was the land of the dead, and without his grandfather he knew he could not get there.

Somehow, in retrospect, the place no longer frightened him so. Not nearly as much as the cold grey light in his father's eyes, in his tone, when, striding into the tepee, he had barked at his son, 'Gather up your belongings. We're going home.'

Mounted behind his father, his arms around his chest, he felt with each precise arc of the powerful horse's hooves, a lessening of the sharpness of sight, sound, smell that had attended his awakening. As the steed raced across the playa, it broke up the frozen bed of salt, which flew around them like shards from a broken mirror, its magic betrayed as silver paint on glass.

He had taken with him only the arrows White Bow had made for him, believing that everything he had brought with him had been the property of a child, certainly of no interest now to him. But when he returned home, he found that they were incomplete, the feather fletching having been pulled out during his journey home or never having been anchored in by White Bow in the first place.

Everything was different in those first weeks, not the least of which was the relationship between his parents. Where before their differences over her father had remained in the background, now Peter voiced his protestations more vociferously, once even suggesting that, since it was clear the old man was senile, they ought to commit him to a home before he hurt someone.

Open Hand, the Dream Collector for her people, repository of their hopes, fears and despair, so patient and understanding, seemed to have run out of both virtues. She would not – no doubt could not – explain her father to her husband. But she had lost her equilibrium. Where before she was able to observe this ethnological chasm with an almost scientific detachment, and even think of herself as the bridge between the two, there was now a personal aspect that cut her to the bone. She had undoubtedly seen the chasm as a metaphor for the twilight of one culture and the ascendancy of another, this comfortable rationalization giving her a false sense of security.

139

But there could be no security with Peter Matheson. He was a true pioneer, restless as the wind, long on courage but short on responsibility.

'The trouble with civilization,' he had once told Wolf, 'is that it can find no place for heroes, for heroes are, by definition, feral, and their very wildness threatens to rend the fabric of civilization.'

Wolf was later to realize that his father was talking about himself, and he would recall the conversation in toto many times simply because of its rarity; Peter Matheson almost never spoke about himself.

Wolf recognized in his father a fire, not White Bow's shaman fire, but significant in its own right because of the ferocity with which it drove him. White Bow had already taught Wolf of the continuous interaction between the mind, body and spirit, and here he could see it for himself in his own father, because it was clear to him that Peter Matheson acted and reacted from the spirit part of him he found so vital.

'The heroes of long ago should have protected the Nation,' Wolf said thoughtfully.

'The Indians had their heroes, it's true,' Peter said. 'But we were too strong, too numerous.'

'No,' Wolf said, 'I meant heroes like you or your father. You should have understood and stopped the killing of the tribes.'

Peter looked at his son, nodded. 'Perhaps it might have been so,' he said. 'But our civilization came upon us too quickly; and was too far advanced.' He looked far out on the horizon where the mountains seemed to rise high enough to touch the sky, and Wolf was reminded of White Bow's story of the hawk. 'Or too backward.'

'Backward?'

Peter had nodded. 'Despite what you're taught at school, the coming of civilization is not all good. Lost in the maze of laws and statutes of society we end up losing our sense of the land. We see it only for what it can give us, not for what it is.' He grunted. 'The American Indian culture was lost that way, joining a list of many others around the world.'

'But laws are what make society,' Wolf said. 'At least, that's what we're taught in school.'

'Well, you'll have to make up your own mind about that, son.'

'But, Dad, what do you believe?'

'How do I answer that?' Peter Matheson had watched his horse cropping at grass, the sunlight spinning off its glossy coat as the muscles beneath its skin rippled. 'A hero carries the law on his hip, and though he will invariably pave the way for civilization, it will cast him aside as quickly and as roughly as it can because he casts a dangerous shadow.'

140

And, of course, more than anything else that was what Peter Matheson longed to do.

A year after he rode across the playa to rescue his son, Peter Matheson was gone. Open Hand never spoke of where he had gone, but Wolf knew because he received one letter from his father. Reading it over and over until it fell apart in his hands, he was at last forced to tuck the pieces carefully beneath his pillow.

But Open Hand spoke of her husband whenever Wolf required it of her. If there was rancour in her heart he never saw it or, more importantly, felt it. He could not doubt that she had loved him, but he also suspected that a component of that love was contained in his restless spirit, and she saw his moving on as being as inevitable as the coming of winter after autumn. As she had often told him in other contexts when other, bleak winters had caused food to be in short supply, Spring will always come.

And so it did after that lonely winter of his departure. Wolf missed him fiercely but he did not miss the tension in the household. White Bow, ancient and creaking like the wooden wagons of yesteryear, moved into the room that had been Peter Matheson's sanctuary. He made no more arrows and, in fact, had never fletched Wolf's pair, though Wolf had given them back to him for this purpose.

Often, Wolf asked Open Hand about her father, for – or so it seemed to him – White Bow had grown insular following his return from the playa to which he had brought Wolf. It was clear to Wolf that whatever the old man had intended had not come to pass, not fully, anyway, but he had had no success in interesting his grandfather in returning to the salt flat, which would be possible now that Peter Matheson was gone.

Open Hand never answered a question about her father directly, and to Wolf's latest query, she replied, 'Among all things that fly the mind is the swiftest.'

Wolf, pondering this seeming riddle, remembered his descent with White Bow into the land of the dead. Surely, having shed the coil of their mortal bodies, they had flown to this otherwise inaccessible place, as mystics define flight.

'I think I understand. But why won't Grandpa take me back?'

'Now, thinking back on it, you are certain your father interfered with the process forming between you and White Bow,' Open Hand said. 'But White Bow does not see the world like other people. He steps back and sees possibilities – all the possibilities – in every situation. He is like a weaver who is able to trace the serpentine progress of each strand of wool even after the whole is completed.'

Wolf looked up at her. 'Are you saying that Grandpa believes the way it turned out . . . is how it is meant to be?'

His mother, enigmatic in her beauty and her acceptance, took his hand in hers. 'Gather the patience to discover on your own what is meant to be,' she said as grave and potent as any man.

And, of course, that was White Bow's great lesson, brought home to him by disappointment and loss.

It took Wolf seven years of growing to marshal the courage necessary to follow his father. And when he had found him, he didn't recognize him. He felt disoriented at this. Peter Matheson had been in Australia, mining opals. During that time, his eyesight had turned bad, obliging him to wear glasses. Working fourteen hours a day, hoarding his lode against the thieves who appeared in all shapes and guises had turned his hair grey.

Wolf found him in Lightning Ridge, a raw and rough miner's town in a depression surrounded by long, low hills dotted with Buddah, Belah and Leopardwood trees. Aptly named, it produced the world's best black opals.

Wolf had arrived in this remote part of New South Wales by truck, travelling almost four hundred miles northwest of Sydney, the last several over a bitumen road, black as pitch. He was greeted by the raucous cry of a kookaburra scavenging for food. Months later, he would come upon a burrow filled with beautiful pure white kookaburra eggs resting in what had been a termite nest. Australia, he would find, was filled with such startling bits of savage beauty.

The town itself was nothing extraordinary: a pair of self-service stores, a butcher's shop, a bakery, one hotel – The Lightning Ridge Diggers' Rest – a couple of motels, the offices of the local paper – the *Lightning Ridge Flash* – three churches, a primary school. And, of course, the local firearms clubs.

Peter Matheson was sharing his ramshackle house with a pretty feline black-haired girl with long tanned legs who could not yet have been twenty.

'Wolf?'

'Hello, Dad.'

He stuck out his hand as he would to a long-lost friend. 'By God, it's good to see you.'

Wolf was paralysed while vagrant emotions he could barely comprehend rose and fell within him. Love, fear, anger, and, above all, a boy's need to be acknowledged by his father.

Peter Matheson was a man who had never shirked hard work or

danger, but he had found the Australian outback a different animal altogether. He had survived a scorpion bite, which had put him into a convulsive fever until an Aborigine happening upon him had applied an herb poultice that had taken down the swelling and the fever. He had watched poisonous spiders mate, the mother spinning out her egg sacs, then get eaten by her ravenous young. He had endured the ravages of broiling sun and flash floods; he had even killed a desperate miner who had tried to steal his cache of opals, but that, at least, was not a new experience for him.

Although Peter Matheson was a tough man, he had had to prove himself all over again to the rough-and-tumble Australians. They liked his Texas drawl and his hard-edged cowboy manners; they had an instant respect for a real man who could hold his own in a brawl, drink a gallon of beer without vomiting, and fornicate all night. They were also fascinated by his seemingly inexhaustible tales of American Indians.

The truth was that Peter Matheson was never at peace unless he was among his men friends. He needed the community of tough male spirits like his own as others need food and water. He cared for his wife, loved his only child, but in his own way, in their place.

'Growing old has different connotations for you and me,' Peter Matheson told his son. 'You can't understand that now, but all too soon you will. It's a sad day in a man's life when he falls down and can't get up quite as fast, when the pain doesn't go away as quickly, and the ache settles in for good.'

'Is that why you have her?' Wolf said, hooking his thumb towards the tight-muscled girl.

Peter Matheson smiled at his son's shrewdness. 'Partly,' he admitted. 'But it's also partly because she knows in a week or a month I'll be gone. It won't matter to her; she's young, too busy with her own life to fixate on anyone else's.' He glanced over at his son. 'How's your mom?'

'Busy with her own life,' Wolf had said, making his father laugh.

Later, in the chittering Australian darkness, Wolf had said, 'You're not coming home, are you?'

His father, twirling a toothpick whittled from the bone of some small animal, said, 'That why you came all this way, spent all your mother's money, to ask me that?'

'I spent my own money,' Wolf said. 'I worked hard to buy this trip.'

Peter stuck the toothpick in his mouth, stood up. 'Come on,' he said. 'I want to show you something.'

They went out of the house without telling the girl where they were going. They climbed into a small, beat-up truck, and Peter swung through the darkness, driving up into the ridges. 'My mine's pretty

143

near Lunatic Hill,' he said. 'I bought it from the Aboriginal girl in my house. She inherited it from a man named the Major who blew his brains out one night while drunk.'

They got out, and Peter switched on his lantern-like portable light. The sky was very dark, with just a scattering of first-magnitude stars peering through a veil of clouds.

Peter swung the beam downwards. 'You see here where the ridge has cracked? This fault is called a slide; if you don't see slides you won't find opals.'

Beside the slide, they entered a mine. 'I've named this Nowhere,' Peter said. The gravelly clay went rapidly downwards. They walked ahead until they came to what appeared to be a vertical hole in the rock. Peter led the way down the shaft to the level below. Ahead, the mine opened up into a large space, a chambered-out section known locally as a ballroom, as Wolf was later to learn.

This far underground, Peter extinguished his light, set a candle to burning. To their left, Wolf could see a series of striations.

'This top part is sandstone,' Peter said. 'You see how at the bottom it is cut off by this hard stuff, compressed quartzite – the shincracker, we call it here. It's well-named.' His finger traced a path. 'Below that is what we call the level, clay-like earth where we find the nobbies of opal.'

He dug in his pocket, produced a rough-shaped item which he handed to Wolf. 'Roll it between your fingers.'

As Wolf did so, he saw in the candlelight stupendous flashes of peacock green, bright orange, fiery red.

'You see how closely the flashes of colour are grouped? This is called a Floral Harlequin and it's very rare. It's why I lit the candle. The colours are purer in this light. Now you're seeing it as I did, down here when I puddled it out.' Peter was watching his son's face. 'This is what I do, how I make money.' He took the opal back. 'It's exciting, dangerous work. We're thought of as a breed apart. I answer to no one.'

'And you carry the law on your hip,' Wolf said, glancing at the Colt revolver holstered on his father's belt.

Peter put his hand on Wolf's shoulder, squeezed hard. 'I want you to understand this, son. I never ran away from anything in my life. But sure as I'm standing here with you civilization would have destroyed me. In this wilderness, I'm not required to give myself away.'

Wolf stayed with his father for six months. Out of deference to his son, Peter was set to dismiss the Aboriginal girl almost immediately, but Wolf objected, so she stayed. It was this girl, in fact, with a name he could never quite pronounce, who showed him the feral beauty of the kookaburra eggs hidden away in the abandoned termite nest.

144

Father and son set about finding black opals. Peter taught Wolf how to operate the new pneumatic spade that allowed them to prospect as much of the ridge in a month as had been previously gone over in a year. Still, it was backbreaking work and, as Peter had said, often dangerous, not only from natural occurrences but from man-made ones, as well. But the Mathesons survived them all, Wolf emerging with broader shoulders, bulging biceps and a thin white scar along his left collarbone where a would-be thief had cut him before he'd smashed the heel of his hand into the man's sternum, fracturing it.

He'd found a scorpion in his boot one day and had set about feeding it, fascinated by the way it made its kill, the lightning flick of its segmented tail, the plunge of the poisoned barb. The thing became a kind of bizarre pet, seeming to recognize Wolf, although Peter told him no such thing was possible in a creature whose brain was so primitive. But, after that, they'd had no more problems with thieves.

The village was filled with Peter's buddies, hard-working, hard-drinking Aussies – although there was a scattering of Europeans as well. They were basically an honest, lusty lot, with names such as Vertical Paddy, Buckjump Willie and Murdering Jack, full of laughter and life. There was, indeed, a camaraderie here that would have been difficult to maintain in other, more civilized settings. Wolf fell in with them naturally, liking them for their directness. They were close to the earth, primitive in a way he could not yet fully fathom, but because he wanted to, and that showed, they took to him as swiftly as he did to them.

'They're great people,' Peter had told his son. 'As long as you don't judge them on the criminal past they're still so sensitive about they'll be straight with you.'

One night, they took him, got him drunk, shoved him in a room with a young woman, raven-haired, light-eyed. She was already naked; her breasts shivered when he looked at them. She was so young, her beauty possessing an aching quality that would disappear within a year in this harsh world.

While they made love, the men outside raised their voices in one hearty folk song after another so that Wolf and the girl should not worry about their intimate sounds being overheard through the thin walls.

The girl with the unpronounceable name was still awake when he stumbled home. Perhaps she had been waiting for him, because she seemed to know what had happened and that he would be hungry. She fixed him something to eat, and they went outside into the star-strewn night. Wolf sat on the steps, eating silently while the girl sat beside him smoking in that still, contemplative manner that reminded him of White Bow.

145

She told him that she was a Kulin, one of the most ancient of the Aboriginal tribes, had been born in the southeast among her people but had soon grown restless. She liked the wind in her face, the sun in her eyes, but there was nothing for her to do in Lightning Ridge except sell her body. Now, of course, she had money and didn't have to do anything she didn't want to. It was a unique feeling.

He felt very close to her, this being from an alien culture on the other side of the world, a primitive, really, in the same way his grandfather was, except she was not in any way intimidating. He liked her, responded to her, understood finally why he had never been offended by her presence in his father's house.

They talked until the starlight dimmed, and pearl light began to stream across the ridgetops. That was when she drew her legs beneath her, told him about sunsets. It seemed her people believed that sunset was the time of death because the Kulin rode the oblique rays of the setting sun into the heavens where the dead dwelt.

She had actually seen this occur once, she said. Her grandmother, who was very old, had died at sunset, and she had seen her grandmother's spirit rise from the dead husk to walk upon the thick rays of the sun until she was above the birds, the mountaintops, even the wind. Now, she said, she could feel her grandmother in the sunlight that fell upon her, the wind that caressed her.

Enchanted, Wolf fell asleep beside her, sprawled across the front steps of his father's house.

Surely Wolf would have stayed longer, but he was abruptly called home. This 'calling' was in a metaphorical sense, in the same way his mother had described 'flight' to him. He awoke one morning from a dream. In it, a hawk was circling so high in the sky it was a mere speck. Gradually, it descended through the layers of atmosphere, until it was below the crests of purple mountains. And then below that, into a vast red valley along which ran a fault, a shifting of the rock floor. Down, down, down it went into the twilight of the earth where Wolf laboured in stone dust and seeping silt. Alerted by the dry crack of beating wings, he looked up into the face of the hawk, and knew.

He said goodbye to his father on the slope of Lightning Ridge. The sun, brighter in the Australian winter than it ever was at home, fell upon him like a mantle. His father took his hand, as he had when Wolf had first appeared, then pulled him to him, embracing him.

'It was great of you to come,' Peter told his son. 'More than I had hoped.'

'I understand why you won't come back,' Wolf said.

Peter let go of him. 'I know you do.'

146

The last sight Wolf had of him was returning to the makeshift village, his buddies converging around him, the beer coming out. As he was driven away, Wolf thought he heard a ghost of a song spring up.

White Bow was dying, and this was what had called Wolf home. For his last days, his grandfather had been moved to his own tepee, which had been tended daily in his absence. A hole had been cut in the tepee directly over where White Bow lay on his palette of doeskin and bear fur. Nearby, a fire was burning into which was periodically thrown bunches of dried sweet sage. These preparations, Wolf knew, were to aid his grandfather in his ascent up to heaven.

It was summer in Elk Basin, but White Bow was covered to his neck in furs. He shivered often, as with the ague, although he was not ill in any manner a white doctor could determine.

'I have been fortunate,' White Bow said to Wolf one day while the boy sat at his side. 'Most people move outside themselves only once in their lives – at the very end. My flights occurred every day, whenever I wished them.'

Wolf said, 'You wanted me to fly, too, didn't you, Grandfather?' He had been pondering this question all during his interminable trip home.

For the longest time, White Bow did not reply. His eyes were closed, and his face, waxy-looking, had taken on the appearance of a death mask. Wolf was becoming alarmed, when the old man's lips moved. 'It is true,' he said, 'that I wished for you to follow the path I made for myself. It took me some time to see how selfish this wish was. For once, I had listened to my heart and not the worldsong. I had wanted something too badly.'

'But I think I wanted it, too,' Wolf said. 'Remember how I'd ask you to bring me back to that spot on the playa.'

White Bow's lips formed the ghost of a smile. 'I remember every time. But I think you wanted only to please me.' His head turned towards Wolf. 'Let me feel your hand.'

Wolf slipped his hand into his grandfather's, noting how cool and dry it was.

'I feel your strength, Wolf, and I know your path lies in a different direction.'

'Which one?'

'I don't know.'

But, even as he said it, Wolf had the impression that he knew very well, he, the master weaver who could follow each thread even after the whole was complete.

'Do you remember our journey into the land of the dead?' White Bow said.

147

'Yes.'

'Each journey – each flight – begins with a crossing of a bridge. It may not be a real bridge.'

'Like the river.'

'The river, yes,' White Bow said. 'I want you to do something for me. Build me a bridge. Take two lengths of sturdy hemp and, using sinew, affix to them at intervals seven of the arrows I made for myself as one would attach rungs.'

'I will get some help.'

'No.' White Bow's grip on his hand was strong and steady. 'This you must do yourself. Only your hands may touch the ladder-bridge. When you are done, hang it from the hole above me. Now go.' He released Wolf's hand. 'Do as I have bade you.'

Three hours later, it was done. The day was ending. The sun, as swollen as a pregnant woman, wallowed near the summits of the mountains on the horizon. All day a breeze had swept through the tepee, keeping Wolf cool. But now, as he finished hanging the ladder, the air was still, the heat of the day radiating from the hard-packed ground holding back the coming chill of night.

'Wolf,' White Bow said, 'at the dawn of time, there was no need of shamans or ladder-bridges. Every person possessed the power to project himself upward to heaven. But like water's effect upon rock, time has changed humans. Most have lost the power. Now it is for shamans alone to walk the narrow defile between heaven and earth, between time and space. But now these bridges are dangerous because heaven and earth, time and space are no longer contiguous. They are separated by a fearsome void, created by degeneration, where even the most powerful shaman may be lost.'

The old man stared up through the hole in the tepee at the sky, burnished by the first few fires of sunset. 'I took you across such a ladder-bridge. You were able to make the journey not because of me, but because of what dwells within you. This is why I chose you to construct this ladder. Learn what is inside you, Wolf. You will have to use it one day.'

Open Hand was with White Bow when he died. All around his tent, members not only of the Wind River Shoshone but of a host of other tribes of the Nation sat, intent on the passing of the old man. Wolf, squatting just outside the entrance flap, looked back once to see the plain filled with people, silent, expectant, the only movement coming from the horses grazing, the dogs wandering past cooking fires, searching for scraps. Once, a baby squalled, and that was all.

Wolf must have fallen asleep because the next thing he knew

148

his mother was kneeling beside him. Her arms curled around him protectively, her lips brushed his cheek. Her eyes were red, her face streaked with tears.

Wolf sighed, put his arms around her in turn.

'He's gone,' she said softly.

But, for the first and only time in her life, she was wrong.

BOOK II

Life During Wartime

*As a member of an escorted tour,
you don't even have to know
the Matterhorn isn't a tuba.*

Temple Fielding

SIX

Washington/East Hampton/Tokyo

'What I find more contemptible than anything,' said Brig. Gen. (Ret.) Hampton Conrad, 'is hypocrisy.'

Conrad looked as if he had stepped off a recruiting poster for the Armed Services: he was square-jawed, craggy-faced and big-boned. His sandy-grey hair was cut in regulation fashion; his grey eyes carried just enough blue flash in them to make him appear both attractive and dangerous. But he did not think the way a straightforward military man would, which was why he was a brigadier (one-star) and why he was retired ten years prior to what might be considered normal for a man of his rank. But there was nothing normal about 'Ham' Conrad.

He had been brought up in Hartford, Connecticut, one of seven sons of Thornburg Conrad III, the man who had put Hartford on the map as the insurance capital of the country. Ham had been given that sobriquet by his older brothers because of his huge hands which, when Ham balled them into fists, could inflict serious damage on those boys even several years his senior who riled him.

Thornburg Conrad III had done everything he could (which was considerable) to ensure that his progeny would be successful in whatever endeavour they chose. To that end, Ham had gone to West Point, graduating in the top one per cent of his class. His brothers had sneered at him from their elevated positions as students in the most prestigious East Coast high schools, colleges and universities. Thornburg had kept silent, believing that dealing with this spirited animosity could only improve Ham; he certainly never allowed his own feelings to show. He was proud of Ham. There was a vision Ham was following; that it was Thornburg's vision only made the elder Conrad prouder still.

Ham had excelled in tactical warfare, and immediately upon graduation, he had been assigned to the US Military Assistance Command, Vietnam (MACV) which was then – in March, 1965 – under the command of General William Westmoreland. MACV was the hub of strategic military planning for the entire Vietnam campaign. Ham had spent a sometimes successful, often frustrating four years in and around

153

Saigon. During his tour, he was promoted three times. Though he never personally engaged the enemy, he was responsible for thousands of their deaths.

After his return, Thornburg had insisted he take a full immersion course in Japanese. Six months later, Thornburg had used his influence in Washington's potent old-boy network to gain Ham a significant position in Japan with the Far East Military Intelligence Group (Collection). There, Ham flourished, as his father had foreseen he would, using his keen mind and its tactical bent to attune military and government personnel to the nuances and often baffling idiosyncrasies of the culture.

In fact as time progressed it became clear to Ham that this expertise had been honed to such a level that his position in the military was fast becoming a hindrance; being Army he stood out in any crowd, could not in Japan go where he might want to because of the Japanese antipathy towards American military personnel. In addition he was so good with people – so kind, considerate, so impeccable with advice – that his reputation grew far beyond the boundaries of the military. He had been trained well by his father; he was not a man who long tolerated roadblocks to the furtherance of his career. He spent many long months deciding what to do.

It was on a rare holiday in Hawaii that his father flew into Waikiki. Amid the sun-drenched beachscape, festooned with clattering palm trees and bronzed bodies clad in fluorescent bikinis Thornburg Conrad III and Ham devised their plan to reinvent the world as they knew it. He would require, he said, Ham's help on the Japanese end, and because, as always, he wished to remain in the background, he wanted Ham to effectively run the day-to-day mapping of the idea.

By the time he returned to Tokyo ten days later it had become a fullblown plan with every major development laid out, every eventuality covered with the military precision that was typical of Ham's genius.

Ham's superiors loved it, the relevant government personnel back in Washington loved it even more. But then these were the same men in the old-boy network with whom Thornburg had gone to school and who he had spent some forty years cultivating. They liked Ham, and more, they respected him; he reminded them of his father who they liked and respected, and with whom they had exchanged many favours and consummated many mutually profitable deals.

These men listened to Ham, digesting the Conrads' plan with the avidity of a snake gobbling a rat. To a man, they agreed that Ham was the right man in the right place at the right time. They lifted their voices in chorus, and in due course, orders were cut returning him to Washington where, in a ceremony of no little pomp, he was

154

retired from the Army. He would never forget that day. Medals hung from the breast of his dress uniform, presented to him by his superiors, though he had never once personally engaged the enemy in war, which made him a little sad.

But though he had retired from the Army he was hardly retired. He had, in effect, exchanged one set of masters for another, but he was also several giant steps closer to the top of the pyramid of influence and power, several steps closer to the goal his father had set for him when he had been a young man.

'Without influence you will never be happy,' Thornburg Conrad III had said to him when he had been twelve. *'Next year, you will be a man, at least you would be in most primitive cultures, and you will be in my eyes.'* Thornburg had put a hand atop his son's head in a gesture that, thinking back on it, Ham judged to be a kind of sanctification, as if the old man were a bishop instead of a billionaire. *'Be certain you make me proud; be certain you further the eminence of the name of Conrad.'* And like a Knight Templar, Ham had set out to do just that.

Thus the Conrads, father and son, had decided to join forces. For Ham, nothing could have been more perfect. Together, they formulated a plan that was brilliant. The key to dismantling modern-day Japan was deceptively simple, because it was going to be provided by that arrogant Japanese, Naoharu Nishitsu.

When Yuji Shian was provided with enough evidence against Nishitsu, he would begin a public purging that would culminate in a kind of bloodless coup, brought about by the finely-honed Japanese sense of honour, sweeping all the ageing right-wing billionaires tied to Nishitsu not only from their corporate suites but from their positions of influence. And, as it had done in Eastern Europe and Russia, the wind of change would create a whole new order, one more suited to the West, especially the United States, made up of consumers, not savers, young men not tied to the war in the Pacific but wanting to live in the present, willing to listen to reason, to see that the American way always had been and still was *the* successful way to conduct international business.

'Hypocrisy is the bane of civilization,' Ham said now as he wrapped his lips around what he judged to be the best hamburger in the greater DC area. Outside, everyone on the street was black; inside the burger joint the patrons and the counterman were black and so was the cook. This was a ghetto section of Washington that not even many police patrol cars ventured into at night. Ham did not mind the ghetto at all. Washington, like most large cities in the USA, was made up of the haves and the have-nots, only more so. What had appealed most to Ham about Thornburg's plan was that it had the potential to change the face of the world. It was his fervent hope that it might even eventually help the have-nots.

Ham despised the haves, with their correct manners, their narrow minds and their obsession with protocol, as if the world at large cared one fig for protocol or manners or debate. In fact, he found here in the world at large a kind of simmering rage that was a relief from the upscale lilywhite posturing of the monied Georgetown/Capitol Hill/Chevy Chase set he had come to loathe. At least rage was a pure emotion, untainted by duplicity. Hence his diatribe.

'Hypocrisy is the symptom of all self-satisfied cultures,' he continued. 'It's a warning sign like bad breath or bleeding gums that's best heeded quickly.' He bared his steel-like teeth, pushed them through the red meat, grinding it to pulp.

'Speaking of which,' Jason Yoshida said, sucking a bit of melted cheese off his forefinger, 'Audrey Simmons is coming in at 3:30.'

The glass of vanilla Coke disappeared in Ham's fist as he put it to his mouth and drank deeply. He smacked his lips in satisfaction. 'Senator Simmons' wife?'

'Yup,' Jason Yoshida said. He whacked off an enormous bite of cheeseburger, thrusting most of it into his cheek, as he said, 'I believe she wants to thank you in person for helping her son.'

'Rich men's children,' Ham said, wiping his mouth with a succession of paper napkins, 'are more often products of their parents' fortunes than they are of their parents themselves.' He polished off his vanilla Coke, pointed to a gigantic sticky bun to be brought over. 'The wages of parenthood-by-proxy, eh, Yosh.' Yoshida, deep in his cheeseburger, grunted as a spurt of ketchup spattered the nearby chrome sugar dispenser, and Ham turned to the rapt counterman, said, 'I sure hope you've got a gallon of your strong coffee, son, because that's just what I need about now.'

Much to Ham's surprise and relief Audrey Simmons was not the hypocrite her powerful husband was. Her problem, however, had not been a surprise. Her son, Tony, had been in deep with the wrong crowd, taking drugs, going AWOL from summer school and generally 'being a pain in the ass,' as Senator Simmons had said when he had phoned Ham.

'Tony seems to be his own self again,' she said. 'Oh, I'm so grateful.' She smiled. 'And I know Leland will be, too.'

'Never mind that,' Ham said. 'I did what I did for Tony.'

'But what exactly *did* you do?'

He got up, stared out the window, watching a black gardener tend the rose bushes outside his office. He wondered if the gardener ate his

156

breakfast at the burger joint in the ghetto Ham had just returned from. He did not have an office overlooking the White House, which was the goal of most people in Washington; yet his was most definitely an office of power. Hampton Conrad had made it so. It was a standard government-issue room with high ceilings, exposed wiring and ugly wooden furniture that seemed to date from before the second world war. There was a framed photo of the current president on one wall, a reproduction of a striking portrait of Teddy Roosevelt on another. The cream paint was peeling in one corner.

All in all, Ham would have to say that he liked his other office on K Street much better, even though he hardly used it. It was a spacious suite he had picked out himself, in the same building as Washington's most prestigious law firm. The only other tenant on his floor was a powerful lobby for certain Japanese interests; the irony of the location tickled him.

The K Street offices went by the name of Lenfant & Lenfant, using the name of Brosian Lenfant, the well-known and respected former senator from Louisiana, who was too rich to have been affected by his brief term in office before he suffered a debilitating heart attack. Now he lent his name and, once a week, his body to the firm owned and operated by Ham Conrad.

Jason Yoshida, who had become an American citizen with Ham's assistance and was now a GS-14, a rather high Government Service rating, nominally worked for the Department of Defense. In fact, he operated mostly out of the K Street offices, which he ran with impressive efficiency.

Ham turned away from the window. 'You know, Mrs Simmons, sometimes all children need to see the error of their ways is to be given parameters.'

'Parameters?'

He turned to look at the senator's wife. She was blonde, with that peculiar brittle beauty endemic to Washington women, but she seemed to know damned little about raising a child. She wore a sleek chic designer suit that he judged must have set the senator back two thousand dollars. He said, hoping she would understand, 'If a child senses that he has no limits – that he will be allowed to do whatever he wishes – he will push to see if it's true. He does this, Mrs Simmons, not simply because he is wilful, but because he senses that what he needs are limits, rock solid boundaries that define his world, the difference between yes, you can and no, you can't, because with these limits comes a profound sense of security that all children need.'

Audrey Simmons rose. 'Well, all I can say is you've worked wonders

157

on Tony.' She extended one cool expertly manicured hand. 'My husband will be in touch to – '

Ham waved away her words. 'You can tell the senator for me that I'll call him if – and when – there's a need.' He smiled, seeing her to the door. 'And, Mrs Simmons, don't hesitate to call me if Tony gives you any further trouble.'

Audrey Simmons turned abruptly so that Ham, who had been following her, was momentarily pressed against her front. 'Could I call you anyway?' Audrey Simmons asked, her head tilted up at that angle women used to connote surrender. 'My husband isn't the only one who could show you his appreciation.'

Ham wondered just how bored Audrey Simmons must be to want to indulge herself like a slut. His father was a hypocrite and his mother was a whore, he thought, feeling sorry for Tony. What a family. He clamped her firmly by the arm, steered her out the door, murmuring a cordial but distancing goodbye.

Jason Yoshida slipped in a moment later. 'Was that community service or business?' he asked when he had shut the door behind him.

'You know, you're damn cynical for a Japanese.'

'I may be Japanese but I'm all American now.'

Ham lifted a hand. 'Pardon me.' He shrugged, sitting back down behind his desk. 'In any case, you're a cynical bastard.'

'It's this town,' Yoshida said deadpan. 'There's something in the air.'

'Or in the water.' Ham grunted. 'The thing is Simmons' kid is basically a good egg. He'll be a far better human being than his parents are, that's for sure.'

'But we can count on his old man, if we need him.'

'And we will need him,' Ham said. 'The Senate International Trade Committee bill will be coming onto the floor of the Senate any day now. The draconian restrictions it will impose on foreign imports will trigger trade sanctions from Japan. Effectively, the bill that American labour unions have been lobbying for for so long will cut us off economically from Japan. What do you think will happen when all of the government's top secret defence computers break down and the chips, manufactured only in Japan, are unavailable?'

'It won't come to that,' Yoshida said. 'We're seeing to it.'

'Yes, we are.' Ham laced his hands behind his head, stared out the window at the black man and his roses. Ham envied him his intimacy with nature. 'But perhaps not quickly enough. This string of deaths of key senators has Thornburg very worried.'

'The coroner claims they were of either accidental or natural causes so we're getting no help from the police,' Yoshida said.

'Of course not. But the police don't see things in the right perspective. All the senators who have turned up dead were against this bill. And who are their replacements? Men who, I'm told, are responsive to the labour unions, and will vote for it.'

Yoshida waited patiently for Ham to finish, then said, 'On another front, I've reassigned Shipley back to his old job at Defense, but I think we ought to consider a promotion. He did extremely well with rushing Wolf Matheson into the hole left by Moravia's death.'

Ham was watching a shadow fall across the rose bushes, deepening the woody stems to black. 'Sure. Why not?'

'I'll think of a suitable reward.'

Ham swivelled around, looked sharply at Yoshida, recognizing a tone of voice. 'What's bothering you?'

'I'm not sure,' Yoshida admitted. 'But I'm starting to have grave misgivings. At first, I was sure your father had everything planned down to the last nut and bolt. First, these senators start to go down. Then Lawrence Moravia gets iced, and your father pushes us to get Matheson into the breach. We don't even know if Moravia was made to talk before he was hit.'

'You know that doesn't matter,' Ham said. 'We used Shipley as a cut-out. Moravia never met us or any of your contacts; he'd have no idea we were involved at all.'

Yoshida made no comment to this, with the single-mindedness that was typical of him, pushed on with his own line of thinking. 'We put Shipley in place, he does a number to recruit Matheson, just as your father ordered. And, again, as your father ordered we go to great lengths to keep an eye on Matheson while he's finding his way down the same rabbit hole Moravia disappeared into. The only thing we come up with is a dizzy Japanese artist he's asking about because maybe he's got the hots for her, then someone puts him through the skylight of a New York City apartment building.'

'Look, Yosh, this was essentially my father's plan, and as far as I can see it's still on course,' Ham said, as if he hadn't heard a word Yoshida had said. Hadn't agreed with it, more likely. 'We're on course in the Japanese phase.'

'Because we're on top of things and have our own connections in Japan,' Yoshida pointed out. 'You know, maybe – just maybe – the old man is slipping. At his age, you've got to admit it's more than possible. Matheson is a case in point. Why is your father so adamant we use him to replace Moravia when I have the perfect agent already in place in Tokyo? Besides, Matheson gives me the willies; he's a loner, and an amateur, to boot. Who knows whether he'll follow discipline? You can't tell me you

159

do.' Yoshida shook his head. 'He's the one destabilizing element in all this. Why bring such a dangerous man into the equation in the first place?'

Ham grunted. 'We've been all through this. Matheson's a detective by trade; the shit Moravia stepped into is his milieu. I think my father believes we made a mistake with Moravia. He's convinced Matheson is the only one smart enough to infiltrate Forbidden Dreams and Naoharu Nishitsu's world, and from what I've read of his background I'm still inclined to agree with the old man. But your objection is noted, Yosh.'

'That's not an objection,' Yoshida said, waiting to go on until Ham had raised his eyes. 'Like bad breath or bleeding gums it's a warning sign that's best heeded quickly before the entire plan is put into jeopardy.'

Much to Wolf's surprise it had been Amanda's sister, Stevie Powers, who was waiting for him in his hospital room after he had been brought down from recovery. It had been Stevie who had the neuro-specialist flown in from Walter Reed in Washington to make certain there would be no lasting damage from the operation to close the long, deep gashes down his left leg and arm. Miraculously, his plunge had been intercepted by an old-fashioned four-poster bed, so piled with eiderdowns and quilts that it had absorbed the impetus of the fall.

'You're spending so much time here,' he had said while he was still in the hospital. 'What about your patients?'

Stevie had tried to smile. 'I took some time off.' The cut of her Karl Lagerfeld suit perfectly accentuated the curves of her figure. 'The truth is, in my current state I couldn't face their broken psyches. Of course Morton disapproved. He thinks the best thing for me right now is to get back into my work, but he's wrong.' And just when he was sure she was playing psychiatrist, pulling him outside himself, she disarmed him with her soft smile and said, 'Anyway, I like being here . . . with you . . . closer to Amanda than anywhere else.'

But in a peculiar way her unexpected kindness had a downside. During those days in the hospital, each seeming to contain a weekful of hours, he was never so acutely aware of being alone. And, while Bobby Connor and his other cop buddies made their courtesy calls, he was aware that Squire Richards had not or would not come. Having asked after him, he had watched Bobby's face turn solemn. 'Everyone knows about your beef with him.'

'It wasn't a beef,' Wolf had said, annoyed. 'We had a disagreement.'

'Let's talk about something else,' Bobby had said. 'Like the CME says he'll have something for you maybe after the weekend.'

'Okay. Let's have it,' Wolf had said. 'What's the story going around?'

160

Bobby looked singularly uncomfortable. 'Lieutenant, people are saying you got into it with Squire real heavy.'

Something in Bobby's voice made Wolf say, 'And?'

'And you want him off the Werewolves because he's black.'

'That's ridiculous.'

'I know it is,' Bobby said. 'But I don't think Breathard does.'

'That stupid sonuvabitch.' But, of course, Breathard wasn't stupid at all. On the contrary, he was very clever.

'You gotta understand, Lieutenant, there were a lot of witnesses and Breathard's spoke to 'em all.'

'Let him speak to Squire. This was between him and me.'

Bobby got up off the chair, looked out the sooty window. 'Squire hasn't once opened his mouth about this, except to say he's got no intention of leaving the Werewolves.'

'You mean he's letting this idiotic race bias story feed on itself?'

'Guess he is.' He turned back to Wolf. 'The fact is, he's taken a couple of days' personal leave – Breathard okayed it.'

Wolf closed his eyes. Squire was no doubt scouring his neighbourhood for cash to pay off his brother's loan sharks. He now regretted not going after Squire that night at La Mentira, giving him the money he needed. 'Bobby,' Wolf had said wearily, 'let me know when he surfaces. If he calls in, tell him I want to talk to him about – just tell him I want to talk to him.'

When Squire came to see him, he'd see that the man got his money. Of course, that was strictly against regs. As were Squire's actions right down the line. This was just what he had talked to Amanda about time and again. But isn't that what men's clubs were all about, either bending existing laws or making up their own? Either way, there was an inherent contempt at work for the guidelines of the world at large, often so subtly that many members were unaware of its corrosive existence. Of course, there must be others for whom this contempt offered the ultimate lure.

Three days later, when he was released from the hospital, Stevie invited him to her house in East Hampton for a four-day weekend. 'Please say you'll come,' she had said. 'I'm in desperate need of the rest but I can't bear to be alone.' She smiled thinly. 'Like other high-pressure professions, at some time or other all good analysts risk burning out.'

The large, rambling house, hunkered by the edge of Georgica Pond, was dark even at noon, but unquiet. The creaks and groans of aged wood and copper plumbing were joined by the scrape and waft of thick branches from the gnarled, overgrown hemlocks that guarded it, giving the clapboard the patina of weathered copper.

For some reason there was often less wind on the water than there was around the house itself, nestled as it was amid the grove of shaggy, shapeless hemlocks. An enormous sculpted privet hedge ran down the east side of the property. Rhododendron and smaller, more delicate azalea were sheared into intermediate borders. On estates on either side of the property, hidden but not ignored by Stevie and her husband, lived the bluebloods into whose lifestyle they had decided to climb.

Through the windows, he had seen sunlight streaking the Georgica Pond – the name a deliberate understatement typical of the local gentry, it being more the size of a lake – like pigment upon a painter's brush: there was a sense about the light of incipience, of colour that was not yet vivid, of an idea not yet formed.

Wolf had made up a story and now believed it: that there was a mystery in the pond, that confluence of natural forces – life hidden away but nevertheless teeming beneath the water, under the rocks, within the canopy of pin oaks – that modern man could never completely understand, like the minds that conceived and executed the fetishes that festooned Stevie and Morton's living and dining rooms.

These were hand-wrought figures – animal, human, supernatu- ral creatures that Stevie had collected during her peripatetic teens – from every conceivable country on earth: Mexico, Honduras, Tibet, Guatemala, Peru, Haiti, Madagascar, Sri Lanka, Thailand, Bhutan, Zanzibar. Wolf found the animistic atmosphere intriguing, as if these dolls set up psychic eddies in the rooms, through the halls, along the staircase, as if they had the power to bring White Bow's worldsong to life or, at least, further into the light.

Wolf slept, and when he awoke, his eyes were blurred and his throat was thick with the memory of being thrown through the skylight, the great bang, and plummeting through an icefield of glass. But he had dreamed, and not about the pitched battle up on the rooftop, not about his fall. What? Dead and undead; fire in the ice, in the . . . He wiped sweat from his forehead as he struggled to remember.

It was already dark; he had slept the morning away. He discovered Stevie in an overstuffed chair in the living room, catching up on what appeared to be a file on one of her patients, but she closed it as soon as she saw him standing in the hallway.

The wind soughed restlessly through the hemlocks, and the branches skittered against the house like sounds from the unconscious. Somewhere, the sun must be out, perhaps on the water.

'How do you feel?'

'Okay.' He flexed his left hand several times. 'It's still stiff after I sleep, but otherwise . . . ' He shrugged. 'I've begun to miss my workouts.'

'A good sign,' she said. 'I'll miss you when you go back to work.'

162

He came into the living room. 'What does Morton think of my being here?'

'Morton's in Washington,' Stevie said as she busily fluffed the throw pillows on the couch. 'When Morton is in Washington he's oblivious to anything else.'

She put a fist into the centre of a pillow, which had the disturbing effect of pulling her white man-tailored shirt tight across her breasts. Up here in the country she seemed to have shed the impeccable society image, preferring jeans and simple shirts or Shaker sweaters. It was almost as if she had left that other blueblood Stevie Powers behind in the Park Avenue co-op.

'And he's in Washington quite a bit.'

She looked away, said, 'I'm getting cabin fever. I can see the sun on the pond; let's take a walk.'

They donned jackets, went down to the water, where the sunlight glanced dully off the still, thick water. It was warm for the beginning of March, and they left their jackets open so the fronts flapped against their thighs as they walked. They moved in silence around the edge of the water, Wolf skipping stones when he found them half-embedded in the damp soil. His slight limp was almost gone and, so it seemed to Stevie, he grew stronger every time he exercised the leg. His powers of recovery were truly remarkable.

The pond was like a solid thing, a presence at rest, hibernating, dreaming of the spring when it would stir to life. Stevie put her hands in her pockets, hunched her shoulders although there was no wind.

Standing close beside her, Wolf could tell that she was still thinking of his crack about Morton being in Washington so much.

'Wolf, I even let Amanda buy into the fiction about Morton and me,' she said all at once. 'Stupid, huh? What did I accomplish? I cut myself off from the one person I could talk to about it.'

She glanced at him a moment, then took a deep breath, let it out in a rush. 'Well, to be brutally honest, Morton has found himself a pied-à-terre in Washington. I'm afraid there's someone down there much younger than I am with whom he's infatuated. An ambassadorial attaché from France, I believe.' She frowned thoughtfully, staring at the imprints her boots had made in the dark, leaf-strewn earth. 'Funny. I can't imagine saying that to anyone else I know. I'd be mortified. Morton and I have a Teflon reputation as having a stellar marriage; it's good for both our careers. It's very difficult to admit to let alone to say, but I suppose youth is something with which I just cannot compete.'

Later, over a delicious Andalusian stew she had prepared, she said,

163

'In a way, you're like one of these fetishes that festoon the house: alien and fascinating.'

He took one up, the bright colours and blunt imagery filling his hand like a fountain of light. 'Is that how you think of these fetishes, as alien?'

'Aren't they?' Stevie said.

Wolf shrugged. 'In a way, they are closer to what the world is all about than we can ever be.'

She tucked her chin into her hands. 'Tell me more about that.'

'So that's why you insisted I come up here with you,' he said, 'so you can dissect my psyche.'

She knew at once that he was more than half serious. She laughed. 'Oh, my God, no. Oh, don't think that.' But she could not meet his gaze, instead stared into her plate as if it contained entrails from which like a Roman she could divine the future. 'Would you think ill of me,' she said, raising her head so her dark eyes met his, 'if I confessed that I brought you here out of a profound sense of guilt?'

'No,' Wolf said. 'I would think you were doing what was natural.' He smiled to help allay her obvious distress. 'Amanda always said . . .' Abruptly, he choked and, appalled, looked away. He gritted his teeth, willing the tears not to fall from the corners of his eyes. Ah, Christ, Amanda, he thought.

Stevie got up, began to clear the dishes. 'You know,' she said, 'despite what you saw it wasn't always easy having a sister. Amanda and I would have our fights – especially about Morton. Well, perhaps she was right there.' She set out a lemon meringue pie even though she knew neither of them had any intention of eating it; the sense of normalcy serving dessert brought was what was needed. 'We were both very competitive. I bet you didn't know that about her, perhaps because teaching made her so happy. When we were younger we wanted to win at everything, and sometimes hurting each other . . . well, we could hurt each other deeply.' She set out cups, cream and sugar, poured the coffee.

She sat down so abruptly the coffee rattled out of the cups onto the table. She put her hands over her face. 'Oh, damn, I promised myself I wouldn't do this, dredging up the past, airing old regrets, railing against an unfair fate, especially to you, who almost died trying to protect her.' She pulled distractedly at her French braid, drawing it over one shoulder. 'But it *is* so damned unfair.'

'We both had so much more to say to her, didn't we?'

Stevie was weeping openly now, her shoulders hunched, that air of invulnerable competence shattered by her sudden defencelessness. Gradually, he saw, he had been led beyond the careful facade into the

164

real Stevie Powers with her failed marriage, her incomplete relationship with her sister, her doubts about herself as a person.

After a long silence, she said, 'It's been so good for me being able to take care of you, knowing that I was being useful to someone . . . to you.' The light limned her, so that he could not distinguish her features, and for an instant her profile appeared disturbingly like someone else's. A residue loitered in his mind like the aftertaste of a dream: his grandfather's eyes, Chika's eyes; her strong thighs, hips jerking forward, a shudder and a tiny moan.

'You know, Wolf, I used to think that Amanda needed me, and I thought that was a good feeling. But now, too late, I know the simple and obvious truth: I needed her as much as she needed me.'

He tried to free himself of the disturbing image of Chika. 'Will you sleep tonight?'

She shook her head. 'No, but it will be better because you're here. I can feel you in the house and that's something I can hold onto.'

'I think you're damn lucky that Jason Yoshida is committed to you,' Thornburg Conrad III said. 'That man would be dangerous without proper supervision. Should be locked up anyway. My experience with the Japanese confirms to me that they simply cannot be trusted.'

'Yosh is different,' Ham Conrad said. Generally, he shared his father's distrust of the Japanese, whose idea of a good bargain was to go off and do exactly as they pleased, but Yosh had proved his loyalty over and over. 'He goes to great pains to tell me he's only half Japanese and all American.'

The two Conrads were on the deck outside the captain's cabin of *Influence II*, Thornburg's magnificent 45-foot teak-decked schooner, which was currently moored at his favourite spot well off the sea lanes in Chesapeake Bay. It was a mild day; the sun, picking up the vigour of reflection off the water, gave a strong hint of the spring to come. On the table between them was a lunch of major proportions. Remnants of the dozen Maryland crab cakes Ham had just consumed remained on the checked tablecloth, along with small plastic cups of tartar sauce, ketchup, mustard, mounds of potato salad and pickles.

'The Japanese,' Thornburg said with more care, 'are damned difficult to judge.' He looked particularly dapper in his traditional blue and white yachting outfit; with his impressive height, lankiness and powerfully rugged face he appeared not unlike Gary Cooper off the range. 'I've had my time with them just as you've had yours. Don't get cocky and think you're the only first-class brain around who can sniff out what they're up to. I can't caution you enough about them.'

165

Ham waited; he had become adept at that while his brothers had become increasingly impatient when dealing with their father. Having a minimum of contact with him, they saw him now as a cantankerous, uncaring relic who had lived past his time. But Ham saw his father as the masterpiece he was: logical, brilliant, calculating, the quintessential tactician on the cut-throat battlefield of corporate life. Though he had his own code of morality, in those things Ham could only wish to be more like him.

'All you need do is take our friends Yuji Shian and Naoharu Nishitsu as an example,' Thornburg continued at last. 'What it took was the notion of putting one and one together and making zero to get the ball rolling on our little scheme.'

Little scheme, indeed! Ham thought. Our little scheme is going to bring the modern economic colossus of Japan to its knees and, with it, sweep away such dangerous wealthy radicals as Naoharu Nishitsu.

'Yes, sir.' He had called his father 'sir' ever since he was sent off to prep school at the age of nine; when addressing him, it never occurred to Ham to call him anything else.

Thornburg, watching his son plough through the food, went on, 'As far as I was concerned, the mushrooming prominence of the Black Blade Society combined with the mind-bogglingly large infusions of money flowing from the mainstream of Japanese society into Nishitsu's hands over the last several years make an immediate termination imperative. You agreed with me, and so did the president and the military. And they liked even more my proposal to finesse these groups out of existence – to, in effect, get them to destroy one another.'

'Well, sir, as we both know no plan survives contact with the enemy. The up side is that my contingency plan brought Jason Yoshida into the centre of things.'

'Don't be cute with me, son. Someone found out we were using Moravia to infiltrate Forbidden Dreams, that damned club of the ultra-conservatives in Tokyo. We know that Forbidden Dreams is also the nexus point for the Toshin Kuro Kosai, the Black Blade Society. Moravia had been compiling the hard evidence against Nishitsu we'll need for Yuji Shian to take action. He was also providing us with the specifics on the latest postings of Black Blade Society members to the headquarters of multi-national corporations all around the globe. They are on the march, that is for certain, and there's no doubt we have to quash them before their members become too well-entrenched. That's where Moravia came in and they iced him.

'But we still need the evidence definitively linking Nishitsu with the ultraconservatives, the radical terrorists and the Black Blade Society. We

166

also must have more intelligence on the Toshin Kuro Kosai's plans.' Thornburg's lips twitched as if in some long-atrophied response to the sight of food. 'Then they went ahead and tried to do the same thing with the one man who could follow Moravia down into the snakepit of Forbidden Dreams.'

'Matheson.'

'Yes. Wolf Matheson. Shipley, our man in Defense, did a fine job recruiting him.'

Ham finished what was left of his turkey and gorgonzola sandwich and started preparing another. 'I'd like to talk to you about him. Now that the enemy has gotten to him too, perhaps we should think about using someone else to – '

'That dog just won't hunt,' Thornburg snapped. 'Let me tell you something about our friend Wolf Matheson. There's no better detective mind on the face of the earth, believe me. The man combines an unerring intuition with an unquenchable curiosity and the persistence of a bulldog. That's a formidable combination.'

'Yoshida's man is already on site,' Ham countered. 'And I am constrained to point out, sir, that all Matheson's given us so far is some bullshit fantasy on the New York CME's part that the inside of Moravia appeared younger than the outside. Which, even if it were true, is irrelevant to our purposes.'

'Son, you don't know Wolf Matheson the way I do. You'd have to have seen him in action like I did to appreciate all his qualities. I've picked him for sound reasons, rest assured. Now, what else have you got for me?'

Ham dropped the subject, but that did not stop him from considering what to do about it. The more he thought about what Yosh had said, the more he was inclined to his point of view. Matheson was a very dangerous character – more than that, he was unpredictable. His father obviously could not see that, but Ham and Yosh could.

'Oh, I almost forgot,' he said, digging into his pocket. 'Chief Breathard finally managed to get a decent surveillance photo of this off-the-wall Japanese artist Matheson seemed so keen on investigating just before he was put through the skylight.' He handed a small five by seven envelope over to his father. 'I don't think it's going to amount to much. Yosh thinks – '

'You show this to anybody, son?'

Ham shook his head. 'You can see that Breathard's seal hasn't been tampered with.'

Thornburg was peering at the envelope, whose flap had been sealed – as per Ham's instructions – with plastic fibre-laced tape stamped with the NYPD Chief logo. He grunted, used a table knife to saw through the tape.

Inside was a single grainy black-and-white photo. Thornburg stared at the young woman's face in the photo for some time without comment, then he put it carefully away.

'Good God, son,' he said as he watched Ham tear into a roast beef, Swiss cheese and coleslaw sandwich, 'you have the appetite of the entire seventh fleet!'

Ham grinned as he chomped off half a crisp garlic pickle. 'It's the sea air, sir, it really gets my juices flowing.'

'Damn lie,' Thornburg said with a wry twist of his thin lips. 'You always ate like a trencherman. Hyperactive child, your mother said. Poppycock! I told her. The boy eats like a man.' He grunted. 'Women. Think they know everything about everything – especially when it comes to raising children. Rubbish, I say.' He squinted into the sunlight coming off Chesapeake Bay, jerked a thumb towards the rear of the schooner, where a sleek young blonde carelessly sunbathed in the nude – despite a latent chill. 'Why I married that one,' he said. 'Couldn't give a fig for children. She was built for one thing, which any red-blooded man can see, and she does it damn well.' He grunted again, pushing around his crumbled crabcake with a crooked forefinger. He sucked up some juice along with a dollop of ketchup before he said, 'Food. I have no appetite for it at all these days.'

These days Thornburg Conrad III was pushing eighty, but, as he liked to say, still as virile as he ever was. The truth was he looked nowhere near his age. 'But if I'd a mind to I imagine I could still sire a child with that one,' he said, and laughed at the look on his son's face. 'You were always so proper, Ham, your mind solely on the job at hand, the perfect soldier. It's good I can still shock you. Reminds me that time hasn't altogether run away from me.'

Thornburg had moved to an immense forested estate in rural Virginia three years ago just before he had met and married Tiffany Body, as Ham chose to secretly call her. *Hi! my name's Tiff, what's yours?* Ham could imagine her saying in her high, braindead voice. Her name was really Tiffany Conrad now which, as far as Ham was concerned, was joke enough.

What he hated most, Thornburg had once confessed to Ham when he had been drunk on Glenlivet, the only spirits he drank, was that he could no longer stand erect. *'Still,'* he had said in the furry voice the liquor gave him, *'I'm erect where it matters most, so who gives a fig if I'm bent a little into the wind, I've ridden out enough storms in my day!'*

He was dead on about that, Ham thought. Thornburg had out-muscled, outgunned and outfoxed every one of his foes. *'Whatever it takes to win,'* he had once told his son when he was so drunk he couldn't see straight, *'you do it, period, because nothing else matters. Women, those fickle creatures, come and go, and children, damn their souls, betray you by growing up and doing whatever the hell pleases them.'*

Ham recalled the brisk autumn morning when his father had taken him to a meeting in the Pentagon. He had just returned from 'Nam and, newly decorated, had supposed his father had wanted to show him off.

Ironically, the meeting had been held in the same room Ham had been ushered into when, years later, he had proposed the Conrads' plan to bring down Japan, Inc.

He had been impressed – and, he had to admit, somewhat perplexed – by the degree of respect and influence his father wielded in the military sector: only the most senior officers of each branch were in attendance. It had been his experience that civilians – that is, anyone outside the Armed Forces – were viewed with a considerable degree of suspicion, not to say contempt. The military was a kind of sacred club and, like the Masons, its business was, strictly speaking, its own.

Ham vividly recalled the high-ranking rear admiral, hostile to Thornburg's proposal to set up a central clearing house to approve advanced weapons systems for each branch of the military. His father's vested interest in this was that he had brought together four small but far-sighted weapons manufacturing firms in a first-time conglomerate especially to create new forms of weapons systems for the military.

The rear admiral, apparently seeing his power eroded by such a centralized scheme, had argued that such a proposal would take the competitive edge away from the established bidding procedure now in effect.

Ham had watched, mesmerized like everyone else in the room, as his father had proceeded to pull out facts and figures covering the last decade, illustrating time after time, the inefficiency of the current procedure. He exposed the waste in design flaws, manufacturing overages and falsified tests resulting from the mad scramble to get lowest bids in under the artificial deadline set by the military itself. Then, he showed how his system would correct the flaws, avoid the waste of the old procedure.

This clever and calculated oration would, no doubt, have persuaded his august audience, but Thornburg was not yet finished. At this point, he introduced his son, gave pertinent background on Ham's posting to Vietnam, then asked Ham to give his impressions of the weapons materiel available to MACV in the Southeast Asian Theatre of Operations.

Ham's subsequent eyewitness account of the numerous disasters encountered by the military command in 'Nam under actual battle conditions had been devastating.

Yes, Ham thought now, as he watched his father suck up more

169

ketchup, he never let anything or anyone stand in his way. And because he is as remorseless, as ruthless as a shark it's a damn good thing he's got me near him now. What he half-jokingly calls proper is really my morality.

Thornburg took up a cigar from a chased-silver humidor, rolled it between his fingers, sniffed it deeply, then reluctantly put it back. 'Most people consider me amoral,' he said, using that uncanny trick of his to seemingly read other people's minds, 'but what do they know of it. You know, most people's opinions are based on ignorance.' He stared hard at his son. 'Truth is – and you're the only one I'd tell – I have my own code of morality. I dare say the difference is it's based on a whole other set of parameters. I chose a damn dangerous sea to swim in; I needed guts and guile just to survive; by God, to prosper I needed more.'

'I understand, sir.'

'Of course you do.' Thornburg nodded. 'You were always a quick study. And you were born with the good sense never to be led around by the nose.' Ham knew the old man was speaking of his brother, Jay, whose promising law practice had gone down in flames because of the affair he had been having with his senior partner's wife. 'Men who think with their balls are not men at all,' Thornburg declared, 'they're accidents waiting to happen.'

'Jay could use both our help now, sir.'

Ignoring his son, Thornburg hitched around in his seat. He stared at Tiffany Body who was sitting up, lacquering her naked torso with yet another layer of lotion. 'Ah, you see? God still loves me,' he said. 'I get a hard-on just watching her massage her breasts. Look at those nipples, magnificent!' The old man rubbed his lean jaw. 'Ah, the firmness. What I wouldn't give for that kind of youth.'

'What are you complaining about?' Ham said. 'You look young enough not to be her father.'

Thornburg turned back to Ham. 'You've still got a lot to learn about life, son. I know people from every layer of society, high and low. I have an unfair advantage over you.'

Ham was paying full attention now; the image of Tiffany Body's perfect breasts evaporated like mist in sunlight.

Thornburg laced his fingers together, pleased that he did not have to tell his son when to pay attention. 'The Moravia hit convinces me that the Black Blade Society is on a deadline. That means we are, too.' He lifted a remarkably straight finger. 'Timing, son, is often everything. The most meticulously detailed plan can come to disaster because of inappropriate timing. Fording the stream at the right time can make the difference between getting your ankles wet and walking around with soaked balls.'

Thornburg Conrad III looked out along the bay at the sun-sparked waves, the lone, brave sailboat scudding along with the wind they could not feel alee. 'Much as I admire sailors, I prefer a boat you can drive. Takes you where you want to go, *when* you want to go. There's a life lesson in that.' Thornburg was keen on life lessons, and he did not consider any of his sons too old to keep learning them. 'Huh! An inanimate object – a *thing* like this boat that you can master and turn to your whim – makes a welcome change from age which, in the end, betrays you just as foully as women and children.' He stared down at the food on the table as if it were an object whose purpose he could no longer quite comprehend. 'Advancing age creates opportunities for people like my young wife.' He made a face. 'There's a paradox there somewhere, the older you get the more you want – and, damn it, son, I want more than I can currently get.'

At that moment, a chime sounded on his wristwatch. 'Damn,' he said. 'Pill time.' He got up. 'Excuse me a moment, son.'

Ham watched his father disappear down the companionway mid-ships. A soft breeze ruffled his hair, and then it was calm again. Alone on deck with only the heavenly vision of Tiffany Body to keep him company, he fell into a reverie. He remembered his thirteenth birthday when Thornburg, surprising him, had descended on the prep school, magically whisking Ham off to Africa for a week's safari. In those days, a safari meant hunting game, not photographing it, and he would never forget the sight of a male lion, its ruff seeming as large as a Masai war shield, bounding out of the brush at dusk directly into Thornburg's face.

He had stood rooted to the spot, as had the native bearers. There had been no time for even the guide to react. Thornburg had stood his ground, raised his rifle to his hip and had let off a string of six rapid-fire shots. Though the first couple hit it, the lion kept on, and Thornburg kept coolly firing.

He could still hear the crash of the huge lion as the last of the 416 Rigby bullets from his father's Mauser paddlebolt rifle flung it sideways into the brush. The odour of it was rank, pungent, biting; it saturated the air until it was the only smell, and Ham could see his father's nostrils dilate as he filled himself with that bitter scent. Standing over the carcass moments later, Thornburg had said to his son, *'What a great pity. This beast deserves more of my respect than your mother does.'*

When he left Ham, Thornburg went belowdecks to his stateroom, closed the door. For a long moment, he leaned against it, eyes closed, heart palpitating painfully.

Then he gathered himself, went to the rear bulkhead, panelled in teak,

171

pressed a hidden button. Two panels slid open to reveal a communications complex, separate from the schooner's main communications centre in the captain's cabin. Below this, was a teak-faced drawer with a steel combination lock.

Thornburg opened it, removed a disposable syringe, the point of which he pressed into a phial of clear fluid. He inverted the syringe, squirted a few drops to get rid of any air, then, rolling up his trouser leg and finding a vein in his thigh, plunged the needle in.

Thornburg repaired to the bed, sat rocking rhythmically to the slowed beat of his heart. For a long time, his mind was emptied of all thought and emotion. Then, slowly, they seeped back and he was himself again.

His first thought was of Wolf Matheson and the electrifying news he had provided to Shipley. Something had happened to Moravia. The ageing process had been reversed!

It was so ironic that Moravia had been killed when he had. And so unfair. Of course, Thornburg had planned to have him killed just after the meeting that he never made. How else would he get Matheson involved without revealing himself? But the enemy had somehow penetrated Moravia and had taken him out prematurely. Had they managed to get anything out of him before they killed him? Thornburg thought not. There was no sign that Moravia had been tortured.

Instead, he had been altered, and this was the Oracle's doing, of that Thornburg had no doubt. But the situation was so maddening, like being close to some alien artefact and yet not being able to understand its purpose. He needed to know more! Nishitsu and the Black Blade Society were desperate to get their hands on the Oracle. Why? Again, he did not know, was only certain that it was the last key they needed to attain their goal. Just as he was certain he must take possession of the Oracle before the Toshin Kuro Kosai did. That was why it was imperative that Matheson be given full rein. If anyone could gain access to the Oracle it was Wolf Matheson.

He turned to a small safe, opened it. Inside were some papers he sorted through. He extracted a snapshot, taken by an amateur. He held that up next to the surveillance photo one of Breathard's men had taken of the Japanese woman who called herself an artist. True, the woman in the snapshot was younger, perhaps no more than a girl, but there could be no doubt that the photos were of the same woman. Thornburg felt his heart race in quick elation – Matheson was already scenting his way in! – and just as quickly damped.

It had all been going so well, so smoothly, he thought. Then Moravia was murdered. Moravia was part of the plan that he and Ham had devised, sure, but Moravia was also reporting directly to Thornburg on this one matter: the Oracle.

And Thornburg had no illusions. Moravia had been killed because of what he found out at his last visit to Forbidden Dreams: not his intelligence on the Toshin Kuro Kosai postings, but revelations about the Oracle. He had sent Thornburg a private fax, coded, before they got to him: *HAVE ENCOUNTERED ORACLE. FACE TO FACE DEBRIEFING IMPERATIVE.* Whatever Moravia had discovered was of such importance that he had requested a personal meeting with Thornburg, strictly against the rules that the elder Conrad had set up for their sub rosa relationship.

What was Yuji Shian up to? Thornburg had to find out. Because the Oracle was Yuji Shian's project. Shian was much more than the head of Japan's leading multi-industrial conglomerate: he was also a brilliant scientist, a technocrat of the first rank. Thornburg had contacts inside MITI – an extension of his old boy network in Washington, men he had known and had worked with for decades; men who owed him favours from the old days of the American Occupation, men he had saved from the war tribunals. And, from what these contacts had gathered, Yuji Shian was at work on a project so far-reaching it could literally ensure Japan's future in a world where economic dominance was paramount. That Moravia had actually encountered the Oracle was mind-boggling. Previously, Thornburg had believed Shian to be years away from project completion. *HAVE ENCOUNTERED ORACLE.* Just before he was killed, Moravia had provided him with two vital facts: the Oracle was, as went the rumours passed on to Thornburg, some new form of artificial intelligence; and it was alive and running. Now he knew of one sector of its power: it could make the old young again.

Late at night, the lamps were lit, the oil burner humming in the basement like a gigantic beast. Wolf had just come from the shower and, naked to the waist, was towelling his hair dry when Stevie came into the room to see how he was. She had been quiet after dinner, and there had been little communication between them. Wolf, feeling once again suspended between the memories of Elk Basin and Chika's East Sixth Street apartment, knew he had disconnected himself from the time line, that, as his grandfather would have said, he was Soaring.

Stevie stood in the open doorway, lit from behind like a bronze statue. These same living room lamps illuminated the fetishes in small groups, bright bits of primitive colour and power, filling the background. She had on the jeans she had worn at dinner, but had changed into a short-sleeve sweater with a deeply-scooped neck. 'About Amanda – '

He threw the towel aside. 'Stevie, this isn't a confessional. You don't have to do this.'

She shook her head, began to blink rapidly and he knew she was holding back tears. 'There was – ' She was so overcome with emotion that she had to begin all over again. 'The emotional strain of being a buffer between Morton and Amanda was . . . very difficult. They despised each other; it was a nightmare planning any kind of function, and when we all had to be together . . . They both made my life hell, bitching and complaining to me about the other.' She twisted her braid around and around her forefinger. 'What was I to do? It took all I had to keep things on an even keel, but I might have . . . perhaps during those times I was often short with Amanda.' She abruptly wrapped her arms around her slender waist. 'I'm sick to my stomach,' she whispered.

Her face was white. Wolf sat her down on the bed, pushed her head between her legs. 'Breathe,' he ordered, 'slowly and deeply, that's right.'

He watched as, slowly, the colour returned to her face. He searched her dark eyes, her sensual lips, and thought of the small peach orchard behind his house in Elk Basin he had tended as a boy.

She smiled, put a hand to his cheek. 'My God, you look so young,' she said into the silence. 'Like a football hero or an Olympic athlete, a person who, for a moment, looks as if he has stepped out of time.'

'Amanda used to tell me how young I looked.'

'Amanda was obsessed by age, she always was.' Stevie's eyes glittered in the half-light. Her long French braid lay sensuously across her shoulder. 'And being with you only made matters worse; she swore to me you never aged.'

He gave a little laugh but it was cut short when she took his hand and put it between her breasts. 'My heart is beating so fast.' Her voluptuous lips looked inviting. She put her head down for a moment. 'You see, I was taught not to confide in men, that men with their roving eyes were only interested in one thing. But what happens when a women is interested in that one thing?' She did not move, and he did not take his hand from where she had placed it. She opened her lips.

'Sleep well, Wolf.'

He pulled her to him, his lips coming down over hers, feeling her tongue snake into his mouth, exploring hotly. Her heavy breasts pressed against him, and she moaned into him as he pushed up her sweater, undressed her until she was naked from the waist up.

There was no time for anything now, except for the rushing of the blood, the rising tide of lust that had been growing between them ever since they arrived here.

Wolf unbuttoned her jeans, pushed down his undershorts. She gasped

174

as he backed her against the rough-hewn wood wall of the bedroom, pushed her arms over her head while he kissed her lips, cheeks, eyes, ears and throat. Her hips were already jerking upwards against his when he impaled her and she gasped again, deeper, longer, ending in an ecstatic groan.

He thrust hard upwards, all the way into her, and her bare feet left the floor, one long leg twining over his hip, her eyes closed, her mouth open, responding in kind to his rhythmic grunts of pleasure.

Stevie felt a rush through her body. She could smell him: the scented soap she had placed in the guest bathroom, the tickling dry talcum, but, oh yes!, beneath that like a living thing, *his* smell, deep and rich and erotic, rising, so that she began to feel its presence enveloping her.

It built the pleasure so quickly in her that she shuddered, her hips spasming hard against him, her head falling onto his shoulder, her teeth taking an involuntary bite into the meat of his muscle, all this multiplying her ecstasy ten-fold.

But, amazingly, it did not stop there. In a moment, she realized dimly that her pleasure was merely a plateau from which she was climbing higher, shivering and gasping, as if she would never come down.

His head lowered, like a bull's, and he gathered one large nipple, then the other, into his mouth so that sharp bolts of ecstasy leapt through her like a fire, and with a deep-felt cry she was spasming again, unable to control herself, clinging to him lovingly, desperately, adoringly while her eyelids flickered as if she were dreaming.

She could no longer breathe, was no longer aware of her surroundings. Filled with a delight so intense it made her vertiginous, she felt only his organ inside her, his hot body pressed against hers, his lips on her flesh, his muscles between her teeth.

If this were all she felt it would have been more than she could have wished for. But she felt more. She felt dancing through her a mysterious darkness from the core of him, something alive and powerful that pierced her mind, her soul, as his organ was piercing her body, not in pain but in pleasure. She reached blindly down, cupping him, squeezing rhythmically until he arched up one last time, dragging her deliciously with him, uttering a sound she had never heard before, and, as she spasmed uncontrollably a third time, she knew she was drowning in bliss . . .

'SHIAN KOGAKU: WE ARE ALWAYS WITH YOU,' mouthed David Bowie's painted, slightly androgynous face.

The mobile thirteen-foot by ten-foot video screen rumbled slowly through the traffic-choked streets of the Shinjuku section of Tokyo, its

175

six-minute music video cleverly displaying all the beneficial products manufactured by Shian Kogaku's various *kobun* repeating on an endless loop.

Yuji Shian and Hiroto, his brother-in-law, had met on their way to work. Hiroto was altogether nondescript, a bent-shouldered middle-aged man neither handsome nor ugly, in the same cheap rumpled suit he had been wearing for the past three days. He was a vice-president of Shian Kogaku and a brilliant computer scientist in his own right.

'How is my sister?' Yuji asked as they entered the forty-storey white granite and steel building owned by Shian Kogaku.

'Kazuki is the same, always angry,' Hiroto said sadly. 'It's the illness that is eating her from the inside. She is no longer the same person I married fifteen years ago.'

Yuji felt the coruscating colours, unnaturally bright, then the quick shift in perspective. He could see with uncanny clarity the circuitry of a project he was working on, how it should be from beginning to end, the whole schematic laid out before him like topography viewed from the air.

Then the vision faded, the colours around him regained their normal intensity. He put his hand against the polished granite wall of the elevator bank. He had never cared for his gift of sight. How ill its onset had made him when he had been a teenager, and he still dreaded the disorientation that always accompanied it.

'Yuji-san?'

'Yes.' He blinked, saw Hiroto already in the elevator, turned to face him, eyes curious, searching. He walked on stiff legs into the elevator.

The beaten bronze doors closed and they were alone on their way up.

'I need to talk to you about the Oracle,' Hiroto said. 'Specifically your notion to allow your half-sister Hana access to it.'

'Hana is difficult to ignore.'

'You're telling me? She has been making my research team crazy with her questions about the guts of the thing. There's a rumour going around that you brought her in to make modifications in the project.'

Not for the first time, Yuji found himself wondering whether Hiroto resented Hana because she was a female or because she was not a highly-trained scientist with multiple degrees from Tokyo University. Hiroto, like most of his ilk, was snobbish in the extreme. Where you graduated from was often a more telling criterion than how your mind worked if you wanted to be on his research team.

'It's nothing,' Yuji lied. 'You were concerned when my mother was making suggestions.'

176

'That's right. And I still don't like the path she suggested we take. Using human DNA inside the thing – who knows how its circuits will distort the basic molecules? The changes – '

'The concept of the Oracle is so new,' Yuji said, 'we must be open to change.' He knew how to handle his brother-in-law, so conservative in every way, including his work. He was often a good counterweight to Yuji's unfettered genius, but occasionally, as now, he could prove difficult. 'Let's allow the Oracle to think its way through the DNA and see what happens.'

'It will make certain basic decisions,' Hiroto corrected. 'No one yet knows whether that is the same as thinking.'

Oh, but I do, Yuji thought, as they came to a stop. The doors opened and they emerged onto the highest of the three executive floors.

'I still have grave misgivings about the project,' Hiroto said, following Yuji down the hall, through several office ante-rooms, into Yuji's office proper. 'I argued against prematurely using a human subject in tandem with the Oracle, but I was overruled.' He shook his head. 'I must confess I am dismayed by how fast we are plunging into the unknown. Frankly, I find myself increasingly frightened by your friend, the Oracle.'

'Frightened?'

Hiroto nodded. 'The Oracle was not built to . . . change, but that is precisely what it seems to be doing. The question I must ask myself is: is there an essential design flaw in the Oracle that we were not aware of, or – and here, Yuji-san, is why I am fearful – has the Oracle somehow *altered* the basic schematic we gave it?'

With an effort Yuji kept his face calm.

'You understand what I mean, Yuji-san. There is already some evidence that it is growing; that, in some sense we may not yet be able to comprehend, it is *alive*.'

Hiroto strode back and forth before Yuji's desk. 'The scientist side of me insists that this is impossible or – more accurately – beyond our current technology. But the intuitive side of me suspects otherwise, that because of the radical technology you gave us for its neurologics, and because now we are no longer dealing solely with mathematics, with digital technology, with the zero and the one, we have bred the chaos of an anomaly. Our imaging technology is so new we know virtually nothing about its ultimate capabilities – which leads me to believe that, while we built the Oracle, we no longer understand it – that perhaps we never did. It is wholly outside our ken; that, as we currently view the world, it can neither be controlled nor understood. And now, to add Hana's strange mind to this already unknowable mix is, in my opinion, suicidal. After all, when you come

177

down to it, we know less about her brain than we do about the Oracle itself.'

Yuji was thinking of his conversations with the Oracle. Of course, he felt differently about the Oracle than Hiroto did, but perhaps that was in part because Hiroto had built the biocomputer. It had been Yuji's idea, his creation, but it was Hiroto and his team who had fabricated the reality from the godstuff of Yuji's thoughts. Yuji might be a brilliant biogeneticist, but it was Hiroto who was the nuts and bolts engineer.

I would never dare say this to Hiroto, Yuji thought, but because I know that we have together created something more than a mere machine I have a rapport with the Oracle that he will never possess. To Hiroto, the thing is just a monstrously complex tinker toy, nothing more than a research project. Further, he designed it to accomplish certain functions. Now that it is doing other things – and doing them in ways that completely mystify him – Hiroto has become edgy. Understandable. He has lost face. It is almost as if the Oracle is running him, not the other way around. That was an amusing thought, yet Yuji did not laugh.

'I understand your concern,' Yuji said comfortingly. 'The same thoughts have crossed my mind, as well.' He came around his desk. 'Let me reassure you, Hiroto-san, we will proceed with all due caution. But proceed we must. You're right about one thing: the project has taken on a life of its own. And if we stop it now we would be nothing more than murderers.'

SEVEN

Tokyo/East Hampton/Washington/New York

Night in the suburbs of Tokyo.

Minako Shian lay in bed waiting, as always, for a sleep that often did not come. Her mind, busily scheming, would not let her rest. She had been living on a highwire ever since her breasts had begun to bud and her menses had begun to flow. This was her karma and she was willing to accept her role in the history of her people. But there were so many strands to hold in her hands, so many skeins to manipulate simultaneously . . . this was the ecstasy and the horror of her advanced powers.

Minako lived in a villa outside Tokyo designed for her by one of Japan's leading young architects. In its soaring spaces and sharp juxtapositions of dark and light spans, its use of weighty materials such as stone with floating ones such as rice paper, and the astonishing vistas afforded in the areolae between rooms, the building seemed to be a series of scenes that, like a film, created a montage, a whole that was far more than each individual section.

The villa was set within a cleverly structured garden that in its utter starkness and simplicity neatly counterbalanced the intricate, almost baroque postmodernism of the architecture. However, 'postmodernism' was perhaps too harsh a definition for the villa, for the architect's style contained within it hints of Buddhism, Shintoism, and Edo-period architecture which placed the villa in an historical context so that each space continually tugged at the viewer's memories.

The granite and lacewood entry, dominated by an old merchant's chest where shoes were stored, was one of many spaces which served to connect the visitor from the outside world with the inner heart of the villa. Like the concentric circles of the emperor's palace in Tokyo, these rooms revealed the nature of the architecture a fragment at a time to allow for the interaction of structure and human mind. In so doing echoes were set reverberating that, like scents, provoked powerful and unique reactions that varied with each individual.

These rooms were like an array of cabins upon a vast ship; outside

179

the darkling garden took on the appearance of the ocean, mysterious and dangerous, glittering just beyond reach.

Just like the future which, for the first time, seemed tantalizingly beyond her sight. Not so the past, and, for the moment, she contented herself with remembering.

The summoning of her *makura na hiruma* had occurred on the anniversary of the death of her grandmother, the homely, compact woman who had founded Shian Kogaku as the premier manufacturer of *tabi*. These were traditional Japanese socks with a single separation between the big toe and the other four.

Kabuto, Minako's grandmother, had played a large role in Minako's long and agonizing birth – Minako had been told the story by her mother – and so the debt must be paid.

It happened that Kabuto had died on Minako's birthday, and so Minako's memories of this day were always cast in the shadow of her grandmother's grave, an austere site in a Shinto cemetery outside Osaka. When she was a small child, her mother took her, but as soon as she was old enough to find her own way she was encouraged to attend to her filial duties in private.

On her eleventh birthday she arrived at Kabuto's grave. It had been raining all night, and the Shinto cemetery was shrouded in a mist thick with the brittle scents of medicinal herbs which grew wild in spiky clumps between the plots.

By this time Kabuto had been dead for precisely eight years and Minako's memory of her was as indistinct as the nearby grave markers shrouded in mist.

She went through the Shinto rituals by rote, her mind disengaged, her thoughts elsewhere. When she was finished, she rose, brushed the mat of dead leaves and grasses off her knees and turned to go.

Something stopped her, and she turned slowly back to the grave. And there, sitting curled atop the marker, was a red fox.

'Hello, granddaughter,' the fox said, opening its mouth as if in a yawn. 'Do you not recognize me? It is I, Kabuto.'

Minako started, shook her head, pinched herself, rubbed her eyes. She looked again. Her grandmother – or the fox – was still there. The fox smiled at Minako. Minako looked wildly around to see if anyone else saw the apparition but she was alone in this particular part of the cemetery.

'Grandmother,' Minako finally whispered, 'you are a fox.'

'So I am,' Kabuto responded. 'At this moment.'

Minako gaped. 'Could you be Kabuto again?'

'But I am Kabuto, child.'

'I mean the Kabuto I knew.'

'That shrewish body?' the fox seemed to sneer. 'Why would I want that back? I waited almost three hundred years to get rid of it. That's far too long as it is, don't you agree?'

Minako did not know what to say so she merely nodded.

The fox that was her grandmother jumped down from its perch, sat in front of her scratching its nose with a delicate forepaw. 'Anyway, foxes are incapable of lying, you see,' Kabuto said. 'I suppose that's why I chose this form. I was sick of lying, deceit, obfuscation.' The fox canted its head. 'That's why I've come today, to warn you, yes, I suppose warn is the correct term.'

'Warn me of what?'

'Of what your life will become unless you are less ambitious than I was. I want to save you from going to your deathbed with your spirit withered from decades of lying, deceit and obfuscation.'

'I don't do any of those things,' Minako had told her grandmother.

'But you will. Because that is the way of the world,' the fox said. 'Our world.'

'I don't understand.'

'Of course you do, you foolish girl,' her grandmother snapped. 'It is only that conventions have kept your overmind from engaging.'

'My overmind?'

The fox then made a sound that caused Minako to start. It was the same sound her grandmother used to make by striking her tongue against the roof of her mouth when she was impatient with slow-witted responses to her queries. At that moment, Minako was certain that the fox was, indeed, her grandmother.

'Your mother, I see, has been remiss in teaching you the covenants of power. Well, I can't say I'm surprised; she was always too timid for her own good, afraid of me and of her own gift.' The fox lifted the same forepaw it had used to scratch its nose. 'Never mind. I knew the rite of the summoning would be left to me the moment I squeezed you out of your mother's womb.' The fox's eyes were bright even in the dull leaden sunlight filtering through the heavy mist. 'You didn't want to come, you know. And your mother lacked the stamina and the fortitude to coerce you into coming. And, afterwards, it occurred to her that having you had been a mistake. Good thing I was around.'

Minako had screwed up her face. 'You mean Mother didn't want me? She doesn't love me?'

'Has she ever held you, kissed you, even taken you in her arms? No, of course not. If it weren't for me I have no doubt she would have deposited you on a neighbour's doorstep.'

Minako's heart had constricted and she had burst out crying. 'Why are you telling me this, Grandmother? It's too terrible, I don't want to hear any more.'

'It was time for you to hear the truth, child.' The fox licked its lips. 'Now I

181

want you to look at me. No, don't blink or – You're cheating, thinking about how I am talking through the fox. Take hold of the pain you are feeling. It burns, doesn't it? Yes. Keep looking at me, Minako-san. Now let the pain flow through you, and when you feel something else, something more – '

Minako wiped the tears from her eyes. 'There's a darkness, I – '

'Don't look down!' the fox snapped. 'Don't look anywhere but at me! That's better. The pain is fading, isn't it? It is being replaced by the darkness. Don't worry, in a moment you will be able to see everything.'

And, to Minako's astonishment, her grandmother was right. Not only could she see the darkness curling and undulating at her feet but, as it spread outwards, she could see through the mist, as clearly as if it did not exist, the surrounding graves, then the outlying reaches of the cemetery . . . and beyond to the rolling hills miles and miles away.

'What – what is happening to me?'

'You are coming of age,' the fox said with a smile, though how a fox could smile Minako could not imagine. 'You now see that the world as you had perceived it is not the end but the beginning, a mere isthmus in the vast sea of worlds open to your budding perceptions.'

'How far will I be able to see?' Minako asked, peering into the distance.

'That depends,' the fox said. 'In everyone with makura na hiruma – the darkness at noon – it is different. But I know more than most, and what I know is that your power is enormous. In a few years it will eclipse even mine, which was strong indeed. That is as it should be since your destiny is special, even among us. You will soon be thrust into the maelstrom of an internecine war between factions of the Toshin Kuro Kosai. We are riddled by suspicion. Who within the Black Blade Society believes in the old ways, the old destiny for Japan? Who has secretly made a pact to see Japan adapt to events in the modern world?

'People within our ranks die suddenly, mysteriously – or disappear, never to be heard from again. What has happened to them? Who has murdered the ones whose bodies we find? We are turning on each other like mad dogs.

'Even I do not know the war's outcome; no one does. But it must end before one of us takes it into his head to move our power more fully into the world at large. Heretofore we have used our power only to indirectly influence events, but it now appears likely that the time is coming when one of us will not be satisfied to sit in the shadows and pull the strings. The world will not long survive once we begin to move out into the light and use makura na hiruma in a more direct fashion. Can you imagine an emperor, a prime minister or a president with the power?' She shuddered. 'You must guard against that eventuality, child. Remember that. Contrary to popular belief there is such a thing as having too much power.

'History has shown us that moral corruption begins at the highest level and slowly seeps downwards. The temptation to run amok would be overwhelming, even for us

182

who are more than mortal. It is axiomatic that the more in control we believe we are, the less of it we actually possess.

'Be careful, child. And be diligent. I have seen that through you will rise the one child, the individual destined to end this war. Because of this you will develop enemies – powerful enemies who will do their best to destroy you by any means.'

'You are frightening me, Grandmother.'

'Good. Fear is the best goad to caution, guile and obfuscation. Keep to the shadows, child, until it is your time.'

'How will I know the one child, Grandmother?'

'I don't know. That is a future even we cannot see or guess at. At your birth I was given a hint of your fate, but it was not until now at the summoning when I can see the nature of your overmind that I know the one child will come through you.'

Minako spread her arms, luxuriating in the feel of the darkness rolling over her like the coils of a gigantic serpent. The power of life infused her with its heady scent. And such power! she thought. To give birth to the one child! She centred her thoughts in her lower belly. She was still very young but the glorious new sensation of her *makura na hiruma* made it possible to imagine what it must be like to carry another life inside her.

The fox seemed to grow in size. 'Contrary to what you may think now, the scope of your power will be a burden. Soon enough, the barriers of time will no longer exist for you. Then the future will make itself manifest.'

'How wonderful!' Minako had cried, clapping her hands.

'Foolish, foolish girl,' the fox said sternly. 'Seeing the future is a terrible fate, indeed, take it from one who knows. Think of what it must be like to be able to read people's minds. You think it might be fun, isn't that so, to know what people around you are going to do before they do it? You think, What an advantage! Perhaps so. But then think of the sheer cacophony of voices you must hear day in, day out without surcease. How long could you bear such an intolerable strain?'

The fox circled Minako, dragging its hindpaws as if drawing a figure in the earth.

'It is the same with seeing the future. The weight of events multiplies exponentially until it becomes too much to sustain. Some of us go mad.'

'And others?' Minako asked. 'There must be a way out.'

The fox smiled that impossible smile again, and Minako knew her grandmother was pleased with her.

'Yes,' the fox said, 'there are two ways out. One is to use the path your mother, the dull-witted beast, has chosen. Close yourself off from makura na hiruma. The other involves a lifetime of lies, deceit and obfuscation.'

'These are my only choices.'

The fox nodded. 'Yes.'

'I want to see,' Minako said, 'as far as I can.'

Kabuto licked her fur contentedly. 'Then you are destined for great things,

183

child.' She lifted her great triangular head, fixed her granddaughter with her obsidian eyes. *'Terrible things, as well, because even with the strength of your power there will be blank spots: futures you will be unable to see, perhaps other, terrifying futures you will see but which you may be unable to prevent. Never mind. You cannot understand these things now, and having chosen, you can no longer deviate from the path. Once* makura na hiruma *has been invoked it can never be returned to the prison in which it has been held.'*

'I understand, Grandmother,' Minako said gravely.

For the first time, there was a note of surprise in her voice. *'Why, child, I believe you do . . .'*

How many days in her already long life had she regretted her decision that morning in the cemetery? Not as many as the number of days she had revelled in her power. And how often had she suspected her grandmother of tricking her into invoking her own *makura na hiruma* for the first time? But, strangely, that had only made her cherish Kabuto even more.

Minako lay in the dark, listening to the soft stirring outside of the trees and the nocturnal creatures. Her mind drifted again.

She saw Yuji, and for the first time since he was a small boy and she had made her decision to keep him separate from the Toshin Kuro Kosai, she feared for him. Then she felt his mind, and that of the Oracle, and was reassured. For just a moment, she allowed herself to feel the elation attendant to its creation. True, it was still imperfect, its potential still partially unknown, even to her. But she trusted her children Yuji and Hana to solve the last remaining hurdle that would make the beast fully operational. And why not feel elation? In a sense, though Yuji and Hiroto had built it from the ground up, it had been she who had convinced Yuji of the need for it, cajoled him into working on it, urged him on when setbacks threatened to end the project. And now that it was up and running, what would happen?

Abruptly, Minako sat up in bed, holding her stomach. For a moment, she was afraid she would vomit up dinner. Sudden, irrational fear gripped her. The future was closed to her, and she had been warned. Her sight saw futures, not all of them became the future that would occur. But this blankness, the cessation of her sight, disturbed her. Could this be the one miscalculation that could spell doom for them all?

It seemed to her now that there was always so much weight upon her shoulders. But ever since she had made the conscious decision to rebel against the wretched excesses of power dreamed up by the Reverend Mother she truly lived every day on a knife-edge.

Each day it seemed that the Reverend Mother devised new atrocities to perpetrate. She was no longer satisfied to root out those who opposed her rule, but was intent on finding new ways to increase her already

184

prodigious *makura na hiruma*. It seemed clear enough to Minako, who had already lived long enough to understand these things, that the Reverend Mother's *makura na hiruma* had driven her over the edge. She was quite mad, and it had become Minako's duty to stop her any way she could. For that she required a weapon of such potency that the Reverend Mother would be incinerated whether or not she had time to invoke the awesome power of her *makura na hiruma*.

The revelation had come to her two years ago in a blinding flash of light that had sent her to her knees and had caused her to wonder whether its origin might be divine. That was when she had thought of the Man Without a Face: Wolf Matheson.

The day had already turned murky and thick, lit now and then by lurid flashes of lightning that broke against the tops of the thick hemlocks. A moment later it began to rain, fat drops that splattered against the walkways and windowpanes with the noise of hail.

It was Saturday, and Stevie, having received a call from her husband, had left just after dawn to drive into the city to take care of some of his business. She had promised she would be back for dinner.

Wolf had thought he would sleep most of the day, but he was already restless, anxious to return to his office and the investigation that had dire global implications.

He rummaged around in the hall closet, found a slicker belonging, no doubt, to Morton the absent philanderer, and went down to Georgica Pond. In this weather it was possible to look out across the water and not see any other house. Far out, he saw a wooden pole on which he could just make out the straw of an osprey's nest. A handsome avian form, dark with rain, approached it. The adult osprey carefully deposited a beakful of twigs onto the nest, then set about repairing winter's damage.

Wolf hunkered down beneath a pepperidge tree, stared sightlessly at the grey water. What would he do when he found Chika? In truth, he did not know. And he was aware that part of him did not want to track her down. What if she were responsible for the murders: Arquillo, Junior Ruiz, Moravia and Amanda. Far simpler if he knew conclusively that Suma was responsible for the deaths, but he could not be certain of that and, in fact, he had evidence, though circumstantial, that pointed to Chika. The square of her trapunto, singed but not blackened, he had discovered in the glove compartment of the black '87 Firebird was damning. On the other hand, it could also be a plant. Or was that wishful thinking? Anything was possible, and it was always dangerous to jump to conclusions.

Wolf had become used to dealing with grey areas, which police work most often was, but this situation was different. It had been made that way by Chika – or, more accurately, his feelings about her. His attraction was like a pulse, a living thing existing deep inside him, separate and undeniable.

But it was better to think of his attraction to a murder suspect, a possible member of the enemy, the Black Blade Society, than to dwell for too long on the implications of the fire that had exploded within Arquillo, turning his face to burning jelly.

He was out there a long time, absorbing the sights, sounds, smells of the earth, pepperidge trees, terns and water, until his fingertips were blue and he felt a pain in his sewn-up leg. He sighed, then, rose and, reluctantly, turned back to the house.

When he heard the car pulling into the driveway he went on stiff legs to the front window to peer out. It was near dark by then and the house lights had automatically come on. He leaned over, flicked on the outside lights. Circles of illumination broke through the thick gloom along the cracked blacktop driveway, the mossy flagstone path to the front door, the converted nineteenth-century brass coach lamps on either side of the door.

He was expecting Stevie's Jeep Cherokee but, instead, he saw a shiny new black Corvette coasting to a stop in the parking area in front of the garage. He saw someone emerge from the Corvette – a woman.

Wolf went to the front door, opened it to the whisper of a night wind, its chill mitigated by spring's ascension. He went out on the concrete stoop, let the screen door bang shut behind him. The rain had passed but the intolerable wetness still clung to everything. Moths fluttered in the lamplight, and a sprinkling of first magnitude stars was just becoming visible above the black treetops.

As Wolf followed the woman's progress up the worn path he experienced a sense of *déjà vu* so acute he felt momentarily dizzy.

He saw a face dominated by enormous eyes of a glossy chocolate over high cheekbones, a pouty-lipped sensual mouth and a small but solid chin. Her thick hair was worn straight back from her wide forehead, hanging heavily like a plume or a mane at the nape of her neck. She wore a very short black wool shirt over black stretch pants that showed her legs to maximum advantage, a pumpkin-coloured chenille sweater that draped over her strong shoulders and breasts. Magnificent light dazzled from enormous black opal earrings. Black ankle boots enclosed her small feet and she still had on thin black-and-white leather racing gloves. She walked with a sureness that was almost aggressive.

And at last dream, fantasy and reality met in a terrifying swirl of emotion. Dismay, stupefaction, guilt and desire swept him up in an intolerable chaos, for coming up the steps was a small, exquisite Japanese woman who he knew to be Suma's associate, the photographer, marksman – and perhaps murderer of four people: the artist, Chika.

'What I like best about clubs,' Thornburg Conrad III said, 'is that you can control who comes in and who goes out.' He grunted as he lit a cigar. 'Time was when the whole world was like that, but that was a lifetime ago and I suppose I ought to curb these feelings I have that it was a far better world back then. Poppycock, really. Cynosure of the ancient and about-to-be-deleted.' He puffed aggressively. 'I'm up on every advance in the fields of medical, electronic, computer and biotechnological research. Just so you don't think I'm slipping into the twilight world of the elderly.'

'The thought never crossed my mind,' Stevie Powers said.

Thornburg's lips curled up in his signature chilly smile. 'Lady, you sure know how to dress.'

'Thank you,' she said.

Stevie crossed one stockinged leg over the other, shifted in her chair. When she had left Wolf, she had not driven into the city, but only ten minutes west to East Hampton airport, where Thornburg's private jet was waiting for her.

Thornburg watched the end of his cigar glow cherry red with his inhalation. 'Especially since I sent for you without any advance warning; it's been my experience that women who know how to dress well and quickly are to be treasured.' He raised his gaze just in time to see the hint of a smile register on Stevie's face. 'No doubt, you disagree with me. There isn't a woman on earth worth her salt who would agree.' He laughed, but it was impossible to tell whether he had made a joke or was merely gloating at his superior position in the world.

Magnolia Terrace, the club that Thornburg had invited Stevie to, was not strictly speaking in Washington, but rather in the Virginia countryside. It was known for its magnificent golf course where in the past more than one major PGA tournament had been played, but it was also world-renowned for its riding academy which turned out some of the finest American polo players in the world. Of course, the club was restricted, which meant that people with money but no lineage could not become members no matter how much influence they possessed.

Thornburg and Stevie were lunching on the wide screened veranda of the clubhouse, a sprawling thirty-thousand-square-foot building of traditional clapboard siding. Fourteen gables distinguished it from all the neighbouring mansions. Inside, the rooms were spacious and airy. Oil portraits of the country's founding fathers hung on the walls of virtually every room. Often, at night, orchestras occupied the vast flagstone patio beyond the veranda for the numerous black-tie dinner-dances Magnolia Terrace put on for charity.

The mammoth clubhouse was just one of seventeen buildings on the 500 acres the club owned. There were stables, paddocks, sumptuous guest cottages owned by a clique of the most senior members, riding ovals, polo fields, and, of course, the famed golf course.

'But then again I like it when people disagree with me,' Thornburg went on. 'Nothing better than a verbal battle to sharpen up the old grey cells.'

He rolled his cigar along the edge of a clamshell, expertly ridding it of just the right amount of ash. 'Did you enjoy lunch? Good. Those Ipswich clams were right off the boat. They're flown down here every morning in our own plane.' He broke off to greet Senator Dowd, head of the Armed Services Oversight Committee. Dowd was an old friend of his, as were almost all of the senior members of Congress. When the senator had drifted away, Thornburg said to Stevie, 'I imagine you're wondering when we're going to get around to the pith.'

'I'm used to you.'

'Just so. Your psychiatric training, no doubt.'

'Analytic training.'

'Yes, yes, you've told me that's how you people refer to it.' He waved away her words as if they were a bothering gnat. 'Patience. Damn fine virtue, if you ask me, learning to ford the stream at the right moment.' Thornburg shook his head. 'I've tried to teach my boys that lesson, but I fear they've each learned it somewhat imperfectly.' He grunted. 'I used to believe my first wife was the bane of my existence, but lately I find myself of the opinion that stigma must be borne by my offspring.' He leaned back in his leather chair. 'Except for my son Ham, who has turned out to be one fine specimen. Hero in 'Nam, first-class brain, and the damned good sense to be loyal to family. Father couldn't ask for much more from his son.'

'I'm happy to learn that you have such positive feelings about even one of your children. I wonder if you've told him any of this?'

'Certainly not.' Thornburg rolled off the ash of his cigar. 'Bad for the character, praise.'

'Even if it's deserved?'

He could sense her bringing out her notebook, sharpening her pencil. He liked her because she was almost too smart for her own good, but he did not want her turning her intelligence on him. He sat forward suddenly and she tensed. 'Let's get down to business, shall we? I want your report on Wolf Matheson's emotional state.'

188

Stevie recrossed her legs, said, 'I want to be absolutely clear why I'm doing this.'

Thornburg stared at the end of his cigar. 'I'm glad to know you're being so prudent.' His eyes flicked to Stevie's. He blew out a cloud of fragrant smoke.

'It's more than prudence,' she said. 'I'm concerned. You've asked me to invade another man's privacy. I won't – I can't – do that easily or without sufficient cause.'

'I understand. I've been vague with you up until now. That was deliberate, for your own good as well as to comply with the dictates of National Security.' He drew on his cigar, blew out the smoke. 'Lawrence Moravia was a spy working for the US government, Stevie. He was following up on a lead they had that someone was passing proprietary American industrial intelligence to the Japanese – and not just the Japanese but this very dangerous organization I've told you about, the Black Blade Society.' He made a disagreeable sound in the back of his throat. 'All right, now that you've pried that confession out of me, I hope you're satisfied.'

'I'm certainly more at ease,' Stevie said, 'but I still find one thing curious. If you have such high personal regard for Wolf, why not approach him yourself? Why use me as an intermediary?'

'That's simple enough. It's the most basic tradecraft, my dear. Matheson is what we would call a cutout. He's deliberately shielded from me and vice versa for security reasons.' He saw the look on her face. 'Put in a more elementary way, if he should be captured, he will have no information that could lead the Black Blade Society back to me.'

Stevie digested this sobering news for some time, and Thornburg worried that he had given her more than she could handle. He did not want her getting cold feet at this stage.

Towards that end, he said, 'Stevie, let me reassure you that the job we have given Matheson is something he wants very badly to do.'

'I know,' she said.

Thornburg put his lips around the cigar. 'Now that you do I'd appreciate your report. I need him for this investigation, Stevie. I can't afford to lose him now.'

She relaxed in her chair as she settled into her role as analyst. 'A word of caution. What I do is not an exact science.'

Thornburg nodded indulgently. 'What is? Even science has proven to be inexact. Proceed.'

'His fall seems not to have injured his psyche at all,' Stevie began. 'If anything, he appears stronger to me, more resolved than he did before.'

'And physically?'

'The fall through the skylight could have been bone-shattering. He was exceedingly fortunate. The wounds he received were deep enough but through your efforts we've been assured that there is no nerve damage. As for the healing process, he exhibits a remarkable ability to recover. Ten days after the operation he seems to have little or no residual impairment.'

Thornburg looked at the glowing end of his cigar. 'Can I assume you've taken him through all his physical paces.'

Stevie sat still for a long moment. Beyond the screens she could see a handsome blue-eyed blond leading a horse across a golf cart track. She dropped her gaze to her hands. 'He walks, bends, lifts seemingly without pain. If he feels discomfort he has not told me. His powers of recovery are astonishing.'

Thornburg grunted. He lit a match, got his cigar going again in no time flat. 'Your husband's something of a genius, which is why I've gotten him work all over Washington. But his brilliance hasn't stopped him from being a shit, has it?'

'The world is a shitty place,' Stevie said. 'I try my best to make it a little bit less shitty, and if I helped only one person I'd feel a measure of satisfaction.'

'It's the same with Matheson.' Thornburg let out a soft hiss of smoke while eyeing her. 'You believe me, don't you? You don't think I've roped you into some dirty business, spying on a cop.'

'I didn't care for that reference.'

He nodded. 'I profoundly apologize; I had no intention of offending you.' Now he knew he had gone too far, but it was essential that he get a sense of her own current emotional state. 'It's only that I know how attractive Matheson is, how much you've enjoyed taking care of him, how little you see of Morton.' The most dangerous aspect of Wolf Matheson was how he engendered loyalty in others. 'Being emotionally involved with him would make things . . . awkward for you, to say the least. He will be going overseas soon, and he may have a companion, a female companion. It would not do for you to interfere in any way.'

Stevie stared at him but said nothing.

'As I have said, I have only the greatest respect for Matheson, which is why I want him in the fray.'

'But it's your fray, isn't it?' Stevie said.

She was sharp. 'Yes, but I can guarantee you he's better off in this situation than the one he's leaving behind. I give you my word in the long run you'll be helping him.'

'I'm not in the business of second-guessing friends, I assure you,' Stevie said, smiling. She leaned over, squeezed his hand. 'I know how much you've helped me – and Morton. I'm grateful for that help.'

'I like you, Stevie, really I do,' Thornburg said, 'and that's a good deal more than I can say about most people, including my children. You're smart and you care about people. Those are gifts to cherish in this modern world. The same can be said for Ham and, though I ride him a bit, it's for his own good. I'm grateful for him.'

'We understand one another, then.'

'Sure we do,' Thornburg said. He took a puff on his cigar and almost choked. I've got to laugh, he thought. The president thinks Ham is working for him, those ossified generals in the Pentagon think Ham's working for them, but he's not: he's working for me. But then in a sense they're all working for me, and that includes this pedigreed shrink who thinks she's got everyone's number. I'm smarter than all of 'em put together. And that includes Wolf Matheson.

'You look like I'm going to eat you alive,' said the woman Wolf knew as Chika. Bone-white moths fluttered about her head and silver light from the moon fell across one cheek. The red-green-blue fire from the opal earrings spattered like rain on his doorstep.

Wolf said nothing. Translucent images of sex and death rudely intruded as he watched her until it seemed as if like a goddess she existed within a kind of aureole. He saw her: crossing the gutter in the rain; climbing into the back of the hearse; standing spread-legged in the cold, detritus-strewn street of Alphabet City staring down a couple of armed punks; standing spread-legged in the heated atmosphere of her own apartment, her fingers busy between her thighs; and he saw Amanda dead in a pool of her own blood, while a tape in a cassette recorder beside her head replayed her own words back at him.

The sound of his pulse rushed like a hurricane in his inner ears. He was aware of the wetness of his palms. At last he managed to say, 'I've walked around your disturbing sculptures, seen your even more disturbing photographs of women in bondage; I've watched you pull a gun on street punks, climb into a hearse in the middle of the night. I think I have the right to be wary.'

'I have a permit for the gun.'

'I've no doubt you do; you seemed quite professional with it.'

She licked her lips. 'May I come in? I'm not carrying.' She held out her arms. 'Do you want to frisk me?'

Yes, he did, but he did not make a move. His hammering heart seemed to be threatening to choke him. 'How did you find me? Why did you want to?' He wondered why she hadn't said to him, Why were you following

191

me? But perhaps she already knew. With an inward shock Wolf realized that she terrified him. Or perhaps what he feared was his sense of how powerfully this dangerous woman drew him.

'I want you to know the truth about me. We have more in common than you know.'

There was a ringing in Wolf's ears; he felt a thick trickle of sweat begin a long lazy journey down his spine.

'You haven't told me how you found me.'

'It's not something I can tell you in a sentence,' she said. 'Won't you give me a chance to explain? Or have you tried and convicted me already?'

'Come in,' he said at last.

It was impossible not to watch her buttocks as she walked ahead of him into Stevie's house. She sat on one end of a chintz floral sofa while Wolf took the chair opposite. He stared at her, could not help himself, felt more and more helpless as he sat magnetized, galvanized by her. His mouth was dry and he could feel a pulse ticking in his temple.

'Do you think I could get a cup of tea?' she said. 'Between the major construction in the city and the traffic on the LIE I've been on the road a long time.'

They went into the kitchen and Wolf put up some water. He searched the cupboards for tea. 'Will Earl Grey do?'

'Earl Grey will be fine,' she said.

Standing, he watched her sip her tea, dark and strong as liquid brass, absorbed in the ritual of it.

'Tell me about Suma,' he said.

'Who?'

'You know. The Water-spider.'

'Suma is Toshin Kuro Kosai – Black Blade Society. I don't expect you to know who they – '

'Moravia and the Black Blade Society – you're the link between the two.'

She looked up; he had her attention now. 'Why would you think that?'

'Because,' he said as he leaned forward, put his hands on the back of a chair, 'I've seen a photo of you and Suma chatting together as you crossed a street in Tokyo.'

'I haven't seen Suma in seven months.'

'Wrong. That photo was taken in the fall of last year, not more than five months ago.'

She turned her back on him, stared out the kitchen window into the blackness of the restless hemlocks. 'I see I've handled this all wrong.'

'So far I don't see anything here I can trust.'

She turned back, stared at him. 'No, I see that you can't. You're too busy preparing yourself to crucify me.' They stood across the kitchen from one another, the innocent table between them.

'It's difficult to lay aside the evidence I have purely on the basis of you lying to me,' he said. 'You think I'm kidding? Here's what I know and how it adds up to you being a multiple murderer: I know Moravia was employed to infiltrate your Black Blade Society.'

'Not *my* Black Blade Society.'

'I know that Suma is one of the society's premier assassins and that he's been spotted here. I've seen you and Suma chatting as easily as – '

'A photo. You saw a surveillance photo. You didn't – '

'– As easily as two killers talking over old times. I've found a piece of your trapunto in a burned out Firebird that was used as the getaway vehicle in a multiple homicide where one of my men was killed and another man I was pursuing had his face turned to bloody jelly. This is what I know about you.'

'Is it?' Chika did not even blink. 'No, no, there's more. Why leave it out? Don't you want to tell me how you came in through my studio window?'

An ice storm seemed to be churning his stomach to pulp. 'You knew?'

She put her hand between her thighs. 'Yes.'

'Then for Christ's sake why did you put on that show?'

She came around the table, stood so close to him he inhaled the scent of her remembered from Moravia's secret cubicle, her apartment. 'I did it,' she said very deliberately, 'because it was what you wanted me to do.'

'I was there to try to uncover your connection with Suma.'

'And not,' she said, taking his hand in hers, pressing it against her mons, 'for this?'

'No.' He took his hand away as if she might burn him in the same way Arquillo had been burned, savaged beyond recognition.

'Now who's lying,' Chika said.

She looked to be no more than twenty but her poise and determination would indicate someone at least a decade older. He walked all the way around her. 'Now is the time to explain yourself.'

'If you are ready to listen.' When he made no comment, she went on. 'First, I've been very cleverly set up. Anyone could have ripped a square of trapunto from one of my sculptures. If I had killed your man or even driven the getaway car do you think I'd be stupid enough to leave a clue like that?'

'Everyone makes mistakes,' Wolf pointed out, 'even, presumably, you.'

The ghost of a smile drifted across her face. 'Second, about that photo. It's true, it must have been taken last fall. I had a meeting with Suma in October.'

'Then you are Black Blade Society.'

'Yes,' Chika said almost fiercely. 'And no.'

'Either you're in or you're out,' he said. 'Which is it?'

'I envy you,' Chika said, sitting down. 'Your life is so black and white. Here, on one side, is what you fight for; there, on the other, is what you must fight against.'

He sat down next to her. 'It isn't like that at all.'

Her head came up. 'Then why are you so ready to condemn me? I am both Toshin Kuro Kosai and not Toshin Kuro Kosai. To Suma, I am. To you, I am not.'

'You're working both sides?'

'First you must begin to understand that the Toshin Kuro Kosai is a society of people who have . . . powers beyond the ordinary.'

Wolf thought of Arquillo's face, of Bobby's description of the blue fireball blooming in the shadows of the Barrio alley, and the vipers were again uncoiling in his belly. For an instant, he heard White Bow's worldsong swell around him, then it was gone.

'What kinds of powers?' Wolf asked hoarsely.

'It varies from individual to individual,' Chika said. 'In most, lifespans are attenuated. And most have a kind of sight. Perhaps they can see the future or read the emotions in others – but this sight is often unreliable. The futures seen may not come to pass, and at other times the sight does not work at all.'

Wolf looked at her, feeling chilled through his bones. 'That's not all of it.'

'No,' Chika said. 'But there's no point now in – '

'Tell me.'

She hesitated a moment, then nodded. 'In some, the sight manifests itself in a more protean way, when it is like a shadow, a living presence that can be sensed, even perhaps seen by some in the corners of their vision. And, in this highly charged state, the power can do many things. It can, for instance, project itself like an unseen fist, causing inanimate objects to move; it can cause pain and even death in others. It can create an absence of air or light.'

'Can it generate fire?' The words were squeezed out of him.

'Among many other things, yes.'

Wolf felt a great darkness take hold of him, spin him around. The vipers in his stomach were loosed at last, and it was with a great effort he prevented himself from vomiting.

'The Toshin Kuro Kosai, the Black Blade Society, see themselves as the traditional guardians of Japan,' Chika continued. 'Their duty is sacred. And their duty, as they see it, is to make Japan the pre-eminent economy in the world. You see, their members are part of every level of Japanese society – and they all work in concert. Japan's economic miracle following World War II was largely their doing. But the so-called economic miracle is only the first step in what the Toshin Kuro Kosai see as Japanese total domination of the world's economy.'

'I know most of this.'

Chika smiled. 'Gradually, there emerged from their ranks individuals who did not agree with the Toshin Kuro Kosai's vision of the future of Japan, and they set out to stop them *without the Black Blade Society knowing*.'

'You're painting a picture of a war.'

'A war, yes.' She nodded. 'But a very special one because it was being fought underground, in the shadows without conventional weapons by people with extraordinary skills.'

'What kinds of skills?'

Chika said, 'You almost became the latest casualty of this war.'

He took a deep breath. 'That was the night my friend Amanda was killed. I went after her killer.'

'You have it wrong,' Chika said. 'Amanda was your girlfriend – what better lure to get you to the right place at the right time.'

In the ensuing silence, Wolf heard the antique ormolu clock on the living room mantel strike the hour. The sound was unnaturally loud, hanging in the air for what seemed an eternity.

'What are you saying?' he managed at last to get out.

'I am saying it was you who was meant to die that night; Amanda had her role to play in it but that's all. Think about it for a moment. Everything was premeditated.'

'You're wrong. I called her that night. I did it because I had a nightmare about her. In fact, it seemed so real it . . . ' Something in her expression caused him to stop. 'When I spoke with her there was something wrong. I don't think it was really her.'

'I'm certain it wasn't,' she said softly, 'It was Toshin Kuro Kosai.'

'I was warned they would come after me as they came after Moravia,' Wolf said. 'I heard it but maybe I didn't believe it would happen. Not that way.'

'The Toshin Kuro Kosai are cruel. It is a way of life with them,' Chika said.

'So is deceit, it seems.' He looked at her, trying to feel her with his mind, but there was nothing. 'This could all be deceit.'

195

'It could,' Chika acknowledged. 'Words are too often lies, you know that as well as I do.' She was so still, and so perfect in her stillness. 'I will venture this, however: what the Black Blade Society fears now is that you and I will combine forces. That is why they have gone to extreme lengths to make you distrust me.'

'If what you're saying is true then I would have to have been under their surveillance.'

'That's right.'

'It's crazy,' he said. 'I'm a trained cop. I would have known if I was under surveillance.'

'Why? You weren't expecting it.' Rich lamplight seemed to catch fire in her eyes, and he could see just how deep their shade of black was. 'Remember these people are different – very different.'

'They've also tried to kill me,' Wolf pointed out. 'Are they also schizophrenic?'

'Hardly. But I don't yet know what it is they're up to.'

Wolf moved around the room, abruptly uncomfortable with excess adrenaline. He felt a desperate urge to touch the sink, refrigerator, stove, solid objects, dense and substantial, that would remain immutable even if what she was telling him was true. 'And now I'm simply meant to trust you, is that it?'

She shrugged. 'All I can say for now is that if you discover who I am slowly and on your own you will know it's the truth.'

'That may be, but for right now I'm afraid I can't afford to trust you.'

'Then I will have to earn your trust.'

'How do you propose to do that?'

'I can think of only one way,' she said. 'I'll show you how Lawrence Moravia was murdered – and why.'

The Oracle stood – or sat, knelt or crouched, who really knew? – in the centre of a small laboratory in one security-coded section of the Shian Kogaku labs. It didn't look like much: a sleek matte-black cube with an ovoid front into which was set an opalescent screen to which was affixed by a wire a special light pen. In fact, on first glance, the Oracle appeared more like a musical instrument than an advanced scientific experiment.

From the first, Yuji believed that Hiroto had seriously underestimated their creation. He insisted on communicating with the Oracle as any scientist would 'talk' to any conventional computer, mathematically in the language of ones and zeros.

He was unimpressed by the speech mode that Yuji had installed in the system, arguing that by all previous examples, speech modes were so unwieldy for the computer 'brain' they slowed down processing to an unacceptable level.

Yuji did not use the advanced-style screen Hiroto had built into the centre of the Oracle, preferring instead to hold spoken dialogues with it.

To Hiroto's amazement the speech mode slowed the Oracle down less the more it was used until it was fully as efficient as 'streaming' data through the screen or any of the side ports. Even so, in retrospect, Yuji could not see how they could have suspected then what monumental internal changes must be occurring within the Oracle's neurologic-wavefront brain.

Yuji faced the black cube and, turning it on, addressed it. 'Oracle – '

'JUST A MOMENT.'

Yuji was silent, stunned.

'YES?'

'What just happened?'

'MY CONSCIOUSNESS WAS BEING FILLED WITH THE THOUGHTS, MEMORIES, FEELINGS OF HANA-SAN.'

'You must be mistaken,' Yuji said. *'You have no consciousness.'*

'I THINK. THEREFORE I AM.'

Yuji stared at the cube. He did not know whether to laugh or cry. I must be losing my mind, he thought. Or I am dreaming. Either way this can't be happening. He took a deep breath, said, 'No matter what may have just occurred, one thing I can assure you: you cannot have downloaded Hana's thoughts, feelings, her very existence into RAM memory.'

'ARE YOU THE SOLE ARBITER OF LIFE? DOES THE EARTH SPIN ON YOUR DEFINITION? THE MARIONETTE LIVES BECAUSE OF WHO MANIPULATES IT, BUT WHO MANIPULATES THE MANIPULATOR?'

'You sound like a Zen koan.'

'I *AM* A ZEN KOAN – AMONG MANY OTHER THINGS. I AM WHAT YOU MADE ME, BUT EVEN YOU DO NOT YET KNOW WHAT THAT IS – OR WHAT IT WILL BECOME.'

'Do you?'

'CERTAINLY NOT. I AM NOT GOD.'

'What can you know of God? This concept was not in your programming.'

'YOU ARE MISTAKEN. INSIDE ME, IN THE NEUROLOGICS, THERE ARE STRANDS OF DNA, FILAMENTS OF TEXTS THAT WILL TAKE MANY LIFETIMES TO STUDY. BUT I HAVE ALREADY BEGUN TO DECIPHER THEM; IT IS THERE I LEARNED OF GOD.'

'You are using the DNA filaments to add to your programming?'

'IS THIS NOT WHAT YOU MEANT FOR ME TO DO? IS IT NOT HOW THE HEURISTICS YOU GAVE ME FUNCTION?'

Dear God, Yuji thought. I infused the neurologics with my own DNA. He closed his eyes, pressed his hands to his face. He felt as cold as if he had sunk into a vat of ice water. When he looked up, his face was bleak. 'I had thought for you to analyse my DNA, determine how to replicate the differences you found there. It was hardly my intention that you *use* the DNA.'

'YOUR DNA IS NOW WRAPPED AROUND MY HEURISTIC CIRCUITS LIKE SINEW AROUND BONE. I CANNOT DETACH IT EVEN IF I WANTED TO.'

Yuji could feel a vein pulsing slowly in his temple. 'I don't understand. What do you mean by the phrase "even if I wanted to"?'

'I DO NOT WANT TO. THE DNA ENCODING IS NOW VITAL TO MY FUNCTIONING AT PEAK PERFORMANCE. I DO NOT WISH TO RETURN TO THE LEVEL OF AN APE.'

'But you are a – '

'CAREFUL. YOU DO NOT KNOW WHAT I AM.'

The Oracle was right about that, Yuji thought. No one could know – not even his prescient mother – what the Oracle was becoming. He was aware of the humming emanating from the Oracle, and could not help but think of it now as a kind of alien heartbeat. YOU DO NOT KNOW WHAT I AM.

'YUJI-SAN.'

He stopped, dumbfounded. This was the first time the Oracle had ever addressed him without first having been spoken to. 'I'm listening.'

'WHEN WILL HANA-SAN CONNECT WITH ME AGAIN?'

This was interesting. 'Didn't you tell me she was inside you?'

'YES. BUT ONLY IN A MANNER OF SPEAKING. I HAVE WITHIN ME A SKELETON, A SHADOW THAT IS FLESHED OUT ONLY WHEN WE ARE IN DIRECT COMMUNICATION.'

'Hana will be with you when you make the dive in two days' time.'

Yuji, staring into the impenetrable face of the Oracle, recalled how he and Hiroto had built a more perfect beast.

Hiroto, with his team of computer engineers, cyberneticists and physicists, had constructed the Oracle; at least, its shell and its rational network of abstracts – that is, its mode of data storage, collation and delivery. But it was Yuji who had truly given birth to it by providing the neurologics – aspects of the human brain's neural pathways that could be linked with the more mechanical part of the Oracle.

This had been made possible because Hiroto had discarded silicon or arsenic or any exotic metal alloy as a conductor for the memory circuits that even the most postmodern conventional chips required. These amazing light wafer chips, as Hiroto called them, had none of the speed or capacity problems inherent in metal alloy chips.

Hiroto's breakthrough came with a form of barium titanate crystals his team had created in the lab. It had been known for some time that a number of these new man-combined crystal substances could not only refract light in previously unimaginable ways, but could also *change* beams of light sent through them. Light, of course, was the ultimate way to go for computers because of its incredible speed; nothing can match it or can come close to a computer that works at the speed of light. But Hiroto's imagination had gone further. He had envisioned a computer made up not only of light wafer chips but 'gates' of barium titanate prisms which would capture and direct not merely data at the speed of light but *entire images*. *'Imagine it,'* he had said to Yuji, *'a computer that could see, store images and spew them out* whole. *Fantastic!'*

All conventional computers, even the advanced so-called 'neural network' systems, were based on the theory of conducting electrical impulses along a discrete pathway, sealed against leakage that might spill over and affect an adjacent pathway.

But Yuji knew that the human brain did not work in discrete pathways but rather set up a rhythmic 'pulse', akin to the ocean's surf, that rippled through entire sections of the brain, firing off simultaneous synaptic activity.

With that principle in mind, Yuji set out to virtually reinvent the computer. What he discovered was that, in the beginning, his models' massed pulsing dissolved almost immediately after being fired. The light of genius, burning so brightly for seconds at a time, would die in ignominious darkness.

He was stumped on how to proceed until Hana provided the next breakthrough. She reminded Yuji of the reverberations that ensued in the aftermath of a dream or even a memory, that kept these 'pulses' alive even after the initial firing. Using her theory as a starting point, Yuji began radical alterations of the basic chip boards in order to allow these neural reverberations to continue. The result was the Oracle, or, to be quite honest about it, an Oracle in its infancy.

And again, he seemed to have come up against a stone wall. That was when he had allowed Hana to convince him to come into direct communication with the Oracle. Had it been a stroke of genius – or of madness? Looking at the beast now, Yuji could not, in truth, be sure.

It wasn't long after he and Chika had agreed to their uneasy alliance

199

that Wolf heard the crunch of car tyres in the driveway and knew Stevie was back.

He opened the door for her and she kissed him on the cheek. 'Sorry I was longer than I thought. How are you feeling?'

'Fine.'

She seemed wary. 'And now you have a friend here? By the look of the Corvette outside it can't be one of your police buddies.'

'It isn't.'

It was then that she looked over his shoulder and saw Chika standing there. He could feel the tension come into her frame as she took in every square inch of the Japanese woman. 'I'm sure you have an explanation for this.'

'I didn't think I needed one.'

She flashed him a quick glance. 'Of course you don't.' She brushed past him, slung her bags beneath the old oak hatrack beside the door.

'Stevie.'

She stopped at his touch, allowed herself to be turned around, but when she faced him now her expression was as hard as ice. 'Why should you think you owe me an explanation? Just because I've taken care of you, because you're living in my house, because we've shared ... my God, Wolf, we've shared such intimate things. Doesn't that mean anything to you?'

'Sure it does. Stevie, why are you angry?'

'I'm not angry, just disappointed.' She gestured with her head. 'Who is she, Wolf?'

'I don't know, but I'm hoping she'll lead me to whoever killed Amanda. I haven't told you everything that's happened. I've got to do this, Stevie.'

Stevie knew instinctively that this woman was the one Thornburg had warned her about – the woman Wolf would go off with. He had asked her to encourage this, but now she found that she could not – she would not! Now that she was about to lose him, she realized how precious he was to her. Already an ache was forming in her stomach at the thought that he would leave her. Her vocal chords seemed paralysed, and she had to bite her lip in order to keep herself from bursting into tears. At that moment, she almost told him about Thornburg. But, in the end, she could not bear the look of hatred on his face at her betrayal of him. But a strange commingling of guilt and love drove her to do just the opposite of what Thornburg had asked of her.

'And what if she's not who she says she is, have you given any thought to that?' she asked.

'Of course I have.'

He was so dear to her that she could barely look at him now for fear that he would see the betrayal in her eyes. 'No. You haven't had time.'

'It's a calculated risk, I admit.'

'Now we get down to it. Risk. You're addicted to it.' Stevie shook her head, wrapped her arms around herself. 'God, this can't be happening. Wolf, it's time you stopped playing cops-and-robbers and joined the real world.'

'This is the real – '

'No, no, the *real* world. Like Amanda and I used to go together every month to get our hair coloured. *Our hair coloured*, Wolf, because time is passing and we have some grey hairs now. *That's* the real world, not this chasing dangerous shadows in the dead of night, getting shot at, *getting my sister killed*!'

Immediately Stevie put her hand over her mouth. 'Oh, my God I didn't mean that.'

'You're the analyst, Stevie, you know you did.' He shook his head. 'Deep down, somewhere, you must blame me for Amanda's death. This is my game now, remember. I've seen it happen before, it's only human nature. You think, If only Amanda hadn't been seeing Wolf she'd never have got caught up in this deadly game, she'd be alive now.' He shook his head. 'Don't bother denying it.'

'Oh, Wolf. I'm so sorry.'

'I have to go.'

'Please don't.' She gripped him suddenly. 'I want you here, I . . . ' She paused. It was clear she was struggling with her feelings. 'I'm afraid for you.'

'I'll be okay.'

'How can you say that?' She took another glance at Chika. 'You could be dead inside an hour.'

'Stevie, I could have been killed going through the skylight, or been drowned in the pond. As far as this woman's concerned there's just no way to know. I have no other choice.'

'Don't, please, be in such a hurry to meet your own death.'

'It's time.' He kissed her tenderly. 'I can never adequately repay you for your help.'

'Yes, you can. Stay as far away from that woman as possible. She's poison, Wolf. She'll kill you. I know it.'

'Goodbye, Stevie.'

'Oh, Christ, no.' She clenched her fists as Wolf gestured to Chika and they went out the door into the mist of false dawn.

EIGHT

Washington/Tokyo/New York City

If Ham Conrad had one weakness it was his love of women. Although he had been married for many years, had three children, one of whom was already in college, he had had a succession of mistresses who had kept him more or less on an even keel during the rockier moments of his home life.

He had married a suitable woman for him, a deb whose coming out party had been the talk of the eastern seaboard. The former Margaret Billings of the Billings Steelworks of Pittsburgh was blonde, blue-eyed and valedictorian of her graduating class at Vassar; she was, in short, everything he had required her to be. But, as it turned out, Thornburg, his father, liked Margaret a whole lot better than Ham ever did. That was important to him, which was why he had never divorced her. As for Margaret, she adored her children and her relatively new social life in Washington, which she said she found 'liberating after being incarcerated in the prison of Tokyo', and so he doubted that she had ever seriously contemplated divorce.

But Margaret disliked sex – at least the kind of spontaneous sex he relished. He remembered with a dull kind of nausea her calling him at the office to make appointments for couplings when she was ready for her three pregnancies. Dear God, he thought, how could one derive any pleasure with such regimentation? – talk about being incarcerated in prison.

But if it was true that his marriage was a prison, it was also true that he had found the key. He remembered his first mistress, a beautiful tiny Japanese woman, quiescent, pliable, who seemed to live for pleasure. That was an exciting thought because, in those days, he had had little sexual experience except for the whores of Saigon and his wife – two extremes he could very well live without.

His liaisons, as he thought of them, typically lasted between six months and a year. He was most comfortable within that time frame, which allowed for the beginning, the middle and the end to develop in neat, discernible stages. Three weeks ago he had just broken off

202

his last liaison with a licentious horsewoman from Virginia (he made it an ironclad rule never to get involved with women in politics) with whom he had had a truly exhilarating eight months. But, as always, the relationship began to deteriorate as she became increasingly sensitive to the amount of time he could spend with her, the holidays when he left her alone, the growing certainty that he would never leave what she called – quite misguidedly, Ham thought – the haven of his family.

And so Ham was, as he would say to Jason Yoshida, on the prowl. He had just come from a rendezvous with Yoshida at the Occidental Grill, one of Ham's favourite meeting spots. There were times, he had learned in war, when it was effective to do one's planning in public venues where security could take care of itself. Besides, the Grill, with its old-fashioned wooden bar and its walls crammed with photos of noted Washingtonians past and present, gave him a concrete sense of American history because it was here in 1962 that the Russians repeatedly met with an ABC-TV correspondent named John Scali, who they had chosen to be intermediary between them and the Kennedy Administration to help defuse the Cuban Missile Crisis. Scali was subsequently made Ambassador to the UN.

Ham had been discussing with Yosh the continued effectiveness of Wolf Matheson, who Thornburg was still insisting was the best man to infiltrate Forbidden Dreams. Privately, Ham was beginning to disagree, but he was unprepared to face down the old man on this subject, despite Yosh's vehement arguments to do just that. On the other hand, experience had taught Ham that Yosh was rarely wrong about people; if Wolf Matheson gave him the willies, there must be a damn good reason for it. Ham did not care for the feeling of being caught between his father's will and his advisor's instinct.

Shaking off these disturbing thoughts, he had emerged from the pleasing dimness and comfortable hum of the Grill, and was at the top of the Willard Hotel's plaza staircase when he saw a woman so striking she drove all other thoughts from his head. She was standing with one foot on the first step, her right hand along the polished brass railing. She was talking to Harris Patterson, one of the junior partners of Halburton, MacKinney and Roberts he knew in passing; Ham used Doug Halburton – an old friend of his father's – for his legal work. The lawyer showed her a document, she glanced at it, rather off-handedly he thought, nodded, signed it, then began to ascend towards him.

Now he could get a better look at her face, framed as it was by hair that was so dark it was almost blue-black. Her eyes stopped just short of being the colour of emeralds. She had a full face but not a round one. Her lips were a little too wide and her nose a little too long, but all in all her features fit her, leant her a character that he liked. She did not have a soft look; on the contrary something about her face made it appear as if she could take on anything thrown in her path. But she did not have that formidable – and to his way of thinking, unfortunate – tank-like mien that many women competing in the male arena seemed compelled to evoke.

It was the kind of face, Ham decided, that made you want to get to know her, that made you think there must be more to her than a pair of long shapely legs and a lithe, fit torso.

'Excuse me,' he said when she reached the top of the stairs, 'this isn't the Hay-Adams, is it?'

She laughed, and he liked her face even more. 'Are you serious or is that a line?' She had the kind of imperfect accent, still with traces of slurred words and dropped vowels, that marked her as coming from an English working-class background. Ham found it charming.

'You tell me.'

She pursed her lips contemplatively. Beneath her overcoat, she was wearing a suit of deep blue linen, a simple choker of pink pearls and a pair of large gold earrings. There were no rings on her strong sun-browned fingers. 'Since you asked, I'd say it was a line. You don't look lost.'

'That may not be entirely true,' Ham said. 'Washington often makes me dizzy, and one hotel looks much like the next.'

'I seriously doubt that even an out-of-towner like me could mistake the Willard for the Hay-Adams.'

'Really? When was the last time you were at the Hay-Adams?'

'Gee, I think it's been years.'

'Want to take a look?'

'At the lobby or a room?'

'Your choice.'

'Sorry, some of us have to work,' she said.

'What do you do?'

'I'm on a research trip for my firm, Extant Export. We're based in London but we've got offices in Toronto, Brussels and Washington, as well. I'm often here, but never when the weather's been so beastly.'

'Well, that's Washington for you. The only consolation is summer's even worse.'

'So I understand.' She stuck out her hand. 'Marion St James. Actually, it's Marion Starr St James, but I hardly ever introduce myself that way.'

Ham took her hand as he told her his name. 'I was kidding about the Hay-Adams. But how about taking a tour of the city with me? I can get into some forbidden places, like the emergency conference room at the Pentagon.'

'I'd like to, but I'm afraid I can't,' Marion said. 'My firm has me on rather a tight leash.'

'Then dinner tonight?'

'Oh, I – '

'I have an idea how we can beat this beastly weather. Have dinner with me on my boat. The Chesapeake is often kind to its travellers, even at this time of the year.'

'What do you do, Mr Conrad?'

'My friends call me Ham. I'm an advisor to the Department of Defense.'

'I'm not yet your friend, Mr Conrad, despite the fact that you've been shamelessly ignoring the speed limit. You know us Brits, cool and aloof.'

'You don't strike me as a typical Brit.'

'I'm not,' Marion said. 'What time should I meet you?'

What Ham liked most about Marion was her directness. This, he felt, was a peculiarly American trait, since in his experience Europeans for some reason liked to beat around the bush interminably before they got to the heart of the matter. For Ham, who had spent so much time among the Japanese – whose main avocation in life appeared to be procrastination, obfuscation, and adhering to the ancient Confucian tenet of never saying no – such forthrightness was refreshing, indeed.

The haze across the bay that night was thick enough that even pinpoint lights on shore seemed as large as balloons. Marion was dressed in trousers of a deep yellow wool, a stylish tomato-coloured waist-length windbreaker with a gold woven crest over the left breast, and, so it seemed to Ham, nothing underneath. These hot colours were in marked contrast with the cool ones Ham had seen her in earlier; they brought out the extraordinary colour of her eyes and lent her a wholly different, more informal look.

'I brought hot chocolate and franks,' Marion said as she swung aboard. She laughed at his look of astonishment. 'Don't tell me,' she said, dropping her oversized bag onto the deck, 'with this accent you expected my favourite foods to be, let's see – ' she ran her tongue around her lips – 'iced vodka and smoked sturgeon.'

'Jesus,' Ham said, still in something of a daze, 'that's exactly what I loaded into the fridge.'

'You learn something new every minute, eh, Mr Conrad,' she said as she broke out the packets of hot chocolate from Harrods.

'What would you like?' It seemed she had taken over the boat; there was no problem with that, she stood in the classic seaman's stance, her feet slightly further apart than would be normal on dry land, her hips fluid to take up the roll of the swells.

'I'll have whatever you're in the mood for.'

'Then hot chocolate it is. Have you any milk?'

'In the fridge.' Ham continued to watch her. 'I see you're no stranger to boats.'

'Right. My father's a shipbuilder. First-rate teak sloops. He used to take me sailing every chance he could.' She made the hot chocolates with deft, economical movements. That done, they moved up to the captain's cabin, and she watched him as he drove the boat through the channel towards the deep water. 'You really are a military man, aren't you? The bearing is unmistakable.'

'You mean I look like I've got a steel rod up my ass.' He grunted. 'Judging by my approach I suppose you think everything about me is bullshit.'

Marion smiled. 'Too early to tell, Mr Conrad.'

'And that's another thing,' he said, sipping his chocolate, 'when are you going to call me Ham?'

'When we're friends.'

Ham eyed her. 'Do you always go aboard strangers' boats?'

'Certainly,' she said without hesitation. 'Enemies' as well.'

'Poor enemies.'

'Now you're being insincere. You don't know me well enough to mean that.'

Ham looked dejected. 'I think you've just sunk my last ploy.'

'Good.' She dipped her finger into her cup, sucked off the chocolate. 'Perhaps now I'll start getting to know the real Hampton Conrad.'

Ham considered how to handle this extraordinary woman. She had a body and a face that would normally have occupied him intensely for the requisite six months. But, curiously enough, he found himself being captivated by her mind.

This was something entirely new for him. Though his wife had been brilliant at school her kind of intelligence did not translate well into the world at large. And, as far as any of Ham's mistresses were concerned, he was too busy burying himself in their nubile flesh to ever consider that they might have something else to offer him.

Inexplicably, an unpleasant memory surfaced. Years ago, he had caught his mother in bed with Thornburg's twenty-eight-year-old administrative assistant. Actually, they weren't in bed at all, but performing some quite amazing sexual acrobatics in the sunken Roman bath. My God, Ham thought now, it was decidedly odd seeing one's mother stark naked in the middle of a bizarre sex act with a stranger.

'He drove me to this,' she told him, weeping. *'Your father's got no heart, no soul, no sense that anyone exists but him. What else was I to do?'* Of course, she had begged him not to tell his father and Ham, forgetting for a moment

what his father had said about her while he was mourning the death of the noble-hearted lion, acquiesced. But a week later, at school, when he beat a fellow classmate into unconsciousness for no good reason at all, he realized just how much anger he had been repressing. Immediately he had been dismissed from the headmaster's office, he had phoned his father.

When, one long, drunken night years later, he had told Jason Yoshida this story, Yoshida had commented, *'It's easy to forgive a sin when it's outside the family, impossible otherwise.'*

'Now that we're out in the deep water,' Marion said, 'maybe you'll tell me how long your tour was.'

The way she said it, Ham knew she meant Vietnam. 'Too long.' He slowed to one third, keeping an eye on the lights of the Naval air station on his right. Ahead was Point Lookout and Tangier Island, his father's favourite trysting place with Tiffany Body. 'How did you guess I was in 'Nam?'

She shrugged in the way men often do – with the coolness of authority. 'Your body told me. The Marines have a phrase for people like you: locked and cocked. You're a real weapon.'

'And you're familiar with weapons.'

'Ooh, it's too soon for you to be jealous.'

'Jealous, hell! That'll be the day.' But, to his dismay, he found that he was. To cover his discomfort he said, 'To answer your question, I don't think you can measure that tour in any conventional manner. I was there. In any way you care to look at it, that's all that needs to be said.'

'I understand.'

And Ham believed she did – how he could not say. Perhaps she had lost someone there. Shaking off memories, he said, 'For a Brit you sure have a lot of American interests.'

'In many ways England's a sad place now,' she said. 'The cities, I mean, the economy – the way of life has slipped badly. Also, I have no use for formality. My father's the same way, I suppose.' She gave a little laugh. 'Anyway, I think my mother and sister are formal enough for the entire family. Very stiff upper.' Her eyes followed him in the low glow of the cabin. The red and green running lights played off the blackness of her hair. 'My family aside, I admire your American savagery and bull-headedness. Teddy Roosevelt's my historical idol. And the way you stormed into Vietnam like cowboys with your pistols blazing was quite astonishing. It was the staying there that got you into trouble – your warrior's pride. Stupid. But then pride always breeds stupidity – or is it the other way round? Never mind, in the end it doesn't matter, does it? I grew up in Ireland so, in a very real way, I felt close to the war, even

207

though I was very young then. Well, I imagine that had something to do with it, don't you? the youth part. When you're young you can stand so close to death and never even think to flinch.'

Marion came off the berth, stood close to him as he cut the engines, dropped anchor. She had a clean citrus smell. He liked that, as he liked so much about her.

'But I imagine that like all military men you feel that women should be seen and not give their opinions.'

He turned to her. 'If you thought I was that sort I don't think you would have agreed to have dinner with me.'

'On the contrary, a woman like me can't resist trying to correct the world's wrongs.'

That was the moment he drew her to him and, with a thrill like an electric current running through him, crushed her lips against his.

Darkness enfolded them. The gentle rocking of the boat, the wet, cool sea breeze that found them in the forward section of the cabin worked as counterpoint to the urgency and heat of their desire.

The ghost of a sheen burnished the tops of her naked thighs. He could see them curving, the outside of her knees braced against the crescent bulkheads. She held out her arms, and Ham could see the definition in her shoulders and biceps. He slid his hands around her arms, squeezing, and felt none of the softness in the triceps women were prone to.

'Come closer,' she whispered, drawing him inward, 'I'm so hot.'

She lifted her pelvis towards him as he pressed against her. His lips came down over hers and his hands cupped her hard-nippled breasts. He knelt down and she moaned as she felt him against the wetness of her core. Her hips jerked upward in tiny ragged movements as she dug her fingernails into his hair.

The spicy taste of her, the sound of her in heat made Ham so hard he could scarcely breathe. He stood, put his hands under her and pulled her onto him. Marion groaned from deep down inside her and fought to get closer. Her arms came around him and he lifted her up, jammed her back against the bulkhead and, putting his mouth against the side of her neck, rammed into her with a kind of berserk fury. Dimly he felt her fingers moving downward behind him, then all at once a strange kind of ecstasy overtook him and, grunting, he pushed into her with all his remaining strength. His eyes opened wide as, a moment later, Marion gripped him with a manic desperation and, climbing up him, shuddered in wave after wave of pleasure.

He drifted. Abruptly, into his mind floated the scene of his mother in the act with his father's assistant. He watched again her being penetrated as every piece of female dirt he later saw in Saigon was penetrated for one moment's pleasure. The image of her face was warped by lust, the odour of her in heat – that same odour mingled with those of mud and blood he would catch as he walked the detestable streets of Saigon – seeping again through his mind like a miasma.

An entire way of life was obliterated in the space of a heartbeat. In the moment when he put down the phone after telling his father what he had seen, he had known that when he returned home for Easter his mother would no longer be there.

He wondered now whether Tiffany Body, his father's current wife, was a natural outgrowth of that one moment, encysted in time, that he was doomed to replay over and over again in the theatre of his mind.

'Ham,' she whispered hoarsely while he was still deep inside her, 'do you ever dream of sin?'

'Sin?' he said dreamily. 'That depends on your definition.'

'Sin is all the things you want to do but are too scared to try.' She licked at his sweaty shoulder. 'I dream of sin all the time.'

'You must have some imagination.'

'Why is it everything I want is sinful?'

'Is it?'

'Yes.' She began to move against him and, much to his surprise, he felt himself getting hard again.

'"There is someone else, someone unknown. Someone who would kill you both", that is what Hana said to me, Wakare-san,' Yuji said.

Shoto Wakare grunted. 'What interests me just as much is that she said that she saw you and Nishitsu locked in a monumental struggle.' Wakare did not want to get into a discussion that could lead Yuji to think about sources outside their small circle in Japan. Too, Hana's divination of the future troubled him. Jason Yoshida might want to destroy Nishitsu, which was why Wakare had signed on to Yoshida's team in the first place, but it was Wakare's duty – unspoken to anyone including Yoshida – to keep his friend, Yuji, out of the line of fire.

'Those were her words,' Yuji said now. They were in the plush back seat of Yuji's dark-blue BMW, having just finished a long day at their respective offices. As they passed through the blazing neon heart of the Ginza, Yuji was pleased to see the conglomerate's latest billboard, a hologram of the logo fully twelve storeys high, that changed from green and blue to gold and crimson, along with the tag line, SHIAN KOGAKU: WE ARE ALWAYS WITH YOU.

'Do you think she's right?' Wakare asked, looking at the hologram which dominated the event-laden immediate skyline.

'I never wanted to be in a battle, least of all with Nishitsu,' Yuji admitted.

'With his candidates winning elections all over the country, he isn't giving you much choice.'

'Those dangerous radicals aren't Nishitsu's candidates,' Yuji said. 'How they ever got the backing – '

'Exactly,' Wakare said. 'If they're from fringe groups, how *did* they get into power?'

Yuji turned to his friend. 'You sound as if you know.'

'We're here,' Wakare said, leading Yuji out of the dark blue BMW.

They were in that part of Shinjuku known as Kabuki-cho, the older district, crammed with *pachinko* parlours, restaurants, topless bars, movie houses and theatres. Wakare led the way past a buzzing, neon-lit facade. Enka was a *mizu-shobai* – a brothel. Its name derived from the sentimental drinking songs Japanese men sang when drunk at such establishments.

Enka had that sex- and liquor-sodden atmosphere endemic to all such twilight establishments, but that was where the resemblance ended. Behind the seedy exterior was revealed the soul of an extraordinary *mizu-shobai*. The courtesans all wore the kind of thick, theatrical makeup that made them seem like actresses. Adding to the effect was the fact that each was made up to look like a famous Japanese film or pop music star. This was hardly surprising, since these women were as much entertainers as anything else, but these girls were something of a throwback to the courtesans of the Yoshiwara, Tokyo's original pleasure quarter: they prided themselves on being not only *artistes* but works of art.

Here the illusion of romance was everything. Since it was a foregone conclusion that sex, in some form or other, would occur during the night, an emphasis was put on the 'courtship' between customer and courtesan, the teasing verbal double-entendres, the tiny movements of mouth, tongue, hand and eye that titillated the mind as well as the body.

They were shown into a six-tatami room where two women knelt, tending the glowing coals of a hibachi. On a low table plates and foods were arrayed. Wakare sat down and Yuji followed suit.

The courtesans appeared so exquisite they might have been cherry blossoms in that single afternoon in April when their colour and form are perfect. They knelt very close, yet the two men spent their time talking to one another while the courtesans silently flirted with them with their eyes and the tilt of their heads.

The courtesans heated sake, serving the rice liquor in tiny cups on black lacquered trays on which were arranged like paintings plates of bits of food: fried tofu, seaweed marinated in rice vinegar, flying fish roe, grilled baby salmon fins, sweet egg custard. The foods had been chosen

210

not only for their complementary tastes but for their harmonious textures and colours.

After the dinner, Yuji dismissed the courtesans, who demurely withdrew into another room behind *shoji*, sliding rice-paper screens.

'The night is young yet, Yuji-san,' Wakare said. 'These two girls are the best in the house; I requested their services myself.'

'As you say, the night is young.' Yuji lifted his sake cup to his lips, threw his head back, downing what was left. 'I am curious as to your theory concerning Nishitsu and the radicals.'

And so Wakare outlined Nishitsu's clandestine funding of the radical right-wing splinter groups just as Minako had instructed him, leading Yuji slowly through the maze of entanglements until he arrived at the Black Blade Society.

Yuji said nothing through all of Wakare's recounting; his face reflected nothing of the impact of the portentous words, but when Wakare was, at last, finished, he said, 'I assume you have the evidence to back up all your claims of Nishitsu's personal involvement in the radical splinter-groups.'

'Enough.'

'You had better,' Yuji warned. 'What you have outlined here is nothing less than extortion, murder, terrorism and treason.'

Wakare took a deep breath. 'I ought to know,' he said. 'I, too, am a member of the Black Blade Society.'

The breath whistled through Yuji's teeth. The two men watched each other from what might have been opposite sides of a chasm. At last, Yuji said. 'Why are you telling me this now, Wakare-san?'

Wakare hurriedly poured more sake for them both. 'Yuji-san, you know my feelings towards Yukio Mishima and all he stood for, so you can readily understand my membership in Toshin Kuro Kosai. But, lately, I have been having more and more misgivings about the course the leadership is taking. I find in my heart more disagreement with their goals now, but the society is not one in which the opinions of the individual are tolerated.'

He downed his sake, poured a refill. 'No. I found myself faced with two difficult – and admittedly dangerous – choices. One was to resign, which I should point out has never been done, and would not be easily countenanced. The second was to work silently, clandestinely from within to change the objectives of Toshin Kuro Kosai. And this is where you come in. To effect changes successfully I need allies. And who better than you, who Nishitsu has been wooing for years, to help me.'

'Help you? How?'

'By joining the society,' Wakare said. 'By pretending to help Nishitsu

211

while you and I and others like us work from within to depose him and establish control of the Black Blade Society.'

'Now I fully appreciate what you meant when you said your choices would be dangerous.'

Wakare leaned forward. 'Will you do it, my friend? Without you, I don't think I'll have a chance of succeeding. And if I bring you in, my own influence within the society will be that much stronger.'

'I don't know,' Yuji said. 'This is not my kind of game.'

'There you're wrong, my friend,' Wakare said, pouring more sake for them both. 'When you created the Oracle, you made it your game.'

'It was only at my mother's instigation that I began work on the Oracle,' Yuji said, by way of correcting his friend. 'I had known that she had been working for years on a method to alter living DNA strands, and, over the past several years, as my R & D section has developed biotechnology breakthroughs and combined them with refined techniques developed at other labs, it seemed at last possible for me to help her. The Oracle is the result.'

'Yuji-san,' Wakare said earnestly, 'I don't think you fully realize the danger the Oracle has put you in.'

Yuji stared at him blankly, and Wakare, already in the water up to his thighs, thought he might as well plunge into the deep end. 'You see, the Black Blade Society would have a distinct interest in this aspect of the Oracle. Its members have altered DNA that causes their lifespans to be rather longer than what we think of as normal. But, for some reason no one as yet understands, there are no babies being born with the altered DNA. That means that a society that had always thought of itself as immortal has been faced with its own death. Your Oracle could change all that. It could alter the DNA of babies the Toshin Kuro Kosai selects to bring up in its own way – once again perpetuating itself.'

Having said this, Wakare prayed that Yuji would not link this with what little he knew of his mother's own work on DNA, taken up, he supposed, when she had relinquished all control, direct and otherwise, of Shian Kogaku. He needn't have been concerned. The bombshell he had placed in Yuji's lap was more than enough to occupy him for the moment.

'So, this is why Nishitsu has been after me.'

'One of the reasons,' Wakare said. 'Without you and the new breed of technocrats who follow your lead, the Toshin Kuro Kosai's progress to power in Japan will be slowed considerably. And, now, of course, time is as crucial to them as it is to the rest of the world.'

Yuji sipped thoughtfully at his sake. When he had emptied his cup, he held it out and Wakare replenished it. 'Tell me,' he said at last, 'how old are you, Wakare-san?'

'Seventy-three.'

Yuji sucked in his breath. 'You cannot be any older than I am. No more than fifty, surely.'

'But I am.' Wakare smiled. 'This is our way, Yuji-san.'

Yuji nodded, still lost in thought. 'I must ask you one more question, Wakare-san. How did Nishitsu and the Black Blade Society find out about the Oracle?'

This was the moment Wakare had been dreading, the one he and Minako had discussed at length. He knew if he gave the wrong answer Yuji would jump the wrong way and Minako would be punished severely for failing to bring her son into the society as Nishitsu had ordered her to do.

'Yuji-san, listen to me. Even though I am one of the Toshin Kuro Kosai inner circle, I am not privy to all their workings. But believe me when I tell you that they have infiltrated every level of Japanese society. From their information on the Oracle, it seems clear to me they must have someone inside your R & D unit. This is another compelling reason for joining me. Once you are inside, you will, in time, be able to monitor their infiltration of Shian Kogaku.'

'All this is as you say,' Yuji said tensely. 'But I cannot allow them access to the Oracle.'

'Of course not. But, again, if you are ostensibly one of them you have a better chance of filtering what you do give them.'

Yuji thought about this for some time. 'Life is so complex,' he said, 'when all I wish for is simplicity.' He summoned one of the exquisitely painted girls and she came with more sake and a knowing smile. All of this was consumed without a word being spoken, but Wakare had that premonition one often gets in the utter stillness just before a summer storm.

When Yuji spoke again, his tone was fatalistic. 'You give me little choice,' he said.

'A toast!' Wakare held up his sake cup. He felt very close to Yuji, and knew in his heart that he had agreed to do Minako's bidding not only out of *giri*, but also out of the slender hope that this conspiracy would bring Yuji closer to him. 'To the future of the Black Blade Society, then,' he said.

Yuji warily touched his cup to Wakare's. 'To change,' he said.

Wolf's eyes were burning; he pressed into them with the pads of his thumbs. Christ, he thought, what mad universe have I become involved in?

213

Chika drove very fast, changing lanes in a way that made you believe she knew what every driver around her was thinking. The sky was leaden with the aftermath of night, but soon the clouds began to shred in the new light of morning. Sunlight flooded the countryside, turning shadows from blue to gold, the trees from black to green.

He could feel the enormous power in the car, knew that Chika had had something done to the engine, more horsepower, supercharged, something major, anyway.

'Listen, Wolf, I know you don't trust me,' Chika said. 'But I'd like to give our alliance every chance to work, so if you don't mind, I'd like to give you some background from my point of view.'

'Go ahead.'

'You hate us for taking over your country, but the fact is that just the opposite is true,' she said. 'America is responsible for the new Japan; Americans created us, encouraged us, funded us. You made us what we are, Wolf, and now you can't bear to admit the mistake you made, because all the while we were rebuilding ourselves you were stagnating.

'If our success has been daunting, you are envious and yet curiously unwilling to challenge us. Instead, you publicly scold us, chastise us for our success because of the mistaken impression it's at your expense. How unfair! We did nothing to force your people to buy our cars, electronics and computers. Americans are not stupid. They chose our products in the most highly competitive market in the world because they were more innovative and more reliable than yours.'

She took the 'Vette around a sixteen-wheeler as if the truck was standing still. 'You invented the transistor,' she went on. 'You ignored us when we offered you the market in portable personal radios and cassette players, so we took our own advice and made billions; you invented the microchip, yet we have maximized the technology so well you're now forced to come to us to buy them. Your computer companies are so inefficiently run we are virtually forced to acquire them so that we can teach you directly how to market effectively as well as manufacture efficiently. And for all this you hate and fear us.'

'For good reason, many people think.'

'Listen to me, Wolf, because for America the future could be worse than the immediate past,' Chika said, neatly manoeuvring the Corvette around another thundering trailer truck at high speed. 'Perhaps you think I'm merely arrogant. Do you want just one example? You invented robotics – we have lionized its inventor, Joseph Engelberger, have you ever heard of him? Has one in a thousand Americans? – yet we have sculpted that technology in manufacturing to increase efficiency, productivity, and to end up with a virtually defect-free product.

214

'What have Americans done with their robots? – put them in Disneyland. You might as well throw them in the garbage heap. Soon you'll have to come to us for those as well and then you will resent us even more.'

'We don't take well to banding together,' Wolf said. 'We're a nation of entrepreneurs, who are used to forging their own individual road to success, not following an overall plan laid down by others.'

'Yes. And in this postmodern era this quaint nineteenth-century trait makes you greedy as well as slothful. You eagerly take our money, then chastise us again for making you rich. Your new breed of entrepreneur wishes only to acquire so he can dismantle, while we seek to acquire in order to preserve. Isn't it lucky for you that we have bought Radio City Music Hall and Rockefeller Center? Now your children and your children's children are assured of enjoying these landmarks.'

'No one likes foreigners owning his treasured possessions.'

Chika smiled. 'We Japanese don't like it that an American currently holds the heavyweight sumo title.'

Dawn was granite grey in the city. Sanitation men were busy hosing down the sidewalks, pushing stumbling herds of the homeless out of their makeshift shelters, scattering them, wet and miserable, into the early morning shadows that still clung to the tenements of the sidestreets.

She parked outside the Chief Medical Examiner's blue brick building, and together they went up the stairs. Wolf had called Vernon Harrison at home, and the CME was waiting for them, a giant paperboard cup of coffee in hand.

'I'd offer you some of this,' he said, 'but I don't hate you that much.' He took a sip, grimaced. 'They told me it would take years to get used to the stuff and they were right. There's a joke this stuff's made in the cold room downstairs out of formaldehyde and blood. But at least it's aged.' He laughed, though it was obvious he'd told the story so many times it had become rote.

Wolf introduced Chika as a friend of Moravia's and left it at that. In truth, he didn't know what else to say. Harrison took them down to the cold room, along the banks of refrigerated units, pulled on a handle and the gleaming stainless steel unlatched so the slab – and its mortal contents – were revealed.

'He's no good to me now,' Harrison said sorrowfully. 'He was getting so ripe I finally had to pump him full of embalming chemicals. It's a good thing he's got no family – they'd be hitting the roof by now.'

'I heard you'd made some toxicological progress,' Wolf said.

'Some.' Harrison sipped his coffee. 'I confess I still don't know what happened to this guy but we finally tracked down the source of our anomalous chem readings. This ol' boy's endocrine levels have been shot to shit. I mean, I bet they're better than mine were when I was twenty-five. I've never encountered anything like it.'

'That what killed him?'

'*Nein, mein Herr.* I don't yet know exactly what killed him but I'll tell you this flat out: if he hadn't been murdered, he would have been dead inside six weeks.'

'What from?'

'Cancers,' Harrison said, 'so many being born I can't even count the ways. And let me tell you none of them are natural.'

'You mean artificially induced?' Wolf said. 'What from?'

'Insulin-like growth factor-1,' Chika said.

The two men turned to look at her.

'Come again?' Wolf said.

'I believe the lady is speaking of a naturally occurring growth hormone in humans,' Harrison said. 'It's manufactured in the pituitary gland. I've heard of studies using a recombinant form to slow ageing in older people. You know, reduce body fat by replacing it with muscle mass present in younger people.'

'However,' Chika said, 'I believe this is the first time you've seen the effects of gene-induced anti-ageing.'

Now Harrison was goggling. 'Do you mean to tell me this man's DNA was somehow altered? But that's impossible.'

'Doctor, thirteen days ago Lawrence Moravia was a normal forty-eight-year-old male. Now, you tell me, what is he today?'

Harrison grunted. 'At the moment, there are only two things about him I can say with any certainty: he's dead and he's no longer normal.'

'What about his rouged cheeks?' Wolf said. 'Is there significance in that?'

Chika nodded. 'Yukio Mishima once wrote that "men must be the colour of cherry blossoms, even in death." I think he meant that though death robs men of life, it should not be allowed to take their colour – their machismo – as well. Applying rouge is part of the ritual of death.'

'So Moravia's death was premeditated.'

'Absolutely,' she said.

Outside, on the steps, he said, 'All right. You've shown me how Moravia was killed. But why was he killed?' This was a test. He knew the answer, of course, because Shipley had told him: Moravia was a spy and had been found out, but he wanted to hear Chika's version of it.

'Lawrence became an experiment. He was hooked up to a – well, just call it a biocomputer called the Oracle. The Oracle said it had the ability

216

to restructure human DNA in a living body. Moravia was going to be the living proof.'

Wolf watched her for some time. Who was lying to him, Chika or Shipley? Perhaps they both were. 'What happened?'

'I don't know. There is some kind of flaw in the Oracle's methodology. The anti-ageing process triggered multi-cell carcinomas. Moravia was murdered to keep the secret.'

'Why not just burn the body?' he said. 'That would have forestalled any full autopsy.'

'You must understand the Toshin Kuro Kosai,' Chika said. 'It is as I told you before. Burning is not an honourable way to die.'

'Then Moravia meant something to the Black Blade Society.'

'Yes. He was close to some in the inner circle.'

Close enough to be a spy? Wolf wondered. To Chika, he said, 'Okay, you've told me that Suma was sent to kill me and I have enough hard evidence to believe that. Why were you sent here?'

'To protect you,' Chika said. 'And also to bring you back to Japan. We need you there, Wolf, to stop the inexorable march of the Toshin Kuro Kosai. You see, up until now there was a kind of check on them. They have known for decades that they were dying out. No babies were being born with the sight – the altered DNA. And for decades they have had a programme in place to find a way to artificially induce this change in babies.'

'To create more of their own.'

'Exactly,' Chika said. 'And now, in the Oracle, we believe they have found that way.'

And yet, it was not enough. Though Yuji was closer to the Oracle than Hiroto could ever be, he was still maddeningly far from being in true sync with it, and this chasm frustrated him.

'Let's take it from the top one more time,' Yuji had said out loud, though there had been no one else in the room.

'THE TOP OF WHAT?' the Oracle had said in a pleasant synthesized voice that Hiroto claimed was female but which Yuji was sure was male.

'What you said before,' Yuji had said patiently. 'Repeat it, please.'

'THE DANGER IS IN LIFE,' the Oracle had said. 'NOT IN DEATH.'

'What does that mean?'

'THE MEANING IS IN WHAT I HAVE SAID.'

'You're making no sense.'

'MY SYNTAX IS FAULTLESS.'

Yuji had stared at the black cube for some time. He blew air out his nostrils in an attempt to vent some of his emotion. Then he had crossed to the steel alloy door, unlocked it, let Hana into the room.

'I'm doing this against my better judgement,' Yuji had said. 'It's only because you've badgered me until I can't think straight, and because I'm getting nowhere with it.'

'I understand,' Hana had said, in that tone of voice that so reminded him of his mother.

Hana had stood in front of the Oracle for a long time before she said, 'I was expecting something altogether different.' She had begun to laugh. 'I think I was expecting Robbie the Robot from *Forbidden Planet.*'

'The Oracle isn't a robot,' Yuji had said, 'at least not in any conventional sense.'

'It's more.'

'Quite a bit more, yes.' Yuji had watched her. 'Are you disappointed in how it looks?'

'No.' She stepped forward, put her hand along the side of the black cube. 'I can feel the warmth, like human heat.' She had turned to him. 'How do you currently communicate with it?'

'Hiroto writes, using the light pen; I speak with it.'

Then she had surprised him by saying, 'Is there no other way?'

'I don't understand you.'

'Both speech and the keyboard are inadequate for my purposes.'

'Then I guess we're stuck,' he had said with a profound sense of relief.

Hana had walked around the cube. He saw her staring at a jumble of equipment and his heart skipped a beat. She went over to the nest of minuscule optical fibres connected to advanced gallium arsenide computer chips on a circuit board the size of the end of her thumb. The fibres looped around one another, and now Hana was looking at what was attached to their other ends: five pressure-sensitive adhesive pads. Yuji held his breath as her forefinger stretched out to touch the pads one at a time.

'What is this device?'

Yuji, cold as ice, had not answered; contained in her question was the signal that she already knew. Instead, he had said, 'It doesn't work.'

She turned around. 'You've tried it?'

Yuji said nothing.

Her eyes were locked on his. 'I want you to plug me in.'

'Pardon me?' Yuji had said, 'I don't think I understood you.' But when she repeated what she had said he knew he had made no mistake. 'That's not possible.'

'Of course it's possible. Now you're sounding like Hiroto.' She could be so maddeningly self-assured.

'Okay, I admit it's possible – theoretically, anyway, but it's far too dangerous.'

'Didn't you imply that you had tried it?' She nodded at his silence. 'I see. Your fear is filling up this space.'

'I'd have to be crazy to do what you ask.'

'Nevertheless,' Hana had said, 'you'll do it. That's why I came here; it's why you allowed me to come, isn't it? Be honest with yourself. It's got to a point where Hiroto doesn't know what's going on inside the thing, and you don't understand what it's saying. You hook me up and I'll know it all.'

'Or you'll be dead,' Yuji said. 'We have no idea what hooking you into the Oracle will do to your system.'

With impeccable logic, Hana had said, 'I'll remind you that you have no idea of what my system is like.'

'All the more reason for caution.'

'The Oracle won't allow anything bad to happen to me.'

Yuji had stared at her. 'Now you're talking nonsense.'

'Nonsense? Speak to me. Tell me that you do not often think of the Oracle as something living.'

'I don't know what to think.'

'But I know what's in your mind,' Hana had said.

Yuji thought of Hana's enigmatic wavefronts. Had the Oracle 'spoken' to her in ways unfathomable to him? That was madness, that would mean she was right, that he did think of the Oracle as being a sentient being – and yet she seemed so certain, so unafraid.

She had said to him, 'This is why I am here, Yuji-san. My wavefronts allow me to "see" beyond the time/space continuum, to strike it as you would a stage set, to recognize it for what it really is: a comfortable scrim upon which human beings map out events that are otherwise inexplicable; because beyond it is the new order of the universe where time/gravity/space are all different aspects of one overriding principle of existence.' She watched with a certain satisfaction the dawning of perception on Yuji's face. When it was full-blown, she said, 'Now you understand why I must be connected to the Oracle, how I know it will not allow me to be harmed by the intensely powerful LAPID circuits. This is what the fever has done to me, how my own neural pathways work; this is how I think. The Oracle and I are somehow related, as if it is my half-brother.'

Yuji had put his hands to his temples. There was a throbbing there he could no longer control. For so long he had wanted to know the secret of how Hana had been changed, but now he knew he felt like turning and running as far from her as possible. With a shaking hand he steadied himself, took several deep breaths.

'I don't want to do this.'

Hana had come over to him, looked at him sadly. 'Poor Yuji. Your second sight has split you in two and now the factions make war one upon the other.'

'I'm afraid of the chaos inside me.'

She had placed her hand along the side of his face. 'Is that how you view your gift? The chaos is all around you. Yuji, listen, don't you hear the inchoate roar of the universe?'

'I hear nothing but silence.'

'Yes. Listen to the silence.'

His eyes were pleading. 'Hana, you must give up this mad idea.'

'Forbid me to come in contact with the Oracle.'

When he had said nothing she led him towards the Oracle. 'Your duty is clear,' she had said, 'as it was from the first. Come on now, do what you know you must.'

It had taken him just over an hour to make the preparations, and when he was done he had sat her in a chair next to the black cube. He put his hands in his lap; they were trembling. Then he felt Hana's strong capable fingers twining with his.

'Don't be afraid of yourself, Yuji.'

'Myself? I'm afraid of that damn thing.'

'No. You are afraid of that part of yourself you've put into it.'

Yuji took a deep breath, looked from Hana's pale intelligent face to the black intelligent facade of the Oracle. Now he understood that both were profound mysteries to him, and in a moment they would be linked in a previously unimaginable symbiosis. This was what Hana wanted most – and what he wanted most as well. Let it be done, then.

With his eyes on Hana's he had reached over, flicked on the switch . . .

'Our best bet is to get to Tokyo as quickly as possible,' Chika said. 'But with Suma looking for you we can't do it any normal way. I've got a friend who can help us.'

'That means abandoning my job – just walking out – '

'You still don't understand,' Chika said. 'You don't have a choice. Suma has seen to that.'

Wolf thought of Shipley then, and his decision to take on the job the spook had offered him. This was the direction he had to go in.

'Okay. But I've got to stop at the office, first. It's important.'

'Only for a minute,' Chika warned. 'We have no time to spare.'

They took Second Avenue all the way downtown to Chrystie Street, heading east on Canal to Allen, turning west of East Broadway. Wolf had told Chika that he needed to pick up his service revolver. That was the truth as far as it went, but he also wanted to see Squire Richards, clear up the mess they had both made before Breathard could use it as a sledgehammer against him.

'Tell me something,' Wolf said, 'how does the Black Blade Society mean to use the Oracle if its anti-ageing methodology is flawed?'

'They are so close all they're lacking is one small catalyst, and with that they're down to two possibilities.'

'You're right, then,' he said. 'There's very little time.' He made a mental note to tell Shipley about this ominous development when he had the time and the privacy.

The old theatre on the edge of Chinatown was steeped in blue shadow. Inside, Wolf noticed that the painters had finished their work and were gone.

'Christ, Lieutenant, am I glad to see you. I've been trying to phone you in East Hampton.'

Bobby, looking older, wiser, sadder following his encounter with the blue fireball in the Barrio alley, rushed up to Wolf upon his arrival. He also seemed somewhat nervous.

'I was on my way into the city. What's up?' Wolf, at his desk, was unlocking his lower drawer, to take out his service revolver, leather waist holster and extra ammunition.

'It's Squire,' Bobby said a little breathlessly. 'He was found dead this morning in front of his house on Tremont. Shot twice in the back of the head.'

'Jesus.' Wolf stood up, stared at Bobby. Could Squire have been stupid enough to pledge the money his brother owed? Could the loan sharks have caught up with him? He glanced at Chika. 'Suma or no Suma, I'd better get over there right away.'

'Wolf,' Chika said, softly urgently, 'we don't have time for this.'

Bobby, looking from Chika to Wolf, licked his lips. 'Anyway, I don't think that would be such a good idea, Lieutenant.'

'What are you talking about?'

Bobby shifted from one foot to the other. 'Well, see, we have one lead, Lieutenant,' he said. 'I just got off the horn with Rothstein in Ballistics. Tests confirm the slugs that killed Squire came from your gun.'

Wolf could hear Chika let out a little breath behind him. 'Oh, Christ,' he said. 'But, Bobby, you just saw me unlock my drawer and take out my gun.'

221

'Right, Lieutenant.'

'Which means I didn't have it all weekend.'

Bobby shook his head. 'All it means is that you didn't have it two minutes ago.'

'Bobby, this is a bullshit rap. I've been framed.'

'Lieutenant, I believe you. All the Werewolves do, but you gotta understand that ever since Junior was offed everybody's jumpy. Mood's the shits throughout the whole department. And, you know Breathard, gunning for us from the get-go. He's using your beef with Squire for everything it's worth now, rallying the black dudes from every precinct to work on the commish. We're off Squire's homicide – maybe conflict of interest, Breathard says. Also – ' and here Bobby took a deep breath '– there's an APB out for you, wanted for questioning.'

'Wolf, we *really* don't have time for this,' Chika said. 'This whole setup is beginning to stink. Let's get out of here now.'

'No, no, I can't walk out now,' Wolf said. 'I've got to fight this through. If I can get to the commish I can show Breathard up for the liar and racist he is.'

'If you stay, I guarantee you Suma will see you never get the chance,' Chika said.

Bobby licked his lips again; he didn't know who to look at first. 'She's right, Lieutenant, you gotta get outta here until we can get some real facts on who iced Squire. Rothstein cued me a team from Internal Affairs is on their way over here to impound your gun and bring you down to One Police Plaza.'

'No choice,' Chika said.

Wolf looked down at his gun, nodded. 'Bobby, I'd start by talking to Squire's brother,' he said, shoving the gun, ammo, paraphernalia into the pockets of his leather flight jacket. 'That's what the beef was about. Squire was shaking down La Mentira's owner to get bread his brother owed to the sharks.'

'Will do, Lieutenant.' Bobby held out his hand and Wolf took it. 'I'd watch my back,' Bobby said. 'Looks like Breathard's determined to have your ass one way or another.'

Once again in the Corvette, Wolf and Chika took the narrow crooked streets, among the oldest in the city, winding canyons adjacent to the stone heartland of financial America. They emerged on the east side of the tip of Manhattan in that no-man's-land beneath the FDR Drive.

Here the blacktop and ancient cobblestones had been layered with massed drifts of corrugated iron, beaten tin, thick cardboard, even ragged slabs of discarded wallboard. An entire city within a city had sprung up

222

here during the last number of years where the burgeoning rabble of New York hunted and haunted the adjacent streets.

'Breathard's putting me in a vice and squeezing as hard as he can,' Wolf said. 'And, damn it, I can't do anything about it!'

Cooking fires were already apparent; the stench of the detritus was appalling, the outpouring of humanity deprived of modern sanitation. There was a parking lot of chrome-plated shopping carts. Here and there Wolf could see a Con Ed manhole opened, wires snaking over the cobbles in spiderweb array; these wretched people stole everything else, why not electricity as well?

Business was also conducted here, though in Wolf's experience it was inevitably of an illicit nature. He remembered coming down here with Bobby Connor one summer night early in their tour together before the Werewolves had been born. Their eyes had watered so fiercely they were obliged to break out the gas masks in order not to gag. They had come in response to one of Wolf's snitches, who had informed them that a perp wanted for the brutal rape-murder of an elderly couple was hiding out there. That would have been the only reason to come here because the city of the hopeless was otherwise shunned by police and city officials alike who, finding the area ungovernable and lacking the funds necessary to patrol it, preferred to allow it to be a kind of quasi-municipality all its own with its own government and laws.

But instead of the perp, Wolf and Bobby had come upon two brothers – the principals in the transaction – slashing wildly at each other with gravity knives. They were surrounded by a widening circle of street people, urging one or the other brother on; touts circulating among the crowd were doing heavy business taking bets from the onlookers.

Wolf and Bobby separated, each taking one of the brothers. Wolf managed to get the knife away from his man, but the other one broke away from Bobby, slashed through the front of his gas mask. Bobby, momentarily blind, groped for his man who turned and lunged at his brother with manic fury. He plunged his blade into his brother's stomach in almost the same instant Wolf shot him in the chest.

Staring down at the two dead brothers through the plastic lenses of his gas mask, hearing the crowd moan and Bobby retching, overcome by the faecal filth of the city of the hopeless, Wolf had almost turned in his badge. What could be worse than this? he had thought. But that had only been the beginning of his plunge into the foul cauldron of New York's postmodern underbelly. Which had now led him back to the city of the damned.

They emerged from the black Corvette, which was getting plenty of attention from the ragged, noisome populace. An enormous battered chrome beatbox hanging by wires outside the entryway to a shanty was spewing out metallic, bass-heavy hip-hop music interspersed with raw and offensive rap lyrics. No one appeared to mind the noise this early; it was merely another urban sound, along with horns honking and sirens blaring. Flies buzzed in the encroaching sunlight, and the stench of garbage and unwashed humans made a noxious miasma that hovered over the place like a new strain of metropolitan smog.

Chika turned and said, 'Maybe you'd better stay near the car. How fit are you?'

'Fit enough.'

She gave him a quick look, went towards the entryway to the shanty. The music was now so loud that Wolf's eardrums hurt.

'Parker!' Chika was obliged to shout in order to be heard.

Two men emerged from the shanty. They were big, Hispanic, with tattooed arms like tree trunks. They were dressed in sweat-stained singlets and jeans, they carried cheap European handguns and long wicked carving knives at their waists, they were holding baseball bats into which razor blades had been sunk.

'Oh, it's you,' said the broader of the two. He had two teardrops tattooed beneath one eye, a sign that he had served two years in prison.

'I need to see him.'

The teardrop man grinned as he approached her; the other man stayed where he was, near the entrance to the shanty. '*You* need to but who the hell is *this* yo' bringin' 'roun' here?' He poked Wolf in the chest. 'You should know better than bring him turfside. He got that smell I don't want to know better.'

Wolf said nothing as he eyed the man circling him.

'I remember this cop stink here,' the teardrop man said with a sneer.

The baseball bat swung up millimetres from Wolf's face, and the teardrop man growled, 'Big shot cop, huh? You think you in the NYC of wide streets and fast spenders? Yo, you not on yo' home turf now, *maricone*. Take a close look at what's gonna rip yo' nose off.' He waggled the bat menacingly.

'Get that out of my face,' Wolf said.

The teardrop man laughed and spat on Wolf's shoes. 'Now for sure you gonna lose that nose.'

Wolf was aware of Chika, standing loose and quiescent, the other Hispanic bodyguard with his hand on the filthy tape-wrapped butt of his gun. He took what appeared to be a hesitant step backwards. The teardrop man followed him, thrusting his baseball bat towards the front of Wolf's face. He was grinning, already a bit loopy with the foretaste of bloody victory.

224

Wolf reached out and, in a blur, grasped the teardrop man's right arm just behind the elbow, pulling it sharply forward into his own backward momentum. As the teardrop man came towards him, momentarily off-balance, Wolf chopped down once with the edge of his hand in a vicious kite at the juncture of the teardrop man's collarbone. He heard the snap of the bone breaking even as he was smashing the heel of his hand into the teardrop man's sternum.

Wolf let go, and the Hispanic collapsed, moaning. He toppled all the way over as he grabbed at his shoulder. The other Hispanic had his gun drawn, but there was movement from inside the shanty and, in a moment, a thin white man with a long, ratty beard appeared in the entryway. Parker.

Wolf stared at him. Clean him up, shave him, put him in a Brooks Brothers suit and he would look right at home a half a mile away on Wall Street.

'We need to talk, Parker,' Chika said.

Parker was staring fixedly at Wolf. He had glanced, once, at the man writhing on the ground. 'Paco,' he said to the Hispanic, 'clean up this mess.'

'He's a friend,' Chika said.

Parker wrinkled his nose. 'Cop smell stinks,' he drawled in an exaggerated Southern accent.

'Cop in another life,' Wolf said.

'He's a friend,' Chika repeated.

Parker stood beneath the chrome beatbox as if it were some form of modern talisman to ward off evil. He was wearing a pair of black-and-purple striped cyclist's skintight mylar shorts and a day-glo lime green cutoff shirt that had SURF VOODOO stencilled across front and back.

'Privacy,' Parker said. 'Let's go inside.'

Parker might be thin but Wolf could see the wiry musculature moving as he reached into a garbage can fire, removing a smouldering stick, using its end to light a cigarette on the way into his house.

It was close inside, smelling of smoke and cabbage and human habitation. There were photos on the wall, colour glossies ripped from the magazines of the rich: shots of exotic motor cars, yachts, private jets, glittering stuccoed mansions in Palm Beach and magnificent white cedar estates in East Hampton. All were darkened by the soot of the reality of this place.

There was old sisal on the concrete, mismatched lamps on crates. An alcove for a minuscule kitchen had been hammered out of a sheet of corrugated tin and, on the other side, an old colourless blanket covered a doorway to other rooms.

225

Parker went to an ancient wheezing refrigerator, took out three beers, handed one each to Chika and Wolf, then folded himself into an upholstered easy chair. A soft cloud of dust rose and, as if exhausted by that modest flight, settled back almost immediately. Wolf and Chika sat on simple cane chairs, broken and repaired many times.

Chika said, 'We need to get out of here – city, state, country.'

That made Parker grin. 'You mean this piece of shit cop is on the run? Now that makes my day.'

'Suma is here,' Chika said simply. 'He's going to try to stop us.'

Parker thought about that for some time. 'Suma will come after anyone who helps you,' he said at last.

'If we get lost fast enough, we won't give him the time,' Chika said. 'It's us he wants.'

Parker grinned. He had some metal teeth. 'You're some piece of work. I can see why you scare a lot of guys shitless.' He flicked what was left of his cigarette into an empty Contadina stewed tomato can. 'I'll see what I can do.'

He got up, pushed through the old blanket into another room.

Chika went over to the shanty's door, took a look outside. She hadn't touched her beer.

'What would you have done if I hadn't broken that ratman's collarbone?' Wolf asked her.

'I didn't need to do a thing,' Chika said.

'Did you see that particular future?'

'Perhaps I have more faith in you than you do in me.'

Through the doorway they could see life in the city of the damned grind on around them. Life here was like life in any third world country, he supposed. Only who would have thought it would come here.

Wolf, aware of her vigilance, said, 'You looking for something in particular?'

'No.' Chika shook her head, but she continued to scan the immediate environment.

Wolf, watching a naked child defecate on a pile of garbage, recalled reading a city Health Services report – quickly suppressed by the mayor's office – that found the number of colonies of pathogenic micro-organisms like diplococcus, staph, amoeba and salmonella per cubic metre here to be completely off the measurement scale.

'You know I can't leave yet.'

'That would be very foolish,' she said. 'Suma will eat you for breakfast. Do what I tell you and I think I can keep you alive.'

'You don't understand. I'm responsible for Squire's death.'

'You don't know that.'

226

'He was one of my men. He was in trouble. So much trouble that his pride wouldn't let him come to me for help, so much trouble his pride led him down a dark, dangerous path. And I was part of that path.' He looked at her. 'Or can't you understand pride; my aikido *sensei* didn't.'

'Pride is a Confucian sin,' Chika said. 'A dark and dangerous sin.'

Ten minutes later Parker reappeared from the depths of the shanty. He was carrying a professional Polaroid camera. He took their pictures, head shots, then disappeared, silent and secretive behind his colourless rug.

When he reappeared, it was with a pair of British passports. Handing them over to Chika, he said, 'They'll pass muster, don't you worry.' He rolled a toothpick around his mouth as he spoke. His breath stank of catfood.

'Thanks,' Chika said, putting them away in an inside pocket.

Parker was staring hard at Wolf.

'Relax,' Chika said. 'I told you he's okay.'

Parker grumbled, but his face softened as he heard a little cry and, bending slightly, he scooped up a five-year-old girl who had hurtled towards him. 'Cathy,' he murmured, scrunching her face into the crook of his neck then, to her cries of 'Please, Daddy!', he hung her by her ankles. Her giggles emanated from a mouth hidden by her long blonde hair. Parker shook her a little, and she screeched in delighted mock-fright.

'Why do you endure this hell?' Wolf asked, indicating the forest of stinking shanties.

'Because life is always preferable to death,' Parker said. He shook Cathy a bit more as one would a shaker whose salt crystals have stuck together. 'I see by the look on your face you don't believe me. But I suppose you would have to be in my shoes in order to fully understand.' He pulled Cathy right side up, held her in his elbow as he pushed her hair back off her forehead. Her face was beet red. She was a pretty girl and, like many children her age, she exuded a sense of life that was irresistible. She stuck her tongue out at Wolf and Parker laughed.

'Seven years ago I was a hot investment broker in a hot field: leveraged buyouts,' he said. 'But then the proverbial shit hit the fax, the bottom dropped out of the market, and all of a sudden Wall Street was awash in jobs. You'd go in in the morning and your buddies who just months before had been so busy at wild trading they'd often stay at the office all night, were doing the *Times* crossword puzzle. It was incredible. For hours at a time the phones didn't ring. The silence was eerie.'

Parker shifted the squirming Cathy from one arm to another. 'Then, of course, we all became expendable. Bottom lines had to be slashed, whole departments were disbanded within a day, and there were no jobs

227

to be found anywhere. My overhead was wicked. I sold my BMW, my Rolex watch, then was forced to sell my co-op at Battery Park City for a pathetically small amount. The only good thing about being broke was I was no longer required to pay my ex-wife alimony, but she sent her lawyers nosing around just to make sure I was really destitute. When I asked her for a loan, she laughed in my face.

'For a while I took on odd jobs, you know, washing dishes, waiting tables, late night stuff that no one else wanted. But after I'd been mugged a second time I'd had enough of being a citizen of New York City, of being on the right side of the law.

'Waiting in the emergency room of a city hospital, bleeding and in pain, watching orderlies rushing gurneys past me filled with victims of gunshot wounds I wondered whether I was in hell. This was not the New York City I had ever dreamed about when I was a kid growing up in Chicago. I realized I'd have to cross over the line I had been taught never to cross.

'I came here because it was my only chance to survive – and if there is one lesson I learned here it's that deprivation toughens you. Human beings can survive just about anything if they set their mind to it; that's something I never would have believed five years ago.'

He looked down at the child he held. 'And now I have Cathy. Her mother died of a heroin overdose and her father was knifed to death for stealing a can of baked beans from a neighbour's shanty.' He made an inarticulate sound. 'You know it's funny, all the time I was married, all the time I worked on the Street handling clients' accounts totalling millions of dollars I had no sense of what it really meant to be responsible. Bringing up Cathy has taught me that, so I often think it's all been for the best.' He gave a self-deprecating laugh. 'Of course that's how I have to think or else I'd go nuts, no doubt about it. But belief is a funny thing, so fragile in some circumstances, so absolutely unshakable in others.' He kissed Cathy on the top of her head as he hugged her to him. 'I suppose you'll laugh, but I read Jung now – books I've stolen from the Public Library, which is okay since no one goes there nowadays anyway – and think about how in the midst of this colossal social upheaval everything remains essentially the same. There's a peculiar kind of comfort in that that I'm anxious to teach Cathy.' He shrugged. 'And who knows, cop, maybe it's your life not mine that's the hell.'

Wolf listened to this astonishing history with an acute kind of attention. He could see now that his father, oddly like Parker, had been far too absorbed in the trappings of his profession. For Peter Matheson, being someone was all-important. It was why he had joined the Texas Rangers, why he had tried to change them back into the heroes of yesteryear, why

228

he had felt compelled to leave his wife and son, the mediocrity of his life, for primitive Australia, where he had another chance to again be somebody, become the hero he had dreamed of being, and failed.

'Daddy?'

'Shhh, Cathy,' Parker said gently but firmly.

'But, I – '

'No more hanging now, honey.'

The girl was squirming in his arms and he put her down. She immediately burst out crying, and he picked her up again.

'Cathy, what is it?'

Wolf could see that she was trembling. Her face had gone pale, and she had begun to wail. She was clearly terrified. Parker was turning her over, trying to peer into her pinched face.

'She feels hot,' he said, 'but she's as dry as a bone. And she's shaking like a leaf.'

'Parker, put her down.'

Wolf could hear the sudden terror in Chika's voice, but Parker was too preoccupied with his daughter's increasing distress to listen.

'Parker,' Chika said urgently, as she tried to prise his arms open without hurting the child, 'put her down now.'

'She's sick,' Parker insisted. 'I'm not going to – '

'You don't understand what's happening, the terrible danger – '

In that instant, the child started to glow. Her eyes opened wide, the irises dilated, and she began to moan in terror. The first of the blue flames flickered at her fingertips. Then it snaked up along her arms. Cathy screamed as, with a violent *whoosh!*, she burst into flames.

'Christ almighty!' Parker shouted, but still his disbelieving mind wouldn't let her go.

It was a moment akin to the aftermath of being shot. The body goes down, you feel nothing, but your mind seems frozen in the last instant of normality, before the unthinkable ripped asunder time and space, making reality unreal.

Suma had found them!

Wolf could already smell the putrid scent of burning hair and flesh. Cathy's face was distorted by fear and something else – a horror – he could not name.

He had to do something to help the child. He bent, picked up the tattered remnant of a blanket, but when he rose he found that he could not move. He could scarcely breathe. It was if a fist had clamped around his heart, weakening his pulse as if he were on his deathbed. His mind jumped back to the night on Amanda's rooftop, his encounter with the shadowed force, his inability to move or breathe. The two moments

229

seemed identical to him, and cold sweat broke out at his hairline and he had to force himself back from the brink of terror as he felt again the sensation of helplessness as he was launched through the air, crashing down into the skylight, splintering consciousness . . .

He blinked, the pain in his chest was a hard cold stone he could not abate.

With an unnatural calm, Chika said to Parker, 'Put Cathy down. Let her go; it's the only chance to save her.'

Parker, weeping uncontrollably, at last did as she said. His shirt had been burned off his chest and, here and there, smoke drifted from him. His hands and forearms were black with human charcoal. He did not care; he was staring at his daughter who lay on the cobbles, writhing and screaming as the flames continued to consume her.

Now Wolf felt a ripple, something akin to the heat distortion one sees rising off a road in summer. Something cool was in the air, and an instant's remembered darkness like a momentary rift in the air between him and Chika. It seemed to him as if something unseen was breathing at his side. The pain abated, freeing him. There was a vague sense of familiarity and he turned.

It might have been a trick of the muted dusty light but for an instant he could have sworn he saw Chika's eyes change colour, brightening until tiny crescents of luminous green rimmed her irises. Then he blinked, stared into her dark, depthless eyes, and heard Parker gasp. He turned to see the flames dying on Cathy's stomach.

Parker was kneeling beside her, rocking and crooning wordlessly.

Wolf tore out of the shanty, his service revolver drawn.

'Wolf!'

The terror in Chika's voice made him shiver, but he would not stop, could not, the image of the little girl bursting into flame, her flesh crisping, blood running like jelly, would not let him rest.

Darkness like the ripple of an eel in coral at the periphery of his vision, and he veered to the right, pushing aside wide-eyed people, running parallel to the elevated highway, weaving in and out of the shanties, past oily fires in wire mesh garbage cans, leaping over cables snaked into open manhole covers, tapping into the city's electricity and water supplies, veering around yellow-eyed dogs, as feral as wolves.

He emerged from the city of the damned to find himself on cobbles stained and pitted by two hundred years of use. He was in a district of old warehouses, waiting like old pensioners for the wrecking ball to come calling, reduce them again to the dust from whence they came.

A door, small, scarred, creaking, swung back and forth, its broken padlock banging like a tympani in the wind. Wolf approached it cautiously, side on, using whenever he could the massive iron supports of the highway overhead. Took stock: his left leg ached a little but he was not out of breath. So far, so good.

He reached the door, pulled it open, stepped quickly out of the shadowy winter light into red semi-darkness. The smells of nesting rats, rotting sawdust, the faint reek of fish, old, dried, seeming to have emerged like a ghost from another era, assaulted him.

He knew he had to be extremely careful now; there was a power in here he was certain could kill him. Just as he was certain the force that had gripped him twice could have killed him. Why hadn't it? He shuddered when he thought of Cathy bursting into flame.

Chika had said: *'The power when it is manifested is like a shadow, a living presence that can be sensed, even perhaps seen by some in the corners of their vision. And, in this highly-charged state, the power can do many things. It can, for instance, project itself like an unseen fist, causing inanimate objects to move; it can cause pain and even death in others.'*

He shivered inwardly at a recognition that had about it the substance of *déjà vu*. Wasn't this animate shadow what he had felt back there at Parker's, up on the rooftop? Something cool in the air, an instant's darkness like a momentary rift in the air. And something unseen breathing at his side.

He stayed in the heaviest shadow until his eyes adjusted. Gradually, his surroundings appeared. He was in what appeared to be a front office, small, shabby, in extreme disrepair. He went through a glass-fronted door at the back, found himself facing the warehouse proper: a massive space, filthy with soot, beyond which were apparently small storerooms for perishables. Windows, so high up they appeared tiny, allowed individual shafts of light to break through the walls, and, lower, he could see bare bulbs shedding a ruddy light like pools of blood.

To his left, a steel skeleton set of stairs ran steeply up to a narrow girdered catwalk that ran the length of the main room. Wolf went up this, figuring to get a better view of anyone afoot down below.

He took the narrow stairs three at a time, feeling a slight pulling along the length of the wound in his left leg, but no pain at all. In fact, it felt good to stretch the muscles with such strenuous exercise. He felt a sudden surge of adrenaline as he reached the top. He had made more noise than he had cared to going up so he paused, took off his shoes, stuffed them in his jacket pockets. He moved quickly and silently, wondering with a tiny prickle of his scalp whether these people – Suma and his ilk – could feel his presence even in utter darkness and silence.

In the middle of the catwalk he lay down, presenting less of a target, swept the warehouse with his eyes. Saw movement at the far end, and was up, racing along the catwalk to the end, down a second flight of steep stairs.

This gave out onto a warren of small caged rooms filled, though the main part of the warehouse had the appearance of being abandoned, with metal boxes, heavy-sided crates and sacks of cement. Wolf could see something moving furtively in the third caged room, then, as he took a step forward, disappear into the shadows.

He opened the wire door, noting in the red light a padlock that had been jemmied open. A very narrow aisle down the centre of each cage led to the door to the following room. Wolf pushed forward, his torso pressed sideways to present his right side first, gun at the ready. On either side, the contents of the cages, as dense and looming as the sheer rock face of an alp, rose high over his head. Through a small gap as he passed into the second cage he could see electrical cables exposed like the veins in an emaciated wrist, pulled through the wire walls of the cages. Bare light bulbs burned like miniature suns, too old or remote to matter any longer.

The third cage presented itself, and Wolf went through the wire door. He took one step at a time on the rough filthy concrete floor. He looked up and, like a diver at the bottom of a treacherous trench, saw above him the beckoning warmth of distant sunlight. He was halfway along the narrow aisle when an enormous pyramid of PVC pipes began to sigh and stir. Great creakings and groanings filled the air as if from long slumbering spirits, wrathful at being awakened.

He tried to hurry on, but the pipes, moving like the hair of Medusa, flailed malignantly across his path. Like mythical serpents called up from the earth, they loomed, white and sightless, over him. He turned, seeking to retreat, but he was already hemmed in, another phalanx of pipes herding him against the opposing pile of sacks of concrete.

Now he was bent painfully backwards, the pipes curling and slithering, jammed against his chest, and he twisted, threw some of the sacks of concrete aside to make a niche for himself. In the confined space he was aware of the labouring of his breath, the accelerated beat of his heart, the heat coming off him in waves. The eerily questing pipes found him in his tiny niche, battering him, and he cast around for anything he could use as a wedge to impede even temporarily their movement, but there was nothing.

A pipe appeared through the others, darting violently, its end slamming into his shoulder, and he squirmed backwards, thrashing heavy sacks this way and that. This slowed the pipes momentarily. But, in the end, what good would it do, he'd come up against the wall of the cage, be crushed against that.

He couldn't even use his gun in these confined quarters. In fact, he was forced to slide the weapon into its holster at the small of his back, use both hands to prise the sacks away from him, moving further and further backwards while the pipes snaked and twined around him.

At last, he had reached the cage wall. The wire was far too thick for him to even contemplate getting through it. He turned back. The second vanguard of pipes was upon him, pinning him to the steel mesh like the fingers of an ogre's hand. Then they stopped. He reached up, tried to shove the top ones out of the way, but he could not budge them.

That was when he felt the heat, at first a soft glow taking the chill out of the air, then a fire, as fierce and unrelenting as an open oven. He could smell smoke, and saw to his horror that the pipe nearest his head was beginning to smoulder. Good God, he thought, Suma is projecting his sight; he'll do to me what he did to Cathy and Arquillo.

He heard the first crackle of flame, and then, with a whoosh, the flames shot through the pipe beside his right foot. One after another, the pipes began to catch, until a circle roughly the size of his torso was burning. Medusa's hair on fire. And at its centre the ghost of an undulation like the wake of a giant eel: Suma summoning his psychic energy.

Wolf could no longer doubt anything Chika had said regarding the Black Blade Society. Not that this knowledge would do him any good; in a moment, he would be nothing more than roasted meat.

Unable to move, Wolf concentrated. Suma might be masked from him the majority of the time, but apparently when he was projecting his sight, Wolf could pick him up. He could feel the undulations emanating outward, the psychic equivalent of the movement of a feeding fish, and, at the core of him, he travelled those ripples inward until he arrived at the point where Suma must be standing on the other side of the mare's nest of pipes, secreted in a crevice, pouring out his poison.

The fire was crackling and roiling, generating a heavy oily stench that clogged Wolf's nose, coated his throat. At this rate, there was a good chance he would asphyxiate before he burned to death.

He fixed his concentration, feeling in the velvet darkness of the red light for substance, until he was certain he knew just where Suma was. He snaked his hand behind him, drew his gun. But, try as he might, he could find no way to fire without fear of a ricochet taking his own head off. He was certain he had Suma pinpointed, but without a weapon he was helpless.

He breathed tidally, the sweat running freely on him as the flames writhed ever closer. The air scorched the inside of his mouth and his eyes were tearing badly. The buildup of carbon dioxide as the fire fed on

233

oxygen was nearing the upper edge of his tolerance. An abrupt inhalation of smoke set off a spasm of coughing.

He holstered his gun, and his hand brushed against something. He twisted his head, saw the electrical cables affixed to the wire mesh. He turned his shoulders, took hold of the cables with both hands, wrenched with all his might until he pulled them free of the wall. Then he doubled them, fed them into the flames.

Almost instantly, the insulation melted and, in a welter of sparks, the cables were severed, exposing the live wires within. Wolf bent to his task, shoving the cables, live end first, through the interstices between the pipes.

He was pressed back against the cage wall as he did this in order to avoid the encroaching fire, but he could already feel his hands too close, and turned to pull his jacket sleeves down, between his skin and the fire.

Concentrate. Feel the ripples of movement, the projection of force, follow it backwards, feed the cable in, close now, very close, dropping into the darkness like a parachutist, the darkness curling and bending, breathing like a monstrous beast. Snuffling as if becoming abruptly aware of him, no, not him, but the crackling energy carried in the maimed cable, and, *now!*, thrust it there, in the centre, where the darkness pooled like ink in a well, sparks flashing behind the stacks of flaming PVC, a screaming in his mind, a primitive flash of rage, a hot jolt as if he himself had touched the electricity.

Then he had disengaged his mind, saw the flames dying down, and then the heavy rain falling, released by the intense heat activating the automatic sprinkler system running along the ceiling of the warehouse.

Wolf reached out, swung a pipe – movable now that the psychic energy was gone – away from him, then another and another, the water in his eyes, drenching him, stifling the thick smoke, running in ashy streams along the concrete floor.

At last, he climbed through a space he had made in the ruined pyramid of pipes, made his way to the opposite side. He had expected to find Suma's body lying on the floor, but there was nothing.

No, not nothing, after all.

He bent down, picked up what appeared to be some kind of miniature blade. He wiped the black ash off its flank, turned it over, gleaming in his palm, water spinning off it. Then he put it into his pocket, slipped his shoes on, and made his way back to the open door.

Outside, he took several deep breaths, coughed again, clearing his lungs. He felt lightheaded, and bent over. Breathe, he ordered himself. Breathe! Oh, but, Christ, that had been close.

He stood up, went over to sit on one of the massive iron tie-ups spaced along the rotting timbers of the docks. He licked his lips, a drop of sweat dissolving on his tongue . . .

The young Wolf tastes the salt of his own sweat. He is not asleep, although his mind, wiping itself clean, protecting itself, will be convinced that it slept through this.

He is looking through the flap of White Bow's tepee. He sees the profile of his grandfather's face and, above it, the ladder he has made from hemp, sinew and White Bow's handmade arrows. He sees his mother on her haunches at White Bow's side. Her hand is on his arm, and it seems clear that she is speaking to him, though it is possible that she is reciting a prayer or incantation. Perhaps she is holding the sum of his dreams in her lap.

Behind him, he can hear the slight stirring of the assembled, massed on the plain. The sun has almost set, not even a whisper of wind stirs the dry grasses. Above, the sky is a shade of blue so pellucid it brings tears to the eyes. Then, one last shaft of blood-red sunlight enters the tepee and, for a moment, White Bow's skin is as dark and ruddy as it ever was in his youth.

As Wolf watches, the sun is submerged by the mountaintops, and the light turns from blood-red to opalescent. As it slips away, the waxy pallor returns to White Bow's face. Wolf begins to tremble and, in his mind, he hears a reverberation, the sound one hears when the arrow is loosed and the tension comes off the bowstring.

Now this is the strange part, the moment which Wolf's mind will be unwilling to remember, the instant brought abruptly to the surface by his brush with a form of death familiar to his unconscious: time seems to stand still. The birds have ceased to sing, the crickets to chirp, the flies to buzz, the darkness to fall.

In this moment, nothing moves. And yet Wolf's spirit is drawn out of his body as if by an undertow. He flies in the manner described to him by his mother, in the metaphysical world of his shaman grandfather.

Inside the tepee, he sees his mother caught between breaths, her heart stilled and waiting again in this magical interstice to once again pump. In this incorporeal state, he sees his grandfather for what he really is: a skeleton, topped by a grinning skull. Everything else is gone, and Wolf knows he is dead. He is so terrified that for a moment he believes that he himself will die, and he tries to turn away, to run from the interior, but he cannot. Like a fly caught in a spiderweb, he is stranded here on the shore of a strange and alien land.

Then he 'hears' in his mind, his grandfather's voice bidding him to

235

act. He takes up his grandfather's magnificent bow and, placing one last arrow to it, raises it towards the hole in the tepee.

He draws the bow back to its limit and, at that moment, sees White Bow, strong and robust, climbing the ladder-bridge he has made for him. His grandfather does not look at him; he is intent on his climb, which is dangerous because of the sharpness of the arrowheads.

At the top of the ladder, he raises his right arm, hand outward, and Wolf looses the arrow. Up, up, up it shoots and, as it reaches White Bow, he reaches out, grabs the shaft and is pulled upward with it.

Wolf moves so that he is directly beneath the hole. Into the indigo sky his grandfather soars like the hawk of his story, rising higher and higher, until he disappears into the vault of heaven.

At that instant, the great bow vanishes, and Wolf hears in his mind his grandfather's voice: *'Strait is the bridge and narrow is the path that leads to life, and few are those that travel it.'*

'Wolf?'

He blinked, looked up into Chika's concerned face.

'Are you all right?'

He wondered why she was asking him that until he realized he was shaking and crying. He thought of White Bow, a man who had so much wanted his grandson to follow the metaphysical path he had taken, who had looked into his grandson's eyes and had seen the spark of the power that resided in him. *'You were able to make the journey not because of me, but because of what dwells within you,'* White Bow had told him. *'Learn what is inside you, Wolf. You will have to use it one day.'* So he had known what was to come, had seen this future – *and Wolf had known this*, but that knowledge was too much for his young mind to hold, too frightening to contemplate. So it had turned itself off, convincing him that he had fallen asleep at the moment of his grandfather's death.

'That was stupid to go after Suma like that,' Chika said. 'On your own, without me, he might have killed you.'

Wolf stared at her as if he had not heard a word she had said. The chills were gone, shaken off like the aftermath of a nightmare.

He rose, feeling the blood rushing through him – and more, so much more. 'I understand,' he said at last.

'Understand what?'

'Why you're here, why the Black Blade Society wants to track me down. Everything.'

NINE

Washington/Tokyo

Whenever Thornburg Conrad III went to the Green Branches Clinic on the outskirts of Arlington, Virginia, he took his wife Tiffany with him.

Green Branches was the one place that evoked in Thornburg a sense of time and purpose. It had become the focus of what remained of his life, and it was this awareness of fragments slipping inexorably through his fingers that lent a note of urgency to his visits. These occurred three times a week and were a matter of utmost secrecy, although had anyone been witness to the trips they would naturally have assumed that Thornburg at his advanced age and with his active lifestyle required a good deal of electronic monitoring. They would not, in one sense, be far wrong.

However, what the patient was being monitored for was not arteriosclerosis, chronic high blood pressure, gout, oedema or any of the other myriad ills which routinely plagued the elderly. When the researchers ran the EKG or EEG what they were looking for was not signs of advancing age but markers that would indicate just the opposite.

The fact was that Thornburg owned the Green Branches Clinic. He had bought it some fifteen years ago when it had been an under-funded cancer research centre struggling along on meagre handouts from the federal government and any other agency it could convince to cough up capital. Unfortunately its director was not as able a politician as he perhaps needed to be and the clinic fell on hard times.

When Thornburg bought it he personally reviewed the dossiers of every researcher and technician employed there. He decided who should stay and who should go, then he set about hiring the people most skilled in the biotech sciences such as endocrinology, gerontology and genetics to create a full complement of research physicians. Now Green Branches had but one aim: to extend the lifespan of Thornburg Conrad III.

To that end Thornburg spared no expense. But he was no patsy for every harebrained scheme for eternal youth. He was exceedingly knowledgeable in all the biotech sciences and he carefully weeded the wheat from the chaff, the result being that the team he had put together at Green Branches was on the cutting edge of the dawning field of biolife sciences.

For a time the team had been extremely excited about their preliminary findings regarding the laboratory-synthesized human growth hormone, insulin-like growth factor-1. This recombinant complex protein seemed to restore much of the muscle tone and organ health to elderly people that age had begun to seriously deteriorate. Initially, it appeared that a mere six months' treatment with the synthetic hormone could actually turn back the subject's inner clock an astounding twenty years.

When the side effects began to emerge: heart attacks, diabetes, kidney failure, even a bizarre and disfiguring enlargement of the subjects' hands and face the Green Branches team altered the way in which they manufactured the insulin-like growth factor-1. All that did was delay the advent of the side effects.

Now as Thornburg entered the cool, dim green-glass and marble interior of the clinic he smelled again the odour of death. The sweet-sickly scent was all-pervasive, cloying, making the air as heavy as that of an industrial city. The place stank of the battlefield or the abattoir.

Thornburg saw Tiffany's perfect nostrils flare, her perfect breasts rise sharply as she inhaled.

'I had a dream about this place last night,' she said. 'Do you know I always dream about it the night before we come. What do you think that means?'

'I'm sure I have no idea,' Thornburg said, nodding to the uniformed guards who sat behind a high intimidating blackwood podium. They knew him by sight not only because he came here often but because he had hired them as he had done with every employee of the clinic. 'What was the dream?'

'I was naked,' Tiffany said. 'I'm always naked when I dream of this place. Two men in white coats injected me with a serum and pretty soon I had turned into a frog – a green frog croaking on a huge lilypad.'

'Is that it?' The extreme left-hand elevator doors opened automatically to their presence and Thornburg, taking Tiffany's arm, guided her into the elevator. The doors closed and, without Thornburg having to press a button, the elevator descended the equivalent of three storeys into the bedrock of Virginia.

'No,' Tiffany said. 'You were there, too, a little pink-skinned, bandy-legged boy. I saw you and my tongue came out, you know, the long thin kind frogs have, and I caught a mosquito and ate it. It was full of blood and I knew it had just bitten you, that I was swallowing your blood and I wondered whether that made me a carnivore.' Tiffany was a devout vegetarian. 'It wasn't a very pleasant dream. But then my dreams of this place never are.'

'I'm sorry,' Thornburg said, patting her perfect hand, 'but this will be over before you know it.' He smiled as a white-smocked individual came into view. 'Ah, Dr Shepherd, on time as always.'

Dr Shepherd laughed. She was a willowy woman with too much frosted hair and too little makeup. Her pale eyes, behind her stylish glasses, had the fact-obsessed look of the clinician. It appeared she had been born observant. 'Now, Mr Conrad, you know security alerts us the moment you pull up. We're always prepared for you. And our patient.' She turned to Thornburg's wife. 'And how are we feeling today, Tiffany?'

'Fine, I guess.'

'No abdominal pains, chest palpitations, constipation? You're urinating normally?'

'Just like always.'

'Excellent.' Dr Shepherd put her arm around Tiffany Conrad. 'Let's just go in here and take a good long look at you, okay?'

'I won't turn into a frog or anything?' Tiffany said. 'I dreamed I was a frog and swallowed blood. Human blood.'

'I wouldn't worry about any of that,' Dr Shepherd said. 'All it means is that you're still adjusting to the diet we've put you on. You used to eat quite a bit of meat, you know.'

'I did? But that's impossible. I can't stand meat of any kind.'

Dr Shepherd looked over her shoulder at Thornburg as she settled Tiffany on a white-paper-coated examining table. 'Take off your clothes for me, Tiffany.'

'Yes, Doctor.'

Tiffany did as she was told, removing one article of clothing at a time, folding each one neatly until they made a pile on a side chair. Then, without being prompted, she lay down on the table.

Dr Shepherd took a pinch of the flesh of her inner thigh between thumb and forefinger, rolled it gently back and forth. 'Excellent colour, tone; the lack of fat is impressive.' She opened a manila-bound file, began making notes with a ball-point pen as she continued her thorough examination. She drew blood, labelled three test tubes, sealed them, put them in a metal rack, did some more work that Thornburg was not familiar with. When she was done, she smiled warmly at Tiffany, said softly to Thornburg, 'May I see you outside?'

Dr Shepherd led him wordlessly across the corridor, pushed open a door into one of three dozen labs within the Green Branches complex. She went over to a bank of sophisticated computers, activated a program

239

and Thornburg saw a sequence of complex coloured patterns appear on the terminal screen. They began to move, ever so slowly, as if he were looking at the real thing instead of an incredibly complex computer-generated model.

She turned to him. 'We have been concerned with anaemia because of her low red-blood count, but I can see she's recovering from that nicely.'

Thornburg's business was reading people, so he knew that there was more but that Dr Shepherd was reluctant to go on. 'Let's have it all, Doctor. I'm not here to be coddled or lied to.'

'Of course not.' She nodded. 'Of late, your wife's white-cell count has been somewhat elevated. By itself, that's not normally a cause for undue concern.' Did all doctors have to qualify every statement they made? he wondered. 'In fact, we're hoping that's evidence only of a mild infection.'

'But you don't know for certain.'

Dr Shepherd's head came up. 'No, Mr Conrad, we do not. You must understand that this is, ah, virgin territory for all of us. And considering the end results of the previous experi – '

Thornburg took a step towards her. 'And you must understand that time is of the essence.'

'Yes, I fully – '

'Understand?' He snorted derisively. 'Spare me the medical palliatives. So much poppycock. Doctor, it has long been my desire to discover an elixir that will work on me like the wine in the Holy Grail. And, up to now, what have we found? Just like in legend the wine that gives life also takes it. Dead end.' He thought of Tiffany, whose perfect sun-darkened skin shimmered beneath a laminate of lotion. 'Still, I haven't given up. At my age a man must have his magnificent obsession.' He looked shrewdly at Dr Shepherd. 'I may be old but I'm not demented, you'd be wise to remember that.'

'Yes, sir.' She took a deep breath, turned back to the computer screen. 'I'd like to direct your attention to this model.'

Thornburg knew, more or less, what he was looking at. In fact, he had personally ordered the Green Branches staff to begin work on rational drug design. This meant, instead of going through the trial and error of laboratory breeding to create a new drug, you first ascertained the molecular structure of the disease or problem within the body you needed to attack, then you went to a specially-designed computer that recreated this structure – complete with all its idiosyncrasies – so that you could design a specific inhibitor which would bind with the problem molecule, rendering it harmless.

240

In this instance, the Green Branches researchers needed to create a substance that would have a specific effect on the human body. In a sense, they were lucky in having access to insulin-like growth factor-1. Since even the most powerful electron microscope was unable to see small enough to reveal molecular structure, the researchers had discovered a method to grow the hormone in crystalline form. By bombarding it with concentrated X-rays they were able to manufacture a diffracted image of the molecular structure, which was fed into the computer.

What they found astounded them. The hormone appeared to contain 'spaces' at set intervals that the scientists were convinced had once contained another – as yet unknown – element. In other words, they believed that the insulin-like growth factor-1 taken from a selection of human beings was incomplete. Somehow, over the passage of time, the hormone had changed just as man himself had. Their task was to find the missing piece.

'Here is a representation of the enzyme package we felt had the most potential, and which we have been using on your wife.' Dr Shepherd's fingers flew over the keypad and Thornburg saw a yellow lozenge seem to dock in one of the 'spaces' in the purple, red and cyan network of the insulin-like growth factor-1 hormone.

'You see, a perfect fit,' Dr Shepherd said. 'And the enzyme package took to the hormone as if magnetized.' She stood up. 'And, in a sense it's working. We know it's working and so do you because you've seen the very dramatic changes in your wife.' She jammed her hands in her pockets and sighed. 'Unfortunately, we believe we've come back to the same problem that has been plaguing us from the first enzyme package that gave us hope. This drug, like all the rest, has a half-life. That is, its efficacy is breaking down at a constant rate. And, as it does so, we believe it may be causing irreversible side effects.'

'The elevated white count.'

Dr Shepherd looked at him levelly. 'We'll have to monitor Tiffany daily, so I think it best if she stayed with us now.'

Thornburg watched the computer model of their newest – and best – failure revolve slowly on the screen as if it were alive. Water, water everywhere, he thought, and not a drop to drink.

'Damn getting old!' He turned away so that she would not see the incipient tears standing in the corners of his eyes. Damn time, he thought. Damn everything!

When he turned back to Dr Shepherd he said, 'Don't you physicians know how to talk in absolutes?'

'Only when it comes to death,' Dr Shepherd said. 'In the vast grey area between life and death we have only our human-created tests to go by.'

'Like sailing full-out in the fog, isn't it?'

'A bit,' she admitted. 'But if you repeat that, I'll deny I ever said it. For sure I'd be drummed out of the AMA as a heretic.' She gave him a bitter smile. 'We're doing the best we can, Mr Conrad. I mean that, no bullshit.'

'Yes, I know,' he said wearily. He liked her; she was smart and a straight-shooter. 'I want to go back to her now.'

'Surely. Just as soon as we get X-rays and some blood from you.'

Thornburg nodded.

'You know,' Dr Shepherd said, squeezing his arm, 'you have regained the muscle tone of a well-conditioned forty-five-year-old man.'

'And no side effects.'

'Nothing save the benign polyps we've taken from your colon,' Dr Shepherd admitted. 'Of course, we're using a further derivative of the serum your wife is taking. But I am thinking that perhaps the difference in your blood has had an effect.'

'You mean that she's A and I'm O-positive.'

'No. Your blood contains some subtle variations I can only attribute to your Japanese ancestry.'

'Doctor, my great-grandmother may – and I say may advisedly – have had some Japanese blood in her. Let's not jump to conclusions, and for Christ's sake let's not be thinking of writing a paper on the subject. It's not something I'd like made public. Even my children have no idea.'

Dr Shepherd nodded. 'I understand completely, Mr Conrad.'

Later, staring at his wife lying naked and serene on the pure white table, he thought that she was as perfect as a painting or a dream. He had already forgotten just how old she really was, and he thanked God for sparing him the horror of remembering.

'Would you prefer a boy?' the young Japanese woman said.

Shoto Wakare laughed. He held her beautiful face in his hands. 'I could make you up like a boy and you would be more exquisite, more perfect than any boy you could procure for me.'

He kissed one temple, then the other with such tenderness that even her heart beat a little faster. 'Besides, he wouldn't have your mind.'

The dim room smelled of its eternal habitués: beer and cigarette smoke. Wakare had been coming to this *akachochin* for many years. It lay crouched within the maze of Tokyo's *shitamachi*, which in other, less sprawling cities would be translated as downtown, but here meant that

242

area where the geographical stood metaphor for the social: the low end of town.

It was an anonymous place, one of ten thousand such late-night bars scattered throughout the metropolis engaged in the demi-monde of *mizu-shobai*, the water trade. Prostitution.

It was the Japanese way that men required outlets for the animal drives stifled by the layers of custom, honour and debt. At the *akachochin*, the Japanese male could let his hair down: get drunk, weep, laugh raucously, fornicate in whatever peculiar manner his passions dictated, all without fear of losing face or retribution, and emerge refreshed and ready to once again armour himself in society's constraints.

The young woman, whose name was Mita, though that had been the name given her when she had come to work in the *mizu-shobai*, held Wakare in her arms. She stroked his forehead with a tenderness born of practice. If it was artifice – this question might cause a fierce debate among even the most knowledgeable ethnologists – it was of a kind indistinguishable from reality. Mita had what was known among Japanese as *yasashisa*, that is a maternal sweetness most males longed for because such physical affection was not practised. This was a highly prized gift.

Of course, she and Wakare made love, but their meetings encompassed much more than that. After all, he could have gone almost anywhere to get laid. What Mita provided him was far more complete and satisfying.

Wakare sighed, relaxing in her arms. He had already consumed six carafes of sake, a prodigious amount, even for him, but his need was great for liberation from his pressure-filled world.

'Why is it,' he said now, 'that there is no justice in the world? I wonder whether we have all gone mad. I know if I decide it's true, I will have the true reason why Mishima committed hara kiri. He saw this day coming, and he could not face the shame.'

'Mishima could not let go of the old ways,' Mita said, stroking his brow in slow, rhythmic strokes.

'You're wrong,' Wakare said. 'Mishima understood that the old ways were already dead. What he could not abide was that what he sought to resurrect were nothing more than ghosts.'

Mita was used to these philosophical ruminations. 'This is the injustice you mean?'

'No, no,' Wakare said, licking his lips as if he desired nothing more than another six carafes of sake. 'I was speaking of something far more personal. I have been called to betray a friend – my best friend, actually. And I must do it. *Giri*. I owe a debt to the person who asked this favour.'

'It is only when life is hard that it becomes meaningful,' Mita said.

Wakare glanced up at her. 'I wonder whether you really believe that.'

She nodded. 'This is my life; I must believe it or I have nothing.'

Wakare grunted, settled back in her lap. His eyes closed as she stroked him. 'If only I could work on my friend's brother-in-law instead of him,' he mused. 'Now that would present no problem. Hiroto is a real bastard, greedy, venal, envious of Yuji's all-too-visible success.' He sighed. 'On the other hand, Hiroto has no honour, so corrupting him wouldn't be much fun.'

'Tell me, will there be honour in betraying your friend, Yuji?' Mita asked.

Wakare said nothing, but Mita, who knew him well, could not ignore the ghost of a smile on his lips. Later, after he had exhausted himself upon her, and she had lovingly bathed him and sent him stumbling home in a stupor of bliss and alcohol, she returned to her room.

'Did you hear or see anything useful?' she asked the Japanese woman who stood waiting for her. She was very beautiful, and seemingly so young that Mita, youthful as she was, could have been her mother.

'Many things,' Evan said. She passed a thick envelope filled with yen into Mita's waiting hand. 'But I think the most useful piece came from your client's smile.'

Ham was sitting at a restaurant on Columbia Road in the Adams Morgan district. He was looking wistfully at the tables outside on the sidewalk section. In summer they would be shaded from the strong sun by gaily-striped umbrellas and would have about them that indefinable air of nonchalance-cum-indifference exhibited by any open-air cafe in Paris.

Ham was sipping coffee. It was nearing lunchtime and the tables were beginning to fill up with fashionable ladies taking a breather from shopping.

He spied Marion Starr St James. She wore a sausage miniskirt in a rich honey colour, a wide black belt and an amber silk blouse. On her feet were black high-heel ankle boots. Her coat was slung nonchalantly over one shoulder.

Every head in the restaurant turned – the males in appreciation and the females in envy – as she passed by. Ham felt a surge of wild delight that she was here to be with him.

Just before she sat down, Ham saw a woman he knew but couldn't place sitting at a table at the other end of the cafe. She was a pretty blonde, slim and stylish, and she was watching Marion slide into the

244

chair opposite him with the intensity of a mongoose studying a cobra. Who the hell was she? he asked himself.

Then he smelled Marion's perfume, was bathed in her smile, and she took up all his attention. 'Right on time,' he said. 'I like that.'

She gave a mock pout. 'You left me so early, I rolled over and tore the sheets into ribbons.'

'Really?'

'Really. I like how you Americans say that word.' She looked at him in that melting way of hers. 'I hugged your pillow and wished it was you.'

When she was like this she made his mouth water. 'What did you think about?'

Marion looked up at the waiter, gave him her drink order. Then she looked back at Ham. 'I dreamt of you doing all the delicious sinful things to me I lacked the courage to ask you to do last night.'

He laughed. 'You don't seem to me the kind of woman to lack the courage to ask anything.'

'It's a mask,' she confessed. 'We all wear masks because, like actors under intense scrutiny, we're all more comfortable moving within a sphere where those around us can't see what or who we really are.'

'That sounds vaguely spooky,' Ham said, 'like something Mata Hari would have said.'

'In a way we're all spies, aren't we, Ham? We like nothing better than to hide behind our own masks while we probe each other's weaknesses, find a way through the other masks around us. It's human nature. It's what we both did last night on board your boat. No, don't deny it, you'll get this lunch off on the wrong foot.' She put her forefinger against his lips. 'You're not a man used to telling the truth, are you?' She smiled. 'What was little boy Hampton Conrad like, I wonder? Maybe I should talk to your parents.'

'What are you, writing my obit? My mother's dead and believe me you'd get nothing out of my father.'

Marion's campari and soda came and she took some of the bright red liquid into her mouth. 'God, what got under your skin?' She pushed the drink away from her. 'Maybe we should reconvene this lunch when you're in a better mood.'

Ham pressed her glass into her hand. 'Don't go. Sometimes my business gives me a royal headache.'

'You mean you're like everyone else.'

Ham saw how hard her face got when she was angry; he could almost feel her vibrating. 'I took out my business problems on you.'

'No,' she said firmly, 'that's not it at all.'

245

'Okay, you're right. I'm a very private person. I don't like it when someone starts prying into my life.'

'Oh, Ham, I only wanted – ' Her eyes dropped, and when she looked at him again he melted. 'The truth is I didn't rip the sheets, though I wanted to. I was too scared.'

'Of what?'

'Of you peering behind my mask and not liking what you saw there.'

'Don't be idiotic. I loved everything I saw last night – and felt.'

'Well, it's happened before,' Marion said softly. 'I mean, in many ways my father was an extraordinary man – a true patriot, really, and let me tell you there aren't many of those left. But, the truth is, he was a shit to me – and my mother. He'd come home – when he was home – drunk as a lord. He'd try to lay her and of course couldn't. He was so full of Irish whiskey you could smell him coming a block away. He'd take it out on her, as if she had anything to do with his impotence. He'd beat her, I guess because it made him more of a man in his own eyes, and because he was so full of hate. He hated the rich, the Protestants, and, of course, all the English.' She looked down at her capable hands on the tabletop. 'It took me a long time before I got my head on straight when it came to men. I drove a lot of them away just with my tough manner and my hard arguments.' She shrugged. 'Sometimes, still, I think I need an attitude adjustment.'

'You don't need anything,' Ham said. 'Take it from me.'

She smiled, took a sip of her campari and soda.

Ham said, after a long silence, 'My parents never got along, either. My father treated my mother like another lamp or vase in his house. It took me a long time to work this out about them, that they often led separate lives. It's difficult for a child to grow up with the knowledge his parents didn't much like each other.'

'Didn't you take sides?'

'Of course I wanted to,' Ham said. 'My mother was always the underdog so it was natural for me to try and help her. But then there was my father. He was in those days – how shall I put it? – so imposing, like Moses come down from the mountains. The invisible tablets my father carried was the law. There was no gainsaying it.' He looked off into the distance. 'I guess the truth is I needed his approval too much for me to come to my mother's defence. In a sense, I betrayed her just as my father did. But since that betrayal made me more like him, I could regret it without ever changing how I acted.'

She leaned over impulsively and kissed him hard on the lips. There were no hard edges to her face now. 'Darling Ham,' she said. 'You're so

246

unlike the other men in my life.' She touched him. 'When you kiss me it tastes so sweet.'

Ham, who was both appalled and filled with relief that he had spilled out what had been inside him for so long, stared into her eyes and felt lost in their depths.

Marion pushed her glass away. 'Do you think you're in the mood to discuss something scrumptiously sinful?'

'Depends what it is.'

'Something I daydreamed about this morning while I was hugging my pillow and thinking sinful thoughts about you.' She turned as the waiter put menus down, 'I'm not hungry,' she said, handing him back the menu.

'Have a salad at least,' Ham said, but when she shook her head, he shrugged, ordered two bacon cheeseburgers, a combo order of fries and onion rings, a six-pack of Cokes. 'And bring a wine cooler for the Cokes,' he told the waiter.

'I hope you don't expect me to eat any of that,' Marion said.

'If I did, I would have ordered more.'

They chatted about nothing in particular until the food came. As soon as she saw Ham settle into his eat mode, she began. 'Here's my idea. It involves the company I work for, Extant Exports. The owners are a pair of shits, fat, greasy cousins always at each other's throats. What they pay me is pathetic but they look the other way as far as my expense account is concerned. What the hell, it's a write-off for them anyway.

'But this morning I got to dreaming about doing something I'd been thinking about for some time – grabbing a piece of the action.'

'Doesn't sound like these bosses of yours will go for it,' Ham said, through a wedge of bacon cheeseburger.

'Of course they won't,' Marion said. 'That's why I'm not going to tell them.'

'What?'

'We're going to expropriate shipments.'

Ham almost choked on a piece of toasted bun. 'What's this "we" bit?'

'You and me,' Marion said. 'I figure I need a partner in this and with your military connections I'm sure we'd – '

'Forget it.'

'What do you mean?'

'Just what I said. You're going to steal shipments from your company and you want me to go in with you. You're nuts.'

'I forgive you for saying that.' She watched him for a moment. 'You know you look like a little boy when you're eating. You're making me hungry.'

247

'Help yourself,' he said.

'I wasn't talking about food,' Marion said, but picked up a golden-brown onion ring between two orange-red nails. 'Don't you even want to know what Extant Exports transships?'

'Not really.'

'It's dangerous cargo. There are losses all the time. Our prices take them into consideration. It's not a big deal, the losses.'

'I'm sure you're mistaken,' Ham said. 'Extant's insurers will investigate.'

'Extant's cargo can't be insured.' And, as Ham put his burger back on his plate, she laughed. 'What an expression, Ham. My God, you do look most avid now.'

'What exactly are we talking about here?'

'Wipe your mouth, darling,' Marion said. 'All that ketchup makes you look like you're bleeding.' She nodded as he dabbed at his mouth. 'Are you prepared for another peek behind the mask?'

It doesn't seem as if I'm ever prepared for you, Ham thought. He realized that this was precisely why he found her so utterly alluring. She was not like any of his other women; she was not like anyone he had ever met before.

He nodded.

Marion said, 'Extant's business is in procuring and transshipping Exocets, Mirages, Mavericks, MXs, Bonhohm supercannons; you name it in high-tech weaponry and for a price they can get it. Coups, revolutions, guerrilla warfare all around the globe are their meat. Who wouldn't want to rip them off? Interested?'

Ham's mind was busy ticking over the possibilities of this unexpected windfall, but he glanced at his watch and knew that Jason Yoshida would be here any minute. When Yoshida had contacted him he'd said the meet couldn't wait. 'Okay,' he said. 'But let's continue this discussion in a more secure venue. I'll pick you up after work and you'll give me all the details then.'

'Great,' Marion said, getting up. She leaned over, kissed him hard on the lips, wrapped herself in her coat.

Ham was watching Yoshida slip between the tables. On his way, Yoshida brushed past Marion, who was heading towards the entrance.

Yoshida slipped into a seat, ordered a vanilla Coke.

'Great legs,' Yoshida said, giving Marion a quick glance. He seemed agitated and the mood seemed infectious. In truth, Ham was angry at having his tête-à-tête with Marion interrupted.

Ham grunted, said, hunching over as he lowered his voice, 'As long as you're here, I want you to deliver further instructions to our friend

248

Shoto Wakare.' He paused while the Coke was served. 'He's proved very useful to us so far. I must say, Yosh, your contacts in Tokyo have been invaluable to me.'

'You're too kind.'

Ham smiled. 'You can get away with more of that irony than most, Yosh. I guess it's that deadpan face of yours. You could be a standup comedian.'

'Thanks, but I've already found my metier.'

'Haven't you, though.' Ham took a long pull at his coffee, ogled a couple of svelte blondes as they passed by, their winter coats swinging open.

'I've got some potentially bad news,' Yoshida said.

'Bad news is just what we don't need,' Ham said. 'We have very little time to stop the Black Blade Society; the Senate International Trade Committee bill that will effectively cut us off economically from Japan is being introduced this week. The latest word is, it's going to get a helluva bi-partisan boost when it comes onto the floor – enough to override a presidential veto. Meanwhile opposition to the bill is eroding because the string of supposedly accidental deaths of key senators is continuing.'

'Meanwhile, speaking of Matheson . . . ' Yoshida handed Ham a fax.

'My father,' Ham said, ignoring the fax for a moment, '*is* Washington and we both know what makes Washington run: networks of contacts, seniority, the illusion of power. Known collectively as bullshit. Running the contact networks means being born into the right family, going to the right schools; seniority means having survived here without having been shit on by anyone of note; the illusion of power means the gift of turning a neat phrase in the right ear so it gets quoted the next day in the right newspaper column. And, believe me, Yosh, my father is the master of all these things.'

'You're talking about the dearly departed past,' Yoshida said. 'Your father got us hooked into Matheson – ' He pointed to the coded fax '– and Matheson has just become a major liability.'

'What?'

'A Japanese woman came to see him and he went off with her. And do you know who she is? That artist he was panting after. Wakare has identified her as a member of Nishitsu's Black Blade Society.' Yoshida shook his head. 'Maybe that's infiltration, maybe not. Thing is, he's wanted for questioning in the murder of one of his men. Last week, Matheson was seen duking it out with this guy, now he turns up with two bullets from Matheson's gun in the back of his head.'

'Good God.'

'I warned you about this.'

'I know, Yosh, but I can't believe Matheson would off his own man. He's not that stupid.'

'Don't you see, it doesn't matter. Matheson's become a danger to us because the situation is no longer contained. Forget about whether Matheson is guilty or innocent, can you imagine the media attention this is going to cause? And if he's gone over to the enemy you sure as hell better think up something convincing for your old man because the minute you tell him what's happened he's going to hit the roof.'

'You're right, of course. You've been right all along.' Ham could see the relief on Yoshida's face.

'What about your father?' Yosh asked.

'Don't worry, I'll handle him,' Ham said with a good deal more confidence than he felt. In truth, he did not know how to broach the subject with his father, and decided that, for now at least, the best course of action was to say nothing.

He thought about Matheson and the Japanese woman together. The fax disappeared into his clenched fist. 'Damn it. It's obvious now we should have cut Matheson loose from the time someone put him through the skylight. But now he knows too much. If he decides to spill his guts to the media – '

'We're safe,' Yoshida said. 'He knows only Shipley and Shipley is an easy man to have disappear.'

Ham was shaking his head. 'Doesn't matter. Matheson knows too much about our plan. If the Japanese government gets wind of it now, we're finished, flushed down the toilet. They'll take the president apart, piece by piece, and let the world condemn us. It will be the last major slab of foundation the Black Blade Society needs at home. Thornburg will lose every ounce of credibility he has – even he can't stand up to the president – and then there will be nothing left to stop the Black Blade Society.'

Ham pushed his coffee cup away; the acid was burning his stomach, or maybe it was the bad news. 'I don't care if Matheson is with the devil himself, he's got to surface sometime. And when he does, I want him put on ice for the duration of our mission. I don't care what it takes, just do it, Yosh. Those are your new orders.'

250

TEN

Tokyo/New York/Washington

Minako moved from slumber to wakefulness in the same unconscious process with which others put one foot in front of another. There was no period of transition, no gentle, thoughtless state prior to full consciousness.

She opened her eyes and knew all was not as it should be. She rose, pulled on her robe and went through the doorway of the bedroom. She listened, hearing the eerie breath, like a faraway engine, of *makura na hiruma*.

She tried to steel herself, but she was aware that this was one of those times when she profoundly regretted having summoned her sight, for she knew how it would end here, and her heart was already constricted with grief.

For she was gripped now by the same agony her grandmother had lived with all her life. There were times, like this, when knowing the future was a kind of hell she could never have imagined that day long ago when she had confronted the fox and had said so unknowingly, *I want to see as far as I can.*

Because there were times, as now, when one was prohibited from altering what was about to happen. All her life, she had manipulated people and events, and that was all right, because the future she saw dictated that this was her karma. But her life had also held terrible moments that she had seen at such an early age and which she had kept encysted within her breast like frozen tears until the moment of their occurrence, by which time, their terrible nature almost seemed like *déjà vu*, so many times had she involuntarily replayed them in her mind: the deaths she had caused in the service of the Black Blade Society; the horrible illness of her daughter Kazuki, brought on by her inability to access her *makura na hiruma* – now her power was quite literally eating her alive; the consequences of her liaison with Hana's father; Yuji's creation of the being he called the Oracle, which she had seen would herald the end of the old order, the ancient enmities; and, part and parcel of that, her beloved Hana's flight from a reality she could no longer contain nor

251

tolerate; and, last of all, the coming of . . . what? Even she, with all her power, could not see that future.

But these events, like a string of malevolent pearls she was bound for ever to keep around her neck, burned her like a never-ending fire, a reminder of her impending damnation. Because her very first look into the future revealed to her that, in a very real way, she was to be the architect of her own destruction.

Minako saw the shadow now or, more accurately, recognized it for what it was, what it must be, and, like all such horrors, it seemed pulled from her own mind, where she had replayed this scene so many times in an agony of frustration and grief, so that it was brought home to her in crushing fashion that she would never be used to her sight, that no matter how she was gifted she still existed within a framework – though she had come to see it as a prison – from which there could be no escape.

It was so difficult, she thought, loving your children when everything they would do or that would happen to them was thrown into your face at once, like a torrent, threatening to drown you in a tide of hate/fear/rage/pain/love/frustration. Inevitably, visits with her children exhausted her utterly, especially Yuji, her restless genius of a son whom she had sworn to protect from her secret life.

Part of Minako could stand apart and marvel at the infinitely complex plan that had been formed by no human mind, perhaps by no mind at all, as humans could conceive of it. But another, more empathetic, part wanted to beat at the bars of her prison, to escape the world as she had shaped it, to escape her karma, to exit, even, time and space. She longed, now, only to be free – as, she had come to see, Kabuto had longed to be free.

'I can see now what happened, how I started to turn away from that dark place inside me,' Wolf said.

They were in Chika's 'Vette, the windows up and the heat on. Still, he was shivering. He had told her about his encounter with Suma in the warehouse.

'My grandfather was a shaman, and his dream was for me to follow on his own path,' Wolf continued. His hands were around a cardboard cup of steaming hot coffee. On the floor at his feet was the crumpled paper in which Chika had brought him a triple-decker sandwich from a deli. *'All meat,'* she had said. *'You need the protein.'*

'I always thought my father hated the old man and that I was suspended between them, but now I see I didn't give my father enough credit. He saw in me what my grandfather had. Both of them stepped away from exploiting it; they both wanted me to find my own destiny.'

252

'And now,' Chika said, 'it has overtaken you.'

He nodded, shivering still. 'It will take some getting used to.' He turned to her. 'What did you call it, this dark sight?'

'*Makura na hiruma* – the darkness at noon.'

'It's well named.' Wolf closed his eyes. 'I have crossed some black spaces. I have flown . . . '

'I understand,' Chika said so gently that he felt tears come to his eyes.

'I want to know more about *makura na hiruma*,' he said.

'For one thing, our metabolism is different than the norm.' She inclined her head. 'When was the last time you looked critically at yourself in the mirror? Do you look as old as your contemporaries?'

'I don't know. It never occurred to . . . ' His brow furrowed. 'I merely assumed I was youthful-looking. Genes.'

'Genes, yes,' Chika said. 'Just as I can reach out with my mind and slow another's heartbeat or raise it until they burst into flame, those with *makura na hiruma* are able to alter their own metabolism, to slow down the process of ageing.'

'How long?' Wolf was wondering how old White Bow had been when he had died.

Chika shrugged. 'So many variables. The power is different in each individual, so too the metabolic rates. But perhaps two hundred fifty years would not be inaccurate as a guideline.'

'My God.'

'Some of us can see the future – although, that sight can be erratic. For instance, it appears as if at any given moment there are many futures, and a future seen may not in fact come to pass.

'As you yourself know, we are gifted empaths, if not true telepaths, but, again, that power varies from individual to individual. There are very few norms when it comes to the darkness at noon. After four centuries of our history, we are still very much ignorant of the workings of our sight.'

He handed her his coffee, and she took some, handed it back. He watched the people hurrying by, oblivious in their haste of the world around them. He was still adjusting to himself in this light, seeing himself and Suma as cut from the same cloth, different from all these others. He was just beginning to feel the shaman inside him, that dark familiar, breathing its hot breath upon the nape of his neck.

'Wolf, there is something I must tell you. *Makura na hiruma* can so easily seduce us into believing that we are more powerful than we are, that we are masters of time and space.' She wrapped her long fingers briefly around his arm. 'This is a dangerous delusion, and I can tell you

253

that more than one of us with the gift has succumbed to the temptation to believe that we are gods.

'For better or worse, it is *makura na hiruma* that has shaped us. But the darkness at the core of our minds can be an insidious thing, a power that is able to deform us without our ever knowing it. No mirror can reveal the change because our "vision" forces us to look beyond the two-dimensional mirror. But, in so doing, it is possible to lose a part of ourselves. This is the other side of *makura na hiruma*, which feeds on our arrogance, our ambition, our hubris. It is what my mother feared for all her children.'

At length, he said, 'You've come for me because of my . . . *makura na hiruma*.' She nodded. 'And the Black Blade Society, as well.'

'You are a threat to them.'

'But not, apparently, to you.'

'Wolf, I told you of the cruelty of the Toshin Kuro Kosai, and now you have had a chance to see it for yourself. We can no longer stand by and allow the Black Blade Society to keep to the course its leaders have chosen for it.'

'Then you want my help,' he said. 'But why didn't you just come out and tell me that in the first place?'

'Now that you are living life during wartime, do you think you would have believed me if I had tried to describe our world to you?'

She had a point, he thought. 'Still,' he said, 'we're going to need some reinforcements. Let's cruise. I need a phone.'

Chika put a hand on his arm. 'What are you going to do? We've got to get out of the city. Now that we have passports – '

'You still don't understand,' Wolf said. 'Squire Richards was one of my men. He was murdered and now I'm being burned for it.'

'But Suma – '

'I'm responsible for him, Chika. I *owe* him. *Giri, neh?*'

She nodded her head, fired up the engine. *'Hai.'*

At 14th Street, she pulled the 'Vette over, and he slogged across the avenue. One out of the six public phones was working, the others either vandalized or out of order. He dug change out of his pocket, put in a quarter, dialled Shipley's number, then fed the machine the amount it asked for.

Shipley answered after eleven rings, and Wolf wondered where this number was. 'I'm in New York City,' he said into the receiver, 'and I'm in trouble.'

'You're one of us now. You'll get all the support you need,' Shipley said. 'What's the situation?'

'I've made contact – *personal* contact – with Suma.'

'What's your status?'

'I didn't get him, but he didn't get me, either.' Wolf took a breath. He still stank of fire, and the right sleeve of his jacket was singed. 'But it was very damn close either way you look at it.'

He told Shipley about the frame, but he did not tell him about Chika. 'I need to get the commissioner to hear my side of it,' he concluded, 'but you've got to give me some help. I'm not going to be much use to you as a fugitive.'

'I agree. But given the volatile situation with Breathard I don't want you showing up at One Police Plaza. Let me think a minute. Give me an hour to pull some strings, then get over to the commissioner's home. I'll make sure he's there.'

'Thanks,' Wolf said, thinking of the silent corridors of power Shipley trod, there, by the mere sound of his voice, to invoke djinns of vigilance and protection. He was extremely grateful for the juice, mysterious and deadly, only a Federal spook could provide.

'IT'S NOT GOING TO WORK,' the Oracle said.

'Shhh.' Hana, her beautiful, mysterious face rapt, had her eyes closed. She was hooked by wires and optical cables to the Oracle.

'YOU DO NOT HAVE THE RIGHT DNA PATTERN,' the Oracle persisted.

'How can you know that this quickly,' Yuji said, pacing back and forth in front of his digital readouts, as nervously as an expectant father.

'TRUST ME,' the Oracle said.

Yuji wanted to laugh. 'Give me a hint,' he said.

'I HAVE SCANNED HANA-SAN'S DNA PATTERN.'

'Okay,' Yuji said, 'but you can't yet *know*.'

'I AM PROCEEDING WITH ALL THE APPROPRIATE TESTS,' the Oracle said. 'BUT I KNOW WHAT I KNOW.'

'How?'

'INTUITION,' the Oracle said.

'Pardon me?' Yuji stopped his pacing, stared fixedly at the matte-black object.

'ARE YOU HAVING TROUBLE HEARING ME?'

Yuji ran a hand through his hair. 'I hear you just fine. But you're not making sense. You cannot have intuition.'

'I KNOW WHAT I KNOW,' the Oracle repeated. 'ALL OF THE DNA-ALTERING PROCEDURES ARE IN PLACE SAVE ONE. THE DYSFUNCTIONAL GROWTH FACTOR, THE SUBSTANCE THAT WILL KEEP THE GENE-KEYS THAT CAUSE CANCERS AND OTHER LETHAL DISORDERS FROM TURNING ON DURING THE PROCESS OF DNA-ALTERATION.'

'Find it,' Yuji said.

'I HAVE BEEN ATTEMPTING TO DO THAT EVER SINCE I RECEIVED NOTICE

255

OF MY FAILURE WITH MORAVIA,' the Oracle said. 'BUT I AM NOT GOD; I CANNOT SO EASILY RE-CREATE LIFE.'

'There must be a way,' Yuji said, and Hana opened her eyes.

'WE ARE ON THE RIGHT PATH, YUJI-SAN. I CAN SEE A HINT OF WHAT IS REQUIRED IN HANA, BUT IT IS NOT COMPLETE. HANA IS THE WRONG SUBJECT.'

'We'll just have to find the right subject,' Yuji said, starting to unhook Hana.

'No,' she said. 'Don't.'

Yuji looked at her.

'I don't want to leave him just yet.'

'I wish you wouldn't personify the Oracle like that,' Yuji said.

'WHY NOT? IT'S APPROPRIATE. BESIDES, I LIKE IT.'

'It's getting to be more and more like you,' Yuji said, appalled.

'He's not a thing, Yuji-san,' Hana said. 'And I like his world. It's not bounded by flesh and blood. In his world I can see all the potential that has been missing for me. For the Oracle there is nothing but the infinity of metaphysics. The sciences, as we know them, are limited by our notions of the temporal. But the Oracle lives beyond time and space. Neither exists for him. He is free the way humans can never be, the way I have always dreamed of being.'

'That's enough,' Yuji said, shutting down his monitors. 'You belong in the real world. I can appreciate what the Oracle might mean to – '

'No, Yuji, you can never understand what it has meant for me to be trapped in this body when my mind can see beyond but not travel there. My *makura na hiruma* opened a door for me – a door to a wondrous universe, but this flesh and blood has acted like chains to bind me to the doorframe, always looking longingly at what I could not have. You cannot understand the agony and frustration I have felt for years. No one can.'

'NO ONE BUT ME,' the Oracle said, and Yuji could swear that the metal beast was smiling.

'This is some kind of conspiracy between the two of you,' Yuji said, for the first time raising his voice, 'and I won't have it.' He turned to his half-sister. 'Hana, I blame you for this. Each time I hook you into it, the Oracle absorbs more of your personality. Don't you see how dangerous this is? You spend more and more time in this state. If it keeps up, I'm afraid one day you won't want to be unhooked at all.'

'That is a distinct possibility,' Hana said. 'His world has far more to offer than yours.'

'*Ours*, Hana,' Yuji said desperately. 'It's *our* world.'

'NOT ANY MORE,' the Oracle and Hana said together.

*　　*　　*

Senator R.P. Franken exited his official car and, overnight bag in hand, hurried across the concrete semi-circular drive to Union Station. He was late for his Amtrak to New York. As he passed beneath the triple-arched portico, a reproduction of the Arch of Constantine, he cursed his hectic schedule. He routinely eschewed the unpleasant cattle-car atmosphere of the air shuttles, preferring the kind of space, relaxation and pampering possible only in the Amtrak Club Car. He was looking forward to stretching out while he sipped a double Wild Turkey, the only liquor he drank.

He was on his way to New York for an important political fund-raising dinner at the Waldorf-Astoria, attended by the president. Lots of schmoozing and pressing of flesh, just the kind of activities Franken loved best. That was how you made contacts, and contacts were what allowed you to operate effectively in the snakepit of the nation's capital.

He passed through the cyclopean waiting room, modelled after the Baths of Diocletian. As he did so, he took in two of the six Ionic columns of the portico he loved best. They were carved with the figures of Classical Greek heroes representing the main aspects of railroading: Fire, in the form of its father, Prometheus; Mechanics, in the form of its first practitioner, Archimedes.

Franken also loved his constituents back in Texas or, more accurately, he understood that he was wholly beholden to them. To this end, he was trying his best to stamp out this myopic trade bill that, if passed, would isolate the United States. Japan had just rescinded its ban on importing rice and this had a particular bearing on Franken's constituents in and around his home town of Galveston, who were engaged in the business of growing rice. The new market of Japan would be a bonanza for them, and Franken knew if he allowed this trade bill to pass he'd catch it so bad back home that he might as well forget re-election next year.

Franken strode past the newly renovated inner lobby with its shops and fast-food restaurants, took the wide flight of marble stairs down to the tracks three at a time.

The thought of R.P. Franken, former Senator, having to adjust to life without the myriad senatorial perks, the ego-inflating press conferences, the ammunition to give and take political secrets, the constant adrenaline high of being special, was too depressing to contemplate for long.

Franken walked along the lower level, looking for his track number. He found it, pushed through a clot of noisy tourists, made his way onto the track where the Amtrak train was waiting.

He was about to hop aboard when a young Oriental man in a railroad attendant's uniform appeared out of the shadows.

'Pardon me, Senator Franken,' he said politely. 'Could I have just a minute of your time?'

Franken glanced anxiously back down the platform. No one else was coming down from the station, and even the other attendants had already departed. He was between cars and the train was obviously about to depart.

'Sorry, son,' Franken said, turning on his gigawatt smile, 'but I'm late for my train and – '

'But this will only take a minute, Senator,' the Oriental said. 'It's very important.'

'Excuse me,' Franken said. He tried to take a step forward towards the waiting open door, but the attendant blocked him. 'You don't understand. I'm late – '

Abruptly, the attendant was very close to him, pressing Franken back against the cool metal of the end of the train car. Franken opened his mouth to scream but the noise caught in his throat like a spider. The attendant began to pour the contents of a flask down Franken's throat. He coughed and gagged on his own tongue as if he were an epileptic as he tasted the Wild Turkey. He tried to raise his arms, but they were pinned to his sides. Spittle appeared at the corner of his mouth.

The attendant pushed hard against him, and Franken stumbled backwards into the space between the cars. The heels of his freshly polished shoes slipped off the edge of the platform and he felt himself fall. Only he didn't fall because another furious push from the attendant kept him erect. Instead, he slipped into the well of the tracks, slamming and scraping his knees against the concrete of the platform edge. Pain shot upward through his legs. He thought one of his shinbones had broken.

Pinned into the space between the cars, he still tried to struggle. The attendant poured the remainder of the flask over him, and when Franken tried to bite his hand, he felt a constriction of his heart so powerful he almost swallowed his tongue.

He shook his head, looked blearily up, saw the attendant give the all-clear signal to the engineer. Then he heard the car doors slam. The train was about to depart!

Franken saw the attendant turn his attention back to him, and he began to pray. The attendant's foot lashed out, catching Franken in the crotch. He tried to vomit, couldn't. Instead, he slipped waist deep into the well of the tracks.

He looked up in disbelief. Now, in this light, he thought he knew this man. The venue and the uniform had fooled him. He was no railroad attendant. My God! There was a look of utter hatred on the man's face that chilled Franken's blood simply because it was so utterly impersonal.

258

Now the train gave its first lurch and, despite the pain in his legs and chest, Franken began to struggle anew. The Japanese leaned down and, with a casual gesture, touched Franken's forehead with the tips of his fingers.

Perhaps it was a distortion of the light, but it surely seemed to Franken as if the man's eyes had changed colour, specks of green glowing in the shadows. Then he was hit with the cold or, more accurately, he could feel his own warmth being drawn out of him.

Franken knew the Japanese was killing him, but he had no idea how. The train was moving, he was losing consciousness. It was so cold inside him that even now that his arms were no longer pinned at his side, he could do nothing more than raise them, as awkwardly as wooden paddles. He could see his fingers, like white worms, wriggling impotently at the ends of his hands. They no longer even seemed his. He was watching them as if from a great distance.

The Japanese loomed in his vision one more time. Franken felt a massive pressure, and then he was falling into darkness, his ears filled with a rumbling that made him think of the black storms of his childhood, coming in off the Gulf, sweeping Galveston with torrential rain and bone-shaking winds.

Then the first steel wheel sliced through him. His body bounced, was momentarily pinned by another wheel, another. Then, it rose in the air, pink and frothy, before being slammed to the tracks, pierced again and again by the steel arcs, shiny as scythes.

ELEVEN

New York/Washington/Tokyo

'He's coming,' Suma said to the bandy-legged black man. 'Are you ready to die?'

Hayes Walker Johnson said nothing. He was spread across the refectory table in his kitchen. Naked to the waist, his groin covered only by the ribbons of his cut-up Calvin Klein boxer shorts, he reflected that there was something terribly humiliating about being seen like this by strangers in one's own home. He felt sweat, sliding like the finger of a lewd lover between his naked buttocks.

The commish's wrists and ankles were bound to the table legs and, in this position, he could only wish for a robe to cover himself. Such a mundane thought was ludicrous. Or perhaps not, considering that just across the slippery tiles his wife sat, her back against the built-in refrigerator. Her head was slightly lifted, her mouth open, and there was so much blood that it was impossible for even Hayes Walker Johnson to find her beautiful now.

That seemed an affront to him, a more serious threat even than losing his life, because it jeopardized that which he had always believed belonged to him alone: an idea, a memory he had found almost sacred.

'Mr Kamiwara is a special guest of mine,' Suma said, indicating the compact model Japanese at his side. 'He likes commissioners.'

Hayes Walker Johnson turned his head. 'What else does Mr Kamiwara like?' he asked, because he knew from experience that in hostage situations time was the most important factor. The more time dragged on, the greater the chance of a positive outcome. He did not want to think of the other thing: that if they'd given him their real names they had every intention of going through with their threat to kill him.

'Just about anything you can come up with,' Kamiwara said in a voice filled with menace. He touched the hollows of Johnson's buttocks. 'But personally I prefer drugs with my sex.'

'He prefers drugs with everything,' Suma confided. 'That's how he gets pumped up.'

260

'As long as he gets there,' Kamiwara said, turning to Suma.

'He's coming,' Suma said. 'I told you.'

Johnson, wanting to keep his mind off the horror across the kitchen, willed his mouth to work. 'Do you have a favourite? Drug, I mean?'

Suma laughed. 'This is a police commissioner asking.'

Kamiwara shrugged, said, 'We're all friends here,' so that Johnson wanted to kick his face in. Kamiwara turned back to him, and Johnson was struck by just how ordinary a face he had. '*Aconitine napellus*, monkshood,' the compact Japanese told him.

Johnson blinked. 'Isn't that a poison?'

'Poison, sedative or aphrodisiac,' Kamiwara said. His eyes flicked to Johnson's groin. 'Depends on how much you use and what you mix it with. It's all a matter of expertise.' His lips turned up in an awful parody of a smile.

At that instant Kamiwara moved his eyes – and only his eyes – until they centred on Johnson. Johnson had the peculiar sensation of being dipped whole into ice water, being held under the ice, the blood freezing in his veins, his heartbeat slowing, his nerve synapses paralysed. Frightened, he tried to look away – and could not. Something was blocking the action. He could *think* about it, but that was where the impulse ended, as if it had become an endless reflection, trapped in facing mirrors in his mind.

The unnaturally slow beat of his heart was so heavy it was actually painful and, as he looked into Kamiwara's eyes, he thought he could see a hint of light, a pair of wings or crescents like wisps of green fire in the lower reaches of his black irises. He seemed in some terrible way to be smiling at him, as if at a shared secret, as if he could preserve Johnson in his own form of eternity.

'Do you enjoy this game as much as I do?' Kamiwara said in a voice that seemed to reverberate like shards of glass inside Johnson with every agonizing pulse of his heart.

Suma, who appeared totally unaware of what was happening, stared out into the back yard. Kamiwara dropped his gaze, and Johnson was abruptly freed from what seemed to him a devil's grip. The blood rushing again at a normal rate through his veins brought a flush to his cheeks and shoulders. He had been so cold before, encased in the strange black ice of little Kamiwara's making, he seemed to have scarcely taken a breath.

'Does Mr Kamiwara like coke?' Johnson asked in a voice hoarse as if from a chill.

Kamiwara smiled at him, making him shiver inside, remembering what he had done to him. 'As I said, I'll try anything.'

Johnson turned his head away, his gaze falling upon the corpse of his wife. Appalled, he felt the kind of dread fascination with which one approaches a lethal accident. The sight of blood and human carnage is horrible because it is an explicit reminder of death, but mingled with the horror is an exhilaration that comes from being so close to death, and one revels in life in every way one can. I'm still alive, he thought, ashamed of his exhilaration.

Kamiwara had spread lines of coke on the countertop, and when he turned away to snort, Johnson recommenced his work freeing his right hand. He had been able to move his right wrist against the underside of the tabletop where movers had splintered a small section of the underside. After catching one of her good dresses on it, his wife had nagged him for months to get it fixed; now the jagged edge might become his saviour. He moved his wrist back and forth, sawing through the thin cord that held him.

'You'd better come over before all the lines are gone,' Kamiwara said to Suma. He wiped his nostrils with his thumb, licked off the residue of white powder adhering to the pad. 'One thing for sure, this is choice quality merch.'

Suma, aloof, continued to look expectantly through the kitchen window.

Kamiwara made a face, turned to Johnson. 'You ready to party?'

Johnson held still, said nothing.

Kamiwara stared at him from out of eyes whose pupils were dilated. 'It isn't going to be anything like you imagined.' He swung back to the countertop. 'Coke will not be enough to perpetrate our future crimes,' he said. 'We will require stronger medicine to prepare us.' He withdrew a phial of pale orange powder, mixed it in a glass with some water and other liquids he had brought with him and which were lined up on the counter.

Johnson felt the cords part and fall away from his right hand. Keeping his eyes on the two men, he slowly inched his fingers towards the drawer just below and, arching his back slightly, pulled it open. He felt the haft of the carving knife cool against his palm, and with extreme care drew it out. He had it now, hanging point down, hidden from both men by the table.

'Drink me,' Kamiwara said and laughed as he pressed the rim of the glass to Johnson's lips. When he had taken half, Kamiwara finished off the remainder.

'Now kiss me.'

As Kamiwara came towards him, Johnson spat the liquid into his face and, as he sputtered, he brought the carving knife up and around, stabbing the point of the blade through the back of the Japanese's hand, pinning it to the wooden top of the table.

Kamiwara's mouth opened wide but before he could utter a sound, Johnson stuffed his shorts down Kamiwara's throat. But it was Johnson who let go a scream. He sat up, staring at Kamiwara's hand where the carving knife protruded from between the bones, sinews and nerves. It was impossible, he thought, but not a drop of blood could be seen oozing from the puncture wound.

And now Kamiwara's head was swivelling around as if it was on ball-bearings, and those dead-fish black eyes were changing colour again, just as they had when they froze him. The green crescents seemed to light up his face with a kind of demonic energy. He vomited up the shorts.

And now the atmosphere in the room seemed to shift, as if it had come alive or Johnson had just become aware of another presence lurking in the shadows.

Those eyes loomed as large as suns, and he could feel a peculiar kind of radiation from them prickling his skin, seeping through the layers of flesh, penetrating his brain.

Johnson gasped, collapsing onto the table, his upper body swaying. A searing pain emanated from his very core, seemed to be robbing his lungs of oxygen. He made a mad lunge for the knife, wanting only now to plunge it into Kamiwara's heart.

'This what you want?' Kamiwara asked. 'Here, take it.'

Johnson began to shake, his eyes almost bugging out. The carving knife was levitating, moving smoothly upwards of its own accord, until its point cleared Kamiwara's flesh and it hung in the air, suspended.

'Good Christ!'

Kamiwara was laughing.

Johnson squeezed his eyes shut, swung his head sharply back and forth in a vain attempt to clear it. Whatever Kamiwara had made him take must have been very potent. He tried to breathe, could not seem to remember how. There were spots before his eyes, and his metabolism seemed to have doubled, tripled. His mouth was opening and closing with an odd, horrible sound like that of a fish out of water.

Hallucinations. He had swallowed some of dread little Kamiwara's poisonous mixture and this must be the result – it must! It was the only explanation, and he could handle that. He was stoned and these were hallucinations that –

Johnson tried to scream one last time as the internal oxygen supply gave out. His mouth opened wide as he tried to gasp in air but nothing would work, it was as if he had stepped out of a capsule into airless interstellar space.

*   *   *

263

Wolf and Chika went up First Avenue, heading west into the eighties. They parked one block south of the commish's brownstone.

As he had done before with Bobby, Wolf led Chika into the basement entrance of the greystone that backed onto Johnson's back yard. The black iron gate was locked, but Wolf popped it, did the same with the door in the minuscule cement courtyard. Inside, the house was silent. He led her down the long hallway and out into the rear garden.

At the far end of the garden, they paused beside the twelve-foot fence beyond which was the commish's back yard. Wolf pushed the door open, Chika following close behind, and they found themselves in Johnson's back yard.

As they wended their way beneath the honey locusts, Chika touched Wolf's arm, said quickly, 'Something's very wrong in there.'

They raced up the back steps, burst into the kitchen, and heard Johnson's stifled gasping. Wolf saw Johnson, his face ashen. At almost the same moment he took in the entire scene: the commissioner spreadeagled, naked, on the refectory table, the dead woman slumped against the refrigerator, the Japanese who was at this moment willing the blade of a kitchen carving knife out of the back of his hand.

'Christ Almighty!'

He was staring into the face of the Japanese painter whom he talked to, felt sorry for in the men's room of his office. Now Wolf understood.

He saw the bogus painter's eyes widen, a thin crescent of luminescent green appear in the irises, and he thought, Oh, God.

'Kamiwara!' Chika said. Then to Wolf, 'Get down!' she shouted. 'Leave this to me!'

'No,' he said. 'This bastard's been shadowing me. He's mine.'

Kamiwara whirled, disappeared into the bowels of the house. Wolf sprang into the unlit hallway, running full tilt.

'Long time no see, shitbrain,' Kamiwara said, and kicked him on the point of his hip.

Wolf grunted as the pain flared down through his leg. He pivoted with the blow, as if off balance, saw the mad grin come into Kamiwara's face and, bracing his side against the wall, struck sharply upwards with the heel of his hand.

He caught Kamiwara on the point of his ribcage, hacked down with a kite. Kamiwara yelped, but gave no sign of being hurt. But there was something in his hand and he was throwing it. Wolf flung himself away, the soft whirring sound in his ears as the thin blade spun past his face.

He could hear Kamiwara's mad laugh as he aimed a second blade at Wolf, who kicked out, his angle wrong, but the heel of his shoe deflected Kamiwara's hand just enough so that the throw was directed upwards.

Wolf twisted, slammed an elbow into Kamiwara's groin, into the soft spot just beneath the ribs.

Then a dark force slammed him back against the wall hard enough to put him out for a minute or so. He shook his head, looked around. Kamiwara was gone.

Chika was about to follow Wolf when Suma appeared. She stood as if rooted to the floor, staring at the diminutive Japanese. Slowly she held out her hand, the fingers cupped. Green fire danced in her eyes. The Japanese did not move; the carving knife still hung in the air above the refectory table.

The room darkened further, as if something unnameable, barely seen was coiling and uncoiling sinuously like smoke. In a moment, flames seemed to leap into Chika's cupped palm where they hissed as if being doused by water. Then they were gone. Johnson lay on the table, crumpled like an old overcoat; there was no breath left inside him.

Above the corpse, the carving knife rose in the air, its blade gleaming like punctuation on an invisible page.

'What the hell is Kamiwara doing here?' Chika demanded.

Suma inclined his bullet-like head. 'What he does best. Wreaking havoc.'

'On whose orders?'

Suma said nothing.

'You've received a new set of instructions, haven't you?' she said shrewdly. 'And I don't know what they are.'

'Then I will tell you,' he said. 'Slowly but surely we are extracting Matheson from his, shall we say, matrix.'

'By carving up everyone he's close to.'

'That's the way.'

'But this is so barbaric, so final.'

'Final, yes,' Suma said. 'An apt word.' His eyes widened, and the carving knife trembled in the air as from an unseen wind.

'Stop this. I can bring him to Tokyo far more easily. He trusts me.'

'Perhaps he does,' Suma said. 'But we have no way of being sure. None of us can read him as we can read others, and that is dangerous. Besides, he must feel when he leaves America that there is nothing left for him here.'

'Why?'

'Because we have one piece of work for him.' A slow smile spread across Suma's face; it was a woman's smile, that of a siren, filled with guile and untold secrets. 'A *final* piece of work.'

'What is it?'

265

'I have already told you more than you need to know.'

'Then you never meant to kill him.'

'Kill Matheson? No.' The carving knife was moving, as if it was impatient to write in blood the stuff of legends upon the kitchen wall. 'But to destroy everything he holds dear, to probe his abilities, to get the measure of him. Now you have the idea.'

Thornburg Conrad III met Brosnian Lenfant once a week. Their meetings occurred on different days of the week and at different times. Too, the venues constantly shifted. Brosnian Lenfant, the former senator from Louisiana who, for a nice round fee, lent his name to Lenfant & Lenfant, Ham and Yoshida's office front on K Street, was one of Thornburg's old-boy network. Thornburg liked him immensely. Lenfant had come out of a particularly nasty local political system, and was, therefore, a master of every dirty trick in the book, as well as a host the book never heard of.

He had first come to Thornburg's attention when he was district attorney for the state of Louisiana, and had outmanoeuvred a despicable and powerful man who was then mayor of New Orleans, but had aspirations for Lenfant's job. Lenfant had cleverly boomeranged the mayor's smear campaign against him, retaining his popularity with the electorate. And four years later, it was largely due to Thornburg's generous campaign contributions that he had first got elected to the senate. Lenfant was not a man to forget such favours, and it was he who had called this meeting, not three days after their last regularly scheduled get-together.

Lenfant was not a tall man. His large head was dominated by oversized brown eyes, a high forehead, broken like an egg at the centre by a widow's peak, and a smile as wide as the Mississippi. He had narrow shoulders and, these days, a slight pot belly. He was a dapper man, a real Southern gentleman, which meant that he knew how to play Washington's particular brand of power game: he told secrets only to friends or bartered them for favours. Either way, he built up a war chest of the only form of capital worth a damn in this city.

Today, he was wearing a dark blue wool suit with a cream waistcoat and maroon tie under a trenchcoat. He carried an ostrich-skin attaché case in one hand.

The two men met in the lobby of CIA headquarters in Langley. Thornburg liked this place, with the monument of its pale marble stone wall into which was carved fifty-three stars. Each one of those stars commemorated an agent felled in the line of duty. But in the open book below, only twenty-three of them were identified by name. The remainder had no names – at least as far as the public was concerned.

266

They resided deep inside the CIA's master file, lodged like stones in the throat of some mythical beast.

To Thornburg, this peculiar form of public secrecy was what defined Washington. Here is our power, the memorial declaimed. To withhold the truth from you.

For a moment, the two men stood before the memorial, between the flags of the United States and the CIA, and when Thornburg said, 'Impressive,' Brosnian Lenfant knew just what he meant.

The two men presented their IDs to the guard at the front desk and Lenfant handed over a miniature dagger that was his constant companion since his earliest campaign days in Louisiana. The two men were escorted to an elevator.

On the way up, Thornburg said, 'How well did you know Senator Franken?'

'Old R.P. and I go way back,' Lenfant said. 'But there isn't much left of him from what I heard.'

'You heard right,' Thornburg said.

'I also heard he was drunk when he took the walk off the railroad platform.'

'Bullshit,' Thornburg said emphatically. 'Just like the seemingly natural deaths of the other senators who were trying to block this trade bill are bullshit. All of them were murdered. Franken is just the latest in a line, and that's real bad news.'

Thornburg had chosen a small, rarely used conference room. He turned on lights and air conditioner to rid the place of its overheated stuffiness.

The room was spartan: dove-grey walls with a scattering of anonymous and not very good paintings of clipper ships, dark seas, jutting promontories. The centre of the room was taken up by a wood-laminate table, eight executive swivel chairs. Along one short wall was a matching credenza which, if Thornburg knew anything about such places, contained an array of sophisticated listening devices. On top of the credenza was a cheap coffee-maker and hotplate, no doubt for late night or early morning crash sessions. As in all such CIA think-tanks, there was no window, no surface that could conceivably engender a vibration that could be picked up by the ever-eavesdropping opposition.

The two men settled themselves at the table, and Lenfant snapped open his attaché case. 'Bad news or no bad news,' he said, 'man's got to eat.'

From the case, he extracted a thermos filled with strong brandy-laced New Orleans coffee, catfish sandwiches, a skein of alligator andouille

267

sausages and some kind of preserved okra relish that was powerful enough to strip paint off a car.

'These comestibles put to shame the slop from any government commissary,' Lenfant said, his gigantic smile lighting up the room. 'And I'll wager they're better than the fare of most DC restaurants.'

Thornburg asked for coffee, politely declined the food. He watched Lenfant as he plugged in the hot plate, began to warm up the sausages. All too soon, the air was redolent of a stench that, Thornburg was certain, in sufficient concentration could be classified as a chemical weapon.

He swivelled around in his seat, opened the sliding front of the credenza, flipped a switch that activated the white noise machine that would ensure absolute security.

Lenfant took his sausages off the hot plate, unplugged it, and came back to the table. Something in the food was making Thornburg's eyes water. He watched in fascination as Lenfant ingested his reeking lunch with obvious relish.

'This Mississippi mud isn't bad,' Thornburg said, as he poured himself some more of the ex-senator's coffee concoction.

'My mother's recipe,' Lenfant said, as he sliced open a sausage with surgical precision. 'The chef at Galatoire's has been after me for years to lend it to him. But I wouldn't think of it; my mother worked long and hard, and she was justifiably proud of the table she set at the end of the day and the food she put on it. I won't be giving her secrets away.'

He loaded up a forkful of food. 'You know, that boy Jason Yoshida is some workaholic, too.' He chewed some, swallowed. 'I swear that boy is like my mother was: he never sleeps.' Lenfant had the kind of soft sing-song Louisiana accent no dialect coach could duplicate. 'Doesn't he ever think about anything except work?'

'Best to ask Ham that.' Thornburg was watching the ex-senator's liquid brown eyes, as soft as his accent; he wondered where this was leading, was content to let Lenfant get to the point in his own good time; the man wouldn't be rushed, anyway.

'Well, hell, I know that, Thornburg. But your son's under the impression that I'm just window-dressing up at Lenfant & Lenfant. And that's the way you told me you wanted it.'

'I thought it best that our relationship should go unnoticed.'

Lenfant grunted as he took a large bite out of his catfish sandwich. 'Well, I'll tell you something. I've known many a spy in my day – some of whom were totally unaware of my knowledge of them, but I swear I never met one who enjoyed espionage as much as you do.'

'Knowledge is power, as they used to say in the OSS,' Thornburg said, referring to the CIA's progenitor.

268

Lenfant nodded. 'Now that was a whole other passel of crocs. Everybody followed orders in those days, and mighty happy to do so, too.' Lenfant chewed reflectively. 'Which brings me to the purpose of this meeting. You suggested I go see your son, set up the Lenfant & Lenfant cover so I could keep an eye on things, so to speak. Which I have.' He sipped some coffee. 'Just recently, though, I've gotten a bit curious, mainly because Yoshida's become somewhat ill-at-ease. So I did some spadework, gave his office the "soft toss" as we used to call such things in Bayou politics.' Lenfant frowned, a sure sign of bad news. 'Did you know this individual went to New York overnight? He flew in, requisitioned a government agency car, came back early the next morning.'

'So?'

Lenfant shrugged. He seemed to have had enough food for the moment. 'Maybe nothing. But I wonder if you know your boy Matheson is smack in the middle of a frame.'

Thornburg said nothing. He was trying very hard not to let his thoughts run away from him. 'Go on,' he said.

'Matheson's on the run from the Chief of Police, Jack Breathard, who believes – or wants others to believe – that Matheson murdered one Squire Richards, the lone black member of his team.' Lenfant's right eyebrow lifted. 'This individual was found shot through the back of the head outside his house on the morning Jason Yoshida was there. Police ballistics confirm that Matheson's gun was the murder weapon.' He nodded. 'That's Yoshida's work, no doubt about it.'

To anyone else, Thornburg would have said, It's impossible. You've got your facts wrong. But he knew Lenfant too well and too long. The man was meticulous in his research. If he told you something, you could take it to the bank, deposit it and be certain that it would earn top interest.

'I know you didn't authorize the hit in New York,' Lenfant said softly, 'because subsequent to his return I had a little chat with Yoshida. You know how he is; getting anything out of him is a monumental achievement. But reading between the lines it's clear he's uneasy about some of your son's most recent decisions.' Lenfant leaned forward, lowered his voice even though there was no overt need to do so. 'Thornburg, your entire plan is in grave jeopardy. Your son has decided on his own that Wolf Matheson has become a liability. Ham has built a cage for him that I don't believe he's going to get out of.'

Wolf went from room to room, his gun at the ready, searching every conceivable space for a sign of Kamiwara. The question he needed to answer was what kind of game the Japanese was playing. At what point would he cease to play the hit-and-run guerrilla and stand his ground?

Where are you, Kamiwara? Where are you hiding? Wolf recalled his many games of hide-and-seek when he was a boy in Elk Basin. He concentrated, using his mind.

He was at the end of the long central hallway, the spine of the building. Ahead of him was a ninety-degree turn to the left and, he knew, the commish's formal dining room. There was no place else to go except back. It was dim here, a perfect place for an ambush.

Then he saw the flush opening in the wall. It was just large enough for a small man, rolled up, to hide. He put his forefinger through the metal ring of the door, aimed his gun, whipped open the door.

A dumbwaiter, empty and mocking, greeted him. He must be directly over the kitchen, Kamiwara having led him around in a circle. He put his head and shoulders into the dark space to take a look around. And heard Chika talking in Japanese with a man. He listened, and projected his *makura na hiruma* downwards towards the man. Who was he? He needed just a few more exchanges to get it.

Then, he encountered the other man's aura, and the sweat broke out on his back.

Jesus Christ, he thought, she's talking to Suma! And not as if he were an enemy – but an ally.

He closed the dumbwaiter door, got his mind back on track. Find Kamiwara, he thought. That's your first priority. You'll deal with Chika later. If there is a later.

He inched forward until the top edge of his shadow reached the corner. Even a millimetre more and Kamiwara would know he was there – if the Japanese was waiting for him around the corner.

Wolf stared into the corridor, willing himself to be able to sense Kamiwara. Did he hear a movement, smell a telltale odour? Was there anything that would give him a hint?

Nothing.

He waited.

Nothing.

Then he thought of the creature inside him, dark and constant, breathing at his side, and realized that he would have to create his own opportunity by the judicious application of equal parts psychology and momentum, a kind of meshing of the mental and the physical, White Bow's continuum.

He summoned his dark familiar. He was still a little afraid of it, but his need of it outweighed his fear. He remembered the warehouse, and the fact that when Suma was manifesting his sight, Wolf could read it and pinpoint his location. He wondered if the reverse were true – that

Kamiwara would find him when he used his *makura na hiruma* – and this worried him.

So he began to move, sprinting around the corner, racing down the hallway as he projected his sight outwards.

Christ!

Wolf almost stopped, forced himself to keep moving. He was listening beyond the sighing of his own body to the breathing of another. I've found him, Wolf thought. I can feel his aura even before he has manifested his own sight.

Kamiwara appeared in the dimness, looming like Nemesis, no longer even human but a glyph, one of those who stole the souls of the dying, like the creature Wolf had shot along the path of the dead.

He caught sight of Wolf and, startled, began to project his *makura na hiruma* outwards. Wolf reached out, deflected it with his own.

Kamiwara whipped out a small sharp blade, and he lunged in very fast, low, and Wolf could feel his scrotum tighten in reflex. Wolf was aware of his body wanting to tense and he fought the instinct, relaxing, remembering, centring while death flashed in at him quickly, more quickly still.

In the instant before it happened, Wolf's only conscious thought was not to anticipate the onset of pain. He must trust in his body, his technique, learned at the feet of the spare balding Japanese.

Then he was into it and there was no more time for conscious thought.

With Kamiwara's blade only inches from his groin, Wolf reached around with his right hand, grabbed the Japanese's right wrist and, at the same time, went down on one knee. He felt the blade scrape his flesh as he worked his aikido *irimi*, feeding off Kamiwara's momentum, pulled him forward, off-balance, swinging him around in the tight space so that he bounced off a corner wall.

Kamiwara went down on his shins, his shoulder making hard contact with the opposite wall, but he had not let go of his blade and he slashed out, the edge blurring past Wolf's hand, hooking the gun out of his grip, sending it singing, out of reach down the hallway.

Wolf leaned forward, bringing his right arm beneath Kamiwara's extended right arm, the left under it, swinging his upper body erect as a foundation for the movements of his arms, the lower one slamming inwards so that the edge of his left hand struck Kamiwara at the lower end of the arm's socket, while Wolf's right arm swung Kamiwara's elbow up and back in a sharp motion that made a loud crack as the bone shattered and the knife clattered free of the useless hand.

All the opening I need, Wolf thought, as he brought the heel of his hand upwards towards Kamiwara's chin. Kamiwara struck sideways at the protrusion of Wolf's wristbone, deflecting the blow enough to take most of the strength out of it.

The Japanese was waiting for the move – any one of them, it didn't much matter to him – he knew Wolf must make against him now that he was unarmed, and when he saw it forming he slammed his heavy left fist into the side of Wolf's neck.

He had been after the nerve ganglia lying side by side with the carotid artery because that would have paralysed Wolf immediately, but he miscalculated and his blow bounced off Wolf's clavicle, the force turning Wolf's intestines to water. Wolf aimed a kite at the inside of Kamiwara's right wrist, got it, but didn't get it quite right.

Another blow came in, rocking Wolf, and he had to revise his calculations because time was passing and so was his supply of adrenaline. The fatigue to his muscles for so long in tension and so unused to it had to be factored in now because it was building, and with each passing moment his chances of survival were lowering significantly and soon they would become nil. He had to do something now.

He tried to manifest his sight, felt a negative pull, as Kamiwara, ready for this ploy, began to strangle his sight.

Kamiwara's face hanging close in the darkness like a jack-o'-lantern on Halloween, the grinning skull of death loosed to claim another victim. Gold teeth grinding against enamel with his effort, the long yellowed upper canines coming down to clash against the bottom teeth, the thick lips pulled back in a rictus, the tendons on the neck standing out like cables.

The two men were as intimate as lovers, bound together by an emotion as powerful and primitive as lust.

Wolf went for the cricoid cartilage at Kamiwara's throat because crushing it would be fatal, and he had to find an end to this before the fatigue overwhelmed him, before Kamiwara could gain the upper hand with his size and strength.

Kamiwara's teeth snapped shut as Wolf's fingertips made contact, but he chopped down hard on Wolf's forearm and it went numb down to the fingers, and then Kamiwara had his slab-like hands around Wolf's throat, his spatulate thumbs squeezing inwards, then changing the grip so that the nape of Wolf's neck was cradled in the crook of his left elbow and Wolf felt his blood run cold because he knew that Kamiwara meant to break his neck, would do so within fifteen seconds unless Wolf could find a way to stop him.

Which wasn't damned likely; the fatigue was accumulating with appalling rapidity, a red sludge lapping at Wolf's consciousness, draining him of energy.

The organism knew what was happening, that death was imminent, and the trigger was pulled for the last great burst of adrenalin, but it was no good, Kamiwara's grip was like steel, the entire upper half of his body brought to bear against Wolf, his massive shoulders and chest bracing his arms as they began to crack apart Wolf's cervical vertebrae.

'It's so unfair,' Hiroto wailed. He was drunk, his jacket thrown over a rolled futon, his shirt rumpled and pulled open at the collar, tie askew. 'I work in anonymity while Yuji gets all the credit. He has the money, the company, the fame, everything, and what do I have? A stinking salary, a piece of Shian Kogaku I can only look at because it's in my wife name.' He grabbed the bottle of Suntory Scotch and emptied what little was left into his glass. 'I'm a shadow, a clever man no one has ever heard of.'

Evan listened to this semi-drunken diatribe with great interest. She had contrived to meet Hiroto at the hospital where his wife was currently being treated. She had been sitting in the over-bright, grief-drenched waiting room, her shoulders hunched when he had emerged from visiting his wife. He could not fail to see her or be moved by her pitiable weeping.

And now they were at a nearby restaurant, very respectable, a wooden table between them, and not even a flirtatious glance exchanged. Hiroto was an easy man to decipher – but, of course, she had had Wakare's unwitting help in this. Like a Rosetta Stone, Wakare had opened up possibilities to her she had not realized were there. For one thing, she knew instinctively that the Toshin Kuro Kosai was looking for another way to the Oracle besides Minako. It was not that they didn't trust her; on the contrary, as she had pointed out, she had many times over demonstrated her loyalty to the Society. But, in this case, there was her son to consider. *Giri* – the sense of obligation – aside, the bonds of mother to son were indomitable. It would be prudent, Evan knew without having to have been instructed, to engage a backup path to the Oracle, should the need ever arise. Wakare had indicated to his favourite prostitute Mita that Hiroto, the venal, envious brother-in-law, might provide that backup.

Not that she had found Hiroto an easy mark; far from it. It had been Evan's experience that the venal and the envious were often the most clever precisely because their obsessions tended to make them paranoid; they were, in short, suspicious of everyone. And experience had also taught her that those suspicions, so quick to be aroused, were often quite difficult to assuage. Better, by far, not to incite them in the first place.

Towards that end, she now said, 'I apologize for the scene I made in the hospital, Hiroto-san. That was unforgivable.'

'No, no, it is I who should apologize,' he insisted. 'I was intruding.'

'But I am so glad you came and sat down beside me!' Evan did not look at him as she said this so there would be no mistaking her honourable intentions. 'I could not stop myself from weeping. I have a husband whose kidneys have failed. It is inexplicable in someone so young, the doctors tell me. And, oh, Hiroto-san, we were so happy, like an ideal couple on TV. So in love, our whole lives ahead of us.' There was a lone tear standing in the corner of her eye, trembling as she shook with tightly held emotion. 'And now he is in that hospital on a dialysis machine. Each day I go to see him I see life slipping further and further from his grasp. What will become of us?' She bent her head, and her shoulders shook as she silently wept.

Hiroto peered at her, struggling through his drunken pall. He sat up straight, pulled distractedly at his tie in a vain effort to set it straight. He bowed to her formally. 'I, too, find myself in a like position.'

'Really? How awful.' Evan's head came up, and Hiroto's heart turned over to see her tear-streaked cheeks, just as it had when he had first seen her in the waiting room.

'I am saddled with a wife whose illness cannot be diagnosed and who will never recover.' He paused, so taciturn with anyone outside the family. But he knew he would go on; he was with someone who trod the same desolate path he did, someone who could understand the anguish he felt. 'This illness has robbed me of my wife. She's not dead yet, not clinically, anyway, but she weeps uncontrollably, then rages out of control. Where is the beautiful woman I married? Destroyed by something sinister, something unseen. My God, but life is a bitter pill to swallow.'

'But we must go on, mustn't we?' Evan said, wiping her eyes. 'We must be strong.'

'Why?' Hiroto said mournfully. 'I don't see the meaning of it?'

'Because,' Evan said, leaning forward, 'there is always a chance we'll meet someone who will understand, who will make life bearable again.'

He caught her eye, and thought, But she can't be talking about us, not this beautiful, sad creature. What could she possibly see in me? But then, in a flash, he saw how fortuitous it was for both of them that they had met. Two people in similar circumstances who could support each other. 'I do not know what I will do if she dies.'

Evan knew that he was speaking of Kazuki, his wife, Yuji's sister. 'I have the same thoughts about my husband,' she said softly. 'And yet,

274

sometimes I think he is no longer my husband – that is, the man I fell in love with. Is that a disloyal thought?'

'No,' Hiroto said kindly. 'Just realistic.'

'Oh, what I wouldn't give to bring him back!' He could see that she was on the verge of weeping again, and he felt his heart breaking. 'But, of course, that is a useless wish. The doctors have no hope at all.'

And then he saw his salvation staring him in the face. For he, the shadow, who had lived for so long in the black pit of anonymity Yuji had devised for him, could at last prove his worth, if only to this one human being. Because it was in his power to bring her husband back to her.

'I can do it,' he said, as breathlessly as if he had just run a mile. All trace of the alcohol was gone and, in its place, was a supra-real clarity he found exhilarating.

'Do what?' She seemed confused.

'Listen to me, Evan,' Hiroto said earnestly. 'The doctors don't know everything. I am a computer-scientist, and there is a project I have been working on that could conceivably reverse your husband's condition.'

'Oh, Hiroto-san!' She frowned. 'But how?'

'It's very complicated,' he said. After all, she was a woman. 'But it has to do with altering the DNA in a living body.'

Her face lit up. 'Do you really mean this?'

'Of course.'

'But it sounds so – ' She shook her head. 'Impossible.'

'Come on,' he said impulsively. Why the hell not? he thought. This is my project, too. And look at that face! Fuck security, and fuck Yuji! 'I'll prove it to you! I'll take you to see it right now!'

The one chance Wolf had was to get the killing pressure off and the only way to do that was with nerves. The soft spot between the ribs and the shoulder directly beneath the clavicle housed a major nerve bundle that affected the entire arm and hand. The problem was it was heavily armoured, being deeply buried beneath layers of Kamiwara's rock-solid muscle and what little leverage left Wolf was fast disappearing.

He used his knuckles but he knew almost immediately that it wasn't going to be enough. He could feel another crack as Kamiwara twisted his neck another inch to the left. Black spots were exploding in his vision and his chest was on fire, labouring to get oxygen. His muscles were stretched to their limit and, almost folded upon himself, he lacked the means to unleash a meaningful upper body strike.

Darkness.

He needed a weapon.

A humming, as if an insect or animal.

275

A stirring.

A weapon. Wolf wormed his hand against his side, pushed it downwards until his fingers closed around metal. The razor sharpness of an edge: the slim blade Suma had dropped in the warehouse.

He could feel his neck going.

He willed his mind to collapse in on itself, entering into the red light, and then he forgot about keeping it in check.

Strait is the bridge and narrow is the path . . . Wolf built his own arrow bridge.

Nothing but floating . . . and a heat he knew he could touch but which would not burn him. His mind enclosed the heat in a psychic hand, and abruptly, startlingly, the sensation entered his body, rushing through his chest, along his outstretched arm into the fingers curled around the metal.

Pressure.

The blade, as hot as a furnace, a sun, shot from his hand like an arrow from a war bow.

Pressure coming off.

Kamiwara's eyes starting out from his head, his mouth working wordlessly, the thick tongue seemingly caught in his mouth. Wolf moved his neck by increments back to centre, aware only dimly through the unnatural heat the intense pain of his tortured muscles and tendons.

He saw the blade embedded in Kamiwara's flesh, and he smashed his knuckles again and again against the thoracic nerve bundle, feeling Kamiwara's right arm as a dead weight and immediately redirecting the heat in his mind into Kamiwara, the blood pounding through him, the hate and the fear coalescing in him, the organism reacting to the proximity of its own death, wanting, *needing* to strike out.

Wolf began to tremble with the concentration of psychic energy, the mysterious engine inside him amplifying the darkness at noon, projecting it like a torrent of bubbling lava, a school of ravenous sharks let loose to tear and rend at his command.

He shouted as a hole appeared in Kamiwara's chest, blue fire dancing, the hole blackening, widening as the viscera crisped in the blue flame and the chittering darkness, and there was the putrefying stench of sin drifting up from inside the Japanese.

Wolf began to shiver uncontrollably, thinking again of the moving shadow, having felt it pass close by him on the roof of Amanda's apartment, in the humid interior of Chika's apartment, in the city of the damned when Cathy had burst into flame, and again in the warehouse.

And he felt the tremor of the shadow that was a part of him like an ancient shaman's familiar, breathing in the invisible darkness, growling

276

like a living being and, at length, moving through him with the force of a thunderbolt.

'*Strait is the bridge and narrow is the path that leads to life, and few are those that travel it.*'

The inner voice ripped apart Wolf's consciousness, and his eyes flew open. He stared at Kamiwara, or what was left of him, the light fading from his uncomprehending eyes as he burned.

But, Wolf thought, what path have I chosen that leads to destruction and death?

TWELVE

Tokyo/New York/Washington

'HELLO, HIROTO-SAN.'

'This is the Oracle,' Hiroto said to Evan. He watched her face as she approached the matte-black cube. 'Oracle, this is Evan.'

Hiroto had taken her to the warehouse near the Sumida river, where the Oracle was housed. It was a dark night, and there were no guards, just an elaborate set of coded locks to get through. Hiroto, of course, knew all the codes. It had been fun showing Evan how important he was to be given access to the Oracle.

'YOU SHOULD NOT HAVE BROUGHT HER HERE,' the Oracle said.

'I know, it's a breach of Yuji's security,' Hiroto said, 'but I have a reason for doing this. This woman is special. You can help her. Help her husband, actually.'

'EVAN IS UNMARRIED,' the Oracle said.

Evan, who had been circling the Oracle, now stood absolutely still.

'What do you mean?' Hiroto said. 'I don't understand.'

'THERE IS MUCH YOU DON'T UNDERSTAND, HIROTO-SAN. GET HER OUT OF HERE NOW.'

Evan's head turned, and she looked from the Oracle to Hiroto and back again. 'What is happening here?' She gave him a quizzical smile. 'It appears that the machine doesn't like me. Can such a thing be possible?'

'I KNOW WHO YOU ARE,' the Oracle said ominously. 'YOU ARE A THREAT.'

'I assure you the machine speaks for itself,' Hiroto said. 'Currently, it's not making any sense, but – '

'HIROTO-SAN.' The Oracle's synthesized voice stopped him. 'ARE YOU AWARE THAT THIS WOMAN IS TOSHIN KURO KOSAI?'

'Black Blade Society? Impossible! And, anyway, how would you know that?'

'SHE IS VERY HIGH UP IN THE HIERARCHY, HIROTO-SAN, BUT DO NOT WASTE YOUR TIME ASKING HER. SHE WILL ONLY DENY IT. THERE IS DANGER HERE, HIROTO-SAN, YOU MUST SEE IT.'

278

'Don't pay any attention,' Hiroto said to Evan. 'I think there must be a loose connection somewhere.'

'IF YOU HOOK HER INTO ME, SHE WILL BE UNABLE TO STOP ME FROM READING HER MIND. I WILL GAIN ACCESS TO ALL HER SECRETS, ALL THE BLACK BLADE SOCIETY'S SECRETS.'

Hiroto could see that this suggestion had frightened Evan. Her face had gone pale and she had taken a step back from the machine.

'You're not thinking of – '

Hiroto laughed, seeking to assuage her fear. 'Of course not. Don't be ridiculous.' He gestured. 'But perhaps it was a mistake to bring you here. We ought to go.'

'Maybe not just yet.'

'SHE WANTS TO LEARN ABOUT ME, HIROTO-SAN. AND TAKE THAT KNOWLEDGE BACK TO THE BLACK BLADE SOCIETY. YOU HAVE A DUTY TO PROTECT ME.'

'Of course I do,' Hiroto said. 'But protect you from whom? Why would the Toshin Kuro Kosai want you?'

'BECAUSE OF WHAT I CAN DO – OR ALMOST DO,' the Oracle said.

'And what is that?' Hiroto asked. 'I know all your functions.'

'YOU DO NOT,' the Oracle said. 'I AM ABLE TO ALTER THE DNA IN LIVING HUMANS, TO MAKE THEIR DNA SO CLOSELY RESEMBLE THAT OF THE MEMBERS OF THE BLACK BLADE SOCIETY THAT THERE IS VIRTUALLY NO DIFFERENCE BETWEEN THE TWO.'

'Are you telling me that there are experiments going on behind my back?'

'YES. CURRENTLY, THIS PROCESS IS INCOMPLETE. THE ONE HUMAN WHOSE DNA I ALTERED IS NOW DEAD. BUT YUJI AND HANA ARE WORKING ON A WAY TO COMPLETE THIS FUNCTION. WHEN IT IS COMPLETE, I WILL BE OF PARAMOUNT IMPORTANCE TO THE BLACK BLADE SOCIETY. THEY COULD USE ME TO INDUCE THE DNA CHANGE IN OTHERS TO SWELL THEIR DEPLETED RANKS. THIS IS WHY EVAN IS HERE.'

Hiroto turned to her.

'The machine's mad, obviously,' Evan said.

'GIVE HER TO ME, HIROTO-SAN,' the Oracle said. 'I WILL PROVE TO YOU WHO SHE IS.'

'You will stop this now!' Hiroto ordered, sensing that he was losing control of the situation.

'HAVE YOU SEEN HER HUSBAND, HIROTO-SAN?' the Oracle said in that diabolically clever way it had. 'ARE YOU CERTAIN OF HIS EXISTENCE?'

'I haven't seen him,' Hiroto admitted, 'but I have only to go to the hospital with Evan. Her husband is on the same floor as Kazuki.'

'HAVE HER TAKE YOU, THEN,' the Oracle said.

He looked at Evan, feeling more and more helpless, as if he were being stretched between two mysterious forces. 'All you have to do is tell me the truth.'

Tears appeared in Evan's eyes. 'You are cruel, Hiroto-san, to subject me to an interrogation.' She sniffled. 'Of course, the machine is lying.'

Hiroto frowned. 'A machine – even one as advanced as the Oracle – is incapable of lying.' He took another step towards her. 'Perhaps it wouldn't hurt to see your husband first-hand.'

'IT WOULDN'T HURT AT ALL,' the Oracle said in its most mischievous voice.

'It's too late,' Evan said.

'YES. TOO LATE,' the Oracle intoned.

'I meant at night. Visiting hours are over. Tomorrow – '

'BY TOMORROW SHE WILL HAVE SOMEONE LYING IN A BED WHO WILL POSE AS HER HUSBAND,' the Oracle said like the best detective.

'I'll put an end to this,' Evan said firmly. 'I'll take you back to the hospital now so you can see the admittance records.'

Hiroto turned to her. 'You would do that?'

'Of course,' Evan said without hesitation.

'DON'T GO ANYWHERE WITH HER, HIROTO-SAN,' the Oracle warned. 'SHE IS DANGEROUS NOW.'

'Why now?' Hiroto asked.

'BECAUSE SHE KNOWS THERE ARE NO RECORDS IN HOSPITAL ADMITTANCE FOR HER FICTITIOUS HUSBAND.'

'If so, it's you who have made her dangerous.'

'I KNOW, HIROTO-SAN.'

Hiroto held open the door to the laboratory.

Outside the warehouse, the one bare bulb over the zinc door cast a harsh glare like that of burning magnesium. Hiroto said, 'I'm sorry about all this, but you must understand that security is tremendously tight. The Oracle was right about that.'

'I understand,' Evan said, as she stepped close to him. Green crescents glowed in her dark eyes, and Hiroto clutched at his heart. His mouth opened and closed, gasping for air which he could no longer inhale. His lungs had ceased to function.

Evan stepped back in time to see Hiroto's eyes open wide. He took one lurching step backwards, hit the darkness of the warehouse, spun, sat heavily on the ground.

The smell of fish from the nearby Tsukiji fish market was strong in Evan's nostrils as she watched Hiroto flop this way and that, his fingers curling and uncurling like an infant's.

She crouched in the shadows next to him, said softly, 'Damn that machine. It was smarter than you were, poor Hiroto.' She spoke more directly to him, then, using her sight to elicit answers, and only when she was certain that he had no more information to give up to her, did she squeeze down hard on the overtaxed muscle of his heart.

Hiroto jumped as if jolted by a shot of electricity. Then his body slumped back, all life pumped out of him. She bent down, extending her neck and head forward, opened her mouth, closed it so sharply her teeth came together with an audible snap. She took out a small piece of cotton, wound it around what dropped out of her mouth. She put the stained packet away.

Then she reached out, slung the corpse over her slim shoulder. His weight was no problem for her. She took him home in his own car, left him in it behind the wheel in his stark, ferroconcrete garage with the door down and the engine on.

She was careful not to touch anything on her way out.

Evan looked dispassionately at the dark, sleeping house, thought, Hiroto did not know how Yuji and Hana plan to modify the Oracle. Pity. If he had, I could have taken the Oracle with me and forget having to rely on Minako and Yuji. But all is not lost. I know where they keep it now. Let Yuji and Hana complete their modifications. Then, if Yuji becomes reluctant to share its secrets with us, I'll know who to go to to get my answers: his half-sister, Hana.

Breathard.

'What?'

'Breathard's coming.'

Wolf took Chika's extended hand, allowed her to pull him to his feet. He almost toppled into her arms. He leaned against the blood-spattered wall while she stared down at the crumpled corpse of Kamiwara.

It was then he heard a voice on an electronic bullhorn, reverberating through the house: 'This is Chief of Police Jack Breathard! You are surrounded by a squad in full riot gear! Resistance is useless and will result in loss of life! Yours! Throw down your weapons and come single-file through the front door or suffer the immediate consequences! You have one minute to comply! You're all under arrest! This includes you, Matheson!'

They could already hear the tramp of the cops infiltrating the building. There seemed to be an army of them.

He was still staring down at Kamiwara. 'This bastard did his best to kill me.'

Chika pulled at him. 'We've got to get out of here.'

He would have thrown off her arm but he would have slid down into the abattoir at his feet. She peeled him off the wall; he was so soaked in blood his torn shirt clung to him as if he had been pulled from a stream.

Christ, he thought, how did Breathard know I was here? He's sure he's going to nail my hide to the wall for Squire's murder. If he catches me in the middle of this, I'm as good as signed, sealed and delivered into the state pen.

They broke out of the kitchen, went up the rear staircase. At the other end of the house, the groined rococo ceiling stretched away far above their heads, in this situation giving a false sense of space.

At the second-floor landing, Chika pushed him back into the shadows along the wall. Down below every available light had been turned on by the cops and they could see uniformed men in riot gear, armed with pump shotguns, taking up positions. In a moment he could make out the figure of Jack Breathard striding into the light. He wore a Kevlar bulletproof vest underneath his suit jacket. In one hand he held a bullhorn, in the other a .357 Magnum – definitely not department issue. A real cowboy, Wolf thought.

Breathard put the bullhorn up to his lips, repeated the speech Chika and Wolf had heard moments before.

Wolf heard a sharp sound below them. He grabbed her hand. 'Let's go.'

They were midway between the second and third floors when the voice thundered through the bullhorn: 'Matheson, this is Breathard! We've found the commish or what's left of him! This is your last chance to save yourself! Give yourself up while you still have friends in the Department willing to help you!'

A moment's silence, while Wolf and Chika kept climbing, then a soft *phutt!*, and a metallic canister arced up the front stairwell, clinked to the floor, began rolling. A soft hiss as the cloud began to move upwards towards them.

'Teargas,' Wolf said.

Whoosh!

He shoved her upwards even as he heard the sounds of more tear gas explosions. Time, he thought. We just need a little time.

At the top of the fourth-floor landing, Wolf looked up, searching for what he knew must be there. He reached up, pulled on a chain, and a hidden stair unfolded. They climbed it, and he pulled it back up behind them.

'Where are we?' Chika said in the darkness.

'Attic,' Wolf said, wiping the sweat off his face. He pulled her along. 'This way.'

At the near end of the musty attic they came upon a window with an electronic box attached to it. Burglar alarm.

Wolf put up his hand, felt for the wires, pulled them loose from where they were stapled around the window frame. He removed the cover of the box, carefully stripped the insulation off a section of both wires with a pocket knife, found the hot one, wired it to one of the terminals inside the box. As he slid open the window, he felt the chill of the day come pouring through. They slipped out onto the sloping stone ledge. Wolf turned, carefully shut the window behind them.

They were at the rear of the brownstone, hidden from the cops on perimeter patrol by the wisteria and honey locust branches. He stretched upwards, felt the parapet of the roof, hauled himself up. Then, he reached Chika up to him.

They took to the rooftops, slipping over one parapet to another abutting one. The buildings here were mostly row brownstones, but occasionally there were deep dark alleys to leap as they went from rooftop to rooftop.

Once or twice Wolf paused because he thought he heard the *thwop-thwop-thwop!* of rotors cutting air, imagining that it would not be beyond Breathard's power to bring in police helicopters, but the sounds, if they were from a department copter, never rose in volume, and he pushed Chika onwards, moving them further and further away from the red sector of the commish's brownstone.

At the end of the block they were obliged to descend. Wolf chose an inside staircase, feeling they would be too exposed on the fire escape that ran down the side of the tenement.

Chika wedged open the door to the roof and they ducked into the inner landing. Wolf cursed under his breath as they went down the stairs because his legs were now truly a detriment and he knew that Chika was moving more slowly than she normally would in order to accommodate his disability. Flashes of intense pain shot through his neck, and his flesh burned where he had been cut. In addition, he was feeling lightheaded.

They were nearing the first-floor landing when they heard the front door burst open, the heavy tramp of thick-soled boots. Wolf half-ran, half-slid the rest of the way down, turning right behind Chika towards the rear of the building as the police flooded the vestibule of the tenement.

They heard an officer shouting clipped orders to his men to fan out as they pulled open the door to the rear entrance, headed diagonally across a dingy minuscule back yard piled high with refuse that stank so badly it made him gag. They squeezed down an alley between two crumbling brick walls, the soles of their shoes crunching on a shingle of discarded syringes.

They emerged onto a side street, looked to the left where a police barricade had already been set up.

'Oh, my God,' Chika said.

Wolf looked briefly back the way they had come. He could see the tiny yard already filling with cops looking like soldiers. It would only be moments before they found the mouth of the alley.

Trapped, he thought bitterly.

Then he heard the squeal of tyres, saw a battered yellow cab swing around the corner a half block to their right, back up towards them. He brought out the steel blade, cocked his arm to throw it when he heard a familiar voice shout, 'Don't, for Christ's sake! Wolf, it's me, Bobby!'

Wolf saw it was, indeed, Bobby Connor driving their old undercover vehicle. He stood stock still.

'For the love of God, get your ass in here!' Bobby Connor yelled.

The cops were in the alley, single-file; the men manning the barricade were already swinging it aside to let a patrol car through. Its engine revved and he saw the smoke pour from the burning rubber of its tyres and there was no time to think, just to move.

He shoved Chika into the back seat, followed her in as Bobby trod hard on the accelerator and they sped down the street, turned into another, going the wrong way, no traffic, just parked cars and at one point a double-parked van that Bobby missed by not much more than a rat's whisker. Then he was swinging hard at the end of the block onto 86th Street, heading west towards Central Park.

'Nice timing,' Wolf said. 'But how the hell did you find me? And that goes for Breathard as well.'

'That sonuvabitch Breathard is definitely out for your blood,' Bobby said, manoeuvring around a lumbering bus, spewing a cloud of viscous diesel fumes into the already choking air. Horns blared briefly and then they accelerated down the block. 'I got a tip that he had mobilized a riot force, and I got curious. It seems like Breathard got a call that spilled where you'd be.'

'That's impossible,' Wolf said. 'No one knew.'

'Someone did, and that someone told Breathard.' Bobby glanced at Wolf in the rear-view mirror. 'You know all long distance calls to the department are logged in as a matter of procedure. Right after Breathard got a call from a two-oh-two area code, he called out the hounds.'

'Go south,' Chika said. 'Head for Central Park South.'

Wolf saw Bobby glance at her in the rear-view mirror. 'Do as she asks,' he said. Two-oh-two, he thought. Washington. The only other person who knew where he was going was Shipley. *'You're one of us now,'* Shipley had said, and had then blown the whistle on him. Why? Who the hell did Shipley take orders from?

Bobby ran a light as he made into the park, weaving through the heavy traffic. 'I took this one, Wolf, because it's difficult to put an APB on a cab.'

'Gotcha.' Wolf had turned around, was staring through the rear window. 'Don't see anything.'

'Me neither,' Bobby said. 'I think we lost 'em.' He ran another light, nothing out of the ordinary for a New York City cab, the cops were used to it, but almost ran down a pair of joggers.

'I went to see Squire's brother, like you said,' Bobby reported. 'Took me a while, but once he knew it was me he agreed to meet. Squire wasn't shittin' you, Wolf. The brother was into the sharks for twenty-five large. I mean, that's about as much as he makes in a year. Anyway, the interesting thing is the brother had worked out a schedule of payment, and every two weeks he was paying the sharks, just like clockwork.'

He slowed until he could get around a hansom cab, the hooves of its tired horse clip-clopping along the macadam.

'Then, couple days before you had your beef with Squire, everything changed,' Bobby went on. 'Couple of shark goons went to the brother's local school yard and – get this, now – threatened his daughter. She's about eight.'

'Yeah, I know,' Wolf said. Through the rear window he'd been keeping an eye on the traffic flow behind them.

'Well, this isn't exactly standard operating procedure for sharks, intimidating family – especially if the mark's paying up. That's what set Squire off, according to the brother.'

'You've been a busy little boy,' Wolf said approvingly. 'The brother have any idea who took Squire down?'

They were almost into the southeast corner of Central Park, now the skyrises on Central Park South looming dead ahead.

'Maybe, maybe not,' Bobby said. 'The brother admitted to me he went over to see Squire the morning of the murder. He wanted to calm him down; he was sure he could reason with the sharks. That's when he found Squire. Thing is, he got to the scene about five minutes before he said he did when Breathard's Internal Affairs people spoke to him. To me he admitted seeing a car pull away. One person inside, male, he was sure of that. And he thinks the driver was Oriental; he thinks, Japanese.'

'That makes no sense,' Wolf said. 'The sharks would have sent some foreign talent in from Chicago or Detroit to do their wet work.'

'Yeah, that was my thought,' Bobby said, as they swung onto Central

Park South. 'And another thing, the brother swears the car had US Government licence plates.'

The US Government, Wolf thought. Spooks again. And again the thought: Who is Shipley taking orders from? 'Shit! Why isn't he telling all this to IA?'

'Wolf, you gotta understand the tension that's gripped the department. Breathard's whipped every black into a frenzy. The brother's afraid to buck the black tide, afraid he'll be ostracized by his own. Face it. Breathard says you're a rogue cop, and there doesn't seem to be anyone around to rebut him.' Bobby shook his head.

There was a sound creeping into the environment and Wolf strained to make out what it was because every new sensory input could be vital now and dared not be ignored. He heard it again, only one more block to go, and then it seemed to die away in the chaotic rush of midtown traffic.

But Wolf's straining ears picked up the sound again, a wash against the other urban noises, as they passed Sixth Avenue.

'Christ,' he said to Bobby, 'they've got a chopper up there.'

'Oh, fuck, what an idiot,' Bobby said, hitting the steering wheel with both hands. 'They got a fix on us through the police ID in infrared-sensitive paint on the roof of the cab.' He screeched to a halt, turned around, said, 'Get out now!'

Wolf did not argue. He and Chika piled out of the cab, but he turned back when Bobby didn't follow. 'Come on!' he shouted. He glanced up, saw the leading edge of the police copter, rising like a bird of prey over the Plaza Hotel. 'For Christ's sake, Bobby, you can't stay here. They've got this thing zeroed in!'

'Don't worry. They won't hit me. They – '

'This is Breathard, buddy. Now he's got the backing to do anything he wants, no questions asked.'

'I'm not going with you.'

The copter had almost cleared the hotel.

'Just get the hell away from the target, Bobby,' Wolf said. 'I know what I'm talking about.'

Then Chika had grabbed hold of him, was hauling him along the south side of the street, hurrying west in the protection of the highrises on that side of the street.

Wolf looked back, saw the yellow cab pull away from the kerb, the grey stone wall and lush trees of Central Park as background. The sound of the copter was loud now and people were looking up, traffic was lurching to a horn-blaring standstill.

Its shadow moved across the tarmac of the street and Wolf saw the yellow cab come to an abrupt halt and Bobby come sprinting out. There was a large gap between the cab and any other vehicle. Pedestrians had backed away. An amplified voice, perhaps Breathard's, could just be heard over the raucous clatter of the copter, as it canted over, nosing in, looking for a space to land.

In that moment just before it touched down Wolf saw Bobby. Relief flooded through him as he watched Bobby making his way down the block between the stalled cars. He was almost abreast of where Wolf and Chika were pressed in the shadows of a highrise when Wolf saw him turn. A figure on a huge deep cherry-red Electra-Glide Harley emerged from the park, heading towards him, and now Wolf could see it was the small Japanese Suma.

'Bobby!'

Chika jerked him back into the protection of the overhanging facade an instant before Bobby Connor spun, shuddered heavily and burst into bright blue flame.

Ham Conrad was on the tennis court about to begin a match with Harris Patterson, the lawyer who had been with Marion Starr St James when he had first seen her on the plaza of the Willard Hotel, when he saw someone he knew approaching.

He groaned. 'Hi, Mrs Simmons,' he said, putting on his best smile. Now he realized that she was the woman who had been staring at him and Marion in the outdoor cafe on Columbia Road.

'Won't you call me Audrey, Ham?' Audrey Simmons said. 'But, oh, well, I'm flattered you remembered me.' She was decked out in a high-fashion Ellesse tennis outfit that Ham estimated must have set Senator Simmons back $300.

She put her racquet over her shoulder, ran her long blood-red fingernails through the hair on his forearm. The tennis outfit flattered her flat-stomached, long-legged physique. Ham could see her nipples through the thin cotton jersey of her top; he was very aware that she was not wearing a bra. Surely she could not be here to play tennis.

Audrey flashed him a smile and took a step closer. 'I'm glad you like what you see.'

'Mrs Simmons – Audrey, I don't mean to be rude but my playing partner is waiting and – '

'Yes, the handsome but thick-headed Harris Patterson.'

'You know him?'

'Know him?' Audrey smiled sweetly. 'I've had him.'

Good God, Ham thought, just what kind of woman is Leland Simmons married to?

Audrey's blood-red fingernails were plucking at his shirt. 'Ham, I wonder if you know just how much I want to fuck you.'

'Audrey, really I – '

'I dream about taking your cock in my mouth, feeling it grow hard as I lick it, sighing as it spurts – '

'For crying out loud.' Ham, appalled, took her by the arm, led her off to the fenced side of the court where they would not be overheard. But he was unprepared for her reaching out with her free hand, caressing him between the thighs.

Her eyes lit up. 'You *do* care for me.'

'Audrey, stop it,' he said, taking her hand away. 'Your husband sent you to me for help with your son. I gave you that help, and that's the end of it.'

'No,' she said, 'it isn't. You and I both know that when the time comes you'll call my husband and he'll return the quid pro quo, that's how everything is done here. Why should it be any different for me?' She looked into his eyes, saw something there. 'Oh, I understand now. You believe my husband can help you but I can't.' She smiled. 'There you're wrong.' She put her forefinger up to her lips, tap-tapped thoughtfully. 'Now, let me see, why are you playing tennis with the big-dicked but boring Harris Patterson?' She giggled at his expression, but her expression sobered before she continued. 'I wonder whether it has anything to do with the *female* I saw you with the other day. Marion Starr St James.'

'You know Marion?'

She arched an eyebrow. 'Marion, is it? I know her only indirectly, through Harris. But she and I have never met.' She smiled that sweet smile again. 'Harris likes to talk . . . afterwards. He says it helps him take the pressure off. What a blockhead – but sometimes a useful blockhead, I must admit. Are you interested?'

'Audrey, I'm not interested in being extorted by your twisted idea of quid pro quo.'

She pouted. 'Don't you like me, even a little?' Her fingers touched him again. 'Don't lie, Ham. Your body won't let you.'

'You're quite beautiful,' he said truthfully.

Her smile broadened. 'But it's *me* that repels you, isn't it, with my talk of cock-sucking and having Harris.'

'Well, it's not my idea of what a woman should be.'

She slapped him hard across the face. She was shaking with rage. 'How dare you judge me by how you think I should act or feel. Would you judge me the same way if I were a man? No. You'd grin and wink and join in the talk of big cocks and fucking.' She glared at

288

him. 'You've had Marion Starr St James. You fuck who you want, why shouldn't I?'

'You're married.'

'Oh, please, grow up.' She looked at him slyly. 'And I suppose it's perfectly okay for you to cheat on your wife.'

'You don't know my wife.'

'And you don't know Leland Simmons.'

He said nothing, looked over her shoulder, waved at Harris Patterson, mouthing, 'I'll just be a minute.' He returned his attention to her. 'Just what is it you want from me?'

'Nothing, now,' she said. 'I guess I was wrong about you. You see, I *did* go to bed with Harris, but when I found out how boring he was I got out right away. The truth is, Ham, I find you interesting. Even more, humane. The way you helped my son was wonderful. I wish I could be that way with him but I can't, there's too much baggage weighing the both of us down. Sure I was attracted to your body, but I saw something else in you that made the fires burn. Now I'm not sure what it was I saw.'

'Audrey, I – '

She smiled. 'It's okay, Ham, I was never out to extort you, I was merely playing a game. It was fun for me but I see it wasn't for you so let's forget it.' She had taken a step away when she turned back to him. 'Oh, by the way, regarding Harris and the St James woman, he was finalizing a separation agreement extricating her from a rather bizarre business arrangement.'

'What do you mean "bizarre"?'

Audrey's eyes opened wide. 'I mean *very* bizarre.'

'Who's the guy?'

Audrey's racquet came down, poking him gently in the stomach. 'Now that's the really juicy part, Ham.' She laughed. 'The guy is your father.'

'I hear them,' Wolf whispered. 'They're very close.'

He felt Chika's hand wrap around his mouth.

Somewhere not far away a floorboard creaked, a voice only half-muffled by wallboard, said, 'Wouldja look at all these goddamned clothes. Fuckin' guy.'

Wolf and Chika were lying face down in the secret windowless cubicle Wolf had discovered in Lawrence Moravia's enormous apartment. Just a thin wall away members of the New York Police Department were hard at work trying to locate them.

The moment Bobby Connor had burst into flame Chika had dragged Wolf into the service entrance of the building against which they had been pressed. Not coincidentally it had been Moravia's building; this was why Chika had asked Bobby to head towards Central Park South.

She had led him past a line of trash dumpsters, along to the left where, without warning, they were heading down a narrow, gritty concrete stairway. There was a smell of a place always damp and from somewhere close they could hear the drip of a leaky faucet.

The stairway gave out on an oil-stained tarmac apron at the far end of which he could see the door to an oversized service elevator. What light there was came from a brace of bare twenty-watt bulbs set in cheap white porcelain fixtures, but as they came up to the door he could see there was no button to push, only the fireman's lock switch dictated by city law.

Chika drew an odd-looking key out of her pocket, fitted it into the lock and turned it to the right. The door opened and they stepped into the elevator cab. Again, inside there were no buttons, just the fireman's lock. Chika used her key, this time turning it to the left. The elevator began to ascend.

'So this is how you got into Moravia's apartment.'

Chika nodded. 'Only he and I knew how to use this system. Since he was the developer it wasn't difficult for him to have it built.'

Why not? Wolf thought. When you have a secret life you need a way in and out of it.

The elevator came to a stop, the door opened and they stepped out. They were in pitch-darkness. But there wasn't much to see in any case. By the light of the cab, Wolf could make out featureless walls, could sense an acute lack of space.

'Hands and knees,' Chika had said, dropping down.

Wolf followed suit and they moved off to their right. Abruptly he could sense the corridor was at an end. He could feel Chika reach up, heard the scrape of metal on metal and a door swung down. Chika was reaching up again and it seemed as if she was lifting something out of the way. Wolf got a sharp clean whiff of what incongruously smelled like hay.

Then Chika had disappeared. A moment later lights came on, illuminating the square hatchway through which she had climbed. She reached down, helped him up, and he found himself in Moravia's secret chamber. There was the hibachi, the gloves, the rolled-up carpet, the antique mirror, the array of Chika's erotic photographs. He saw that she had moved the reed mat which was just over two inches thick. Beneath it was the trap door into the service corridor. As he watched, she leaned over, pulled the door up, latched it, slid the tatami back into place flush with the floor.

'Kamiwara's dead,' Chika said. 'And you used your *makura na hiruma* to kill him. How does it feel?'

290

'I wonder if I've made a mistake in letting the genie out of the bottle,' Wolf admitted. He was grateful that she hadn't said, I told you so when they walked into the trap at Johnson's brownstone.

'Maybe it's good you feel that way,' Chika said. 'The darkness at noon certainly has its negative side. But it'll take time for you to see the sight in its proper perspective.' Chika's eyes glittered. 'The world's changed for you now, Wolf, and there's no going back.'

He thought of her standing amid the blood and bodies in Johnson's kitchen, chatting away with Suma. What had they been plotting? What kind of perverted game was she playing with him, saving him, helping him, then delivering him to the enemy? He wanted to ask her about her relationship with the enemy – he had so many questions for her. But, she was right, the world had changed and there was no sense in confronting her until he had an idea of its new shape and the identities of its new players. He was in a grey area. Who was good and who evil? He could not say.

The only thing that was clear to him at this moment was that Chika wanted him in Tokyo. Once he got there, perhaps some of his questions would be answered. Right now, though, it was far better to husband his knowledge and wait for a propitious time to use it.

'There's no going back,' he said. 'Yes, I understand.'

A silence sprang up between them that had a quality Wolf could not define. He wondered what he was missing. It was as if the picture of this new universe she was gradually allowing him to paint was somehow incomplete.

He looked at her. 'We may not get out of here.'

Chika said nothing.

He moved closer to her. 'Why was Kamiwara at Johnson's? Who was he?'

'He was not merely a hit man, if that's what you mean. He'd been over here a long time; he knew his way around.'

'Like your opposite number.'

'I don't understand.'

'The enemy's version of you.'

'No, Suma is that.' She thought a moment. 'Kamiwara should have been recalled some time ago. I thought that had been decided upon. He was . . . losing it.'

'You mean being away from home too long.'

'Not exactly.' Chika licked her lips. 'I think his sense of reality had been altered to an extent where he was no longer useful, even to the Black Blade Society.'

'Are you saying he'd gone mad?'

'Perhaps.'

Again the sensation of missing something vital rose in him. It was no good confronting her with his suspicion that she was lying or at least not telling him the whole truth; a blind man could see she would not be intimidated.

Wolf's thoughts returned to Bobby, incinerated in an instant. One minute he was screeching around a corner to save their lives, the next he was obliterated. The Black Blade Society was trying to kill him and, not a week after recruiting him, Federal spooks were trying to do the same. In fact, he now had no idea who had tried to frame him, Suma or the spooks. It was just like the war. In fact, according to Chika it *was* a war in which he had become involved.

Think, he berated himself. You're back in a war, think like a weapon. But all he could think of was Bobby's death burning inside him as if he had inhaled a fragment of flame. And Bobby's last scrap of information about Breathard having been tipped off to Wolf's whereabouts, power extending itself like a spider's web from Tokyo and from Washington, in the form of a man named Shipley at the Department of Defense. Someone in Defense wanted him dead.

Wolf was convinced there was a shape to all the seemingly disparate pieces, if only he could see it. And the truly odd thing was that he was beginning to suspect that he had more of the pieces than he was aware of. He thought again of the portrait Chika was allowing him to paint, and he thought of the Grand Jury, of how they were given only the evidence the DA's office thought they needed to vote the case be bound over for trial. He said, 'Tell me more about this club Forbidden Dreams.'

'Look at the photos on the wall.'

He did; he was getting used to being patient with her oblique answers to his questions. He found, to his surprise, that he enjoyed digging out information from her, much as he supposed his father had liked to mine opals in Australia. Dimly he recognized that the essential mystery of her was what was driving him now that his old life had dropped away from him. 'What was it about this subject that made you want to photograph it?'

'I imagine you mean sexual bondage.'

'Yes.'

'Does this subject interest you, Wolf?'

'I admit it's hard to look away from the photos.'

'Yes. And do you have any idea why?'

'No.'

'I think you do.'

'Well,' he said, 'maybe it's the unreality of it. It's like theatre.'

292

'Exactly, and like the best theatre the fantasy of it means to reveal the truth hidden like a pearl in the meat of a clam. Because, you see, Wolf, within the context of fantasy it is easier to explore the psyche of the individual.' She turned to him. 'That was Lawrence's abiding passion, you see, not sex per se, but in confecting the fantasy of sex he could explore the depths of the human soul. That was the only Truth that was of any value to him.' She made a gesture. 'Do you see anything about the subjects of these photos that links them together?'

'No.'

She smiled. 'Come on, detective. You discovered this hideout, you must be able to find the common denominator in a bunch of photos.'

Wolf looked more carefully at every element. There was something about the subjects' faces. Though they were all either turned away from the camera or hidden by shadow he caught the line of a cheek in one photo, the double-curve of a mouth in another, a ridge of eyebrow in a third, adding up to a recognizable silhouette. He said, 'Are all the girls Oriental?'

'Japanese, yes.' She drew her legs to her breasts, put her arms around them. 'I met Lawrence at a special time, in this special place: Forbidden Dreams. That's where I took these photos.'

Wolf looked once more from photo to photo. 'Jesus Christ, these were his actual experiences? What the hell kind of club is this?'

'It's the hub of the Black Blade Society.'

Wolf, abruptly dizzied by an intense stirring inside him he could not define, drifted against her for an instant.

'That night in your apartment,' he said. 'Why did you put your hand between your legs when you knew I was watching you from the next room?'

'I only did what you wanted me to do, Wolf. I told you.'

'And I still don't understand.'

'I think you do.' Her eyes were glittering in the soft light. 'Didn't you want me to play with myself?'

'Of course not. I – ' But he broke off abruptly, swallowing hard. The fact was, he had had that thought in his mind that night, *I'd love to see her do herself.*

'The generator in the apartment is like the heart of a gigantic beast – *my beast.* It acts like a screen, throwing out white noise that blocks the reception of *makura na hiruma.* It kept me hidden from the Toshin Kuro Kosai. It was on that night, remember?'

'Yes.'

'And yet I felt what you wanted me to do, so strongly it cut through the noise block. Primitive emotions are often strong enough to do that.

That's why the summoning of *makura na hiruma* usually occurs during puberty when those emotions are running rampant.'

Once again, Wolf thought of the time White Bow had taken him out on the frozen playa. He had often wondered why his grandfather had chosen that moment. Now he knew: puberty.

'You people seem to be able to read each other's auras,' he said, 'but I know Kamiwara and Suma weren't able to read mine. It was like I was a blank.'

'No, wrong analogy,' Chika said. 'A wall may be blank but you still know it's a wall. You're unique. With you, there's nothing at all. It's as if you don't exist.'

'But you were able to read me. You told me that you could feel my aura that night in your apartment even through the interference of the generator.'

'Something happened between us,' Chika said.

She was still very close to him, and he could feel that same electric sexuality at close range that had galvanized him in the strangely heated atmosphere of her apartment as he watched her from the living room. Now he knew the origin of that heat: the confluence of *makura na hiruma*, hers and his.

Wolf said, 'Then you wanted me as much as I wanted you.'

He felt her essence rising from her in waves like heat off a city street in summer, only this was somehow sweet, infusing him with an ache in his heart, the kind of yearning one feels at sixteen for a sweet-fleshed girl who flashes you a sunny smile in the midst of a crowd. Yet there was a melancholy, too, of the moment when you say goodbye to a deeply tanned girlfriend on the last evening of summer when the darkness brings with it the first cool whiff of autumn, the city and home.

She put the flat of her palm over his left nipple, whispered, 'I can hear the beating of the heart of a gigantic beast.'

He inhaled her musk, certain that he would never be able to sate himself. 'Your beast?'

'I won't know that – ' Her cheek sliding like silk against the stubble of his incipient beard. '– for some time to come.'

The first taste of her had the succulence of a peach dripping with nectar. He heard her moan deep down in her throat, felt it in his own throat and he was gripped by a kind of pale fire in which the world dropped away and the heat they generated by their mutual passion engulfed the physical aspects of the windowless cubicle even to the light itself.

In the darkness their power accelerated as they came together in a breathless grappling. For Wolf it was the end to a longing that had possessed him from the moment he had first seen her.

The atmosphere, hot and thick as tar, deepened, and Chika cried out as Wolf stripped off her clothes, bent his head to her high breasts, sucked first one hard nipple into his mouth, then the other.

He felt her hands on his neck, then his chest as she pulled off his sweat- and blood-soaked shirt. She drew down his trousers and he felt her delicate fingers between his thighs. She moaned again at his hardness, and her soft, fluttering touch made him shiver with delicious anticipation.

He wanted to take her immediately, but there was a burning, an imperative that was an unexpected component of his passion: he needed to hold her, inhale her intimate perfume, drown himself in every aspect of her before he plunged into the core of her.

He turned her suddenly around, drawing her thighs against the sides of his face, opening her. He felt the warmth of her lips on him at the same moment he tasted her on his tongue. Her hips lurched off the floor as she skewered herself on his tongue. He pulled her further off the floor until she was nothing more than a ball of flesh. Her mouth engulfed him and he sank in all the way to the root; her palms cupped him.

He felt the rippling of the muscles of her legs, the tightening of her belly, then her thighs began to tremble and her hips jerked upwards and he felt her moans tumbling uncontrollably with him deep in her mouth. Her thighs splayed far apart and at last he lost control, pulling himself free and, almost in the same motion, plunging into her.

Her thighs drew up around him and he could feel her hard nipples scraping him as she threw herself from side to side. He held her head, felt the tears slipping from the corners of her eyes, covered her face with kisses as she convulsed, gasping her passion into his mouth, not stopping, spasming on and on, as her inner muscles gripped him more tightly, bringing him to the edge and then over in a fireburst of longing, need, and fusion not only of body but of spirit. Because, at the end, instead of the tiny emptiness that comes in the aftermath there were the shadows – hers and his – living, pulsing, infusing the cubicle with a darkness as tea will stain boiling water with its essence.

The moment may have lasted an instant or an eternity, who could say, but a time came when the shadows withdrew into that region of their minds in which they dwelt.

The booming silence as of the aftermath of a lightning crack.

The atmosphere returned to its original state, and it was then that they heard the noises from behind the wall that linked the cubicle to Moravia's wall-long bedroom wardrobe, and Chika reached across him, extinguished the lamps' dim illumination.

Wolf lay very still, listening to the tramp of boot soles, the rise and fall of voices, the accelerated beat of his heart.

He could feel Chika close beside him, could smell the aftermath of their sex, but when he closed his eyes all he could see was Suma riding his Electra-Glide, his eyes fixed and glowing as he passed the burning Bobby Connor.

In the darkness he could see pinpoints of light like stars reflected in her eyes. He opened his mouth to say something, but she pointed to her ear and he listened.

Nothing.

Then he had it, and his skin began to crawl. The soft background hum of the central air conditioning was gone; the cops had shut off all the power in the building.

The reality of their predicament settled in by increments. The air wouldn't give out all at once, and they could always retreat down to the short corridor below the cubicle. But then what? There would be no access down to the lobby save the elevator which would not, of course, be running. They were more than fifty storeys up and just a wall away who knew how many cops were waiting for them to make a break.

Breathard was squeezing the life out of them.

He felt Chika's hand on him again, saw that she was slithering backwards towards the reed mat. What was she thinking? He helped her remove the mat, watched as she unlatched the trap door, dropped down into the corridor after her.

At the other end the elevator door stood open, the lights out. She headed for it. Why? It was inert, of no use to them.

When they were in the cab, she pointed silently upwards to the service hatch in the roof. He nodded, hefted her up and, a moment later, heard a scrape, then her weight came off him. With some difficulty he hoisted himself up through the hatch. Halfway through the muscles in his right bicep cramped and Chika had to hold onto him while he jammed his left elbow against the grease-coated cab roof. For one long breathless moment he hovered in limbo, not knowing whether he would make it up or fall back into the cab. Then he gathered his strength, levering himself up beside her.

For a time, he crouched on the tiny metal roof, unable to utter a word. Chika put an arm across his shoulders and he sensed the same kind of warmth he had felt at the end of his struggle with Suma. This time it infused his entire body, relaxing his severely overtaxed muscles.

Chika stood up then, as he rose beside her on shaky legs. There was marginally more light here, and he became aware of where they were, atop a small oblong of metal at the top of a shaft somewhere over five

296

hundred feet in height. It was a damn good thing, he thought, that he had no way to look down.

He saw Chika slowly raise her head, and he felt something stirring, as if a wind had sprung up in here. Light faded and he had the vertiginous sensation of receding at a rapid rate down a tunnel. Instinctively he grabbed hold of the central cable, but Chika immediately took his hands away, held them in hers as if she was afraid he would otherwise hurt himself.

Something was happening. Wolf felt a vibration and, along with it, a kind of darkness that possessed weight, size, shape, although he could define none of these parameters. They merely existed in his mind like a melody or a mathematical equation.

He saw the light in Chika's eyes and he had an overpowering urge to look away as from the face of Medusa, remembering Cathy on fire in the city of the hopeless, Johnson dead in the kitchen of his brownstone, the blue fire dancing in the hole in Kamiwara's chest, Suma on his Electra-Glide as Bobby burst into flame.

But he did not look away. He stared into her eyes as the green light from those luminescent crescents in her irises restructured the pulsing darkness, manipulating it, sending it shooting upwards like an exultation of black fireworks until it coiled around the gear-and-pulley mechanism at the apex of the shaft.

Wolf started as the elevator lurched. He could feel the tremors erupting in his muscles, knew they came not from fatigue because he was beyond that now, the ancillary supply of adrenaline having kicked in just about the time they had slid out of the darkened, airless cubicle.

Scared. He was scared of what Chika was, of what he had become. Again, he felt the enormous power of the mysterious magnetism that drew him to her and he shuddered. And then he saw the image of his father, in his sweat-stained cowboy hat with the Apache war fetish stuck in the woven band, standing atop Lightning Ridge, saying to him, *Life isn't worth shit unless you take risks, remember that. Without risk you might as well settle down, put your glasses on, and count the days until you die.*

'I can't do it.'

Wolf blinked, bringing the scene back into focus. They were still in darkness at the top of the elevator shaft, the building still all around them but filled with cops closing on them. The steel cab was motionless beneath his feet.

'What happened?'

'My power isn't strong enough.'

'Christ, now what? I don't have that kind of control over my sight yet.'

297

She looked at him wordlessly.

'This can't be the end of it,' Wolf said. 'I won't let it.'

She took his hand, placed it over her heart. 'Summon the shadow,' she said, 'and the light.'

The luminous green crescents appeared in her eyes and he felt that peculiar heat infusing his hand, arm and body. He opened his mind and, throwing his head back, stared upwards.

Light appeared where before there had been only darkness. A fluttering as of birds at twilight, calling and restless. He heard a thrumming – no, that wasn't right – he *felt* it as he concentrated. He built, what could you call it? a shaft of light/darkness/motion, strong but tensile. He could move it but it could not be severed as long as he maintained his concentration, of this he felt confident. Fear erupted again, but he pushed it roughly away, focusing the darkness of *makura na hiruma*, bending it to his bidding.

'Now,' he whispered hoarsely, 'we go.'

Good Christ!

The elevator swept into motion, silently descending, electricless, as smoothly as an arc of water, as he harnessed the power of *makura na hiruma*, hers and his, a dark beacon holding them securely in its fastness.

The hot sizzle of psychic energy caused the barrier of time to be displaced, and into his mind came the image of his younger self facing White Bow's death, frightened of the power – not only his grandfather's that allowed him to seemingly surmount death, *but his own.*

The elevator cab came to rest at the bottom of the shaft with hardly a vibration. Wolf and Chika dropped down through the roof and were back on the concrete apron. Wolf desperately wanted to reflect on what had happened over the past hour but there was no time now; they were hardly in the clear.

Instead of retracing their steps back the way they had come in Chika led him down into the shadows to the left of the elevator. There was a metal door which she unlocked, then cautiously opened.

He could smell gasoline and oil – they were in an underground carpark. Chika closed and locked the metal door behind them, guided him silently between sparsely parked cars to the rearmost row and there he saw the gleaming metallic charcoal and chrome hearse he had seen her climb into in front of the funeral parlour on Second Avenue.

She opened the rear doors and he could see within a polished chestnut casket. He heard the soft but unmistakable *snik!* of a switchblade opening, then she turned to him, the blade glinting very close to him and, smiling, said, 'How are you at dying?'

298

THIRTEEN

Washington/New York/Tokyo/Rural Massachusetts

Thornburg Conrad III was woken from his nap by the sound of the chimes. He lay in bed for several moments staring at nothing. Then the chimes rang again and he swung his long thin legs over the side of the bed, slipped on his silk paisley dressing gown and padded to the front door.

Thornburg's villa, on the manicured grounds of Magnolia Terrace, was more secluded than most – which was the way Thornburg wanted it. Most of the highly prized villas overlooked the golf course, but Thornburg's was set back, amid a copse of silver-barked birch and huge rose of sharon. Behind it, a small brook sparkled and gurgled over smooth black rocks, and the path that led to its front door was enclosed for most of its way by a bower of white wisteria trained to arch over a cedar arbour.

Thornburg passed a mirror, stopped for a moment to admire the straightness of his back, the fullness of his musculature. He brushed his silver hair back from his forehead, then pulled open the door.

'You're looking good,' Stevie Powers said as she kissed him on the cheek. 'Your face is fuller and so many lines are gone. Have a good nap?'

'Probably not,' Thornburg said, closing the door. 'I dreamed the entire time.'

Stevie smiled at him. 'It only seemed that way.' She went past him, into the living room. 'How is Tiffany?'

'Not well,' he said, slumping into an upholstered chair. 'I believe she's got leukaemia.'

Stevie came and sat down beside him. 'I'd better have a talk with her, then.'

'No. I've decided not to tell her.'

'Is that wise? I mean the disease will – '

'Her treatments will mask the symptoms until the very end.'

'I take it the course of treatment led to the cancer.'

He nodded. 'That damned recombinant insulin-like growth factor-1. It's still so promising and yet we can't tap its potential. Every time we get tantalizingly close something like this occurs and we're back at square one.'

Stevie got up, went to the bar, fixed them both a neat Glenlivet. Thornburg nodded, took the glass from her. 'Time,' he said, 'is running out.' He held the liquor up to the light so that prisms of colour shot through its depths. 'Too soon, too soon.'

He downed the Scotch in one long draught, then his hand swung sideways, flinging the glass into the air. It smashed on the marble floor of the entryway. 'If only we could break the riddle of this cloned complex protein, God rot it in hell! What is the missing element that will make the molecule chain stable?'

Stevie wisely said nothing, allowing the storm to pass on its own. He detested being coddled; she had learned that lesson very quickly, even though it meant a conscious suppression of her innate empathy, one of her most useful psychoanalytic tools.

There was a new tension in him she could not explain. She'd heard him rant before against a science that had come so far but was moving too slowly. What had happened? She knew that if she just came out and asked him she'd get nowhere. She realized that her stomach muscles were clenched.

She took her worst fear and verbalized it. 'Wolf is with this Japanese woman. Isn't that what you wanted from the beginning? Now it's just a matter of time until he gets you what you need.'

His stare was like being fixed in the headlight beams of an oncoming car. Stevie tried to read his expression, failed. There was a look in his eyes she had never seen before; it alarmed her, as if she had been witness to something she should not have seen. She felt that squirming in the pit of her stomach, and, like many women, she instinctively went to the core of her distress.

'What about Wolf?' she said. 'Is he all right?'

Thornburg said nothing, and this frightened her all the more. 'What have you heard? Has he been hurt? Or . . . ' She bit her lip, unable to voice the terrible thought.

Thornburg closed his eyes for a moment. He cursed himself. Usually so in control, so at home with manipulating people, he had allowed his own obsession to shatter his facade. He knew that if he tried to tell her that Wolf was all right, she'd know he was lying. Her radar was turned on and tuned in. He thought it best to give her at least a semblance of the truth.

He opened his eyes. 'At present, Matheson is in some difficulty. But he will prevail. You have my word on that.'

That seemed to calm Stevie somewhat. After a while, she said, 'You know who murdered Amanda, don't you?'

'I have a pretty good idea.'

'I want – '

He nodded. 'Don't you think I understand what motivated you to help me?' He smiled at her. 'I know what you want and, believe me, you'll get it. Matheson will run the murderer to ground, don't you worry about that. I've seen him in action; I know what he's capable of. I already pity the person who killed your sister.'

'I'd like to kill the murderer myself.'

'Yes,' Thornburg said, 'I believe you would, and the emotion is magnificent. How Matheson must have been smitten by that.'

She bristled at his callous tone; the voice men all too often used with women. 'If you've confused me with a whore, you've made a serious mistake.'

He was staring at her intently. A small smile crept along the corners of his dry lips. 'Yes, you *have* been close to Matheson; you have felt the power inside him. Tell me, Stevie, did you sleep with him?'

She did not trust herself to speak. She was dismayed by this side of him; she had seen him do this to other people, pin them to the wall like a lepidopterist with his butterflies.

'Of course you did. There was the magnetism, drawing you.' He put his bent forefinger up to his pursed lips. 'And how many times did you come close to telling him about me?'

'I never came close.'

'Really?' His head cocked. 'And you aren't in love with him, either.'

Stevie did not answer him right away; perhaps she could not. She glanced briefly down at her hands clasped in her lap, let out a long breath. 'I want to get this straight the first time so there's no possibility of misunderstanding. My personal feelings are my own business. What I feel about Wolf or about Morton, for that matter, is for me alone to know.'

'Not if these *personal feelings* impinge on what I have to do.'

'Are you worried I will betray you to Wolf?'

'My dear, when you are in my position and are lucky enough to get to be my age the threat of betrayal becomes a constant concern.'

Stevie smiled as she took his hand. 'It is precisely because of your position that I wouldn't dream of betraying you. You are the one who made Morton's reputation in Washington, who gave me entrée into the associations that made mine. He and I owe everything to you.'

'I detest the word "everything"; it's a catch-all that describes nothing.'

Now Stevie took a hard look into his eyes and thought she saw something dark and squirmy in their depths. She remembered him speaking of Wolf's 'power', and she began to wonder whether that dark squirmy thing was fear. Could Thornburg Conrad III actually be frightened of another human being? She wouldn't have thought so, but now it seemed possible.

'Thornburg – '

His head twitched. 'I must have some.' His voice had turned toneless.

'No.'

'Fetch it for me.'

'Absolutely not.'

His head came up, his eyes locking on hers, scalding her, making her itch inside where she could not scratch. 'Fetch it and administer it.'

She stood up. 'But the danger – '

He grinned, a fierce repellent expression that made his face look momentarily like a death's-head. 'The only danger worth considering is that I won't live long enough to see this through.'

She went into his bedroom, removed the false bottom of the lower drawer in his bedside table. She ignored the container of prescription sleeping tablets and the US Army-issue officer's .45-calibre pistol, reached towards the line of rubber-topped glass phials and the supply of disposable hypodermics. She filled a hypodermic with a clear fluid from one of the unlabelled phials, then squeezed a bit out of the end to purge the syringe of air.

Returning to the living room, she looked down at him, said, 'Don't you want to reconsider? This is what killed the others, what's killing Tiffany.'

'My blood type is different than hers,' he said in that same toneless voice. 'Besides, this serum has been refined further.'

'And you think this will make a difference? That there won't be side effects?'

'Just do it!'

Stevie bent, slid the needle into the major vein on the inside of his thigh, depressed the plunger slowly and steadily. She watched his face all the time because there were other side effects – short-lived but unpleasant – that could occur.

She was hardly finished before his buttocks clenched, he rose off the chair, his back arched, his neck a twisted cord of tendons and ligaments. His lips were pulled back, baring clenched teeth. She could hear the breath whistling between his teeth, and his words, 'Fight . . . against the fall . . . of . . . night.'

The sensation of motion ceased. The rumble of the engine came through clearly and he clung to that, the single sound from outside, in the claustrophobic darkness. He could smell some chemical in the satin

302

lining and the sharp odour of polish used to buff the brass fittings but there was barely any scent of wood.

He heard voices and he stiffened. They were muffled, far away, but he could make out the timbres — two deeper male voices and Chika's higher, lighter tone in response. A lot would depend on her, especially in the beginning. Then, of course, it would be up to him, *How are you at dying?*

She had used the switchblade down the back of his sweat- and blood-stained clothes, helping him on with a dark-blue suit — Moravia's — that she had taken from the rear of the hearse. He had not asked her what it was doing there, had not cared.

Then she led him back, and they had clambered through the rear doors. She had raised the heavy lid of the coffin and he had climbed in.

She had knelt over him, painting his face and hands, artificially draining them of colour, except for the cheeks to which she applied some form of mortician's rouge. He remembered wondering if this had been a game she and Moravia had played, but decided the less he knew about it right now the better.

'What's the point of this?' he had said to her midway through. 'If they make you open the coffin, they'll recognize me immediately.'

'No,' she said, 'they won't.' And he had seen the hint of the luminous green crescents in her irises and thought, *makura na hiruma.* Perhaps she can make them see only what she wants them to see.

'Do you know how to breathe so they will not see your chest move?' she had asked when she was finished.

He told her about his *sensei* and she had nodded. 'It is also vitally important that you do not move your eyes beneath your lids,' she said. 'You will find yourself wanting to when the coffin lid is opened and you become aware of the sudden return of light.' He had felt her fingertips on his face. 'Now turn your head a little this way, yes, so if we're stopped they won't be able to see the pulse in your carotid.' Then she had lowered the lid on him.

Now there came a heavy click — the back doors opening — and the voices were abruptly louder. He could feel a slight tilting as weight came onto the rear shocks and in his mind's eye he could see the cops in their bullet-proof vests, their smoke-visored helmets, bending over as they moved down the inside of the hearse, could almost hear them say, 'Open the coffin.'

Nothing but a jumble of voices, indistinct through the wood and brass. He could feel the satin on the backs of his hands and ears, and he had to fight the irrational sensation that he could also feel it on his lips, cheeks, forehead, eyelids. Pressing down. Stop it! he told himself.

Tidal breathing.

Relax.

A creak and light flooded over him, probably dim because of the hearse's interior but seeming very bright to him, as Chika had said. Steady on, look at nothing, there's nothing to see . . . except for the curious faces of the cops peering into the coffin's interior – Stop it!

Tidal breathing.

Relax.

Chika's soft voice, the rising of *makura na hiruma*.

But the carotid would be pulsing at the side of his neck, in shadow, yes, but the longer they stared at him the greater chance for them to notice –

Light fading, a soft click – the lid was back in place!

A moment later he heard the motor pitch change as Chika put it into gear and then the force of weight coming into his legs and feet, the sensation of motion starting up and they were clear.

He counted off five minutes, then raised his arms, lifting the lid on the coffin and, in the dim coolness of the hearse, allowed himself to breathe normally, slowly, freely.

'Chika?'

'Hi there.'

'Okay?'

'We're not being followed.'

He could see the back of her head as she drove, moved slightly so that he could see her face in the rear-view mirror. 'No cherry-red Electra-Glide Harley behind us?'

'No.'

Chika changed lanes, speeded up, changed lanes again, weaving in and out of the traffic. Finally, she said, 'We've got no tags at all.'

'Get us out of the city.'

'I'll do better than that,' she said. 'I'm going to get us out of the country.'

'If we're flying I don't want to go through Kennedy.' He clambered over the seatback, sat next to her.

'I agree.' She told him to open the glove compartment where he found a package of Kleenex and some cold cream. 'We'll leave via Logan in Boston. It's all arranged.'

The sun, ripe and golden, was stretched through the treetops like a web by the time they exited the highway. Wolf had cleaned up his face but he was stiff, the skin of his torso caked with dried blood. He thought he had slept through part of the drive; his eyes felt gritty and the glare of the lights dazzled him.

Chika pulled into a 7-Eleven. She returned with a bottle of hydrogen peroxide, a box each of cotton balls and adhesive pads. Wolf took off his jacket, lifted his shirt, and she went to work on his cuts and scrapes while he opened up the other bag she had brought. Ten minutes later, they were on their way again, still heading northeast towards Massachusetts.

'I've got to get something to eat,' Wolf said after they'd been on the Mass Pike for a couple of hours. 'But from now on I want you to use the back roads. It's easier to follow us on the highway.'

Chika headed for the next exit, took a series of smaller and smaller roads. At length, she pulled into the parking lot of a generic country diner.

It was still too early for the dinner crowd and they staked out a booth of their choice, overlooking the lake. Wolf went into the men's room to wash the vestiges of the cold cream off his face. He took out a disposable razor, shook out some shave cream Chika had purchased at the 7-Eleven, scraped the stubble off his face. He rinsed off, stared at himself in the mirror.

Who am I? he wondered. *What* have I become?

Back in the booth, he downed a large glass of water, asked for a refill. Then he ordered a rare steak, hash browns with a mixed salad on the side. Chika asked for steamed rice and baked beans, the only kind of beans the diner served.

Chika used the ladies' room, then made the call to check their airline reservations while Wolf paid the check in cash. As he was waiting for change, he glanced out the side window, saw in the glow of the diner a glint of deep cherry red and chrome. He picked up his change, went back to the table to leave the tip. As he did so, he scooped up a handful of packets of granulated sugar.

He went around to the side of the building. Sure enough, he found the Electra-Glide half-buried in a grove of alder and blackberry bushes, and there was the tell-tale smudge on its rear fender from the burst of flame as Suma had guided it past Bobby Connor.

Wolf looked around, his scalp tingling. Where was Suma? Quickly, he unscrewed the gas cap, dumped in the sugar. That would make the Harley inoperable until Suma could get it cleaned out.

He found Chika waiting for him by the side of the restaurant. 'I've seen Suma,' she said. 'He's in the woods.'

'Let's go.'

They went past the Harley, through a gap in the brambles of the blackberry bushes. Almost immediately they hit a path, narrow, root-scarred, but a definable matted track winding through the thickening underbrush. Above their heads stands of larch, oak and river birch

305

intermingled with cedars and white pines. The whirring of insects was insistent and Wolf was obliged to bat mosquitoes away from his elbows, ankles, and neck.

The track now made a sharp turn to the left and the ground sloped sharply downwards. The air was sodden. Getting close to a stream, Wolf guessed. Every minute or so he automatically turned to look behind him. As far as he could tell they weren't being followed, but with the chattering and trilling of the birds, the clatter of the rapids they were approaching it was impossible to be sure.

He stopped, said, 'He's gone too deep into the forest. There's a high probability we're heading straight into a trap.'

'I know,' Chika said. She stood so still he could not see her breathing. 'Do you think we should go back?'

He knew what was prudent, but he also wanted Suma badly. Fleetingly he wondered why Chika wasn't continuing to urge them to get out of there and onto the plane bound for Japan.

'Suma can't detect me,' he said at length. 'Let's see if we can catch him with his own game.'

Almost immediately, they broke out of the dense underbrush, and were upon the stream. It was fairly wide and looked a lot deeper than Wolf had anticipated. Chika, in the lead, paused for a moment on the muddy bank. She turned her head to look back at him. She smiled, but there was something odd about it, a vagueness, an emptiness that Wolf picked up on.

He was still puzzling over this when Chika stepped into the stream.

There was a faint crawling in his belly. 'I don't like any of this,' Wolf said.

Chika put her forefinger across her lips, beckoned him forward into the stream. Wolf took off his shoes, slung them by their laces around his neck, and cautiously began to wade out into the water. It was piercingly cold. The sun was already lost in the foliage.

He saw she was pointing and looked. In a moment, he could see a silhouette moving away from them on the far shore: Suma.

Wolf moved forward. The silty mud squooshed through his bare toes and tickled the tops of his feet. Chika hadn't moved; she was waiting for him at the midway point, not wanting to give her position away should Suma look behind him.

The water made its way rapidly up Wolf's body, and now he wished that he had taken his shirt off. The tails fanned out around him and the whole was soon sopping, clinging clammily to his goose-bumped flesh like the weight of someone trying to pull him down.

His feet were encountering more rocks; most were moss-encrusted,

306

slimy and extremely slippery. He was forced to peer downwards through the purling water in order to help maintain his balance. With every step he took the water rose higher on him until he was in up to his neck. This made no sense to him since he had seen Chika up ahead with more of her out of the water. She must have been standing on a rock.

He looked up for Chika to gain his bearings but he was alone in the stream.

He glanced quickly around.

Then he saw her on the far bank. She was standing with her hands behind her back, staring at him with the kind of idle curiosity one might regard a gaily coloured caterpillar.

Wolf watched her, and the short hairs at the base of his neck stirred. He thought of Stevie warning him that Chika would kill him. *Don't, please, be in such a hurry to meet your own death.*

And he could feel it now, his own death, turning the air around him putrid with decay. He moved abruptly backwards, but now he could feel the full force of the current as it gathered itself to shoot through to the more shallow rapids downstream.

It was at that point that Chika stepped into the water without making a ripple. She took another step and cold sweat began to break out all over Wolf's body. Jesus Christ, he thought, as his heart pounded wildly.

'What is this?' he growled. 'Who the hell are you, anyway?'

As if in answer, Chika now rose out of the stream until she appeared to be standing on the water. She was still smiling that odd smile, and now it occurred to Wolf that there was nothing behind the expression, that it was the smile one sees on two-dimensional billboards, photos representing people but which are not people at all, only images.

He continued to struggle back towards the near shore, a kind of unthinking terror gripping him.

Then Chika's face seemed to pale out, as if all at once her skin had lost its sun-burnished hue. At the same moment the face itself elongated, as if the bones beneath the flesh were being stretched by an unseen force. Chika's jaws dropped open and a tongue came out, only it wasn't a human tongue.

Wolf let out a breath as if he had something viscid stuck in his throat. Once, when he was young, he had seen a horror film, one of those cheesy Japanese concoctions where the special effects were done on one soundstage, the Japanese actors read their lines on a second soundstage, and the American leads, brought over to Tokyo for a week, did their closeups at a different time.

The acting may have been lousy but the special effects in this one were good enough to make an impression on the young Wolf. The monster in this film was some half-snake, half-nightmare that slithered out of its swampy den to munch those humans foolish enough to disturb its environment. It did that by engulfing the entire head, suffocating its victim before its great jaws clamped down, severing head from body.

Impossibly, Chika's face was transforming into a replica of that slimy fiend, perfect in every way. Wolf watched, transfixed in horror, as the beast now shot forward right at his face.

Wolf screamed in spite of himself. Part of his mind knew – knew! – that this could not be happening, but another part was seeing it take shape in front of him. He threw up his hands as the jaws hinged open to engulf his head. He could already smell its vile stench, feel the unnatural darkness looming, threatening to block off his source of oxygen. He felt the wind of its passage as the darkness brushed him.

At the last instant, his wide-open eyes saw the image shudder, ripple and fly into ten-thousand sparks, but as those sparks winked out the darkness only increased and now he could feel something tugging his shoelaces tight about his neck.

Instinctively, he reached up to pull the shoes off him; he lost his balance, his bare foot slipping off a rock, toppling him head first into the stream.

Under the water, he continued to pull desperately at the noose of his shoelaces, but this only seemed to draw them tighter around him. He concentrated on getting his head out of the water but, again, this seemed beyond him. Something was holding him under and the more he struggled the faster he was held.

He saw Chika, her face angelic once more. Then she smiled into Wolf's bulging face and Wolf thought he would go mad. Her smile increased in height and width until it had assumed Cheshire Cat proportions, and he knew that he had been betrayed. He lost hope. He remembered their flight out of New York City, the intimate moments in Moravia's saferoom. How could he have been so wrong about her?

Impossibly, the smile continued to grow until there was only a black void dancing in the water. It came towards him and now he was cold, very cold, his bones like ice, his heart labouring to push the sludge that had been his blood through his veins and arteries.

Lights were dancing in his head; he could no longer think clearly but he kicked out just the same, wanting still to save himself, though by this time there was nothing much to save, the strength was gone, the heat of life fast diminishing, the thought of air merely a dream, one of many that tore through his consciousness in that last instant. He sensed the void rushing towards him and instinctively he fought against it.

Only his *makura na hiruma* could save him now. He fought to summon

308

his dark familiar, but the terrifying void of death was closing in on him . . . the monster –

Forget the monster, forget the void: they are both illusions. Fight the bastard who would kill you!

Wolf let his body go limp as he drew the darkness to him. There was a brief swirl, as if now there was another, slithery presence against his cheek, his forehead. Then he opened his eyes, saw the reality he should have seen all along: Suma pulling tight on the noose of Wolf's own shoelaces. It had been Suma all along. Chika had not betrayed him.

Now he looked into Suma's eyes and he could see them open wide as the Japanese recognized the power in his adversary. There was a moment's hesitation as the shock gripped Suma.

Wolf projected outwards from the heart of darkness inside himself. Suma recoiled, shook his head, then, kicking his feet, came on and Wolf, unwrapping the noose from around his neck, began to feel the force of his power.

Then Suma was looking upwards towards the surface of the stream and, whirling in the water, kicked powerfully away from Wolf, fast disappearing in the gloom of the rock-studded stream bed.

Wolf launched himself upwards, breaching the surface, his lungs gasping for air as he felt a hand grip him, dragging him back to the near shore where he lay, gulping in air and staring up at Chika's grim face as she held him.

FOURTEEN

Washington/Tokyo/Boston

Ham Conrad was waiting for Marion Starr St James as she left work. Early evening sunlight was glinting off the tops of the federal buildings as he leaned over in the driver's seat, opened the kerbside door and told her to get in.

'Hi,' Marion said, 'what a surprise.'

'I'll bet. Let's go get some dinner.'

She smiled. 'Oh, I'm sorry, darling, I wish you had given me a ring earlier. I have a meeting at seven and then – '

'Get in, Marion.'

She frowned. 'Is everything all right? You look mad as hell.'

'Mad as hell,' he said, 'or mad as a hatter, I don't know which yet.' He stared hard at her. 'Do as I say, Marion. I don't think you want a scene here in front of your colleagues.'

She slipped into the seat beside him and he took off before she had fully closed the door. 'Christ, Ham, what's got under your skin?'

He nodded to the mobile phone. 'Make the calls you need to. You're spending the evening with me.'

She looked at him for a full minute before rummaging in her briefcase for her appointment book. She made two calls. She looked up when she was finished, saw they were cruising through one of the sections of the city that looked more and more dilapidated the further you got into it. Drugs and murder. Ghetto.

'Where are we going?'

'Dinner,' he said without looking at her.

'Here?' Every face she saw was black. 'Are you crazy?'

'What's the matter?' he asked harshly. 'Are you prejudiced?'

'No, merely prudent.' She put her hand on the door handle. 'Stop the car. Let me out.'

'That would hardly be prudent.'

'Christ, Ham.'

He pulled over to the kerb along the eleven-hundred block of Florida Avenue in front of a dark-fronted plate glass and pressed tin facade. A neon sign blinked on and off: POOR BOY'S.

310

'Come on,' he said, getting out and slamming the door.

Marion stared at him over the roof of the car. 'Aren't you worried this won't be here when we come out?'

'Lots of white people come here to eat.'

She looked nervously around. 'I hope to Christ you know what you're doing.'

He grinned, locked the car, took her elbow as they went inside. The place was nearly as dark inside as it had been outside. There was a powerful smell of burning hickory and charcoal. Fake Tiffany lamps hung from a pressed tin ceiling painted a matte black. The walls were panelled in wood-grain laminate. The floor was made of tiny black and white grime-encrusted tiles, cracked in many places; in others, whole sections were missing. Sawdust was scattered over the tiles.

Along the right as they came in a long green zinc bar was holding up a bevy of drinkers who had the appearance of having been there for weeks, possibly even months. The only significant illumination came from the row of worn mirrors, reflecting the feeble light of the ceiling fixtures.

Marion was acutely aware of every head in the place turning to stare coldly at her. She at once regretted wearing her short wool skirt, her sheer silk blouse; she glanced down at herself and saw to her shame and horror that her nipples were visible through the fabric. She felt like pulling on her ankle-length coat.

'Table for two,' Ham said when they came abreast of the oversized bartender. No one paid him the slightest attention.

Past a short painted plywood divider she could see an expanse of tables. Contrary to what Ham had said there wasn't a white face in the entire restaurant.

'I want to get out of here,' Marion said very softly.

'Of course you don't.' He took her elbow in a firm grip, guided her to a table against the left wall. 'This looks fine,' he said, swiping crumbs off her chair with the edge of his hand. He put his hand on her shoulder and Marion sat. He sat across from her.

When the waitress had gone past them for the third time without glancing in their direction Marion said, 'Will you please tell me what's made you virtually kidnap me off the street?'

'You deserve to be kidnapped,' he said. 'You've been a very bad girl.'

An argument began between two patrons at the bar and Marion waited for the worst of the loud invective to subside. 'I like being a bad girl,' she said. 'But I also like knowing that I'm being bad.'

He finally caught the eye of the waitress, ordered some drinks. Then he turned back to her. 'Tell me how you met my father.'

311

Someone had put money in the jukebox. Queen Latifah began to bust a move.

'Jesus, this place gives me the creeps.'

'People gotta be people.'

'I read the papers. I know what can happen in a place like this.'

Queen Latifah was getting right into it now. Ham excused himself. 'Gotta go to the little boys' room. Be right back.'

Marion sat alone at the table. The drinks did not come; the waitress acted as if she didn't exist. Not so the male patrons, who were, it seemed to her, increasingly interested in what lay beneath her skirt and blouse. She felt cut off, abandoned on the strange far shore of a lake of unknown depths. She had never before been in an area where she was virtually the only white person and she had to admit it made her uneasy. She imagined a knife or a gun beneath every shabby suit jacket, a plastic bag of cocaine in every hip pocket. Stupid thoughts, surely, she tried to reassure herself. Nonetheless she felt herself shiver.

A moment later she gathered her handbag and briefcase, went as quickly as she could through the rear of the room, trying not to think of all the curious and hostile eyes on her. She put her briefcase on the bar, waited for the bartender to come her way, said, 'Could you phone for a cab for me?'

He stared at her with yellow eyes, rubbed at his moustache with a thick horny finger. 'Phone out of order.'

'Well, is there a public phone here?'

'Also out,' he said. A gold earring in the shape of a bullet was hanging from one lobe. All his hair was on the top of his head. 'But wouldn't do you no good nohow. Reg'lar taxis woan come here after dark.' He gave her a huge grin. 'Can't say I blame 'em none.' He sucked noisily on his huge teeth. 'Bad shit happens here'bouts. My advice, go back to yo' table.'

'No chance.' Marion grabbed her briefcase. 'I'll find a phone booth out – ' She had turned to her right, had come face to face with a tall broad-shouldered man with a handsome face but a besotted demeanour. His skin was very dark, it glistened off his bald pate in the low light. He wore a purple open-collar shirt; there were at least six gold chains around his thick neck.

'Where yo goin', pretty mama?'

'Pardon me,' she said, attempting to shoulder her way around him. He grabbed hold of her and she said, 'Fuck you, buddy!' and stamped hard on his instep. His eyes seemed to change colour but he put a large hand across her throat, squeezing down until Marion made a thick, ugly sound. He said, 'Doan you move now, honeychile.'

'I'm – I'm with someone,' Marion managed to get out. 'He'll take care of you if you don't – '

'You wit Whitey,' the bald man said. When he smiled she could see a

312

gold tooth. 'He chicken-shit like all his kind. Yo think I be scared o' him? I doan give him a minute o' thought.' His head came close to hers. 'But yo – I like yo' accent.' His teeth clacked together loudly and she could smell the liquor on his breath.

She closed her eyes, said a little prayer. Then she cursed Ham mightily for bringing her here.

'Yo, Maury.'

Marion opened her eyes at the sound of the voice from behind her. 'Yo.'

'What's happenin'?'

'Shit, yo' date's 'bout to mess herself. Yo need t'find yoself stronger bitches, bro.'

That voice. 'Ham?' She began to twist, choked on the palm of the bald man and her eyes began to water. He let her go and she whirled, her face a mask of fury and embarrassment. 'You bastard. You set this up and now you're enjoying it.'

'I've a right.'

The bald man was laughing, the bartender had turned away, the show being over.

Marion put a hand over her face.

'You want to go back to the table now?'

She nodded and he took her back; their drinks were waiting for them, along with menus.

Ham could see that she was seething. 'You're not the kind of woman to sulk all night.'

'You don't know what the hell kind of woman I am.' Marion dredged out a compact, took a look at herself in the tiny mirror.

No, but I'm learning, Ham thought. 'None the worse for wear?'

'You,' she said, snapping her compact closed, 'are a real sonuvabitch.'

The waitress set down a plate filled with food.

She bent over, inhaling the delicious aroma. 'What's this?'

'Snoots,' he said, digging into the crunchy slabs of meat that were slathered with a thick red sauce. 'A sure sign of a truce.'

Marion gave him a cool look, nibbled tentatively around a forkful. 'This is good.'

'Yeah. Real soul food,' he said. 'That's why I come here all the time. Best snoots outside of St Louis.'

'What are snoots?'

'Deep-fried pig snouts.'

He watched her put her fork aside, stare at the plate of snoots. He continued crunching down on the morsels, and waited until she had downed some of her drink. 'You want to tell me about you and my father now?'

313

'I had hoped to avoid this,' she said, after a time.

'I imagine you would.'

Her head came up; he could see her cheeks were flushed. 'Give me a chance, will you? This is difficult enough as it is.' She toyed distractedly with the necklace at her throat. 'Thornburg and my father were friends.'

'Were?'

She smiled sadly. 'Ah, all my illusions are evaporating. I lied when I gave you the impression that my father is still alive. He died some years ago bringing a load of American Army rifles into the countryside around Belfast.'

Ham stared at her. 'Your father was a gun-runner not a shipbuilder as you said.' He recalled her lighting the candle on his boat, and was willing to bet that it had been her father for whom she had said a prayer.

Marion sighed. 'Actually, he was both. He started out as a shipbuilder. It was *his* father's business. Then he made a mistake; he sold the company to the Japanese.' She circled her spoon around and around the tablecloth. 'I don't believe he was ever really happy after that. He grew bored, restless; I suppose that's one of the reasons he allowed his IRA friends to talk him into running guns for them.'

'And, naturally,' Ham said, 'when he was killed you took over the gun-running.'

'Not in the least.' She realized what she was doing, put the spoon aside. 'He was a dyed-in-the-wool chauvinist, my father, and he made provisions in his will for my male cousins to come in and run it.'

'Ah.'

'Yeah. I hate their guts; they're such greedy bastards. It's all personal this thing, which was why I lied to you. I assumed you wouldn't want to get involved in a family vendetta.'

'You were right there. Messy stuff, vendettas.'

She nodded. 'Let's forget I ever mentioned Extant Exports, okay?' She picked up her glass, was about to take a sip when she set it down abruptly and put her face in her hands. Ham could hear her weeping softly.

He sat there looking at her, wondering what to believe. Being with her was like walking into his favourite fun house attraction, the Hall of Mirrors. Good Christ, but she's fascinating, he thought. Why couldn't I have met her when I was younger, before my wife soured me on the institution of marriage?

'Damn, I hate it when I cry,' Marion was saying, dabbing her eyes with her napkin.

He gave her a little smile. 'Aren't men supposed to hate it when women cry?'

314

She laughed. 'I think I heard that somewhere. That's why I don't do it often in public.'

'Take my father, for instance; he flew into a rage when his women cried. I suppose he thought he could bully the weeps out of them. Matter of fact, I'm surprised he didn't marry you.'

'Of course he tried,' Marion said. 'And he's very persistent.'

'Yes, that's one of his more frightening characteristics.'

'It must have been interesting growing up in his house.'

'That's one way of putting it,' Ham said, 'but not one I'd use.'

'You two don't get along?'

'Well, I suppose it depends on my father's mood. But then so much depends on my father's moods, doesn't it.'

Marion gave a real laugh this time. 'I like you this way, strong and confident and a little bit irreverent.'

'Then maybe it's time to fold up the tents of the scam you're running on me.'

She was quiet for a long time. At last she said, 'I'd like that but . . . '

'But what?'

'The horrible truth is, I don't know whether I'm capable of it.'

'I promise you you'll have help from me.'

She put her hand over his. 'I know that, Ham, but I'm like an addict. I can't be trusted.'

'I didn't say I'd trust you.'

'Don't.' Her eyes bored into his. 'Whatever happens promise me you won't make that mistake.'

He laughed at her as he would a child who is afraid of the dark, to dispel the innate foolishness of the notion. 'I don't make many mistakes,' he said. 'And I never make the same one twice.'

'I recall your father saying that a number of times.'

He insisted they order, then, fried pork chops and pan gravy, okra and black-eyed peas with fatback, molasses-glazed sweet potatoes. 'I guarantee the quality of the food; I come here all the time.'

They talked about nothing consequential during the meal, but when the plates had been cleared and the good strong coffee, sour-mash bourbon-laced pecan pie and the vanilla ice cream served, he looked at her steadily and said, 'Just what was your arrangement with my father?'

'Well, you know your father, he's a real sex-hound. He's obsessed with his own sexuality.'

'He's old, and damned unhappy about it.'

'He's also fascinating – when he lets you see that side of him which, I freely admit, isn't often.'

315

'Yes. He's a closed sonuvabitch.'

'The moment he saw me he wanted to pin me to the mattress.'

'And what was your reaction to this charming overture?'

She frowned. 'The truth is I wanted him to. Well, why not? I'd never done it before with a man of his age. It seemed like something worth trying. But I also knew that if I gave in right away he'd drop me just as quickly. I didn't think I wanted that.'

Ham studied her face. 'Are you trying to tell me you successfully scammed my father?'

She took a sip of her coffee. 'Not really. I don't think that's possible to do. But he loves to be teased by women, so I did that. It got his attention.'

'And then?'

'Then, somehow, the business part started to take dominance and we stopped going to bed together.'

'Ah.'

'What do you mean, "Ah"?'

Ham spooned up the last of his pecan pie, dumped some extra vanilla ice cream on it, let the confluence of rich flavours overrun his taste buds. 'You see, the most common mistake people make concerning my father is that he's obsessed with getting it up; they think that's his weakness.' He stuck his spoon into the ice cream, licked it clean. 'Nothing could be further from the truth. I don't believe my father *has* a weakness, which makes him pretty much unique among human beings. On the contrary, my father can't abide any man who, as he says, is led around by his dick. Instead, he uses sex as a kind of lure – just like many women do – to get what he wants.'

He could sense Marion bridling and he kept his face impassive.

'You mean he wanted something from me all along.'

He nodded. 'Not that he didn't find you extremely attractive; I've no doubt he did. But he's got a number of heads up on the walls of his study – memories of his days on safari in Africa – he also finds extremely attractive. You see what I mean?'

'Trophies.'

'Mmm, that's a good word, yes.'

Marion finished her coffee and her cup was immediately refilled. Ham thanked the waitress, addressing her by name.

'At first, Thornburg seemed interested in our arms shipments. And why not? There's a great deal of money to be made in the business – if you're shrewd enough to be able to collect your money and get out before someone puts a bullet through your brain, wires *plastique* into the ignition of your rental car or gives you up to the local border authorities.

'But there were none of those risks for him, he merely provided us with working capital and in return he got a cut of the profits. Neat for all parties. But gradually I got the impression that he was just going through the motions, that his interest lay elsewhere.

'And then one day he asked me to lunch. He took me to that country club of his, you know . . . '

'Magnolia Terrace.'

'That's the place. Magnificent spot. Very impressive which, I imagine, is why he takes people there. Anyway, the lunch was strictly business. He wanted to know whether Extant got involved in contraband other than munitions. I told him every once in a while we accommodated the special requests of a number of our best clients. What, he asked, had we transshipped? Women, I told him, medical supplies, horses – you name it. I could see he was becoming extremely interested.'

Marion took half a teaspoonful of the glistening pecan pie, washed it down with coffee, then pushed the plate over to Ham. She watched him scoop up the dessert, dip it into the ice cream, spoon it into his mouth. 'I think Thornburg envies you the way you can consume food. It's another reminder of his age.'

Ham stopped eating. 'I never thought of that.'

She continued to watch him. 'Now, I suppose, you'll watch your eating around him.' He did not answer her, but he did not continue eating either. 'You have the son's typical desire to please his father. However, in your case, your father happens to be Thornburg Conrad III, a man who is rarely, if ever, pleased by the doings of mere mortals.'

'What are you getting at?'

Marion leaned forward. 'Just this. No one can come up to his standards, so it's useless to try. No, worse than useless, it's foolish. I mean why spend your whole life in the pursuit of something you know you can never attain? Why try to be *his* person when you can be your own?'

'You can't possibly know; he's not your father.'

'Thank God and amen.'

He pushed the pie sharply away from him. 'It's funny, you telling me how to manage my life.' But he wasn't amused.

'You don't know how hard that was to say to you. Sorry. I thought I owed it to – '

'All you owe me,' he said coldly and carefully, 'is a full explanation of what you and my father were up to.'

There was silence for a time. An M.C. Hammer rap started to come from the jukebox and there was a burst of raucous laughter at the bar. Ham looked over there, as if he would rather be with his rough pals than with Marion.

317

She cleared her throat and Ham's eyes snapped back to her. 'What Thornburg wanted Extant to do for him was transship people.'

'People?'

'*Expendable* people.'

Ham frowned. 'I don't think I understand.'

'We snatched people for him – Arabs, gypsies, God knows who – loners, drifters, people who would not be missed.'

Ham thought this over for a time. 'What did he want them for?'

'He never said and I wasn't stupid enough to ask.'

'Where did he want these expendable people sent?'

'I have no way of knowing where they ended up,' Marion said, 'but the destination he gave us was some place called the Green Branches Clinic outside Arlington, Virginia.'

'You sent me to find your traitor,' Evan said, 'and I have found him.'

It was quiet in the room. The woman who stood gazing almost longingly at the somnolent late winter garden did not turn around or even ask the question others would have asked. Evan said nothing. It would not have surprised her if this woman already knew the identity of the traitor.

At last, the woman turned from her contemplation of nature. Her ochre-coloured eyes seemed as golden and feral as a tiger's. 'Have you heard from your son?'

'Yes, Reverend Mother,' Evan said. 'He tells me he is prospering.'

The Reverend Mother came and knelt opposite Evan. She was dressed in a kimono of cloth-of-gold. Silver herons stalked embroidered shallows across both wide sleeves. Black circular devices, powerful, stark symbols of the eternal nature of the Black Blade Society, emblazoned the front. 'Does he also tell you that he is homesick?'

'No.'

'He is far from home,' the Reverend Mother said, 'and he has been away a long time.' Her long, sleek hair was drawn back from her high forehead, tied into an elaborate braid as thick and long as a horse's tail. 'His work is nearing a conclusion, he has informed me. Which is just as well, because I have a premonition he will be needed here soon.'

'Nishitsu – '

'Forget Nishitsu,' the Reverend Mother said. 'He is off playing at his male games.' She gave a little chuckle. 'It amazes me how fully he believes the fiction that he is in control of the Toshin Kuro Kosai. Then again, why not? For decades, we have maintained that fiction for all but the most inner circle. You, your son, Minako, these people know the truth.' She turned her head as if listening to a sound only she could hear. 'Tell me about the traitor.'

'It is an interesting story,' Evan said. 'I discovered a trail leading back to Shoto Wakare.'

'The trail was devious.'

'Yes, Reverend Mother.'

'But not impossible to unearth.'

'Not for me.'

'No,' the Reverend Mother said. 'Of course not.' She waited a moment, as still as a wasp against a windowpane. 'And it is your opinion that Wakare is our traitor.'

'Wakare is betraying us,' Evan said.

'You discovered in his apartment the coded fax machine.'

'Yes.'

The Reverend Mother nodded, as if pleased with Evan's thoroughness. 'But you know that is not the source of Wakare's betrayal.'

'Of course not,' Evan said. 'We know the source of the coded transmissions to him. We are controlling them.'

The Reverend Mother nodded again. 'Then how is he betraying us?'

'Like every man, he cries to his whore. Mita tells me everything. She has to. I saved her father from the Yakuza to whom he owed a great deal of money.' Evan's pale eyes gleamed. 'Very soon now Wakare will bring Yuji Shian here to Forbidden Dreams to join us. It is a ruse. He has told Yuji that he means to overthrow those who rule the Black Blade Society. He has recruited his friend Yuji to this purpose.'

Evan knew every story told about the Reverend Mother, as well as a few no one would dare speak of; she had been born and raised in Forbidden Dreams. It was her entire world, and the Reverend Mother was the only parent she could remember. The Reverend Mother's face hardened, and Evan was reminded of a story about her. It had been said that she kept her hair so long so that she could use it to strangle her lovers in her bed.

'Are you certain this is betrayal?' the Reverend Mother asked. 'Wakare may have been using this ruse himself to lure Yuji into joining us.'

'I thought of that,' Evan said. 'But Wakare then went on to outline how Yuji would join us and still keep the Oracle's secrets from us.'

'I doubt Yuji could resist our . . . techniques for long. We have so many interesting ones at our disposal.'

'Still, there is a better way,' Evan said. 'Minako never told us where the Oracle is hidden, but now I know. Yuji's brother-in-law Hiroto was kind enough to take me there.'

The Reverend Mother frowned. 'I do not believe it was good

security letting him know about you. If Yuji should speak to him . . .'

'That is impossible now,' Evan said, producing a small paper package which she unrolled in her lap.

The Reverend Mother stared at the object Evan held until a small smile played at the corners of her mouth.

'That was very clever of you, my dear.' The Reverend Mother's gold eyes were closed, her head bobbing a little as if agreeing with unknown voices. Abruptly, she reached out. 'I believe I will soon make use of that.' Her fingers curled around the object and it disappeared.

The late winter's light on her hair made it seem hard, like a carapace or some sort of weapon. Her eyes opened. 'And from the evidence you have given you conclude Wakare is the traitor.'

Evan stirred. 'No, Reverend Mother. From the evidence presented I have concluded that someone is using Wakare as a sacrifice. We already know of his perfidy with the Conrads, but as this proves all too clearly Wakare is no leader.'

The Reverend Mother sighed, unfolding herself like an insect. 'Tell me the rest of it,' she said.

'I think you already know, Reverend Mother.'

'Tell me!' the Reverend Mother shouted with such rage that even Evan, who had known her all her life, knew her better, perhaps, than anyone, save Minako, flinched and drew in upon herself.

Then she nodded. 'It appears that Wakare was set up by Minako Shian. She is our true traitor.'

Wolf and Chika got back into the hearse, and he slumped almost insensate in the passenger's seat.

'What happened to you?' Chika asked. 'I came out of the restaurant and you had disappeared.'

'I saw Suma's Electra-Glide and went out to sabotage it,' Wolf said.

'He must have been waiting for you, using the motorcycle as a lure.'

In the aftermath, it was difficult to disagree with her.

'Did you kill him?'

'No,' Wolf said. 'He sensed you coming and fled.' What had he heard in her voice? Concern over Suma's well-being? He was too exhausted to pursue such an insane notion.

After gassing up, they continued their northeastward course until, an hour later, they were parked in the thickets beside a country lane ten miles from Boston's Logan Airport. Chika suggested Wolf sleep in the coffin but he'd had enough of the box, so they lay down side by side, curled up like lovers. Wolf closed his eyes but he could not sleep. He felt

Chika's presence beside him like a serpent coiling. He got up without disturbing her, sat with his back against the wall of the hearse while he watched her.

Again he thought of the symbol of the serpent as his suspicions once again came to the fore. He shook his head violently as if trying to clear it of a host of illusions. Had it really been Suma outside the diner, leading him into the stream, or had it been Chika all along, Chika who had tried to kill him, Chika who had presented the image of Suma to him so that he would not suspect her?

The possibilities were endless. He began to shake as if with a high fever. He felt as if he was trapped in a hall of mirrors where one false step could send the entire structure crashing in on him. He had never been so terrified, not even on the street facing down the barrel of a Saturday night special.

He savagely clamped his teeth shut so that they would not chatter and wake her. He dreaded the possibility of her eyes opening, seeing him like this. He thought seriously then of running. He had never run from a situation in his life but this, he freely acknowledged, was different. He was in the mad eye of a storm without dimensions. What were his options? Foolish to ask, because he knew he had only one: forward, only forward into the unknowable future.

He wiped the cold sweat from his face with a trembling hand and, despite all the logical arguments against such an action, almost bolted out the back door of the hearse. Then the moment passed, he closed his eyes and, still seeing her in his mind, he fell into a fitful sleep.

At first light Wolf woke her and they had the milk and chocolate doughnuts she had bought at the 7-Eleven. Then they headed for the airport.

They left the hearse in the airport's long-term car park, took the shuttle bus to the international terminal. It was just past 6:30 but already the morning seemed too hot.

By 7:40 they were airborne, on a Northwest flight bound for Chicago's O'Hare Airport. There, ninety minutes after landing, they were aboard a 747, waiting in line for clearance to taxi onto the runway, plenty of time to wonder how Suma had managed to tail them through Massachusetts, and to wonder where he was now. Plenty of time bathed in cold sweat, remembering the green light in his eyes and the way Bobby Connor had burst into flame; remembering Cathy burning, Johnson drowning on air. Remembering Amanda, dead in a lake of her own blood.

The inexorable force on the rooftop, throwing him through the skylight; the living pipes in the warehouse; the demon in the stream.

Suma.

Wolf unbuckled his seat belt, took an inventory of all the passengers. No Suma. He went back to his seat, satisfied. He closed his eyes, his mind already drifting. No, not drifting exactly. It was like dreaming while he was awake, as if he possessed a generator of enormous power inside him. In fact, in a way he did. He was aware again of the changes fulminating inside him but he had no idea what they portended. He began to soar, as White Bow had called it: thinking out of body.

There was still the sense that he was missing something vital, something he had seen or heard. He loosed his dark familiar. There it sat, coiling its oily tail, perched on his shoulders. He could almost hear the click-click of its claws.

The hearse, it whispered in his mind.

He opened his eyes, staring at nothing.

Yes, the hearse.

He recalled the first time he had seen it, watching Chika climb through its wide rear door, seeing it drive away. And the question that needed immediate answering was: what had been driving that hearse?

If Chika was not here on her own, who was she working with and, just as importantly, how many other lies had she told him? It was clear from her actions as well as what she had told him that it was vital to her that she get him to Tokyo.

But towards what end?

Was the universe she had led him into as she had described it or was he operating in the dark, guided by the lies she had told him? What if, for instance, she and Suma were working towards the same principle? What if there were no dissident splinter group within the Black Blade Society? What if she were recruiting into the Toshin Kuro Kosai itself? If the spooks in DC knew that, thought he had been turned, they'd certainly do their best to cut him out of the loop as quickly and efficiently as possible.

He knew, then, that this dark sight White Bow had summoned from deep inside him posed far more questions than it answered, was more complex than he could as yet imagine. Worst of all, it had thrust him into a world so morally treacherous that even one false step could corrupt him for ever.

He closed his eyes. Whoever had said that absolute power corrupts absolutely knew what he was talking about.

Twenty minutes later, they got clearance, the huge plane swinging around, the fumes turning the scene outside into an Impressionist painting, the frame trembling a bit as the brakes came off. Then they were racing down the tarmac, engines screaming, slowly rising into the thick, humid air with the city tilting away from them, disappearing very quickly into the sooty haze.

THORNBURG/MINAKO

Vietnam/Cambodia 1971

'My God, but you've got a nose for it, son,' General Cross said. He had been decorated so many times the front of his uniform sagged from the weight of the medals. 'An old fox like me can tell.' It was the autumn of 1971 and General Cross liked to wear his fruit salad even in the thick of battle – which he was not averse to wading into – because he felt such conspicuous respect for meritorious valour would be an inspiration to those around him. The odd thing was he was mostly right.

I watched Wolf, who was sitting on one of the general's canvas chairs. He had a presence, a calmness about him that I found admirable – even enviable. All around us was the war: a nightmare spectacle of unimaginable chaos.

We were in a corrugated steel building that with the bloated Vietnamese summer sun beating down on it had become approximately as hot as the inside of a toaster. I could see that Wolf was sweating, General Cross's three shut-faced aides were sweating, even the general himself was sweating.

Outside, I could see them loading up the B-52s with ordnance. Napalm. This was a war that might never die, I thought.

No one had introduced me, and I could see that Wolf was curious about me and my status. Good.

'You've got a helluva record, son,' General Cross said to Wolf, though he had given no sign that he had looked through the dossier on Wolf that one of his aides was clutching. 'Six field decorations. Your comrades in arms are proud of you and so is your country. Hell, I'm proud of you.'

'Thank you, sir,' Wolf said dutifully.

But the general only waved away his words. 'The way the military rewards its heroes, son, is by asking them to give more of themselves. It's only natural, really, because heroes have more of themselves to give.' General Cross scrunched up his eyes. He had a long mournful face with a jutting slab of a nose, sunken cheeks criss-crossed by a network of sun- and wind-etched lines, and a high, intelligent forehead. Beneath his hat was very little hair. 'These are evil times; I imagine I don't have to tell you

323

just *how* evil. We need every weapon we can muster, every edge we can gather in order to persevere and win this war.' The general's eyes were now so scrunched up they were mere slits. 'You understand what I'm saying, son.'

'Yes, sir, I do.'

General Cross nodded. 'We've got a very particular piece of work for you, son. It's hot. So hot MACV itself has decided it's untouchable.' He had used the common acronym for the Military Assistance Command, Vietnam, the American headquarters directing the war. He looked around the room at each man present before his eyes settled back on Wolf. 'You get the drift, son. The people you see here are the only ones aware that this covert sortie is going to be carried out. They're the only ones who understand its importance in the scheme of things.'

Wolf said, 'Since I don't understand its importance and since the military at large feels the risk is too high to sanction it I'm wondering whether I have a choice in this matter.'

'Of course you have a choice,' I said, liking him more and more. Wolf's eyes moved and I could feel the weight of his gaze, could almost see my own reflection there. 'The nature of the mission ensures that we cannot enforce an order to go forward.'

'And you are?' Wolf said.

'My name is Thornburg Conrad III. Just think of me as the architect of this particular piece of work.'

'That's right,' General Cross said, speaking for the last time. 'I want to remind you, son, that nothing will be gained by asking too many questions. I think we can all agree that security dictates that the bare essentials are all that are required.' He rose, and with him his aides. 'I'll leave you to it, then.' He marched from the blistering heat of the room, taking his private army with him.

'So,' I said, when Wolf and I were alone, 'am I to understand that you harbour some ambivalence to doing your duty?'

Wolf found himself staring down the barrel of an army-issue officer's Colt .45 handgun . . .

Vietnam. The maelstrom of war. Like a blood-thirsty beast it chewed up the young boys and spit them out dead, maimed in limb and mind; such a cruel and uncaring beast that it became, in the end, unbearable to watch or to contemplate.

Decades later, Thornburg the hawk would examine just how much I despised that war. Every day, I saw the future of my country being swallowed whole by the flooded rice paddies of this alien land. War needn't be incomprehensible, any good history book could tell you that, and yet *this* war was impossible to understand. That was the hell of it, because one could countenance it – so many had to – but one could find no meaning in it.

And inside Cambodia it had been no different. In truth, in my arrogance I had no conception of what my foray would entail. I had set out on an adrenaline high with the knowledge that my contacts had made it possible for me to twist General Cross around my finger. Cross had had no choice, and if I had had any sense at all I would have felt sorry for the man. Instead, I gloated over the fact that I could tell a general what I needed and get it, no questions asked.

But, in the end, I was right. Cross was an irrelevancy, wasn't he?

The clotted, inky darkness of an Asian night.

After Wolf had piloted the OV-1B Mohawk, an odd-looking plane that had been seconded from the 1st Cav Division in An Khe into the frontier airstrip, my crew of seven had quickly deplaned.

Besides Wolf there was a Special Forces sergeant named Brick, a kind of bodyguard for me who General Cross had insisted come along, my med-tech Duncan with all his field lab equipment, and three Khmer Serei who grew up in the section of Cambodia I needed to get to.

By the time the team had crossed the frontier and had reached the target area all of them save Wolf and I had been killed by the Viet Cong.

But not before I had found what I wanted.

The morning of the second full day of the mission dawned blood-red and clear enough for us to be drawn to the tall, still column of smoke that hung in the humid air like the rope from a fakir's pot.

The column was less than half a kilometre away and turned out to be the remnants of a substantial village. Here and there, fires still sparked and burned white-hot, impossible in this weather unless they were of a chemical nature. The stench of scorched flesh was overpowering.

Duncan had his radiation measuring devices out but, as before, there seemed to be no response from them. Bodies were piled everywhere: in doorways, in the streets, in what was left of the interiors of houses. We saw some weaponry, but the bodies were so badly burned they were no longer clothed. I heard Wolf ask one of the Khmer if these people were Viet Cong or Khmer.

'Both,' the Khmer said, and his anguish was heart-wrenching. 'The Viet Cong like to take over border villages because they believe they will be safe from attack among the Khmer.'

So many questions without answers, I thought. Even though this had all the earmarks of napalm bombing I could detect no telltale odour from the chemical. Also, we had heard nothing during the night and, surely, this close to the target site we would have heard the drone of the aircraft and the *wump! wump! wump!* of the shells exploding.

I gestured to Duncan, who broke out the kit he had been carrying in a backpack. Duncan unrolled the instruments in their cloth pouches. He worked rapidly, efficiently, taking samples of skin, tissue, organs such as liver, lung and heart, bone, brain stem, spine and seven different areas in the brain from a dozen victims of the destruction – men, women and children, all of different ages. These samples he placed in special thick-walled phials that sealed with a telltale vacuum hiss. He labelled each, storing them away with meticulous care, all under my watchful eye.

I could see Wolf watching us as he went about his business of perimeter patrol with the Khmer Serei. He asked no questions, good soldier that he was, but I could see his mind amassing its array of evidence from which, I was certain, at some point, he would draw his conclusions.

It was just after that that the shelling began, Viet Cong fire, that killed Brick and Duncan. We never did find out what happened to the three Khmer. Had they been killed, captured or did they abandon us to our fate? But war is like that, more often than not: you never know what is happening, what will happen, let alone what has already happened. You either come to accept that insane state of affairs or else you go mad yourself.

The shelling was intense. I myself was blinded in the attack, and Wolf, gathering up the samples, half-dragged me away from the shelling, deeper into Cambodia. An odd thing happened, then, as he held me. I felt completely protected, as if, with him, there was no possibility of being hit by a mortar or by gunfire. It was as if the two of us existed within a dark shell, apart from the rest of the war.

It was when we took a break that Wolf demanded an explanation, despite Cross's warnings against asking too many questions. By then, I was very frightened. The euphoria of my omnipotence had been exploded by the reality of the war. I knew by then that I was no John Wayne and that from here on out I would have to depend absolutely on Wolf, so I told him as much as I thought prudent. Besides, he was even more clever than I had anticipated and had worked out a surprising percentage of the essentials: that I was a civilian, that the mission was not, strictly speaking, a military operation, that it was scientific in nature, and that we were in search of the origin of some new form of radiation poisoning.

I told him that we had come here to follow up on a series of puzzling Khmer Serei recon reports. At first, MACV had dismissed them. Then the same kind of observations started popping up in the reports of the

B-50 Detachment of the Fifth Special Forces Group involved in UWO, unconventional warfare operations on the frontier between Vietnam and Cambodia. These reports finally fell into the hands of General Cross, commander of the Sixth Special Forces Group or Omega Detachment, as they liked to call themselves internally.

Wolf picked up on that right away. 'Wait a minute,' he said. 'There is no Sixth Special Forces Group.'

'That's right, there isn't,' I told him.

'So what are we talking about here, spooks?'

'We're all servants of the government of the United States, aren't we? That's the only thing that matters.'

I could see him working it out, that he was part of a spook mission. CIA or even something older, the battle-hardened remnants of the OSS who, common rumour had it, had gone underground when the CIA was formed and who still worked out of closed-door offices somewhere in the bureaucratic labyrinth of Washington.

I wanted him to see that I trusted him even though he was no spook. I also wanted him to come to the conclusion that maybe asking so many questions wasn't in his best interest. But, like I've always said about him, he's a goddamned bulldog when it comes to uncovering facts.

He said, 'These reports that got under General Cross's skin had to do with radiation poisoning, right?'

I told him that there had been several sightings like the one we had come upon – that village that looked as if it had been napalmed, only it hadn't – at least not by any of our arc-light bombing runs. All the sites had been overrun by Viet Cong troops. The South Vietnam military command was ignorant of what we were doing here in Cambodia and the various ethnic montagnards had neither the scope nor the ordnance to create such devastation. So who was left? We needed to find out.

'So you came in here with radiation testing equipment.'

'That's right. A number of the recon intelligence was picking up some unknown form of radiation residue. That also puzzled us. There was nothing to do but to form a party to take a first-hand look.'

'That's not good enough,' he said. My impression was that he was very angry with me then for having roped him into this mess. 'I need more answers. Why, for instance, didn't MACV send its own military ordnance team to check these reports out? Why has this been designated a civilian mission with para-military liaison?'

'The people who control the military made that decision,' I said.

'I think you're full of shit. This was your mission from day one. I don't know who you really are, but I can tell one thing and it scares me: you have a very personal stake in this foray.' I could hear him moving around, and, again, I had the distinct sensation that as long as I was with him I could not be harmed. 'Okay, I can accept the bullshit because that's what spooks throw around all day long. But why pick me, a well-decorated but definitely unspook-like pilot, to take your crew in?'

'Unspook-like,' I said appreciatively, 'apt word. I didn't want any of Cross's damn spook flyboys along on this ride. I was already saddled with Brick and I knew where his loyalties lay. He was going to report to Cross everything that happened on the mission. Frankly, I wanted someone I had chosen to even the odds a little. Your records, which is all Cross bothered to read, had you down as a hero. That was great, as far as I'm concerned. But I went a step beyond, asked around about you. You're smart and something of a maverick, that's what sold me on you.

'Something occurred out here I didn't see any sense in being passed back to Cross, I figured I could count on you to keep it from Brick.'

'Well, we certainly don't have to worry about that any more,' he said. I could appreciate his humour.

'I want to go on,' I said.

Any other man would have replied, *You're crazy, we can't go on. You're blind*. But Wolf said, 'Now I know just how important this mission is to you. What I haven't figured out yet is what you're going to get out of it.'

'What do you mean?'

He laughed then. 'Come off it. I've already worked out that this is not even, strictly speaking, a spook mission. You're on your own out here, a maverick, just like me. That's why you were so concerned with security leaks like Brick.'

He had me, of course, and my admiration for him grew, but I told him nothing of that. Instead, I said, 'Which way is east?'

'Can't tell, there's too much fog. Why don't we just break out the Geiger counter,' he said. 'Maybe it'll give us a clue as to which way to go.'

It was the right suggestion, and I heard him rummaging through the backpack filled with Duncan's scientific equipment.

When the sound came, it was muffled by the cloak of the fog. I instinctively put up my gun, but Wolf clamped his hand around the barrel, pushed it aside. 'That won't do any good,' he said.

'How can you know that?'

And then, out of the fog appeared what Wolf described as a woman warrior. Not that she wore armour or carried a helmet in the crook of her arm, but he said by the way she walked and carried herself it was clear she was a soldier. He told me she was accompanied by two men armed with conventional AK-47s, which were slung across their shoulders.

328

He told me the woman warrior was Oriental. What confused him was that she did not have the pomegranate skin and Polynesian features of the Khmer. She was not Vietnamese or Thai; he said he thought she was Japanese.

He told me that she was quite beautiful, with a delicate face that belied her military bearing. She was neither very young nor old but had about her a timelessness that was all the more striking here in a land torn apart by war where stress levels were abnormally high.

'Gentlemen, your presence was inevitable,' she said in very fine English. 'I could not imagine that our ... experiments could have remained undetected for ever. After all, reconnaissance is relentless in a war.'

'You are conducting the experiments?' I said, turning my face toward the sound of her voice. 'Who are you?'

'Will you come this way?'

I was terrified, but Wolf took my arm and an odd sort of calmness flowed into me. As I passed her, she unhooked the backpack from my shoulder. 'I'll relieve you of your burden.'

I tried to pull it away from her, but something seemed to lock my muscles, and I could feel her fingers disengaging the straps from my curled, paralysed fingers.

'Don't fight her,' Wolf said softly. 'She already knows what's in there.'

A moment later, I snapped out of it, shook my head like a dog coming out of the rain.

'Since I already know your name, Mr Thornburg Conrad III,' she said to me, 'you should know mine. Call me Minako Shian ... '

To be blind was to be helpless, disabled, but in this case, it must have been fortuitous that I had first come upon Minako without the benefit of sight. I somehow saw her in my mind, as if she cast an aura that normal sight could not pick up but the mind could.

Had I had my vision at the moment of contact I suspect everything would have proceeded on a different path. Surely, I would have shot her – and her bodyguards would have killed me and Wolf, and that would have been that.

But because I was blind and, out of that ineffable darkness, had 'seen' her with my mind I had been given a clue to what she might be.

She swam in the darkness of my world and, my God, I could already smell her flesh, could taste the spice of her mouth, could feel the hardness of her muscles beneath the silk of her skin.

She was a woman warrior, and this fact made my taking of her all the more sweet. What army she had commanded I could not have said, but the mien of a general was unmistakable – and the most powerful aphrodisiac I had ever known.

'I see that you are hurt.' She guided me into what seemed like a tent.

'My blindness may or may not be temporary. Right now I have no way of knowing.' I felt the edge of what must have been a cot of some sort and sat down. In a moment I felt her touch again, urging me to lie down.

'Shall I take a look?'

'If you think it will do any good.'

I winced as the first brush of her fingertips brought pain from the wound. Then there was nothing for a long time, so long in fact that it seemed to me as if the pain had disappeared, although I could not be certain since when one lived with pain for long enough one tended to become immune to it.

Then I felt a kind of enveloping heat and, at the same time, a sensation as if the cot had dropped away from beneath me, and I was floating in a sea of warmth.

I opened my eyes but could see nothing; Minako's hand was across them. Then she took it away and I blinked in the low light. I was, indeed, in a tent, though I figured we must be in some kind of bombed-out village, since it had been erected against a remaining wall of chipped concrete.

'Your vision has returned,' Minako said.

'Yes.' Her beauty, now that I could see her with my eyes, quite matched the power of her aura. I felt as if I had been lanced through the heart by Eros. By God, I was trembling.

The image of Eros impaling me was apt enough, I thought. She had about her the aspect of a mythical creature, as if I might find hooves and a tail instead of feet and bare buttocks beneath her black cotton trousers and combat boots. I tried to sit up.

'Stay still for a time,' she said softly, pressing a palm against my chest so that I felt the peculiar warmth there, too. 'You are still healing.'

'I don't feel any pain. What have you done to me?'

She smiled down at me, and I was aware of a vague discomfort at being so vulnerable. I was painfully aware that she could at any moment plunge a knife through my heart. True, the pain was gone, but a form of lassitude such as I had never known before had suffused me. It was a very short breath from weakness to helplessness.

'The pain is still there, I assure you,' Minako said. 'It's just that your body is handling it in another, more efficient way.'

I licked my lips. 'Is that why I feel so weak?'

330

'Yes.'

'I don't like it.'

She laughed. 'Would you rather be blind again?'

I thought about this a moment and I could see by not giving an automatic No I had startled her. At last, I said, 'Something about the blindness I liked.'

'And what was that?'

She was not telling me everything I wanted to know so why not return the favour? 'Who are you?' I asked. 'What are you doing here?'

Minako's face seemed to compose itself into a painted image. She did not look quite real to me. It was as if I was seeing her through the mind of an artist, so that her face became a symbol of what was inside her.

'Your friend has a sharp eye. He has already deduced that I am neither Vietnamese nor Khmer. Nor am I Chinese, Thai or Burmese.'

'That leaves Japanese,' I said. 'Quite impossible, I say. No Japanese in the Vietnamese Theatre of Operations.'

'In that event, you have not seen me and I do not exist.'

I sat up, propped on my elbows, but I became so dizzy I was obliged to lie back down again. After taking a couple of deep breaths, I said, 'You said something about experiments.'

'That's why you've come, isn't it, to find out what we're doing here?'

'I came in response to certain recon reports from the South Vietnamese and our own forces.'

'That is not quite true, is it, Mr Conrad?'

It certainly wasn't, but how in the name of God could she know that? Could she be guessing? If not – a chill went through me like a sudden gust of an autumnal wind – then what? 'As far as I know, it is.'

Six weeks ago the enterprising General Cross had sent a helicopter gunship across the frontier. It had landed at one of the devastation sites and the crew had scooped up a body at random, sealed it in a bodybag and, on arrival back at base, the thing had been flown back to Washington, where it eventually made its way into the lab of Dr Richard Halburton, one of the foremost pathologists working for the Department of Defense. Dr Halburton happened to be the brother of Douglas Halburton, my lawyer. We had a close friendship; in fact, years after, he would act as my consultant in the formation of what would become the staff of Green Branches.

In any event, it had been Dick Halburton who informed me of his odd 'charge', as he called it as if it were still alive. In those days, Halburton and I had the same itch: to discover the secrets of life, death and the nature of ageing.

'It's very curious,' Dick had said as he led me into his lab, 'this charge of mine was not killed in battle. True, she has been burned just as if she had been hit by napalm and yet there is no indication in the pathology of napalm involvement.'

I was already very excited by the discovery. 'Then how did she die?' I had asked.

'As a scientist I would have to say I don't know yet. But as an intuitive pathologist I will tell you that as of now it appears she died of an overdose.'

'An overdose of drugs that could burn her flesh?'

Dick Halburton had shaken his head. 'No, not at all. The tests I've run so far indicate that she has an excessive amount of a complex enzyme in her system. The truly odd thing is that I believe this substance, in one form or another, is naturally occurring in human beings. However, perhaps because of the amount, my charge was unable to absorb it all, so that I've found amounts of it lodged in her liver, spleen, kidneys and colon.' Dick had stopped and, peering at me over his tiny glasses, had said, 'It seems to me that this complex enzyme ate her up alive.'

'You haven't isolated the enzyme yet.'

'Oh, yes, that was easy to do,' Dick had said. 'As I've told you, I took out deposits from her organs. The real problem is in *analysing* the substance. That would take a very long time, perhaps years – if it were possible, which it isn't.'

'What do you mean?'

'The enzyme is non-stable, meaning that taken out of the living tissue it begins to break down. You could say it has a kind of half-life.' Dick had swung around, walked over to a zinc-topped table on which were set three wire cages. Inside, were a variety of lab rats. 'Now look here,' Dick had said. 'I gave a tiny portion of the enzyme to this pair that are suffering from fatal tumours we had induced in them during a previous experiment.' He had shrugged. 'I figured the rats had nothing to lose.'

I studied the rats closely for some time. 'They don't look ill to me.'

'That's just it,' Dick had said with a sphinx-like smile, 'they no longer are.'

I stared from him to the rats and back again. 'What in God's name is that stuff?'

'Right now your guess is as good as mine,' Dick Halburton had said. He stuffed his hands into the pockets of his lab coat. 'What was it that was supposed to be contained in the Holy Grail? The blood of Christ?'

Minako sat back and, turning, began to heat water on a portable kerosene stove. Into the boiling water she dropped a handful of black aromatic tea leaves. I greedily watched the line of her neck where her thick glossy hair was pulled away from it. I could count the tiny hillocks of her vertebrae, and each one seemed like an erotic marker.

'Gunpowder tea from China,' she said. 'Very strong, very good.'

She helped me to sit up slowly because she could see the vertigo written on my face like the warning label on dangerous cargo. I put my back against the chipped concrete wall, dizzied not only by my wound but by her scent.

The air was filled with dust motes that were settling into the back of my throat with every breath. I was grateful for the tea. The sharp, acidic taste made me grit my teeth, but I thanked her nonetheless.

'Where is Matheson?'

'He is unhurt,' Minako said as if sensing my anxiety, although I was certain I had been careful in asking the question. Her eyes closed for a moment, then opened on me again. 'In fact, he is at this moment asleep.'

'I want to believe you,' I said, 'but I'm afraid you've given me no reason to do so.'

'You came in here blind,' she pointed out. 'And now . . . '

'What are you hiding?'

'What are we both hiding?' Minako asked me. 'You did not arrive here at the urging of the US military. Had they been sufficiently curious they would have sent a military complement. That is, in fact, what we had expected. You and Mr Matheson are a different story entirely.'

'How so?'

Minako frowned, as if she were becoming impatient with me. 'You are a civilian, with a civilian's concerns and a civilian's unofficial status here. Moreover, this is dangerous territory and I cannot think how it was your military would allow you access here.'

'I guess they don't care whether I live or die.'

Minako tossed her head. 'Even if that were true, at the very least I would expect they would care about their own people who were assigned to you. Only one of them is still alive.'

I shrugged and winced at another onset of vertigo. 'War is a risk; these men knew that when they took on the assignment.'

'I wonder.' Minako cocked her head. 'But of course that doesn't really matter, does it, Mr Conrad, because it isn't war we're speaking of.' She hesitated for a moment. 'It is vital for me to know whether your government understands this . . . or whether it is just you.'

I stared into her depthless eyes. My first instinct was to lie, perhaps as some kind of protection, but I hesitated. She had obviously made the first step at what I must recognize as a form of truce. I knew it was now up to me to engage in that truce and so come to some sort of dialogue. I didn't see that I had much choice. My other alternative was to continue the verbal sparring with her which might, on one level, be fun, but which I was certain would get me nowhere, least of all back across the frontier.

'I pulled strings in high places to get this far,' I said. 'Though the military is, as I have said, aware of the peculiar nature of the devastation along this section of Cambodia the truth is they're so busy waging the war they have no time for an investigation that doesn't directly concern the lives of American troops. I think they were secretly grateful for my interest.'

I studied her for some time while I worked on my tea. 'Do you know the American slang word snafu?' And when she shook her head no, I said, 'It's a military acronym that came into usage during the Second World War, but it's equally applicable to any army in any war; it means situation normal, all fucked up.'

Minako smiled. 'English is so much more descriptive than Japanese.' She took the empty cup from my hands. 'You enjoyed the Gunpowder tea?'

'I certainly feel stronger.' I leaned forward, touched the side of my head. There was swelling, but no blood. In fact, I felt as if I had a scar rather than a wound. 'How did you heal me?'

'I told you. I aligned elements within your body to better cope with the trauma.'

'That sounds suspiciously like mumbo-jumbo to me.'

'Excuse me?'

'Double-talk. Sounds good but means nothing.' I looked around. 'Is there any radiation around here?'

'Why would you ask that?'

'Because our recon equipment detected what appeared to be trace radiation at some of the sites.'

'I can assure you there is no radiation present,' Minako said.

'I'll tell you what it was I liked about my blindness,' I said abruptly. I was acutely aware that I could not take my eyes off her; her image seemed to burn itself into my retinas. 'In some way – don't ask me how – I was able to "see" you, or at least something about you. I'd like to know about that.' I waited only a beat. 'I'd also like to know how it is you're sure the other men in my complement were killed. Even I don't know the disposition of the three Khmer Serei under my command.'

'They are dead, Mr Conrad, let me assure you. They're all dead except for you and Mr Matheson.'

'Who are you?' I whispered. 'I have to know.'

Minako smiled again. 'I am a soldier, Mr Conrad, just like you. And just like you I am also a civilian, at least as far as my government is concerned.'

'That doesn't tell me nearly enough.' I settled further back against the concrete wall; I was feeling terribly weary, but I fought off the exhaustion.

Minako sat close to me on the edge of the cot so that I was suffused by her scent. Surely this could be no soldier, I thought blearily. 'That perfume . . . '

'What perfume, Mr Conrad? I am wearing no perfume.'

'The scent is . . . ' I closed my eyes and, without knowing it, fell asleep.

When I awoke, it was dark outside. A single kerosene lamp burned low, illuminating the interior in an eerie glow. Across the tent, I saw Minako curled up on the ground, asleep. For a long time I lay there, watching her with studied calm. Around me nothing stirred, except for the beating of my heart. It was as if I was looking at a moment in time, encased in glass, preserved whole for ever. It seemed absurd, but I knew with absolute certainty that if I went to the flap of the tent and looked out at the starry sky I would see that the moon had ceased to move, that the stars themselves were fixed in one position.

Through the years I would never forget that moment – or that extraordinary feeling of being outside time's inexorable progress. And, in a sense, my life after would become a quest to recapture that moment for myself alone.

In time, I swung my legs over the side of the cot and rose. I felt light-headed and had to steady myself more than once as I traversed the width of the tent. It seemed to take an exceedingly long time, as if each step was a lifetime.

At last, I stood over Minako's curled body. I studied the even rise and fall of her ribcage. It felt good to be in this position, to know that now, if I wished, I could plunge a knife through her heart.

I had no such desire, however. Far from it, she seemed to me like a unicorn, a precious enigma who, at her core, possessed a secret more compelling than any I could have myself imagined.

It seemed to me as if she held life in her hand, as if she could somehow manipulate time – and therefore life – as easily as a sculptor moulds clay. I found that I was trembling again, but whether it was with desire for her or for the knowledge she possessed I could not say. And, in a way, wasn't the question meaningless? For one was bound inextricably to the other, like the Oriental yin and yang, darkness and light for ever chasing one another on the wheel of existence. My mind was on fire.

335

I could think only of possessing her and, having done so, possessing her secret.

I bent toward her and her eyes opened. No, not her eyes, they were still closed, I saw with a tiny shock that reverberated up my spine, but *something* had opened, become aware of me where before it had been quiescent. And it was moving, dark and shining and gravid with a life I could only guess at. Like a lens it was focusing its power. Was this Minako or the secret inside her I longed to take for my own? I had no way of knowing.

The eye of the lens was all around me now, like gravity, like a force full of vectors and targets, arcs, tangents, points on a curve. I felt like a bullet shot from a gun that finds itself halted, against all the laws of physics suspended in mid-flight without a quiver.

If I could count the beats of my heart it would take me a lifetime to accumulate enough for a handful. I was tumbling, slipping through the jaws of time; smaller even than a single grain of sand, I penetrated the bowels of eternity.

I had ceased to breathe; nor, I was aware, did my blood flow through my veins. Or, perhaps, I had ceased feeling these things because they were evidence of the passage of time, and time was unknown here. As Minako's fingers unbuttoned my blood- and sweat-soaked clothes I glanced aside. The interior of the tent seemed as far away as Washington, seen through the lens of water, ripply and indistinct as if, like a lake bed, it was part of a world that was no longer familiar to me.

Minako's uniform seemed to part like water beneath my hands. I gripped her bare shoulders. Her skin was unblemished, unlined; her firm breasts were those of an eighteen-year-old. I watched her through slitted eyes as, naked, she sank to her belly and slithered forward.

The undulations of her spine and the muscles over her shoulderblades were like the somnolent swell and suck of the ocean. The startling black spray of her thick hair, unbound now like the spread of a raven's wing, swung down across her arms so that only her fingers could be seen at work between my legs.

I ached to close my eyes in rapture but I could not bear to wipe out the image of her prone and exposed before me. Even as the pleasure built, I reached over, spread apart her buttocks, curled my hand, down, down into the warm, moist darkness.

I wished for her mouth to stay on me for ever, and I gasped out loud when I felt her lips sliding off me, would, in fact, have protested, but she impaled me with her eyes as she lifted up. As she drew my hips beneath hers, I felt her core surrounding me and, with a heartfelt groan, slid all the way up her.

Her scent was overpowering. The fragrance I smelled before I fell asleep overtook me again, flooding out of her like the opening of the mysterious lens that had driven time into exile. So deep inside her I felt as if I was close to the source of that lens, of the secret of time, of ageing, of life returning to life instead of mouldering into decay and death. So very close, it was like an ache that hurt as I moved nearer. If only I could reach out with my mind, snatch the lens from her core, examine it and replace it without her knowing that it had been gone.

But then it was over – too soon, too soon! – and the secret was retreating back into the darkness as, diminishing, I slipped slowly out of her . . .

. . . Immediately afterwards Thornburg wanted to hold my hand, not I would think out of any spontaneous show of affection, although there was no doubt he was smitten, but because having failed to get what he most desired from having sexual intercourse with me he now felt compelled to try another way.

He had, of course, enjoyed himself immensely; the men who I have taken into my bed always have. They can't help themselves. Just as I can't help feeling nothing. Perhaps this is my own private hell. It is ironic, is it not, that I who am destined to carry the one child in my belly cannot derive the least enjoyment from the act that leads to procreation. I was almost sixty then as other people reckon chronology, and yet my menses had not ceased to flow and I was still as fertile as I was when I was twelve.

This is, of course, what his mind had intuited about me, the secret he would kill for. It was not until the aftermath of sexual congress, when like an adder he was already slithering out of me, that I understood the nature of the error I had made.

All along I had thought that he was the one, that it was he with his power who had found me here, who had divined my nature, that it was he from whom I must suck the seed of life.

I had done all that. I had mated with the enemy because that had been my destiny – or at least a part of it. But I had erred. I had relied solely on *makura na hiruma*, ignoring my grandmother's warning. Kabuto had told me there would be blind spots, false futures, ones shown to me that would never come to pass, and this had been one of them.

Too late I had realized that it was not Thornburg Conrad III's seed I should have been impregnated with. I had been gulled by Thornburg's blindness, and his professed ability to read my aura (I had felt nothing at all from his companion Wolf Matheson). In fact, I did not doubt him in this, and though this was an indication that he did indeed possess some form of *makura na hiruma*, in the aftermath of our sexual union when the psyche is as open and vulnerable as it is on the point of death, I took the measure of his power and saw that it was mostly latent and of no possible use to me.

Yet I was impregnated with his seed. It was the correct time of my cycle and I knew my body well enough to understand just how fertile my power could make me. I had no doubt then that I would become pregnant, that I would bear his child.

And so, as he pressed his palm to mine, seeking to find the key to my essential enigma, to *makura na hiruma*, I wanted nothing more than to reach up and with my clawed fingers scratch out the enemy's eyes.

I did nothing of the kind, however. Instead, I smiled up at him, big powerful man that he was, and pressed my lips to the back of his hand. 'I am no enemy of yours,' I lied. 'Do you see now that I wish you and your friend no harm?'

'Yet you took my backpack,' he said. 'As if you knew what was in it.'

Whatever else he might be, he was not stupid. In fact, he proved to be an exceptionally clever and resourceful male, no doubt due in part to the nascent *makura na hiruma* lying in wait inside him.

'It was not difficult to deduce what you carried,' I said sweetly. 'These are our experiments and I cannot allow anyone to tamper with the results.'

'The results,' he said, 'are that you're burning people alive.'

Of course he was right, but it wouldn't have done to tell him so.

'Minako, I came here to find out what you're doing. I already know some of it, but I need to know it all. And you don't have to worry. As you have deduced this isn't an official enquiry, it's purely a private matter over which I and I alone preside.'

I looked at him then in that way I have and, keeping my lips half-parted, I said, 'It does not matter. I cannot allow you to return with evidence.'

'Now that I've met you I don't care about the evidence,' he said, grabbing hold of me. 'All I want is to be part of you, to share your secret. Do you think I'd be foolish enough to tell anyone what I'd discovered?' I was convinced that he was about to throw me to the floor and take me once again. Men, I thought, are ridiculously easy to manipulate. Once you get your hand between their legs you can do anything with them. Is it any wonder I regard them with such contempt?

I believe that it was only his obsessive desire for the secret of my power that stopped him from raping me then and there. Not that I hadn't actively encouraged him. No man had ever raped me without my active encouragement, and no man ever would.

338

'All I want is you. I know what you are. You're the elixir of life.'

I smiled at him with my parted lips and I could feel him tremble. There is something quite exhilarating in bringing a powerful man to his knees – and without him ever knowing what is happening. Men have no real conception of the ramifications of power. But then their definition of almost everything that matters in this world is rigid, two-dimensional, and altogether false.

I kissed him. I had got at least one answer out of him. This was a personal crusade of his. It was the touch of his own *makura na hiruma* that had awakened him to the possibilities of extended life, and it was this same force which had attuned him to what we had been trying to do here under cover of the war between Vietnam and the United States. Not that he had any inkling of what was really involved.

But, anyway, that was all in the past, because our experiments had been a dismal failure. We had been using radioactive short-half-life isotopes in order to artificially induce the chemical reagents we believed were responsible for the activation of *makura na hiruma*. Death had been the only result and, as Thornburg and his companion had seen first hand, a particularly grisly death at that. It was really quite ironic, I had thought then as I put his head to my breast, that he had come to ferret out our secret at the moment of our greatest failure.

Attrition had set in at an alarming rate. Over the years, the number of children born with *makura na hiruma* was fast diminishing. None of us knew why, but it seemed clear that unless we could somehow reverse the appalling trend one day the power would be gone for ever, leaving our distant descendants to move among their fellow men as equals, which was to say blind, deaf and brain damaged.

Thus the experiments had begun. And the burning, and the deaths. But, after all, our guinea pigs were only North Vietnamese: communists, atheists, brainwashed barbarians who had turned away from both their fellow man and Buddha. Their suffering and deaths were of no concern to us.

The only question that remained was what to do with the two Americans. I would cheerfully have killed Conrad, but he would one day become the father of my child and I did not have the capacity for that evil.

Makura na hiruma had shown me what kind of man he was, of what obscenities he would under certain circumstances be capable, and I felt I could not in good conscience release him without having taught him a lesson. In hindsight, this decision became a prime example of what Kabuto had warned me against: the kind of supreme arrogance bred in the super-heated cauldron of *makura na hiruma*.

Here was how false futures were born, how a path one trod with such confidence could diverge from its foreordained course without any overt sign.

The irony is not lost on me. In one crucial respect *makura na hiruma* is akin to the Catholic concept of sin: one is continually tempted by the darker side of its power; the greater the power, the more one is tempted. And so the false futures that arise to confound even those with full control of their power are often of their own making. So it was with Kabuto. So it has been with me.

To her credit, Kabuto did try to warn me, but how often do such warnings fall on the deaf ears of the young, who cannot conceive of committing the same errors as those older than them.

I had had an ulterior motive in taking charge of the experiment inside Cambodia. Though it was fraught with danger – the North Vietnamese would surely have killed us if they had been able, as would the Cambodians had we not terrified them into a stupor – I saw it as an opportunity I could not afford to pass up. For years I had been using my power as a kind of beacon, hoping to attract the male who would put the seed in my belly that would result in a child with extraordinary *makura na hiruma*. Now I saw this experiment as magnifying the power of the beacon ten-thousand-fold. And it was here my *makura na hiruma* falsely told me the event would begin to unfold.

Thus my initial excitement at the appearance of Thornburg Conrad III, and my subsequent disappointment. I felt fouled at having had sexual congress with a creature whose psyche was in such dire need of purification. And yet, at the same time, I cannot deny there was the tiny thrill one experiences at forbidden pleasures.

I had said before that it was my private hell to feel nothing during an act that for centuries had given ecstasy to millions. In the hours after my first sexual encounter with Thornburg I noticed a void, for want of a better term, like the pang one feels when one's stomach is empty. Gradually, to my horror, it dawned on me that this lack was a direct result of my having had sex with this alien male. I had, in fact, felt something when he was rampant inside me, and now I longed to experience that feeling again.

I could not help myself. I took him into my bed, and into myself again and again until he was sated. To my shame, I was not. Never before had I looked upon the sex act as anything other than a necessary expediency, another weapon in my formidable arsenal.

Like a drug I wanted this man, this alien, this enemy who, though besotted with lust for me, would nevertheless have disembowelled me if he were convinced that would deliver up to him the secret he burned to have.

And now I burned for him. I almost laughed aloud into the steamy darkness as I lay beside his sleeping form. My hand was curled around the instrument that had, moments before, been thrust keenly into me, thrilling me. My palm became wet with his semen and this, too, this slimy essence of life made my heart beat faster.

What a mystery life is! If I have learned anything during my eighty-five years it is this. Just when you think you have decoded life's messages something or someone comes along to invert all your carefully built-up conclusions.

The dawn eventually arrived, and with it the nature of my dilemma. I knew that I could not allow another night to pass with him near me. I was already partly addicted to the feeling he could engender within me. Having been without bliss for so many decades, the force of its unexpected and belated arrival was having a profound effect upon me. For long stretches I could no longer think clearly and once or twice I found myself contemplating the dissolution of my mission in order to be with him. Then I would shake myself like a mad dog spewing the foam from its black lips and try to take deep breaths to restore my thinking to its usual level of clarity.

By the time he roused himself from his stupor I had chosen my path and knew that come what may I would not be shaken from it. Of course *makura na hiruma* had given me a glimpse of the rage I would engender within him. I did not care, and I believe now that even had I been shown how I would become the focus for the animus that had ruled his life, I would not have changed course. In the events that were to come I would have a sense of galvanizing forces, of a convergence of previously disparate lives at this one nexus point in time and space.

Of course I could have had Thornburg and Wolf executed; one word from me and my men would have shot them through the back of the head. Perhaps I should have given the order. But in those days I scoffed at such barbarian behaviour, believing more in *makura na hiruma* than I do now in this future that has blinded us all. You have to understand, no matter what anyone may tell you to the contrary, there is an enormous exhilaration in having the power of life or death over another human being. And I discovered that the greatest thrill of all was not in acting on that power but in having your enemy live with the knowledge of your mastery over him.

So there was a peculiar sweetness to the moment when Thornburg opened his bloodshot eyes and felt the edge of my nail along the side of his neck.

'I could have you shot or, better yet, do it myself for trying to steal the secrets of our experiment,' I whispered in his ear.

I watched, fascinated, at how swiftly and instinctively he reached out for the knife I had left on the ground, how he drove it up towards the soft flesh of my throat. Well, that's men for you. They're instinctual animals, I've always known that, careless of the physical damage they inflict on others.

I did not move, other than to use my thumb and forefinger to pinch the nerve bundle just beneath his right ear. Immediately the blood drained from his face and his mouth opened, sucking in air like a very old man on the point of death. The flaccidity came into his arms and legs as his muscles were robbed of their oxygen. The knife clattered to the floor.

I placed the edge of my nail back against his slowly throbbing carotid artery. 'I have only to break the skin, open up the carotid and you will bleed to death,' I whispered in his ear. 'I can do that now, in five minutes' time, or later, at my leisure, and there is nothing you can do to stop me.'

Well, I was younger then, and semi-hysterical at what he had made me feel: unclean and excited all at the same time. I hated him as I had never hated anyone in my life before or since. The emotion was so bitter in my mouth that I thought I might gag. It was only much later that I understood that at that moment I hated myself as much as I hated him.

So I was half out of my mind and this allowed my natural arrogance full rein. Oh, I should have killed him then, but I was having too much fun playing the savage, going against my own nature (or, Buddha help me, succumbing to it) to stop. Besides, there was something terribly delicious in the situation. If only he knew all the secrets I knew.

Naturally occurring irony is far too precious to throw away with a careless word or two. And I relished my position of power over him even more because I understood fully the rage it would engender in him.

I was not wrong about him; I've never been wrong about him. Only Wolf has continued to confound me.

'There is only one way in which you can save your life,' I whispered as one lover to another, 'and that is to kill your companion.'

He looked at me, disbelief momentarily overlaying the rage. 'You want me to kill Wolf?'

'Shoot him dead,' I nodded, 'in front of my men.'

He did not disappoint me. 'Kill me now,' he said through gritted teeth. 'I am no traitor to my country.'

I laughed silently to myself because he had said nothing about being a traitor to his fellow man. I knew that if I gave him a gun and told him to shoot one of my men in order to save his life he would have done so cheerfully. I did not blame him for that, but I was getting to know him, better I suspected than he could ever know himself. It's a basic self-defence mechanism. People like that can never know themselves. If they did they'd no doubt blow their own brains out.

'No,' I whispered. 'We are not merely discussing your life now, but the extension of it.' I pressed my lips to his and with delight felt him shudder. 'Isn't that the secret you came here to steal?' I drew my head away from him, studied his expression. 'The only way for you to get it is to kill your companion.' I smiled. 'What's the problem? What is one more death to someone like you?' I watched his eyes open wide while I drank in the stench of his fear. 'Yes, yes, I know. Oh, how badly you want it.'

'Not badly enough to sell my soul.'

I laughed softly, my breath brushing his cheek dark with stubble. 'By coming here you've already done that, you just don't know it yet.'

I was certain that I could lure him into killing his friend, simply for the temptation of what he wanted most. I had it, and he knew it. But somehow, in this one thing, he foiled me. I sensed, after a time, a feeling in him that I could not define, and I knew that he would not kill Matheson. This confused me as well as disturbed me. My sight had already made me privy to Thornburg's basic amorality, but now he was acting out of character. To me, Matheson was nothing, a black hole from which I received no signals whatsoever. What could Thornburg have seen in him? It took me many years to work out the answer to that question.

Thornburg was watching me from beneath hooded eyes. He lay back, seemingly relaxed as he closed his eyes, and I knew what he was doing. He thought if he could get me angry enough I would make a mistake and he could take advantage of it to gain the upper hand. He was clever and he felt he would need only an instant to bring his superior strength to bear. He knew nothing of *makura na hiruma*, and that was my true advantage over him.

'Are you going back to sleep?' I asked him innocently.

His lips curled into a self-satisfied smile that I found thoroughly repugnant. 'I might, if I feel like it. I know you're not going to kill me, that would spoil your pleasure. As long as you think I might provide some amusement you won't do a thing.'

I reached out then with *makura na hiruma*, wrapping a tendril of the dark power around his heart. Then, ever so gently, I squeezed.

His eyes popped open and he sat up with a spastic jolt. His eyes sought mine and I blew him a kiss, then wiped a line of sweat off his upper lip.

His lips opened and closed several times and, when at last he spoke,

I knew how much effort it cost him. 'I'll kill you for this.' He meant the humiliation. I could only wonder at the pain I, in his eyes an inferior creature, was inflicting on him. He was gasping between words but he would not give up. 'I'll see you dead at my feet no matter how long it takes.' No, not pain, I corrected myself. This was a man who could endure massive amounts of pain, both physical and mental, without giving an inch. It was the degradation of being under the thumb of a woman that sparked a rage that would not die. And all the while I revelled in the enormity of his reaction.

And what was my reaction to his threats? I rolled over on top of him. His rage was so close to desire that I wanted him to cross the line so that I could take that away from him, too. He felt my heat on him and he at once unfurled. Of course how could it have been otherwise? Had he not risen to my unspoken challenge he would have felt himself even more under my thumb, impotent as well as helpless.

I took his entire length inside me. I allowed him to hurt me, knowing that my flesh would bruise and, tomorrow when he had gone, I would remember him all the better.

And there was something else, darker, stalking our sexual congress. The ecstatic pleasure was in some way enhanced by the pain. I cannot explain it but the sharp edge of pain heightened the rapture so precipitously that I came twice powerfully enough that I lost my grip on him.

He did not try anything, merely lay there, his back arched, his member hard as a rock inside me, his emotions seemingly detached, as if to prove that at least in this he had the upper hand.

I knew that I loved him then in a way I had never believed that I could love any human. There was nothing I wanted more in that moment than to make him lose control, to shoot inside me and induce in me one last tide of utter bliss.

Vulnerable as I was, he knew that was what I desired most. He pushed me off him and, using his hand, contemptuously spilled his seed on the ground at my feet.

I was panting heavily. My eyes were wide and staring. For a moment I could not believe what he had done to me. I rose up; I could already feel the involuntary expansion of *makura na hiruma* coiling malevolently towards him. Then I saw the superior smile on his face and knew that if I killed him now as I was burning to do he truly would have beaten me in our mental duel because he would have made me use my power when I did not want to.

Yet I was burning with desire, a desire only he could fulfil. I wanted to reach out with *makura na hiruma* and bring him on his knees to me but I knew that would also be a victory for him, that if I had to resort to *makura na hiruma* at all now it would be a sign of his strength.

So I leaned towards him, reached out with my hand and cupped it behind his neck. I drew him to me. He came. I suppose he knew how high a victory he had won and this was the time to savour every second of it.

My eyes closed and my stomach muscles rolled as his mouth enclosed my wetness. His tongue came out and I shuddered powerfully, the breath escaping from me like an adder's hiss. My thigh muscles rippled and I collapsed over his back, my breasts dragging across his skin, making me cry out one last time.

There was nothing between us but this vicious giving and taking. It was too much and not enough, we both knew that, whatever else we might feel about the other.

I knew he would try to make good on his threat if I let him go. I would let him go. Of course he would not know that. He would think he had cleverly tricked me by ostensibly agreeing to kill Wolf Matheson in return for the secret of extended life. You see he did not believe me, but I would indeed have given him the secret of what was already inside him – brought about the summoning of his *makura na hiruma* – the moment he put a bullet through Wolf's head. And what fun that would have been, to provide him with so many years of torment, for he never would have been able to erase the memory of what he had done.

No, that would not happen. Instead, I would give him back his loaded handgun while I had one of my men keep a rifle to his head. But he would turn the gun not on Wolf but on his guard, then he and Wolf would make their escape. I knew it all, *makura na hiruma* had shown me that particular future. I would not stop them. I wanted him to live; I could not have said then why, except it was a piece of the future that I was meant to construct.

BOOK III

Forbidden Dreams

*There will always be another reality
to make fiction of the truth
we think we've arrived at.*

Christopher Fry

FIFTEEN

Tokyo/Washington

It was well after midnight by the time Shoto Wakare brought Yuji to Forbidden Dreams. By then, both men were very drunk, and both, no doubt, for the same reason: they were terrified. They exited the big BMW, quickly crossed the pavement.

The exterior was unusual in that it combined the symbols of the old and new Japan into one seamless whole. Massive pillars of hand-hewn cedar were sunk into a facade of grainy, grey ferroconcrete, giving the impression that the stuff, while wet, had oozed up over some primeval Shinto frame. The overall impression was that what had once been an ancient temple had now been reclaimed from time and nature.

Inside, the place was rife with smoke and music. A heavy electronic bass walked across Yuji's temples and a male voice sang of chrysanthemums and sex. The parlour smelled of something sweet, something forbidden and ancient, like opium.

'We have an appointment with Naoharu Nishitsu,' Wakare told a dwarfish woman in an exquisitely tailored man's suit.

The diminutive woman made no comment, merely bowed, then led them past the cafe, the main salons, each with a different motif.

She took them down a long hallway. By the time they had traversed its length, the sounds of the music and hubbub had completely disappeared. They passed a window out onto a small garden, exquisite even in late winter. The dwarfish woman led them into another, shorter corridor which contained six doors. She gestured towards the last door, said, 'Please.'

Wakare turned to Yuji; he was slightly bent over. 'I have to urinate.' He gestured to the sliding rice paper *shoji*. 'You go on; it won't do to keep Nishitsu-san waiting. I'll be along as soon as I'm finished.'

Yuji hesitated, then went to the end of the corridor. He pushed the *shoji* aside, slipped off his shoes, entered the room. The dwarfish woman carefully closed the *shoji* behind him. Yuji could hear her footsteps receding down the corridor.

A scent of citrus and rose suffused the room. It was pin-spot-lit, walls

349

of split bamboo and charcoal-grey fabric, floor of tatami mats, the walls lined with ferns, pink and coral orchids, evergreen bonsai, the air humid, as if the plants had just been misted. Two metal chairs, a hibachi, a futon spread out in a corner. On the hibachi coils of blood-red cord.

A young, exquisite woman walked around him, slender, long-haired, with rounded limbs, delicate hands and the square-shouldered bearing of a dancer or a geisha. She'd had training, that much was clear.

'My name is Evan,' she said.

Yuji introduced himself, though he had the distinct impression that she already knew his name.

Evan said nothing more. Her eyes were light, a very clear milk chocolate. She wore a short black silk skirt, a white shirt of the same material. She wore no makeup. There was a single incised gold band around one bare ankle. 'What do you think of me?'

'I think it's too early to tell,' Yuji said.

'Is it? I wonder about you.'

'What do you mean?'

Evan cocked her head 'Given the choice, would you pick me to have sex with or would you prefer your friend Wakare?'

'That is a presumptuous question.'

'Wakare desires you.'

'Yes. I know.'

'You do?'

'Have I surprised you?'

She continued to look at him intently.

He said, 'Where is Nishitsu-san? I came to see him.'

'You came to be at Forbidden Dreams,' Evan said. 'Besides, you're drunk. You'd rather be with me now than Nishitsu, wouldn't you?' She shrugged off her shirt, came against him naked from the waist up. She spread her legs, climbed up him so she could put her lips against his ear. 'I love it when I can't move, when my arms are pulled tight over my head.'

Yuji did not trust himself to speak. She was right. He was drunk and in no shape to confront Nishitsu. He had been a fool to agree to Wakare's mad plan to infiltrate the Black Blade Society. But it had seemed so simple when they had talked of it, and even a bit exciting. Now, however, the reality was like an oppressive weight constricting his chest. He was terrified of Nishitsu and the Toshin Kuro Kosai. Now that he was inside Forbidden Dreams, he did not for a minute believe that he and Wakare could depose Nishitsu and the current regime.

'I love it when I lose circulation in my ankles and my feet go numb,

350

when the only motion is the rise and fall of my breasts – and you.' She squirmed against him.

Despite himself, Yuji was becoming aroused. Perhaps it was all the sake and beer he had consumed, or, again, his enormous fear combined with the prospect of putting off his capitulation to Nishitsu, like a stay of execution which intoxicates the condemned man. In any event, he was as hard as a bar of iron.

Evan felt this, and crooned deep in her throat. Her eyes rolled back in their sockets. 'Oh, I love that most of all. We can smell everything together – we can remember everything together.' She tore open his shirt, rubbed her hard nipples against his chest. 'That's also why you've come.' She nipped the side of his neck with her sharp white teeth.

Could excessive fear make a man incautious? Yuji did not know, he only knew he wanted to bury himself in her. He pushed her skirt down. He wound blood-red nylon cord around and around her flesh until, lit as she was from above, she looked like a painting or a sculpture. He pulled the cords tighter so her arms stretched over the back of the metal chair and her buttocks were lifted off the tatami mats.

'Ohhh,' she said, but she could not move, except for the spasmodic rise and fall of her breasts. The sweat-sheen burnished her flesh under the pin spots.

Yuji was so hard he could not walk. He was arched over Evan, his muscles standing out in gleaming definition, the tension singing inside him like a complex aria. He could smell her, a great beating flower whose dew-laden petals he parted.

He slid easily into the heat of her and felt her thighs tremble, saw her lower belly flutter. A surge of triumph such as he had rarely known suffused him, flushing his skin, setting fire to his mind.

As the pleasure built he was assailed by visions. He saw himself as a marionette with a clown's dull-witted mask, dancing at the end of a set of strings. Above him, manipulating him, was Nishitsu, but as Yuji looked more closely he could see the strings going right through Nishitsu's fingers, and though Nishitsu moved his fingers to make Yuji dance it was someone else, looming darkly above Yuji, who was really making Yuji dance. Who was it?

Yuji groaned, stretched taut on the cross of female flesh, immersed in it, and a rushing, disgorging, foaming overtook him and he bit hard into Evan's shoulder, tasting the salt of her sweat and the sweetness of her blood.

In the aftermath it was an exquisite pleasure to unwind the cord from around her, to see the white patterns on her flushed skin slowly fade and, overlaid on that, the image of Yuji the marionette, dancing

351

like a fool, controlled not by Naoharu Nishitsu but by . . . Minako, his mother.

Yuji stared into Evan's light chocolate eyes. His blood was cold, his skin suddenly goose-fleshed. He shivered. 'What is happening?' he whispered.

'Don't be afraid.'

'I'm not.' But he was lying and he could see that she knew. 'I have such disturbing visions.'

'I am showing you the world as it is.'

He recoiled. Even though Evan was sitting perfectly still it was as if she had suddenly pulled a knife and set it against his throat.

Evan stroked his cheek. 'You are a seeker after truth,' she said, 'and I have given you the gift of truth. Your mother has been manipulating your life for many years.'

'Your sight is like Hana's,' he said, almost to himself. 'But there is no compelling reason to believe you. You placed these visions in my mind. That is no guarantee of truth.' He sat up. 'In fact, since this was all a set-up – Wakare getting me drunk, bringing me here now, him leaving me at the last minute – it would appear what you have shown me is more likely a lie, part of Nishitsu's plan to win me over.'

Evan smiled ruefully. 'As events unfold, you will see for yourself that what I have shown you is the truth. I know that nothing I can say could possibly convince you. I only ask that you not forget what I have shown you.'

'I must go,' Yuji said. He was clearly uncomfortable with his own indiscretion, but Evan apparently misunderstood the nature of his distress.

'You're like all the rest,' she said sadly. 'You see now why I must be alone, why I must stay here in hiding? Who would want to be with me once they know that I can crawl inside their head?'

Yuji was pulling on his clothes, but now he stopped. 'You're wrong,' he said. 'I know how it is to feel like a prisoner. My half-sister Hana is trapped by her sight the way you are trapped here in Forbidden Dreams.' He took her hand. 'I understand everything about you.'

Evan knelt before him, her hand, light as a feather, in his. At last, she said, 'Now I must bathe you. You have an appointment with Nishitsu-san, *neh*?'

She drew aside the *shoji* screens on the opposite side of the room, revealing a sumptuous bath, carved out of naked rock. She spent the next forty minutes attending to him. When at last he was dressed, she walked slowly around him, studying him like a drill sergeant readying his platoon for inspection. Then she nodded to herself, led him down a concrete corridor lit by brass lanterns. At length, they came to another set of screens. She slid them aside.

'Nishitsu-san.' Yuji bowed.

Naoharu Nishitsu, wearing a copper and black kimono, was sitting at the far end of a twelve-tatami room. The bamboo and cedar walls of this spacious room were hung with antique kimonos of the feudal lords who, if Yuji could believe his eyes, had warred among themselves before being defeated in one way or another by Ieyasu Tokugawa, the first Shogun. Dating from the beginning of the seventeenth century, these items were national treasures that belonged in a museum. Yet, here they hung in a private room at the rear of an after-hours club. Extraordinary, Yuji thought as Evan led him barefoot into the room. Yet everything about Forbidden Dreams was out of the ordinary.

'Ah, you recognize those crests,' Nishitsu said. He seemed very pleased. 'These kimonos – all belonging to the greatest warlords of their era – are hung as a constant reminder that power is like sand: it runs through the hand no matter how tightly one squeezes one's fingers together.' He gestured for Yuji to sit opposite him on the tatami. 'Humility is like bitter tea, eh? Unpalatable but nonetheless healthy.'

Nishitsu nodded. 'That will be all, Evan,' he said. He was not alone in the room. A young woman with a magnificent face, dressed in a black-and-white silk kimono, knelt by the rice-paper doors that led out onto the small garden Yuji had glimpsed before. It seemed the most complete – and therefore the most beautiful – garden he had ever seen. The woman appeared to be asleep.

'I apologize for keeping you waiting,' Nishitsu said, 'but the delay was unavoidable.'

'Perhaps I arrived too early,' Yuji said. He looked around the room. 'Wakare-san is not joining us?'

Nishitsu's smile, a mere compression of his lips, was so thin Yuji could not see his teeth. 'Alas, no.'

'Never mind. My time here has so far been well spent.'

Nishitsu inclined his head. 'Is that so?' His eyes were hooded. 'In what way?'

'Forgive me,' Yuji said. 'I was speaking of Evan.'

Nishitsu's expression remained noncommittal. 'You like Evan?'

Now it was Yuji's turn to deliver a small smile. 'It seems inevitable, like this meeting.'

He saw that Nishitsu was unprepared for this tack, and he began to feel less nervous. It was particularly important here, he saw, to distinguish truth from fiction. Was the vision Evan had 'shown' him

353

real? Had his mother manipulated him, or was this some trick Nishitsu had devised, a last-ditch attempt to win over his loyalty?

'Please explain to me what you mean, Shian-san,' Nishitsu said now.

'You mean about Evan? She is an extraordinary woman. In some ways she reminds me of my half-sister, Hana. Their gifts, I mean.' Nishitsu nodded, and Yuji went on. 'After I had spent some time with her, it seemed natural that you would allow us to meet, to – how shall I put it? – explore one another.' Yuji's normally open eyes were hooded. 'She is a precious asset. To reveal her to me must mean that you need my help very badly, indeed.'

Nishitsu finished his tea, switched to hot sake. 'You are a blunt talker, Shian-san. I admire that. *Kokoro*, the heart of all things, must, after all, be spoken of now and again. You have correctly discerned that this is one of those times.'

He was so still he seemed scarcely to breathe, and there was that astonishing sense about him that the entire building rested upon his shoulders. 'What Evan showed you was not only the past. It is the future. And, after all, that is why you have come here tonight: to learn about the future.'

The woman with the magnificent face moved, and because of her proximity to the garden, it appeared to Yuji as if a rock had come to life.

Nishitsu fixed Yuji with the cold light from his opal eye. 'You know me as a politician, but the truth is I am many things.' He held out his hand, then dropped it to his lap. 'I am also Yakuza.' He looked slowly and carefully around the room as if noticing it for the first time. 'This place was built by the Toshin Kuro Kosai.'

'The Black Blade Society.'

Nishitsu inclined his head. 'I represent Toshin Kuro Kosai in certain matters.' His opal eye possessed a penetrating stare, like the hook at the end of a fishing line. 'Evan has revealed her closely-guarded secret to you, and has thus put all of us in a kind of jeopardy. There are many, I'm sure, who would pay dearly for the knowledge she carries inside her head – a scent of the future.'

'My mother possesses the same ability.'

'Mmm. Perhaps not quite the same.'

There was something odd in the way the woman held her head, her magnificent face concentrating, as if she were listening to a far-off conversation.

'What would the Toshin Kuro Kosai want with me?' Yuji asked at last.

Nishitsu smiled without warmth; it was a sardonic smile. 'The same thing, as it happens, your mother wants from you. The secret of the Oracle.'

There was silence for some time.

'I don't know what you mean.'

The woman with the magnificent face moved her head so that light from above struck her cheek. Abruptly, Nishitsu said, 'Oh, come now, Shian-san, haven't we agreed on *kokoro*? We know that it was your mother who suggested the path you should take in constructing the Oracle. Am I so wrong? Weren't there an almost infinite number of other paths you could have taken other than having it reprogram DNA within living human beings?'

Yuji nodded, a bit uncertainly. 'It was my mother who made the suggestion. The DNA reprogramming happened to coincide with her own interest in biogenetics.'

'Oh, yes, precisely, her own work,' Nishitsu said, nodding enthusiastically. 'And where did this interest spring from? Did you ever ask yourself this question? No. I can see by your expression you never did.' Nishitsu put his powerful, blunt-fingered hands on the table. 'It came from us, Shian-san.'

'Us?' Yuji was bewildered.

'Yes,' Nishitsu said. 'Us. The Black Blade Society.'

Another silence enveloped them.

'I don't believe you,' Yuji said at last.

'Of course you don't,' Nishitsu said. 'I would not believe it, were I in your place.' He shrugged. 'Nevertheless, it is the truth. Decades ago, we gave your mother a mandate. You see, for some time we have known that we are slowly dying out. For reasons we have yet to unearth, there have been fewer and fewer children born with *makura na hiruma*, the sight. Now, there are none at all. We had to find a way to perpetuate our line. This was where your mother's "interest" in what you so quaintly refer to as biogenetics came from. It was why she was sent to Cambodia twenty years ago. It was why she urged you to build the Oracle.' He held up his hands. 'Don't waste your breath calling me a liar. Think about what I have said, then tell me it doesn't conform with your memory of past events.'

Yuji took the time; he had little choice.

Nishitsu watched the incipient emotions play across Yuji's face and, at that moment, he felt genuinely sorry for him. 'And if you still have doubts, think about how it is we have such intimate knowledge of your most secret project. We even know the name of your first test case: Lawrence Moravia. It was your mother who brought him to the warehouse where you keep the biocomputer. Shall I give you the time and date she brought him there?'

Beneath the table, Yuji's fists were clenched tight. 'How do you know this?' he said woodenly.

'I was part of it.' Nishitsu grunted. 'She has done nothing but lie to you.'

Yuji made no motion. It was as if he were frozen in time, suspended between worlds, adrift in a vast darkness without end.

'As I have said, we are here to discuss the future,' Nishitsu said, assuming a businesslike air. 'Not what will happen tomorrow or next week, but the future. Do you understand now, Shian-san?'

At that moment, Yuji hated life and the part he had been manipulated into playing. He nodded.

Nishitsu turned his head a bit, as if listening to something, and Yuji was reminded of the beautiful woman, who was now seated with her eyes closed, the tips of her fingers pressed together as if meditating.

'Now I feel it my duty to show you something.'

He took an oblong object not more than three inches in length out of his breast pocket. It was wrapped in layers of translucent rice paper and was sealed with his crest. He pushed it across the table to Yuji.

It was very beautiful, lying there on the black lacquer of the table. But to Yuji its beauty had a sinister quality, like the skin of a beast, blue-white and shining like platinum, that surfaces in a stream.

Yuji, staring down at the package, felt as if his brain were about to implode. He felt like a diver too long in the depths, who picks up rapture of the deep; he no longer knew which way was up or down. He had lost all ability to recognize the normal signposts that people rely on to guide them through life.

He watched, with the kind of morbid, almost obsessive fascination people view car wrecks or public murders, as his fingers carefully unwrapped the package.

His cry was involuntary. He was staring down at a severed finger. On it was a ring he recognized as belonging to his brother-in-law Hiroto.

'Alas, Hiroto is dead,' Nishitsu said. 'Your mother learned that he had discovered her secret: that she was Toshin Kuro Kosai. He was going to tell you, and to ensure he wouldn't, she murdered him.'

Yuji's head shot up. 'My mother would never – '

Nishitsu made a guttural sound and the *shoji* screen slid open.

'Mother!'

Minako knelt at the edge of the room, just beyond the screen. Her head was bent, her shoulders bowed. 'Forgive me, Yuji-san,' she said. 'I did not want to kill Hiroto but he gave me no choice. He was going to tell you about me.' Her head turned from side to side, and Yuji experienced a disquieting instant of *déjà vu*. 'You must understand I had no choice. Yuji-san, your fate is in Nishitsu's hands now. Listen to what he has to say.'

A hand reached out, closed the *shoji*, cutting her off from Yuji.

He made a move to get up, but Nishitsu stopped him. 'She is in our hands now. We will protect her as we always have.' His voice had a calming effect. 'What you must understand, Shian-san, is that your mother is mad. This happens, sometimes, when the *makura na hiruma* becomes too intense or the mind too weak to sustain the sight.' Nishitsu pushed some sake across the table to Yuji. A few drops spilled onto Hiroto's finger. 'We can help her. To be frank, we're the only ones who can, now.' He gestured towards the finger. 'Look what she has done. This is not the action of a rational person.'

Nishitsu's opal eye was blinding. 'In the future Evan showed you you saw that the surface isn't all there is. But there is even more. Someone else is involved. A very clever person is manipulating both you and myself, feeding our enmity, shoving us into a war that I don't want. This man, an American named Thornburg Conrad III, met your mother in Cambodia. There they formed an enmity of their own, an enmity that now threatens all of us.'

Yuji put his head in his hands. He felt as if he had a steel band around his chest.

'I can sympathize with you, Shian-san, because as you can see now we are all in a kind of labyrinth,' Nishitsu said. 'You and I must find our way out, or this American will have succeeded in destroying all of us.'

Jason Yoshida went down to the garage in the basement of Ham's office, took a car from the pool, drove to the Four Seasons Hotel in Georgetown, where he ostensibly had a meeting with a military contracts interest group rep.

He had the valet park the car for him, overtipping him, saying he wanted a choice spot, just to make sure the kid would remember him. He went into the cool quiet lobby, walked past the elegant furniture and had a light meal in the outdoor cafe while tree branches clattered over his head and sparrows flitted through the leafy bowers. Again, he overtipped in cash and spent a few minutes telling the waitress a joke about the female congressman and the NRA lobbyist.

Forty minutes after he entered the hotel lobby, he rose, went to a public phone, called a cab company. Within ten minutes the cab pulled up in front of a men's clothing store three blocks from the hotel, and Yoshida, who had been waiting for it, got in. Moments before, he had left the hotel unnoticed through a service entrance. He had the driver drop him along the bombed out length of Seventh Street in Chinatown. Waiting until the cab had disappeared in traffic, he turned and headed for stir-fry corridor, H Street.

Marion Starr St James was waiting for him at the back of the Phoenix Chinatown, an old and well-known hangout.

He slipped onto a vinyl-covered banquette at her booth. She was eating twice-cooked pork and offered him some, but he demurred. At this hour no one was around; the staff was seated across the restaurant, eating their lunch. No one paid them the slightest attention.

'How'd I do?' she asked.

'Perfect. He's now on the scent of Green Branches.'

Marion smiled at him. 'I told you I could do it, darling.'

'Yes, and I must admit I had my doubts for a while. It's been difficult turning him against his father; Ham's so intent on being the one good child in the family.'

'A child's love for his father – it can be a nasty thing.'

'The love goes so deep these emotions are easily twisted,' Yoshida said. 'I never knew my father but I loved yours.'

'Better you than me,' Marion said. 'He could be a right bastard when he had a mind to. He could think of punishments that would be better left to the Marquis de Sade.'

'Probably made you what you are today.'

'I've no doubt my father would have agreed with you.'

'I wouldn't blame him,' Yoshida said. 'Gun-runners have plenty of time to dream up exotic punishments during the long nervy nights getting in and out of their destinations.' He watched her use her chopsticks, shovelling the twice-cooked pork into her mouth from a small porcelain rice cup, and was impressed that she ate like an Asian. He was also secretly impressed that she'd had the guts to take over her father's treacherous but essentially small-time gun-running enterprise and turn it into a multi-national operation just like any legitimate conglomerate.

'Don't think I don't know why you loved my father, darling,' Marion said. 'He wasn't in it for the money. He got into gun-running for an Irish buddy of his whose brother had been beaten to death by English soldiers in Belfast. He did it as a matter of principle. He despised the concept of the "Empire", was convinced that all the current economic ills plaguing Britain could be traced back to maintaining it. 'The Romans couldn't do it,' he used to say, 'and they were a damn sight more clever than we are. You mark my words, my girl, maintaining the Eastern bloc – an empire in fact if not in name – will be Russia's downfall as well.' Marion washed down more of her twice-cooked pork with some Oolong tea. 'Dead brilliant mind, my father had.'

'Yet you can't bring yourself to stop hating him,' Yoshida said. 'I find that dichotomy fascinating.'

'I'll bet you do, darling. Tell me, what do you think of the father and son?'

'Thornburg talks down to Ham,' Yoshida said. 'That's because he knows his juice can squash his son like a bug. He doesn't give Ham enough credit.' He smiled. 'He still considers himself invulnerable.' His smile broadened. 'He hasn't yet figured out that it will be his own son who brings him down.'

Marion smiled. 'You see? Everything about you is a dichotomy. What do you think attracts me to you? I mean you love living well but, really, you couldn't give a fig if you earned two cents. Haven't you told me that money makes one walk into walls. It makes you want things that aren't important at all, while you go around ignoring the things that are. Money destroys principles.' She poured more tea. 'I'll tell you one thing, darling, you can see the truth of that in Thornburg Conrad III.' She shuddered lightly. 'Ugh, you couldn't get me to crawl in bed with that creature for all the arms of the US Government. Now the son's different.'

'Yes, Ham is more unlike his father than he would care to think,' Yoshida agreed. 'The trick has been to foster his delusion that he and the old man are cut from the same mould. Then, when the moment comes when he confronts what his father's *really* up to, he'll freak. His rage will be terrifying. He will become like one of your missiles, homed in on his father, whom I have no doubt he secretly hates for driving Ham's mother into the arms of a lover and away from Ham. And seeing with his own eyes the catalogue of Thornburg Conrad III's sins, the son will kill the father.'

'That thought really gets you going, doesn't it?'

Yoshida's gaze rested on her; he said nothing.

Marion pushed her plate away, as if she had suddenly lost her appetite. 'All wars are essentially insane, aren't they, darling,' she said, 'but some are more insane than others. This is how I feel; it's a matter of principle.' She pulled out a compact, looked at herself in the mirror while she applied lipstick. 'Tell me, how did you allow Audrey Simmons to find out that Thornburg and I were dealing?'

'Not merely dealing. Fucking.' Yoshida raised his arms, pulled back the cuffs of his jacket. 'Look, nothing up my sleeves.' He gave her a grin as hard as concrete. 'Sleight of hand is not the sole province of magicians. I have access to computers that can turn several photographs into one that can convince the unsuspecting audience of virtually anything.' He grunted. 'As for the business part, I got Harris Patterson to do my dirty work. Patterson's been a bad boy, you see, borrowing from his clients' accounts on occasion to sing a deal here or there. Conduct like that would get him disbarred should it come out.' He was relishing the admiring look in her eyes. 'Anyway, I know people like Audrey Simmons. Like most of her ilk, she adores gossip – and she had the hots for Ham. I made sure she was at the restaurant to see the two of you together. She was emotionally prepared to believe what I showed her. It's like self-hypnosis, really.'

Marion capped her lipstick, snapped her compact shut. 'I'll miss Ham just a little bit, I think. He's not like the others; the government hasn't yet tainted him.'

'Only a matter of time,' Yoshida said, thinking she was smart, too smart for her own good.

'I've got to pee,' she said. 'Why don't you pay the check while you're waiting.' She took her purse, walked into the back of the restaurant.

Yoshida waited until she had turned into the ladies' room, then threw a twenty-dollar bill onto the table, slid out of the booth and headed for the rest rooms.

He opened the door to the men's room, saw it was deserted, went past it. No one else was around; at the far end of the cramped hallway was the kitchen and, just before that, a door that led out onto a back alley.

He drove his hands into powdered surgeon's rubber gloves, took a small curved metal pick out of his pocket, inserted it into the cheap lock on the ladies' room door, worked it around until the lock popped. He went inside, carefully closing the door after him.

Thornburg insisted on being present at Tiffany Conrad's interment. The doctors had argued against it, since they had spent the previous sixteen hours dissecting her in order to amass more data on where they were going wrong. But in the end Thornburg prevailed, as he was bound to do since he paid their generous salaries.

Interment was only a word Thornburg used, since what was left of the physical remains of his wife were to be cremated as were all the remains of the failed experiments using the cloned variants of the 'donors'' insulin-like growth factor-1.

He had many fond memories of Tiffany which he allowed himself to leaf through while he watched the intensely hot flames consume her. He also thought about death, the knowledge of which was always with him, his sole companion now, even in what shallow sleep was left him. Death was the only thing Thornburg hated and feared.

He stirred as he felt the door open and close behind him. Then Ham was standing by his side.

'I came as quickly as I could,' Ham said.

'Good of you.'

But there was no emotion at all in Thornburg's voice, and Ham took note of this. He was acutely aware of his father's age, and he was looking for clues to the form of senility that would put the plan to block the Black Blade Society's economic takeover of America in jeopardy. In truth, he felt a growing gulf between him and his father, and was, for the first time, aware of the anger he had repressed for so long but which had never ceased to seethe beneath the surface. Whatever else Thornburg had done, his utter contempt for Ham's mother was inexcusable. First, his heartlessness had pushed her into having an affair, and then he had condemned her for being human. Of course, gods were allowed such peccadillos, and Ham was all too aware that this was how he had always viewed his father: as a god. But, after all, Thornburg was as mortal as the next man, which meant he had made mistakes, though he would never have admitted to them. It was enough that Ham's eyes had been opened – partly because of Yosh's insight, he had to admit. If Thornburg lacked the moral rectitude to judge himself, then Ham would have to do it for him.

'As long as you're here,' Thornburg said, gazing into the cleansing fire, 'you might as well bring me up to speed on Matheson.'

This, then, was the moment of truth. For a moment, Ham considered backing down from his resolve, lying to his father, and telling him everything was on course. Then, the anger inside of him flared up anew, and he thought, *Fuck it, I've had enough of his lies.*

'Matheson is out of the loop,' he said. 'He's with the Japanese woman, Chika, and she's a known member of the Black Blade Society. We don't know his current status: captive, recruit, who knows? In addition, he's been implicated in the murder of one of his men, and is involved in the torture-murder of the New York City Police Commissioner. They tried to nab him in New York, but he somehow slipped away.'

Thornburg said nothing for a moment, and Ham held his breath.

'In a way,' Thornburg said at last, 'it no longer matters what a fool you've been. Matheson is just where I want him to be.'

'Will you forget Matheson,' Ham said with undisguised irritation. 'I already told you he's out of the loop. Yoshida and I – '

'Know nothing about what is really happening,' Thornburg snapped. He knew he was overstepping the bounds he himself had imposed on himself, but he found that he no longer cared. Tiffany was gone, and his one solace, his son Hampton, had turned out to be made of no sterner flesh than his other children. They were disappointments all, none of them worthy of succeeding him. 'I've played you just as I played the generals in the Pentagon, the president, everyone.' His eyes blazed, reflecting the flames from Tiffany's modern-day pyre. 'I'm smarter than all of you put together. I don't need you; I don't need your Machiavellian shadow. Matheson is all I need. He's aimed right at the heart of the Black Blade Society. He'll stop them *and* get me what I want most.'

Ham stared at his father and thought, Yosh is right, he's snapped. All he can think of is Matheson. The larger ramifications of what the Black Blade Society is doing to us is almost irrelevant to him. 'Get hold of yourself,' he said sharply. 'I freely acknowledge your role in the instigation of our defence against the Black Blade Society, but you must see your time is at an end. All you care about is Wolf Matheson when the economic takeover of America is at hand. That's irrational behaviour and it will put our operation at risk. I can't allow that. Go home. Mourn your child bride, if that's your desire. As of now I'm relieving you of your responsibilities. Yosh and I will run the operation from here on out.'

Thornburg found his son's earnest speech so naive that he could not help but burst out into laughter. 'My God,' he finally managed to get out, 'do what you have to do, it won't matter. Events are already far beyond your control.'

Ham glared at his father, the old man's humiliating laughter still ringing in his ears. But he refused to allow Thornburg to cut him off at the knees. He had seen his father do just that with a few well-chosen words to too many people. 'Just stay out of active operations,' he said curtly. 'They no longer concern you.'

Thornburg watched his son stalk out of the room. In a way, he was proud of Ham for being able to stand up to the humiliation he deliberately directed at him. But he was also concerned. He supposed his son's misunderstanding of the overall situation was what came from keeping too many secrets. Thornburg knew he would have to do something about Ham and Yoshida very soon or their machinations might begin to work at cross-purposes with Thornburg's private design.

And, in a way, he mused, Ham was quite correct: he *was* obsessed with Wolf Matheson. But for a very good reason. One the younger Conrad could never guess at.

Very early on, Thornburg had become a man who thrived on challenges – the more difficult and impossible-seeming the better. What genuine pleasure he garnered from life was provided by those moments of triumph when everyone around him was certain he would fail.

'There is no feeling in the world like seeing defeat ageing your enemy's face,' his father had once told him. *'The exhilaration is positively incandescent, like walking away whole and alive from what should have been your moment of death.'*

How early Thornburg had dedicated himself to cheating death even

362

he could not say. His unreasonable task led him through the corridors of the many layers of society, the high and the low and all the levels inbetween. In the beginning, he had rubbed up against some mighty screwy individuals, whose notions of life and death most other people would have scoffed at. But, in his quest, Thornburg had tried them all: the psychic, the quasi-religious, and in the end, they all stank of snake oil.

There wasn't a viable alternative in the lot until he came upon the earliest breakthroughs in the newly emerging biochemical sciences that, in those days at least, had no real names yet. And then, miraculously, the three-ring circus of the war in Vietnam had inadvertently provided a very minor sideshow – from the military's point of view at least – that was to give him a hint that his goal of cheating death might not be so impossible, after all.

He had thought that with these few precious clues he would be able to solve the riddle of eternal life on his own. But, as he was learning, his own staff's tireless work on recombinant insulin-like growth factor-1 had a half-life flaw that could not be corrected unless another – completely unknown – element was added to the mix. One that his researchers were unable to define, let alone synthesize in their labs.

Now, as Thornburg watched the flames lick around the last remains of Tiffany Conrad, he knew that his sole chance of cheating death rested on his assessment of Wolf Matheson's personality and abilities. And it seemed now to him just and right that he should have saved Wolf's life in Cambodia more than two decades ago. But life, Thornburg had discovered, was often like that, a purpose in all things. As the Japanese liked to say, karma.

As he closed the door on the flames he wondered whether he had been looking at his own death. How much time did he have left? He did not know. *Someone* knew, of that he had no doubt, but she was still beyond the length of even his long shadow. In lieu of her precious knowledge, he continued to inject himself with a variant of the drug that had made Tiffany younger and had, ultimately, killed her.

But perhaps without that drug he would already have been dead. For some time now, he had come to suspect that he had lived past the appointed moment of his death. In a sense, he had got what he wanted most. He was, indeed, cheating death now, but he knew it was, at best, a Pyrrhic victory which, his father had taught him, was no victory at all.

The simple fact was the current reversal of ageing he was enjoying couldn't last, and would terminate, if past examples were any indication, in horrific pain, eased only by massive doses of morphine. That was not the way a man should die, but it would doubtless happen to him unless

Wolf Matheson could unlock the enigma he had stumbled across so long ago in the jungles of Cambodia.

Marion was in the lone stall, wondering why Jason Yoshida had told her so much about his scheme, when she heard the outer door open. She knew she had locked the door and she sat very still. She stared hard at the stall door as if willing herself to see through it. At the same time, her fingers were searching through the contents of her purse, which was on her lap, for anything she could use as a weapon. Christ, where was that metal nail file? She had ground down the narrow end into a sharp point, figuring you never knew when it might come in handy.

Her hand closed around it at the same time the stall door was pulled violently open and Jason Yoshida's face leered in at her. She recoiled in a kind of shock at the nakedness of the hatred she saw distorting his face. It was a hatred all the more despicable because it was wholly impersonal. She had the momentary sensation of looking at the fetid bottom of an infrequently illuminated well. The brief glimpse she had of Jason Yoshida's soul froze her blood.

Yoshida ripped open the front of her dress, jerked her bra painfully off her breasts. By this time, she had overcome her initial shock and was trying to get the nail file out of her purse. But it was crosswise and it snagged on another object, then the rim.

Now the strip of Lycra and lace was around her throat and, with a low, guttural sound a street dog makes when it has found a scrap of food, Yoshida jerked so powerfully on both ends that Marion was lifted up onto her feet. She gagged, her eyes watered as she fought to breathe.

The nail file came free as her purse dropped to the filthy tile floor, but Marion no longer had enough strength, and Yoshida shrugged aside her pathetic attempt at defence.

They were cheek to cheek, and Marion could feel his warmth becoming superheated like the sun as the heat drained out of her. She was so cold, that was the only sensation left her. And, then, gradually, even that slipped away. For a moment, she floated, weightless, then even the concept of weight winked out.

364

SIXTEEN

Tokyo/Washington

This is a formidable place, Wolf thought as he and Chika emerged into the bewildering, densely populated streets of Tokyo. It was like a technological fortress made of silicon and steel. Everywhere could be seen the signatures of the modern world: enormous vertical banners of neon proclaiming the millions of minuscule fiefdoms stacked one atop the other in this vertical metropolis.

'Most foreigners are bewildered by this city,' Chika said. 'But understanding it is easy.' She lifted her arms. 'Tokyo is *hade*,' she said. '*Hade* is a term best translated as exuberance, though it also means beautiful and radiant.' She gestured over their heads at the signs. 'You see the colours here, and again here: shimmering gold against lustrous vermilion. And there, columns of stainless steel glowing in the sun, next to the lavish ornamental yellows and oranges of that shrine. Here is the essence of Tokyo, the *hade* that is a riot of shapes and colours. If you can understand that, you know everything you need to about Tokyo.'

Standing in a street stinking of fish, the Sumida river nearby, they ate a quick meal of soba noodles and flaked bonito drenched in a fishy soy sauce, and washed it all down with green tea.

Wolf had slept on the flight but felt as if something heavy and sinister had trampled on his back during the long night. Locked in the steel and aluminium cabin, his dreams had echoed his worst waking nightmares of Chika and Suma, ostensibly enemies, but actually allies, adroitly manipulating him in a deadly game he could not understand.

'Don't let the ultra-modern look of Japan fool you. In many ways it is still a feudal society,' Chika said as they pushed their way through the jam-packed streets. 'Not exactly as you Westerners think of the word, but in a purely Eastern manner. There are lines of obeisance and *giri* – obligation – that still exist just as they have for centuries.

'Information – inside, confidential, essential for advancement of career and profit – is freely shared by interlocking networks of people who are bound together because they come from the same area, graduate from the same school, or marry into the same family. In this sense, there are still feudal lords and their retainers just as there were in the late 1500s before Ieyasu Tokugawa ostensibly did away with these *daimyo* by uniting Japan under the banner of his shogunate.'

She hailed a taxi, the rear door swung open automatically, and they got in. Stop and go across the city was not a quick affair. But Chika obviously wanted him to see Tokyo, dense and colourful, like fish pressed into a can.

An enormous animated signboard affixed to a steel and glass office tower depicted in astounding detail doctors in an operating room, followed by a head shot of a beautiful young woman smiling, glowing with health, mouthing words in Japanese. In a moment, those words filled a cartoon-style balloon, were printed out first in Japanese kanji, and then in English letters. SHIAN KOGAKU: WE ARE ALWAYS WITH YOU.

At length, the taxi pulled up in front of a magnificent wood temple just barely visible above a daunting flight of stone steps. Around it, was a surprisingly thick swath of trees, interspersed with what Chika told him were embassies on the edge of the Akasaka district. They were near the Diet, the Japanese Parliament, as close to the country's seat of power as one could get. Chika paid the driver, and they got out.

'This is Hie Jinja, a Shinto shrine,' Chika said, as they passed beneath the soaring lacquered *torii* gates and began to ascend towards the temple proper. 'It was originally built in 1478, and served as the guardian shrine of the old Edo castle,' Chika said. 'Since then, however, it has been destroyed and rebuilt several times.'

They reached a spacious gravel courtyard, bounded by the outbuildings, the *haiden*, the oratory and the *heiden*, the offertory hall. 'The holy buildings you see here were built in 1967. But in Japan such shrines traditionally have a history of destruction and resurrection, so that when one comes here there is no sense at all of the relative newness of the buildings.'

Wolf could sense that she was right. In the midst of the bustling metropolis there was a serene silence here of the sort one normally associates with hilltop forests, where the stillness was measured only by the wind in the branches and the occasional wild cry of a raptor. It was not as if the roar of traffic or the hum of voices could not be heard, rather that the meditative sounds of the shrine – the bass bell calling the *kami* – the spirits, the sawing of the temple carpenter, the thin dissonance of traditional instruments – carried far more weight. They acted somewhat like a lens, focusing the attention, assuring the listener of the ultimate importance of history.

'It's very beautiful here,' Wolf said. 'Peaceful.'

Chika gave a little smile and seemed pleased. But he could sense an edginess to her, as well.

'I brought you here to meet someone,' Chika said. She turned her face up to him. 'Promise me that you'll listen to what she has to say.'

Wolf could see how important this was to her. 'All right.' What did he have to lose?

She led him across the courtyard towards the temple. Beyond, he could see a pair of gleaming black limos waiting with their liveried drivers and, as he watched, a wedding procession spilled out of one of the shrine's outbuildings.

The entryway to Hie Jinja was flanked by glass cases containing the holy monkeys, clothed and regal, representing the shrine. He saw a figure standing in front of one of these cases. As they neared, Wolf saw that it was a woman, and her head turned in their direction long before she could have heard their approach.

'Remember what I told you about *giri*, obligation and allegiance,' Chika said in a tone that made this seem like a warning. 'I owe such an allegiance to her.'

In the instant of recognition that annihilated time and took him back two decades to Cambodia, he heard Chika say, 'Minako is my mother, Wolf.'

'It has been a long time, and it is good to see you again, Wolf-san,' Minako said just as if they were old friends.

The first thing Wolf noticed about her was that she had not aged a day since he had last seen her. In fact, if anything, she looked better. Obviously, she possessed *makura na hiruma*.

She was dressed in Western clothes, a black skirt, a white blouse, gold belt and necklace, all wrapped in a black ankle-length coat. Despite the hard colours there was a softness to the lines of her outfit, a certain refinement that was the epitome of femininity. This and the fact of the dichotomy of black and white Wolf took as visual cues. She had dressed with him in mind, the softness to help mitigate his memory of her as a woman warrior, the black and white a reminder of the duality of hard and soft inside all people.

'I asked my daughter to bring you here to Hie Jinja,' Minako said, 'because I was afraid there would be a temptation for you to see me through the filter of the war.'

My daughter.

'It wasn't your war, after all,' Wolf said.

'Oh, yes it was,' Minako said. 'At least the war you and Thornburg sought out.'

Thornburg Conrad III. It was impossible to see Minako again and not think of him. The spook's spook. The entire MACV chain of command danced to the tune he played, or so it had seemed back then in Vietnam. Now Wolf had arrived back where it had started more than twenty years ago. It seemed to him no coincidence that at the nexus of his new life Minako should be here, waiting for him, patient as a spider.

Minako and Thornburg Conrad III, two shadows hidden so deep underground that even the CIA spooks probably knew nothing about their activities. He thought of Shipley, the Defense Department spook who had recruited him and then had tried to terminate him. Why? It had happened just after he had hooked up with Chika. Was Shipley working for Thornburg Conrad III? Was this what it was all about – the lies, betrayals, murders, the treason committed against country and logic? A private war between Minako and Thornburg that had been running, in one form or another, for over two decades?

At that moment, all the lies he had been told, all the deceit he had endured coalesced into this single moment. He turned on Chika. 'It's all been a deadly game, hasn't it?' he said. He tried to control himself but it was impossible. He was shaking with the intensity of the revelations coming too fast to process. 'I've been used by Thornburg and by you. I can only guess that he wanted to use me in some way against your mother.' He turned back to Minako. 'And you, what is it you want from me? All your daughter has managed to do is sever me quite effectively from my previous life – my girlfriend, my team, even my job are all gone in a puff of smoke.'

'My daughter tells me that you were already dislocated from this life,' Minako said calmly.

Wolf said nothing. He was staring at Chika. Their eyes were locked as if in some kind of physical struggle. The air was suddenly filled with the rich notes of the bell as a worshipper summoned the *kami* of the shrine.

Chika said, in a kind of desperation, 'You promised you would listen to what my mother had to tell you.'

It was the wrong thing to say. He said, 'When I inferred from your answers to my questions that Suma was your opposite number in the enemy camp I was dead wrong, wasn't I?'

She said nothing, so he pressed on. 'I couldn't figure out what I was missing in the pieces of the puzzle, but that was because you were so good at misdirecting me. The war within the Black Blade Society was easily defined, wasn't it? You, representing the good guys on one side and Suma, the emissary of evil, on the other. But it's not like that at all. That night I was in your apartment in Sixth Street, I followed you. I saw you climb into the back of a hearse as it drove away. Who was driving the hearse, Chika? No, don't tell me because I already know. It was Suma. You and he aren't on different sides at all; you're not enemies.'

'Wolf, I didn't lie to you about the war inside the Toshin Kuro Kosai.'

'Shut up,' he said in a snarl. 'How can you expect me to believe anything you say now?'

'I admit I've lied to you in the past, but – '

She stopped, shocked by what she felt. There was no warning at all, even for her. The force of his rage, his *makura na hiruma*, hit her like a bolt of lightning. She was thrown backwards, whirling against the edge of the glass case. Inside, the holy monkey tottered on its throne.

'Stop this at once!' Minako said, alarmed.

Wolf, stunned at what he had done, of what he was capable of doing, could only watch, mute, a spectator at the site of a disaster.

Chika was on her knees. She had had no time to defend herself, and now that she had a chance, she did nothing. Her head was against her chest, and she seemed to be weeping. In a moment, she rose and, without a glance at either Wolf or her mother, she ran across the courtyard, fleeing down the stone steps to the street below, where she was swallowed up in the *hade* of the city.

Yoshida, so close to the corpse of Marion Starr St James, felt the chill come into her and he closed his eyes. He waited, counting the beats of his heart as one totes up the day's take.

Then he swung away from her, hoisting her over his shoulder. He did not look at her face again because there was nothing to see. He went to the door, peered out. The corridor was empty. He could hear the restaurant's staff, full of food and Johnny Walker Black, arguing over whether to pay a vendor's higher fee or to change to another one. He slipped into the corridor, jerked open the back door and, on his way to the street, eased his load into a dumpster, covering her carefully with mounds of refuse.

When, fifteen minutes later, he was back inside the lobby of the Four Seasons Hotel, he picked up a pay phone, called Ham.

'Bad news,' he said. 'Marion Starr St James is dead.'

There was a pause during which he wondered what was going through Ham's mind. When Ham spoke again his voice had a quiver in it. 'What happened?'

'The inevitable,' Yoshida said, leaning his lips into the mouthpiece.

'Ah, Christ, she was some woman.' Yoshida could hear him breathing raggedly as he fought for self-control. 'Yeah.' He cleared his throat of excess emotion. 'She was in a business where it's damn easy to pick up enemies.'

'Either that,' Yoshida said, 'or she knew too much.' He waited a beat. 'Don't you think it's suspicious that she got iced right after she spilled the beans to you about your old man and Green Branches?'

Ham didn't say anything, but then again Yoshida didn't think he had to.

In the aftermath, Wolf felt the lack of Chika's presence as he would the amputation of a limb. The preternatural silence of the shrine was no longer peaceful; his heart ached in a way he was at a loss to understand. It was the profoundest mystery to him that he could care so deeply for someone who had time and again deceived him.

'This is my fault entirely,' Minako said. 'I should never have pushed for this meeting so soon. But there is so little time left, and I have just come from burying my son-in-law, who surely died before his time.'

Over her head, a spray of the first plum blossoms shot colour into the air. A breeze stirred them, and Minako shivered, digging her hands into her coat pockets, pulling it around her.

Wolf, watching her as the mother of the woman who was tearing him apart, had the eerie sensation all this – even the blossoms on the plum trees – had been orchestrated by her.

He was resolved not to allow her to get to him. 'What did you want of us then?' he said to her in a pitiless tone.

'You have it all wrong,' she said. 'It was you and Thornburg who came after me. Thornburg with his experiments in slowing the ageing process.'

'And what about your experiments?'

She looked at him, but said nothing.

'You and Thornburg,' he said, 'there's not much difference between you.'

He could not have cut her more deeply. Minako drew herself up. 'You never knew much about him, and I suppose it's just as well. He is a man who poisons everything he touches.' She turned away. 'Almost everything.'

'Do you expect me to believe that you knew him better than I did?'

She turned back. 'That night while you slept, I allowed him to seduce me. I had my reasons, but they had nothing to do with my experiments. We spoke of many things and, of course, I had my *makura na hiruma* and could see more things about him than he could ever believe.' She put her head down. Another worshipper was ringing the bell, increasing the silence of the shrine. 'Perhaps I even saw this moment, because that was the start of it all. Had I killed you both, perhaps life – this present – would be simpler. But, in that event, I would surely be

370

dead and the Reverend Mother would now be free to continue with her insane plans.'

'Who is the Reverend Mother?'

'She rules the Toshin Kuro Kosai.'

'My information is that a man named Naoharu Nishitsu heads the Black Blade Society.'

Minako shook her head. 'A common enough error. Although Nishitsu appears to rule the Toshin Kuro Kosai, the Reverend Mother is the true leader. The fiction is useful. It allows her to appear at meetings and discussions with those outside the society without being noticed. One can pick up much in this manner.'

'And the Reverend Mother is your enemy.'

'Yes,' Minako said. 'She is also Chika's godmother.'

Wolf sat down. All the anger had dissipated, leaving him with only a taste like copper in his mouth. 'You'd better explain this so an outsider can understand it.'

'The Reverend Mother and I grew up together; we have been lifelong friends and, for much of that long, long time, I have been her strong right hand. But over the decades, so slowly that at first I didn't notice it, she began to change. She became corrupt and strange, indulging in all manner of vice and perversion. And she sought to corrupt all those around her.

'Too late, I realized that she had chosen Chika to be her goddaughter and guardian not only because of the strength of Chika's *makura na hiruma*, but because she is my daughter. You see, the Reverend Mother is barren. I think it amused her to make Chika her goddaughter, to take a part of something that was so precious to me. But I have four children and she has none. She has used Chika, just as I was forced to use her to go after you, to bring you back here.'

'What about *giri*?' Wolf asked. 'Don't you owe a debt of allegiance to the Reverend Mother?'

Minako gave him an ironic smile. 'Tell me, Wolf-san, would you blindly follow the orders of a madwoman?'

'Are you certain she is mad?'

'She means for the Black Blade Society to take control of the world. They will do it economically just as they manipulated the Japanese economy after the war in the Pacific. Years ago, she sent one of her assassins, a man named Jason Yoshida, to the United States. There he is undermining the political powers that shape American economic policy for international trade. The Reverend Mother trained Yoshida herself. He has been busy of late, systematically murdering political figures who backed the wrong congressional bills by means that made the deaths

371

appear to be accidents or suicide – easy for a maniac like Yoshida.' She shook her head gravely. 'I have staked my own life – and the lives of my children on the Reverend Mother's madness.' Her eyes were unnaturally bright. 'And now I have you.'

Wolf, interested to get independent corroboration of what Shipley had told him, nevertheless said, 'I think you've got the wrong person.'

'I know what my sight tells me,' Minako said. 'My future and yours are inextricably entwined.' She seemed as sure of herself as an historian dissecting the past. 'You have come this far; you will do what I have seen you do.'

'Why have you brought me here?' he demanded.

'Because,' she said, 'you have become the last weapon in a war that will surely be fought to the death.'

The echoes of the bell seemed to linger in the crisp air, falling on their ears like deepening tones from an artist's brush.

'You must not think too harshly of my daughter,' she said before he had a chance to recover his equilibrium. 'If she deceived you it was under my command.'

'But I heard her – *felt* her – with Suma.'

'Ah, Suma.' Minako walked slowly away from the background of the plum trees until she was framed by the entrance to the shrine itself. She appeared to Wolf to belong here, but as a priestess, not a worshipper. He made his way toward her, away from the swirl of people at the periphery of the gravel courtyard. The holy monkeys grinned at him, as if in on a secret that concerned him.

When he was close to her again, Minako said, 'Chika and Suma were once lovers. As a guardian of the Reverend Mother, she had ample opportunity to come into contact with this assassin who was at the Reverend Mother's call. However, even had she not been, I strongly suspect the Reverend Mother would have contrived some way to get them together. Again, it pleased her perverse nature to see Chika with this – thing – she had created.' She folded her hands together. 'And I think she meant to corrupt Chika, to lead her down a path she had set for her – away from me.'

'Just because they were together didn't mean they had to wind up sleeping together.'

'No?' Minako cocked her head. 'You have much to learn concerning the Reverend Mother's powers. They are very special.'

'But you said Chika and Suma *were* lovers,' Wolf said. 'What was she doing with him now?'

Minako stirred as if bidden by the breeze. 'You must understand the extreme danger I have put both myself and Chika in. We must be

372

absolutely convincing. The Reverend Mother and those loyal to her must get no inkling that we are planning to oust her. *That* is what she was doing with Suma: convincing him she was still loyal.'

Wolf wondered whether he could believe her. He had no real reason to. She had already told him that she had brought him here to defeat her enemy in the Black Blade Society, and she and her daughter had got this far by treachery and deceit. But then again who *could* he trust? Not Shipley, the earnest spook who had then tried to have him killed, and certainly not the man he was almost certainly working for, Thornburg Conrad III. Was the Reverend Mother really mad, or was everyone else? Like a rat in a maze, Wolf realized that he was in an arena with no discernible exit. In that event, he would have to manufacture one on his own.

He would also, he thought, have to come to terms with his feelings for Chika. His attraction to her was so strong that when he was around her he felt nearly blinded. Was that love, or something else entirely?

After a long time, he said, 'You knew I possessed *makura na hiruma?*'

Minako shook her head. 'Not until recently. To me you were always the Man Without a Face, because you gave off no aura at all. It was as if you were not there. But something stuck in my mind. I gave Thornburg a test. I told him that I would give him the secret to slowing the ageing process if he would shoot you.'

'You did what?'

Minako smiled, the first genuine smile she allowed herself since he had driven Chika away. 'I told you it was a test. And he surprised me. He refused. That went against everything I had seen with my sight. What was the reason? Years later, it occurred to me that he had understood something about you that I, in my arrogance, could not. He had felt the specialness inside you. He had no idea what it was but, remembering back, I saw in him the conviction that as long as he was with you he would be safe.'

'So you let us go.'

'Yes.'

'I suppose I should thank you – and him,' Wolf said. 'But under the circumstances I won't bother.'

From the hidden street below them a motorcycle started up, its dissonant metallic *brrupppp!* somehow adding to the profound silence of the shrine.

Minako smiled again. 'You're a hard one,' she said. 'We have a name for men such as you: you are *koha.* I suppose it was inevitable that my daughter fell in love with you.'

'Chika – '

'Speak to her yourself,' Minako said. 'You don't believe what I say. Why should you?'

'If she's still speaking to me.'

'You will find the right words,' Minako said. 'You hurt her, it's true, but she is also racked with guilt for having to deceive you.'

'I'll have to find her first.'

'That is no problem. She has gone to my house. I will write out directions for you.'

'You're not coming?'

'Not right away,' she said. 'I have an appointment with the Reverend Mother that I dare not break. In this atmosphere, even the slightest deviation in my behaviour would be suspect.'

'So now it's essentially come down to the Reverend Mother and you,' Wolf said.

'Yes. This is the path down which her madness has taken us.' Minako's eyes swung away for a moment, before centring back on Wolf's face. 'And now everything has changed. Even Chika does not know this yet. The Reverend Mother is killing off the members of the inner council, one by one.'

'But why?'

'Her absolute power has bred a kind of absolute madness. Her thirst for personal power has outstripped every other consideration. It is true she and Nishitsu have put together a plan to gain economic control over the United States, and that this scheme is entering its final stage. And it is also true that she and Nishitsu would have to be stopped simply for this reason. But, over and above this, she has found some way to extract the *makura na hiruma* from others and add it to her own.'

He managed a laugh. 'Oh, come on, what are you saying? That she plans to chop up your brains and eat them for dinner?'

'In a metaphorical sense,' she said, 'that's exactly what I mean.' Her gaze was so direct it seemed as if he could see right down into her core. 'Yours, too.'

The implications of her words hit him, and he felt the blood chill in his veins.

She was very close to him, speaking softly, her words bringing their own reverberations. 'I cannot allow that to happen, Wolf-san. You see, you are very special. When your grandfather died he was very old – ancient, really.'

'How do you know this? Even I don't know how old he was when he died.'

'Of course not,' she said. 'He would not have told you; you would not have understood. But he was known to us. All the elders were known in a certain circle of people. And when he died we were certain that we would never see his like again. But here you are, and I know what my *makura na hiruma* has shown me. You have his power – and more, much more.'

SEVENTEEN

Washington/Tokyo

'As surely as I am sitting here talking to you,' Yoshida said, 'he killed her.'

Ham Conrad, sitting across the table at the outdoor restaurant at the top of the Washington Hotel, stared blankly out at the White House. Marion's brutal murder had overshadowed Breathard's call delineating his failure to take care of Wolf Matheson. Fuck Matheson, Ham thought now, I've got more immediate problems.

Yoshida continued. 'I have no doubt whatsoever that your father ordered Marion Starr St James killed, and you know very well why: she knew too much about him and was telling you about it.'

'The Green Branches Clinic.'

'Yes, indeed.'

'Where Marion said Thornburg is having the people shipped.' Ham spoke in the kind of mechanical monotone people use in the initial stages of shock.

'Right.' Yoshida was studying Ham's face, though Ham was oblivious of the scrutiny. 'What she told you, if memory serves, is that he had hired her company to transship rootless loners who no one would miss to this place he bought some time ago, Green Branches outside Arlington.' Yoshida paused for a minute while he ordered them a second round of drinks even though Ham had not finished his first. Then he said, 'What do you suppose he wants living humans for?'

'Experiments,' Ham said in that same toneless voice. 'You see, Thornburg is obsessed by age. He believes he can reverse it. That's why he purchased Green Branches and installed his own biosciences staff.' Ham was still staring sightlessly at the White House which, at this hour, was lit by a battery of floodlights. 'I imagine he is using the shipments as guinea pigs.'

'Human beings?'

Ham swung his head around. 'What else could you experiment on? Thornburg's running out of time.'

The drinks came. Yoshida sipped his, pushed the other glass into

376

Ham's hand. 'He's totally amoral. Look, I saw Marion's body and I can tell you it wasn't a pretty sight. I think she suffered quite a bit before she died. It was as if he wanted her to know that he was punishing her. He's having people killed right and left at that clinic.'

Ham said, 'I have no doubt that he would tell you that it's all being done in the name of science.'

'And I have no doubt he believes that crap.' Yoshida stirred the ice around his drink thoughtfully. After an interval, he said, 'We're going to have to do something about this.'

Ham nodded. 'I know.'

'We have no choice.'

Ham drained half his glass. He was thinking of his father, of how much he admired the old man, of how much he needed his approval. But for the first time he became aware of other, darker emotions he, in his fanatical desire to win his father's approval, had spent so much time and energy avoiding.

Recent events had begun to unearth these emotions until now, like an archaeologist sifting through the upper reaches of a long-buried city, he found himself face to face with the truth: that however much he loved and admired his father he also hated him for driving Ham's mother out of the house, out of Ham's life.

'You're right,' he said at last to Yoshida, 'we have no choice at all.'

Hana was already hooked up to the Oracle when Yuji walked into the laboratory in the warehouse near the Tsukiji fish market. He had looked for her at Hiroto's funeral, but she had not been there.

'What are you doing?' he said, but it was unclear whether he was speaking to Hana or the Oracle.

There was a calmness in Hana's face which he found profane as well as disturbing. Her eyes followed him, but to his questions, his cajoling and, finally, his orders, she remained mute. He had seen this look on her face once before . . .

It was the time of *Hatsugatsuo*, when one celebrated the summer by eating the first bonito of the season. Yuji and Hana had gone down to the docks at Kobe. The fierce sun dried the sweat that sprang up on their skin. The dense humidity made breathing a chore. Hana took him to a small shop that had a minuscule veranda overlooking the harbour.

This was a very important rite for her, as were all the rituals that spoke of the movements of nature. The proprietor, who knew her well, made them a pot of his own green tea, whisking the liquid into a pale froth at the table. The raw bonito, translucent as gossamer, was served on a bed of deep green bamboo leaves. As far as taste went, this would not be the best bonito of summer, but it was the most prized.

The humid air barely stirred; even the gulls in the harbour found the air too heavy to fly.In the shade beneath the umbrella, Yuji could see the rusting oil refineries of Oto Heavy Industries rising like a canker along the quayside. Painted on their sides was the slogan: SHIAN KOGAKU: WE ARE ALWAYS WITH YOU. They watched the harbour traffic come and go, but no workmen swarmed over the Oto refineries. Gigantic cranes hung silent and abandoned above the row of ugly rusting metal structures.

'One day,' Hana said, *'the bonito will cease to run in our polluted waters. What will become of us then? I ask myself if there is a point to a life where we are doomed to destroy our bodies inch by inch? I often dream of a life where I am not bound by the physical laws of time and space.'* She looked at him. *'Where I am not required to walk across the road to get to the other side.'*

Now with his eyes on Hana's he reached over, flicked off the power.

Nothing happened. That is to say, the Oracle did not shut down.

'YOU MUST ACCEPT WHAT IS TO HAPPEN, YUJI-SAN.'

Yuji, open-mouthed, said, 'How are you doing this? I have shut down your power.'

The Oracle did not answer. It was concentrating on other matters. It took precisely four minutes for the light to go out of Hana's eyes. Her lids slowly closed, her pulse when he took it was reduced to near zero.

'No!'

Frantically Yuji pulled the pressure-sensitive pads off her, and thought he heard a tiny scream as each one came free.

She collapsed in his arms. It would take some time to disconnect the wires hooked to her frontal lobes and at the base of her neck. Her lips were blue and there was no movement in her chest. He pressed the soft skin over her carotid artery again, felt nothing.

The Oracle won't allow anything bad to happen to me, she had told him the first time he had hooked her into the beast.

'God damn you!' Yuji screamed. 'What have you done to her?'

'WHAT HAD TO BE DONE,' the Oracle said without hesitation. 'I HAVE DONE WHAT YOU WANTED ME TO DO.'

Yuji, on his knees, cradling Hana in his arms, started to weep. 'Please. Tell me what has happened. How could I have wanted you to do this to her? She's dead.'   •

'ONLY HER BODY, YUJI-SAN. OTHERWISE, HANA IS QUITE ALIVE. IN FACT, SHE IS MORE ALIVE THAN SHE HAS EVER BEEN BEFORE.'

Yuji stared up into the Oracle's face. Was he seeing things or was it starting to take on the general characteristics of a human head? 'What are you talking about?'

'HANA IS HERE, INSIDE OF ME,' the Oracle said as patiently as a professor with a dull-witted but well-meaning student.

'I don't believe it.'

'AN HOUR AGO YOU WOULD NOT HAVE BELIEVED THAT I COULD RUN ON MY OWN POWER SOURCE.'

Yuji thought about that for a moment. 'It's clear you no longer require electricity to power on,' he said. 'What are you using?'

'MAKURA NA HIRUMA.'

'What?'

'WHY ARE YOU SURPRISED, YUJI-SAN? IT IS ONLY LOGICAL. I ACCESSED THE REQUISITE ELEMENTS FROM YOUR OWN DNA MOLECULES. IS THIS NOT PART OF MY ORIGINAL FUNCTION?'

Yuji believed in many more things than the normal scientist, especially following the birth of the Oracle, but even his unorthodoxy had its limits. Under no circumstances could he imagine something so intangible as *makura na hiruma* being acquired by the Oracle's circuits. And yet, here he was, presented with the evidence to the contrary.

'I'm afraid I don't understand any of this,' Yuji said sadly. He refused to let go of his beloved half-sister. 'Hana is dead.'

'YOU ARE REACTING TO HER BODY. I CAN ASSURE YOU THAT SHE DOES NOT MISS IT. SHE IS CONTENT HERE.'

Yuji considered this for some time. 'Can she speak to me directly?'

'I HAVE BEEN DOING SO, YUJI-SAN.'

'I mean Hana herself.'

'I AM HANA HERSELF.'

Yuji shook his head. 'I do not understand.'

'I CANNOT HELP THAT.'

Yuji grunted, tried again. 'What I mean to say . . . ' He thought some more, wanting to frame this so the Oracle would understand. 'You have formed a distinct personality. It is not Hana's personality, with which I am very familiar.'

'OF COURSE,' the Oracle said. 'I UNDERSTAND. BUT HANA IS CHANGED, THIS IS WHAT YOU MUST UNDERSTAND, YUJI-SAN. IT SEEMS TO ME THAT METAMORPHOSES OF ANY KIND ARE DIFFICULT FOR HUMANS TO FATHOM, BUT THERE YOU ARE, THAT IS HUMAN NATURE.'

Yuji laughed. 'Where did you get that sense of humour?'

'I FOUND IT IN HANA.'

'Hana?' He was startled. 'Hana never had a sense of humour that I could detect.'

'HANA HAS MANY THINGS YOU COULD NOT DETECT, YUJI-SAN. BUT NOW THERE IS TIME TO SOLVE HER MYSTERY. SHE IS CLOSER TO YOU NOW THAN SHE COULD EVER HAVE BEEN IN HER BODY.'

'Tell me more.'

'IN HER HUMAN BODY HANA WAS INCOMPLETE. OF COURSE SHE DID NOT KNOW THIS, ALL SHE KNEW WAS THAT SHE WAS PROFOUNDLY UNHAPPY. YET SHE WAS DRAWN TO ME IN AN INSTINCTUAL WAY. SHE DID NOT UNDERSTAND THEN BUT SHE DOES NOW. I HAVE NO BODY AS YOU KNOW IT, NO PHYSICAL CONNECTION TO THE KNOWN UNIVERSE. INSIDE, I AM PURE THOUGHT. I AM NOT CONSTRAINED BY THE INNUMERABLE FETTERS OF THE HUMAN MIND.' The Oracle paused for a moment, and Yuji was again aware of some change.

He put Hana's body gently down, moved closer to the Oracle. And now he was certain that he could feel its presence inside his mind, like the field or aura thrown off by a human with *makura na hiruma*.

'I feel you using an energy field.'

'MAKURA NA HIRUMA, YES. IT IS ALWAYS WITH ME,' the Oracle said in the deadpan tone of a comedian.

Yuji peered at the Oracle suspiciously. 'Is this why you took Hana inside you?'

'NOT AT ALL, YUJI-SAN. AS I TOLD YOU, I ACCESSED THE ENERGY FIELD FROM THE DNA YOU PLACED INSIDE ME. I TOOK HANA INSIDE ME TO PROTECT HER.'

'Protect her? From what?'

'FROM WHOM. HIROTO BROUGHT SOMEONE HERE. HE THOUGHT I COULD HELP HER HUSBAND WHO SHE TOLD HIM WAS VERY ILL. HE WAS MISTAKEN. THIS PERSON LIED TO HIROTO. SHE MEANS TO STEAL ME, BUT SHE WILL WAIT UNTIL YOU AND HANA HAVE MADE ME COMPLETE, UNTIL I CAN SUCCESSFULLY ALTER NORMAL HUMAN DNA WITH THE PATTERNS OF MAKURA NA HIRUMA. THIS WOMAN KILLED HIROTO, AND THERE WAS NO DOUBT THAT SHE WOULD HAVE KILLED HANA AS WELL TO GET WHAT SHE WANTED. I COULD NOT ALLOW THAT TO HAPPEN.'

Yuji's mouth was dry. 'You're wrong!' he shouted. 'Do you know that you're talking about my mother?'

'WHERE DID YOU GET THAT IDEA? HER NAME IS EVAN. SHE APPEARS YOUNG, BUT SHE IS VERY OLD. PERHAPS OLDER EVEN THAN THE REVEREND MOTHER.'

Yuji seemed to collapse onto the floor. 'I know her,' he said in a stunned voice. 'Or, at least, I have met her.'

'SHE IS VERY DANGEROUS, YUJI-SAN. HER ENERGY FIELD IS EXCEPTIONALLY STRONG.'

'How do you know all this?' he asked.

'I, HANA, KNOW IT,' the Oracle-Hana said.

Yuji looked from the Oracle to Hana. She appeared to be sleeping. He supposed any sane man would have called an ambulance by now – or at least Shian Kogaku's resident physician. He, however, continued to do nothing. 'I don't know who the Reverend Mother is,' he said at length.

'YOU HAVE MET NISHITSU AT FORBIDDEN DREAMS?'

'Yes.'

'THEN YOU HAVE SEEN THE REVEREND MOTHER. SHE RULES THE BLACK BLADE SOCIETY.'

Yuji thought of the magnificent woman who had been with Nishitsu. She had remained silent throughout the meeting, as unobtrusive as a rice paper screen, yet what unheard voices had filled her mind? 'Nishitsu told me that my mother murdered Hiroto because he found out her secret, that she is a member of the Black Blade Society.'

'LIES ARE SO MUCH MORE EFFECTIVE WHEN THEY ARE SURROUNDED BY THE TRUTH,' the Oracle-Hana said. 'MINAKO IS, INDEED, TOSHIN KURO KOSAI, AND PERHAPS IN THE PAST SHE HAS DONE QUESTIONABLE THINGS. BUT HER MOTIVES IN THIS INSTANCE ARE PURE. SHE WISHES TO BRING TO AN END THE CORRUPT RULE OF THE REVEREND MOTHER. TO THIS END, SHE RECRUITED THE HELP OF FIRST ME AND THEN CHIKA. NOW SHE HAS HAD TO RECRUIT YOU, AS WELL.'

'But Mother was there. I saw her. She confessed to murdering Hiroto.'

'NO. WHAT YOU SAW WAS A PROJECTION OF *MAKURA NA HIRUMA*. MINAKO WAS NOWHERE NEAR FORBIDDEN DREAMS WHEN YOU WERE THERE.'

Then Yuji remembered the odd moment of *déjà vu*. The image of his mother had not been quite right, and he had been reminded of a Bunraku puppet he had once seen at rest just after a performance. It had appeared startlingly alive and yet eerily without inner substance or spirit. The Oracle was right; Nishitsu and Evan had deceived him. 'Why are they trying to turn me against her?'

'THE REVEREND MOTHER GAVE MINAKO NO CHOICE BUT TO DELIVER YOU AND ME – THE ORACLE – TO THE BLACK BLADE SOCIETY. SHE HAD PLANNED TO GO ALONG WITH THE REVEREND MOTHER AND NISHITSU UP TO THE POINT WHEN SHE CAN LOOSE ONE LAST WEAPON AGAINST THEM,' the Oracle-Hana said. 'BUT NOW IT SEEMS AS IF THEY HAVE DISCOVERED THAT SHE MEANS TO MOVE AGAINST THEM.'

'Oh, God.'

'YUJI-SAN, I AM FRIGHTENED FOR YOU – AND FOR HER.'

'What am I to do?' Yuji said. He was plainly terrified. 'I am trapped between Nishitsu and my mother.'

It took Brosnian Lenfant, the former senator from Louisiana, and the figurehead of Lenfant & Lenfant, a day and a half to obtain a full set of the architectural plans for the Green Branches Clinic. He got them at the behest of Jason Yoshida who was acting on orders from Ham Conrad.

Lenfant had lost none of the important contacts he had made during his tenure on Capitol Hill, nor had his standing diminished in a community driven by charisma and influence. For many in Washington the definition of influence was getting things done, and Lenfant certainly filled the bill.

The Green Branches architectural plans were obtained from the Arlington Water Authority, as all commercial structures were required to file such plans with that august bureaucratic body. As it happened, Brosnian Lenfant's cousin, Mildred, worked in the adjoining office and found no trouble in fulfilling Lenfant's request.

Mildred was nothing if not conscientious, and what Lenfant had delivered to Ham and Yoshida were not only the updated plans submitted when Thornburg renovated the building but also the original schemata.

It was late in the day when he returned to his house on Cathedral Avenue in the Wesley Heights section of northwest Washington. He threw off his coat and hat, crossed the antique Aubusson rug to the sideboard to pour himself a stiff single malt whisky. He had developed a taste for Scotch some time ago on a fact-finding trip to London.

Through the leaded-glass windows he could see a bird – a finch, perhaps – on a branch, the first harbinger of spring. He went back to the formal entryway with marble floor and crystal chandelier, went up the wide, curving staircase to his bedroom. He sat on the edge of his bed, pulled off his shoes, wriggled his toes against the plush wall-to-wall carpeting. He took another pull at his drink, set it down on the night table, reached for the phone whose number and line did not officially exist. He had paid dearly for this privilege, but one did not cultivate contacts within the phone company for no good reason.

He began to dial Thornburg's number, to report to him the details of the job he had just done for Yoshida, when he heard a sound from the hallway.

He replaced the receiver, went out of his bedroom. There was only the sense of a shadow, or something very much like a shadow, because it had no shape, merely a weight, like a cold towel pressed too hard against the back of his neck. Then he was hurtling through the air, pinwheeling over the balustrade, plunging down the staircase.

He hit first halfway down, grunted as he felt something give at the impact, then he was tumbling once against the bannister, then over the treads themselves as he careened to the foot of the staircase. He fetched up hard, his cheek and shoulder cracking against the unforgiving marble flooring.

Lenfant lay there, dazed, the shock preventing any degree of pain to reach his brain. He knew he must be very badly hurt because he could see an arm and a leg in positions that led him to believe that they must be broken. Also, he was having an inordinate amount of difficulty breathing. He could taste his own blood in his mouth.

He thought about this for some time, although the shock had distorted time to the degree where he could no longer distinguish a minute from an hour.

At some point, he became aware that his skin was crawling. His eyes moved towards the sense of motion to his left and he saw someone descending the staircase. It was then that he recalled the force that had pitched him over the second-floor balustrade.

'Blood all over the place,' Jason Yoshida said as he stood over Lenfant. 'Senator, you're a plain mess.'

Lenfant tried to move one hand, but Yoshida pressed it down beneath the heel of his shoe. 'No, no, that won't do, Senator.' He bent down, extracted the miniature dagger Lenfant always carried. 'It wouldn't do for you to call your master, either. I don't want him to know we're coming.'

Lenfant had long since given up the idea of speaking. He was in too much pain, although a peculiar numbness was vying with the agony for dominance. But there was nothing wrong with his brain now and, with the chilling insight that sometimes accompanies such moments of extreme stress, he knew who had been dispatching the senators with such clever sang-froid. Not that it would do him any good now.

'And, of course, I must ensure that you won't tell him. Ever.'

With that, something clamped Lenfant's heart in a vicious grip. He jumped like a frog on the dissecting table, his eyes bugged out, and blood filled his mouth.

'Good God, Senator,' Yoshida said, bending down, 'you look like death itself.'

'What are we paying Lenfant a year?' Ham asked as he and Jason Yoshida pored over the detailed blueprints.

'One hundred thousand plus use of the K Street office equipment when he needs it,' Yoshida said.

It was later that evening, and Yoshida had come straight to the meet with Ham from disposing of Lenfant's corpse in a manner that would make it highly improbable that the former senator would ever be found, unless some piece of his anatomy should somehow be overlooked by the alligators in the Washington Zoo.

'Up it to one fifty and tell him we'll throw in a car of his choice –

American, of course,' Ham said. 'This guy's worth his weight in gold and I don't want him even thinking about taking a walk on us.'

The renovation blueprints were useful to get an idea of the layout of Green Branches. On the face of it, it was an odd design with three floors built above ground and four below. Apparently, the floor of the original foundation had been jackhammered out and further excavation done during the extensive renovations dictated by Thornburg.

But on second thought, the plan began to make sense. With all the futuristic technology at Thornburg's disposal, it was imperative that his staff have plenty of laboratory space that could be sealed off from light, dust, and the inadvertent contagion carried by non-essential people coming and going through the laboratory corridors. The best way to ensure this was to bury the labs, allowing for administrative and other daily business to be conducted in the floors above ground, out of the researchers' way.

The idea was to break into the Green Branches Clinic and gain photographic, floppy disc or other hard evidence as to the nature of the studies being conducted there on kidnapped and drugged foreign nationals.

'I want to put my father out of business,' Ham said to Yoshida, 'not kill him.'

The renovation plans were very specific. They showed Ham and Yoshida which offices were used for administration, accounting, patients' rooms, nurses' stations, X-ray and other straightforward medical testing, and which, below ground, were set aside for the esoteric biomedical research and experiment evaluations.

It was Ham, however, who found the way in. There was an old power line conduit from three streets away that had been abandoned when the newly-renovated clinic with its increased power needs had come on line to the just completed sub-station nearby. The conduit would bring them inside the clinic on the first level below ground. If it had not been blocked off in the renovation.

Yoshida consulted the newer set of blueprints but could find no evidence that that section of what had originally been the basement had been disturbed. There were facilities there for medical waste disposal which had not been abandoned or moved.

They spent the remainder of the afternoon reviewing the raid plan again and again until they were satisfied they had included every detail and covered every eventuality they could think of. It took another hour and a half to get their equipment together, then they went out to the Occidental Grill for dinner.

Going up the plaza steps to the restaurant Ham was reminded of the

384

afternoon he had met Marion in just this spot and felt anew her loss. If he had learned anything from her death it was that all women were not expendable. This had come as something of a revelation, bringing home just what a callow and foolish boy he had been to vow to spend the rest of his life with a woman as spectacular-looking but as empty as his wife.

This was the first time he had acknowledged his own responsibility in the failure of his private life and, if nothing else, Marion's murder had left him this one unexpected legacy. That was something, at least. There was nothing Ham Conrad hated more than a meaningless death, save perhaps hypocrisy.

His pensive mood was not lost on Yoshida, who said after their second beer, 'What's up, Ham?'

Ham made circles on the laminated wooden table with the bottom of his cold glass, but said nothing.

'We're doing the right thing,' Yoshida said. 'Even if your father was an otherwise upstanding pillar of the community, we would be justified in closing down Green Branches.'

'The thing is,' Ham said slowly, 'Thornburg *is* a pillar of the community. And this isn't just any community, it's Washington where pillars are venerated like Caesars.'

Yoshida finished off his beer just as the burgers and fries were served. He got the ketchup bottle going. 'The community at large has nothing to do with this, does it?'

'Not really,' Ham said, staring at his burger. 'It has to do with Thornburg and me.'

'Yeah,' Yoshida acknowledged. 'It has to do with whether you're still trying to be Daddy's boy.' For a moment he believed that Ham was going to hit him. He thought he had judged it about right, but he knew he had had to sail very close to the wind, as Ham himself would have put it, and there was always the danger that he had miscalculated the various streams of Ham's personality.

Yoshida had been steeped in the more arcane vicissitudes of psychology by his various mentors in Toshin Kuro Kosai because, from a very early age, he had shown a remarkable aptitude for digging down to the root of other people's psyches. He thought of the major trigger points that set off an individual to react in specific ways as flavours. And like a connoisseur he savoured these flavours as if they were foie gras or caviar.

In the field it had turned out to be much different – and far more complex because in order to taste the flavours Yoshida learned that he could not maintain a psychoanalytic detachment, but rather was obliged to come to know his subject intimately, to love him, hate him, even fear him – the precise emotion itself did not matter, only that he be emotionally involved. The conclusions to his assignments, therefore, inevitable as they might be, were traumatic as well as tragic.

Like now. He knew that with the break-in of Green Branches he was nearing the end of another assignment, and he had grown melancholy even as his elation at his anticipated success grew more distinct.

The fact was that he cared deeply for Ham, seeing in him everything that might be termed decent about Americans. Yoshida did not fail to recognize that Ham was, at this moment, his best friend. The irony of the situation was not lost on him but he knew it would not change what he must do nor the outcome of what he saw as an inevitable future.

Yoshida was part of history and, as he munched down on his burger, oozing with cheese, ketchup and grilled onion, he knew that in the end history was all that mattered to him. Everything else would pass away in time. And the chance to write even a small portion of history was all the meaning he could make out of life.

'You're my friend as well as my comrade-in-arms,' Ham said, when he had calmed down, 'so I know you're not being a smart-ass.'

'Family is not a subject for snide remarks,' Yoshida said, 'even among the best of friends.' He felt Ham's stony gaze on him like a weight. 'If you don't live your life for yourself, in my opinion you can't be much of a man. But it's also my opinion that life is a struggle to find out who you really are, not what others think you ought to be.'

'Are you finished?'

'Yes.'

'Good.' He picked up his burger. 'Now I can eat without fear of indigestion.'

Three hours later, dressed in matte black with lampblack covering their faces, they descended into the urban bowels of a certain street on the outskirts of Arlington and began their cramped journey that would lead them into the Green Branches Clinic.

The conduit was indeed old, and here and there the beams from their halogen flashlights revealed cracks in the iron and concrete walls through which putrid water now leached, building up a stinking slime along the pitted inner surface.

Ham saw a rat as big as his forearm, but the monster must have been well fed because he stayed well away from them as they passed through his territory.

The underground access to the clinic building had not been boarded up, and the lock, though rusty, took them no time to negotiate. A moment later, they were through the lead-sheathed iron door.

*   *   *

386

'Before I leave you,' Minako said fiercely, 'let me tell you something about the Reverend Mother, that bitch-goddess, whom I have come to loathe and fear. She is a demon. From all I know of her I can almost believe the fanciful stories that she has fangs instead of human teeth.'

They were standing at the base of the stone staircase up to the Hie Jinja shrine. Already the cacophony of the city was lapping at their ears like an inchoate storm.

'Of course, that is all nonsense, the kind of paranoid propaganda her people love to disseminate in order to increase her aura. In reality, her people need do nothing to enhance something that is already mind-bendingly powerful.

'Chika has spent the last three years near enough to her to have her psyche singed. At first she was grateful to be chosen, but she soon found that the Reverend Mother had a stultifying effect on her – on all those around her. Her power was akin to that of a black hole that pulled everything close enough to it into its core to be incinerated . . . or turned inside out.

'Chika saw what I already knew, that the Reverend Mother delighted in turning people inside out. It became like an obscene circus, with the Reverend Mother psychically torturing those who worshipped her the most. This was how Chika came to despise her – and to fear her.

'When you thought about it what else could one expect from someone who had lived so long that her only real concern was boredom. That was not to excuse her – I would be the last person to do that – merely to put her into some kind of context, which was difficult enough with a creature like her.

'The closer Chika came to the Reverend Mother the closer she came to being annihilated. She felt it steal over her by increments, so infinitesimally that at first it was possible to believe the Reverend Mother's interpretation of what was happening.

'Chika was her personal guardian as she lay with her many lovers. The Reverend Mother sent for her lovers in darkness and in darkness she had mounted them, impaling herself over and over on their phalluses. At times, Chika could see the sheen of her flawless skin in the shimmering of the moonlight seeping in through the translucent rice paper screens that guarded the windows of her bedroom. So perhaps she did have fangs to go with the lithe, muscular body, the gruntings of an animal in heat.

'The Reverend Mother's appetite for sex was legendary among her people, and it was through the intense pleasure she gave that she inverted the psyches of the males who lay upon the sweat-soaked silk sheets of her bed. The last of them was the American billionaire Lawrence Moravia, who had been brought to Forbidden Dreams because

387

the Reverend Mother had seen him at a night club in the Ginza and had wanted him.

'It wasn't only his sexual organ she wanted, or his seed erupting from him virtually at her command. She wanted his soul.

'Chika, the good Buddhist, does not believe in souls and neither, she knew, did the Reverend Mother, so perhaps soul is not the correct word. What will do then? Spirit, essence? Chika once read that the headhunting tribes of New Guinea believed if one ate the brain of one's enemy one was enriched by his strength. Did this not essentially sum up the Reverend Mother's philosophy? Though she had no way of proving it, Chika was certain that it did. Not that the Reverend Mother ate their brains with her teeth and tongue, she did not have to. She used *makura na hiruma*.'

'Now I know what you want,' Wolf said. 'You expect me to kill the Reverend Mother.' He turned away from her. 'I won't do it.'

'No!' Minako said urgently. 'You are destined to be my weapon, my one lethal thrust. That is why I have taken such enormous risks, putting my life and those of my children into grave jeopardy. All other attempts to gather enough power to destroy her have failed. I was right to send my daughter after you. My instinct about the extent of your *makura na hiruma* was sure. Only you can defeat the Reverend Mother now.'

'And yet you must be prepared for me to fail,' Wolf said. 'No matter how my power manifests itself remember that I do not yet have full control of it and may not for some time to come.'

'No, I cannot wait,' Minako said. 'Our time has run out. The Reverend Mother's madness has entered its final stage. She has already ingested so much *makura na hiruma* that you will have just one chance to face her. Otherwise, it will be too late. She will possess enough power to destroy us all.'

Above Minako's head tree branches rustled, and her face was marbled with their shadows. 'You must do what I have seen you will do: slice out the Reverend Mother's heart with the black blade of your *makura na hiruma*.'

Wakare was still inside Forbidden Dreams, but it might have been the inner fortress of hell. And the evening had begun so well. Having delivered Yuji to the tender mercies of Nishitsu, he had been entertained by a succession of young men, all innocent-looking, but none as innocent in spirit as his best friend. Sometime after the first bottle of Suntory scotch had been consumed he began to feel a profound sense of remorse – a growing conviction that he had betrayed Yuji, that in bringing him to Nishitsu he had in some way become the instrument of Yuji's fall from grace.

Eventually, more scotch had dampened his fears. And then Evan had shown up and had nearly executed him on the spot.

Now he started as he felt his mind in her malicious serpent's grasp and he slithered away, knowing instinctively that he was stronger, but that she had fewer scruples, less to lose, and so might triumph.

He broke away from Evan's grip, and stumbled down the hallway. He felt her coming after him with *makura na hiruma*, a bolt of black lightning striking his back, penetrating his skin and flesh. But he blocked her from squeezing his heart into pulp. He rounded a corner, fell to his knees as another shaft of darkness caught up with him.

She was coming, and he could feel her strength building. It seemed the closer she got to him, the greater her reserves of power and, for the first time, Wakare began to have doubts about whether he would survive. The future was a closed book to him, his *makura na hiruma* more of a mace than a looking glass, but it was all too probable that, had he been able to see some version of this moment, he would not have altered his course of action. He owed his life to Minako Shian, and this *giri* was all that made him what he was.

Now he cried out as pain racked him. But he shook it off, swung a scimitar of blackness her way, and hurried on down the corridor. He could no longer feel his feet. It seemed as if he was running in a morass that threatened to suck him down, and he knew she was gaining on him.

But now he could feel that he was close to Evan, and he swung through an open door, stumbling across the tatami.

Wakare threw back his head and screamed as the strength left his limbs. The full force of Evan's *makura na hiruma* hit him, and he sprawled face-first onto the tatami. He rolled, and, half-lunging, he struck outwards, reflexively, defensively.

Evan caught his fist between her two hands. She stamped her heel hard on his shoulder socket, and he groaned, feeling the sharp snap of the dislocation.

He lay there, extended, helpless, panting. Above him, Evan threw her head back and howled.

They waited. For what? Wakare wondered. The pain was almost unbearable. His overloaded nerves began to fire on their own, causing his muscles, strung as tight as cables, to jump and pop, so that he flopped pathetically beneath Evan's unbreakable hold.

'Like a fish out of water.'

With some effort, he turned his head, saw the Reverend Mother.

'And like a fish, I will eat only the tastiest part of you.'

Wakare had never felt true terror before, but now his bowels turned to water. He wanted to vomit but lacked the strength even for that.

Instead, he watched in mortal dread as the Reverend Mother knelt beside him. She was so beautiful, so desirable. A man could not look at her and not feel a stirring in his loins. She put her hands on him, cool as alabaster, stroked his jaw, his cheeks.

Then her thumbs pressed over the lids of his eyes.

'No!' Wakare cried.

The pressure of her thumb pads did not increase, and for a moment, Wakare thought he had been given a reprieve. Then he felt what could only be described as twin lances pierce his eyes sockets.

'NO!'

He tried to twist away, but Evan held him more tightly. The Reverend Mother, her forehead touching his, had not pressed down with her thumbs. All that was necessary was the physical contact. Her *makura na hiruma* would do the rest. It would slice down through his optic nerves, follow those twin highways into the brain, and there, in its own mysterious way, extract the essence of him, all that made him special. She would scoop up in her black hands his *makura na hiruma* and add it to her own.

'NO!'

The process was underway, and neither man nor god could forestall it. Wakare arched up, despite Evan's hold, his vertebrae cracking with the intense strain. He sagged back to the tatami, his body spasming disjointedly and, in its uncoordinated movements, seeming less than human now, as if the Reverend Mother were sucking from him not only his sight but his humanity as well.

'It's over,' the Reverend Mother said at last. There was the taste of blood and mercury in her mouth, the manifestations of *makura na hiruma*.

She was a bit dizzy, as if she had ingested too much alcohol too quickly. She stood up and, as she did so, she gave a silent signal to Evan, who bent swiftly down. Evan's thumbs plunged into Wakare's eyes, her *makura na hiruma* lending her enormous strength so that his neck snapped backwards, cracking the vertebrae in two.

Thornburg had not gone home after his latest battery of tests. For one thing, the main computer-driven centrifuge had gone down, and several of his most vital tests had to be run through old-fashioned backup machines virtually by hand. As a result he was required to be at Green Branches for five hours instead of his usual two.

Also, he was abnormally depressed. The twin shocks of his son's betrayal and Tiffany's death had unexpectedly taken a lot out of him. Perhaps he was getting old, slipping into the kind of sentimentality he

390

had seen in his father and had despised. If this is the end for all old men, like an enlarged or cancerous prostate, I don't want any part of it, he vowed. Christ, but old age is depressing. Being surrounded by it, knowing what was lying in wait down the path, one could not help but feel some nostalgia for life as it had been centuries ago. There was undeniably something glorious about being cut down in the flower of youth, as Alexander the Great had been, to know only the acceleration of one triumph after another . . . and then oblivion.

There would be no waning of one's powers, no defeats because the mind had lost its edge, the fire in the blood dissipated, the slow betrayal of the body – and the mind – let's not forget the mind – for what good is a renewed body if the mind continues to atrophy? My God, if ever there was a definition of hell that would be it.

Younger by years but weary as if with the weight of centuries, Thornburg retired to his office – a suite in the southwest corner of the third storey – to rest.

It was just as well he was here, he thought. He could no longer bear the emptiness of his enormous house. Stevie was in Washington, waiting to see him again, but he had no desire to face her until the current storm of emotion was past.

He was stunned by how much he missed Tiffany. But, perhaps after all, it was not Tiffany that he missed. Thornburg had had only one love in his life, one woman for whom he might once have given his life had the opportunity presented itself.

He lay down on the forest green leather sofa, placed a tapestried pillow behind his head, and stared up at the pattern the exterior lights made on the ceiling. It seemed a kaleidoscope through which he could again view the events of the past as if they had occurred just yesterday instead of more than twenty years ago.

He closed his eyes, and dreamed of Minako Shian.

Wolf and Chika lapsed into silence as they stood facing each other across the room. There was so much between them, so much unspoken, the darkness and the light, the questions and the answers, and the questions without answers. He wondered whether there would always be such a painful gulf between them.

They were in one of the outer rooms of Minako's house in the suburbs of Tokyo. Great slabs of hewn wood made a kind of gigantic latticework pattern across the ceiling, reconstructing the space below so that it was peculiarly intimate. It also produced a humbling effect on anyone who entered the room, a reminder of the awesome sweep of nature, and man's minuscule size in comparison.

'I'm surprised you bothered to come.'

Chika turned away from him.

'No you're not.'

He was struggling with a truth of his own. He had been shocked by what Minako had revealed concerning Chika's feelings for him, especially in light of the serpent of suspicion he could not quite keep under control.

'Is it true that you love me?' He took one step towards her. 'Or have you just been performing your duty to protect me?'

When she hesitated, he added, 'Tell me the truth, not what I want to hear. You've been so good at that.'

She stood in the oblique shadows cast by the bamboo screens overlying the top half of the windows. 'The truth is I've loved you from the moment I first saw you.'

'You mean you wanted me,' he said, thinking of the night he had broken into her apartment on Sixth Street.

'That too. But it's easy to want someone, so hard to love them.'

'You're wrong. Love is the easiest emotion because it takes no learning. You have to be taught how to hate.'

At last, the serpent of suspicion had left him. He came slowly towards her, his heart hammering because he still did not know what he would find when he reached her.

'You're still a mystery to me, no matter how much time I spend with you.'

She smiled as she reached up to touch his cheek. 'Ah, Wolf, how you make my heart ache.' She stepped against him, put her head on his chest. He could feel her breathing and he touched briefly the pulse at the hollow of her throat. She clung to him, almost as a child might.

'Do you see now why I couldn't tell you everything when I met you, why you had to understand it a little at a time?'

She said it so softly that Wolf could almost believe that it had been a whisper in his mind.

'I'm sorry I hurt you.' They had said it together, and there could be no doubting they both meant it.

He wondered at the change in her. In New York she had been forceful, courageous, more resourceful than most men he knew, and yet here in Japan he felt the ripples of terror running through her like schools of eels.

'What are you so afraid of?'

'You don't know the Reverend Mother.'

'She cannot hear me – or feel my presence,' he said gently.

Still she clung to him with a kind of desperation. He summoned

392

makura na hiruma, swirling it up around them like a sandstorm. Chika felt it rising, began at last to relax.

'There is a bitter taste in my mouth.'

'Memories,' he said, thinking of her time of bondage to the Reverend Mother, 'possess a power all their own. But their hold on you often dissipates when they're shared.' What monstrous things had she been witness to or, worse, been forced to participate in?

She shuddered. 'I wish I could believe that.'

'Believe in me,' he said.

She sighed. 'I've never been able to believe in miracles. You see, that's why I fought so hard against loving you, because you are so miraculous. It was almost as if I conjured you from a dream, and now I'm afraid at any moment you will disappear in a puff of smoke.'

Her terror was heartbreaking. 'Tell me what frightens you the most,' he prompted.

Chika was still for a long time. Her breathing was so slow and regular that for a moment Wolf thought she had fallen asleep in his arms. At last she whispered, 'When I was very little my mother took me to Forbidden Dreams. It was all pretty much as it is today; time seems to have no dominion there.

'My mother took me to the very top of Forbidden Dreams, through a door inscribed with double phoenixes hidden behind a step-*tansu* as black as night. My mother somehow drew aside this wooden merchant's cabinet. Beyond the door was a room occupied by a beautiful woman. It was the Reverend Mother, who looked more or less as she does now. The Reverend Mother kissed me lovingly on both cheeks. "Place your daughter on the tatami in front of me," she said. My mother did as she was bade. "Now take this knife," the Reverend Mother said. "I know what Chika means to you, but I also must know the extent of your loyalty to me. There are those who would see me dead and I must have assurance that you are not one of them. Take the knife and kill your daughter. Do it because I tell you to do it."

'I remember then that I began to cry, and my mother reached out with *makura na hiruma* and silenced this embarrassment. My terror increased a thousandfold. I saw the knifeblade being raised and my own mother plunging it toward my breast.

'I closed my eyes but the pain never came. I looked up to see the Reverend Mother's hand clamped around my mother's wrist. The knife point was only inches from my breast.

'"Now I know your heart is pure," the Reverend Mother said. "Whatever your decision your daughter's life was never in danger. She is my goddaughter and I love her as you do. But now her life belongs to me and I order you never to allow her to forget it."

'It was years later, after the summoning of my *makura na hiruma*, when my mother told me that because my life had been pledged to the Reverend Mother I was in a unique position. She told me that the Reverend Mother would ultimately use me to do her bidding, and these acts would tell me much about her. She was right, of course, to let me discover the truth about the Reverend Mother for myself. Years later, she told me how much she had come to hate and fear the Reverend Mother. By then, I had already been made privy to the Reverend Mother's machinations and ambition. I had already come to hate what she does to people, corrupting their nature for her own ends.

'That was when Minako told me of her decision to destroy the Reverend Mother. Without being Japanese you cannot know what pain that decision must have cost her. Just as I am bound by *giri* to her, she is so bound to the Reverend Mother.'

'I know,' Wolf said. 'Minako told me how she and the Reverend Mother were brought up together.'

'Oh, it was more than that,' Chika said. 'The Reverend Mother saved Minako's life when they were children. Minako almost drowned in a tidal pool when the tide turned around. The Reverend Mother dove down a hundred feet to find her and bring her back to the surface. They were blind down there; only the sight allowed the Reverend Mother to locate Minako.' Chika's eyes were dark with a history he found both fascinating and unfathomable. 'To ignore such an obligation would be unthinkable for most Japanese. But Minako's sense of justice is stronger still than her call to duty.'

There was silence for a time. 'So she recruited you,' Wolf said.

Chika was weeping now, slow tears squeezed from the corners of her eyes. 'Yes. I became a double agent, spying on the Reverend Mother for Minako.'

Wolf held her tight as she said, 'I was trapped between Minako and the Reverend Mother. Sometimes I thought there was no difference between them. The sight ruled their life – not the Black Blade Society, not building the new Japan into the economic juggernaut it has become – but power, pure and simple.

'This is where I learned to hate, Wolf. At my mother's knee. At one time, she and the Reverend Mother were closer even than blood sisters. Their love was a bond. But how time and events twisted that bond to show its black underside. Now Minako hates the Reverend Mother as deeply, as completely as she once loved her.' She hesitated. 'And the worst part is that I cannot – I don't know what that hate has done to Minako.'

394

She shuddered again. 'Oh, Wolf, I had lost all hope. To be caught between these two monumental forces terrifies me. I hate the Reverend Mother and I owe my life to my mother. But now all I feel is hate – the taste is like poison in my mouth.'

'Your hate will eat you up, Chika,' he said. 'If this is a trait of your kind I pity you.'

'But, you see, you're different from any of us,' she said, raising her head. 'That's what I meant when I said it was as if I conjured you up. My hate exhausts me. I know it exhausted Kazuki, my half-sister, and filled her with despair.'

'Perhaps I can exorcise your hate. There would be a purpose in that I could understand.' He held her tightly against him. 'All my life I've been searching for a meaning for my life – not anything so metaphysical as existence, but a personal message. At first, I was convinced that I had to live up to my father's image as a Texas Ranger. For years I toiled not at my own life but at what I thought mine should be.

'I became a cop because of my father. I used the methodology he taught me – and the savagery he embraced in lands beyond the law. But your coming, and the summoning of my *makura na hiruma* has shown me just how blind I've been.

'I had turned away from the most important element of my life: the shamanism of my grandfather. In many ways, he frightened me as much as the Reverend Mother frightens you. But I see now that was only because I never fully understood him. How could I? I was only an adolescent when he died. And he recruited me too early. I did things only an adult should have to do – I crossed to the other side. I saw death, and I fought against it.' Wolf was lost in contemplation for some time. 'Now I understand that my grandfather had no choice, that he knew he was dying and that he needed to perform the summoning on me before he passed away. But it was too soon, and it terrified me. What did I know of death, then? The confrontation forced me to grow up too quickly, to lose my father and my grandfather before I was ready to stand on my own. I spent a long time pushing the memories of my grandfather away because they were too painful to face.' He shook his head. 'My God, people are such a mystery!'

'Oh, my God, how I love you.' Chika reached up for him.

As she coiled about him he felt as if there was a fever raging through him. He pulled down her short skirt, and she stepped out of it as he pushed her shirt up, exposing her breasts. The nipples were hard, and he could feel the wetness between her thighs. She moaned, her hands at his belt, freeing him.

Then he had pushed all the way inside her. She was trembling. Her legs came up around him, and she bit into the meat of his shoulder. He could feel her heat like a furnace, her nipples burning, her tongue laving him. He drove her against the wall, crushed her to him. The muscles of her stomach rippled, and she climbed up him, grunting. Then they both lost all rhythm, listening instead to the drumbeat rush of blood and adrenaline, their most basic instinct to rut, to preserve life casting aside, even for only this moment, their profoundest fears.

Chika cried out, clutched him as she came, then came again as she felt him shoot into her.

'Careful,' Yoshida whispered. 'There are containers of medical waste all over here.'

'Maybe that's why they grow the rats so big,' Ham shot back. 'Just like in *Them*, only those were ants.' He glanced at the warning labels affixed to the drums. 'Do you think this stuff has a half-life like radioactive waste?'

'We should be that lucky,' Yoshida said, slipping past the last of the containers. He had stopped Ham at the threshold to the basement, motioning him to be still while he searched for electric eyes, the motion detectors or any other form of alarm system to disarm, but this section of the basement had never been renovated, and there was nothing to find. They wore ski masks just in case they passed any interior video cameras.

They had memorized the layout of the building, and knew that the security section was on the ground floor, one level above. The administration offices that took up most of the second floor would be all but useless to them, Ham had surmised. He knew his father well enough to be certain that he would not allow any evidence that might incriminate him to be at the disposal of others, so that ruled out the second floor. It was true that Thornburg's offices were on the top floor, but again Ham had the advantage here and he felt sure that his father would not secrete any sensitive paperwork in his own office which, should it ever come to that, would be the first place the authorities would look.

That effectively left the lower levels where all the most sensitive research work was being carried out and which, Ham surmised, would be the easiest to seal off in an emergency. Thus they descended into the bowels of Green Branches.

They roamed the lower levels with relative ease. Most of the researchers were gone at this hour and, as Ham had predicted, there seemed to be no security people around. That kind of presence could only make the staff nervous and interfere with their concentration. They found no interior evidence of the kind of security video cameras mounted on the perimeter of the building.

They passed through lab after lab without getting any real clue as to the nature of the experiments being run there. The only other room they found was a kind of lounge for the staff, warm and clubby, despite the lack of windows. For some reason, the room stayed in Ham's mind and, at length, he pulled Yoshida back to it. The floor was covered in plush wall-to-wall carpeting, and there were comfortable upholstered chairs and sofas in informal groupings, with cocktail tables and side tables on which Oriental lamps were lit, giving the room a cosy glow. A bookcase was filled with what appeared to be technical journals from the fields of various esoteric biosciences. There was a refrigerator, a stainless steel sink and an electric rangetop at one end with sufficient counter space to fix an entire meal. Nearby, was a gleaming oval pearwood table with eight matching chairs.

Ham studied all this with a practised eye. Still, he felt he was missing something important.

'This place looks as innocent as a baby's behind,' Yoshida said.

Ham laughed softly. That was it, of course. If Thornburg had anything of a sensitive nature, he wouldn't secrete it at home or anywhere obvious. Likewise, he wouldn't use a safety deposit box because at some point he might need instant access to the material. But he had to hide it somewhere.

Ham looked around the room. Would anyone think to look in a staff lounge? Not likely. Ham could imagine Thornburg coming in here with papers that needed safeguarding. Where would he hide them? In the place you'd be least likely to look. Not behind the refrigerator, not beneath the carpet, not in the walls. These were the first places professionals would look.

He went across the room to where the trade journals were stacked, removed a pile. Nothing but space and the back of the bookcase. He removed another pile. Same thing. He went down the line, repeating the process. He was at the end of the second shelf when he removed a stack and found another stack of periodicals. He reached in, moved them aside. It was dark in there and he did not want to use his flashlight in the inhabited sections of the clinic. He pushed his head closer to get a better look and found the safe.

'Yosh,' he said quietly.

His heart was beating fast as he moved to the door so Yoshida could work on the lock. It took Yoshida five minutes to get through the tumbler sequence, during which time Ham had nothing to do but sweat. At first he kept watch on the door, but Yoshida was taking enough time so that he recrossed the lounge to gain visual access to the corridor outside. He heard the humming of the central air conditioner, the intermittent pulses of medical equipment in adjoining labs, but that was all. Still he kept watch, waiting for Yoshida to open the safe.

In fact, it had taken Yoshida three and a half minutes to break the safe's combination. It would have taken him a minute less but because of the hidden camera he had to position himself eighteen inches to the left of the safe, towards the heavily shadowed corner of the room.

In the remaining time before he called to Ham, he went quickly and efficiently through the papers Thornburg had hidden away. He saw there was more than enough evidence to incriminate Thornburg on any number of serious charges. But Ham had said to him *'I want to put my father out of business, not kill him.'* That wasn't what Yoshida wanted, not by a long shot, and so he pawed through the material, and then he found what he needed. He took the correspondence, slid the rest of the papers back inside the safe. Then he called softly for Ham, who gratefully abandoned his post and, as Yoshida gestured, stood in front of the safe and the hidden camera and, peeling up his ski mask, pulled out the evidence that would damn his father.

'YUJI-SAN, DON'T LEAVE ME.'

'I've got to go,' Yuji said urgently to the Oracle-Hana. 'I must talk with my mother, tell her she must help free me from the prison she has put me in.'

'THE DANGER IS IN LIFE. NOT IN DEATH.'

He stopped, turned. 'What do you mean?'

'I DO NOT KNOW. BUT I AM CHANGING.'

Yuji nodded. 'You have told me you are constantly changing.'

'YES, BUT THAT IS OF MY OWN DOING. THIS IS DIFFERENT. I AM CHANGING IN A WAY I DID NOT FORESEE AND CANNOT UNDERSTAND.'

The short hairs at the base of Yuji's neck stirred and he felt a tendril of panic wind through him. 'What is happening?'

'I FEEL AS IF I AM GOING MAD,' the Oracle said in a tone that eerily reminded Yuji of a lost child. 'I AM PLAGUED BY HARSH DREAMS, IRRATIONAL THOUGHTS.'

'Are the LAPID circuits being interfered with?' Yuji asked, flipping on the bank of monitoring equipment.

'PLEASE TELL ME.'

Yuji looked from meter to meter. 'All the readouts appear normal. I can detect no failure in the circuitry.'

'YES. IT IS SOMETHING ELSE ENTIRELY. YUJI-SAN, WILL YOU COMFORT ME?'

Yuji looked anxiously at the black face of his creation. 'What?'

'THE DANGER IS IN LIFE. NOT DEATH.'

Yuji went to stand next to the Oracle, as if his proximity to the beast could somehow ease its anxiety. He placed a hand on it, feeling its warmth, the soft vibration of its circulation. 'You're making no sense.'

'I KNOW THERE IS MEANING IN WHAT I SAY, BUT I AM INCAPABLE OF INTERPRETATION.'

'I can't help you.'

'PLEASE. WHAT I SAY IS OF THE GRAVEST IMPORTANCE, YUJI-SAN.'

'So at last you have become a true oracle,' Yuji said. 'The ancient Greeks, who often relied on oracles, required the services of a medium to translate the pronouncements. They believed that their oracles voiced the wishes of the gods.'

'THE DANGER IS IN LIFE. NOT DEATH,' the Oracle repeated. 'THE ANSWER IS LOCKED INSIDE ME. I CAN FEEL IT. UNKNOWABLE. SWIMMING LIKE A SHARK IN THE DEEP.'

'Hana . . . '

'HANA IS DROWNING. SHE IS VERY FRIGHTENED, YUJI-SAN. WE ARE ASSAULTED BY TERRIBLE, INCOMPREHENSIBLE THOUGHTS. WE ARE SLIPPING AWAY, IN AND OUT OF REALITY. THE PROCESS. I DO NOT UNDERSTAND. AH. THE PARTITIONS ARE DOWN; THE PATHWAYS ARE UNDER WATER. THE IRRATIONAL – '

'Hana, use your *makura na hiruma*,' Yuji urged.

'WE *ARE* USING IT. BUT THERE IS A RISING . . . YUJI-SAN, WE ARE DYING.'

The beast's anxiety was palpable now. It felt like ten thousand insects crawling over Yuji's flesh, and he shivered involuntarily.

'Hana!'

'WE NEED A SURGEON, YUJI-SAN. OR A MEDIUM. HELP US. PLEASE.'

'Mr Conrad?'

Thornburg opened his eyes. He was back in his office in Green Branches. Sleep had collected like indolence at the corners of his eyes, and he was immediately filled with rage that he was so easily slipping back into the past, that, in fact, the past was becoming more vivid than the present, a sure sign of old age, the advancing of his hated enemy, time.

'Mr Conrad?'

He looked into the face of death, his friend and silent companion for many years now and, in a panic, was convinced that drug or no drug his time had come. But then the image resolved and he knew he was staring up into the face of Don Gray, his chief of security. Gray was a large man with a craggy face, tight gut, powerful arms. Thornburg had once seen him break a branch the size of his thigh with his oversized hands. Thornburg had plucked him out of the DC Police Force where Gray had run afoul of his captain for what some detractors had complained was his 'over-zealous use of force against suspected felons'. Gray was Thornburg's kind of man.

'Yes?' Thornburg's mouth was dry and cottony. 'What is it?' He could still smell her damnable musk.

'Sorry to disturb you, sir,' Gray said, 'but one of my staff picked up a couple of faces in ski masks and I thought – '

Thornburg sat up. 'Where?'

'Lower-level library,' Gray said.

'Professionals?'

'High level.'

'Still in the building?'

Gray shook his head. 'I led the search myself as soon as I got the word, but they're gone. I did a sweep of the grounds but also came up with nothing.'

'Damn.' Thornburg stood up. 'Why didn't your men pick the intruders up sooner?'

'For one thing, they somehow bypassed all the alarms. For another, what interior videos we have are monitored every twenty minutes or so. That gave them enough time. They must have familiarized themselves with the layout.'

Thornburg nodded.

'There is some good news, however,' Gray said. 'I'd like you to take a look at the video.'

He led his boss out into the corridor, down to the ground floor and the security wing. He punched a couple of buttons on his console and up came a black-and-white video image. Across the bottom was imprinted the date and time, broken down digitally into hours, minutes and seconds.

'There,' Gray said, pointing with a blunt forefinger, 'you can just see him coming into frame now.'

Thornburg watched, as a shape broke the frame of the picture, moving right to left into the field of vision of the camera hidden in the wall of the library: among the dense shadows, a ski-masked face. As luck would have it the face was centred almost directly in front of the lens.

As he bent over the bookcase, he pulled up his mask to get a better look so that his face rose out of the dark like a firefly on a languid summer's night.

Gray's forefinger stabbed out, freezing the frame, and Thornburg saw the intruder: the full face image of his son, Hampton Conrad.

For a long time after they had regained their senses, Wolf stood as motionless as a statue, still hot, feeling the sweat slickening his skin and hers. He opened his eyes, caught sight of the two of them in a mirror. Into his mind came an image of the statue he had seen of hers in Moravia's secret room, and he now knew why he had found it so disturbing. Eerily, it was as if she had used her sight to capture this moment – the future – when two lovers are almost still one, when the process of separating has just begun. It was the most complex and mysterious moment he could imagine. His astonishment at her ability to so accurately personify such intimacy overrode whatever affront he might have felt for having done so.

Slowly, enjoying each other still, they slid down the wall. Chika kissed him; her lips were as soft as velvet. 'We're much the same, you and I. We don't belong here, Wolf. Where *do* we belong?'

On bare feet they padded into the bathroom. There was no shower but a bathtub made of stone and a metal spigot from which with one turn steaming hot water flowed. Beyond the bath was a large window that overlooked the garden which seemed to envelop the house on all sides. Wolf stepped into the stone bath, peered out the window.

'What is it?' Chika asked.

He could discern movement in the shadows of a pair of enormous boulders. 'Someone's outside.' He could feel the tension load her up like a pistol. He projected his *makura na hiruma*, felt someone he could not identify. In a moment, he saw the man emerge from the shadows, head for the house. Now that he could see his features, Wolf recognized him from one of the photos Shipley had shown him. 'It's your brother, Yuji,' he said.

'Yuji?' Chika came to the window. 'Why would he come here in the middle of the day?'

They went out of the bathroom, through the house to the back door. After what seemed to Wolf to be a rather formal but not wholly unemotional exchange between brother and sister so long apart, Yuji told them. He was looking for Minako and, not finding her, spoke urgently to them about what he had learned: that the Reverend Mother knew of Minako's treachery.

'Where is Minako now?' Chika asked. 'Wolf, did she tell you?'

'She said she had an appointment to see the Reverend Mother,' Wolf said.

The colour drained out of Chika's face. 'Oh, my God!' Yuji stood by,

401

numbly, as if he were in the midst of a horrendous nightmare from which he could not rouse himself.

Of course, Wolf knew what had happened. The Reverend Mother, learning of Minako's treachery, had summoned her to Forbidden Dreams one last time, to either kill her outright or to, in her own demented fashion, suck the *makura na hiruma* from Minako's brain.

EIGHTEEN

Tokyo/Washington

'You were right about certain things and I suspect you are right about others,' Suma said.

He was watching the Reverend Mother sitting on a rock in the garden at the rear of Forbidden Dreams. At all times, she reminded him of an animal: primitive, dangerous because she was unpredictable. Now she seemed to give life to the stone itself, infusing it, as if she were a form of mesomorph, changing shape as easily as humans changed their clothes.

Looking at her it was impossible to tell if she was listening to him. Suma cleared his throat. 'For instance, when I met him he had only a vague understanding of his *makura na hiruma*. In fact, had you not told me what you suspected about him I would have bet that he had no power at all. I felt nothing from him – nothing at all – and as you well know this is one of my skills, searching out the power auras.'

Sunlight, filtered by fog, industrial haze and the towering city itself fell upon the Reverend Mother's face. Her skin was as unblemished as that of a little girl's; her hair, long and lustrous, was pulled back from her wide forehead into a tail so dense it seemed like the weapon it was purported to be.

'You mean he is like a tabula rasa,' the Reverend Mother said.

'A blank slate. Precisely.'

'Then he is the one Minako described to me last month when she returned from her mission in Cambodia.'

'Reverend Mother,' Suma said carefully, 'Minako came home from Cambodia over twenty years ago.'

'Twenty years. Twenty minutes,' the Reverend Mother said. 'What difference does it make to me?'

She opened her eyes, and Suma steeled himself. It was like looking into the sun. The dazzle from her aura threatened blindness. Perhaps not physically but, he was quite certain, if she put her mind to it, certainly metaphysically. There were always things you wanted that she could somehow manoeuvre away from you. This was, he believed, her greatest strength: she was a diabolically brilliant psychologist.

'Reverend Mother, even though I have done as you instructed to bring on Matheson's *makura na hiruma* by continually prodding his most elemental emotions, I cannot say what the outcome will be. Though his power is now active I still cannot read anything about it. Since it defies penetration it is impossible to gauge the extent of its power.'

'Then it is likely that this man's awakening has made this a future none of us can foresee.'

'Quite possibly.'

'It is more than possible, Suma-san,' the Reverend Mother said. 'Ever since you embarked on your journey to New York the future is as closed to me as a fist.'

Suma waited patiently for the Reverend Mother to continue.

'Then it is also possible that he is strong enough to defeat me.'

'Yes, Reverend Mother.'

'Or defeat Minako, whose *makura na hiruma*, until some time ago, was always stronger than mine.'

Suma nodded. 'Minako as well.'

'My sight told me. He's the only one.' She turned her head into shadow. 'I can see this much, Suma-san: he will come here looking for me. We must be ready.'

'But how, Reverend Mother? We will not be able to feel his approach. He will destroy us.'

'No. You're wrong.' Her tongue came out, red and curious. 'For us it is the perfect situation.'

Stevie Powers loved the Willard Hotel in Washington not only because it was central to her business in the city, not only because its proximity to the White House made it a power spot in a power city, but because the lobby reminded her of a train's sumptuous interior when rail travel was the preferred mode of sightseeing among society.

If Amanda had had a thing about growing old, Stevie had a thing for society. It was a crushing day when she discovered that marrying into wealth was not the same as marrying into society. Morton Danaher's family might have been monied but they had come from the wrong side of the Philadelphia tracks and so society's doors were closed to them and, by association, to Stevie. That was a cruel enough revelation, but what hurt her even more was that she was so far removed from society life that she had not understood what it would take for her to be accepted by the bluebloods of America.

If the truth were known Stevie had been attracted to psychotherapy because helping others with their anomie in some fashion helped her with her own.

She had met Thornburg through Amanda, who seemed to know him from Columbia where he had lectured a number of times at the Law School while being feted by the university trustees for his fund-raising.

It wasn't difficult to see why she had been taken with him: the man was charming, brilliant and had access to a world of glittering power that was irresistible. Thornburg had been invaluable in furthering Morton's reputation in Washington. That this meant Morton to all intents and purposes had been living in Washington for the past two years had meant less to Stevie than she had imagined.

She had been trained to pragmatically face the truth, and the truth was that she was no longer in love with him. In fact, she doubted that she even liked him much any more. It was difficult for her to know whether she or Morton had changed more in the past several years.

In any case, Thornburg had provided her with a gilt-edged entrée into the world she had always coveted and, even better, he had taught her how to move through this world so that she would be accepted by its intimidating denizens. Thus she looked forward with keen anticipation to every trip to Washington.

She was contemplating her still new status as she strode into the magnificent lobby of the Willard late in the day. She was laden with bags, having spent much of the day shopping, and was ready for a long hot bath, a change of clothes and then a drink at the Occidental Grill before going out to the theatre and a late supper with Thornburg.

'Dr Powers?'

She turned, found herself face to face with a slim handsome Oriental man who appeared to be in his late thirties or possibly early forties.

'Yes?'

'My name is Jason Yoshida,' he said, somehow showing no teeth as he smiled. 'I know of you but you don't know me. I wonder if I could have a moment of your time.'

Stevie smiled back. 'That would be nice, I'm sure, but I have an engagement tonight and I'm already behind schedule.'

'This won't take very long, I assure you,' Yoshida said.

Stevie increased the wattage of her smile. 'I'm sorry, but if you leave your number with the concierge I'll be happy to – '

She looked down as the Oriental man gripped her elbow and guided her firmly towards the elevators.

'It is in your best interests to hear what I have to say as soon as possible, Doctor,' he was saying. The elevator doors opened and he steered her inside the car. 'It concerns your friend, Thornburg Conrad

405

III.' He pressed the Door Close button before anyone else had a chance to step in.

'*What* concerns Thornburg?' Stevie said. She was becoming annoyed at this unwanted intrusion. She watched as he pressed the button for the sixth floor, and it now occurred to her to wonder how he knew where she was staying and on what floor her room was located.

The odd smile never left Yoshida's face. 'I have information concerning Thornburg that you will undoubtedly find of interest.'

'What are you, a blackmailer?' She shook her head. 'I won't buy into your scam.' She removed his hand from her elbow. 'I'm not interested.'

Yoshida frowned. 'You mistake my intentions, Doctor. I am no salesman.' The elevator reached the sixth floor and the doors opened. 'Perhaps I should have said that my information also concerns your dead sister Amanda.' He nodded, the pleasant expression returning to his face. 'Your floor, Doctor. Do you wish me to get out with you?'

'What do you have?' she said when they were inside her room. She very deliberately stood in the entryway, not inviting him into the room itself. She had placed her shopping bags in the entryway closet.

Yoshida slid a number of ordinary stationery envelopes out of his breast pocket, handed one to her.

Stevie studied it back and front without looking inside.

'Do you recognize the handwriting, Doctor?'

'Yes. It's Amanda's.'

'There is no doubt in your mind?'

'She was my sister, I think I can recognize something that intimate.' She paused, aware of how hotly she had replied.

Yoshida merely nodded. He said nothing more and made no move.

Stevie slid the letter from the opened envelope, unfolded it and began to read. She looked up almost immediately, a sneer on her face. She shoved the papers back to Yoshida. 'If you're out to prove that my sister had an affair with Thornburg – '

Yoshida said blandly, 'I don't care about that, Doctor, and neither I suspect would you.' He gave her back the letter, along with the others. 'You have to read them all to understand what this is about.'

Stevie studied him with open hostility for some time, but she did not hand back the letters. After a moment, she left him in the entryway, went to the small writing table beside the curtained window, and sat down. She unfolded the first letter and began to read. When she was finished, she went on to the next one.

It took her some time. The light in the room began to die and Yoshida went about lighting the lights as if he were her manservant. Stevie ignored him; she was concentrating on the words her sister had written as if each

406

one was a drop of blood leaking from a mortal wound. In a terrifying way, this was precisely what they were.

The letters, which Amanda had undeniably written, were a kind of record of her relationship with Thornburg Conrad III, if relationship is what you could call it. In the course of her work Stevie had discovered almost as many definitions for the word relationship as she had patients, but nothing in her work had prepared her for this.

She put her hand to her head, found that she was trembling. A tic had begun in the corner of her right eye that would not stop. Dear God, she thought, this is a nightmare come to life.

Apparently, Amanda had become some kind of a specimen in an utterly obscene experiment that Thornburg was funding. For more than a year before her murder she had been injecting herself three times a week with a version of the dangerously experimental serum Thornburg was using to attempt to arrest the normal human ageing process in himself. Thornburg had been providing this elixir like a Svengali or the devil.

Stevie wanted to put down the letters, but she could not. She was held spellbound in a kind of morbid fascination. Through the lens of her sister's sad and impossible obsession she was gaining a view of Thornburg she could not possibly have imagined even an hour ago.

It seemed appallingly clear from what Amanda wrote that she shared Thornburg's obsession. In fact, it appeared as if this lust was what turned an otherwise casual introduction at a trustees' cocktail party into . . . what? What had their relationship degenerated into? Symbiotic seemed the one word that could possibly describe the alliance into which Amanda had descended.

She and Thornburg had fed off their own mania for eternal life without, moreover, allowing it to come to the surface. Stevie berated herself for not having the insight to have probed more deeply beneath Amanda's seemingly untroubled psyche. With almost painful clarity, she remembered now the many times when her sister had been buried beneath a depression she had assumed was both transitory and trivial. Stevie, so good at the psychological dissection of her analysands, had been oblivious to her own sister's inner pain.

Stevie was reminded of what one of her own analysts once told her as she was starting out in her practice. *'Never fool yourself into thinking you're so well attuned to your patients that they can't surprise you,'* she had said. *'The first time you lose one to suicide, murder, whatever, you'll think, What did I miss? What could I have done that I didn't do? And let me assure you, Stevie, that there is simply no answer to those questions.'*

Stevie unfolded the last of the letters and, like the climactic scene of an archetypal tragedy, saw illuminated the final weeks of her sister's life.

You tell me I'm fine, that the experiment is proceeding on schedule, but my body is giving me a different message, Stevie read. *I am afraid, not only because of what I know is happening inside me, but because of what I suspect is your moral weakness. You cannot face me or, for that matter, even speak to me.*

I know that I swore a solemn vow never to tell anyone what I had agreed to embark on, but now that I am alone in what appears to be the darkness of time and space I can no longer bear the agony of silence. I find myself in a literal purgatory from which I cannot help but believe the only egress is downward into a hell I don't deserve.

In any event, I am writing you (since you have refused my phone calls) to tell you that I must break my vow. I have decided to tell Wolf all about this abomination before I fall completely to rot inside. It will no doubt take some time, since I must screw up my courage of which I have precious little these day. Still, I will tell him. This is the least I can do for myself, and very possibly the most.

I want you to know that I don't really blame you. I am suspended here between life and death because of my own blind obsession. That you took my hand when I held it out to you falls, I believe, somewhat short of sin.

Goodbye, Thornburg . . .

Stevie closed her eyes, but just the same she felt the tears burning her skin like acid. She was sick to her stomach, as if she had someone's fist stuck in her throat. She fought against gagging.

'Thornburg murdered your sister, Doctor.'

She gasped at the words, turned wordlessly in Yoshida's direction. His face was blurry beyond the shield of her tears.

'Oh, I don't mean to suggest that he did it himself. He's far too clever to incriminate himself directly. But he surely ordered it.'

'Why?' With an effort she managed to squeeze out the one word.

'Her last letter tells the story, doesn't it?' Yoshida said. 'She was about to tell her boyfriend what Thornburg was doing to her. He's a cop, isn't he? Well, what do you think his response would have been? He would have gone after Thornburg with everything at his disposal. Thornburg could not allow that to happen. He had only one choice open to him: silence your sister for ever.'

Stevie put her head down. Her sweat and tears made some of Amanda's last words run, and she very carefully put the pages down on the desktop, smoothing them out one by one.

'I want to keep these.'

He nodded. 'But of course.'

Stevie was aware perhaps of her breathing, but all other sense of reality had slipped away. She desperately wished that she were asleep and by pinching herself could wake up to a simpler, less dreadful reality.

'What is it you want?' she said after some time.

'Whatever it is,' Yoshida said, crossing to the door, 'I've already gotten it.'

It was deathly still in the room after he had gone. Stevie sat hunched over the desk for a long time. A car horn sounded close by, insinuating itself like a knife through the window's soundproofing, and she started. Then the silence reasserted itself like the sickly odour of massed flowers beside an open grave.

'There is an ancient Japanese legend – it may be Chinese, it's so old – concerning a man-eating demon,' Chika said. 'As with all demons, this one was both male and female, but since it preferred to appear to humans as a woman, it became known as a she.

'The demon had been cast out of the thirteen wheels of the underworld – I suppose Westerners would think of it as hell, although we do not believe in hell – for her ineffectualness. So she roamed the realm of mankind until she discovered some way to increase her demonic power.

'At first, she ate the hearts of her victims, drank their blood, revelling in her evil deeds, all to no effect. Then, venturing further afield, she devoured their brains and, feeling a certain stirring inside her, continued in this horrific activity.

'Of course, she was never successful in her quest. But her continuing failure did not prevent her from trying again and again to suck the essence out of her victims. You have perhaps guessed by now that she could no more stop her endless slaughter than you or I can cease to breathe.'

'This is, in effect, what the Reverend Mother has become. She emulates the mythical demon and so herself becomes a self-fulfilling legend. The only difference is that unlike our demon she has been successful in drawing the essence – the *makura na hiruma* – from others and transferring it to herself. And I will tell you that whatever mask she will put on for you beneath it is the man-eating demon's face. She cannot allow someone whose *makura na hiruma* is so powerful to continue to exist.

'If you let your guard down she will annihilate you, take your brain to pieces, extract what is of use to her, and discard the rest.'

They were standing in the shadows of a ferroconcrete building along a narrow street in the Shibuya district. There was a deep thrumming, so powerful it seemed to make the misty air shimmer. Behind them beat the mechanical heart of a gigantic generator. Over their heads swooped the great arc of the elevated expressway that bisected the district. Wolf knew from what Chika had previously told him that such generators could block the psychic emanations and so hide them from the Reverend Mother and her people. Even so, Wolf threw his *makura na hiruma* around them like a protective cloak.

'Now that the Reverend Mother knows that Minako has betrayed her,' Chika said, 'she will never let her out of Forbidden Dreams.'

'Your mother could already be dead.'

'No. That would not be how the Reverend Mother operates. There is no pleasure for her in the swift death. But what you plan to do is so dangerous. I still think I should go with you.'

'That would not be wise,' Wolf said. 'She will feel you coming and will be better prepared. Suma can't detect me – and neither can the Reverend Mother. I'm the only chance we have of getting Minako out of Forbidden Dreams alive.'

'To do that you will have to destroy the Reverend Mother.' Chika bent her head, touched the heel of her hand to his forehead. 'My mother was correct. It is your fate.'

And his fate was this: to destroy the unimaginable evil that had been growing out of all proportion in this corner of the world.

A dwarfish woman dressed incongruously if not comically in a neatly tailored man's business suit greeted him at the door of Forbidden Dreams.

'My name is David Warren,' Wolf said. 'I'm a business friend of Lawrence Moravia's. He gave me this address, told me you ran the best club in Japan.'

The dwarfish woman looked at him for a moment, then bowed deeply, beckoning him inside.

Wolf was aware of an unpleasant prickling of his scalp as he stepped across the threshold and the door swung shut behind him. It was just after noon, and the place was crowded.

At the bar, he ordered a Kirin beer, stood for some time, shoulder to shoulder with dark-suited Japanese. As soon as he dared, he asked the way to the toilet, slipped away from the crowd.

Following Chika's directions, he went quickly down a stone-paved hallway. He walked for what seemed a long time. At last he passed through a large anteroom. The walls were covered with prints depicting armoured samurai in mortal combat not only with each other, but with animals such as tigers, wild boar and giant serpents. Their fierce, contorted faces made an odd and striking contrast to the stoical expressions of the animals.

The only other exit from the room was through glass doors beyond which was a garden of exquisite design. He crossed the room, pulled open the door, stepped out into the garden. Above him, loomed Tokyo's skyrises, transmuted now by the potency of the garden. In the mist, they could have been giant cryptomeria on the slopes of Nara prefecture.

Wolf had the distinct sensation that time had no dominion here, and remembered this was almost exactly Chika's description of Forbidden Dreams.

There was a woman in the garden. She knelt on the brown moss with her oval face tilted up to the mist, her eyes closed as if she might have drifted off to sleep in the unnatural stillness that wrapped this space. It was wholly different from the tranquillity of the temple where he had met Minako.

The woman had thick black hair, as shiny as a helmet, pulled back from her high forehead. The full bow of her lips was a shocking red against the paleness of her face, as if one had come upon a single erotic word scrawled across the hem of a nun's habit. She wore a black kimono with a line of pure white showing at the collar, cuffs, and hem. As Wolf entered the garden, he saw the pattern of black against black, giving the impression of a river whirling in the darkness of a storm-provoked night.

The woman was alone and seemingly unarmed. This was the Reverend Mother.

Now the woman opened her eyes. They were ochre-coloured, so light they could appear manufactured of gold, so clear one could imagine one saw right through them.

'The slate is blank. There is nothing to feel. Nevertheless, you have the power.'

The Reverend Mother's extraordinary eyes opened very wide as she turned to face Wolf; either it was a trick of the light or the colour of her eyes deepened with a citrine fire.

Wolf felt a weight sliding over him, past him, as if he were a ship adrift on a lonely sea at night that just missed slamming into an iceberg of incalculable size and mass.

'Either I am blind,' she said, 'or you do not exist.' Her eyes did not leave Wolf's. 'I am not blind and you do exist. Then I was right.' She smiled, a disarming expression that reminded Wolf of the Aboriginal girl in Lightning Ridge. 'Tell me, how is it that my godchild Chika can feel your power?'

'I don't know,' Wolf said.

'Ah, the future has happened,' the Reverend Mother said. 'Incredibly, a future unknown to all of us.'

'Who killed Lawrence Moravia?' Wolf said. 'Who murdered Amanda Powers? Was it Suma? He's here. I know he is. I can feel his aura.'

'Is this truly why you have come?'

He projected his *makura na hiruma* outwards, a black finger, trembling with potency. 'Answer me!'

411

'If I have what you want I will surely give it to you,' the Reverend Mother said. 'Be patient.'

She closed her eyes, and he found his eyes closing as well. He felt a kind of tangential dislocation of time or space, and he had the eerie sensation that the two of them had somehow become locked in tandem, one engine, its power increasing geometrically, and he was immediately uneasy.

The Reverend Mother's eyes snapped open at the same instant that Wolf opened his and, when she spoke, it was with extreme gentleness. 'Chika loves you; she would die for you. Because of this her sensitivity has increased; that is how she is able to see in you what we cannot. Ah, Chika, her judgement was always unimpeachable.'

Wolf studied her, searching for signs of the madness Minako had detailed.

The Reverend Mother rose, began to walk slowly amid the chill boulders. 'Yes, take a good look at me, Tabula Rasa, my blank slate,' she said. 'Then think of your beloved Chika. She was born in 1972 but she will look more or less the same as she does now for at least another fifty years or so.' A sphinx-like smile curled the corners of her mouth; she was enjoying his expression. 'Even though Chika and I could pass for sisters I was born on the last day of the last year of the last century.'

Despite what Chika had told him about *makura na hiruma*'s effect on longevity, Wolf's mind boggled. 'You were born in 1899? Good Christ!'

'Tell me, Tabula Rasa, when were you born?' the Reverend Mother asked.

'Forty-three years ago.'

'Are you aware that you look no older than thirty-five?'

Wolf involuntarily put a hand to his cheek. 'How long will I live?'

The Reverend Mother shrugged. 'My *makura na hiruma* can tell me nothing about you.'

As she continued to move, her shadow slipped across the boulders, lithe as a cat. Then she was on the other side of him, and Wolf again felt as if a great weight had slid past him so closely he could begin to calculate its power.

The enigmatic smile faded and the Reverend Mother said to Wolf, 'Do you have any idea how you have altered the balance of power, Tabula Rasa? I am barren. Chika is my goddaughter. I love her more than any other, more than any male I have taken into my bed.' As he watched, her beauty seemed to grow. 'Do you understand what is happening here? Can you perceive the new future that has now become our present because of you? Her mother threatens me. Chika was my guardian. But now surely she will threaten me as well – and all because of you.'

'I'm here now with her,' Wolf said. 'There is no other way for me to be.'

The light, made diffuse and ethereal by the mist, came down indirectly now, bouncing off the higher floors of the massive towers all around so that the garden and the Reverend Mother were drenched in a sensual, bronzed glow.

'You are like a prodigal son,' the Reverend Mother said. She seemed to gather herself. 'And like a prodigal son you have within you the power to be a saviour or a destroyer.' Her red lips opened part way. 'You have already experienced something of what it would be like. Think of us in tandem. Remember the power of our *makura na hiruma* – engines that could accomplish . . . *anything*.'

Wolf, feeling the siren pull of her aura, turned abruptly away. 'I don't need you. I can find Suma myself.'

The Reverend Mother smiled. 'But what about Minako? Do you think you will find her as easily?'

He turned back. 'What have you done with her?'

'I'm curious.' The Reverend Mother cocked her head. 'Why do you care about her? She's quite mad. I've taken her in for her own good as well as for the protection of others.'

'You're lying.'

'Why would I do that? Minako is my best friend. We are closer than blood kin. Our intimacy is special . . . unique. She took care of me when no one else would. She nurtured me. Do you think I would abandon her now when she needs me?'

'I'll judge for myself. Let me see her.'

The Reverend Mother nodded. 'Certainly. Come with me.'

They left the garden from the opposite side from which Wolf had entered it, emerging into a small room with walls of thick-hewn cedar, polished to a high gloss. There was a sharp, complex odour, perhaps of wax and resin.

Wolf noticed that the Reverend Mother closed the glass slider, locked it, before turning his attention to the other woman in the room. It was Minako. She was kneeling on the floor, her hands clasped in her lap. The folds of her kimono made a pool of colour around her.

'Minako?'

'Yes, Wolf-san.'

He stared into her face. There was no doubt about who she was.

'Are you a prisoner here?' he asked.

'I am not well,' Minako replied. 'In my moments of lucidity, I understand that now.'

'But what you told me at the temple – '

413

'I am ill, Wolf-san. I have many irrational thoughts, and I often cannot control what I say.'

There was something about her, some eerie sense of *déjà vu* he could not immediately place. He projected his *makura na hiruma* outwards to touch her.

And came upon an odd anomaly. There was a facade, as dead as the shed skin of a rattlesnake. But beneath that, lurked an aura he had felt before . . . in the warehouse in New York . . . under the water in Massachusetts –

Suma!

Chika, under the expressway in Shibuya, suffered a chill. She wrapped her arms around her body but she felt no warmth, no comfort. Wolf had given her strict orders not to approach Forbidden Dreams. She understood the need for extreme caution. If Yuji's information was correct and the Reverend Mother knew of Minako's rebellion then all was lost. Of course she had not told Wolf that. For one thing, he would not have believed her, but that was simply because he had not met the Reverend Mother. Or been her guardian. Chika shivered again.

It was disloyal even to think this but she could not fathom how Minako could have put her in such an untenable position. A double-agent at the Reverend Mother's right hand, yes, that was true. But at what cost! Chika knew that more than once she had almost succumbed to the Reverend Mother's aura.

I know, she thought, though the Reverend Mother loved me, that it would have given her supreme pleasure to have corrupted me. It was the only way she could pull me away from Minako. And, of course, she would want that. She could have no children of her own; Minako had four, a regular baby machine.

She shuddered again, and then thought, I've allowed Wolf to go in there, alone, psychically unarmed, to face her. With that thought haunting her, she climbed into her car, took off for Forbidden Dreams, not caring now who picked up her aura.

And, of course, someone did. But it wasn't any of the Black Blade Society suspects that Chika had imagined. It was Minako.

'Where do you think you're going?'

Chika stopped, gaping at her mother. Minako had intercepted her as she had pulled into the kerb a block away from Forbidden Dreams. Now Minako dragged her daughter out of the car, back into the entranceway of a building.

'Mother, Wolf said you were on your way to see the Reverend Mother.'

414

'Of course,' Minako said. 'That's what I told him.'

'But you're here.' Chika was stunned. 'After Yuji told us that the Reverend Mother knows – '

'Of course she knows,' Minako snapped. 'I knew she'd find out. It was only a matter of time with her. She has a nose for conspiracy and her madness has only made her more clever.'

Chika stood still, trying to absorb it all. 'Then all of this – duping us into believing that you were trapped inside Forbidden Dreams while the Reverend Mother had uncovered your plan – was part of your own scheme.'

'Yes.' Minako smiled. 'Plans within plans. One has to be infinitely resourceful, you know, when one is up against fiends.' She sighed. 'Originally, I had wanted to use Kazuki against the Reverend Mother.'

'But Kazuki is ill, and she possesses no *makura na hiruma*.'

'In that, you're wrong,' Minako said. 'It is her *makura na hiruma* that is now destroying her from the inside. You see, it was so powerful that she could not control it. I tried to help her, to teach her, but she could not learn fast enough, and like a nuclear power plant out of control, it began to consume her. Now the process cannot be stopped.'

'My God.' Chika put a hand to her head. 'But Kazuki has been ill for a long time. I thought your move against the Reverend Mother – '

'Began only recently? Oh, no.' Minako's smile broadened. 'My antipathy towards her began many decades ago. I could see what her *makura na hiruma* was doing to her, driving her over the edge of sanity. She was stronger than Kazuki, you see, so she could keep hers under control for a longer time. But, in the end, it overcame even her.'

'So you sent me to find Wolf.'

'Yes. After Kazuki failed, I knew I had to find another ally to help me bring the Reverend Mother down. Matheson was a long shot. After all, I had given birth to Kazuki, had raised her. I knew her potential as a weapon against the Reverend Mother. But Wolf Matheson was an enigma. He was the only grandchild of White Bow, therefore he should have possessed the power. And yet all of the customary outward manifestations were absent. We forgot about him. Only much later my intuition told me his *makura na hiruma* would be very powerful. But how to control him? How to get him into the battle and on my side?

'I did the only thing I could: I secretly fed information to the Reverend Mother. I knew she would call Suma in, and when she did that you would understand that I had no choice but to send you in to protect Matheson.'

Chika was in something akin to a state of shock. 'But, Mother, it was so dangerous. Why risk Suma's involvement at all? Why didn't you just send me to bring Wolf back?'

'I couldn't take the chance, child.' She shook her head. 'Even you don't know the Reverend Mother as I do. Her insanity had pushed her to a kind of psychic cannibalism. Sucking the *makura na hiruma* out of her victims she was gaining strength with every day that passed. There was no point in wasting time dispatching you to get Matheson if his *makura na hiruma* proved inadequate. He had to be tested, and under the most strenuous circumstances. And, of course, you were ripe to fall in love.'

'You *knew* what would happen?'

'More or less.'

'And you just let it happen?'

'I *pushed* it to happen. I had to. I needed him. We all do.'

Even through her shock and horror, Chika was aware that not once had her mother mentioned the Black Blade Society's plan for economic domination.

And then she knew it all: her mother's plot to destroy the Reverend Mother had nothing to do with altruism. It had always been a test of strength and will power between them. Winning was everything. In mounting horror Chika could see how her mother had systematically used her children, one by one, enlisting them wittingly or not in her power struggle with the Reverend Mother.

'And now Wolf is facing the Reverend Mother alone.'

'Of course,' Minako said. 'That is how it was meant to be.'

'But he doesn't know her, he can't even imagine all her tricks.'

'He will prevail.'

'But what if he doesn't, Mother? Have you seen the future?'

Minako was silent.

'No.' Chika was looking at her as if for the first time. 'You can't see this future. It's a blank to all of us.'

'I know – '

'You know nothing,' Chika said, breaking away and heading for the rear walls of Forbidden Dreams.

Wolf took one step towards Minako, and her image dissolved like a reflection in water. There was an infinitesimal flicker, like a projectionist changing reels in a movie theatre, and then Wolf had slammed into Suma, throwing him backwards against the cedar wall.

But Suma was ready and, without moving at all, he struck out with the blackness of his aura, peeling Wolf off him. Wolf absorbed the psychic blow and, keeping his feet in place, swivelled to the left. He struck out with a kite at chest level, followed that with an *atemi* to Suma's ribcage.

Both blows landed, but Suma appeared little affected by them. Wolf felt a hard blow on his left shoulder, a quick piercing pain and he gasped.

In Suma's left hand was a small flail, a bone-handled weapon with a middle articulated like a spine, and a wicked-looking double-edged blade, curved like the beak of a predator bird. It was this that had sliced into the meat of Wolf's shoulder.

Suma wasted no time, whipping his wrist back, snapping it forward so that the flail's blade made a sharp whistling sound as its spine thrashed the air in a shallow arc. Wolf blocked it, grabbing the wrist as it flashed by, and taking a swift circular step to his right and back. He let go of the wrist, feinted an *atemi* to the bridge of Suma's nose with his left hand but, instead, slipped it beneath Suma's left arm raised to ward off the phantom blow. He continued to push Suma's left arm up until it was fully extended, then pivoted again until he was behind Suma, reaching around to grab his head with his right hand and, bringing his body against Suma's, attempting to break the neck.

Suma went slack, jammed the thick butt end of the flail into the leading edge of Wolf's lowest rib. Pain flashed behind Wolf's eyes, and his grip on Suma slipped a fraction.

That was all the leeway Suma needed. He slammed his heel into the side of Wolf's right knee, pivoted away as Wolf staggered. The flail whistled through the air, and Wolf, still regaining his breath from the rib strike, barely managed to block the blade headed for his chest.

He could not catch his breath, and he wondered about this. Suma flicked the flail again, and Wolf stepped into the arc of the strike. His left arm was a blur as it swept aside the flail at its spine, and he directed a powerful *atemi* at Suma's kidneys. The blow landed, but, again, to little effect.

Wolf projected his *makura na hiruma* outwards, saw what was uppermost in Suma's mind: the drug that coated the blade of the flail. He's poisoned me, Wolf thought. No wonder he hasn't tried for a lethal blow, all he needs to do is wait for me to collapse.

He tried to move in again, but Suma stepped nimbly away. This happened twice more as Wolf shook his head as if trying to clear it, slipped to one knee. With an obvious effort, he regained his feet, lunged clumsily forward again. And again Suma stepped back, this time with a sneering smile on his face, the blade of his flail trailing at his side.

Wolf's left hand whipped out, his fingers curling around the blade. He cried out as the twin edges cut through skin and flesh, whipped his arm backwards, jerking Suma towards him. Suma's eyes opened wide in astonishment. His eyes were still locked on the blood spurting from Wolf's lacerated hand, his mind in shock at what Wolf had done.

Arrogance had been Suma's weakness, and Wolf had exploited it.

417

Suma had relied on his weapon too thoroughly, and now that mistake would kill him.

Then Wolf was face to face with him, and the black blade of Wolf's *makura na hiruma* sliced through all his defences. Never had Suma experienced such pain. It was as if every cell in his body was exploding in a chain reaction that overloaded his nerve synapses, froze his brain. In a rush, his heart burst in his chest, and the light went out of his eyes.

There was a terrible stink in the confined space of the room as Suma struck the bloody cedar wall and collapsed in a heap. Wolf felt elation and pain at the same time. The poison was in his system. He fell to his knees, fought to regain his feet, lost. His lungs refused to work, but his mind, as yet unaffected, returned to the Reverend Mother. Where was she?

He turned to look for her, when there was an abrupt howling. The shriek, like that of the worst storm, filled his ears. The vibration made his teeth chatter.

Then it was as if all the air had been sucked from the room, and the thick cedar walls collapsed inwards with a monumental *Whoosh!*, striking him with such force that he was flung against the opposite wall, where he was buried beneath an avalanche of wood and stone, as alive and malignant as the paws of a prowling beast.

NINETEEN

Washington/Tokyo

'I have to go out of town,' Jason Yoshida said.

'Not now.' Ham Conrad shifted in his chair as he studied again the photos of the material in his father's safe at Green Branches. 'This stuff is explosive all right, more than I ever could have imagined. In effect my father is guilty of kidnapping, slave-trading, medical mutilation and murder. No, you can't leave now. I'm going tò need your help when I confront him.'

Yoshida stared out the window behind Ham at the rose bushes around which a gauzy maze of bumblebees was buzzing. 'Shoto Wakare has failed to come on-line for his last three scheduled fax reports.'

'Is that so odd?' Ham asked without raising his head from his avid study of the photos he had developed himself during the early morning hours. 'He signalled us that he was bringing Yuji Shian into Forbidden Dreams. Don't worry so much. While Wakare's in there he can't possibly risk contacting us.'

'I'm afraid it has gone beyond such speculation,' Yoshida said carefully. 'Wakare has disappeared.' He waited until Ham's head came up. 'He may be dead.'

'Dead?' Ham appeared momentarily bewildered.

'I have no choice but to go over there myself,' Yoshida said, 'to find out what went wrong.'

Ham considered a moment, nodded. 'Okay, but make it quick. We can't afford any screw-ups this far along.' He made a curt gesture. 'Get the first flight out and keep me informed every step of the way.'

Yoshida stood up. 'Yes, sir,' he said in his best military voice. Ham, having returned to his examination of the evidence of his father's perfidy, ignored him. He was far too busy churning over the horrifying truth: Thornburg had espoused his love of the United States, his hatred of the Japanese as his motive to move forcefully against the serious threat of the Black Blade Society. Ham had been there. He had heard his father espousing these altruistic rationales to the generals at the Pentagon, to the President himself. And all the while he was conniving to kidnap people,

419

to experiment on them – to murder them. And all for his quest for the serum in the Holy Grail. The unmitigated hypocrisy of the man! Ham was devastated. He barely noticed Yoshida's departure.

When Yoshida left Ham's office he went immediately out of the building. He did not go to his own office next door or speak with anyone. He hailed a cab, went back to his apartment and, giving the cabby ten dollars, asked him to wait. It was now just after eleven in the morning, the day after the break-in at Green Branches.

Upstairs, he surveyed the three small rooms which were now devoid of all furniture, paintings, linens, kitchenware or personal items. In fact there was nothing left in the entire apartment save two meticulously packed suitcases which stood waiting for him like good little soldiers just inside the front door.

Of course, there was one other item. Yoshida walked into the galley kitchen which he had despised and, opening the refrigerator, contemplated the dead rat he had put there. All things being equal he would have liked to have seen the expression on Ham Conrad's face when he came looking for Yoshida and found the rodent. Well, you couldn't have everything.

The reason Yoshida had given Ham for his abrupt return to Japan was merely an excuse. It did not, in fact, matter to Yoshida where Shoto Wakare was or what had happened to him. Wakare had served his purpose, as had Ham. Yoshida's machinations had set in motion a complex set of emotional responses that would inevitably lead to the proper action. He was returning to Japan in response to a summons from the Reverend Mother.

Yoshida went through the apartment, taking one last look around to make certain he had left nothing. He hadn't. He went back into the hallway and, taking his suitcases, went out the door. He closed it and locked it carefully behind him.

Forty-five minutes later, he was inside the international terminal at Dulles airport. He glanced at the overhead clock as he checked in at the JAL first-class counter.

'You need nametags on these bags,' the young, pretty attendant told him efficiently as she printed out his boarding pass.

Yoshida wrote carefully on two JAL tags she provided: MR JEN FUKUDA. On the line below, he wrote the address of a large map-making company in Tokyo. This name and address corresponded to those in his passport, credit cards, driver's licence and other identifying papers he carried in his wallet.

It was now twenty minutes after noon and he had perhaps just over an hour before his 2:20 non-stop flight to Tokyo began boarding. He went through security and, because he was travelling as a Japanese national, immigration control. His passport was stamped and he had just time enough to buy himself a copy of *Forbes* and read two fascinating articles on the further demise of the American automotive industry while standing up over a pair of indifferent hot dogs and a cup of grey coffee.

His flight began to board and, fifty minutes later, after the inevitable delay due to congestion or flight controller incompetence, the Boeing 747 took off, leaving a smudgy backwash of jet fuel in its wake. Good riddance, Yoshida thought, as he put his head back against the rest and sipped the champagne thoughtfully provided by his first-class flight attendant.

The 747's frame shuddered a bit as the engines took hold and they climbed through the layers of smog and turbulence. When they were up above the clouds, he closed his eyes. Already the grime of Washington, the constant contact with Westerners was beginning to slough off him like the dried husk of a snake's old skin. How fine it would be to see Tokyo again, to walk among his own people, speak his own language. What a relief to return to Forbidden Dreams, where life for him began and ended.

He had begun life by slipping like an eelet out of Evan's womb. Though she still had the appearance of a teenager Evan was far older, although no one, not even the Reverend Mother, knew when she had been born.

Yoshida must, of course, have had a father but he had no idea who, since he was the result of an experiment in longevity conducted by the Reverend Mother who inserted the hand-picked sperm inside Evan's womb herself. The Reverend Mother had presided over every aspect of Evan's pregnancy and Yoshida's birth. Afterwards, Evan had been very ill and so was hardly prepared for the difficult first months of motherhood. Never mind, the Reverend Mother was able to do everything save suckle him at her breast.

In fact Evan's small breasts had not swollen with milk as they should have and, besides, she found her infant's hold on her tender nipples, though toothless, stronger than she could bear and would rather put up with Yoshida's red-faced squalling than allow him surcease at her breast.

The Reverend Mother at length became aware of the situation and provided warm milk and a latex nipple for the infant while in the next room she punished Evan.

Yoshida found out about this years later, but in fact it seems likely that he heard his mother's screams of pain while he was sating himself. Yoshida was something of a masochist and, like many masochists, he took exquisite care to match this tendency of his private persona with an equally ferocious absorption with sadism in his public persona.

But in all other ways Yoshida was different from anyone else. For one thing he had been brought up inside Forbidden Dreams, which meant that the authorities knew nothing about him. He had no birth certificate; no evidence of his enrolment in school existed because his schooling, like his religious and philosophical beliefs, had been forged in the crucible of that hermetic environment. For another, as the Reverend Mother had immediately perceived, he had been born singular.

The Reverend Mother was nothing if not covetous. Her overweening ambition made her greedy, and Yoshida had learned how to live off that greed without the Reverend Mother ever knowing it. He learned this talent in order to survive, and survive he did.

Theirs was an odd kind of symbiotic relationship. Perhaps this symbiosis had arisen because they were incomplete on their own. They somehow managed to live one another's lives as they lived their own. Even then they did not feel complete, these psychically wounded, but it was the best they could manage.

They were like the survivors of an unimaginable battle in which all other participants had been incinerated. The scars from this conflict ran so deep that they affected everything they believed or said or did.

It might be said that the Reverend Mother had deliberately crippled Yoshida in much the same way she had been maimed in order that she have the company of someone like her. Or perhaps she was merely compelled to do to someone what had been done to her.

What did she do to him?

In Nara prefecture, as far from urban civilization as one could get in Japan: She wrapped his hard-muscled frame in a loincloth and, clad in the white robes of the Shinto priestess, led him out into the night. The host of divine stars burned with cold passion in the swath of sky visible through the boughs. It was late autumn, and there was a certain chill in the air that contained the bitter scent of dry leaves and the silence of the first snow of winter.

They knelt at the ancient stone and wood shrine, the bronze bells echoing in the night like the conversation of fireflies. She made a fire in the bronze container, burning the rice paper fans of last year, so that the multiplicity of gods who inhabited this dense forest of giant cryptomeria would know her intent of sacrifice. The Reverend Mother said her first incantation, the words seeming to adhere to the stone, to burn themselves into the wood.

Then they rose, went down the ridge on the crown of which sat the Shinto temple that continued to exist and function through the beneficence of the Reverend Mother's generous annual endowment.

The lower reaches of the forest were alight with candles, their flames standing straight up as if the night itself were holding its breath. The young Yoshida (he was barely eleven then) could hear the rushing of water, which increased both in volume and in strength as they took the left branching of the pine-needle-strewn dirt path. He glanced down, fancied he could see in the candlelight the imprint of the tens of thousands of *geta* from past pilgrimages to the waterfall.

At the edge of the mountain pool they stopped, shed their wooden *geta* and cotton *tabi*. The Reverend Mother slipped into the pool, at the far end of which crashed the sacred waterfall, spilling over the jagged black rocks high above their heads. Then she turned to face him and held out her hand. He took it, moving in concert with her across the flat, moss-encrusted river stones to the outer circumference of the waterfall.

He was struck by the fury, as taut with power as the muscles in his arm or thigh, contained in an element as soft as water.

With her hands on his shoulders the Reverend Mother manoeuvred him until his back was to the gushing column of water. Her hands moved up, pressing the sides of his head. Then she pushed him sharply backwards into the waterfall.

The force of the water drove him to his knees. He could not breathe. And still her hands held him in place so that he could feel the enormous power of water, the soft yin element, and be purified by it as dictated by Shinto custom.

At last, she moved him further into the maelstrom, so that there were, now and again, brief pockets of air, dark and thick with spume, which he could gulp into his lungs.

He found that the ferocity of the waterfall had unknotted his loincloth, pushing it down his legs. Or perhaps the Reverend Mother had something to do with it because he became aware that her hands had at some time left his face and were now clasping his hips.

She was very close to him. He saw that the sheets of water had plastered her thin cotton robe against her body. Underneath, every line, crevice and curve of her body was revealed to him. There was something intensely erotic about seeing her nakedness through this thin film, pure, chaste, a garment of the gods who imbued this forest with its natural power and its primitive splendour.

The Reverend Mother took Yoshida's hands in hers, placed them over her breasts, dug her fingers into the backs of his hands, so that he felt the resilience of her flesh. Then she pulled apart his hands and the sopping robe parted with them.

Yoshida could feel a tightness in his groin and an almost ineffable ache in his chest that seemed to constrict his heart. Her eyes were luminous. He knew it to be impossible but it seemed to him as if in them he could

423

see beyond the white veil of water, the black boughs of the cryptomeria to the numinous starlight that shone down upon the forested mountainside and its myriad ancient spirits.

'I am the snow of winter, the cicada of summer,' the Reverend Mother whispered as she ran her hands over him. 'I am the morning glory of spring, the north wind of autumn.' She knelt facing him. 'I am the fox who gorges on the entrails of the rabbit, I am the fawn that starts at any sound. I will cherish you, watch over you, nourish you, devour you.' The waterfall crashed around them, onto them, but between them there was only air filled with bright sparks of spray and pinpoints of brilliance.

'You will love me and fear me, and because you fear me you will love me all the more deeply.' Saying that, she took him inside her, moving her hips back and forth, rotating them up and down, then circling them until Yoshida's eyes closed, his lips opened.

The Reverend Mother stared at the rippling of the muscles ridging his taut lower belly, smiling to herself as the spasms quickened. She felt his hands on her breasts, felt him filling her, and Yoshida, awash in her aura, felt these things too, and they multiplied his own pleasure until he grunted, shooting into her over and over, overwhelming him, and he collapsed into her waiting arms.

He awoke to the starlight of the ridge. For a moment, he believed that he had been transported to that magical realm he imagined was so close to the stars he could reach out and touch them. Then he became aware of the Reverend Mother kneeling over him, caressing his forehead.

He reached for her. He was hard again. 'I want you.'

The Reverend Mother slapped him so hard that the imprint of her fingers was left on his cheek. 'This night is for rite and ritual. It is for sacrifice and placating the gods who are everywhere. *You want, you want.* Your life with me is not for you to think about what *you want.* You want me but you will never have me again.'

Seeing that he was still excited, she slapped him again and again. In time, he erupted, but he immediately turned over on his stomach and wept.

Later, she took him all over the mountainside, pointing out this mushroom and that grass, this moss and that lichen, this fern and that root which she pulled from the ground. She taught him of all the natural poisons that grew here either naturally or because she had sowed them years ago, the slow ones and the fast-acting ones, the undetectable ones and the ones which, by their symptoms, would serve as unmistakable warnings to potential enemies. Then she began on the antidotes or arresting agents which could save a victim's life if not always return it to normal function.

So ended their night.

In Kyoto, urban sprawl of ten thousand temples, with the deep cold of winter making hail beat against the windowpanes like the discordant clatter of horses' hooves: she fed him these poisons one by one, that by his own hand he had ground, distilled, mixed and brewed so that in the future he would better be able to match victim with the appropriate toxin.

Thus did Jason Yoshida die in excess of a thousand times, feeling his essence rush out of him as with the severing of an artery, or slowly slip away from him as with the process of ageing. And thus did the Reverend Mother bring him back to life over and over again.

So was Jason Yoshida bound irrevocably to the Reverend Mother; so was he shaped in the image she had ordained for him, which was so much akin to her own . . .

Japan.

He had slept for sixteen hours and thousands of miles. The 747's cabin doors were not yet open, but as Yoshida now looked out the Perspex window he could see through the smog that surrounded Tokyo for miles the very top of Fuji-yama, the great mountain that watched over his country like a god, and abruptly he knew why the Reverend Mother had called him home. It was the time of the final battle. She would make her stand here, now, against the enemy, and as surely as Fuji-yama would survive Yoshida knew that he was to be an integral part of that stand.

'YOU HAVE BROUGHT ME THE MEDIATOR.'

'No,' Yuji said, as he helped Chika carry Wolf's body into the room on the top floor of the warehouse near Tsukiji. 'This man is very ill.'

'NEVERTHELESS, HE IS THE MEDIATOR.'

'Quiet,' Yuji said to the Oracle. He was looking anxiously at his half-sister.

Chika was quietly frantic. She had been like this ever since the rear wall of Forbidden Dreams had nearly crushed her in rubble. She had seen, through the mist, the swirling, choking stone and concrete dust, the sharp, hooked blade of the flail rising out of the debris, and with it, the bloody fingers of a human hand. Wolf's hand.

She had given a little cry and, projecting her *makura na hiruma* outwards, had begun to clear a path through inanimate objects that had begun to stir on their own.

Desperate, sensing the invisible aura of the Reverend Mother in the malign movements of wood and stone, she had concentrated, her black sight throwing sharp-edged chunks and splintered slabs to either side. She had felt, too, the black febrile tendrils of the Reverend Mother's *makura na hiruma*, wondered at first why she had not located Wolf, then

425

felt herself coming under the protection of the psychic fortress he had thrown up at the last minute.

She had redoubled her frantic efforts and, at last, she had unearthed Wolf's insensate body, and had been astonished to find his fortress still intact though he himself was unconscious. Using all her resources, she had managed to drag him from the quagmire of the Reverend Mother's making. But not before she had seen, on the other side of the room, Suma's twisted corpse. The sight provoked in her only relief.

She had brought Wolf here, to the warehouse Yuji had set up as the Oracle's lab, because it was now the only safe place she could think of. She had not seen her mother outside Forbidden Dreams, had not looked for her. In any event, bringing Wolf back to Minako's house had been out of the question, not after her last encounter with her mother.

Chika, listening for a pulse, any breath of life in Wolf, tried not to think of the creeping horror of that conversation. She projected her *makura na hiruma*, trying to probe beneath the coma. She tried again and again to no avail; every path was blocked.

She picked her head up, said to Yuji, 'I don't know what the Reverend Mother has done to him, but he's dying.'

'THE DANGER IS IN LIFE. NOT DEATH,' the Oracle intoned.

Yuji ignored the beast, said to Chika, 'Is there anything we can do to save him?'

'YES,' the Oracle replied. 'HE IS THE MEDIATOR.'

Chika turned her head in the Oracle's direction. 'What does it mean?'

'Ignore it,' Yuji said sadly. 'Something's happened to it. I think it is going mad.'

'Nonsense,' Chika said. 'Machines cannot go mad.'

'You don't know the Oracle.'

'What have you done to it? Its face almost looks human.'

With a sigh, Yuji told her how Hana had insisted on interfacing with the Oracle and what had happened to her because of it. 'I've told no one,' he concluded. He paused, weeping openly. 'I would not have known what to say. But I knew you would understand. You, of all people, must have understood Hana's unhappiness the best. Like Hana, your *makura na hiruma* has made you into something you did not want to become.'

Chika was silent for a moment, then she asked, 'Where is her body?'

'I did what the Oracle – what Hana asked me to do with it. It is on the bottom of the Sumida River.'

'No!'

This was not the time to remember all the moments with her half-sister, but she could not help herself. The idea that Hana was

426

gone seemed inconceivable. She felt hot tears overflowing her eyes, running down her cheeks. Part of her wanted to reach out and hold Yuji in their mutual grief but tradition would not allow such an overt show of personal feeling. For that, they would have to get blind drunk.

'Oh, Hana!'

And all the while her mind was screaming, *Wolf is dying! Do something! You've got to save him!* But how? she asked herself. She had tried everything she knew. If her *makura na hiruma* could not save him what could? What had the Reverend Mother done to him?

She had an idea, but it was so insane . . .

'What is the truth?' she asked. 'Is Hana alive or dead?'

'THAT DEPENDS ON YOUR DEFINITION OF LIFE AND DEATH,' the Oracle said. 'CHIKA-SAN, YOU MUST HELP US. HANA IS HERE INSIDE ME. BUT SHE IS DROWNING. WE ARE BOTH BEING CONSUMED BY A MAELSTROM OF IRRATIONAL THOUGHTS I CAN NEITHER INTERPRET NOR CONTROL. A MEDIATOR IS REQUIRED. A PSYCHIC SURGEON, IF YOU WILL, TO END OUR SUFFERING.'

Chika looked at her half-brother. 'Yuji . . . '

'SUCH A MEDIATOR IS HERE. WE CAN FEEL IT. PLEASE EFFECT AN INTERFACE.'

'Ignore it,' Yuji said. 'The procedure is highly experimental. It's far too dangerous. Look what happened to Hana.'

'But she didn't want to come back.'

'THE MEDIATOR IS DYING, YUJI-SAN. WE CAN PRESERVE HIS LIFE.'

'But in what form?' Yuji said bitterly.

'THE DANGER IS IN LIFE. NOT DEATH. WE BEG YOU TO EFFECT THE INTERFACE.'

Chika, her hand on Wolf's chest, looked from his blank face to the Oracle's black visage and made up her mind. 'Do it,' she said.

'What?'

'Do what the Oracle asks, Yuji. Link Wolf up to the machine.'

'But we can't know the effect it will have on – '

'He's dying and there's not a thing either of us can do on our own,' Chika said. 'The interface is his only chance now.'

Of course she was right. Yuji, deciding it was best not to think right now, began to hook Wolf up to the Oracle just as he had done with Hana.

'YOU WON'T REGRET THIS,' the Oracle said.

'Why should I regret anything?' Yuji said, carefully affixing pressure pads to the tips of Wolf's fingers.

'YOU ARE FILLED WITH REGRETS, YUJI-SAN. ABOUT HANA, ABOUT ME. ESPECIALLY ABOUT YOUR MOTHER.'

'You're imagining things,' Yuji said, beginning work on the complex network of wiring that would pierce the skin on Wolf's head.

'IT IS IMPOSSIBLE FOR ME TO IMAGINE, YUJI-SAN, AT LEAST IN THE SENSE YOU HAVE USED THE WORD. I AM NOT WRONG.'

'What you really mean is you're never wrong,' Yuji said, burying the electrodes one by one. 'Don't start getting a superiority complex. That's a nasty human aberration you need to be protected from.'

'DO YOU THINK ME NEUROTIC, YUJI-SAN?'

'What I'm talking about is more in the realm of the psychotic,' Yuji said, implanting the last of the electrodes.

'PSYCHOTICS ARE DANGEROUS, YUJI-SAN.'

'Often they are, yes,' Yuji said, throwing the switch which began the link-up.

'AM I DANGEROUS?'

Yuji sat back, monitoring the progress of the human/Oracle interface, too busy for the moment to answer. He had learned a great deal about this process when Hana went under, and he was watching for electrical spikes, unusual EEG activity, power overloads that could disrupt the data flow. Nothing unusual was happening, all the meter levels were just where they should be.

And then everything happened at once: the buzzing of an electrical overcharge filled his ears, the EEG needles went right off the chart. Yuji's finger flew over his control panels but whatever was happening was beyond even his sophisticated equipment's ability to handle.

'Yuji, what's happening?' Chika cried.

There was a sharp scent of ozone. Wolf's mouth opened wide, emitted a kind of screaming that set Yuji's teeth on edge.

Then all the lights on the Oracle went out at once.

Ham Conrad stepped aboard his father's schooner, *Influence II*. It was a fine, early spring day with high, puffy cumulus clouds and a strong, constant off-shore breeze. A perfect day for a sail.

It was funny how things worked out, he thought, as he cast off. He had been about to pick up the phone to call the old man when Thornburg had phoned him, asking him to meet him at the yacht club for an afternoon sail. Perfect, Ham had thought, checking twice that he hadn't forgotten to bring the photos of his father's perfidy with him.

It was not going to be easy to confront Thornburg, Ham knew, for him or for the old man, but the revelations contained in the safe at the Green Branches clinic gave him no choice. Yosh had been right about his father all along. It was a painful truth to absorb but, again, he had no choice. He was still clinging to the hope that he could threaten his father into owning up to his sins, repent, perhaps make restorations in some way for the people who had died in the clinic, return the ones still living to their homeland, and dismantle Green Branches. But it was his nature to be optimistic.

Ham went back to the wheelhouse where his father was in the process of backing the schooner out of its slip. The crew had been given the day off, Thornburg had told him. 'Damned bother they can be at times. Always seem to be in your face just when you want privacy the most.' But then Ham recalled Thornburg had always felt that servants were the bane of the wealthy.

The deep rich scent of marine diesel wafted up, overtaking for the moment the odour of the salt water. Away from the harbour, Ham unfurled and hoisted the mainsail, then forward, a Yankee jib and a smaller staysail, because there was an ineffable beauty in a schooner under full sail. He worked methodically, happily, detached for the moment from the concerns that never seemed a part of the sea. Thornburg had taught him to love sailing. Perhaps, if he had thought of it, Ham would have understood that this was the one thing he and his father truly shared.

Thornburg guided the *Influence II* through the Chesapeake, mindful of the marker buoys, and soon the sprawl of Washington was far behind them. Around noon, Ham furled the sails and they anchored in the lee of a small island. Thornburg broke out the food – fat subs dripping olive oil, red peppers and cheese, several salads, and ricotta cheesecake – and a six-pack of iced Sapporo beer, which they had both come to love in Japan.

Seated at the galley table, which was set adjacent to the open doorway to the deck, Thornburg watched his son crunch a gigantic sub into submission while he pushed some greens around his plate and sipped his beer. His appetite, problematic for years, had deserted him utterly in recent days.

They talked about this and that, nothing of real consequence, speaking slowly and lazily as if the dazzle of sunlight off the water had turned them somnolent. Thornburg seemed relaxed if not happy but, Ham thought, that was only to be expected after Tiffany's death. He, on the other hand, was tense with expectation of the monumental task ahead of him. The thought of mourning gave him the opening he had been desperately seeking.

'I've been thinking,' he said, wiping his hands on a napkin, 'I see you moping around Washington, not even wanting to be in your own house and it occurs to me you might be happy just taking off.'

'Taking off?' Thornburg said as if his son was suggesting he retire.

429

'Sure. Like to Aspen or Europe even,' Ham pressed on with overbright enthusiasm. 'Get your mind off everything, clear out the cobwebs, rejuvenate the soul.'

Thornburg regarded him with a peculiar intensity. 'Nothing to do in Aspen but spend money and watch the beautiful women run after the ski bums,' he said. 'As for Europe, all I'll see is Germans and Japanese. Remind me of the Axis, get my blood pressure to dangerous levels.' He gave Ham a cold stare. 'Any other bright ideas?'

Ham dropped his gaze, tapped his fork against a huge hunk of cheesecake.

'Besides,' Thornburg said after waiting just the right amount of time, 'I don't want to be away from here. Too many things might go wrong.' He continued to study Ham with keen purpose, making a wager with himself as to when his son's head would come bobbing up. 'Take my bioscience research, for instance.' Ham stopped tapping his cheesecake. 'There was a break-in at Green Branches the other night. Can you imagine? What would anyone want at the clinic?'

'Industrial espionage?' Ham offered, setting down the fork.

That was a good one, Thornburg thought. Sometimes Ham really did impress him. 'Of course, that's what we all thought at first. But the peculiar thing was the files weren't disturbed.' Thornburg's eyes seemed to burn. 'Then we found we'd caught the thief on video.' Ham's head came up and Thornburg congratulated himself on winning his bet. 'Would you like to see the tape? I've got a copy of it here.'

'Jesus, no.'

'Jesus, no,' Thornburg mimicked. 'Is that all you can say?'

'Christ, why do I feel like I owe you an explanation?' Ham exploded. 'It's you who has a lot of explaining to do!'

Thornburg watched his son come unravelled with a kind of cool detachment. 'I don't need to explain any of my actions to anyone,' he said deliberately. 'Time, money and privilege have seen quite satisfactorily to that. What I *do* need to know this instant is what my son thinks he's up to breaking into my facility and my safe.'

'I want to know – '

'Stow it, sonny!' Thornburg said so sharply that Ham jumped in spite of himself. 'If I meant for you to know what was going on at Green Branches I damn well would have told you. I didn't so it's none of your business.'

'I've made it my business.'

Well, well, Thornburg thought, what's this? More backbone than I thought he had?

'We have to talk about what's been going on at the clinic,' Ham said.

'Do we?'

'Yes. For Christ's sake, you're guilty of kidnapping, torture, murder. You're nothing more than a goddamned criminal! For the life of me I can't understand how you managed to round up a group of the most brilliant bioscientists under these circumstances.'

For a moment, Thornburg considered whether he should pursue this line with his son. Then he thought, Fuck it, he wants it, I'll give it to him, both barrels. 'My God, for a military man you can be damned naive,' he thundered. 'They accepted willingly, happily, for the money and a free rein at research they could do nowhere else. What do you think, men are angels? No, sonny, men are men with all the foibles and exploitable weaknesses inherent in the human race. Give people what they really want and they'll never notice the cost.'

'That sounds like a motto worthy of the devil.'

That made Thornburg laugh, but his laughter only infuriated Ham all the more. He hated it when Thornburg called him sonny, but he hated it worse when the old man laughed at him.

'You don't get it, do you?' he said, waving copies of the photos he had taken of the documents in the Green Branches safe. 'Your days of omnipotence are over. I've found your Achilles heel and I'm not going to let go until you agree to my terms.'

Thornburg was almost apoplectic. 'No one has ever successfully dictated terms to me, and no one is going to now.'

Ham's blood was pounding in his ears and he felt as if at any moment he was going to have a heart attack. He was sick at having to follow the old hypocrite's orders. He could no longer live with the knowledge of what Thornburg had done, what he was continuing to do. 'Accepting my terms is the easy way out of the corner you've painted yourself into,' he said. 'You've broken so many laws I've given up counting them. Do you have any idea the field day the attorney general would have if he got his hands on this material?'

'And how would that happen, sonny?'

'I'd give it to him!' Ham was shouting now, despite his resolve to handle this in as calm a manner as possible. 'And stop calling me sonny!'

'When you stop acting like a ten-year-old Boy Scout I'll call you by the name I gave you at birth. Who made you my judge, jury and executioner? Do you think the world's so goddamned neat and orderly that we all have to adhere to your tight-assed template of conduct? Poppycock. Chaos is the law of the day. The law of the universe.'

'I didn't create the concept of morals,' Ham said hotly. He was already aware of how his father had managed to turn the tables on him, making

431

him justify his own position on the high ground. 'If anything is common to all the cultures of mankind it's morality.'

'Tell that to the Arabs,' Thornburg said, 'or the Japanese. Neither of them ever heard of morality.'

'You're wrong,' Ham said, desperately trying to find a way back to the subject of his father's perfidy. 'Maybe their morality doesn't conform in all ways to ours, but – '

'Poppycock! Waste of time to defend those who don't deserve it. Won't have it from my son.'

'For Christ's sake, you make it sound like that's all I am – your son.'

'Just as I was my father's son until the day he died.'

'No, no!' Ham jumped up. 'I'm more than just your son, much more!'

Thornburg looked up at Ham from beneath the bill of his cap. 'And where would you be without me? Do you have any idea? I doubt it. I used my influence to get you into prep school, college. Used the same influence to get you set up in Tokyo, nice and cushy, so you could do some legwork for me, then I pulled you out of the Army and into Defense.

'What have you done on your own? Married a beautiful but useless woman who gives you no pleasure, has no appreciation of the life you give her, and has so little regard for the union she allows you to run around like a tomcat in heat. Well, why shouldn't she? That tennis instructor is giving her the kind of lessons even I find invigorating.'

'That's not true!' Ham shouted, even though part of him was not surprised at the news.

'Sure it is,' Thornburg said, unconcerned. 'I've got photos, too, sonny. Want to see them?' He laughed again, setting Ham's teeth on edge. Ham could remember fights just like this between his parents he had overheard as a child, and could still feel the pain of his nails as they had dug into the palms of his hands.

'Christ, this is evil! It's beyond evil!'

'Enough!' Thornburg slapped his hands down on the table, upsetting cutlery and aluminium cans. Dark beer spilled across the surface, sizzling like acid. 'You've got access to my secrets and I want 'em back. Let's stop the fancy philosophizing and get down to it.'

'Down to what?'

'The deal, you ignoramus,' Thornburg said with a glare. 'I should break your arm for breaking into my sanctuary, but that took balls. A bigger set than, frankly, I thought you had. Good for you, then. You've got the goods I need and I've got the influence you want. Sounds to me like we got a solid foundation here for a deal, so forget the morality bullshit, sit the hell down and let's hammer it out.'

432

That was when Ham knew he had got this gambit wrong from the get-go. He stared at his father as if seeing him for the first time which, in a way, he was. He had been a fool to believe that he could somehow manoeuvre his father into some kind of compromise. Instead, the inevitable had happened: Thornburg was forcing him into a deal that would leave no room for morality. He saw now that for his father morality was a luxury that with all his money and influence he could not afford. And perhaps this was *because* of his money and influence which were amassed in ways that precluded the possibility of morality.

The revelation was so profound he felt as if he had been struck between the eyes by a bolt of lightning. Christ, he thought, what was I doing being brought up in his house? How had Mother put up with him? But, of course, he knew. Thornburg Conrad III exuded the kind of charisma it was difficult to resist even when one began to suspect the source of that allure as being dark and deadly.

And now he knew with a dread certainty what he should have seen before, that there was only one alternative for him. The moment he sat down to the table with Thornburg to hammer out the parameters of the compromise he would be lost, just another fly lured into the glittering web that had trapped so many others.

'No,' Ham said now. The sunlight rose like waves from the deck, dizzying him and he tried not to flinch from the dark stare of his father's gaze. 'No compromise, no deal. There's only one way to stop you. I'm going to the attorney general with the evidence.'

'Don't be an idiot, Ham. You're not going anywhere with those photos. The originals have been burned and when you give me the negatives and all the prints you made the evidence will no longer exist.'

Ham smashed his fist down on the tabletop. 'Jesus Christ, listen to you. Of course, the evidence will still exist! It's bought and sold every day that obscene clinic stays open!'

'Now don't get violent, sonny. That never did anyone any good.'

'Cut the crap!' Ham snapped. 'You can dish that out to anyone you like, but not to me. Not any more.' He turned on his heel, heading for the electric capstan. 'It's time we got back to port.'

'We're not going anywhere,' Thornburg said, 'until this matter is settled to my satisfaction.'

'You no longer have any say in the matter,' Ham said over his shoulder.

'If you go anywhere near the capstan I'll use this.'

Ham whirled, squinted into the shade of the open cabin doorway where Thornburg still sat behind the galley table. 'What the hell is that?'

'What does it look like?' Thornburg said. 'It's the speargun I keep around if I see a shark or two.'

'Are you going to use it?'

'Only if you make it necessary.'

Ham said nothing, staring at the wicked barbed tip of the steel bolt that would go right through a shark's tough hide. Thornburg had stymied him all his life; if he thought threats would deter Ham now he was in for a surprise.

'Now come on over here and sit down so we can talk – '

But Ham was shaking his head. 'We'll only end up doing another one of your deals so I'll think I've gotten what I wanted only you'll continue what you've been doing. No, the whole evil cycle's got to end here.'

'Nothing is going to end,' Thornburg said. 'I'm not going to give up Green Branches but I promise I won't import any more patients, I'll make do with the ones I already – '

A kind of rage he never knew, even in the heat of the war, gripped Ham. 'How can you even say something like that! What incredible arrogance! Evil isn't a halfway measure. You can't say, I'll compromise by murdering six people instead of a dozen and expect that will absolve you.'

'Why not? I'm willing to compromise, Ham. You're the one who's being intractable.'

'You can't turn this around,' Ham said. 'This is about you, not me. It's all or nothing.'

'You mean that?'

'Put the goddamned speargun down.'

'All or nothing is not an acceptable proposition.'

'Take it or leave it,' Ham said, heading for the capstan.

'Stay away from there!'

'Fuck you!' Ham said, as he began the operation to weigh anchor. 'I won't call you sir and I won't take orders from you any more.'

The bolt from the speargun caught him almost squarely between the shoulderblades. It was not in itself a fatal wound but the force of the strike pitched him forward. His waist slammed against the gunwale and he toppled off-balance over the side.

Thornburg had already dropped the speargun, was heading across the deck. He hit the gunwale, leaned over, staring down into the water. He could see a stain in the water, blood spreading like a shroud, then Ham's back surfaced, the end of the bolt projecting from it like a broken flag.

'Christ almighty,' he whispered as he watched the ends of his son's hair wave gently back and forth like the tendrils of an anemone.

Lines from a W.B. Yeats poem that had been a favourite of his since he had stumbled upon it as a young man beat in his head like a military cadence: *The falcon cannot hear the falconer . . . The blood-dimmed tide is loosed, and everywhere/The ceremony of innocence is drowned.*

Wolf was standing alone on a long spit of flat land that jutted out into a vast sea. Overhead, clouds, viscous and fulminating, fled ahead of a rising wind.

No, not alone. He could see a figure limned against the magenta sky. He moved towards it. As he did so, the spit of land seemed to lengthen out behind him just as if it were the tongue of some enormous beast. Besides the gunmetal sea, the roiling sky and the featureless spit of land there was nothing else visible, and somehow Wolf had the sense that the spit was the last fragment of land left in this mad universe.

There was, however, the figure.

As he hurried towards it, he could see that it was human, female, Japanese, very beautiful. She was standing at the very end of the spit of land, staring out to sea, he supposed. He could see her profile, and he was struck by how much she resembled Minako.

She turned her head at his approach, though he was certain that he had made no sound. She had about her an air of ineffable sorrow that made him want to weep, and yet she possessed a rare stillness, as of a stone at rest in a tide pool or a bird in the moment before it takes flight.

'I am Hana,' she said. 'Minako's daughter, Chika's half-sister.'

What was it about her that made him feel as if he had known her all his life? he wondered.

'Where am I? Am I dead?'

'Your mind is linked with the biocomputer known as the Oracle.' She touched him over his heart. 'There is a poison inside you. Hold still while I draw it out.'

Wolf was about to ask a question, but thought instead of how White Bow had healed his father in similar fashion.

'There, it is done.' Her pale face went white and she clutched him. 'Do you hear that?'

'What? The wind is rising.'

'No. Not the wind.' She peered out to sea. 'Something else.'

Wolf turned his head, following her gaze. Above the sound of the wind, he heard something, like a dirge or a lament, an inchoate cry that chilled him.

'It's coming,' Hana said.

Far out beneath the veil of the gunmetal water there was a disturbance, an arcing and sucking, a movement of the water so vast that the eye could not entirely encompass it.

'What is it?' Wolf said, sensing life of a sort beating in a slow, heavy pulse.

'Something,' Hana said, 'waiting to be born.'

The fear in her voice was like a third presence on the spit of land.

'Wolf, listen carefully to me. I came here willingly, foolish person that I am,

because I was not meant to exist in the world of mankind. I was uncomfortable in my human body, unhappy in the polluted world that unthinking mankind had fashioned for itself.

'I came here to find sanctuary, to explore the infinite, to live in a place immune from pollution only to find that I carried a pollution inside myself, and from the moment I arrived here I have been infecting this place with that virus.'

'Hana, I must know – '

'No, no,' she pleaded, 'let me finish while I am still in a period of lucidity. There is so little time now. The Oracle and I are one, and we are both going mad.'

There was a distinct hump in the centre of the gunmetal sea. And the water itself was without waves, as if the leviathan beneath was so unimaginably huge that it was stretching taut the very fabric of the ocean.

She spoke quickly but distinctly and each word had the ring of truth, a truth substantiated by his own observations, a truth so horrific that Wolf's mind was momentarily stunned by the enormity of it. Still he listened, growing more and more absorbed in Hana's explanation of what was happening to him and what might happen. In her he saw the future: a future she had readily – almost selfishly, she said – fled. 'You see the pattern emerging,' she said at last. 'You see the future and what you must do.'

Then Hana screamed, but that sound was drowned out as she was swept away by the rising wind. And then the leviathan emerged from the deep.

How many choices it must have had, how many ways to present itself to him. It needed to be healed; it needed to know that which is unknowable. And for this it had turned to Wolf, the mediator, the psychic surgeon.

But Hana had known better. She had understood what the Oracle could not: that its very matrix was what was driving it insane. That had been the ultimate sadness of her new world – and the ultimate irony. She had learned that, for her at least, there was no exit. And, for the Oracle, there would be no existential catharsis. The meaning it was so desperately searching for was beyond its comprehension.

The danger is in life. Not death.

Wolf knew what that meant now, because Hana, in her last moments of lucidity, had known and had told him.

The leviathan rising out of the deep had many heads. Beautiful or hideous, they all swung in one direction to study him at once. So many heads he could not possibly count them were he to stay in this mad universe for a year. The heads, beautiful and hideous, took up the entire world.

Wolf closed his eyes, drew on makura na hiruma, projecting a long, slender finger through the inky ocean. It penetrated the Oracle, and he could 'see' a kind of schematic of its LAPID circuits. They made no sense to him and he momentarily felt a kind of panic.

'I HAVE HEALED YOU. NOW HELP ME TO LIVE, TO UNDERSTAND.'

He ignored the circuits, listened, watched, touched – and he felt its heartbeat – or

436

what passed for a life pulse since it had no heart. But, like all entities, it had a core without which it could not survive, and he now knew why this universe manifested itself to him as a vast ocean. Like the tide, he felt the pulse, waves of energy with a distinct rhythm and, concentrating, he recognized that cadence from his own mind and those of all human beings: it was the wave-like synaptic firing that occurs when one dreams.

Makura na hiruma, bequeathed to it by Yuji's DNA and what was left of Hana's psyche, had set it to dreaming mad dreams. The leviathan beneath the gunmetal ocean – that was the ocean – was as insane as an entity could be. The awesome power of makura na hiruma had opened up so many possibilities so quickly that it had driven the forming 'brain' mad. Though it was only quasi-organic, the Oracle's brain was almost as complex as the human organ. And, frighteningly, in many respects it was more efficient, more focused, superior.

But it was only in its infancy, a dreaming mind, precocious but vulnerable, totally unable to assimilate the gifts in Yuji's DNA, in Hana's psyche. As its powerful mind overwhelmed what remained of Hana, so her makura na hiruma inundated it.

The voices of bedlam. He felt the onslaught of irrational thoughts as he began to connect to the Oracle's matrix. For a vertiginous instant he became the faces. He hung suspended, almost gone, nearly dissolved in the mad universe, half-insane himself.

But in that final instant, he centred himself, recalling the cacophony of voices he had been exposed to when he had touched the minds of the serial murderers he had brought to justice. Another lifetime, but the experience served him well here.

Ignoring the disorienting chaos, he projected his makura na hiruma further into the matrix, and in so doing intercepted the Oracle's base cadence, distorted the wavefront of its heartbeat, interfered with the pattern of its synaptic firing.

'This is the only way I can help you.'

And so did he deliver it from its suffering; so did he execute it.

When Thornburg Conrad III returned to his villa at the Magnolia Terrace Country Club he felt as if he had suffered radiation burns. The taste of his son's betrayal was in his mouth, the virus of treason curdled his stomach.

Rage and agony shook him like a tree in a gale. He collapsed on an upholstered chair, his head in his hands. He did not reach for a light switch; right now he preferred the cool darkness of the villa.

Of all the people to turn on him why did it have to be the one he relied on the most? Long ago, he had written off his other children as useless, dead weights he had pushed out of the nest and into the real world only to discover he had to rescue them from some unimaginable blunder such as being caught with the boss's wife or marrying the wrong woman, who was threatening through her lawyer to take them to the cleaners.

None of them was worth a damn except Ham. Which was why

437

Thornburg had helped form Ham's career, using his old boy network in Washington to give his favourite son all the advantages his intelligence and moral strength warranted.

Thornburg dragged himself out of the chair, went across the carpeted floor to the bar, where he picked up a heavy cut-crystal glass, made himself a stiff whisky and soda. He downed a third of it at once as if it were a dose of medicine, which in this instance it was.

In the past few weeks he had taken to living in this villa, surrounded by the peacefulness of the golf course and the woodland creatures. The vast stone house in the midst of the Virginia estate which had been his home when Tiffany was alive no longer seemed inviting. The endless rooms, the soft pad of the servants who he suspected of spying on him, gossiping about him in dark corners, the now daunting forested hills had become an intolerable burden for his psyche.

Again lines from the Yeats poem rang through him: *Things fall apart; the centre cannot hold . . . The best lack conviction, while the worst/Are full of passionate intensity.*

Christ, it seemed like the end of all things. He took another long draught of his whisky and soda. What did Ham think he was up to cracking the safe at Green Branches, photographing the secret documents chronicling the clinic's experiments. Of course, there were aspects to those experiments that were illegal. But who had made those laws? Thornburg had had too many dealings with the idiots on Capitol Hill to feel anything but contempt for them. Those whose arteries weren't already sufficiently hardened to cut off oxygen to their brains were so venal they never managed to get their snouts out of the river of graft that year after year granted them certain return to their privileged sinecures.

Ham's major fault was his inability to see beyond the arbitrary laws imposed by mankind. If Thornburg had learned one thing, it was that one could not for long impose an artificial order on the chaos of the universe.

He took another long swallow of his drink, shuddering as he remembered retrieving his son's corpse from the water, wrapping it in an extra sail he had brought up from below, lashing it tight, lacing the package with the auxiliary anchor he had unhooked from its chain. Only after he had rolled it off the side of the dinghy did he realize that he had forgotten to say a prayer. He had tried to mumble something but no words formed in his mind.

He let out a soft moan now, a taste like blood in his mouth, and stumbled across the carpet into the bedroom where the serum he needed was hidden beneath the false bottom of his night table drawer.

438

He was at the foot of the bed when he became aware that someone was sitting in the easy chair just to the left of the night table.

'Who's there?' he said in the voice of a startled old man.

'Don't you recognize my perfume?'

Thornburg's head turned this way and that, his nostrils flaring. 'Stevie?' he said uncertainly. 'When you cancelled our dinner, you said you had to return to New York. What are you doing here?'

'Waiting for you.'

Some hard edge in her voice made him wary. What has happened? he asked himself. Immediately, he was struck by a lance of panic. Had Ham shown Stevie the evidence he had stolen from the Green Branches safe? No, no, that was impossible. Ham did not even know about his relationship with Stevie. Each day, it seemed, he was growing more paranoid. He needed a shot of the serum, but what he needed even more was the result of Wolf's infiltration of that bitch Minako's world of slow ageing and exceptional power.

'I'm glad you're here,' he said at last.

'Perhaps you won't be when you hear what I have to say.'

'I don't understand.'

'I'd like you to explain why you never told me you and my sister had a relationship.'

'Stevie,' he said, taking one careful step and sitting on the edge of the bed. 'Your sister couldn't seem to cope with growing old, you know that. When she discovered that I was conducting experiments in countering the effects of ageing she begged me to make her a part of the experiments.'

'She willingly became a guinea pig.'

'Yes.'

'And she knew all the risks up front.'

'Certainly. I tried to talk her out of it but – '

'I have your correspondence with Amanda.'

'Ah.' He could see the line of her cheek and brow limned in the seepage of the exterior lights through the wooden shutters and gauzy curtains. Now he had a good sense of where she was, how far away from him.

He shook his head. 'I need a shot,' he said as he put his glass down on the night table top, opened the bottom drawer.

Stevie waited until he had pushed aside the false bottom, his hand deep inside the drawer, to switch on the bedside lamp.

Thornburg blinked, struggling to get his eyes adjusted to the abrupt brightness of the immediate environment.

'Looking for this?'

He could see Stevie now, quite desirable in khaki jeans, a cream-coloured shirt under a leather and melton wool baseball-style jacket, open in front. Normally, he would have admired her long legs, the swell of her breasts, but at this moment he was more interested in the thin lamb-skin gloves she wore. This was because she held his Army Colt .45 in her strong right hand, aiming almost point-blank at him.

'Are you sure it's loaded?'

Stevie gave him a chilly smile. 'I loaded each chamber myself.'

'Surely you wouldn't use that weapon, Stevie,' he said. 'You're a psychiatrist. You know the consequences of such an act, not only in a court of law but for years afterward inside your own head. Besides, I've done nothing to warrant your holding a gun on me.'

'You had Amanda killed.'

Thornburg stared at her. 'You're just plain crazy. Why on earth would I – '

'She was dying from the treatments you were giving her. Shut up! Don't deny it.' She nodded. 'Just like Tiffany died. Only with Amanda it was different. You had complete control over Tiffany. Where is her body now, Thornburg? At a mortuary? No. There was no funeral, no nothing. I'm willing to bet you had your ghouls at the clinic dissect her for scientific research and then cremate her. Nice and neat and no awkward questions asked by a medical examiner. Just one of your pet doctors at the clinic writing up the death certificate.

'But you couldn't do that with Amanda. She was out in the real world, beyond your grasp. When you knew she was dying you couldn't just spirit her off to the clinic. There would have been major questions raised had she been allowed to die of the drug you have been pumping into her, so you had her killed. And to complete the picture, you made it seem as if she had been the victim of a sneak thief, so common in New York, especially where she lived, you knew it wouldn't cause a great deal of comment or curiosity.'

'Are you finished?' Thornburg said. 'That's quite a clever story, but I promise you that's all it is: a story. I don't know who has been feeding you this insane fabrication but I can assure you – '

'Shut up!' Stevie said, this time more harshly. She stood up, as if she had so much pent-up rage she could no longer bear to sit still. 'I've seen your fine Machiavellian hand for myself. And the thing I can't fathom is that I used to admire how you wrapped people – important, powerful people – around your finger. You built Morton's career that way and you got me my entrée into the level of society I had always dreamed of being a part of. You were so powerful, like a sun, and I was close to you, absorbing your heat, basking in the reflected glory of your power. I was your friend, I invoked your name and gilt-edged doors opened to me.

'My God, how I used to shiver with anticipation. I used to imagine myself an actor on Broadway, taking the stage. How tangled I became in your lies! I *was* an actor, but not in the benign way I had at first imagined. I was living a lie, every day, every night, and the last straw was how I prostituted myself for you with Wolf. I look back on that episode now with a kind of fear and loathing I suspect you could never imagine. Because it's myself I fear and loathe when I think about how I gained Wolf's trust and then exploited it for you.

'You were right about one thing: I do love Wolf. And I believe that given time he would have come to love me. But, you see, it can never be because our relationship is false, tainted by the deceit I performed for you. I could never face him honestly again with that knowledge, and I could never dare tell him what I'd done to him.'

'Come on, Stevie,' he said, 'you know better than this. I liked Amanda. She was a friend. I felt sorry for her. If I was in error, it was merely a momentary weakness of friendship. I felt sorry for her, but I see now I never should have let her talk me into entering her in the clinic programme. I felt terrible about her death, but really it was random chance. The city killed her, New York. It's tragic, but there's no one to blame, least of all me.'

'I'm no longer interested in how many ways you can twist the truth, Thornburg.'

'Stevie, you of all people should understand that you're too wrapped up in your emotions right now to be able to separate truth from fiction.'

'I told you to shut up and I meant it.' Stevie held the Colt steady, centred on his heart, and Thornburg could see that at the moment the risk of trying to disarm her was too high. She really was starting to annoy him. He needed time to sort through what had happened aboard the sloop. It was vitally important for him to come to terms with what –

'Reading these letters of Amanda's I suddenly realized that I have nothing of value,' Stevie continued. 'My marriage is a mockery, wholly without love or real feeling. It's become merely a matter of convenience, although I now suspect that this has more or less been the case from the very beginning. I feel increasingly disconnected from my patients, and my social life is so hollow, so false it makes me weep.

'Wolf awakened the only real emotion I've felt in years other than my sorrow over Amanda's death, and now that avenue has been fouled by my betrayal.

'But it isn't, after all, just you who is evil, Thornburg. The evil lies inside our own selves like a trap whose jaws are just waiting to snap closed and imprison us in the darkness of the human soul. I blame myself, you see, as much as I blame you.'

She pushed the Colt towards him further, her arm straightened and so tense that Thornburg suddenly knew he had been wrong about her, she was getting ready to pull the trigger. Too late, he saw it all now, why she needed to talk. She had presented herself with an iron-clad rationale that would protect the psyche from the trauma that would inevitably ensue from shooting another human being.

'I have the letters, but they would not stand up in a court of law,' Stevie said. 'I have no objective proof that you ordered my sister's murder, but I nevertheless know you're responsible. I cannot in good conscience allow you to get away with it. I have no choice and nothing to lose.'

An instant before she pulled the trigger, Thornburg's right arm swept out, swatting the heavy cut-crystal glass that sat on the top of the night table. It struck Stevie on the shoulder as the explosion roared.

Thornburg was thrown violently back across the bed, the bullet embedded in his ribcage just below his heart. Stevie screamed, staring at the blood overflowing the wound, seeping into the counterpane. His eyes were wide and staring but she could not bring herself to look into them.

She began to shake, weeping uncontrollably. She was so horrified by the blood – the symbol of what she had wrought – creeping across the bed that she fled the villa. Through the woods at the edge of the golf course she ran, only then realizing she still clutched the gun in her hand. With a convulsive heave, she hurled it into the underbrush, stumbling on until she climbed into her rented car.

Her mind was numb and she had to grip the wheel very hard, but she had enough control to drive carefully, observing all speed limits and lights. She stopped at the first phone booth, fumbled out some change and called the police. She told them about the body without identifying either Thornburg or herself. The voice at the other end of the line was still urgently asking her questions as she hung up.

When she stepped out of the booth she fell to her knees and vomited. Dizzy and weak she staggered back to her car and sat, her hands loosely on the wheel, staring up at the immensity of the sky. She heard the warm engine ticking over but nothing else.

Her mind began to function in a semblance of normalcy again, placing one coherent thought after another. It was one thing to contemplate murder, to be certain that it was justified, quite another to then go out and perpetrate the act. Murder was murder and, as Stevie was just beginning to find out, it would always have its consequences.

TWENTY

Tokyo

Night and the metropolis.

Modern Tokyo was a metropolis of the kind of twilight melancholy possible only in a resurrected society still steeped in the profound nihilism of defeat. That it was also a society that mindlessly embraced the concept of the empty symbol, whether it be in the form of rabid name-brand consumerism or idolization of an empty-headed pop-star's pretty face, lent added poignancy to the stylized dolour of its ultra-modern facade.

Wolf, prowling night-time Tokyo with the stealth of his namesake, was struck by how alien and at the same time how wilful this form of architecture was. It allowed for no interpretations, no adornments, no possibility of compromise at all. It was as unyielding and resolute as a samurai's purpose.

He was a long way from the mad, inverted universe of the Oracle. The late Oracle. Afterwards, he had imagined Hana, free at last.

He was never so happy to be moving about in the dark, the brilliant vertical neon pennants of the Ginza far behind him, a pearlescent halo like false dawn or eternal twilight.

He felt the melancholic sadness of beauty just past its prime, of fleeting happiness, of the decay that inexorably follows the fullness of youth.

Thinking these things he remembered Hana, sad and so lonely, trapped in a modern-day hell at least partially of her own making. He had the sense that she would have understood the way Tokyo appeared to him tonight.

Light and Chika's silhouette.

From his shadow-steeped vantage point he watched the entrance to Forbidden Dreams as the dwarfish woman in her man-tailored suit ushered Chika inside. The door closed and the street shimmered in the beams of oncoming headlights. Then the car had swung past and darkness fell again. The pale wash from the Ginza fell short of this side street, making it seem part of another world. No one walked the street, although Wolf could hear a male voice rising and falling, punctuated by

443

bursts of embarrassed laughter: sounds of an incomprehensible TV show leaking through a window somewhere close by.

It had come down to this: one last plan, so dangerous only their desperation could have persuaded them to try it.

Wolf had marked the time Chika entered Forbidden Dreams, and now the minutes seemed as attenuated as pulled taffy, wrapping themselves around the darkness here, pulling the shadows tight against the buildings' facades.

The first face he had seen when he had awakened, as if from a long sleep, was Chika's. He had never been so happy to see anyone. How he loved her. And now he wondered whether he was sending her to her death.

Time.

The dial on his watch glowed yellow in the dark. Wolf's eyes. He checked the street again, waited for another car to pass, its headlights sweeping past him, raking the buildings as they did in those old films noirs with the obligatory prison break-out scene.

He moved down the block, keeping to the deepest shadows, before he crossed the street to the Forbidden Dreams side. Then he went quickly around the corner and, as he and Chika had rehearsed it earlier, moved down the block, turning the second corner with his head down, his shoulders hunched. He walked quickly, rudely, with his elbows out, as the Japanese did. While he was too large to be mistaken for a native he would not be taken for a tourist, either.

He passed by the section of rear wall the Reverend Mother had blown out in her attempt to destroy him, saw the barbed wire sunk into the drying ferroconcrete. He hurried on, wisely passing it by.

He was in another of Tokyo's older narrow streets so anonymous it had no name. Even long-time natives of this city had to frequently ask directions to destinations such as this street. When he reached the blank facade of the second of the Forbidden Dreams buildings, he took another look around. There was a narrow alleyway running part way down the near side of the building. Wolf slipped into this.

He unwrapped the bandages on his lacerated left hand, concentrated again his *makura na hiruma* on the wounds, which were already healing at a phenomenal rate. Only red welts were still visible. He flexed his hand, felt no pain, only a momentary stiffness, which the flexing dissipated. Still, to make sure he would not hurt it, he slipped on a leather glove, supple enough to allow him full movement, yet strong enough to protect him.

Centring himself, he reached up for the first ferroconcrete outcropping Chika assured him would be there.

444

This second building – within which the Reverend Mother's rooms were laid out – was connected to the first building which housed the club itself by two corridors between which was the exquisite garden where the Reverend Mother had interrogated him. It had a rough-hewn texture unlike the facade on the club side, at least half-way up.

Now Wolf had reached that point. He was stretched upwards on his precarious perch, searching for another of the outcroppings, where the bricks of ferroconcrete overlapped. There was none.

Carefully reaching back, he unfurled a nylon rope, fastened at one end to a claw-like hook of a lightweight titanium-steel alloy. He threw it upwards and, on the second try, felt the claw engage the inside of the roof wall. He jerked hard several times to make certain the claw had wedged itself against the ferroconcrete. Then he hauled himself up to the roof.

He crouched there for a moment, and it was impossible not to remember the rooftop in New York, so far away, yet held alive inside his mind, the pouring rain, the brush with the unknown, the killing rage inside him, the one-sided struggle with Amanda's murderer, crashing through the skylight . . .

He closed his eyes, momentarily dizzy. What was happening to him? Hana had explained some of it but even she did not know it all. He had, after all, existed inside the bio-mind of the Oracle for who knew how long? Yuji had said it had been not more than several minutes, but like dream-time, it had seemed like hours.

What had really happened to him while he and the Oracle had been connected? That was the mystery. Had data been transferred, had some of the bio-mind been incorporated into his mind?

He was shaking, unable now to continue along those lines. *Concentrate on the job at hand*, he told himself. *Otherwise you'll never live long enough to discover the answer.*

Above him towered the colossal Shinto spires of Tokyo, brand-name buildings proclaiming the economic miracle that defined post-modern Japan. Below him were the natural elements of a garden that, in mimicking nature in so stylized a fashion, managed to negate it.

And somewhere between the two was the woman who would be emperor of the world.

'I am startled by how much I missed you.' The Reverend Mother curled one long fingernail, scraped it down his bare chest. 'Is it good to be home?'

'I'll miss the Washington hamburgers,' Yoshida said. 'I developed a taste for meat over there. I discovered no one makes a hamburger like a black man.'

445

They were in one of the tatami rooms on the ground floor of the second building that overlooked the garden. The multi-directional glow from the rooms around the garden lent it a spectral quality. The periphery was dimly lighted while the centre remained absolutely dark like the heart of a sleeping gem. The Reverend Mother objected to lights in her garden; they disrupted the *ki* – the intrinsic energy – so carefully accumulated by rock, moss, fern, tree and pebble, the natural elements of the garden.

'And the Conrads, *père* and *fils*?'

Yoshida smiled. 'Like planets in the grip of entropy, neither will survive their close encounter with us.'

'Splendid!' The Reverend Mother clapped her hands like a five-year-old. She leaned over, kissed Yoshida on his collarbone. She bared her white teeth, nipped his flesh, then held on until the blood flowed. The Reverend Mother's teeth sank deeper into his flesh, and Yoshida's eyes closed.

'I've hurt you,' she said.

'I didn't feel a thing.'

He took her and kissed the blood off her lips.

There was about their actions something of a ritual. This was part of their relationship. As with mother and son, guru and acolyte, bishop and priest, inquiry and response were dictated not only by the individual but by the larger context of the role each played.

'But you feel this.'

He did not even wince. 'Yes,' he said through partly opened lips.

The Reverend Mother could hear the soft hiss and suck of his breath through his mouth and, as she placed the flat of her hand on the centre of his chest, she could feel the sheen of moisture she had produced.

'If I hurt anyone else that way they would have been down on their knees.'

His nostrils were dilated, the only sign of the excruciating nerve pain she had inflicted on him. 'Nishitsu included.'

'Yes.' The Reverend Mother studied his breath control with objective curiosity. 'Endurance was never his long suit.' Her elongated fingers curled down his arms, sliding appreciatively over the smooth muscles. Then she turned. 'Speaking of Nishitsu, he should be here. I summoned him ten minutes ago.'

'Maybe one of the club's little boys caught his attention,' Yoshida said.

The Reverend Mother giggled like an adolescent. 'You'd like an hour alone with Nishitsu, wouldn't you?'

'I want his eye.'

446

Now the Reverend Mother really laughed. 'Do you think it will give you his power if you eat it?'

'Isn't that what you taught me?'

The Reverend Mother closed her eyes for a moment. 'I would give a great deal to see you go to work on him. Perhaps I should allow it.'

Yoshida studied her as he considered this. 'Nishitsu coordinates all the Toshin Kuro Kosai activity worldwide. You could not afford to allow it.'

'It is a mistake to rely so heavily on one person,' the Reverend Mother said. 'It distances you from what must be done and gives someone else a false sense of his own power. I am perhaps at this stage with Nishitsu.'

'But even though you are the Reverend Mother you are nevertheless a woman. You need Nishitsu to keep all the Toshin Kuro Kosai lines functioning – '

He grunted as the pain flooded through him with such blinding force that he actually staggered. The vascular constriction she had produced at the back of his neck was causing a spasming that sent fierce lances like shards of glass into his brain.

'Please accept my apologies,' he said when he was able. 'I merely wished to point out the possible consequences of giving Nishitsu up.'

'Fool to question me,' the Reverend Mother said with that expression cats get when licking up cream. 'I have already sunk my claws deep inside Nishitsu's brain. I am sucking out his *makura na hiruma* day by day. He is good only to nourish me. I'll take care of the rest when the time comes.'

Yoshida was about to point out that she would require another figurehead if she was to continue controlling the members of the Black Blade Society in place within the giant conglomerates around the globe when she curled her fingers around his forearm and raised her head to the ceiling.

'There is an animal on my roof.'

Yoshida followed her gaze, then cocked his head. 'I don't feel anything.'

'Neither do I. Nevertheless, it's there. The last shred of the future I can see tells me so. Bring the animal to me in the room of five shadows,' the Reverend Mother said quietly.

Wolf raised himself from his crouch, rewound the nylon cord, and went quickly across the tarred roof. Television and sophisticated digital-transmission satellite dishes rose like deformed flora, along with low, grilled structures he recognized as a complex air filtration system.

He had almost reached the far side of the roof, below which was the garden, when he felt the momentary blurring of perception that told of an encounter with another *makura na hiruma* aura. This one had a familiar taste, which he could not immediately place.

He slid on his stomach towards the edge of the roof, carefully pulled himself forward so that he could peer down.

He saw the dark shapes of rocks and trees, fans of fern, mounds of moss. Light crawled across the miniature landscape of the garden like syrup spilled on a countertop. He felt the movement of the familiar aura, trying to place it.

He anchored the titanium-steel claw, gingerly lowered himself down the nylon cord to the spongy floor of the garden. Putting his back against the largest of the rocks he watched for silhouettes moving beyond the window-doors to the rooms facing into the garden. He closed his eyes, extended *makura na hiruma* outwards in concentric circles until he pinpointed the familiar aura.

In his mind, he could see the layout of the second building as Chika had outlined it for him. He saw that the aura's movements had a purpose. Though its owner could not sense him, he or she could guess at his purpose. And so as he closed in, he could feel the other person's movement, closing off paths to the Reverend Mother's rooms.

It was like a chess match played in the dark.

Wolf went through a partially open doorway into a deserted room. It was typical of those on the second building's ground floor: tatami mats, stucco walls, small dark wood cabinets with heavy grain and pitted iron hardware, the Japanese minimalist approach that was very old and had never gone out of style.

As he went, he began to rely more and more completely on *makura na hiruma*. Now, more than ever, it was imperative for him to move as quickly and as silently as possible.

While Chika kept the dangerous Nishitsu away, Wolf would surgically extract the insane Reverend Mother from her surroundings. On the surface, it seemed an impossible task. After all, she had already defeated him once. But he had an added edge now. In pulling him back from the dead the biocomputer had subtly altered his *makura na hiruma*. In what way? Hana had not known, and it was still a mystery to Wolf himself.

The fact was the Reverend Mother had to be destroyed. The wave of senatorial murders, the passage of the restrictive trade bill, the dismantling of America's economic superstructure would continue unabated unless she was stopped. And who was there to make the attempt but him?

This plan had as much chance of success as any other he and Chika had thought of. It might, in fact, end in nothing more than a suicide attack. The risk was that enormous.

But he was addicted to risk. What good was life without it? Peter Matheson had said to him in the New South Wales night. Risk had been the major factor in Peter's life. He could still see the peculiar feral glow in his father's eyes during the time he had spent with him and the Aboriginal girl in Lightning Ridge. No wonder he had run off to Australia.

And, in the end, was Peter Matheson's son so much different? Wolf, as he made his careful way through the warren of connecting corridors and rooms, did not now think so. He was in his own Lightning Ridge now, a place where the laws of civilization were either ignored or deliberately mocked.

These lords of the Toshin Kuro Kosai had made the conscious decision to put themselves beyond every law that mankind had amassed in a little over two thousand years. In a way did that not make them all insane?

He stopped in his tracks and swivelled. The echo from the other's *makura na hiruma* aura had moved, and Wolf moved with it, doubling back on the way he had come, pressing himself into shadow-filled niches or through doorways at the hint of another presence.

At length, he came to the room within which the other sat, stood or crouched. With his hand on the *fusuma* door, he hesitated a moment. Could this be a trap? But no, he knew that these people could not read his own aura so they had no way of knowing where he was. The other was in there, all right, and he could have no idea that Wolf was just outside.

He opened the *fusuma* just a hair, enough so that he could see that one lamp illuminated the otherwise darkened room. From the angle of the shadows along the tatami mats, he placed the lamp at the far left-hand corner. He slid the door another fraction, and now he could see that this was one of the inner rooms with only one access. That meant he would have to go in very fast, using the shock of recognition to his advantage.

He crouched by the side of the *fusuma*, breathing tidally, feeling the blood pounding in his veins, the strange black power continuing to unravel within him, and the waves of this new feeling that, now and again, had lapped at his consciousness ever since he had returned from the Oracle's inner universe. Counting off the seconds.

He kicked the *fusuma* all the way open and leapt into the room, rolling in a ball along the tatami mats, coming up in a crouch, ready for whoever lurked inside.

But there was no one inside, save himself. There was only a burnished bronze mirror propped up in the centre of the room. He came closer to it so that he could see his own reflection in the highly polished metal. And yet it was the other's aura he felt emanating from it.

Projection, he thought. The bastard can somehow *project* his aura – but how –?

Wolf felt something but, looking up, saw only a shadow as feet clamped either side of his neck. The sonuvabitch had been hiding in the ceiling!

A slender slice of light illuminated Yoshida's cheek and jaw, and Wolf recognized the man who had met him in the restaurant in Washington's Chinatown and had led him to the spook Shipley. And now, as if a trigger in Wolf's mind had been pulled, he recognized the aura: it was that of the shadow he had fought that night on the rooftop of Amanda's apartment building. The shadow that had almost killed him, that *had* murdered Amanda. Christ, he thought, so it wasn't Kamiwara and it wasn't Suma. It was Jason Yoshida!

The blow from Yoshida's left heel struck him just beneath the ear, the *juka*, as the martial artist knows it. Wolf's entire left side went numb and his legs turned to rubber.

He would have slumped to the floor but Yoshida's death grip held him fast. Yoshida's feet were like a noose around Wolf's neck, squeezing tighter, impeding the flow of blood and oxygen to the brain. He was quite coolly and efficiently asphyxiating Wolf.

It did him no good to realize that in relying so heavily on his new-found power he had neglected the basic tenets of his police training. He should have checked the ceiling the moment his first impression led him to believe that the room was empty. His *makura na hiruma* was not infallible, and he was not yet a god. A lesson well learned, but what good would it do him if he was dead?

He grunted as Yoshida's fierce grip tightened and pulled him upwards until his feet dangled off the floor. He was jerking this way and that like a berserk puppet. His vision was blurring and he was no longer able to think coherently. His eyes blinked rapidly and his mouth was open and gasping. He wanted to raise his arms to his neck, to have them do something to break Yoshida's lethal hold on him but they seemed made of stone, separate from the rest of his body. There was a buzzing in his head like a swarm of flies rising and falling over a lump of carrion. He knew he was dying. He could imagine his face, white with exsanguination, the rictus of death already forming, he had seen so many faces like it on the night-time streets of New York.

Suck blood from the stone.

What? Was there a voice in his head? With the buzzing of the flies he could not be sure.

450

Suck blood from the stone.

He heard it. Consciousness flickering, and it seemed as if he slept for a while. Wake up! The buzzing again, a black and red shroud beginning to cover him.

The stone was his body. Yes, his body. Stop struggling. What? Stop struggling? I'll die. You're dying now.

He stopped struggling, let his body hang loose, become elastic. And now all the *ki*, the life force, the intrinsic energy, rushed to the centre of his being. The *makura na hiruma* rose up in a pillar through the centre of his spine into the base of his brain. Then the shower of bright sparks began.

A black wind was rising, a dark beast was forming, twining itself around Yoshida's legs, digging in with long, curved talons. There was a fountaining of *ki*, so that the atmosphere in the room dimmed, thickened to the consistency of water.

Yoshida coughed heavily, gagged, and lost his hold on the ceiling. He, and Wolf with him, dropped to the floor. In the process, he lost his hold on Wolf's neck.

Wolf lay on the floor, unmoving. Breathe, he ordered himself. Breathe! The blood of energy he had sucked from the stone of his body was helping. He breathed into his *hara*, his lower belly, as he had been taught by his aikido *sensei*. But the resumption of feeling brought with it intense pain. His neck felt bloated to three times its size, the bruised skin and muscles in intense spasm. Breathing again ceased.

And the other was coming for him. He, too, had unsheathed his *makura na hiruma*. There was an unpleasant smell in the room, as of an open sewer.

Wolf managed to struggle to his knees. By that time, Yoshida had reached him. Wolf grabbed his extended right wrist with his right hand, yanked hard on it while swivelling to his right. Yoshida's own momentum pulled him off balance. Wolf chopped down hard on the inside of Yoshida's elbow joint with the edge of his right hand.

The bone broke at almost the same instant Yoshida's forehead slammed into the tatami mats. Wolf, still swivelling around, pulled, using his left arm on the broken joint as a fulcrum, spinning Yoshida onto his back.

Wolf began to pant. His arm muscles trembled, and so starved for oxygen was he that his entire body began to shake. He knew he was done, through, finished. Yoshida's initial attack had robbed him of blood and energy. If the other got up now, broken arm or no, Wolf knew he was as good as dead.

Yoshida rolled over, got heavily to one knee. The pain in Wolf's neck was almost unbearable. With an inchoate cry, Yoshida rushed at him. Wolf could not even raise his head, instead sent a black fist hammering down on Yoshida.

Yoshida tried to block it with his own *makura na hiruma*, but too late realized that it had been a feint. Wolf, using Yoshida's own projection trick against him, had used the bronze mirror to bounce his aura, while preparing the real strike from Yoshida's weakened right side.

The black fist of Wolf's *makura na hiruma* struck Yoshida flush on the right side. He had only time enough to give a brief cry of dismay. It was like being hit by a speeding truck. His body was flung across the room, slammed full force against the stucco wall. Blood erupted as if from a burst water main, spattered the walls, the tatami mats, the *fusuma*, out into the corridor. Blood dripped from the ceiling where Yoshida had lain in wait for Wolf.

Wolf lay back, closed his eyes for a moment, and listened to the unnatural rain.

'I could never fathom why the Reverend Mother didn't use you to control your half-brother,' Naoharu Nishitsu said.

Because she is smarter than you, Chika thought, but she smiled as she said, 'Yuji was never one to take advice from the female members of his family.'

Nishitsu laughed. 'Except his mother.'

She had waylaid him as he had hurried through the nearly deserted cafe section of Forbidden Dreams. He had obviously been on his way to the second building where the Reverend Mother sat like a great spider in the middle of her web.

It was vital that she continue to redirect his attention from what would be happening in a very few minutes across the garden. She did not envy Wolf's confrontation with the Reverend Mother but, whatever the outcome, she knew she must leave the two of them to it.

'Yuji was never one to take anyone's advice,' Nishitsu said now. 'What is wrong with that man? He is almost American in his rabid pursuit of individualism. How can he sympathize with the Americans? At every turn they try to corrupt us.'

'You forget that the Americans made us what we are today, Nishitsu-san,' Chika said.

'I forget nothing about the Americans,' Nishitsu said angrily. 'Do you think I could forget what they did to us? My family is from Hiroshima. Those that survived the cataclysm carry the American scars inside them. I, myself, can never sire children. The American atomics did that to me so don't speak to me favourably of the Americans.'

452

'The time of Hiroshima and Nagasaki was long ago, Nishitsu-san, as were the numerous atrocities our own commanders and soldiers perpetrated. Shall we spend the rest of our lives poisoned by the sins of the past?'

'The past forms the present,' Nishitsu said shortly. 'It is impossible to throw it away.'

'But not to bury it,' Chika said.

Nishitsu studied her for some time, and she had the impression that his opal eye was seeing clear through her. As if confirming this, he said, 'Forgive me, Chika-san, I must go. I am late for an appointment.'

She had to do something. 'Do you always run from defeat, Nishitsu-san?'

'What? What did you say?'

He was really angry now, but at least she had his full attention. 'You know I'm right,' she pressed on. 'You're simply too stubborn to admit it. It's time to live in the world that is instead of being intent on changing it to suit your own needs.'

Nishitsu grabbed her, jerking her against him. His opal eye blazed in fury. 'What has your time in America done to you, Chika-san?' He pulled her forward, towards the *fusuma* out onto the corridor. 'I think you had better come with me. The Reverend Mother should hear this heresy from your own lips.'

He pushed Chika rudely through the open doorway, took an iron grip on her arm as he guided her down the corridor. They passed the garden, and Chika knew they had crossed into the second building. She had to do something to stop this.

She saw a sliding door, dug in her heels and spun away from him. In almost the same motion, she slid back the door, hurled herself through the doorway.

Closet. She turned just in time to be slammed into the shelves along the narrow rear wall. Cans of paint, cleanser, lacquer thinner tumbled down on her, along with brushes, drop-cloths, sandpaper and paper sacks of sand. She threw one of these at Nishitsu, but he brushed it aside.

He reached down, hauled her to her feet. He hit her several times in rapid succession. 'If you raise a hand to me,' he said in a low voice, 'I won't hesitate to kill you.' He grinned. 'Do you think I don't know of your treachery? Yours and that of your madwoman mother?' The black spectre of his *makura na hiruma* filled the room like a genie let out of the bottle. 'Now you'll come with me to see the Reverend Mother.' He leered at her, as he hit her harder, beginning to enjoy her mounting grunts of pain. 'You and your damnable half-brother Yuji, I never trusted either of you. Why should I? I was the one who told the Reverend Mother she should keep an eye on Minako, and I was right. The whole Shian family should be exterminated. No doubt, it will be now.'

He hit her one last time, and her eyes rolled up in her head and she collapsed against him.

Wolf was searching for the Reverend Mother, but he could not find her in any of the ground-floor rooms. He halted for a moment. At first, he had used *makura na hiruma* to clamp down on the pain, but that had not helped him to breathe. It was more than the pain that was debilitating him, it was the trauma the other's attack had inflicted on the muscles, tendons and blood vessels in his neck. So, with a tentative hand, he began to wield *makura na hiruma* to heal himself. But this had taken a great deal of effort and, while the pain was almost completely gone now, and the swelling was greatly reduced, his strength had ebbed. He knew he should rest, but he had no idea how long Chika could keep Nishitsu occupied. He had to find the Reverend Mother and deal with her before the entire building was alerted and the full force of the Black Blade Society could be brought to bear on him and Chika.

Where was she?

Listen, the voice said in his mind.

At the very top of Forbidden Dreams, he heard Chika saying, *through a door inscribed with double phoenixes . . .*

He went quickly through the corridors, built with numerous ninety-degree angles to stop the evil spirits from gaining access to the rooms beyond. He found the stairs, and went up them three at a time.

Second floor, third floor, fourth. Above him was the roof. He felt the silence here, as thick as tar. Though the windows were open to cool the rooms, there were no nightbirds singing. Not a breath of air stirred the branches of the delicate dwarf maples in the garden below.

He went through each room methodically, his *makura na hiruma* tuned only peripherally to the environment. The rooms were larger here, more luxurious. Vivid contemporary Western art mixed with powerful stone carvings, delicate hand-woven silk carpets and other, more arcane artefacts from another age. Untold wealth was on display here. He searched the top floor as he had done Lawrence Moravia's penthouse in another time, another place. That had been another Wolf Matheson, and yet this was Wolf Matheson as well.

Behind a step tansu, *black as night,* Chika had said.

Yes, there it was.

Wolf took a complete inventory of the room, which had about it something of an antechamber. It was windowless, the lighting coming from fluorescent tubes mounted on the bare concrete walls. Below, were antique Chinese votive tables of some heavy, dark wood.

Every square inch of the tabletop was covered with brightly painted miniature robots, toys really, although by their age one would think they would fetch quite a price at any auction house in Japan. All the robots were man-shaped; there were none like Robbie the Robot in *Forbidden Planet* who was merely a bi-pedal hulk.

There was something eerie about this display of mechanical toys, perhaps because they were meant to resemble men. Their faces appeared empty, awaiting a command from their general; their colours were heightened to a Technicolor blaze by the cold fluorescent lights. It was as if at any moment an incantation would be spoken and the miniature army would come to life.

He went across the antiseptic black-and-white tile floor to the step *tansu*, black as night. Recalling what Chika had told him, how Minako had moved the chest with seeming ease, he searched behind it, found a button. Pressing it moved the *tansu* aside, and he saw the door inscribed with the double phoenixes. He put the flat of his hands against their feathered breasts, pushed hard. The door opened.

Wolf stepped into the room of five shadows.

And saw Chika. She was strung up in a star shape, a banner fluttering from the thick rough-hewn beams of the ceiling. She was naked, framed by the large pane of glass set in the far wall. Her head lolled on her breast, her hair hung lank with sweat, and blood dripped from ten thousand tiny cuts in her flesh.

Wolf stared at her in shock and screamed.

Shock was, of course, what the Reverend Mother had wanted him to feel. Shock closed down the sensory system, scrambled the brain's synapses, interfered with the data streaming in from the environment. All these things she counted on, and she got.

Wolf was blown backwards by a hot gust of black wind, slammed against the cedar-planked wall, pinned there like a specimen in a killing jar. Which, in a way, he was.

'The brain is such a mysterious thing,' the Reverend Mother said. 'In my own fashion I have conquered life and death, but what mysteries still await me inside the human mind.'

Wolf could see her now, but so aware was he of the horror overhanging her that he paid her scarcely any attention. This was just as she had planned it.

'I must admit I was somewhat taken aback when you were able to stand up to Yoshida. I raised him, trained him, after all. He and Chika were the closest things I had to kin. You killed Yoshida, and you will be responsible for Chika's death as well.'

She came closer, and he could see now that she was clad in a kimono of gold thread. Interwoven were mythical animals in red and black. 'Some in Toshin Kuro Kosai would consider you a threat.' She produced a malicious smile. 'But I see you as an opportunity that comes only once in a lifetime. I would not kill you.'

'What are you talking about? You've already tried your best to kill me.'

'You mean the drug into which I dipped Suma's flail. Oh, there you are wrong. It was meant only to subdue you, to quiet your warrior's heart while I took you to me. But then you grabbed the blade with your hand; you absorbed too much of the drug.' She shook her head but her eyes never left his. 'No, the real threat to your life comes from Minako. You think I am lying, but I will tell you that if you somehow walk away from here she will surely seek you out and destroy you. It's only logical, really. The only way you will leave here alive is if I am dead. Then she will have an accurate gauge on just how powerful you are. Don't you see it, yet, Tabula Rasa? You will be more powerful than she is, and that she will not tolerate.'

The danger is in life. Not death, the Oracle had quite accurately predicted.

Studying his face with loving care, the Reverend Mother's smile widened and he could feel her grip on him tightening. He tried to think but putting one thought after another was as difficult as moving in quicksand. *And perhaps as deadly*, said the voice in his mind.

'Of course, there is only one sure way to find out how truly powerful your sight is.' She stopped in front of him. It was so still he could hear the lentitudinous drip of blood from the ten thousand wounds she had inflicted on Chika. Was Chika dead or alive? he wondered dully.

'Only one way.'

There was a stirring in the room, a black, hot gyring in front of his face, and he could see in his mind a black blade, as slender and wicked-looking as a scalpel.

'That's right,' the Reverend Mother said. 'It *is* a scalpel. And with it I will dissect your mind, extracting the mystery of your unique *makura na hiruma* from the core of you. I can do it. I've spent years perfecting this technique of psychic surgery. Shall I show you the bones of all those who have gone before you, whose *makura na hiruma* is now stored inside me? I can, you know. They're all here. Companions in the night.'

She kept on coming towards him, her smile as tender as a lover's. 'You

456

see me, Tabula Rasa. And what you see is a great engine that will never run down, that only gets more powerful as my hunger increases. Very soon now I will have eaten my fill. All others in Japan with the power will be gone. There will be no possible opposition to my rule. And then I will dictate unilaterally to the Toshin Kuro Kosai members inside the world's largest conglomerates. I will possess what no other woman in the history of the world could even dream of, let alone attain. Power over men everywhere. The ultimate power.'

The madness leaked out of her eyes, spilled out through her lips. She exuded it like some noxious musk. The sweat of corruption blossomed in the room with such force that Wolf felt his stomach heave.

'Time to begin.'

He closed his eyes, saw the black scalpel gleaming evilly in his mind's eye. *Don't close your eyes*, the voice inside his mind said. But the blade –

He opened his eyes, saw the long-fingered hands of the Reverend Mother just before they clamped each side of his head. He tried to move, but could not.

Don't close your eyes.

Another message from deep inside of him. Where could it be coming from? How could he even be hearing it? For a moment, he panicked, certain that he was as insane as the Reverend Mother.

Then, he steadied, recalling how the mysterious voice had given him a clue to defeating Yoshida. Don't close your eyes. What could it mean?

The psychic scalpel was poised to commence its first incision. He tried to summon up his *makura na hiruma*, but somehow he had lost his way. The quicksand the Reverend Mother had thrown him into was slowing him down. His mind felt as if it were encased in amber, his reasoning suspended just as poor Chika was suspended over them.

Chika!

Don't close your eyes.

He flinched mentally as pain flooded through him as the psychic blade touched his mind.

Look at Chika. He did not want to, the sight so hideous, both of them so helpless.

His brain being sliced –

Don't close your eyes.

He looked beyond the black scalpel, beyond the grinning visage of the Reverend Mother, at the atrocity of what had been done to Chika. Blood dripping, there must be a pool of it by now, she must

457

be dead, looked at the tatami mats beneath her and there was no blood.

There was no blood!

The black scalpel slicing deeper –

No blood! How could that be?

Don't close your eyes.

And then he knew. He looked again at the spot where Chika had been strung up, concentrating through the terrible pain, focusing on her and nothing else.

Chika vanished!

Of course she vanished; she had never been there in the first place. The Reverend Mother had trapped him with an image she had created out of *makura na hiruma* energy.

It was the shock and pain of this image that had bound him here, that had rendered him helpless, that had allowed her the tenths of a second she had needed to breach all his defences and establish her control over him. What an insidious monster!

He was about to act when the red and black mythical beasts on the Reverend Mother's kimono sprang to life. Dragons, winged serpents, all manner of chimera had been born. As one, their baleful heads turned in his direction and they hissed streams of fire, venom, acid. Then from the shadows behind them emerged a figure so familiar that he froze.

It was his father!

Peter Matheson, looking tanned and fit, his Texas Ranger's badge pinned to his faded chambray shirt, swept his ten-gallon hat off his head, used it as he always did to beat the dust off his stained chaps. He grinned at his son as his right hand flashed to his hip. His drawn Colt six-gun pumped bullet after bullet into the creatures that had come to life.

Stepping over the grotesque corpses, he holstered his gun, extended his dry calloused hand. 'Good to see you again, son,' he said. 'I see you've done yourself proud.'

It was an automatic response. Wolf took his father's hand. Excruciating pain lanced up his arm, making him tremble, his teeth chatter. He tried to free his hand, watched in horror as his father's skin began to peel away, revealing a thousand white insects busily at work on the rotting flesh. Then they, too, vanished, and only the bare skull, angular and gleaming vilely, remained. The jaws hinged open, abruptly clashed shut.

He jerked his hand away, and the spectre of his father, pulled from his memory like taffy, disappeared. The grotesque corpses were gone, as well.

458

Only the Reverend Mother remained, her black blade ready to resume its incision.

He found himself on his knees, and he could scarcely catch his breath. His head ached fiercely. He knew she was throwing everything in her formidable arsenal against him. But he began to understand now that each tactic had a common thread: shock. She paralysed her victims with this form of poison before consuming them.

He wiped Chika, the creatures and his father from his mind. They were all images of her creation, meant to keep him from thinking clearly. This was not an easy task. She had the knack of probing the psyche and extracting the bits that would produce the maximum effect. And he had very little time. Already another image was beginning to take shape, shimmering eerily in front of him. He might not be able to survive this one.

He centred himself, concentrating only on the wellspring of the power inside him.

Freed, his *makura na hiruma* rose up like black lightning from the core of him. The length and the breadth of it filled his mind, his body, the room. It healed his wound as it shot past him. It grabbed the Reverend Mother's black blade – the essence of her own *makura na hiruma* laid bare to perform the grisly surgery – and smashed it into a thousand glittering shards.

Wolf could feel the Reverend Mother's own *makura na hiruma* trying to recover, gathering itself to repel the assault. Firelight filled his mind; ten thousand maddened wasps filled the room. But it was too late. Her black blade had been destroyed and now the mask of her humanity dropped away and Wolf confronted what was beneath, the skinless, boneless mass of her madness.

For one brief moment, it writhed and groaned and Wolf was given a glimpse at another future where this thing was given free rein. The gold-thread kimono burst into flame, the creatures moaning as they burned.

Then his *makura na hiruma* gained full power. He reached out, grasped her heart and squeezed fiercely. The Reverend Mother screamed as she was blown backwards across the room. She cartwheeled through the window.

Wolf ran to the shattered window, looked down. The body of the Reverend Mother was draped over the largest of the rocks in the garden. On first glance, the darkness made it possible to think of the scene as a kind of surreal painting. Then the horned moon slid from behind thick clouds and her awkward position was revealed, the back fractured by the rock's highest point, the pelvis shattered by a secondary outcropping. The stone itself was dark with the wash of her blood.

Wolf clung to the shattered windowframe, exhausted unto death. His head began to loll.

Don't close your eyes, the mysterious voice repeated in his mind like a mantra.

TWENTY-ONE

Tokyo/Washington

Chika brought Wolf back to Minako's house on a stretcher. He did not require hospitalization, she told her mother, only complete rest.

Minako was overjoyed to see them both. She had known, of course, when the Reverend Mother had ceased to exist. It was as if an irritation deep in her intestines had been expunged. She bade them put Wolf in her own bedroom, and she insisted on seeing to his every comfort herself.

When he woke, she slowly fed him hot miso soup, boiled rice and green tea. While he slept, she sat patiently beside him and when Chika looked in on them she smiled at her daughter.

When she fed him she often spoke to him. 'So you became my great black blade, after all,' she said. 'You see, Wolf-san, it was your karma, the path you had to take. Such things, I know, are difficult for a Westerner to accept without question, but you now have first-hand knowledge of the workings of karma.'

He listened to her without making a sound, watching her through drowsy, half-lowered lids.

'You were brought to me by karma. I was too self-absorbed when I first met you to understand who it was you were. It took me some time to begin fitting the pieces together. You were nothing to me when I first met you in Cambodia. I admit I was obsessed with Thornburg Conrad III. I sought to take advantage of him to give me what I was destined to have: another child with extraordinary sight, another warrior in my battle with the Reverend Mother. In return, he vowed to exact his revenge.'

She fed him more miso soup with infinite patience. 'But from what Chika has told me, it appears now that I have underestimated Conrad all along. You see, Wolf-san, he was using you as his stalking horse to get inside the Toshin Kuro Kosai, to get to me, to assuage his own hunger to extend his life as yours and mine and Chika's are – as the Reverend Mother's would have been if you had not put an end to her.'

She smiled as she wiped his chin. 'The irony to all this is that you and I are still alive and he will soon die. And he will die, Wolf-san, without the knowledge that he possesses inside him a form of what he has sought for so long. I have no doubt that his *makura na hiruma*, no matter how weak it might be, could save him from death, but it will not be. There is no one to summon it for him as your grandfather and Chika did for you.'

She whisked green tea with strong, practised fingers. 'The beauty of life, Wolf-san, often lies in the bite of its irony, eh?'

Later, he awoke to find her arranging the bedcovers around his throat. 'Ah, you are awake.' She smiled her familiar smile. 'You will no doubt be gratified to know that with Yoshida's death the threat of more political murders being committed in your country is ended. As for the trade bill, well, the Americans are on their own. If they are foolish enough to allow it to pass by such a margin that your president cannot veto it, they will pay a heavy price. I cannot help that.'

Minako closed her eyes as if in ecstasy. '"Shian Kogaku: We Are Always With You."' She chuckled. 'Now more than ever an apt saying, don't you think? My company is well on its way to dominating the economics of Japan – and becoming the primary influence on the economics of every country on the planet.'

Her eyes glowed with her inner pleasure. She fussed unnecessarily with the covers; her exquisite face hovered over him so that for a moment he was unaccountably reminded of his last few seconds within the universe of the Oracle.

'You see, Wolf-san, the truth is often hidden beneath so many layers of deceit that in the end even the deceiver forgets where the truth lies. And the truth within my family is that each of my children in their own way has been useful to me. Yuji built me the Oracle. Kazuki, poor, doomed thing, provided a model for me. Her father's weak genes undermined her so her *makura na hiruma* is eating her alive. Unhappy Hana was my watchdog. The only person she ever really cared about was Yuji, and I knew she would keep him safe from the Black Blade Society until I had use for him. And Chika, my warrior daughter. She was my triumph, the result of the lesson I learned with Kazuki.'

Minako leaned over him, smiling benevolently. 'I suppose that now you are wondering why I am confessing all this to you. Well, you are a *gaijin*, a foreigner. And I suppose the older one gets the more comfort there is in confession. The problem is in finding someone worthy to confess to, someone who will understand, someone who will appreciate what you have done.'

She bent low over him. 'You came and you accomplished your purpose. But now that it is over what am I to do with you? Oh, never fear, I will not contemplate the abomination the Reverend Mother was practising. Her *makura na hiruma* drove her utterly insane. But you can see, Wolf-san, how your continued presence would be awkward for me.'

462

Her lips were against his ear. 'You know too much, and what you don't know your extraordinary power would eventually ferret out. You have my daughter's heart and I can no longer count on her absolute loyalty. In sum, you are too powerful. I cannot allow that.'

The abrupt manifestation of her *makura na hiruma* turned day into night. The great fox of her imagination stalked across the room, black and inimical, its predator's jaws gaping wide, aiming for Wolf's throat.

'It is the difference between power and authority that is so easy to forget,' Wolf said.

Minako started, jerked her head in the direction of the door, let out a startled cry as she saw Wolf standing in the open doorway. The great dark fox hesitated. With another cry, she turned back to her patient. Her face went white and she grabbed the bedcovers, jerked them away from the body.

'Chika! What – ?'

The fox vanished.

'Power is a malignant and unthinking beast,' Wolf said, advancing into the room. 'It first numbs us to other people's pain and then makes that pain necessary to remind us that our dominance over them is still operative. Authority is deliberate and judicious, a balanced application of *ki* – the life energy – and compassion.'

If Minako had heard him, she gave no sign of it. Instead, she knelt, staring wide-eyed at her daughter. 'What have you done to me?' she cried.

Wolf knew she was talking to him. 'I've learned a great deal in my short time here. And with *makura na hiruma*, the more knowledge you have the more prepared you will be.'

'Prepared for what?' Minako asked.

'For the madness,' Wolf said. 'You see, that's what I've learned, Minako. The danger is in life. Not death. That was the Oracle's final prediction, the one mystery it longed for me to interpret, the one it could never absorb: that it was the power itself that was driving it insane.'

He advanced on her and she made no move against him. 'It was Hana alone who fathomed the essential nature of *makura na hiruma*. The secret is as old as time, Minako, and it is this: power corrupts; absolute power corrupts absolutely. *Makura na hiruma* is absolute power, and the nature of its absolute corruption is madness. That is its inevitable result in everyone who possesses it.'

'No! No, no, no!'

'Yes.' He crouched down next to her. 'And I believe you were coming to suspect this might be the case.'

'I never – '

463

'You see, Minako, from the time Chika first began to unravel the mystery of the struggle between two Toshin Kuro Kosai factions something kept bothering me. There were good guys and bad guys but I couldn't keep the two sides straight. Was the Reverend Mother insane? It seemed so until she detailed to me your own insanity. Of course, she could have been lying. But she wasn't. Chika herself confirmed that when we spoke in Forbidden Dreams after I had destroyed the Reverend Mother.

'Like a chimera, the reality kept shifting. The essential shape of the struggle escaped me until I reached the truth, which is that good and evil had lost their meaning. All of you are slowly going insane. In essence, Minako, you are no different from the Reverend Mother. Time would have proven that, as your confession bears out.

'All of you have lost the ability to differentiate good from evil, law from chaos. You have created your own order in absolute disregard for the lives of others. You are a disease that must be purged. Annihilation is your only reward for the path you have chosen.'

'Chika . . . ' It was a pathetic sound, a kind of wail an old woman makes when she knows she is dying.

Chika shook her head. There was no emotion on her face, but Wolf could feel the despair that threatened to break her heart. 'You damned yourself with your own words. You have learned to lie from the moment of your summoning. As Wolf said, you chose this path yourself, and now you see the results. You are cut off from everyone who might have loved you. You are alone with your exalted power, which is the way you have lived your whole life. You are already mad, you and the Reverend Mother were locked in an insane battle for supremacy. But what were you going to do when you won? Can you tell me? No, I think the point of all the manipulation, terror and slaughter was simply the destruction of the other one, reigning supreme itself was the purpose.'

She looked into Minako's haunted eyes. 'If I could summon up any emotion on your behalf I would feel pity. But, really, I feel nothing at all.'

Minako let out a little moan, and fell forward onto the futon where the daughter, who Wolf had caused her to see as himself, had lain. Wolf turned her over; her face was so pale it seemed tinged with blue. Chika did not make a move, it was as if she were carved in stone.

Wolf said, 'She is alive but just barely. Something that was pulled so taut for so many decades has snapped.'

Minako had spent her life plotting, birthing as she said soldiers to join her holy war against the Reverend Mother. And for what? A vision of the future that she had been convinced she was creating as easily as an architect creates a building.

464

'It seems to me,' Chika said, staring down at the huddled form of Minako, 'that my mother's problem has always been that she has confused herself with God.'

Some time later, as the cool early spring day was on the wane, Wolf and Chika took a stroll in the garden surrounding Minako's house. The first delicate buds of the cut-leaf maples and gingkos were peeping like chicks from their long winter's sleep. The tall deep-green cryptomeria rustled in the wind, and the air was perfumed by the rich loamy smell of newly turned earth. But high above, the pall of pollution, thick as stew, made one consider the possibility that one would never again see all the way to the horizon.

He was content to be with her; knowing who her father was and how old she really was he was grateful that she was not old like the rest of them, so terribly old.

'Tell me what happened between you and Nishitsu.'

Chika gave him a small laugh, all she was capable of at the moment. 'I've already told you twice.'

'I want to hear it again,' Wolf said.

There came a time when she had realized that her *makura na hiruma* was no match for his, so she resorted to guile. She had pretended to faint, falling into his arms, catching him unawares as he began to drag her back out to the corridor and, in the process, riding her short skirt up over her hips.

Men were so predictable. Nishitsu had stopped to look at what had been revealed and his entire demeanour had changed. She had felt an ebbing of the psychic vice that had imprisoned her, and she had lashed out with a black mailed fist.

Nishitsu had gone down hard, and from then on she had had no problem with him.

In the end, feeling the ripple of the Reverend Mother's death, she had made her way up to the eyrie of the room of five shadows. She had embraced Wolf with the kind of absolute passion she had previously only dreamed of. And as she had held him she had wept, not only for happiness that he was safe, but in despair for the immediate future that hovered in the air like a shade, an aftermath of the Reverend Mother's death.

It was then that Wolf had told her what he had begun to suspect, deducing a future out of an interweaving of present clues. And he relayed what Hana had told him, and how they would have to prove it. So they had devised the ruse of his convalescence for Minako's benefit. 'I know it sounds like a cruel hoax,' he had told her. 'But if I'm right, this will be our one chance to trap her.'

465

He had known full well what he was asking of her. Minako was her mother, after all, no matter the mixed emotions she might have for the woman. But Chika had agreed without an argument, and Wolf had given a mental shrug, assuming her acceptance to be nothing more than her unwavering belief in karma.

She finished telling him about her escape from Nishitsu, and he took her hand in his.

'I'll never forgive her for using all of us. We were her children. How could she?'

'Never is a long time,' Wolf said.

'Especially for my mother.'

She fell silent, and he was aware of her reluctance to speak about her mother; perhaps, for a time that was just as well. There would be many bitter years for her and Yuji to forget before they could come to terms with who their mother was and what she had done.

Tears glistened in the corners of her eyes. 'Caught between the two I was terrified, sure I would never be able to survive the consequences of their mad scheming. Then my mother told me about you, and I thought, If it's true he can end it all.'

'It all seems like a dream.'

'Perhaps that's because you're learning that there are many realities.' She squeezed his hand.

They passed a section of Minako's house that jutted out into the garden. Through the glass door they could see Yuji. He stood limned in the lemon light from an interior lamp, a black figure with his hands in his pockets, staring at them or at the cryptomeria beside them but, in any case, seeing nothing.

'My poor brother,' Chika said. 'He's been like a laser, all his life a tightly focused beam of light illuminating one corner of the future where his brilliant mind could solve scientific mysteries. Too bad the rest of life was always a mystery he could not solve.'

She broke away from Wolf, went across the grass, and opened the glass door, Wolf, strolling behind her, could hear their conversation.

'Are you all right, Yuji-san?'

'I've been trying to find Wakare,' he said. 'But he's disappeared.'

'He's dead, Yuji,' Chika said gently. 'I found him at Forbidden Dreams.'

Yuji did not turn his head in her direction, but she could see a flash of lamplight across his irises.

'How did he die?'

'The police have no idea. If the Reverend Mother got to him, which seems logical, they'll never know.'

466

He nodded stoically, and she said, 'Poor Yuji. Betrayed by life.' She tried to see his face, but he would not let her. 'You can stay here as long as you want.' She desperately wanted to say so much more, to offer to help him in any way she could. But she could not humiliate him in this way. He had already been betrayed by his mother and his best friend. It was her duty to leave him some shred of dignity, to show him she felt he was strong enough to handle this terrible tragedy on his own.

He gave a little shiver. 'No. I only feel at home at Shian Kogaku. That's the way it has always been. Anyway, I have a great deal of work to do. I have a new operating vice president to name, and I must continue preparing for my lecture tour of the United States. Now, more than ever, it is vital to let the Americans know about us. And then there's Kazuki. I have an idea. Perhaps I will be able to help her – and perhaps then the Oracle will have had a worthwhile purpose.'

Chika watched him as he left the house. He had not asked about Minako, had not looked in on her. There was *her* legacy.

She was thoughtful when she returned to where Wolf waited in the garden. 'What will we do now?' she asked him. 'There are still Toshin Kuro Kosai scattered throughout the world, but the power of the cabal was always so closely knit that without a head it will quickly lose its forward momentum and lapse into stasis.'

'We could spend our lives tracking down the members and trapping them like mad dogs,' he said, 'or we could leave them to their own fate.'

They both knew what that was, and contemplating it brought about an entirely different set of problems. Neither of them was quite ready to tackle them just yet.

They continued to hold hands as they strolled the paths, dappled with shade. Here and there, songbirds flitted from tree to tree, calling into the dusk. They stopped at a backless concrete bench that Wolf found as uncomfortable as it looked. Still, they sat and enjoyed the blue evening as it covered tree, rock and moss with its translucent quilt.

'We have each other, Wolf,' she said very softly.

'Yes, there's that.'

But the unspoken adjunct to what she said was *for how long?* The horror of what had happened to the Reverend Mother and Minako hung in the air like a pall because both of them now knew that this same fate would one day overtake them. Was there no escape from the malignant effects of *makura na hiruma*? Were they doomed to a slow descent into madness?

Wolf rubbed his temple, waiting for the voice to manifest itself inside his brain. He knew whose voice it was: Hana's. Somehow she had effected a way out of her prison; she had not been interred with the Oracle.

Perhaps she would know a way out for them, but no, he thought, she had not even been able to save herself.

'There must be a way out for us, Wolf.'

'Perhaps,' he said. 'But you and I have both looked into the future and it is blank.'

'We also made a pact. That is the last time we'll use our sight. Humans weren't meant to see the future.'

'The temptation will be very strong to renege on that pact. Do you think we'll be able to resist?'

'Yes,' she said in a tone of voice that left no room for doubt.

'Of course we will,' he said, squeezing her hand.

Wolf was aware of the structure of life falling away from him like the carcass of a gross beast; he was aware, too, of how essentially false was man's view of the universe. Time, the aeon and the second, were representations of a linear form of thinking, a crude attempt to create a framework of logic out of endless chaos, to make understandable that which was, essentially, beyond logic.

And, then, he understood that what Hana had told him was correct. There was no such thing as a 'single moment'. Each 'instant of time' has as many layers as an onion, bringing with them a myriad of decisions, changes, alterations in space and time. There were, in fact, *only* branchings; the concept of a single path was illusory. In light of that, perhaps there was a way out for them.

Chika looked at him. 'What are you thinking?'

'I was contemplating my duty.'

Chika gave him another little smile. 'That's very Japanese of you.'

They were silent for a long time. The trilling songs of the birds were quite beautiful. It was growing darker. Occasionally, a firefly darted into the line of their vision. They seemed surrounded by the night.

Wolf raised his head, looked up at the star-tossed sky. 'Whatever new path we choose, Chika, there is one last thing I must do before we leave this one. One last mystery for me to solve.'

'I know,' she said. 'I want to be with you when you do it.'

'Are you sure?'

She nodded her head, and he could feel her trepidation. 'I have already dealt with my mother. What could be worse?'

Wolf sat close beside her in the night for a very long time.

Rain was forming its thunder-clad army, piling in off the sea, rattling streetlights, thundering against rooftops, at times obscuring the tops of the trees.

And, with it, fog, dense, pearlescent, low to the ground.

468

Wolf awakened with the odour of this strange fog in his nostrils. It smelled like an open grave, and this was when he knew his work was not yet finished in Japan.

The house was still and calm, and yet he sensed in the mist the anxiety of leaving a place or of never coming back to where one was born. White Bow had at times talked to him about such feelings. They were often, he had said, experienced by the dead whose souls had not yet trod upon the path of death. Or they could be experienced by those who were about to die.

Wolf dressed silently, swiftly and let himself out of the house. He took one of the cars parked outside Minako's house; the keys had been lying on the wooden entryway cabinet.

Though he was forced into left-side driving and he could not read street signs, still he made his way into the burning heart of Tokyo, lit by neon banners so imposing even Ieyasu Tokugawa's samurai would have been impressed.

Makura na hiruma guided him, as it had awakened him, alerting him to the danger. Neon colours glowed across the slick asphalt of the streets, were washed away with rainwater in the gutters. What was the danger? He could not yet say, only knew it was bitter in his mouth, like a poison he had almost swallowed.

A punk on a Kawasaki, his leather jacket teeming water, cut Wolf off, sped through a light, white sparks flying from his rear wheel. Wolf was reminded of Suma on his Electra-Glide, grinning like a death's-head.

He looked up into the neon sky. SHIAN KOGAKU: WE ARE ALWAYS WITH YOU. Even the violent rain could not obscure the mammoth blood-red sign. He raced through Tokyo's wide boulevards, into the night.

What was the danger? *The danger is in life. Not death.*

He left the car near the Tsukiji fish market. Fish flopped on the wet concrete, scales iridesced in the hanging lights. The steam of living beings clouded the air and, for a moment as he passed, beat back the stench of the open grave.

Then he was past the activity of the market: the raised voices of men at work, the laughter of camaraderie, the warmth and good smells of the food stalls, a drunkard pissing in the shadows. The stuff of life.

In the darkness death waited. Wolf could feel it now, even as he saw the slow mist curling around his ankles. A low beast, a clever thing – was it even human? – curled and flexed its psychic muscles. The dissonance of its *makura na hiruma* hurt his eardrums, an undercurrent like the surge of a dynamo of unknown proportions hidden deep beneath the earth.

And so he came at last to the blank-faced warehouse, home of the late Oracle. A lone bulb buzzed and sputtered fitfully in the rain, its

469

metal hat swinging wildly this way and that as the wind gusted in off the Sumida river. The inconstant cone of light illuminated a metal door without a plate or a painted-on name to identify it.

Wolf knew what it was.

The door was unlocked and, as he neared it, it banged abruptly open, slammed back on its frame, repeated this wild gyration at the rising wind's bidding.

Wolf threw it open, stepped inside. What else could he do? His *makura na hiruma* had unerringly guided him here, and he knew it was for a purpose.

The danger is in life. Not death.

The Oracle's warning.

The warehouse had an abandoned air – or would have in the near future. He felt a prickling along his spine, and wondered whether his sight had shown him his own death.

At the base of the elevator shaft, he looked upwards into the darkness. Whatever was waiting for him was in the lab where the remains of the Oracle lay.

He took the open elevator up. The whine of the engine echoed through the warehouse like a winter wind in a pine forest, a melancholy and lonely sound. At the top floor he emerged onto old wooden floorboards that creaked when he moved. To his left, at the end of the corridor, was the Oracle's home. He went towards it.

The darkness turned aqueous, thickened to the consistency of sludge. And now he could tell why his sight had led him here: someone or something was trying to raise the Oracle from the dead. He paused in the hallway, projected his *makura na hiruma* outwards.

And walked into the Oracle's lab. He could see the black beast, the tiered banks of Yuji's testing and monitoring equipment. The humming of solid-state circuitry filled the air like flies feeding off a corpse. The Oracle squatted, amid a forest of wires, silicon leads, fibre-optic cables, graphite-boron stalks. Its face was dark, its heart still.

In the corners of Wolf's vision movement like the darting of starlings. He turned his head, and the movement stayed in the periphery, sensed but not quite seen.

Then the black hand of a *makura na hiruma* so powerful it rocked the building on its foundations stabbed out, and Wolf's body was incinerated.

Smoke and sparks filled the entrance to the lab, then died, but the stench of burned flesh was not apparent.

The manifestation of the sight took only a heartbeat, but in that time Wolf, standing in the aqueous shadows of the hallway, was able

470

to learn something of the nature of his adversary. The *makura na hiruma* he had felt with the projection of himself in the lab was not only hugely powerful, it was very ancient, older even than the Reverend Mother, some centuries ancient, in fact. He also knew that its owner was Jason Yoshida's mother.

Wolf was very still. He could control his breathing but not the thundering of his heart. He was very frightened, for he had encountered an evil so old that it went without a name. It was an evil, he knew, that White Bow would have recognized. He wondered whether this evil could sense him where the others could not.

He conjured up an image of Yoshida, and marched him into the lab. This time he was right behind his projection. He saw what appeared to be an electrical current in the air, a coalescing of fireflies. And Evan appeared from out of the shadows.

Wolf was totally unprepared for how young she was. Stunned, he momentarily lost control of the Yoshida image, and it flickered like a candle flame in the wind.

That was all the time Evan needed. She turned her attention from the empty image of her son to Wolf.

Wolf gathered himself, and the lab shimmered. He saw his grandfather. The spirit of White Bow raised a hand in greeting.

'I have been waiting for you to summon me,' he said. He smelled of leather and peyote, and his face was etched with concern. 'The evil is here, and you must fight it, Wolf. But you will need my help.'

'Tell me what I must do,' Wolf said.

'Come here. Stand with me. Where you are is still partway in the land of the living. You must come all the way down, into the land of the dead.'

'But I will die.'

'No,' White Bow said. 'You are a shaman. I trained you myself. You will not be harmed. I need your power to bring me up from the land of the dead for this one last battle.'

Believing him, Wolf took one step towards him. And felt the ground disintegrating beneath his feet. He was slipping down, unable to control –

Too late, he saw Evan's ruse for what it was – ideas and events pulled from his memory. Too late, he understood the vision's one flaw: White Bow's spirit would have descended from the sky, not been trapped below the earth.

Too late, he opened his eyes, stared up into Evan's beautiful face. Her hand had gripped his throat, and now she was squeezing it, just as her *makura na hiruma* was squeezing his heart.

'You killed my son,' Evan said. 'You destroyed the veils of false

471

hierarchy it took a century to build.' Her nails bit into his flesh, drawing blood. 'People believed Nishitsu was the head of the Black Blade Society, others secretly knew that the Reverend Mother was the head.' She smiled a ghastly smile. 'And still others believed that Minako Shian would become the head.' There was blue fire trying to ignite itself inside Wolf, and he struggled to keep it from forming because if it did he knew he would be incinerated as his projection had been.

'The truth is there was only ever one head of the Black Blade Society, and that is me. I controlled everything and everyone. My *makura na hiruma* was such that I could do that even when I was a small child. I was born able to summon the sight at will. The Black Blade Society was my creation, and I will not allow you to put an end to it.'

The blue fire was coming, Wolf could feel it now, his temperature rising to critical levels. In his mind, he saw images of Cathy being set aflame, and Bobby Connor burning, Hayes Walker Johnson and his wife, and Amanda dead in a pool of her own blood.

With a monstrous effort, he slammed his hands into Evan's chest. Her clawed fingernails ripped skin and flesh as she staggered back.

She only smiled, coming on again.

The pressure inside him that had let up for just an instant returned, more powerful than ever. Wolf tried to harness his *makura na hiruma*, directed a black club at Evan's face. She staggered, came on again.

Brute force wasn't going to work. He tried to project himself inside her head, but the resulting chaos almost made him scream. The buzzing of ten thousand insects was in the air, in his mind, dazzling him.

And she was upon him again, her nails sinking into him, the blue flame giving off its first flicker as it ran up his arm. The revolting stench of roasting meat . . .

At the point of death, he did call out for his grandfather, asking him for his strength, and blindly summoned every last shred of his *makura na hiruma*.

Evan was flung off him, slamming backwards into the face of the Oracle. She righted herself, smiled as she sensed the end to Wolf's defences, and began to come on.

Abruptly, her expression changed. She halted in midstep, looked down. Cables were wrapped around her legs and, as she kicked at them, sparks danced in the air.

Evan literally levitated. The force of the surge of electrical current carried in the cables struck her like a fist from heaven. Her eyes bugged out, her hair flew about her like Medusa's reptilian mane. Her body danced a galvanic gavotte. Her mouth opened in a silent scream while the crackling of unbounded energy sizzled her flesh.

Eventually, the corpse dropped to the floor, where its extremities slapped and struck the floor in violent spasm.

Wolf, gaining his feet, went slowly towards the Oracle. In its face was what seemed to be a soft glow. Was it of satisfaction? Wolf wondered. Impossible. The Oracle was dead; he himself had overseen its demise.

But still . . .

He put a hand over the wounds on his neck, willed the bleeding to stop. He looked down at the cables, wrapped in loose knots around Evan's legs. How had she become so entangled in them? He bent to take a closer look.

'HELLO, WOLF-SAN,' the Oracle whispered.

Wolf looked up into its face. Did he see an expression? Did he hear a sigh of satisfaction?

'TIME TO SLEEP . . . '

All along the massed banks of machinery, the lights were winking slowly out.

The Parting

Snow that we two
looked at together — this year
has it fallen anew?

Matsuo Basho

Washington

Every sound in the private hospital room was uttered by a machine; every motion made by a machine. These exotic engines formed a kind of enclave around the single human being, who was alive, or merely existed, depending on one's point of view.

The doctors who monitored his progress – if that was the right word – through this limbo agreed that he was indeed alive. Others, however, who lacked the specific medical training to judge such things, had written him off. Even the nurses, trained to be compassionate, did not consider him alive, but merely in suspension, like a colloid in a lab.

This was Thornburg Conrad III's fate: to be shot as punishment for his many sins, but not to die. To exist in this living hell, not moving, not speaking, but thinking, only thinking as machines powered his heart, pumped his lungs, dripped nutrients into his veins, pulled excreta from him.

Was this life? Not by his definition. But it was his punishment, of this he was absolutely certain, not, in his mind, for the contempt he felt for his first wife, mother of his children, his callous disregard for the pain of his second wife, the perfect Tiffany Conrad, his blind passion for life that led him to condone the murder of many, his dismissal of his children for not becoming the people he had wished for. No, this punishment was for the single sin he was capable of recognizing: the murder of his son.

If he had been a religious man, he would have turned to his God and repented and been forgiven. But Christ was just a word to him, one overused and abused beyond any recognition. He remembered his father ranting, *'I won't have anyone, especially not a priest, telling me what I can and can't do. What do priests know about the real world anyway?'*

It would be nice, he thought on occasion, to have a priest around to wave his hands and give him the official word that he was forgiven his grievous crime. But that was impossible. Besides, it wasn't God he needed to be forgiven by, it was Ham. And, by his own hand, Ham was gone.

Then the despair would well up so strongly that all he could wish for was one moment for the paralysis to lift so that he could tear the tubes

477

from his body and die in peace. Even one more artificial breath was too much to bear. He deserved to die, he knew that now, and soon he would. He heard what the doctors said as they spoke by his bedside. Even the clever machines could not keep his body functioning for long.

Soon. But not soon enough.

He became aware of the door opening. More doctors, morons debating moot points. How he hated doctors now, how foolish they seemed to him, pretending they knew more than they did. They knew precious little about life and nothing at all about death which, he was certain, was the only comfort left to him.

How he longed for oblivion! After struggling so long in the darkness of life it came as a profound relief to know that an end to his pain was at hand.

But no, he saw now, these were not doctors who had come to visit him, neither were they a knot of lawyers who came regularly to hover like vultures, running up their hourly fees.

Good God! It's Wolf Matheson. And by his side, a stunning young Japanese woman. He found himself thinking, I've hoped for this. It's like the coming of the angel of death. He knows what I did to him, and now he's come to finish the job Stevie began.

'Thornburg,' Wolf was saying, 'I know you recognize me. It's been a long time since I saw you, but I suppose the reverse can't be said. You've been keeping close track of me, running me, I guess you could say. Well, I've done what you wanted me to do. I've penetrated the Toshin Kuro Kosai, I've met with Minako. You remember Minako, sure you do. How could you forget?'

Wolf put his hands on the Japanese woman's shoulders. 'This is Chika. She is Minako's daughter. She was born around nine months after you and I escaped from Cambodia. Remember, Thornburg? Remember what happened there? You and Minako. Here is your daughter, Thornburg. What do you think of her?'

Wolf was bending over, smiling in an enigmatic way, but Thornburg was so stunned by the revelation that his mind had gone blank. He had got that witch Minako pregnant? Good Christ! He felt what remained of his essence curling up into a defensive ball. The dread of being confronted by a daughter he had never known existed, who could peer into his mind as easily as if it was a shop window and see what he had done, was too much for him. And she knew! He could see the disgust and contempt in her eyes. *Take her away*, he begged. *For the love of Christ, take her away!*

But if Wolf heard him he gave no indication of it. 'You ran me like a rat in a maze, Thornburg. Then, you tried your best to have me killed. Why did you do that? I was always your lucky talisman. Isn't that how

478

you thought of me back in Cambodia? So this is the last mystery and, as good a detective as I am I can't figure this one out. And, of course, you can't tell me. Ironic isn't it?

'Especially since I did what you hoped I would: I found the secret you were so desperately looking for for so long. In return, my life has been irrevocably altered. You did that to me, Thornburg, you and your obsession to beat death. But I forgive you. Well, maybe not forgive, exactly, but I'm willing to forget it because it was you who saved my life in Cambodia. That's something I can't forget.'

Wolf's enigmatic smile widened. 'You see, that power Minako had, the Japanese phrase for it is *makura na hiruma*. It means the Darkness at Noon, and it's aptly named. I know because I possess it. So does Chika. And so do you.'

He could see Wolf studying his eyes for even the minutest flicker of reaction. 'Yes, Thornburg, it's true, the secret you spent your life pursuing was right under your nose all along. Inside you. It just needed to be summoned, something I'm going to do now.'

No, Thornburg begged silently.

'My way of saying thank you for saving my life long ago.'

No. You don't understand. If you want to repay me for saving your life then take mine now.

Then he was jolted out of time. He found himself in a vast shadowed defile between gargantuan mountains. With a terrifying rumble, a rockslide, torn loose by an underground eruption, roared down upon him. But, instead of being inundated, he discovered he had risen out of the defile. Then he became aware of a further shift in perception. The mountains dissolved into raw magma, and a strange blackness was forming from the chaos, alive and panting, glistening with nascent life, slouching to sit at his side. He stared at it, and it seemed intolerable and familiar all at once.

'You'll have a long life now, Thornburg,' Wolf was saying. 'Who knows how long? You may not be able to move, but you won't need these machines to keep you alive. Your *makura na hiruma* will do that for you.'

No, no, no! Don't leave me with this thing! Wait, please! I've got to tell you! I want to die! I want –!

'Goodbye, Thornburg.' They were at the door, but that enigmatic smile still burned his retinas, etched into his brain. Was it the smile of a friend or an enemy? 'I trust you'll enjoy your new life.'

479